TALES OF MYSTERY & THE SUPERNATURAL

General Editor: David Stuart Davies

SCOTTISH GHOST STORIES

SCOTTISH GHOST STORIES

Selected by
ROSEMARY GRAY

From ghoulies and ghosties
And long-leggedy beasties
And things that go bump in the night,
Good Lord, deliver us!

WORDSWORTH CLASSICS

For my husband
ANTHONY JOHN RANSON
with love from your wife, the publisher.
Eternally grateful for your unconditional love,
not just for me but for our children,
Simon, Andrew and Nichola Trayler

Readers who are interested in other titles from
Wordsworth Editions are invited to visit our website at
www.wordsworth-editions.com

For our latest list and a full mail-order service, contact
Bibliophile Books, 5 Datapoint, South Crescent, London E16 4TL
TEL: +44 (0)20 7474 2474 FAX: +44 (0)20 7474 8589
ORDERS: orders@bibliophilebooks.com
WEBSITE: www.bibliophilebooks.com

First published in 2009 by Wordsworth Editions Limited
8B East Street, Ware, Hertfordshire SG12 9HJ

ISBN 978 1 84022 168 8

Text © Wordsworth Editions Limited 2009

Wordsworth® is a registered trademark of
Wordsworth Editions Limited,
the company founded by Michael Trayler in 1987

Typeset in Great Britain by Antony Gray
Printed and bound by Clays Ltd, St Ives plc

CONTENTS

The Watcher by the Threshold

JOHN BUCHAN

A chill evening in the early October of the year 189— found me
driving in a dogcart through the belts of antique woodland which
form the lowland limits of the hilly parish of More. The Highland
express, which brought me from the north, took me no farther than
Perth. Thence it had been a slow journey in a disjointed local train,
till I emerged on the platform at Morefoot, with a bleak prospect of
pot stalks, coal heaps, certain sour corn lands, and far to the west a
line of moor where the sun was setting. A neat groom and a
respectable trap took the edge off my discomfort, and soon I had
forgotten my sacrifice and found eyes for the darkening landscape.
We were driving through a land of thick woods, cut at rare intervals
by old long-frequented highways. The More, which at Morefoot is
an open sewer, became a sullen woodland stream, where the brown
leaves of the season drifted. At times we would pass an ancient lodge,
and through a gap in the trees would come a glimpse of chipped
crowstep gable. The names of such houses, as told me by my
companion, were all famous. This one had been the home of a
drunken Jacobite laird and a kind of north-country Medmenham.
Unholy revels had waked the old halls, and the devil had been toasted
at many a hell-fire dinner. The next was the property of a great Scots
law family, and there the old Lord of Session, who built the place, in
his frouzy wig and carpet slippers, had laid down the canons of Taste
for his day and society. The whole country had the air of faded and
bygone gentility. The mossy roadside walls had stood for two
hundred years; the few wayside houses were toll bars or defunct
hostelries. The names, too, were great: Scots baronial with a smack
of France – Chatelray and Riverslaw, Black Holm and Fountainblue.
The place had a cunning charm, mystery dwelt in every cranny, and
yet it did not please me. The earth smelt heavy and raw; the roads
were red underfoot; all was old, sorrowful and uncanny. Compared
with the fresh Highland glen I had left, where wind and sun and
flying showers were never absent, all was chilly and dull and dead.

Even when the sun sent a shiver of crimson over the crests of certain firs, I felt no delight in the prospect. I admitted shamefacedly to myself that I was in a very bad temper.

I had been staying at Glenaicill with the Clanroydens, and for a week had found the proper pleasure in life. You know the house with its old rooms and gardens, and the miles of heather which defend it from the world. The shooting had been extraordinary for a wild place late in the season, for there are few partridges and the woodcock are notoriously late. I had done respectably in my stalking, more than respectably on the river, and creditably on the moors. Moreover, there were pleasant people in the house – and there were the Clanroydens. I had had a hard year's work, sustained to the last moment of term, and a fortnight in Norway had been disastrous. It was therefore with real comfort that I had settled myself down for another ten days in Glenaicill, when all my plans were shattered by Sibyl's letter. Sibyl is my cousin and my very good friend, and in old days when I was briefless I had fallen in love with her many times. But she very sensibly chose otherwise, and married a man named Ladlaw – Robert John Ladlaw, who had been at school with me. He was a cheery, good-humoured fellow, a great sportsman, a justice of the peace, and deputy lieutenant for his county, and something of an antiquary in a mild way. He had a box in Leicestershire to which he went in the hunting season, but from February till October he lived in his moorland home. The place was called the House of More, and I had shot at it once or twice in recent years. I remembered its loneliness and its comfort, the charming diffident Sibyl, and Ladlaw's genial welcome. And my recollections set me puzzling again over the letter which that morning had broken into my comfort. 'You promised us a visit this autumn,' Sibyl had written, 'and I wish you would come as soon as you can.' So far common politeness. But she had gone on to reveal the fact that Ladlaw was ill; she did not know how, exactly, but something, she thought, about his heart. Then she had signed herself my affectionate cousin, and then had come a short, violent postscript, in which, as it were, the fences of convention had been laid low. 'For Heaven's sake, come and see us,' she scrawled below. 'Bob is terribly ill, and I am crazy. Come at once.' To cap it she finished with an afterthought: 'Don't bother about bringing doctors. It is not their business.'

She had assumed that I would come, and dutifully I set out. I could not regret my decision, but I took leave to upbraid my luck. The thought of Glenaicill, with the woodcock beginning to arrive and the

Clanroydens imploring me to stay, saddened my journey in the morning, and the murky, coaly, midland country of the afternoon completed my depression. The drive through the woodlands of More failed to raise my spirits. I was anxious about Sibyl and Ladlaw, and this accursed country had always given me a certain eeriness on my first approaching it. You may call it silly, but I have no nerves and am little susceptible to vague sentiment. It was sheer physical dislike of the rich deep soil, the woody and antique smells, the melancholy roads and trees, and the flavour of old mystery. I am aggressively healthy and wholly Philistine. I love clear outlines and strong colours, and More with its half tints and hazy distances depressed me miserably. Even when the road crept uphill and the trees ended, I found nothing to hearten me in the moorland which succeeded. It was genuine moorland, close on eight hundred feet above the sea, and through it ran this old grass-grown coach-road. Low hills rose to the left, and to the right, after some miles of peat, flared the chimneys of pits and oil works. Straight in front the moor ran out into the horizon, and there in the centre was the last dying spark of the sun. The place was as still as the grave save for the crunch of our wheels on the grassy road, but the flaring lights to the north seemed to endow it with life. I have rarely had so keenly the feeling of movement in the inanimate world. It was an unquiet place, and I shivered nervously. Little gleams of loch came from the hollows, the burns were brown with peat, and every now and then there rose in the moor jags of sickening red stone. I remembered that Ladlaw had talked about the place as the old Manann, the holy land of the ancient races. I had paid little attention at the time, but now it struck me that the old peoples had been wise in their choice. There was something uncanny in this soil and air. Framed in dank mysterious woods and a country of coal and ironstone, at no great distance from the capital city, it was a sullen relic of a lost barbarism. Over the low hills lay a green pastoral country with bright streams and valleys, but here, in this peaty desert, there were few sheep and little cultivation. The House of More was the only dwelling, and, save for the ragged village, the wilderness was given over to the wild things of the hills. The shooting was good, but the best shooting on earth would not persuade me to make my abode in such a place. Ladlaw was ill; well, I did not wonder. You can have uplands without air, moors that are not health-giving, and a country life which is more arduous than a townsman's. I shivered again, for I seemed to have passed in a few hours from the open noon to a kind of dank twilight.

We passed the village and entered the lodge gates. Here there were trees again – little innocent new-planted firs, which flourished ill. Some large plane trees grew near the house, and there were thickets upon thickets of the ugly elderberry. Even in the half darkness I could see that the lawns were trim and the flower beds respectable for the season; doubtless Sibyl looked after the gardeners. The oblong whitewashed house, more like a barrack than ever, opened suddenly on my sight, and I experienced my first sense of comfort since I left Glenaicill. Here I should find warmth and company; and sure enough, the hall door was wide open, and in the great flood of light which poured from it Sibyl stood to welcome me.

She ran down the steps as I alighted, and, with a word to the groom, caught my arm and drew me into the shadow. 'Oh, Henry, it was so good of you to come. You mustn't let Bob think that you know he is ill. We don't talk about it. I'll tell you afterwards. I want you to cheer him up. Now we must go in, for he is in the hall expecting you.'

While I stood blinking in the light, Ladlaw came forward with outstretched hand and his usual cheery greeting. I looked at him and saw nothing unusual in his appearance; a little drawn at the lips, perhaps, and heavy below the eyes, but still fresh-coloured and healthy. It was Sibyl who showed change. She was very pale, her pretty eyes were deplorably mournful, and in place of her delightful shyness there were the self-confidence and composure of pain. I was honestly shocked, and as I dressed my heart was full of hard thoughts about Ladlaw. What could his illness mean? He seemed well and cheerful, while Sibyl was pale; and yet it was Sibyl who had written the postscript. As I warmed myself by the fire, I resolved that this particular family difficulty was my proper business.

The Ladlaws were waiting for me in the drawing-room. I noticed something new and strange in Sibyl's demeanour. She looked to her husband with a motherly, protective air, while Ladlaw, who had been the extreme of masculine independence, seemed to cling to his wife with a curious appealing fidelity. In conversation he did little more than echo her words. Till dinner was announced he spoke of the weather, the shooting, and Mabel Clanroyden. Then he did a queer thing, for when I was about to offer my arm to Sibyl he forestalled me, and clutching her right arm with his left hand led the way to the dining-room, leaving me to follow in some bewilderment.

I have rarely taken part in a more dismal meal. The House of More has a pretty Georgian panelling through most of the rooms, but in the dining-room the walls are level and painted a dull stone colour. Abraham offered up Isaac in a ghastly picture in front of me. Some photographs of the Quorn hung over the mantelpiece, and five or six drab ancestors filled up the remaining space. But one thing was new and startling. A great marble bust, a genuine antique, frowned on me from a pedestal. The head was in the late Roman style, clearly of some emperor, and in its commonplace environment the great brows, the massive neck, and the mysterious solemn lips had a surprising effect. I nodded toward the thing, and asked what it represented. Ladlaw grunted something which I took for 'Justinian', but he never raised his eyes from his plate. By accident I caught Sibyl's glance. She looked toward the bust and laid a finger on her lips.

The meal grew more doleful as it advanced. Sibyl scarcely touched a dish, but her husband ate ravenously of everything. He was a strong, thickset man, with a square kindly face burned brown by the sun. Now he seemed to have suddenly coarsened. He gobbled with undignified haste, and his eye was extraordinarily vacant. A question made him start, and he would turn on me a face so strange and inert that I repented the interruption.

I asked him about the autumn's sport. He collected his wits with difficulty. He thought it had been good, on the whole, but he had shot badly. He had not been quite so fit as usual. No, he had had nobody staying with him. Sibyl had wanted to be alone. He was afraid the moor might have been undershot, but he would make a big day with keepers and farmers before the winter

'Bob has done pretty well,' Sibyl said. 'He hasn't been out often, for the weather has been very bad here. You can have no idea, Henry, how horrible this moorland place of ours can be when it tries. It is one great sponge sometimes, with ugly red burns and mud to the ankles.'

'I don't think it's healthy,' said I.

Ladlaw lifted his face. 'Nor do I. I think it's intolerable, but I am so busy I can't get away.'

Once again I caught Sibyl's warning eye as I was about to question him on his business.

Clearly the man's brain had received a shock, and he was beginning to suffer from hallucinations. This could be the only explanation, for he had always led a temperate life. The distrait, wandering manner was the only sign of his malady, for otherwise he seemed normal and mediocre as ever. My heart grieved for Sibyl, alone with him in this wilderness.

Then he broke the silence. He lifted his head and looked nervously around till his eye fell on the Roman bust.

'Do you know that this countryside is the old Manann?' he said.

It was an odd turn to the conversation, but I was glad of a sign of intelligence. I answered that I had heard so.

'It's a queer name,' he said oracularly, 'but the thing it stood for was queerer. Manann, Manaw,' he repeated, rolling the words on his tongue. As he spoke, he glanced sharply, and, as it seemed to me, fearfully, at his left side

The movement of his body made his napkin slip from his left knee and fall on the floor. It leaned against his leg, and he started from its touch as if he had been bitten by a snake. I have never seen a more sheer and transparent terror on a man's face. He got to his feet, his strong frame shaking like a rush. Sibyl ran round to his side, picked up the napkin and flung it on a sideboard. Then she stroked his hair as one would stroke a frightened horse. She called him by his old boy's name of Robin, and at her touch and voice he became quiet. But the particular course then in progress was removed, untasted.

In a few minutes he seemed to have forgotten his behaviour, for he took up the former conversation. For a time he spoke well and briskly. 'You lawyers,' he said, 'understand only the dry framework of the past. You cannot conceive the rapture, which only the antiquary can feel, of constructing in every detail an old culture. Take this Manann. If I could explore the secret of these moors, I would write the world's greatest book. I would write of that prehistoric life when man was knit close to nature. I would describe the people who were brothers of the red earth and the red rock and the red streams of the hills. Oh, it would be horrible, but superb, tremendous! It would be more than a piece of history; it would be a new gospel, a new theory of life. It would kill materialism once and for all. Why, man, all the poets who have deified and personified nature would not do an eighth part of my work. I would show you the unknown, the hideous, shrieking mystery at the back of this simple nature. Men would see the profundity of the old crude faiths which they affect to despise. I would make a picture of our shaggy, sombre-eyed forefather, who heard strange things in the hill silences. I would show him brutal and terror-stricken, but wise, wise, God alone knows how wise! The Romans knew it, and they learned what they could from him, though he did not tell them much. But we have some of his blood in us, and we may go deeper. Manann! A queer land nowadays! I sometimes love it and sometimes hate it, but I always fear it. It is like that statue, inscrutable.'

I would have told him that he was talking mystical nonsense, but I had looked toward the bust, and my rudeness was checked on my lips. The moor might be a common piece of ugly waste land, but the statue was inscrutable – of that there was no doubt. I hate your cruel heavy-mouthed Roman busts; to me they have none of the beauty of life, and little of the interest of art. But my eyes were fastened on this as they had never before looked on marble. The oppression of the heavy woodlands, the mystery of the silent moor, seemed to be caught and held in this face. It was the intangible mystery of culture on the verge of savagery – a cruel, lustful wisdom, and yet a kind of bitter austerity which laughed at the game of life and stood aloof. There was no weakness in the heavy-veined brow and slumbrous eyelids. It was the face of one who had conquered the world, and found it dust and ashes; one who had eaten of the tree of the knowledge of good and evil, and scorned human wisdom. And at the same time, it was the face of one who knew uncanny things, a man who was the intimate of the half-world and the dim background of life. Why on earth I should connect the Roman grandee* with the moorland parish of More I cannot say, but the fact remains that there was that in the face which I knew had haunted me through the woodlands and bogs of the place – a sleepless, dismal, incoherent melancholy.

'I bought that at Colenzo's,' Ladlaw said, 'because it took my fancy. It matches well with this place?'

I thought it matched very ill with his drab walls and Quorn photographs, but I held my peace.

'Do you know who it is?' he asked. 'It is the head of the greatest man the world has ever seen. You are a lawyer and know your Justinian.'

The *Pandectae* are scarcely part of the daily work of a common-law barrister. I had not looked into them since I left college.

'I know that he married an actress,' I said, 'and was a sort of all-round genius. He made law, and fought battles, and had rows with the Church. A curious man! And wasn't there some story about his

---

* I have identified the bust, which, when seen under other circumstances, had little power to affect me. It was a copy of the head of Justinian in the Tesci Museum at Venice, and several duplicates exist, dating apparently from the seventh century, and showing traces of Byzantine decadence in the scrollwork on the hair. It is engraved in M. Delacroix's *Byzantium*, and, I think, in Windscheid's *Pandektenlehrbuch*.

selling his soul to the devil, and getting law in exchange? Rather a poor bargain!'

. I chattered away, sillily enough, to dispel the gloom of that dinner table. The result of my words was unhappy. Ladlaw gasped and caught at his left side, as if in pain. Sibyl, with tragic eyes, had been making signs to me to hold my peace. Now she ran round to her husband's side and comforted him like a child. As she passed me, she managed to whisper in my ear to talk to her only, and let her husband alone.

For the rest of dinner I obeyed my orders to the letter. Ladlaw ate his food in gloomy silence, while I spoke to Sibyl of our relatives and friends, of London, Glenaicill, and any random subject. The poor girl was dismally forgetful, and her eye would wander to her husband with wifely anxiety. I remember being suddenly overcome by the comic aspect of it all. Here were we three fools alone in the dank upland: one of us sick and nervous, talking out-of-the-way nonsense about Manann and Justinian, gobbling his food and getting scared at his napkin; another gravely anxious; and myself at my wits' end for a solution. It was a Mad Tea-Party with a vengeance: Sibyl the melancholy little Dormouse, and Ladlaw the incomprehensible Hatter. I laughed aloud, but checked myself when I caught my cousin's eye. It was really no case for finding humour. Ladlaw was very ill, and Sibyl's face was getting deplorably thin.

I welcomed the end of that meal with unmannerly joy, for I wanted to speak seriously with my host. Sibyl told the butler to have the lamps lighted in the library. Then she leaned over toward me and spoke low and rapidly: 'I want you to talk with Bob. I'm sure you can do him good. You'll have to be very patient with him, and very gentle. Oh, please try to find out what is wrong with him. He won't tell me, and I can only guess.'

The butler returned with word that the library was ready to receive us, and Sibyl rose to go. Ladlaw half rose, protesting, making the most curious feeble clutches to his side. His wife quieted him. 'Henry will look after you, dear,' she said. 'You are going into the library to smoke.' Then she slipped from the room, and we were left alone.

He caught my arm fiercely with his left hand, and his grip nearly made me cry out. As we walked down the hall, I could feel his arm twitching from the elbow to the shoulder. Clearly he was in pain, and I set it down to some form of cardiac affection, which might possibly issue in paralysis.

I settled him in the biggest armchair, and took one of his cigars.

The library is the pleasantest room in the house, and at night, when a peat fire burned on the old hearth and the great red curtains were drawn, it used to be the place for comfort and good talk. Now I noticed changes. Ladlaw's bookshelves had been filled with the *Proceedings* of antiquarian societies and many light-hearted works on sport. But now the Badminton Library had been cleared out of a shelf where it stood most convenient to the hand, and its place taken by an old Leyden reprint of Justinian. There were books on Byzantine subjects of which I never dreamed he had heard the names, there were volumes of history and speculation, all of a slightly bizarre kind, and to crown everything, there were several bulky medical works with gaudily coloured plates. The old atmosphere of sport and travel had gone from the room with the medley of rods, whips and gun cases which used to cumber the tables. Now the place was moderately tidy and somewhat learned, and I did not like it.

Ladlaw refused to smoke, and sat for a little while in silence. Then of his own accord he broke the tension.

'It was devilish good of you to come. Harry. This is a lonely place for a man who is a bit seedy.'

'I thought you might be alone,' I said, 'so I looked you up on my way down from Glenaicill. I'm sorry to find you feeling ill.'

'Do you notice it?' he asked sharply.

'It's tolerably patent,' I said. 'Have you seen a doctor?'

He said something uncomplimentary about doctors, and kept looking at me with his curious dull eyes.

I remarked the strange posture in which he sat, his head screwed round to his right shoulder, and his whole body a protest against something at his left hand.

'It looks like heart,' I said. 'You seem to have pains in your left side.'

Again a spasm of fear. I went over to him and stood at the back of his chair.

'Now for goodness' sake, my dear fellow, tell me what is wrong. You're scaring Sibyl to death. It's lonely work for the poor girl, and I wish you would let me help you.'

He was lying back in his chair now, with his eyes half shut, and shivering like a frightened colt. The extraordinary change in one who had been the strongest of the strong kept me from realising his gravity. I put a hand on his shoulder, but he flung it off.

'For God's sake, sit down!' he said hoarsely. 'I'm going to tell you, but I'll never make you understand.'

I sat down promptly opposite him.

'It's the devil,' he said very solemnly.

I am afraid that I was rude enough to laugh. He took no notice, but sat, with the same tense, miserable air, staring over my head.

'Right,' said I. 'Then it is the devil. It's a new complaint, so it's as well I did not bring a doctor. How does it affect you?'

He made the old impotent clutch at the air with his left hand. I had the sense to become grave at once. Clearly this was some serious mental affection, some hallucination born of physical pain.

Then he began to talk in a low voice, very rapidly, with his head bent forward like a hunted animal's. I am not going to set down what he told me in his own words, for they were incoherent often, and there was much repetition But I am going to write the gist of the odd story which took my sleep away on that autumn night, with such explanations and additions I think needful. The fire died down, the wind arose, the hour grew late, and still he went on in his mumbling recitative. I forgot to smoke, forgot my comfort – everything but the odd figure of my friend and his inconceivable romance. And the night before I had been in cheerful Glenaicill!

He had returned to the House of More, he said, in the latter part of May, and shortly after he fell ill. It was a trifling sickness – influenza or something – but he had never quite recovered. The rainy weather of June depressed him, and the extreme heat of July made him listless and weary. A kind of insistent sleepiness hung over him, and he suffered much from nightmares. Toward the end of July his former health returned, but he was haunted with a curious oppression. He seemed to himself to have lost the art of being alone. There was a perpetual sound in his left ear, a kind of moving and rustling at his left side, which never left him by night or day. In addition, he had become the prey of nerves and an insensate dread of the unknown.

Ladlaw, as I have explained, was a commonplace man, with fair talents, a mediocre culture, honest instincts, and the beliefs and incredulities of his class. On abstract grounds, I should have declared him an unlikely man to be the victim of hallucination. He had a kind of dull bourgeois rationalism, which used to find reasons for all things in heaven and earth. At first he controlled his dread with proverbs. He told himself it was the sequel of his illness or the light-headedness of summer heat on the moors. But it soon outgrew his comfort. It became a living second presence, an *alter ego* which dogged his footsteps. He grew acutely afraid of it. He dared not be alone for a moment, and clung to Sibyl's company despairingly. She went off for a week's visit at the beginning of August, and he endured for seven days the tortures of the lost. The malady advanced upon him with swift steps. The presence became more real daily. In the early dawning, in the twilight, and in the first hour of the morning it seemed at times to take a visible bodily form. A kind of amorphous featureless shadow would run from his side into the darkness, and he would sit palsied with terror. Sometimes, in lonely places, his footsteps sounded double, and something would brush elbows with him. Human society alone exorcised it. With Sibyl at his side he was happy; but as soon as she left him, the thing came slinking back from the unknown to watch by him. Company might have saved him, but joined to his affliction was a crazy dread of his fellows. He would not leave his moorland home, but must bear his burden alone among the wild streams and mosses of that dismal place.

The 12th came, and he shot wretchedly, for his nerve had gone to pieces. He stood exhaustion badly, and became a dweller about the doors. But with this bodily inertness came an extraordinary intellectual revival. He read widely in a blundering way, and he speculated unceasingly. It was characteristic of the man that as soon as he left the paths of the prosaic he should seek the supernatural in a very concrete form. He assumed that he was haunted by the devil – the visible personal devil in whom our fathers believed. He waited hourly for the shape at his side to speak, but no words came. The Accuser of the Brethren in all but tangible form was his ever present companion. He felt, he declared, the spirit of old evil entering subtly into his blood. He sold his soul many times over, indeed there was no possibility of resistance. It was a Visitation more undeserved than Job's, and a thousandfold more awful.

For a week or more he was tortured with a kind of religious mania. When a man of a healthy secular mind finds himself adrift on the terrible ocean of religious troubles he is peculiarly helpless, for he has not the most rudimentary knowledge of the winds and tides. It was useless to call up his old carelessness; he had suddenly dropped into a new world where old proverbs did not apply. And all the while, mind you, there was the shrinking terror of it – an intellect all alive to the torture and the most unceasing physical fear. For a little he was on the far edge of idiocy.

Then by accident it took a new form. While sitting with Sibyl one day in the library, he began listlessly to turn over the leaves of an old book. He read a few pages, and found the hint to a story like his own.

It was some French *Life of Justinian*, one of the unscholarly productions of last century, made up of stories from Procopius and tags of Roman law. Here was his own case written down in black and white, and the man had been a king of kings. This was a new comfort, and for a little – strange though it may seem – he took a sort of pride in his affliction. He worshipped the great emperor, and read every scrap he could find on him, not excepting the *Pandectae* and the *Digesta*. He sent for the bust in the dining-room, paying a fabulous price. Then he settled himself to study his imperial prototype, and the study became an idolatry. As I have said, Ladlaw was a man of ordinary talents, and certainly of meagre imaginative power. And yet from the lies of the *Secret History* and the crudities of German legalists he had constructed a marvellous portrait of a man. Sitting there in the half-lighted room, he drew the picture: the quiet cold man with his inheritance of Dacian mysticism, holding the great world in fee, giving it law and religion, fighting its wars, building its churches, and yet all the while intent upon his own private work of making his peace with his soul – the churchman and warrior whom all the world worshipped, and yet one going through life with his lip quivering. He watched by the threshold ever at the left side. Sometimes at night, in the great brazen palace, warders heard the emperor walking in the dark corridors, alone, and yet not alone; for once, when a servant entered with a lamp, he saw his master with a face as of another world, and something beside him which had no face or shape, but which he knew to be that hoary evil which is older than the stars.

Crazy nonsense! I had to rub my eyes to assure myself that I was not sleeping. No! There was my friend with his suffering face, and this was the library of More.

And then he spoke of Theodora – actress, harlot, *dévote*, empress. For him the lady was but another part of the uttermost horror, a form of the shapeless thing at his side. I felt myself falling under the fascination. I have no nerves and little imagination, but in a flash I seemed to realise something of that awful featureless face, crouching ever at a man's hand, till darkness and loneliness come, and it rises to its mastery. I shivered as I looked at the man in the chair before me. These dull eyes of his were looking upon things I could not see, and I saw their terror. I realised that it was grim earnest for him. Nonsense or no, some devilish fancy had usurped the place of his sanity, and he was being slowly broken upon the wheel. And then, when his left hand twitched, I almost cried out. I had thought it comic before; now it seemed the last proof of tragedy.

He stopped, and I got up with loose knees and went to the window. Better the black night than the intangible horror within. I flung up the sash and looked out across the moor. There was no light; nothing but an inky darkness and the uncanny rustle of elder bushes. The sound chilled me, and I closed the window.

'The land is the old Manann,' Ladlaw was saying. 'We are beyond the pale here. Do you hear the wind?'

I forced myself back into sanity and looked at my watch. It was nearly one o'clock.

'What ghastly idiots we are!' I said. 'I am off to bed.'

Ladlaw looked at me helplessly. 'For God's sake, don't leave me alone!' he moaned. 'Get Sibyl.'

We went together back to the hall, while he kept the same feverish grasp on my arm. Someone was sleeping in a chair by the hall fire, and to my distress I recognised my hostess. The poor child must have been sadly wearied. She came forward with her anxious face.

'I'm afraid Bob has kept you very late. Henry,' she said. 'I hope you will sleep well. Breakfast at nine, you know.' And then I left them.

Over my bed there was a little picture, a reproduction of some Italian work, of Christ and the Demoniac. Some impulse made me hold my candle up to it. The madman's face was torn with passion and suffering, and his eye had the pained furtive expression which I had come to know. And by his left side there was a dim shape crouching.

I got into bed hastily, but not to sleep. I felt that my reason must be going. I had been pitchforked from our clear and cheerful modern life into the mists of old superstition. Old tragic stories of my Calvinist upbringing returned to haunt me. The man dwelt in by a devil was no new fancy, but I believed that science had docketed and analysed and explained the devil out of the world. I remembered my dabblings in the occult before I settled down to law – the story of Donisarius, the monk of Padua, the unholy legend of the Face of Proserpine, the tales of *succubi* and *incubi*, the Leannain Sith and the Hidden Presence. But here was something stranger still. I had stumbled upon that very possession which fifteen hundred years ago had made the monks of New Rome tremble and cross themselves. Some devilish occult force, lingering through the ages, had come to life after a long sleep. God knows what earthly connection there was between the splendid Emperor of the World and my prosaic friend, or between the glittering shores of the Bosporus and this moorland parish! But the land was the old Manann! The spirit may have lingered in the earth and air, a deadly legacy from Pict and Roman. I had felt the uncanniness of the place; I had augured ill of it from the first. And then in sheer disgust I rose and splashed my face with cold water.

I lay down again, laughing miserably at my credulity. That I, the sober and rational, should believe in this crazy fable was too palpably absurd. I would steel my mind resolutely against such hare-brained theories. It was a mere bodily ailment – liver out of order, weak heart, bad circulation, or something of that sort. At the worst it might be some affection of the brain, to be treated by a specialist. I vowed to myself that next morning the best doctor in Edinburgh should be brought to More.

The worst of it was that my duty compelled me to stand my ground. I foresaw the few remaining weeks of my holiday blighted. I should be tied to this moorland prison, a sort of keeper and nurse in one, tormented by silly fancies. It was a charming prospect, and the thought of Glenaicill and the woodcock made me bitter against Ladlaw. But there was no way out of it. I might do Ladlaw good, and I could not have Sibyl worn to death by his vagaries.

My ill nature comforted me, and I forgot the horror of the thing in its vexation. After that I think I fell asleep and dozed uneasily till morning. When I woke I was in a better frame of mind. The early sun had worked wonders with the moorland. The low hills stood out fresh-coloured and clear against a pale October sky; the elders sparkled with frost; the raw film of morn was rising from the little loch in tiny clouds. It was a cold, rousing day, and I dressed in good spirits and went down to breakfast.

I found Ladlaw looking ruddy and well; very different from the broken man I remembered of the night before. We were alone, for Sibyl was breakfasting in bed. I remarked on his ravenous appetite, and he smiled cheerily. He made two jokes during the meal; he laughed often, and I began to forget the events of the previous day. It seemed to me that I might still flee from More with a clear conscience. He had forgotten about his illness. When I touched distantly upon the matter he showed a blank face.

It might be that the affection had passed; on the other hand, it might return to him at the darkening. I had no means to decide. His manner was still a trifle distrait and peculiar, and I did not like the dullness in his eye. At any rate, I should spend the day in his company, and the evening would decide the question.

I proposed shooting, which he promptly vetoed. He was no good at walking, he said, and the birds were wild. This seriously limited the possible occupations. Fishing there was none, and hill-climbing was out of the question. He proposed a game at billiards, and I pointed to the glory of the morning. It would have been sacrilege to waste such sunshine in knocking balls about. Finally we agreed to drive somewhere and have lunch, and he ordered the dogcart.

In spite of all forebodings I enjoyed the day. We drove in the opposite direction from the woodland parts, right away across the moor to the coal country beyond. We lunched at the little mining town of Borrowmuir, in a small and noisy public house. The roads made bad going, the country was far from pretty, and yet the drive did not bore me. Ladlaw talked incessantly – talked as I had never heard man talk before. There was something indescribable in all he said, a different point of view, a lost groove of thought, a kind of innocence and archaic shrewdness in one. I can only give you a hint of it, by saying that it was like the mind of an early ancestor placed suddenly among modern surroundings. It was wise with a remote wisdom, and silly (now and then) with a quite antique and distant silliness.

I will give instances of both. He provided me with a theory of certain early fortifications, which must be true, which commends itself to the mind with overwhelming conviction, and yet which is so out of the way of common speculation that no man could have guessed it. I do not propose to set down the details, for I am working at it on my own account. Again, he told me the story of an old marriage custom, which till recently survived in this district – told it with full circumstantial detail and constant allusions to other customs which he could not possibly have known of. Now for the other side. He explained why well water is in winter warmer than a running stream, and this was his explanation: at the antipodes our winter is summer, consequently, the water of a well which comes through from the other side of the earth must be warm in winter and cold in summer, since in our summer it is winter there. You perceive what this is. It is no mere silliness, but a genuine effort of an early mind, which had just grasped the fact of the antipodes, to use it in explanation.

Gradually I was forced to the belief that it was not Ladlaw who was talking to me, but something speaking through him, something at once wiser and simpler. My old fear of the devil began to depart. This spirit, the exhalation, whatever it was, was ingenuous in its way, at least in its daylight aspect. For a moment I had an idea that it was a real reflex of Byzantine thought, and that by cross-examining I might make marvellous discoveries. The ardour of the scholar began to rise in me, and I asked a question about that much-debated point, the legal status of the *apocrisiarii*. To my vexation he gave no response. Clearly the intelligence of this familiar had its limits.

It was about three in the afternoon, and we had gone half of our homeward journey, when signs of the old terror began to appear. I was driving, and Ladlaw sat on my left. I noticed him growing nervous and silent, shivering at the flick of the whip, and turning halfway round toward me. Then he asked me to change places, and I had the unpleasant work of driving from the wrong side. After that I do not think he spoke once till we arrived at More, but sat huddled together, with the driving rug almost up to his chin – an eccentric figure of a man.

I foresaw another such night as the last, and I confess my heart sank. I had no stomach for more mysteries, and somehow with the approach of twilight the confidence of the day departed. The thing appeared in darker colours, and I found it in my mind to turn coward. Sibyl alone deterred me. I could not bear to think of her alone with this demented being. I remembered her shy timidity, her innocence. It was monstrous that the poor thing should be called on thus to fight alone with phantoms.

When we came to the House it was almost sunset. Ladlaw got out very carefully on the right side, and for a second stood by the horse. The sun was making our shadows long, and as I stood beyond him it seemed for a moment that his shadow was double. It may have been mere fancy, for I had not time to look twice. He was standing, as I have said, with his left side next the horse. Suddenly the harmless elderly cob fell into a very panic of fright, reared upright, and all but succeeded in killing its master. I was in time to pluck Ladlaw from under its feet, but the beast had become perfectly unmanageable, and we left a groom struggling to quiet it.

In the hall the butler gave me a telegram. It was from my clerk, summoning me back at once to an important consultation.

Here was a prompt removal of my scruples. There could be no question of my remaining, for the case was one of the first importance, which I had feared might break off my holiday. The consultation fell in vacation time to meet the convenience of certain people who were going abroad, and there was the most instant demand for my presence. I must go, and at once, and, as I hunted in the timetable, I found that in three hours' time a night train for the south would pass Borrowmuir and might be stopped by special wire.

But I had no pleasure in my freedom. I was in despair about Sibyl, and I hated myself for my cowardly relief. The dreary dining-room, the sinister bust, and Ladlaw crouching and quivering – the recollection, now that escape was before me, came back on my mind with the terror of a nightmare. My first thought was to persuade the Ladlaws to come away with me. I found them both in the drawing-room – Sibyl very fragile and pale, and her husband sitting as usual like a frightened child in the shadow of her skirts. A sight of him was enough to dispel my hope. The man was fatally ill, mentally, bodily, and who was I to attempt to minister to a mind diseased?

But Sibyl – she might be saved from the martyrdom. The servants would take care of him, and, if need be, a doctor might be got from Edinburgh to live in the house. So while he sat with vacant eyes staring into the twilight, I tried to persuade Sibyl to think of herself. I am frankly a sun worshipper. I have no taste for arduous duty, and the quixotic is my abhorrence. I laboured to bring my cousin to this frame of mind. I told her that her first duty was to herself, and that this vigil of hers was beyond human endurance. But she had no ears for my arguments.

'While Bob is ill I must stay with him,' she said always in answer, and then she thanked me for my visit, till I felt a brute and a coward. I strove to quiet my conscience, but it told me always that I was fleeing from my duty; and then, when I was on the brink of a nobler resolution, a sudden overmastering terror would take hold of me, and I would listen hysterically for the sound of the dogcart on the gravel.

At last it came, and in a sort of fever I tried to say the conventional farewells. I shook hands with Ladlaw, and when I dropped his hand it fell numbly on his knee. Then I took my leave, muttering hoarse nonsense about having had a 'charming visit', and 'hoping soon to see them both in town'. As I backed to the door, I knocked over a lamp on a small table. It crashed on the floor and went out, and at the sound Ladlaw gave a curious childish cry. I turned like a coward, ran across the hall to the front door and scrambled into the dogcart.

The groom would have driven me sedately through the park, but I must have speed or go mad. I took the reins from him and put the horse into a canter. We swung through the gates and out into the moor road, for I could have no peace till the ghoulish elder world was exchanged for the homely ugliness of civilisation. Once only I looked back, and there against the skyline, with a solitary lit window, the House of More stood lonely in the red desert.

The Outgoing of the Tide*

JOHN BUCHAN

Between the hours of twelve and one,
even at the turning of the tide.

Men come from distant parts to admire the tides of Solway, which race in at flood and retreat at ebb with a greater speed than a horse can follow. But nowhere are there queerer waters than in our own parish of Caulds, at the place called the Sker Bay, where between two horns of land a shallow estuary receives the stream of the Sker. I never daunder by its shores and see the waters hurrying like messengers from the great deep without solemn thoughts, and a memory of Scripture words on the terror of the sea. The vast Atlantic may be fearful in its wrath, but with us it is no clean open rage, but the deceit of the creature, the unholy ways of quicksands when the waters are gone, and their stealthy return like a thief in the night watches. But in times of which I write there were more awful fears than any from the violence of nature. It was before the day of my ministry in Caulds, for then I was a tot callant in short clothes in my native parish of Lesmahagow, but the worthy Dr Chrystal, who had charge of spiritual things, has told me often of the power of Satan and his emissaries in that lonely place. It was the day of warlocks and apparitions, now happily driven out by the zeal of the General Assembly. Witches pursued their wanchancy calling, bairns were spirited away, young lassies selled their souls to the Evil One, and the Accuser of the Brethren, in the shape of a black tyke, was seen about cottage doors in the gloaming. Many and earnest were the prayers of good Dr Chrystal, but the evil thing, in spite of his wrestling, grew and flourished in his midst. The parish stank of idolatry, abominable rites were practised in secret, and in all the bounds there was no one

---

* From the unpublished remains of the Revd John Dennistoun, sometime minister of the gospel in the parish of Caulds and author of *Satan's Artifices against the Elect*.

had a more evil name for the black traffic than one Alison Sempill, who bode at the Skerburnfoot.

The cottage stood nigh the burn, in a little garden, with lilyoaks and grosart bushes lining the pathway. The Sker ran by in a line among rowand trees, and the noise of its waters was ever about the place. The highroad on the other side was frequented by few, for a nearer-hand way to the west had been made through the lower Moss. Sometimes a herd from the hills would pass by with sheep, some-times a tinkler or a wandering merchant, and once in a long while the laird of Heriotside on his grey horse riding to Gledsmuir. And they who passed would see Alison hirpling in her garden, speaking to herself like the ill wife she was, or sitting on a cutty-stool by the doorside, with her eyes on other than mortal sights. Where she came from no man could tell. There were some said she was no woman, but a ghost haunting some mortal tenement. Others would threep she was gentrice, come of a persecuting family in the west, who had been ruined in the Revolution wars. She never seemed to want for siller; the house was as bright as a new preen, the yaird better delved than the manse garden; and there was routh of fowls and doos about the small steading, forbye a whee sheep and milk-kye in the fields. No man ever saw Alison at any market in the countryside, and yet the Skerburnfoot was plenished yearly in all proper order. One man only worked on the place, a doited lad who had long been a charge to the parish, and who had not the sense to fear danger or the wit to understand it. Upon all others the sight of Alison, were it but for a moment, cast a cold grue, not to be remembered without terror. It seems she was not ordinarily ill-famed, as men use the word. She was maybe sixty years in age, small and trig, with her grey hair folded neatly under her mutch. But the sight of her eyes was not a thing to forget. John Dodds said they were the een of a deer with the Devil ahint them, and, indeed, they would so appal an onlooker that a sudden unreasoning terror came into his heart, while his feet would impel him to flight. Once John, being overtaken in drink on the roadside by the cottage, and dreaming that he was burning in hell, awoke and saw the old wife hobbling toward him. Thereupon he fled soberly to the hills, and from that day became a quiet-living, humble-minded Christian. She moved about the country like a ghost, gathering herbs in dark loanings, lingering in kirkyairds, and casting a blight on innocent bairns. Once Robert Smellie found her in a ruinous kirk on the Lang Muir, where of old the idolatrous rites of Rome were practised. It was a hot day, and in the quiet place the flies buzzed in clouds, and he noted that she sat clothed in them as with a garment, yet suffering no discomfort. Then he, having mind of Beelzebub, the god of flies, fled without a halt homewards; but, falling in the coo's loan, broke two ribs and a collarbone, the whilk misfortune was much blessed to his soul. And there were darker tales in the countryside, of weans stolen, of lassies misguided, of innocent beasts cruelly tortured, and in one and all there came in the name of the wife of the Skerburnfoot. It was noted by them that kenned best that her cantrips were at their worst when the tides in the Sker Bay ebbed between the hours of twelve and one. At this season of the night the tides of mortality run lowest, and when the outgoing of these unco waters fell in with the setting of the current of life, then indeed was the hour for unholy revels. While honest men slept in their beds, the auld rudas carlines took their pleasure. That there is a delight in sin no man denies, but to most it is but a broken glint in the pauses of their conscience. But what must be the hellish joy of those lost beings who have forsworn God, and trysted with the Prince of Darkness, it is not for a Christian to say. Certain it is that it must be great, though their master waits at the end of the road to claim the wizened things they call their souls. Serious men – notably Gidden Scott in the Bach of the Hill, and Simon Wanch in the Sheilin of Chasehope – have seen Alison wandering on the wet sands, dancing to no earthy musick, while the heavens, they said, were full of lights and sounds which betokened the presence of the Prince of the Powers of the Air. It was a season of heart-searching for God's saints in Caulds, and the dispensation was blessed to not a few.

It will seem strange that in all this time the Presbytery was idle, and no effort was made to rid the place of so fell an influence. But there was a reason, and the reason, as in most like cases, was a lassie. Forbye Alison there lived at the Skerburnfoot a young maid, Ailie Sempill, who by all accounts was as good and bonnie as the other was evil. She passed for a daughter of Alison's – whether born in wedlock or not I cannot tell; but there were some said she was no kin to the auld witch wife, but some bairn spirited away from honest parents. She was young and blithe, with a face like an April morning, and a voice in her that put the laverocks to shame. When she sang in the kirk, folk have told me that they had a foretaste of the musick of the New Jerusalem, and when she came in by the village of Caulds old men stottered to their doors to look at her. Moreover, from her earliest days the bairn had some glimmerings of grace. Though no minister would visit the Skerburnfoot, or, if he went, departed quicker than he came, the girl

Ailie attended regular at the catechising at the mains of Sker. It may be that Alison thought she would be a better offering for the Devil if she were given the chance of forswearing God, or it may be that she was so occupied in her own dark business that she had no care of the bairn. Meanwhile, the lass grew up in the nurture and admonition of the Lord. I have heard Dr Chrystal say that he never had a communicant more full of the things of the Spirit. From the day when she first declared her wish to come forward to the hour when she broke bread at the table, she walked like one in a dream. The lads of the parish might cast admiring eyes on her bright cheeks and yellow hair, as she sat in her white gown in the kirk, but well they knew she was not for them. To be the bride of Christ was the thought that filled her heart, and when, at the fencing of the table, Dr Chrystal preached from Matthew 9, verse 15, 'Can the children of the bridechamber mourn as long as the bridegroom is with them?', it was remarked by sundry that Ailie's face was liker the countenance of an angel than of a mortal lass.

It is with the day of her first communion that this narrative of mine begins. As she walked home, after the morning table, she communed in secret, and her heart sang within her. She had mind of God's mercies in the past; how he had kept her feet from the snares of evil-doers which had been spread around her youth. She had been told unholy charms like the Seven South Streams and the Nine Rowand Berries, and it was noted, when she went first to the catechising, that she prayed, 'Our Father which wert in heaven', the prayer which the ill wife Alison had taught her; meaning by it Lucifer, who had been in heaven, and had been cast out therefrom. But when she had come to years of discretion, she had freely chosen the better part, and evil had ever been repelled from her soul like Gled water from the stones of Gled brig. Now she was in a rapture of holy content. The Druchen Bell – for the ungodly fashion lingered in Caulds – was ringing in her ears as she left the village, but to her it was but a kirk bell and a goodly sound. As she went through the woods where the primroses and the whitethorn were blossoming, the place seemed as the land of Elim, wherein there were twelve wells and threescore and ten palm trees. And then, as it might be, another thought came into her head, for it is ordained that frail mortality cannot long continue in holy joy. In the kirk she had been only the bride of Christ, but as she came through the wood, with the birds lilting and the winds of the world blowing, she had mind of another lover; for this lass, though so cold to men, had not escaped the common fate. It seems that the young

Heriotside, riding by one day, stopped to speir something or other, and got a glisk of Ailie's face which caught his fancy. He passed the road again many times, and then he would meet her in the gloaming or of a morning in the field as she went to fetch the kye. 'Blue are the hills that are far away', is an owercome in the countryside, and while at first on his side it may have been but a young man's fancy, to her he was like the god Apollo descending from the skies. He was good to look on, brawly dressed, and with a tongue in his head that would have wiled the bird from the tree. Moreover, he was of gentle kin, and she was a poor lass biding in a cot house with an ill-reputed mother. It seems that in time the young man, who had begun the affair with no good intentions, fell honestly in love, while she went singing about the doors as innocent as a bairn, thinking of him when her thoughts were not on higher things. So it came about that long ere Ailie reached home it was on young Heriotside that her mind dwelled, and it was the love of him that made her eyes glow and her cheeks redden.

Now it chanced that at that very hour her master had been with Alison, and the pair of them were preparing a deadly pit. Let no man say that the Devil is not a cruel tyrant. He may give his folk some scrapings of unhallowed pleasure, but he will exact tithes, yea, of anise and cummin, in return, and there is aye the reckoning to pay at the hinder end. It seems that now he was driving Alison hard. She had been remiss of late – fewer souls sent to hell, less zeal in quenching the Spirit, and, above all, the crowning offence that her bairn had communicated in Christ's kirk. She had waited overlong, and now it was like that Ailie would escape her toils. I have no skill of fancy to tell of that dark collogue, but the upshot was that Alison swore by her lost soul and the pride of sin to bring the lass into thrall to her master. The fiend had bare departed when Ailie came over the threshold to find the auld carline glunching over the fire.

It was plain she was in the worst of tempers. She flyted on the lass till the poor thing's cheek paled. 'There you gang,' she cries, 'broking wi' thae wearifu' Pharisees o' Caulds, whae daurna darken your mither's door! A bonnie dutiful child, quotha! Wumman, hae ye nae pride, or even the excuse o' a tinkler-lass?' And then she changed her voice and would be as saft as honey: 'My puir wee Ailie, was I thrawn till ye? Never mind, my bonnie. You and me are a' that's left, and we maunna be ill to ither.' And then the two had their dinner, and all the while the auld wife was crooning over the lass. 'We maun 'gree weel,' she says, 'for we're like to be our lee-lane for the rest o' our days. They tell me Heriotside is seeking Joan o' the Croft, and they're sune to be cried in Gledsmuir's kirk.'

It was the first the lass had heard of it, and you may fancy she was struck dumb. And so with one thing and other the auld witch raised the fiends of jealousy in that innocent heart. She would cry out that Heriotside was an ill-doing wastrel, and had no business to come and flatter honest lassies. And then she would speak of his gentle birth and his leddy mother, and say it was indeed presumption to hope that so great a gentleman could mean all that he said. Before long Ailie was silent and white, while her mother rimed on about men and their ways. And then she could thole it no longer, but must go out and walk by the burn to cool her hot brow and calm her thoughts, while the witch indoors laughed to herself at her devices.

For days Ailie had an absent eye and a sad face, and it so fell out that in all that time young Heriotside, who had scarce missed a day, was laid up with a broken arm and never came near her. So in a week's time she was beginning to hearken to her mother when she spoke of incantations and charms for restoring love. She kenned it was sin, but though not seven days syne she had sat at the Lord's table, so strong is love in a young heart that she was on the very brink of it. But the grace of God was stronger than her weak will. She would have none of her mother's runes and philters, though her soul cried out for them. Always when she was most disposed to listen some merciful power stayed her consent. Alison grew thrawner as the hours passed. She kenned of Heriotside's broken arm, and she feared that any day he might recover and put her stratagems to shame. And then it seems that she collogued with her master and heard word of a subtler device. For it was approaching that uncanny time of year, the festival of Beltane, when the auld pagans were wont to sacrifice to their god Baal. In this season warlocks and carlines have a special dispensation to do evil, and Alison waited on its coming with graceless joy. As it happened, the tides in the Sker Bay ebbed at this time between the hours of twelve and one, and, as I have said, this was the hour above all others when the Powers of Darkness were most potent. Would the lass but consent to go abroad in the unhallowed place at this awful season and hour of the night, she was as firmly handfasted to the Devil as if she had signed a bond with her own blood; for then, it seemed, the forces of good fled far away, the world for one hour was given over to its ancient prince, and the man or woman who willingly sought the spot was his bondservant for ever. There are deadly sins from which God's people may recover. A man may even communicate unworthily, and yet, so be it he sin not against the Holy Ghost, he may find forgiveness. But it seems that for the Beltane sin there could be no pardon, and I can testify from my own knowledge that they who once committed it became lost souls from that day. James Denchar, once a promising professor, fell thus out of sinful bravery and died blaspheming; and of Kate Mallison, who went the same road, no man can tell. Here indeed was the witch wife's chance; and she was the more keen, for her master had warned her that this was her last chance. Either Ailie's soul would be his, or her auld wrunkled body and black heart would be flung from this pleasant world to their apportioned place.

Some days later it happened that young Heriotside was stepping home over the Lang Muir about ten at night, it being his first jaunt from home since his arm had mended. He had been to the supper of the Forest Club at the Cross Keys in Gledsmuir, a clamjamphry of wild young blades who passed the wine and played at cartes once a fortnight. It seems he had drunk well, so that the world ran round about and he was in the best of tempers. The moon came down and bowed to him, and he took off his hat to it. For every step he travelled miles, so that in a little he was beyond Scotland altogether and pacing the Arabian desert. He thought he was the Pope of Rome, so he held out his foot to be kissed, and rolled twenty yards to the bottom of a small brae. Syne he was the King of France, and fought hard with a whin bush till he had banged it to pieces. After that nothing would content him but he must be a bogle, for he found his head dunting on the stars and his legs were knocking the hills together. He thought of the mischief he was doing to the auld earth, and sat down and cried at his wickedness. Then he went on, and maybe the steep road to the Moss Rig helped him, for he began to get soberer and ken his whereabouts.

On a sudden he was aware of a man linking along at his side. He cried a fine night, and the man replied. Syne, being merry from his cups, he tried to slap him on the back. The next he kenned he was rolling on the grass, for his hand had gone clean through the body and found nothing but air.

His head was so thick with wine that he found nothing droll in this. 'Faith, friend,' he says, 'that was a nasty fall for a fellow that has supped weel. Where might your road be gaun to?'

'To the World's End,' said the man, 'but I stop at the Skerburnfoot.'

'Bide the night at Heriotside,' says he. 'It's a thought out of your way, but it's a comfortable bit.'

'There's mair comfort at the Skerburnfoot,' said the dark man.

Now the mention of the Skerburnfoot brought back to him only the thought of Ailie, and not of the witch wife, her mother. So he jaloused no ill, for at the best he was slow in the uptake.

The two of them went on together for a while, Heriotside's fool head filled with the thought of the lass. Then the dark man broke silence. 'Ye 're thinkin' o' the maid Ailie Sempill,' says he.

'How ken ye that?' asked Heriotside.

'It is my business to read the hearts o' men,' said the other.

'And who may ye be?' said Heriotside, growing eerie.

'Just an auld packman,' says he, 'nae name ye wad ken, but kin to mony gentle houses.'

'And what about Ailie, you that ken sae muckle?' asked the young man.

'Naething,' was the answer – 'naething that concerns you, for ye'll never get the lass.'

'By God and I will!' says Heriotside, for he was a profane swearer.

'That's the wrong name to seek her in, ony way,' said the man.

At this the young laird struck a great blow at him with his stick, but found nothing to resist him but the hill wind.

When they had gone on a bit the dark man spoke again. 'The lassie is thirled to holy things,' says he; 'she has nae care for flesh and blood, only for devout contemplation.'

'She loves me,' says Heriotside.

'Not you,' says the other, 'but a shadow in your stead.'

At this the young man's heart began to tremble, for it seemed that there was truth in what his companion said, and he was owerdrunk to think gravely.

'I kenna whatna man ye are,' he says, 'but ye have the skill of lassies' hearts. Tell me truly, is there no way to win her to common love?'

'One way there is,' said the man, 'and for our friendship's sake I will tell you it. If ye can ever tryst wi' her on Beltane's E'en on the Sker sands, at the green link o' the burn where the sands begin, on the ebb o' the tide when the midnight is by, but afore cockrow, she'll be yours, body and soul, for this world and for ever.'

And then it appeared to the young man that he was walking his love up the grass walk of Heriotside, with the house close by him. He thought no more of the stranger he had met, but the word stuck in his heart.

It seems that about this very time Alison was telling the same tale to poor Ailie. She cast up to her every idle gossip she could think of. 'It's

Joan o' the Croft,' was aye her owercome, and she would threep that they were to be cried in kirk on the first Sabbath of May. And then she would rime on about the black cruelty of it, and cry down curses on the lover, so that her daughter's heart grew cauld with fear. It is terrible to think of the power of the world even in a redeemed soul. Here was a maid who had drunk of the well of grace and tasted of God's mercies, and yet there were moments when she was ready to renounce her hope. At those awful seasons God seemed far off and the world very nigh, and to sell her soul for love looked a fair bargain; at other times she would resist the Devil and comfort herself with prayer; but aye when she awoke there was the sore heart, and when she went to sleep there were the weary eyes. There was no comfort in the goodliness of spring or the bright sunshine weather, and she who had been wont to go about the doors lightfoot and blithe was now as dowie as a widow woman.

And then one afternoon in the hinder end of April came young Heriotside riding to the Skerburnfoot. His arm was healed, he had got him a fine new suit of green, and his horse was a mettle beast that well set off his figure. Ailie was standing by the doorstep as he came down the road, and her heart stood still with joy. But a second thought gave her anguish. This man, so gallant and braw, would never be for her; doubtless the fine suit and the capering horse were for Joan o' the Croft's pleasure. And he, in turn, when he remarked her wan cheeks and dowie eyes, had mind to what the dark man said on the muir, and saw in her a maid sworn to no mortal love. Yet his passion for her had grown fiercer than ever, and he swore to himself that he would win her back from her fantasies. She, one may believe, was ready enough to listen. As she walked with him by the Sker water his words were like musick to her ears, and Alison within doors laughed to herself and saw her devices prosper.

He spoke to her of love and his own heart, and the girl hearkened gladly. Syne he rebuked her coldness and cast scorn upon her piety, and so far was she beguiled that she had no answer. Then from one thing and another he spoke of some true token of their love. He said he was jealous, and craved something to ease his care. 'It's but a small thing I ask,' says he, 'but it will make me a happy man, and nothing ever shall come atween us. Tryst wi' me for Beltane's E'en on the Sker sands, at the green link o' the burn where the sands begin, on the ebb o' the tide when midnight is by, but afore cockcrow. For,' said he, 'that was our forbears' tryst for true lovers, and wherefore no for you and me?'

The lassie had grace given her to refuse, but with a woeful heart, and Heriotside rode off in black discontent, leaving poor Ailie to sigh her love. He came back the next day and the next, but aye he got the same answer. A season of great doubt fell upon her soul. She had no clearness in her hope, nor any sense of God's promises. The Scriptures were an idle tale to her, prayer brought her no refreshment, and she was convicted in her conscience of the unpardonable sin. Had she been less full of pride, she would have taken her troubles to good Dr Chrystal and got comfort; but her grief made her silent and timorous, and she found no help anywhere. Her mother was ever at her side, seeking with coaxings and evil advice to drive her to the irrevocable step. And all the while there was her love for the man riving in her bosom, and giving her no ease by night or day. She believed she had driven him away, and repented her denial. Only her pride held her back from going to Heriotside and seeking him herself. She watched the road hourly for a sight of his face, and when the darkness came she would sit in a corner brooding over her sorrows.

At last he came, speiring the old question. He sought the same tryst, but now he had a further tale. It seemed he was eager to get her away from the Skerburnside and auld Alison. His aunt, Lady Balerynie, would receive her gladly at his request till the day of their marriage; let her but tryst with him at the hour and place he named, and he would carry her straight to Balerynie, where she would be safe and happy. He named that hour, he said, to escape men's observation for the sake of her own good name. He named that place, for it was near her dwelling, and on the road between Balerynie and Heriotside, which fords the Sker Burn. The temptation was more than mortal heart could resist. She gave him the promise he sought, stifling the voice of conscience; and as she clung to his neck it seemed to her that heaven was a poor thing compared with a man's love.

Three days remained till Beltane's E'en, and throughout this time it was noted that Heriotside behaved like one possessed. It may be that his conscience pricked him, or that he had a glimpse of his sin and its coming punishment. Certain it is that if he had been daft before, he now ran wild in his pranks, and an evil report of him was in every mouth. He drank deep at the Cross Keys, and fought two battles with young lads that had angered him. One he let off with a touch on the shoulder; the other goes lame to this day from a wound he got in the groin. There was word of the procurator fiscal taking note of his doings, and troth, if they had continued long he must have fled the country. For a wager he rode his horse down the Dow Craig, wherefore the name of the place has been the Horseman's Craig ever since. He laid a hundred guineas with the laird of Slofferfield that he would drive four horses through the Slofferfield loch, and in the prank he had his bit chariot dung to pieces and a good mare killed. And all men observed that his eyes were wild and his face grey and thin, and that his hand would twitch, as he held the glass, like one with the palsy.

The Eve of Beltane was lower and hot in the low country, with fire hanging in the clouds and thunder grumbling about the heavens. It seems that up in the hills there had been an awesome deluge of rain, but on the coast it was still dry and lowering. It is a long road from Heriotside to the Skerburnfoot. First you go down the Heriot water, and syne over the Lang Muir to the edge of Mucklewhan. When you pass the steadings of Mirehope and Cockmalane, you turn to the right and ford the Mire Burn. That brings you on to the turnpike road, which you will ride till it bends inland, while you keep on straight over the Whinny Knowes to the Sker Bay. There, if you are in luck, you will find the tide out and the place fordable dry shod for a man on a horse. But if the tide runs, you will do well to sit down on the sands and content yourself till it turn, or it will be the solans and scarts of the Solway that will be seeing the next of you. On this Beltane's E'en, the young man, after supping with some wild young blades, bade his horse be saddled about ten o'clock. The company were eager to ken his errand, but he waved them back. 'Bide here,' he says, 'and boil the wine till I return. This is a ploy of my own on which no man follows me.' And there was that in his face, as he spoke, which chilled the wildest, and left them well content to keep to the good claret and the saft seat, and let the daft laird go his own ways.

Well and on he rode down the bridle path in the wood, along the top of the Heriot glen, and as he rode he was aware of a great noise beneath him. It was not wind, for there was none, and it was not the sound of thunder; and aye as he speired at himself what it was it grew the louder, till he came to a break in the trees. And then he saw the cause; for the Heriot was coming down in a furious flood, sixty yards wide, tearing at the roots of the aiks and flinging red waves against the dry-stone dykes. It was a sight and sound to solemnise a man's mind, deep calling unto deep, the great waters of the hills running to meet with the great waters of the sea. But Heriotside recked nothing of it, for his heart had but one thought and the eye of his fancy one figure. Never had he been so filled with love of the lass; and yet it was not happiness, but a deadly, secret fear.

As he came to the Lang Muir it was grey and dark, though there was a moon somewhere behind the clouds. It was little he could see of the road, and ere long he had tried many moss pools and sloughs, as his braw new coat bare witness. Aye in front of him was the great hill of Mucklewhan, where the road turned down by the Mire. The noise of the Heriot had not long fallen behind him ere another began, the same eerie sound of burns crying to ither in the darkness. It seemed that the whole earth was overrun with waters. Every little runnel in the bay was astir, and yet the land around him was as dry as flax, and no drop of rain had fallen. As he rode on the din grew louder, and as he came over the top of Mirehope he kenned by the mighty rushing noise that something uncommon was happening with the Mire Burn. The light from Mirehope Sheilin twinkled on his left, and had the man not been dozened with his fancies he might have observed that the steading was deserted and men were crying below in the fields. But he rode on, thinking of but one thing, till he came to the cot house of Cockmalane, which is nigh the fords of the Mire.

John Dodds, the herd who bode in the place, was standing at the door, and he looked to see who was on the road so late.

'Stop!' says he – 'stop, Laird Heriotside! I kenna what your errand is, but it is to no holy purpose that ye're out on Beltane E'en. D' ye no hear the warring o' the waters?'

And then in the still night came the sound of the Mire like the clash of armies.

'I must win over the ford,' says the laird quickly, thinking of another thing.

Ford!' cried John, in scorn. 'There'll be nae ford for you the nicht unless it was the ford o' the river Jordan. The burns are up and bigger than man ever saw them. It'll be a Beltane's E'en that a' folk will remember. They tell me that Gled valley is like a loch, and that there's an awesome heap o' folk drouned in the hills. Gin ye were ower the Mire, what about crossin' the Caulds and the Sker?' says he, for he jaloused he was going to Gledsmuir.

And then it seemed that that word brought the laird to his senses. He looked the airt the rain was coming from, and he saw it was the airt the Sker flowed. In a second, he has told me, the works of the Devil were revealed to him. He saw himself a tool in Satan's hands; he saw his tryst a device for the destruction of the body as it was assuredly meant for the destruction of the soul; and there came black on his mind the picture of an innocent lass borne down by the waters, with no place for repentance. His heart grew cold in his breast. He had but one thought – a sinful and reckless one: to get to her side, that the two might go together to their account. He heard the roar of the Mire as in a dream, and when John Dodds laid hands on his bridle he felled him to the earth. And the next seen of it was the laird riding the floods like a man possessed.

The horse was the grey stallion he aye rode, the very beast he had ridden for many a wager with the wild lads of the Cross Keys. No man but himself durst back it, and it had lamed many a hostler lad and broke two necks in its day. But it seems it had the mettle for any flood, and took the Mire with little spurring. The herds on the hillside looked to see man and steed swept into eternity; but though the red waves were breaking about his shoulders, and he was swept far down, he aye held on for the shore. The next thing the watchers saw was the laird struggling up the far bank and casting his coat from him, so that he rode in his sark. And then he set off like a wildfire across the muir toward the turnpike road. Two men saw him on the road, and have recorded their experience. One was a gangrel, by name McNab, who was travelling from Gledsmuir to Allerkirk with a heavy pack on his back and a bowed head. He heard a sound like wind afore him, and, looking up, saw coming down the road a grey horse stretched out to a wild gallop, and a man on its back with a face like a soul in torment. He kenned not whether it was devil or mortal, but flung himself on the roadside and lay like a corp for an hour or more, till the rain aroused him. The other was one Sim Doolittle, the fish hawker from Allerfoot, jogging home in his fish cart from Gledsmuir fair. He had drunk more than was fit for him, and he was singing some light song, when he saw approaching, as he said, the pale horse mentioned in the Revelation, with Death seated as the rider. Thought of his sins came on him like a thunderclap, fear loosened his knees. He leaped from the cart to the road, and from the road to the back of a dyke, thence he flew to the hills, and was found the next morning far up among the Mire Craigs, while his horse and cart were gotten on the Aller sands, the horse lamed and the cart without the wheels.

At the tollhouse the road turns inland to Gledsmuir, and he who goes to the Sker Bay must leave it and cross the wild land called the Whinny Knowes, a place rough with bracken and foxes' holes and old stone cairns. The tollman, John Gilzean, was opening the window to get a breath of air in the lower night, when he heard or saw the approaching horse. He kenned the beast for Heriotside's, and, being a friend of the laird's, he ran down in all haste to open the yett, wondering to himself about the laird's errand on this night. A voice came down the road to him bidding him hurry, but John's old fingers were slow with the keys, and so it happened that the horse had to stop, and John had time to look up at the gast and woeful face.

'Where away the nicht sae late, laird?' says John.

'I go to save a soul from hell,' was the answer.

And then it seems that through the open door there came the chapping of a clock.

'Whatna hour is that?' asks Heriotside.

'Midnicht,' says John, trembling, for he did not like the look of things.

There was no answer but a groan, and horse and man went racing down the dark hollows of the Whinny Knowes.

How he escaped a broken neck in that dreadful place no human being will ever ken. The sweat, he has told me, stood in cold drops upon his forehead; he scarcely was aware of the saddle in which he sat, and his eyes were stelled in his head so that he saw nothing but the sky ayont him. The night was growing colder, and there was a small sharp wind stirring from the east. But hot or cold, it was all one to him, who was already cold as death. He heard not the sound of the sea nor the peeseweeps startled by his horse, for the sound that ran in his ears was the roaring Sker water and a girl's cry. The thought kept goading him, and he spurred the grey horse till the creature was madder than himself. It leaped the hole which they call the Devil's Mull as I would step over a thristle, and the next he kenned he was on the edge of the Sker Bay.

It lay before him white and ghaistly, with mist blowing in wafts across it and a slow swaying of the tides. It was the better part of a mile wide, but save for some fathoms in the middle, where the Sker current ran, it was no deeper even at flood than a horse's fetlocks. It looks eerie at bright midday, when the sun is shining and whaups are crying among the seaweeds; but think what it was on that awesome night, with the Powers of Darkness brooding over it like a cloud! The rider's heart quailed for a moment in natural fear. He stepped his beast a few feet in, still staring afore him like a daft man. And then something in the sound or the feel of the waters made him look down, and he perceived that the ebb had begun and the tide was flowing out to sea.

He kenned that all was lost, and the knowledge drove him to stark despair. His sins came in his face like birds of night, and his heart shrunk like a pea. He knew himself for a lost soul, and all that he loved in the world was out in the tides. There, at any rate, he could go, too, and give back that gift of life he had so blackly misused. He cried small and saft like a bairn, and drove the grey out into the water. And aye as he spurred it the foam should have been flying as high as his head, but in that uncanny hour there was no foam; only the waves running sleek like oil. It was not long ere he had come to the Sker channel, where the red moss waters were roaring to the sea – an ill place to ford in midsummer heat, and certain death, as folk reputed it, at the smallest spate. The grey was swimming; but it seemed the Lord had other purposes for him than death, for neither man nor horse could droun. He tried to leave the saddle, but he could not, he flung the bridle from him, but the grey held on as if some strong hand were guiding. He cried out upon the Devil to help his own; he renounced his Maker and his God: but whatever his punishment, he was not to be drouned. And then he was silent, for something was coming down the tide.

It came down as quiet as a sleeping bairn, straight for him as he sat with his horse breasting the waters; and as it came the moon crept out of a cloud, and he saw a glint of yellow hair. And then his madness died away, and he was himself again, a weary and stricken man. He hung down over the tide and caught the body in his arms, and then let the grey make for the shallows. He cared no more for the Devil and all his myrmidons, for he kenned brawly he was damned. It seemed to him that his soul had gone from him, and he was as toom as a hazel shell. His breath rattled in his throat, the tears were dried up in his head, his body had lost its strength, and yet he clung to the drouned maid as to a hope of salvation. And then he noted something at which he marvelled dumbly. Her hair was drookit back from her clay-cold brow, her eyes were shut, but in her face there was the peace of a child; it seemed even that her lips were smiling. Here, certes, was no lost soul, but one who had gone joyfully to meet her Lord. It may be in that dark hour at the burn-foot, before the spate caught her, she had been given grace to resist her adversary and fling herself upon God's mercy. And it would seem that it had been granted; for when he came to the Skerburnfoot, there in the corner sat the weird wife Alison, dead as a stone.

For days Heriotside wandered the country, or sat in his own house with vacant eye and trembling hands. Conviction of sin held him like a vice: he saw the lassie's death laid at his door; her face haunted him by day and night, and the word of the Lord dirled in his ears, telling of wrath and punishment. The greatness of his anguish wore him to a shadow, and at last he was stretched on his bed and like to perish. In his extremity worthy Dr Chrystal went to him unasked, and strove to comfort him. Long, long the good man wrestled, but it seemed as if his ministrations were to be of no avail. The fever left his body, and he rose to stotter about the doors; but he was still in his torments, and the mercy-seat was far from him. At last in the back end of the year came Mungo Muirhead to Caulds to the autumn communion, and nothing would serve him but he must try his hand at the storm-tossed soul. He spoke with power and unction, and a blessing came with his words: the black cloud lifted and showed a glimpse of grace, and in a little the man had some assurance of salvation. He became a pillar of Christ's kirk, prompt to check abominations, notably the sin of witchcraft; foremost in good works, but with it all a humble man who walked contritely till his death. When I came first to Caulds I sought to prevail upon him to accept the eldership, but he aye put me by, and when I heard his tale I saw that he had done wisely. I mind him well as he sat in his chair or daundered through Caulds, a kind word for everyone and sage counsel in time of distress, but withal a severe man to himself and a crucifier of the body. It seems that this severity weakened his frame, for three years syne come Martinmas he was taken ill with a fever of the bowels, and after a week's sickness he went to his account, where I trust he is accepted.

Skule Skerry

John Buchan

Who's there, besides foul weather?
King Lear

Mr Anthony Hurrell was a small man, thin to the point of emaciation, but erect as a ramrod and wiry as a cairn terrier. There was no grey in his hair, and his pale far-sighted eyes had the alertness of youth, but his lean face was so wrinkled by weather that in certain lights it looked almost venerable, and young men, who at first sight had imagined him their contemporary, presently dropped into the 'sir' reserved for indisputable seniors. His actual age was, I believe, somewhere in the forties. He had inherited a small property in Northumberland, where he had accumulated a collection of the rarer wildfowl; but much of his life had been spent in places so remote that his friends could with difficulty find them on the map. He had written a dozen ornithological monographs, was joint editor of the chief modern treatise on British birds, and had been the first man to visit the tundra of the Yenisei. He spoke little and that with an agreeable hesitation, but his ready smile, his quick interest, and the impression he gave of having a fathomless knowledge of strange modes of life, made him a popular and intriguing figure among his friends. Of his doings in the War he told us nothing; what we knew of them – and they were sensational enough in all conscience – we learned elsewhere. It was Nightingale's story which drew him from his customary silence. At the dinner following that event he made certain comments on current explanations of the super-normal. 'I remember once,' he began, and before we knew he had surprised us by embarking on a tale.

He had scarcely begun before he stopped. 'I'm boring you,' he said depreciatingly. 'There's nothing much in the story . . . You see, it all happened, so to speak, inside my head . . . I don't want to seem an egotist . . . '

'Don't be an ass, Tony,' said Lamancha. 'Every adventure takes place chiefly inside the head of somebody. Go on. We're all attention.'

'It happened a good many years ago,' Hurrell continued, 'when I was quite a young man. I wasn't the cold scientist then that I fancy I am today. I took up birds in the first instance chiefly because they fired what imagination I possess. They fascinated me, for they seemed of all created things the nearest to pure spirit – those little beings with a normal temperature of 125°. Think of it. The goldcrest, with a stomach no bigger than a bean, flies across the North Sea! The curlew sandpiper, which breeds so far north that only about three people have ever seen its nest, goes to Tasmania for its holidays! So I always went bird-hunting with a queer sense of expectation and a bit of a tremor, as if I were walking very near the boundaries of the things we are not allowed to know. I felt this especially in the migration season. The small atoms, coming God knows whence and going God knows whither, were sheer mystery – they belonged to a world built in different dimensions from ours. I don't know what I expected, but I was always waiting for something, as much in a flutter as a girl at her first ball. You must realise that mood of mine to understand what follows.

'One year I went to the Norland Islands for the spring migration. Plenty of people do the same, but I had the notion to do something a little different. I had a theory that migrants go north and south on a fairly narrow road. They have their corridors in the air as clearly defined as a highway, and keep an inherited memory of these corridors, like the stout conservatives they are. So I didn't go to the Blue Banks or to Noop or to Hermaness or any of the obvious places, where birds might be expected to make their first landfall.

'At that time I was pretty well read in the sagas, and had taught myself Icelandic for the purpose. Now it is written in the Saga of Earl Skuli, which is part of the Jarla Saga or Saga of the Earls, that Skuli, when he was carving out his earldom in the Scots islands, had much to do with a place called the Isle of the Birds. It is mentioned repeatedly, and the saga-man has a lot to say about the amazing multitude of birds there. It couldn't have been an ordinary gullery, for the Northmen saw too many of these to think them worth mentioning. I got it into my head that it must have been one of the alighting places of the migrants, and was probably as busy a spot today as in the eleventh century. The saga said it was near Halmarsness, and that is on the west side of the island of Una, so to Una I decided to go. I fairly got that Isle of Birds on the brain. From the map it might be any one of a dozen skerries under the shadow of Halmarsness.

'I remember that I spent a good many hours in the British Museum before I started, hunting up the scanty records of those parts. I found – I think it was in Adam of Bremen – that a succession of holy men had lived on the isle, and that a chapel had been built there and endowed by Earl Rognvald, which came to an end in the time of Malise of Strathearn. There was a bare mention of the place, but the chronicler had one curious note. *Insula Avium*, ran the text, *quae est ultima insula et proximo Abysso*. I wondered what on earth he meant. The place was not ultimate in any geographical sense, neither the farthest north nor the farthest west of the Norlands. And what was the "abyss"? In monkish Latin the word generally means Hell – Bunyan's Bottomless Pit – and sometimes the grave; but neither meaning seemed to have much to do with an ordinary sea skerry.

'I arrived at Una about eight o'clock in a May evening, having been put across from Voss in a flit-boat. It was a quiet evening, the sky without clouds but so pale as to be almost grey, the sea grey also but with a certain iridescence in it, and the low lines of the land a combination of hard greys and umbers, cut into by the harder white of the lighthouse. I can never find words to describe that curious quality of light that you get up in the North. Sometimes it is like looking at the world out of deep water – Farquharson used to call it "milky", and one saw what he meant. Generally it is a sort of essence of light, cold and pure and distilled, as if it were reflected from snow. There is no colour in it, and it makes thin shadows. Some people find it horribly depressing – Farquharson said it reminded him of a churchyard in the early morning where all his friends were buried – but personally I found it tonic and comforting. But it made me feel very near the edge of the world.

'There was no inn, so I put up at the post office, which was on a causeway between a fresh-water loch and a sea voe, so that from the doorstep you could catch brown trout on one side and sea-trout on the other. Next morning I set off for Halmarsness, which lay five miles to the west over a flat moorland all puddled with tiny lochans. There seemed to be nearly as much water as land. Presently I came to a bigger loch under the lift of ground which was Halmarsness. There was a gap in the ridge through which I looked straight out to the Atlantic, and there in the middle distance was what I knew instinctively to be my island.

'It was perhaps a quarter of a mile long, low for the most part, but rising in the north to a grassy knoll beyond the reach of any tides. In parts it narrowed to a few yards' width, and the lower levels must often have been awash. But it was an island, not a reef, and I thought I could make out the remains of the monkish cell. I climbed Halmarsness, and there, with nesting skuas swooping angrily about my head, I got a better view. It was certainly my island, for the rest of the archipelago were inconsiderable skerries, and I realised that it might well be a resting-place for migrants, for the mainland cliffs were too thronged with piratical skuas and other jealous fowl to be comfortable for weary travellers.

'I sat for a long time on the headland looking down from the three hundred feet of basalt to the island half a mile off – the last bid of solid earth between me and Greenland. The sea was calm for Norland waters, but there was a snowy edging of surf to the skerries which told of a tide rip. Two miles farther south I could see the entrance to the famous Roost of Una, where, when tide and wind collide, there is a wall like a house, so that a small steamer cannot pass it. The only sign of human habitation was a little grey farm in the lowlands toward the Roost, but the place was full of the evidence of man – a herd of Norland ponies, each tagged with its owner's name – grazing sheep of the piebald Norland breed – a broken barbed-wire fence that drooped over the edge of the cliff. I was only an hour's walk from a telegraph office, and a village which got its newspapers not more than three days late. It was a fine spring noon, and in the empty bright land there was scarcely a shadow . . . All the same, as I looked down at the island I did not wonder that it had been selected for attention by the saga-man and had been reputed holy. For it had an air of concealing something, though it was as bare as a billiard-table. It was an intruder, an irrelevance in the picture, planted there by some celestial caprice. I decided forthwith to make my camp on it, and the decision, inconsequently enough, seemed to me to be something of a venture.

'That was the view taken by John Ronaldson, when I talked to him after dinner. John was the postmistress's son, more fisherman than crofter, like all Norlanders, a skilful sailor and an adept at the dipping lug, and noted for his knowledge of the western coast. He had difficulty in understanding my plan, and when he identified my island he protested.

' "Not Skule Skerry!" he cried. "What would take ye there, man? Ye'll get a' the birds ye want on Halmarsness and a far better bield. Ye'll be blawn away on the skerry, if the wund rises."

'I explained to him my reasons as well as I could, and I answered his fears about a gale by pointing out that the island was sheltered by the cliffs from the prevailing winds, and could be scourged only from the south, south-west or west, quarters from which the wind rarely blew in May. "It'll be cauld," he said, "and wat." I pointed out that I had a tent and was accustomed to camping. "Ye'll starve" – I expounded my proposed methods of commissariat. "It'll be an ill job getting ye on and off' – but after cross-examination he admitted that ordinarily the tides were not difficult, and that I could get a rowboat to a beach below the farm I had seen – its name was Sgurravoe. Yet when I had said all this he still raised objections, till I asked him flatly what was the matter with Skule Skerry.

' "Naebody gangs there," he said gruffly.

' "Why should they?" I asked. "I'm only going to watch the birds."

'But the fact that it was never visited seemed to stick in his throat, and he grumbled out something that surprised me. "It has an ill name," he said. But when I pressed him he admitted that there was no record of shipwreck or disaster to account for the ill name. He repeated the words "Skule Skerry" as if they displeased him. "Folk dinna gang near it. It has aye had an ill name. My grandfather used to say that the place wasna canny."

'Now your Norlander has nothing of the Celt in him, and is as different from the Hebridean as a Northumbrian from a Cornishman. They are a fine, upstanding, hard-headed race, almost pure Scandinavian in blood, but they have as little poetry in them as a Manchester Radical. I should have put them down as utterly free from superstition, and, in all my many visits to the islands, I have never yet come across a folk-tale – hardly even a historical legend. Yet here was John Ronaldson, with his weather-beaten face and stiff chin and shrewd blue eyes, declaring that an innocent-looking island "wasna canny", and showing the most remarkable disinclination to go near it.

'Of course all this only made me keener. Besides, it was called Skule Skerry, and the name could only come from Earl Skuli; so it was linked up authentically with the oddments of information I had collected in the British Museum – the Jarla Saga and Adam of Bremen and all the rest of it. John finally agreed to take me over next morning in his boat, and I spent the rest of the day in collecting my kit. I had a small tent, and a Wolseley valise and half a dozen rugs and, since I had brought a big box of tinned stuffs from the Stores, all I needed was flour and meal and some simple groceries. I learned that there was a well on the island, and that I could count on sufficient driftwood for my fire, but to make certain I took a sack of coals and another of peats. So I set off next day in John's boat, ran with the wind through the Roost of Una when the ride was right, tacked up the coast, and came to the skerry early in the afternoon.

'You could see that John hated the place. We ran into a cove on the east side, and he splashed ashore as if he expected to have his landing opposed, looking all the time sharply about him. When he carried my stuff to a hollow under the knoll, which gave a certain amount of shelter, his head was always twisting round. To me the place seemed to be the last word in forgotten peace. The swell lipped gently on the reefs and the little pebbled beaches, and only the babble of gulls from Halmarsness broke the stillness.

'John was clearly anxious to get away, but he did his duty by me. He helped me to get the tent up, found a convenient place for my boxes, pointed out the well and filled my water bucket, and made a zareba of stones to protect my camp on the Atlantic side. We had brought a small dinghy along with us, and this was to be left with me, so that when I wanted I could row across to the beach at Sgurravoe. As his last service he fixed an old pail between two boulders on the summit of the knoll, and filled it with oily waste, so that it could be turned into a beacon.

' "Ye'll maybe want to come on," he said, "and the boat will maybe no be there. Kindle your flare, and they'll see it at Sgurravoe and get the word to me, and I'll come for ye though the Muckle Black Silkie himsel' was hunkerin' on the skerry."

'Then he looked up and sniffed the air. "I dinna like the set of the sky," he declared. "It's a bad weatherhead. There'll be mair wund than I like in the next four-and-twenty hours."

'So saying, he hoisted his sail, and presently was a speck on the waters towards the Roost. There was no need for him to hurry, for the tide was now wrong, and before he could pass the Roost he would have three hours to wait on this side of the Mull. But the man, usually so deliberate and imperturbable, had been in a fever to be gone.

'His departure left me in a curious mood of happy loneliness and pleasurable expectation. I was left solitary with the seas and the birds. I laughed to think that I had found a streak of superstition in the granite John. He and his Muckle Black Silkie! I knew the old legend of the North which tells how the Finns, the ghouls that live in the deeps of the ocean, can on occasion don a seal's skin and come to land to play havoc with mortals. But *diablerie* and this isle of mine were worlds apart. I looked at it as the sun dropped, drowsing in the opal-coloured tides, under a sky in which pale clouds made streamers like a spectral *aurora borealis*, and I thought that I had stumbled upon one of those places where Nature seems to invite one to her secrets. As the light died the sky was flecked as with the roots and branches of some great nebular tree. That would be the "weatherhead" of which John Ronaldson had spoken.

'I set my fire going, cooked my supper, and made everything snug for the night. I had been right in my guess about the migrants. It must have been about ten o'clock when they began to arrive – after my fire had died out and I was smoking my last pipe before getting into my sleeping-bag. A host of fieldfares settled gently on the south part of the skerry. A faint light lingered till after midnight, but it was not easy to distinguish the little creatures, for they were aware of my presence and did not alight within a dozen yards of me. But I made out bramblings and buntings and what I thought was the Greenland wheatear; also jack snipe and sanderling; and I believed from their cries that the curlew sandpiper and the whimbrel were there. I went to sleep in a state of high excitement, promising myself a fruitful time on the morrow.

'I slept badly, as one often does one's first night in the open. Several times I woke with a start, under the impression that I was in a boat rowing swiftly with the ride. And every time I woke I heard the flutter of myriad birds, as if a velvet curtain were being slowly switched along an oak floor. At last I fell into deeper sleep, and when I opened my eyes it was full day.

'The first thing that struck me was that it had got suddenly colder. The sky was stormily red in the east, and masses of woolly clouds were banking in the north. I lit my fire with numbed fingers and hastily made tea. I could see the nimbus of seafowl over Halmarsness, but there was only one bird left on my skerry. I was certain from its forked tail that it was a Sabine's gull, but before I got my glass out it was disappearing into the haze towards the north. The sight cheered and excited me, and I cooked my breakfast in pretty good spirits.

'That was literally the last bird that came near me, barring the ordinary shearwaters and gulls and cormorants that nested round about Halmarsness. (There was not one single nest of any sort on the island. I had heard of that happening before in places which were regular halting-grounds for migrants.) The travellers must have had an inkling of the coming weather and were waiting somewhere well to the south. For about nine o'clock it began to blow. Great God, how it blew! You must go to the Norlands if you want to know what wind can be. It is like being on a mountain-top, for there is no high ground to act as a wind-break. There was no rain, but the surf broke in showers and every foot of the skerry was drenched with it. In a trice Halmarsness was hidden, and I seemed to be in the centre of a maelstrom, choked with scud and buffeted on every side by swirling waters.

'Down came my tent at once. I wrestled with the crazy canvas and got a black eye from the pole, but I managed to drag the ruins into the shelter of the zareba which John had built, and tumble some of the bigger boulders on it. There it lay, flapping like a sick albatross. The water got into my food boxes, and soaked my fuel, as well as every inch of my clothing . . . I had looked forward to a peaceful day of watching and meditation, when I could write up my notes; and instead I spent a morning like a rugger scrum. I might have enjoyed it, if I hadn't been so wet and cold and could have got a better lunch than some clammy mouthfuls out of a tin. One talks glibly about being "blown off" a place, generally an idle exaggeration – but that day I came very near the reality. There were times when I had to hang on for dear life to one of the bigger stones to avoid being trundled into the yeasty seas.

'About two o'clock the volume of the storm began to decline, and then for the first rime I thought about the boat. With a horrid sinking of the heart I scrambled to the cove where we had beached it. It had been drawn up high and dry, and its painter secured to a substantial boulder. But now there was not a sign of it except a ragged rope-end round the stone. The tide had mounted to its level, and tide and wind had smashed the rotten painter. By this time what was left of it would be tossing in the Roost.

'This was a pretty state of affairs. John was due to visit me next day, but I had a cold twenty-four hours ahead of me. There was of course the flare he had left me, but I was not inclined to use this. It looked like throwing up the sponge and confessing that my expedition had been a farce. I felt miserable, but obstinate, and, since the weather was clearly mending, I determined to put the best face on the business, so I went back to the wreckage of my camp, and tried to tidy up. There was still far too much wind to do anything with the tent, but the worst of the spindrift had ceased, and I was able to put out my bedding and some of my provender to dry. I got a dry jersey out of my pack, and, as I was wearing fisherman's boots and oilskins, I managed to get some slight return of comfort. Also at last I succeeded in lighting a pipe. I found a corner under the knoll which gave me a modicum of shelter, and I settled myself to pass the time with tobacco and my own thoughts.

'About three o'clock the wind died away completely. That I did not like, for a dead lull in the Norlands is often the precursor of a new gale. Indeed, I never remembered a time when some wind did not blow, and I had heard that when such a thing happened people came out of their houses to ask what the matter was. But now we had the deadest sort of calm. The sea was still wild and broken, the tides raced by like a mill-stream, and a brume was gathering which shut out Halmarsness – shut out every prospect except a narrow circuit of grey water. The cessation of the racket of the gale made the place seem uncannily quiet. The present tumult of the sea, in comparison with the noise of the morning, seemed no more than a mutter and an echo.

'As I sat there I became conscious of an odd sensation. I seemed to be more alone, more cut off, not only from my fellows but from the habitable earth, than I had ever been before. It was like being in a small boat in mid-Atlantic – but worse, if you understand me, for that would have been loneliness in the midst of a waste which was nevertheless surrounded and traversed by the works of man, whereas now I felt that I was clean outside man's ken. I had come somehow to the edge of that world where life is, and was very close to the world which has only death in it.

'At first I do not think there was much fear in the sensation – chiefly strangeness, but the kind of strangeness which awes without exciting. I tried to shake off the mood, and got up to stretch myself. There was not much room for exercise, and as I moved with stiff legs along the reefs I slipped into the water, so that I got my arms wet. It was cold beyond belief – the very quintessence of deathly Arctic ice, so cold that it seemed to sear and bleach the skin.

'From that moment I date the most unpleasant experience of my life. I became suddenly the prey of a black depression, shot with the red lights of terror. But it was not a numb terror, for my brain was acutely alive . . . I had the sense to try to make tea, but my fuel was still too damp, and the best I could do was to pour half the contents of my brandy flask into a cup and swallow the stuff. That did not properly warm my chilled body, but – since I am a very temperate man – it speeded up my thoughts instead of calming them. I felt myself on the brink of a childish panic.

'One thing I thought I saw clearly – the meaning of Skule Skerry.

By some alchemy of nature, at which I could only guess, it was on the track by which the North exercised its spell, a cableway for the magnetism of that cruel frozen Uttermost, which man might penetrate but could never subdue or understand. Though the latitude was only 61°, there were folds and tucks in space, and this isle was the edge of the world. Birds knew it, and the old Northmen, who were primitive beings like the birds, knew it. That was why an inconsiderable skerry had been given the name of a conquering Jarl. The old Church knew it, and had planted a chapel to exorcise the demons of darkness. I wondered what sights the hermit, whose cell had been on the very spot where I was cowering, had seen in the winter dusks.

'It may have been partly the brandy acting on an empty stomach, and partly the extreme cold, but my brain, in spite of my efforts to think rationally, began to run like a dynamo. It is difficult to explain my mood, but I seemed to be two persons – one a reasonable modern man trying to keep sane and scornfully rejecting the fancies which the other, a cast-back to something elemental, was furiously spinning. But it was the second that had the upper hand . . . I felt myself loosed from my moorings, a mere waif on uncharted seas. What is the German phrase? *Urdummheit* – Primal Idiocy? That was what was the matter with me. I had fallen out of civilisation into the Outlands and was feeling their spell . . . I could not think, but I could remember, and what I had read of the Norse voyagers came back to me with horrid persistence. They had known the outland terrors – the Sea Walls at the world's end, the Curdled Ocean with its strange beasts. Those men did not sail north as we did, in steamers, with modern food and modern instruments, huddled into crews and expeditions. They had gone out almost alone, in brittle galleys, and they had known what we could never know.

'And then, I had a shattering revelation. I had been groping for a word and I suddenly got it. It was Adam of Bremen's *proximo Abysso*. This island was next door to the Abyss, and the Abyss was that blanched world of the North which was the negation of life.

'That unfortunate recollection was the last straw. I remember that I forced myself to get up and try again to kindle a fire. But the wood was still too damp, and I realised with consternation that I had very few matches left, several boxes having been ruined that morning. As I staggered about I saw the flare which John had left for me, and almost lit it. But some dregs of manhood prevented me – I could not own defeat in that babyish way – I must wait till John Ronaldson came for me next morning. Instead I had another mouthful of brandy, and tried to eat some of my sodden biscuits. But I could scarcely swallow, the infernal cold, instead of rousing hunger, had given me only a raging thirst.

'I forced myself to sit down again with my face to the land. You see, every moment I was becoming more childish. I had the notion – I cannot call it a thought – that down the avenue from the North something terrible and strange might come. My nervous state must have been pretty bad, for though I was cold and empty and weary I was scarcely conscious of physical discomfort. My heart was fluttering like a scared boy's; and all the time the other part of me was standing aside and telling me not to be a damned fool . . . I think that if I had heard the rustle of a flock of migrants I might have pulled myself together, but not a blessed bird had come near me all day. I had fallen into a world that killed life, a sort of Valley of the Shadow of Death.

'The brume spoiled the long northern twilight, and presently it was almost dark. At first I thought that this was going to help me, and I got hold of several of my half-dry rugs, and made a sleeping-place. But I could not sleep, even if my teeth had stopped chattering, for a new and perfectly idiotic idea possessed me. It came from a recollection of John Ronaldson's parting words. What had he said about the Black Silkie – the Finn who came out of the deep and hunkered on this skerry? Raving mania! But on this lost island in the darkening night, with icy tides lapping about me, was any horror beyond belief?

'Still, the sheer idiocy of the idea compelled a reaction. I took hold of my wits with both hands and cursed myself for a fool. I could even reason about my folly. I knew what was wrong with me. I was suffering from *panic* – a physical affection produced by natural causes, explicable, though as yet not fully explained. Two friends of mine had once been afflicted with it: one in a lonely glen in the Jotunheim, so that he ran for ten miles over stony hills till he found a saeter and human companionship; the other in a Bavarian forest, where both he and his guide tore for hours through the thicket till they dropped like logs beside a highroad. This reflection enabled me to take a pull on myself and to think a little ahead. If my troubles were physical then there would be no shame in looking for the speediest cure. Without further delay I must leave this God-forgotten place.

'The flare was all right, for it had been set on the highest point of the island, and John had covered it with a peat. With one of my few remaining matches I lit the oily waste, and a great smoky flame leapt to heaven.

'If the half-dark had been eerie, this sudden brightness was eerier. For a moment the glare gave me confidence, but as I looked at the circle of moving waters evilly lit up, all my terrors returned . . . How long would it take John to reach me? They would see it at once at Sgurravoe – they would be on the look-out for it – John would not waste time, for he had tried to dissuade me from coming – an hour – two hours at the most . . .

'I found I could not take my eyes from the waters. They seemed to flow from the north in a strong stream, black as the heart of the elder ice, irresistible as fate, cruel as hell. There seemed to be uncouth shapes swimming in them, which were more than the flickering shadows from the flare . . . Something portentous might at any moment come down that river of death . . . Someone . . .

'And then my knees gave under me and my heart shrank like a pea, for I saw that the someone had come.

'He drew himself heavily out of the sea, wallowed for a second, and then raised his head and, from a distance of five yards, looked me blindly in the face. The flare was fast dying down, but even so at that short range it cast a strong light, and the eyes of the awful being seemed to be dazed by it. I saw a great dark head like a bull's – an old face wrinkled as if in pain – a gleam of enormous broken teeth – a dripping beard – all formed on other lines than God has made mortal creatures. And on the right of the throat was a huge scarlet gash. The thing seemed to be moaning, and then from it came a sound – whether of anguish or wrath I cannot tell – but it seemed to be the cry of a tortured fiend.

'That was enough for me. I pitched forward in a swoon, hitting my head on a stone, and in that condition three hours later John Ronaldson found me.

'They put me to bed at Sgurravoe with hot earthenware bottles, and the doctor from Voss next day patched up my head and gave me a sleeping draught. He declared that there was little the matter with me except shock from exposure, and promised to set me on my feet in a week.

'For three days I was as miserable as a man could be, and did my best to work myself into a fever. I had said not a word about my experience, and left my rescuers to believe that my only troubles were cold and hunger, and that I had lit the flare because I had lost the boat. But during these days I was in a critical state. I knew that there was nothing wrong with my body, but I was gravely concerned about my mind.

'For this was my difficulty. If that awful thing was a mere figment of my brain, then I had better be certified at once as a lunatic. No sane man could get into such a state as to see such portents with the certainty with which I had seen that creature come out of the night. If, on the other hand, the thing was a real presence, then I had looked on something outside natural law, and my intellectual world was broken in pieces. I was a scientist, and a scientist cannot admit the supernatural. If with my eyes I had beheld the monster in which Adam of Bremen believed, which holy men had exorcised, which even the shrewd Norlanders shuddered at as the Black Silkie, then I must burn my books and revise my creed. I might take to poetry or theosophy, but I would never be much good again at science.

'On the third afternoon I was trying to doze, and with shut eyes fighting off the pictures which tormented my brain. John Ronaldson and the farmer of Sgurravoe were talking at the kitchen door. The latter asked some question, and John replied: "Aye, it was a wall-ross and nae mistake. It cam ashore at Gloop Ness and Sandy Fraser has gotten the skin of it. It was deid when he found it, but no long deid. The puir beast would drift south on some floe, and it was sair hurt, for Sandy said it had a hole in its throat ye could put your nieve in. There hasna been a wall-ross come to Una since my grandfather's day."

'I turned my face to the wall and composed myself to sleep. For now I knew that I was sane, and need not forswear science.'

No Man's Land

John Buchan

I

THE SHIELING OF FARAWA

It was with a light heart and a pleasing consciousness of holiday that I set out from the inn at Allermuir to tramp my fifteen miles into the unknown. I walked slowly, for I carried my equipment on my back – my basket, fly-books and rods, my plaid of Grant tartan (for I boast myself a distant kinsman of that house), and my great staff, which had tried ere then the front of the steeper Alps. A small valise with books and some changes of linen clothing had been sent on ahead in the shepherd's own hands. It was yet early April, and before me lay four weeks of freedom – twenty-eight blessed days in which to take fish and smoke the pipe of idleness. The Lent term had pulled me down, a week of modest enjoyment thereafter in town had finished the work; and I drank in the sharp moorish air like a thirsty man who has been forwandered among deserts.

I am a man of varied tastes and a score of interests. As an undergraduate I had been filled with the old mania for the complete life. I distinguished myself in the Schools, rowed in my college eight, and reached the distinction of practising for three weeks in the Trials. I had dabbled in a score of learned activities, and when the time came that I won the inevitable St Chad's fellowship on my chaotic acquirements, and I found myself compelled to select if I would pursue a scholar's life, I had some toil in finding my vocation. In the end I resolved that the ancient life of the North, of the Celts and the Northmen and the unknown Pictish tribes, held for me the chief fascination. I had acquired a smattering of Gaelic, having been brought up as a boy in Lochaber, and now I set myself to increase my store of languages. I mastered Erse and Icelandic, and my first book – a monograph on the probable Celtic elements in the Eddic songs – brought me the praise of scholars and the deputy-professor's chair of

Northern Antiquities. So much for Oxford. My vacations had been spent mainly in the North – in Ireland, Scotland and the Isles, in Scandinavia and Iceland, once even in the far limits of Finland. I was a keen sportsman of a sort, an old-experienced fisher, a fair shot with gun and rifle, and in my hillcraft I might well stand comparison with most men. April has ever seemed to me the finest season of the year even in our cold northern altitudes, and the memory of many bright Aprils had brought me up from the South on the night before to Allerfoot, whence a dogcart had taken me up Glen Aller to the inn at Allermuir; and now the same desire had set me on the heather with my face to the cold brown hills.

You are to picture a sort of plateau, benty and rock-strewn, running ridge-wise above a chain of little peaty lochs and a vast tract of inexorable bog. In a mile the ridge ceased in a shoulder of hill, and over this lay the head of another glen, with the same doleful accompaniment of sunless lochs, mosses and a shining and resolute water. East and west and north, in every direction save the south, rose walls of gashed and serrated hills. It was a grey day with blinks of sun, and when a ray chanced to fall on one of the great dark faces, lines of light and colour sprang into being which told of mica and granite. I was in high spirits, as on the eve of holiday; I had breakfasted excellently on eggs and salmon-steaks; I had no cares to speak of, and my prospects were not uninviting. But in spite of myself the landscape began to take me in thrall and crush me. The silent vanished peoples of the hills seemed to be stirring; dark primeval faces seemed to stare at me from behind boulders and jags of rock. The place was so still, so free from the cheerful clamour of nesting birds, that it seemed a *temenos* sacred to some old-world god. At my feet the lochs lapped ceaselessly; but the waters were so dark that one could not see bottom a foot from the edge. On my right the links of green told of snakelike mires waiting to crush the unwary wanderer. It seemed to me for the moment a land of death, where the tongues of the dead cried aloud for recognition.

My whole morning's walk was full of such fancies. I lit a pipe to cheer me, but the things would not be got rid of. I thought of the Gaels who had held those fastnesses; I thought of the Britons before them, who yielded to their advent. They were all strong peoples in their day, and now they had gone the way of the earth. They had left their mark on the levels of the glens and on the more habitable uplands, both in names and in actual forts, and graves where men might still dig curios. But the hills – that black stony amphitheatre before me – it seemed strange that the hills bore no traces of them. And then with some uneasiness I reflected on that older and stranger race who were said to have held the hilltops. The Picts, the Picti – what in the name of goodness were they? They had troubled me in all my studies, a sort of blank wall to put an end to speculation. We knew nothing of them save certain strange names which men called Pictish, the names of those hills in front of me – the Muneraw, the Yirnie, the Calmarton. They were the *corpus vile* for learned experiment; but heaven alone knew what dark abyss of savagery once yawned in the midst of this desert.

And then I remembered the crazy theories of a pupil of mine at St Chad's, the son of a small landowner on the Aller, a young gentleman who had spent his substance too freely at Oxford, and was now dreeing his weird in the backwoods. He had been no scholar; but a certain imagination marked all his doings, and of a Sunday night he would come and talk to me of the North. The Picts were his special subject, and his ideas were mad. 'Listen to me,' he would say, when I had mixed him a toddy and given him one of my cigars; 'I believe there are traces – ay, and more than traces – of an old culture lurking in those hills and waiting to be discovered. We never hear of the Picts being driven from the hills. The Britons drove them from the lowlands, the Gaels from Ireland did the same for the Britons; but the hills were left unmolested. We hear of no one going near them except outlaws and tinklers. And in that very place you have the strangest mythology. Take the story of the Brownie. What is that but the story of a little swart man of uncommon strength and cleverness, who does good and ill indiscriminately, and then disappears? There are many scholars, as you yourself confess, who think that the origin of the Brownie was in some mad belief in the old race of the Picts, which still survived somewhere in the hills. And do we not hear of the Brownie in authentic records right down to the year 1756? After that, when people grew more incredulous, it is natural that the belief should have begun to die out; but I do not see why stray traces should not have survived till late.'

'Do you not see what that means?' I had said in mock gravity. 'Those same hills are, if anything, less known now than they were a hundred years ago. Why should not your Picts or Brownies be living to this day?'

'Why not, indeed?' he had rejoined, in all seriousness. I laughed, and he went to his rooms and returned with a large leather-bound book. It was lettered, in the rococo style of a young man's taste,

Glimpses of the Unknown, and some of the said glimpses he proceeded to impart to me. It was not pleasant reading; indeed, I had rarely heard anything so well fitted to shatter sensitive nerves. The early part consisted of folk-tales and folk-sayings, some of them wholly obscure, some of them with a glint of meaning, but all of them with some hint of a mystery in the hills. I heard the Brownie story in countless versions. Now the thing was a friendly little man, who wore grey breeches and lived on brose; now he was a twisted being, the sight of which made the ewes miscarry in the lambing-time. But the second part was the stranger, for it was made up of actual tales, most of them with date and place appended. It was a most Bedlamite catalogue of horrors, which, if true, made the wholesome moors a place instinct with tragedy. Some told of children carried away from villages, even from towns, on the verge of the uplands. In almost every case they were girls, and the strange fact was their utter disappearance. Two little girls would be coming home from school, would be seen last by a neighbour just where the road crossed a patch of heath or entered a wood and then – no human eye ever saw them again. Children's cries had startled outlying shepherds in the night, and when they had rushed to the door they could hear nothing but the night wind. The instances of such disappearances were not very common – perhaps once in twenty years – but they were confined to this one tract of country, and came in a sort of fixed progression from the middle of the last century, when the record began. But this was only one side of the history. The latter part was all devoted to a chronicle of crimes which had gone unpunished, seeing that no hand had ever been traced. The list was fuller in the last century;* in the earlier years of the present it had dwindled; then came a revival about the 'fifties; and now again in our own time it had sunk low. At the little cottage of Auchterbrean, on the roadside in Glen Aller, a labourer's wife had been found pierced to the heart. It was thought to be a case of a woman's jealousy, and her neighbour was accused, convicted and hanged. The woman, to be sure, denied the charge with her last breath; but circumstantial evidence seemed sufficiently strong against her. Yet some people in the glen believed her guiltless. In particular, the carrier who had found the dead woman declared that the way in which her neighbour received the news was a sufficient proof of innocence; and the doctor who was first summoned professed himself unable to tell with what instrument the wound had

* The narrative of Mr Graves was written in the year 1898.

been given. But this was all before the days of expert evidence, so the woman had been hanged without scruple. Then there had been another story of peculiar horror, telling of the death of an old man at some little lonely shieling called Carrickfey.* But at this point I had risen in protest, and made to drive the young idiot from my room.

'It was my grandfather who collected most of them,' he said. 'He had theories, but people called him mad, so he was wise enough to hold his tongue. My father declares the whole thing mania; but I rescued the book, had it bound, and added to the collection. It is a queer hobby, but, as I say, I have theories, and there are more things in heaven and earth – '

But at this he heard a friend's voice in the quad, and dived out, leaving the banal quotation unfinished.

Strange though it may seem, this madness kept coming back to me as I crossed the last few miles of moor. I was now on a rough tableland, the watershed between two lochs, and beyond and above me rose the stony backs of the hills. The burns fell down in a chaos of granite boulders, and huge slabs of grey stone lay flat and tumbled in the heather. The full waters looked prosperously for my fishing, and I began to forget all fancies in anticipation of sport.

Then suddenly in a hollow of land I came on a ruined cottage. It had been a very small place, but the walls were still half-erect, and the little moorland garden was outlined on the turf. A lonely apple-tree, twisted and gnarled with winds, stood in the midst.

From higher up on the hill I heard a loud roar, and I knew my excellent friend the shepherd of Farawa, who had come thus far to

* In the light of subsequent events I have jotted down the materials to which I refer. The last authentic record of the Brownie is in the narrative of the shepherd of Clachlands, taken down towards the close of last century by the Revd Mr Gillespie, minister of Allerkirk, and included by him in his *Songs and Legends of Glen Aller*. The authorities on the strange carrying-away of children are to be found in a series of articles in a local paper, the *Allerfoot Advertiser*, September and October 1878, and a curious book published anonymously at Edinburgh in 1848, entitled *The Weathergaw*. The records of the unexplained murders in the same neighbourhood are all contained in Mr Fordoun's *Theory of Expert Evidence*, and an attack on the book in the *Law Review* for June 1881. The Carrickfey case has a pamphlet to itself – now extremely rare – a copy of which was recently obtained in a bookseller's shop in Dumfries by a well-known antiquary, and presented to the library of the Supreme Court in Edinburgh.

meet me. He greeted me with the boisterous embarrassment which was his way of prefacing hospitality. A grave reserved man at other times, on such occasions he thought it proper to relapse into hilarity. I fell into step with him, and we set off for his dwelling. But first I had the curiosity to look back to the tumbledown cottage and ask him its name.

A queer look came into his eyes. 'They ca' the place Carrickfey,' he said. 'Naebody has daured to bide there this twenty year sin' – but I see ye ken the story.' And, as if glad to leave the subject, he hastened to discourse on fishing.

2

TELLS OF AN EVENING'S TALK

The shepherd was a masterful man, tall, save for the stoop which belongs to all moorland folk, and active as a wild goat. He was not a new importation, nor did he belong to the place, for his people had lived in the remote Borders and he had come as a boy to this shieling of Farawa. He was unmarried, but an elderly sister lived with him and cooked his meals. He was reputed to be extraordinarily skilful in his trade; I know for a fact that he was in his way a keen sportsman; and his few neighbours gave him credit for a sincere piety. Doubtless this last report was due in part to his silence, for after his first greeting he was wont to relapse into a singular taciturnity. As we strode across the heather he gave me a short outline of his year's lambing. 'Five pairs o' twins yestreen, twae this morn; that makes thirty-five yowes that hae lambed since the Sabbath. I'll dae weel if God's willin'.' Then, as I looked towards the hilltops whence the thin mist of morn was trailing, he followed my gaze. 'See,' he said with uplifted crook – 'see that sicht. Is that no what is written of in the Bible when it says, "The mountains do smoke."' And with this piece of exegesis he finished his talk, and in a little we were at the cottage.

It was a small enough dwelling in truth, and yet large for a moorland house, for it had a garret below the thatch, which was given up to my sole enjoyment. Below was the wide kitchen with box-beds, and next to it the inevitable second room, also with its cupboard sleeping-places. The interior was very clean, and yet I remember to have been struck with the faint musty smell which is inseparable from moorland dwellings. The kitchen pleased me best, for there the great rafters were black with peat-reek, and the uncovered stone floor, on which the fire gleamed dully, gave an air of primeval simplicity. But the walls spoiled all, for tawdry things of today had penetrated even there. Some grocers' almanacs – years old – hung in places of honour, and an extraordinary lithograph of the Royal Family in its youth. And this, mind you, between crooks and fishing-rods and old guns, and horns of sheep and deer.

The life for the first day or two was regular and placid. I was up early, breakfasted on porridge (a dish which I detest), and then off to the lochs and streams. At first my sport prospered mightily. With a drake-wing I killed a salmon of seventeen pounds, and the next day had a fine basket of trout from a hill-burn. Then for no earthly reason the weather changed. A bitter wind came out of the north-east, bringing showers of snow and stinging hail, and lashing the waters into storm. It was now farewell to fly-fishing. For a day or two I tried trolling with the minnow on the lochs, but it was poor sport, for I had no boat, and the edges were soft and mossy. Then in disgust I gave up the attempt, went back to the cottage, lit my biggest pipe, and sat down with a book to await the turn of the weather.

The shepherd was out from morning till night at his work, and when he came in at last, dog-tired, his face would be set and hard, and his eyes heavy with sleep. The strangeness of the man grew upon me. He had a shrewd brain beneath his thatch of hair, for I had tried him once or twice, and found him abundantly intelligent. He had some smattering of an education, like all Scottish peasants, and, as I have said, he was deeply religious. I set him down as a fine type of his class, sober, serious, keenly critical, free from the bondage of superstition. But I rarely saw him, and our talk was chiefly in monosyllables – short interjected accounts of the number of lambs dead or alive on the hill. Then he would produce a pencil and notebook, and be immersed in some calculation; and finally he would be revealed sleeping heavily in his chair, till his sister wakened him, and he stumbled off to bed.

So much for the ordinary course of life; but one day – the second I think of the bad weather – the extraordinary happened. The storm had passed in the afternoon into a resolute and blinding snow, and the shepherd, finding it hopeless on the hill, came home about three o'clock. I could make out from his way of entering that he was in a great temper. He kicked his feet savagely against the doorpost. Then he swore at his dogs, a thing I had never heard him do before. 'Hell!' he cried, 'can ye no keep out o' my road, ye britts?' Then he came sullenly into the kitchen, thawed his numbed hands at the fire, and sat down to his meal.

I made some aimless remark about the weather.

'Death to man and beast,' he grunted. 'I hae got the sheep doun frae the hill, but the lambs will never thole this. We maun pray that it will no last.'

His sister came in with some dish. 'Margit,' he cried, 'three lambs away this morning, and three deid wi' the hole in the throat.'

The woman's face visibly paled. 'Guid help us, Adam; that hasna happened this three year.'

'It has happened noo,' he said, surlily. 'But, by God! if it happens again I'll gang mysel' to the Scarts o' the Muneraw.'

'Oh, Adam!' the woman cried shrilly, 'haud your tongue. Ye kenna wha hears ye.' And with a frightened glance at me she left the room.

I asked no questions, but waited till the shepherd's anger should cool. But the cloud did not pass so lightly. When he had finished his dinner he pulled his chair to the fire and sat staring moodily. He made some sort of apology to me for his conduct. 'I'm sore troubled, sir; but I'm vexed ye should see me like this. Maybe things will be better the morn.' And then, lighting his short black pipe, he resigned himself to his meditations.

But he could not keep quiet. Some nervous unrest seemed to have possessed the man. He got up with a start and went to the window, where the snow was drifting unsteadily past. As he stared out into the storm I heard him mutter to himself, 'Three away. God help me, and three wi' the hole in the throat.'

Then he turned round to me abruptly. I was jotting down notes for an article I contemplated in the *Revue Celtique*, so my thoughts were far away from the present. The man recalled me by demanding fiercely, 'Do ye believe in God?'

I gave him some sort of answer in the affirmative.

'Then do ye believe in the Devil?' he asked.

The reply must have been less satisfactory, for he came forward and flung himself violently into the chair before me.

'What do ye ken about it?' he cried. 'You that bides in a southern toun, what can ye ken o' the God that works in thae hills and the Devil – ay, the manifold devils – that He suffers to bide here? I tell ye, man, that if ye had seen what I have seen ye wad be on your knees at this moment praying to God to pardon your unbelief. There are devils at the back o' every stane and hidin' in every cleuch, and it's by the grace o' God alone that a man is alive upon the earth.' His voice had risen high and shrill, and then suddenly he cast a frightened glance towards the window and was silent.

I began to think that the man's wits were unhinged, and the thought did not give me satisfaction. I had no relish for the prospect of being left alone in this moorland dwelling with the cheerful company of a maniac. But his next movements reassured me. He was clearly only dead-tired, for he fell sound asleep in his chair, and by the time his sister brought tea and wakened him, he seemed to have got the better of his excitement.

When the window was shuttered and the lamp lit, I set myself again to the completion of my notes. The shepherd had got out his Bible, and was solemnly reading with one great finger travelling down the lines. He was smoking, and whenever some text came home to him with power he would make pretence to underline it with the end of the stem. Soon I had finished the work I desired, and, my mind being full of my pet hobby, I fell into an inquisitive mood, and began to question the solemn man opposite on the antiquities of the place.

He stared stupidly at me when I asked him concerning monuments or ancient weapons.

'I kenna,' said he. 'There's a heap o' queer things in the hills.'

'This place should be a centre for such relics. You know that the name of the hill behind the house, as far as I can make it out, means the "Place of the Little Men". It is a good Gaelic word, though there is some doubt about its exact interpretation. But clearly the Gaelic peoples did not speak of themselves when they gave the name; they must have referred to some older and stranger population.'

The shepherd looked at me dully, as not understanding.

'It is partly this fact – besides the fishing, of course – which interests me in this countryside,' said I, gaily.

Again he cast the same queer frightened glance towards the window. 'If ye'll tak the advice of an aulder man,' he said, slowly, 'ye'll let well alane and no meddle wi' uncanny things.'

I laughed pleasantly, for at last I had found out my hard-headed host in a piece of childishness. 'Why, I thought that you of all men would be free from superstition.'

'What do ye call supersteetion?' he asked.

'A belief in old wives' tales,' said I, 'a trust in the crude supernatural and the patently impossible.'

He looked at me beneath his shaggy brows. 'How do ye ken what is impossible? Mind ye, sir, ye're no in the toun just now, but in the thick of the wild hills.'

'But, hang it all, man,' I cried, 'you don't mean to say that you believe in that sort of thing? I am prepared for many things up here, but not for the Brownie – though, to be sure, if one could meet him in the flesh, it would be rather pleasant than otherwise, for he was a companionable sort of fellow.'

'When a thing pits the fear o' death on a man he aye speaks well of it.'

It was true – the Eumenides and the Good Folk over again; and I awoke with interest to the fact that the conversation was getting into strange channels.

The shepherd moved uneasily in his chair. 'I am a man that fears God, and has nae time for daft stories; but I havena traivelled the hills for twenty years wi' my een shut. If I say that I could tell ye stories o' faces seen in the mist, and queer things that have knocked against me in the snaw, wad ye believe me? I wager ye wadna. Ye wad say I had been drunk, and yet I am a God-fearing temperate man.'

He rose and went to a cupboard, unlocked it, and brought out something in his hand, which he held out to me. I took it with some curiosity, and found that it was a flint arrowhead.

Clearly a flint arrowhead, and yet like none that I had ever seen in any collection. For one thing it was larger, and the barb less clumsily thick. More, the chipping was new, or comparatively so; this thing had not stood the wear of fifteen hundred years among the stones of the hillside. Now there are, I regret to say, institutions which manufacture primitive relics; but it is not hard for a practised eye to see the difference. The chipping has either a regularity and a balance which is unknown in the real thing, or the rudeness has been overdone, and the result is an implement incapable of harming a mortal creature. But this was the real thing if it ever existed; and yet I was prepared to swear on my reputation that it was not half a century old.

'Where did you get this?' I asked with some nervousness.

'I hae a story about that,' said the shepherd. 'Outside the door there ye can see a muckle flat stane aside the buchts. One simmer nicht I was sitting there smoking till the dark, and I wager there was naething on the stane then. But that same nicht I awoke wi' a queer thocht, as if there were folk moving around the house – folk that didna mak' muckle noise. I mind o' lookin' out o' the windy, and I could hae sworn I saw something black movin' amang the heather and intil the buchts. Now I had maybe threescore o' lambs there that nicht, for I had to tak' them many miles off in the early morning.

Weel, when I gets up about four o'clock and gangs out, as I am passing the muckle stane I finds this bit errow. "That's come here in the nicht," says I, and I wunnered a wee and put it in my pouch. But when I came to my faulds what did I see? Five o' my best hoggs were away, and three mair were lying deid wi' a hole in their throat.'

'Who in the world – ?' I began.

'Dinna ask,' said he. 'If I aince sterted to speir about thae maitters, I wadna keep my reason.'

'Then that was what happened on the hill this morning?'

'Even sae, and it has happened mair than aince sin' that time. It's the most uncanny slaughter, for sheep-stealing I can understand, but no this pricking o' the puir beasts' wizands. I kenna how they dae't either, for it's no wi' a knife or ony common tool.'

'Have you never tried to follow the thieves?'

'Have I no?' he asked, grimly. 'If it had been common sheep-stealers I wad hae had them by the heels, though I had followed them a hundred miles. But this is no common. I've tracked them, and it's ill they are to track; but I never got beyond ae place, and that was the Scarts o' the Muneraw that ye've heard me speak o'.'

'But who in heaven's name are the people? Tinklers or poachers or what?'

'Ay,' said he, drily. 'Even so. Tinklers and poachers whae wark wi' stane errows and kill sheep by a hole in their throat. Lord, I kenna what they are, unless the Muckle Deil himsel'.'

The conversation had passed beyond my comprehension. In this prosaic hard-headed man I had come on the dead-rock of super-stition and blind fear.

'That is only the story of the Brownie over again, and he is an exploded myth,' I said, laughing.

'Are ye the man that exploded it?' said the shepherd, rudely. 'I trow no, neither you nor ony ither. My bonny man, if ye lived a twalmonth in thae hills, ye wad sing safter about exploded myths, as ye call them.'

'I tell you what I would do,' said I. 'If I lost sheep as you lose them, I would go up the Scarts of the Muneraw and never rest till I had settled the question once and for all.' I spoke hotly, for I was vexed by the man's childish fear.

'I dare say ye wad,' he said, slowly. 'But then I am no you, and maybe I ken mair o' what is in the Scarts o' the Muneraw. Maybe I ken that whilk, if ye kenned it, wad send ye back to the South Country wi' your hert in your mouth. But, as I say, I am no sae brave as you, for I saw something in the first year o' my herding here which put the terror o' God on me, and makes me a fearfu' man to this day. Ye ken the story o' the gudeman o' Carrickfey?'

I nodded.

'Weel, I was the man that fand him. I had seen the deid afore and I've seen them since. But never have I seen aucht like the look in that man's een. What he saw at his death I may see the morn, so I walk before the Lord in fear.'

Then he rose and stretched himself. 'It's bedding-time, for I maun be up at three,' and with a short good-night he left the room.

3

THE SCARTS OF THE MUNERAW

The next morning was fine, for the snow had been intermittent, and had soon melted except in the high corries. True, it was deceptive weather, for the wind had gone to the rainy south-west, and the masses of cloud on that horizon boded ill for the afternoon. But some days' inaction had made me keen for a chance of sport, so I rose with the shepherd and set out for the day.

He asked me where I proposed to begin.

I told him the tarn called the Loch o' the Threshes, which lies over the back of the Muneraw on another watershed. It is on the ground of the Rhynns Forest, and I had fished it of old from the Forest House. I knew the merits of the trout, I knew its virtues in a south-west wind, so I had resolved to go thus far afield.

The shepherd heard the name in silence. 'Your best road will be ower that rig, and syne on to the water o' Caulds. Keep abune the moss till ye come to the place they ca' the Nick o' the Threshes. That will take ye to the very lochside, but it's a lang road and a sair.'

The morning was breaking over the bleak hills. Little clouds drifted athwart the corries, and wisps of haze fluttered from the peaks. A great rosy flush lay over one side of the glen, which caught the edge of the sluggish bog-pools and turned them to fire. Never before had I seen the mountain-land so clear, for far back into the east and west I saw mountain-tops set as close as flowers in a border, black crags seamed with silver lines which I knew for mighty waterfalls, and below at my feet the lower slopes fresh with the dewy green of spring. A name stuck in my memory from the last night's talk.

'Where are the Scarts of the Muneraw?' I asked.

The shepherd pointed to the great hill which bears the name, and which lies, a huge mass, above the watershed.

'D'ye see yon corrie at the east that runs straucht up the side? It looks a bit scart, but it's sae deep that it's aye derk at the bottom o't. Weel, at the tap o' the rig it meets anither corrie that runs doun the ither side, and that one they ca' the Scarts. There is a sort o' burn in it that flows intil the Dule and sae intil the Aller, and, indeed, if ye were gaun there it wad be from Aller Glen that your best road wad lie. But it's an ill bit, and ye'll be sair guidit if ye try't.'

There he left me and went across the glen, while I struck upwards over the ridge. At the top I halted and looked down on the wide glen of the Caulds, which there is little better than a bog but lower down grows into a green pastoral valley. The great Muneraw still dominated the landscape, and the black scaur on its side seemed blacker than before. The place fascinated me, for in that fresh morning air the shepherd's fears seemed monstrous. 'Some day,' said I to myself, 'I will go and explore the whole of that mighty hill.' Then I descended and struggled over the moss, found the Nick, and in two hours' time was on the loch's edge.

I have little in the way of good to report of the fishing. For perhaps one hour the trout took well; after that they sulked steadily for the day. The promise, too, of fine weather had been deceptive. By midday the rain was falling in that soft soaking fashion which gives no hope of clearing. The mist was down to the edge of the water, and I cast my flies into a blind sea of white. It was hopeless work, and yet from a sort of ill-temper I stuck to it long after my better judgement had warned me of its folly. At last, about three in the afternoon, I struck my camp, and prepared myself for a long and toilsome retreat.

And long and toilsome it was beyond anything I had ever encountered. Had I had a vestige of sense I would have followed the burn from the loch down to the Forest House. The place was shut up, but the keeper would gladly have given me shelter for the night. But foolish pride was too strong in me. I had found my road in mist before, and could do it again.

Before I got to the top of the hill I had repented my decision; when I got there I repented it more. For below me was a dizzy chaos of grey; there was no landmark visible; and before me I knew was the bog through which the Caulds Water twined. I had crossed it with some trouble in the morning, but then I had light to pick my steps. Now I could only stumble on, and in five minutes I might be in a bog-hole, and in five more in a better world.

But there was no help to be got from hesitation, so with a rueful courage I set off. The place was if possible worse than I had feared. Wading up to the knees with nothing before you but a blank wall of mist and the cheerful consciousness that your next step may be your last – such was my state for one weary mile. The stream itself was high, and rose to my armpits, and once and again I only saved myself by a violent leap backwards from a pitiless green slough. But at last it was past, and I was once more on the solid ground of the hillside.

Now, in the thick weather I had crossed the glen much lower down than in the morning, and the result was that the hill on which I stood was one of the giants which, with the Muneraw for centre, guard the watershed. Had I taken the proper way, the Nick o' the Threshes would have led me to the Caulds, and then once over the bog a little ridge was all that stood between me and the glen of Farawa. But instead I had come a wild cross-country road, and was now, though I did not know it, nearly as far from my destination as at the start.

Well for me that I did not know, for I was wet and dispirited, and had I not fancied myself all but home, I should scarcely have had the energy to make this last ascent. But soon I found it was not the little ridge I had expected. I looked at my watch and saw that it was five o'clock. When, after the weariest climb, I lay on a piece of level ground which seemed the top, I was not surprised to find that it was now seven. The darkening must be at hand, and sure enough the mist seemed to be deepening into a greyish black. I began to grow desperate. Here was I on the summit of some infernal mountain, without any certainty where my road lay. I was lost with a vengeance, and at the thought I began to be acutely afraid.

I took what seemed to me the way I had come, and began to descend steeply. Then something made me halt, and the next instant I was lying on my face trying painfully to retrace my steps. For I had found myself slipping, and before I could stop, my feet were dangling over a precipice with heaven alone knows how many yards of sheer mist between me and the bottom. Then I tried keeping the ridge, and took that to the right which I thought would bring me nearer home. It was no good trying to think out a direction, for in the fog my brain was running round, and I seemed to stand on a pinpoint of space where the laws of the compass had ceased to hold.

It was the roughest sort of walking, now stepping warily over acres of loose stones, now crawling down the face of some battered rock and now wading in the long dripping heather. The soft rain had begun to fall again, which completed my discomfort. I was now seriously tired, and, like all men who in their day have bent too much over books, I began to feel it in my back. My spine ached, and my breath came in short broken pants. It was a pitiable state of affairs for an honest man who had never encountered much grave discomfort. To ease myself I was compelled to leave my basket behind me, trusting to return and find it, if I should ever reach safety and discover on what pathless hill I had been strayed. My rod I used as a staff, but it was of little use, for my fingers were getting too numb to hold it.

Suddenly from the blankness I heard a sound as of human speech. At first I thought it mere craziness – the cry of a weasel or a hill-bird distorted by my ears. But again it came, thick and faint, as through acres of mist, and yet clearly the sound of 'articulate-speaking men'. In a moment I lost my despair and cried out in answer. This was some forwandered traveller like myself, and between us we could surely find some road to safety. So I yelled back at the pitch of my voice and waited intently.

But the sound ceased, and there was utter silence again. Still I waited, and then from some place much nearer came the same soft mumbling speech. I could make nothing of it. Heard in that drear place it made the nerves tense and the heart timorous. It was the strangest jumble of vowels and consonants I had ever met.

A dozen solutions flashed through my brain. It was some maniac talking Jabberwock to himself. It was some belated traveller whose wits had given out in fear. Perhaps it was only some shepherd who was amusing himself thus, and whiling the way with nonsense. Once again I cried out and waited.

Then suddenly in the hollow trough of mist before me, where things could still be half discerned, there appeared a figure. It was little and squat and dark; naked, apparently, but so rough with hair that it wore the appearance of a skin-covered being. It crossed my line of vision, not staying for a moment, but in its face and eyes there seemed to lurk an elder world of mystery and barbarism, a troll-like life which was too horrible for words.

The shepherd's fear came back on me like a thunderclap. For one awful instant my legs failed me, and I had almost fallen. The next I had turned and run shrieking up the hill.

If he who may read this narrative has never felt the force of an overmastering terror, then let him thank his Maker and pray that he never may. I am no weak child, but a strong grown man, accredited in general with sound sense and little suspected of hysterics. And yet I went up that brae-face with my heart fluttering like a bird and my throat aching with fear. I screamed in short dry gasps, involuntarily, for my mind was beyond any purpose. I felt that beast-like clutch at my throat; those red eyes seemed to be staring at me from the mist; I heard ever behind and before and on all sides the patter of those inhuman feet.

Before I knew I was down, slipping over a rock and falling some dozen feet into a soft marshy hollow. I was conscious of lying still for a second and whimpering like a child. But as I lay there I awoke to the silence of the place. There was no sound of pursuit; perhaps they had lost my track and given up. My courage began to return, and from this it was an easy step to hope. Perhaps after all it had been merely an illusion, for folk do not see clearly in the mist, and I was already done with weariness.

But even as I lay in the green moss and began to hope, the faces of my pursuers grew up through the mist. I stumbled madly to my feet; but I was hemmed in, the rock behind and my enemies before. With a cry I rushed forward, and struck wildly with my rod at the first dark body. It was as if I had struck an animal, and the next second the thing was wrenched from my grasp. But still they came no nearer. I stood trembling there in the centre of those malignant devils, my brain a mere weathercock and my heart crushed shapeless with horror. At last the end came, for with the vigour of madness I flung myself on the nearest, and we rolled on the ground. Then the monstrous things seemed to close over me, and with a choking cry I passed into unconsciousness.

4

THE DARKNESS THAT IS UNDER THE EARTH

There is an unconsciousness that is not wholly dead, where a man feels numbly and the body lives without the brain. I was beyond speech or thought, and yet I felt the upward or downward motion as the way lay in hill or glen, and I most assuredly knew when the open air was changed for the close underground. I could feel dimly that lights were flared in my face, and that I was laid in some bed on the earth. Then with the stopping of movement the real sleep of weakness seized me, and for long I knew nothing of this mad world.

Morning came over the moors with birdsong and the glory of fine weather. The streams were still rolling in spate, but the hill-pastures were alight with dawn, and the little seams of snow were glistening like white fire. A ray from the sunrise cleft its path somehow into the abyss, and danced on the wall above my couch. It caught my eye as I wakened, and for long I lay crazily wondering what it meant. My head was splitting with pain, and in my heart was the same fluttering nameless fear. I did not wake to full consciousness; not till the twinkle of sun from the clean bright out-of-doors caught my senses did I realise that I lay in a great dark place with a glow of dull firelight in the middle.

In time things rose and moved around me, a few ragged shapes of men, without clothing, shambling with their huge feet and looking towards me with curved beast-like glances. I tried to marshal my thoughts, and slowly, bit by bit, I built up the present. There was no question to my mind of dreaming, the past hours had scored reality upon my brain. Yet I cannot say that fear was my chief feeling. The first crazy terror had subsided, and now I felt mainly a sickened disgust with just a tinge of curiosity. I found that my knife, watch, flask, and money had gone, but they had left me a map of the countryside. It seemed strange to look at the calico, with the name of a London printer stamped on the back, and lines of railway and highroad running through every shire. Decent and comfortable civilisation! And here was I a prisoner in this den of nameless folk, and in the midst of a life which history knew not.

Courage is a virtue which grows with reflection and the absence of the immediate peril. I thought myself into some sort of resolution, and lo! when the folk approached me and bound my feet I was back at once in the most miserable terror. They tied me, all but my hands, with some strong cord, and carried me to the centre, where the fire was glowing. Their soft touch was the acutest torture to my nerves, but I stifled my cries lest someone should lay his hand on my mouth. Had that happened, I am convinced my reason would have failed me.

So there I lay in the shine of the fire, with the circle of unknown things around me. There seemed but three or four, but I took no note of number. They talked huskily among themselves in a tongue which sounded all gutturals. Slowly my fear became less an emotion than a habit, and I had room for the smallest shade of curiosity. I strained my ear to catch a word, but it was a mere chaos of sound. The thing ran and thundered in my brain as I stared dumbly into the vacant air.

Then I thought that unless I spoke I should certainly go crazy, for my head was beginning to swim at the strange cooing noise.

I spoke a word or two in my best Gaelic, and they closed round me inquiringly. Then I was sorry I had spoken, for my words had brought them nearer, and I shrank at the thought. But as the faint echoes of my speech hummed in the rock-chamber, I was struck by a curious kinship of sound. Mine was sharper, more distinct, and staccato; theirs was blurred, formless, but still with a certain root-resemblance.

Then from the back there came an older being, who seemed to have heard my words. He was like some foul grey badger, his red eyes sightless, and his hands trembling on a stump of bog-oak. The others made way for him with such deference as they were capable of, and the thing squatted down by me and spoke.

To my amazement his words were familiar. It was some manner of speech akin to the Gaelic, but broadened, lengthened, coarsened. I remembered an old book-tongue, commonly supposed to be an impure dialect once used in Brittany, which I had met in the course of my researches. The words recalled it, and as far as I could remember the thing, I asked him who he was and where the place might be.

He answered me in the same speech – still more broadened, lengthened, coarsened. I lay back with sheer amazement. I had found the key to this unearthly life.

For a little an insatiable curiosity, the ardour of the scholar, prevailed. I forgot the horror of the place, and thought only of the fact that here before me was the greatest find that scholarship had ever made. I was precipitated into the heart of the past. Here must be the fountainhead of all legends, the chrysalis of all beliefs. I actually grew light-hearted. These strange folk around me were now no more shapeless things of terror, but objects of research and experiment. I almost came to think them not unfriendly.

For an hour I enjoyed the highest of earthly pleasures. In that strange conversation I heard – in fragments and suggestions – the history of the craziest survival the world has ever seen. I heard of the struggles with invaders, preserved as it were in a sort of shapeless poetry. There were bitter words against the Gaelic oppressor, bitterer words against the Saxon stranger, and for a moment ancient hatreds flared into life. Then there came the tale of the hill-refuge, the morbid hideous existence preserved for centuries amid a changing world. I heard fragments of old religions, primeval names of god and goddess, half-understood by the folk, but to me the key to a hundred puzzles.

Tales which survive to us in broken disjointed riddles were intact here in living form. I lay on my elbow and questioned feverishly. At any moment they might become morose and refuse to speak. Clearly it was my duty to make the most of a brief good fortune.

And then the tale they told me grew more hideous. I heard of the circumstances of the life itself and their daily shifts for existence. It was a murderous chronicle – a history of lust and rapine and unmentionable deeds in the darkness. One thing they had early recognised – that the race could not be maintained within itself; so that ghoulish carrying away of little girls from the lowlands began, which I had heard of but never credited. Shut up in those dismal holes, the girls soon died, and when the new race had grown up the plunder had been repeated. Then there were bestial murders in lonely cottages, done for God knows what purpose. Sometimes the occupant had seen more than was safe, sometimes the deed was the mere exuberance of a lust of slaying. As they gabbled their tales my heart's blood froze, and I lay back in the agonies of fear. If they had used the others thus, what way of escape was open for myself? I had been brought to this place, and not murdered on the spot. Clearly there was torture before death in store for me, and I confess I quailed at the thought.

But none molested me. The elders continued to jabber out their stories, while I lay tense and deaf. Then to my amazement food was brought and placed beside me – almost with respect. Clearly my murder was not a thing of the immediate future. The meal was some form of mutton – perhaps the shepherd's lost ewes – and a little smoking was all the cooking it had got. I strove to eat, but the tasteless morsels choked me. Then they set drink before me in a curious cup, which I seized on eagerly, for my mouth was dry with thirst. The vessel was of gold, rudely formed, but of the pure metal, and a coarse design in circles ran round the middle. This surprised me enough, but a greater wonder awaited me. The liquor was not water, as I had guessed, but a sort of sweet ale, a miracle of flavour. The taste was curious, but somehow familiar; it was like no wine I had ever drunk, and yet I had known that flavour all my life. I sniffed at the brim, and there rose a faint fragrance of thyme and heather honey and the sweet things of the moorland. I almost dropped it in my surprise; for here in this rude place I had stumbled upon that lost delicacy of the North, the heather ale.

For a second I was entranced with my discovery, and then the wonder of the cup claimed my attention. Was it a mere relic of pillage, or had this folk some hidden mine of the precious metal? Gold had once been common in these hills. There were the traces of mines on Cairnsmore; shepherds had found it in the gravel of the Gled Water; and the name of a house at the head of the Clachlands meant the 'Home of Gold'.

Once more I began my questions, and they answered them willingly. There and then I heard that secret for which many had died in old time, the secret of the heather ale. They told of the gold in the hills, of corries where the sand gleamed and abysses where the rocks were veined. All this they told me, freely, without a scruple. And then, like a clap, came the awful thought that this, too, spelled death. These were secrets which this race aforetime had guarded with their lives; they told them generously to me because there was no fear of betrayal. I should go no more out from this place.

The thought put me into a new sweat of terror – not at death, mind you, but at the unknown horrors which might precede the final suffering. I lay silent, and after binding my hands they began to leave me and go off to other parts of the cave. I dozed in the horrible half-swoon of fear, conscious only of my shaking limbs, and the great dull glow of the fire in the centre. Then I became calmer. After all, they had treated me with tolerable kindness: I had spoken their language, which few of their victims could have done for many a century; it might be that I had found favour in their eyes. For a little I comforted myself with this delusion, till I caught sight of a wooden box in a corner. It was of modern make, one such as grocers use to pack provisions in. It had some address nailed on it, and an aimless curiosity compelled me to creep thither and read it. A torn and weather-stained scrap of paper, with the nails at the corner rusty with age; but something of the address might still be made out. Amid the stains my feverish eyes read, 'To Mr M—, Carrickfey, by Allerfoot Station'.

The ruined cottage in the hollow of the waste with the single gnarled apple-tree was before me in a twinkling. I remembered the shepherd's shrinking from the place and the name, and his wild eyes when he told me of the thing that had happened there. I seemed to see the old man in his moorland cottage, thinking no evil; the sudden entry of the nameless things; and then the eyes glazed in unspeakable terror. I felt my lips dry and burning. Above me was the vault of rock; in the distance I saw the fire-glow and the shadows of shapes moving around it. My fright was too great for inaction, so I crept from the couch, and silently, stealthily, with tottering steps and bursting heart, I began to reconnoitre.

But I was still bound, my arms tightly, my legs more loosely, but yet firm enough to hinder flight. I could not get my hands at my leg-straps, still less could I undo the manacles. I rolled on the floor, seeking some sharp edge of rock, but all had been worn smooth by the use of centuries. Then suddenly an idea came upon me like an inspiration. The sounds from the fire seemed to have ceased, and I could hear them repeated from another and more distant part of the cave. The folk had left their orgy round the blaze, and at the end of the long tunnel I saw its glow fall unimpeded upon the floor. Once there, I might burn off my fetters and be free to turn my thoughts to escape.

I crawled a little way with much labour. Then suddenly I came abreast an opening in the wall, through which a path went. It was a long straight rock-cutting, and at the end I saw a gleam of pale light. It must be the open air: the way of escape was prepared for me; and with a prayer I made what speed I could towards the fire.

I rolled on the verge, but the fuel was peat, and the warm ashes would not burn the cords. In desperation I went farther, and my clothes began to singe, while my face ached beyond endurance. But yet I got no nearer my object. The strips of hide warped and cracked, but did not burn. Then in a last effort I thrust my wrists bodily into the glow and held them there. In an instant I drew them out with a groan of pain, scarred and sore, but to my joy with the band snapped in one place. Weak as I was, it was now easy to free myself of what remained, and then came the untying of my legs. My hands trembled, my eyes were dazed with hurry, and I was longer over the job than need have been. But at length I had loosed my cramped knees and stood on my feet, a free man once more.

I kicked off my boots, and fled noiselessly down the passage to the tunnel mouth. Apparently it was close on evening, for the white light had faded to a pale yellow. But it was daylight, and that was all I sought, and I ran for it as eagerly as ever runner ran to a goal. I came out on a rock-shelf, beneath which a moraine of boulders fell away in a chasm to a dark loch. It was all but night, but I could see the gnarled and fortressed rocks rise in ramparts above, and below the unknown screes and cliffs which make the side of the Muneraw a place only for foxes and the fowls of the air.

The first taste of liberty is an intoxication, and assuredly I was mad when I leaped down among the boulders. Happily at the top of the gully the stones were large and stable, else the noise would certainly have discovered me. Down I went, slipping, praying, my charred wrists aching, and my stockinged feet wet with blood. Soon I was in the jaws of the cleft, and a pale star rose before me. I have always been timid in the face of great rocks, and now had not an awful terror been dogging my footsteps, no power on earth could have driven me to that descent. Soon I left the boulders behind, and came to long spouts of little stones, which moved with me till the hillside seemed sinking under my feet. Sometimes I was face downwards, once and again I must have fallen for yards. Had there been a cliff at the foot, I should have gone over it without resistance; but by the providence of God the spout ended in a long curve into the heather of the bog.

When I found my feet once more on soft boggy earth, my strength was renewed within me. A great hope of escape sprang up in my heart. For a second I looked back. There was a great line of shingle with the cliffs beyond, and above all the unknown blackness of the cleft. There lay my terror, and I set off running across the bog for dear life. My mind was clear enough to know my road. If I held round the loch in front I should come to a burn which fed the Farawa stream, on whose banks stood the shepherd's cottage. The loch could not be far; once at the Farawa I would have the light of the shieling clear before me.

Suddenly I heard behind me, as if coming from the hillside, the patter of feet. It was the sound which white hares make in the wintertime on a noiseless frosty day as they patter over the snow. I have heard the same soft noise from a herd of deer when they changed their pastures. Strange that so kindly a sound should put the very fear of death in my heart. I ran madly, blindly, yet thinking shrewdly. The loch was before me. Somewhere I had read or heard, I do not know where, that the brutish aboriginal races of the North could not swim. I myself swam powerfully; could I but cross the loch I should save two miles of a desperate country.

There was no time to lose, for the patter was coming nearer, and I was almost at the loch's edge. I tore off my coat and rushed in. The bottom was mossy, and I had to struggle far before I found any depth. Something plashed in the water before me, and then something else a little behind. The thought that I was a mark for unknown missiles made me crazy with fright, and I struck fiercely out for the other shore. A gleam of moonlight was on the water at the burn's exit, and thither I guided myself. I found the thing difficult enough in itself, for my hands ached, and I was numb from my bonds. But my fancy raised a thousand phantoms to vex me. Swimming in that black bog water, pursued by those nameless things, I seemed to be in a world of horror far removed from the kindly world of men. My strength seemed inexhaustible from my terror. Monsters at the bottom of the water seemed to bite at my feet, and the pain of my wrists made me believe that the loch was boiling hot, and that I was in some hellish place of torment.

I came out on a spit of gravel above the burn mouth, and set off down the ravine of the burn. It was a strait place, strewn with rocks; but now and then the hill turf came in stretches, and eased my wounded feet. Soon the fall became more abrupt, and I was slipping down a hillside, with the water on my left making great cascades in the granite. And then I was out in the wider vale where the Farawa water flowed among links of moss.

Far in front, a speck in the blue darkness, shone the light of the cottage. I panted forward, my breath coming in gasps and my back shot with fiery pains. Happily the land was easier for the feet as long as I kept on the skirts of the bog. My ears were sharp as a wild beast's with fear as I listened for the noise of pursuit. Nothing came but the rustle of the gentlest hill-wind and the chatter of the falling streams.

Then suddenly the light began to waver and move athwart the window. I knew what it meant. In a minute or two the household at the cottage would retire to rest, and the lamp would be put out. True, I might find the place in the dark, for there was a moon of sorts and the road was not desperate. But somehow in that hour the lamplight gave a promise of safety which I clung to despairingly.

And then the last straw was added to my misery. Behind me came the pad of feet, the pat-patter, soft, eerie, incredibly swift. I choked with fear, and flung myself forward in a last effort. I give my word it was sheer mechanical shrinking that drove me on. God knows I would have lain down to die in the heather had the things behind me been a common terror of life.

I ran as man never ran before, leaping hags, scrambling through green well-heads, straining towards the fast-dying light. A quarter of a mile and the patter sounded nearer. Soon I was not two hundred yards off, and the noise seemed almost at my elbow. The light went out, and the black mass of the cottage loomed in the dark.

Then, before I knew, I was at the door, battering it wearily and yelling for help. I heard steps within and a hand on the bolt. Then something shot past me with lightning force and buried itself in the wood. The dreadful hands were almost at my throat, when the door was opened and I stumbled in, hearing with a gulp of joy the key turn and the bar fall behind me.

5

THE TROUBLES OF A CONSCIENCE

My body and senses slept, for I was utterly tired, but my brain all the night was on fire with horrid fancies. Again I was in that accursed cave; I was torturing my hands in the fire; I was slipping barefoot among jagged boulders; and then with bursting heart I was toiling the last mile with the cottage light – now grown to a great fire in the heavens – blazing before me.

It was broad daylight when I awoke, and I thanked God for the comfortable rays of the sun. I had been laid in a box-bed off the inner room, and my first sight was the shepherd sitting with folded arms in a chair regarding me solemnly. I rose and began to dress, feeling my legs and arms still tremble with weariness. The shepherd's sister bound up my scarred wrists and put an ointment on my burns; and, limping like an old man, I went into the kitchen.

I could eat little breakfast, for my throat seemed dry and narrow; but they gave me some brandy-and-milk, which put strength into my body. All the time the brother and sister sat in silence, regarding me with covert glances.

'Ye have been delivered from the jaws o' the Pit,' said the man at length. 'See that,' and he held out to me a thin shaft of flint. 'I fand that in the door this morning.'

I took it, let it drop, and stared vacantly at the window. My nerves had been too much tried to be roused by any new terror. Out of doors it was fair weather, flying gleams of April sunlight and the soft colours of spring. I felt dazed, isolated, cut off from my easy past and pleasing future, a companion of horrors and the sport of nameless things. Then suddenly my eye fell on my books heaped on a table, and the old distant civilisation seemed for the moment inexpressibly dear.

'I must go – at once. And you must come too. You cannot stay here. I tell you it is death. If you knew what I know you would be crying out with fear. How far is it to Allermuir? Eight, fifteen miles; and then ten down Glen Aller to Allerfoot, and then the railway. We must go together while it is daylight, and perhaps we may be untouched. But quick, there is not a moment to lose.' And I was on my shaky feet, and bustling among my possessions.

'I'll gang wi' ye to the station,' said the shepherd, 'for ye're clearly no fit to look after yourself. My sister will bide and keep the house. If 'naething has touched us this ten year, naething will touch us the day.'

'But you cannot stay. You are mad,' I began; but he cut me short with the words, 'I trust in God.'

'In any case let your sister come with us. I dare not think of a woman alone in this place.'

'I'll bide,' said she. 'I'm no feared as lang as I'm indoors and there's steeks on the windies.'

So I packed my few belongings as best I could, tumbled my books into a haversack, and, gripping the shepherd's arm nervously, crossed the threshold. The glen was full of sunlight. There lay the long shining links of the Farawa burn, the rough hills tumbled beyond, and far over all the scarred and distant forehead of the Muneraw. I had always looked on moorland country as the freshest on earth – clean, wholesome and homely. But now the fresh uplands seemed like a horrible pit. When I looked to the hills my breath choked in my throat, and the feel of soft heather below my feet set my heart trembling.

It was a slow journey to the inn at Allermuir. For one thing, no power on earth would draw me within sight of the shieling of Carrickfey, so we had to cross a shoulder of hill and make our way down a difficult glen, and then over a treacherous moss. The lochs were now gleaming like fretted silver; but to me, in my dreadful knowledge, they seemed more eerie than on that grey day when I came. At last my eyes were cheered by the sight of a meadow and a fence, then we were on a little byroad; and soon the fir-woods and corn-lands of Allercleuch were plain before us.

The shepherd came no farther, but with a brief goodbye turned his solemn face hillwards. I hired a trap and a man to drive, and down the ten miles of Glen Aller I struggled to keep my mind from the past. I thought of the kindly South Country, of Oxford, of anything comfortable and civilised. My driver pointed out the objects of interest as in duty bound, but his words fell on unheeding ears. At last he said something which roused me indeed to interest – the interest of the man who hears the word he fears most in the world. On the left side of the river there suddenly sprang into view a long gloomy cleft in the hills, with a vista of dark mountains behind, down which a stream of considerable size poured its waters.

'That is the Water o' Dule,' said the man in a reverent voice. 'A graund water to fish, but dangerous to life, for it's a' linns. Awa' at the heid they say there's a terrible wild place called the Scarts o' Muneraw – that's a shouther o' the muckle hill itsel' that ye see – but I've never been there, and I never kent ony man that had either.'

At the station, which is a mile from the village of Allerfoot, I found I had some hours to wait for my train for the south. I dared not trust myself for one moment alone, so I hung about the goods-shed, talked vacantly to the porters, and when one went to the village for tea I accompanied him, and to his wonder entertained him at the inn. When I returned I found on the platform a stray bagman who was that evening going to London. If there is one class of men in the world which I heartily detest it is this, but such was my state that I hailed him as a brother, and besought his company. I paid the difference for a first-class fare, and had him in the carriage with me. He must have thought me an amiable maniac, for I talked in fits and starts, and when he fell asleep I would wake him up and beseech him to speak to me. At wayside stations I would pull down the blinds in case of recognition, for to my unquiet mind the world seemed full of spies sent by that terrible folk of the hills. When the train crossed a stretch of moor I would lie down on the seat in case of shafts fired from the heather. And then at last with utter weariness I fell asleep, and woke screaming about midnight to find myself well down in the cheerful English midlands, and red blast-furnaces blinking by the railway-side.

In the morning I breakfasted in my rooms at St Chad's with a dawning sense of safety. I was in a different and calmer world. The lawn-like quadrangles, the great trees, the cawing of rooks and the homely twitter of sparrows – all seemed decent and settled and pleasing. Indoors the oak-panelled walls, the shelves of books, the pictures, the faint fragrance of tobacco, were very different from the gimcrack adornments and the accursed smell of peat and heather in that deplorable cottage. It was still vacation-time, so most of my friends were down; but I spent the day hunting out the few cheerful pedants to whom term and vacation were the same. It delighted me to hear again their precise talk, to hear them make a boast of their work, and narrate the childish little accidents of their life. I yearned for the childish once more; I craved for women's drawing-rooms, and women's chatter, and everything which makes life an elegant game. God knows I had had enough of the other thing for a lifetime!

That night I shut myself in my rooms, barred my windows, drew my curtains, and made a great destruction. All books or pictures which recalled to me the moorlands were ruthlessly doomed. Novels, poems, treatises I flung into an old box, for sale to the second-hand bookseller. Some prints and watercolour sketches I tore to pieces with my own hands. I ransacked my fishing-book, and condemned all tackle for moorland waters to the flames. I wrote a letter to my solicitors, bidding them go no further in the purchase of a place in Lorn I had long been thinking of. Then, and not till then, did I feel the bondage of the past a little loosed from my shoulders. I made myself a nightcap of rum-punch instead of my usual whisky-toddy, that all associations with that dismal land might be forgotten, and to complete the renunciation I returned to cigars and flung my pipe into a drawer.

But when I woke in the morning I found that it is hard to get rid of memories. My feet were still sore and wounded, and when I felt my arms cramped and reflected on the causes, there was that black memory always near to vex me.

In a little term began, and my duties – as deputy-professor of Northern Antiquities – were once more clamorous. I can well believe that my hearers found my lectures strange, for instead of dealing with my favourite subjects and matters, which I might modestly say I had made my own, I confined myself to recondite and distant themes, treating even these cursorily and dully. For the truth is, my heart was no more in my subject. I hated – or I thought I hated – all things Northern with the virulence of utter fear. My reading was confined to science of the most recent kind, to abstruse philosophy and to foreign classics. Anything which savoured of romance or mystery was abhorrent; I pined for sharp outlines and the tangibility of a high civilisation.

All the term I threw myself into the most frivolous life of the place. My Harrow schooldays seemed to have come back to me. I had once been a fair cricketer, so I played again for my college, and made decent scores. I coached an indifferent crew on the river. I fell into the slang of the place, which I had hitherto detested. My former friends looked on me askance, as if some freakish changeling had possessed me. Formerly I had been ready for pedantic discussion, I had been absorbed in my work, men had spoken of me as a rising scholar. Now I fled the very mention of things I had once delighted in. The Professor of Northern Antiquities, a scholar of European reputation, meeting me once in the Parks, embarked on an account of certain novel rings recently found in Scotland, and to his horror found that, when he had got well under weigh, I had slipped off unnoticed. I heard afterwards that the good old man was found by a friend walking disconsolately with bowed head in the middle of the High Street. Being rescued from among the horses' feet, he could only murmur, 'I am thinking of Graves, poor man! And a year ago he was as sane as I am!'

But a man may not long deceive himself. I kept up the illusion valiantly for the term; but I felt instinctively that the fresh schoolboy life, which seemed to me the extreme opposite to the ghoulish North, and as such the most desirable of things, was eternally cut off from me. No cunning affectation could ever dispel my real nature or efface the memory of a week. I realised miserably that sooner or later I must fight it out with my conscience. I began to call myself a coward. The chief thoughts of my mind began to centre themselves more and more round that unknown life waiting to be explored among the wilds.

One day I met a friend – an official in the British Museum – who was full of some new theory about primitive habitations. To me it seemed inconceivably absurd; but he was strong in his confidence, and without flaw in his evidence. The man irritated me, and I burned to prove him wrong, but I could think of no argument which was final against his. Then it flashed upon me that my own experience held the disproof; and without more words I left him, hot, angry with myself, and tantalised by the unattainable.

I might relate my *bona-fide* experience, but would men believe me? I must bring proofs, I must complete my researches, so as to make them incapable of disbelief. And there in those deserts was waiting the key. There lay the greatest discovery of the century – nay, of the millennium. There, too, lay the road to wealth such as I had never dreamed of. Could I succeed, I should be famous for ever. I would revolutionise history and anthropology, I would systematise folklore; I would show the world of men the pit whence they were digged and the rock whence they were hewn.

And then began a game of battledore between myself and my conscience.

'You are a coward,' said my conscience.

'I am sufficiently brave,' I would answer. 'I have seen things and yet lived. The terror is more than mortal, and I cannot face it.'

'You are a coward,' said my conscience.

'I am not bound to go there again. It would be purely for my own aggrandisement if I went, and not for any matter of duty.'

'Nevertheless you are a coward,' said my conscience.

'In any case the matter can wait.'

'You are a coward.'

Then came one awful midsummer night, when I lay sleepless and fought the thing out with myself. I knew that the strife was hopeless, that I should have no peace in this world again unless I made the attempt. The dawn was breaking when I came to the final resolution; and when I rose and looked at my face in a mirror, lo! I looked white and lined and drawn like a man of sixty.

6

SUMMER ON THE MOORS

The next morning I packed a bag with some changes of clothing and a collection of notebooks, and went up to town. The first thing I did was to pay a visit to my solicitors. 'I am about to travel,' said I, 'and I wish to have all things settled in case any accident should happen to me.' So I arranged for the disposal of my property in case of death, and added a codicil which puzzled the lawyers. If I did not return within six months, communications were to be entered into with the shepherd at the shieling of Farawa, post-town Allerfoot. If he could produce any papers, they were to be put into the hands of certain friends, published, and the cost charged to my estate. From my solicitors I went to a gunmaker's in Regent Street and bought an ordinary six-chambered revolver, feeling much as a man might feel who proposed to cross the Atlantic in a skiff and purchased a small life-belt as a precaution.

I took the night express to the North, and, for a marvel, I slept. When I awoke about four we were on the verge of Westmoreland, and stony hills blocked the horizon. At first I hailed the mountain-land gladly, sleep for the moment had caused forgetfulness of my terrors. But soon a turn of the line brought me in full view of a heathery moor, running far to a confusion of distant peaks. I remembered my mission and my fate, and if ever condemned criminal felt a more bitter regret I pity his case. Why should I alone among the millions of this happy isle be singled out as the repository of a ghastly secret, and be cursed by a conscience which would not let it rest?

I came to Allerfoot early in the forenoon, and got a trap to drive me up the valley. It was a lowering grey day, hot and yet sunless. A sort of heat-haze cloaked the hills, and every now and then a smurr of rain would meet us on the road, and in a minute be over. I felt wretchedly dispirited, and when at last the whitewashed kirk of Allermuir came into sight and the broken-backed bridge of Aller, man's eyes seemed to have looked on no drearier scene since time began.

I ate what meal I could get, for, fears or no, I was voraciously hungry. Then I asked the landlord to find me some man who would show me the road to Farawa. I demanded company, not for protection – for what could two men do against such brutish strength? – but to keep my mind from its own thoughts.

The man looked at me anxiously. 'Are ye acquaint wi' the folks, then?' he asked. I said I was, that I had often stayed in the cottage. 'Ye ken that they've a name for being queer. The man never comes here forbye once or twice a year, and he has few dealings wi' other herds. He's got an ill name, too, for losing sheep. I dinna like the country ava. Up by yon Muneraw – no that I've ever been there, but I've seen it afar off – is enough to put a man daft for the rest o' his days. What's taking ye thereaways? It's no the time for the fishing?'

I told him that I was a botanist going to explore certain hill-crevices for rare ferns. He shook his head, and then after some delay found me an ostler who would accompany me to the cottage.

The man was a shock-headed, long-limbed fellow, with fierce red hair and a humorous eye. He talked sociably about his life, answered my hasty questions with deftness, and beguiled me for the moment out of myself. I passed the melancholy lochs, and came in sight of the great stony hills without the trepidation I had expected. Here at my side was one who found some humour even in those uplands. But one thing I noted which brought back the old uneasiness. He took the road which led us farthest from Carrickfey, and when to try him I proposed the other, he vetoed it with emphasis.

After this his good spirits departed, and he grew distrustful.

'What mak's ye a freend o' the herd at Farawa?' he demanded a dozen times.

Finally, I asked him if he knew the man, and had seen him lately.

'I dinna ken him, and I hadna seen him for years till a fortnicht syne, when a' Allermuir saw him. He cam doun one afternoon to the public-hoose, and begood to drink. He had aye been kenned for a terrible godly kind o' a man, so ye may believe folk wondered at this. But when he had stuck to the drink for twae days, and filled himsel' blind-fou half-a-dozen o' times, he took a fit o' repentance, and raved and blethered about siccan a life as he led in the muirs. There was some said he was speakin' serious, but maist thocht it was juist daftness.'

'And what did he speak about?' I asked sharply.

'I canna verra weel tell ye. It was about some kind o' bogle that lived in the Muneraw – that's the shouthers o't ye see yonder – and it seems that the bogle killed his sheep and frichted himsel'. He was aye bletherin', too, about something or somebody ca'd Grave; but oh! the man wasna wise.' And my companion shook a contemptuous head.

And then below us in the valley we saw the shieling, with a thin shaft of smoke rising into the rainy grey weather. The man left me, sturdily refusing any fee. 'I wantit my legs stretched as weel as you. A walk in the hills is neither here nor there to a stoot man. When will ye be back, sir?'

The question was well timed. 'Tomorrow fortnight,' I said, 'and I want somebody from Allermuir to come out here in the morning and carry some baggage. Will you see to that?'

He said 'Ay,' and went off, while I scrambled down the hill to the cottage. Nervousness possessed me, and though it was broad daylight and the whole place lay plain before me, I ran pell-mell, and did not stop till I reached the door.

The place was utterly empty. Unmade beds, unwashed dishes, a hearth strewn with the ashes of peat and dust thick on everything proclaimed the absence of inmates. I began to be horribly frightened. Had the shepherd and his sister, also, disappeared? Was I left alone in this bleak place, with a dozen lonely miles between me and human dwellings? I could not return alone; better this horrible place than the unknown perils of the out-of-doors. Hastily I barricaded the door, and to the best of my power shuttered the windows; and then with dreary forebodings I sat down to wait on fortune.

In a little I heard a long swinging step outside and the sound of dogs. Joyfully I opened the latch, and there was the shepherd's grim face waiting stolidly on what might appear.

At the sight of me he stepped back. 'What in the Lord's name are ye daein' here?' he asked. 'Didna ye get enough afore?'

'Come in,' I said, sharply. 'I want to talk.'

In he came with those blessed dogs – and what a comfort it was to look on their great honest faces! He sat down on the untidy bed and waited.

'I came because I could not stay away. I saw too much to give me any peace elsewhere. I must go back, even though I risk my life for it. The cause of scholarship demands it as well as the cause of humanity.'

'Is that a' the news ye hae?' he said. 'Weel, I've mair to tell ye. Three weeks syne my sister Margit was lost, and I've never seen her mair.'

My jaw fell, and I could only stare at him.

'I cam hame from the hill at nightfa' and she was gone. I lookit for her up hill and doun, but I couldna find her. Syne I think I went daft. I went to the Scarts and huntit them up and doun, but no sign could I see. The folk can bide quiet enough when they want. Syne I went to Allermuir and drank mysel' blind – me, that's a God-fearing man and a saved soul, but the Lord help me, I didna ken what I was at. That's my news, and day and night I wander thae hills, seekin' for what I canna find.'

'But, man, are you mad?' I cried. 'Surely there are neighbours to help you. There is a law in the land, and you had only to find the nearest police-office and compel them to assist you.'

'What guid can man dae?' he asked. 'An army o' sodgers couldna find that hidy-hole. Forby, when I went into Allermuir wi' my story the folk thocht me daft. It was that set me drinking, for – the Lord forgive me! – I wasna my ain maister. I threepit till I was hairse, but the bodies just lauch'd.' And he lay back on the bed like a man mortally tired.

Grim though the tidings were, I can only say that my chief feeling was of comfort. Pity for the new tragedy had swallowed up my fear. I had now a purpose, and a purpose, too, not of curiosity but of mercy.

'I go tomorrow morning to the Muneraw. But first I want to give you something to do.' And I drew roughly a chart of the place on the back of a letter. 'Go into Allermuir tomorrow, and give this paper to the landlord at the inn. The letter will tell him what to do. He is to raise at once all the men he can get, and come to the place on the chart marked with a cross. Tell him life depends on his hurry.'

The shepherd nodded. 'D'ye ken the folk are watching for you? They let me pass without trouble, for they've nae use for me, but I see fine they're seeking you. Ye'll no gang half a mile the morn afore they grip ye.'

'So much the better,' I said. 'That will take me quicker to the place I want to be at.'

'And I'm to gang to Allermuir the morn,' he repeated, with the air of a child conning a lesson. 'But what if they'll no believe me?'

'They'll believe the letter.'

'Maybe,' he said, and relapsed into a doze. I set myself to put that house in order, to rouse the fire and prepare food. It was dismal work; and meantime outside the night darkened, and a great wind rose, which howled round the walls and lashed the rain on the windows.

7

IN MANUS TUAS, DOMINE!

I had not gone twenty yards from the cottage door ere I knew I was watched. I had left the shepherd still dozing, in the half-conscious state of a dazed and broken man. All night the wind had wakened me at intervals, and now in the half-light of morn the weather seemed more vicious than ever. The wind cut my ears, the whole firmament was full of the rendings and thunders of the storm. Rain fell in blinding sheets, the heath was a marsh, and it was the most I could do to struggle against the hurricane which stopped my breath. And all the while I knew I was not alone in the desert.

All men know – in imagination or in experience – the sensation of being spied on. The nerves tingle, the skin grows hot and prickly, and there is a queer sinking of the heart. Intensify this common feeling a hundredfold, and you get a tenth part of what I suffered. I am telling a plain tale, and record bare physical facts. My lips stood out from my teeth as I heard, or felt, a rustle in the heather, a scraping among stones. Some subtle magnetic link seemed established between my body and the mysterious world around. I became sick – acutely sick – with the ceaseless apprehension.

My fright became so complete that when I turned a corner of rock, or stepped in deep heather, I seemed to feel a body rub against mine. This continued all the way up the Farawa water, and then up its feeder to the little lonely loch. It kept me from looking forward; but it likewise kept me in such a sweat of fright that I was ready to faint. Then the notion came upon me to test this fancy of mine. If I was tracked thus closely, clearly the trackers would bar my way if I turned back. So I wheeled round and walked a dozen paces down the glen.

Nothing stopped me. I was about to turn again, when something made me take six more paces. At the fourth something rustled in the heather and my neck was gripped as in a vice. I had already made up my mind on what I would do. I would be perfectly still, I would conquer my fear, and let them do as they pleased with me so long as they took me to their dwelling. But at the touch of the hands my resolutions fled. I struggled and screamed. Then something was clapped on my mouth, speech and strength went from me, and once more I was back in the maudlin childhood of terror.

In the cave it was always a dusky twilight. I seemed to be lying in the same place, with the same dull glare of firelight far off, and the same close stupefying smell. One of the creatures was standing silently at my side, and I asked him some trivial question. He turned and shambled down the passage, leaving me alone.

Then he returned with another, and they talked their guttural talk to me. I scarcely listened till I remembered that in a sense I was here of my own accord, and on a definite mission. The purport of their speech seemed to be that, now I had returned, I must beware of a second flight. Once I had been spared; a second time I should be killed without mercy.

I assented gladly. The folk, then, had some use for me. I felt my errand prospering.

Then the old creature which I had seen before crept out of some corner and squatted beside me. He put a claw on my shoulder, a horrible, corrugated, skeleton thing, hairy to the fingertips and nailless. He grinned, too, with toothless gums, and his hideous old voice was like a file on sandstone.

I asked questions, but he would only grin and jabber, looking now and then furtively over his shoulder towards the fire.

I coaxed and humoured him, till he launched into a narrative of which I could make nothing. It seemed a mere string of names, with certain words repeated at fixed intervals. Then it flashed on me that this might be a religious incantation. I had discovered remnants of a ritual and a mythology among them. It was possible that these were sacred days, and that I had stumbled upon some rude celebration.

I caught a word or two and repeated them. He looked at me curiously. Then I asked him some leading question, and he replied with clearness. My guess was right. The midsummer week was the holy season of the year, when sacrifices were offered to the gods.

The notion of sacrifices disquieted me, and I would fain have asked further. But the creature would speak no more. He hobbled off, and left me alone in the rock-chamber to listen to a strange sound which hung ceaselessly about me. It must be the storm without, like the rumble of artillery rattling among the crags. A storm of storms surely, for the place echoed and hummed, and to my unquiet eye the very rock of the roof seemed to shake!

Apparently my existence was forgotten, for I lay long before anyone returned. Then it was merely one who brought food, the same strange meal as before, and left hastily. When I had eaten I rose and stretched myself. My hands and knees still quivered nervously; but I was strong and perfectly well in body. The empty, desolate, tomblike place was eerie enough to scare anyone; but its emptiness was comfort when I thought of its inmates. Then I wandered down the passage towards the fire which was burning in loneliness. Where had the folk gone? I puzzled over their disappearance.

Suddenly sounds began to break on my ear, coming from some inner chamber at the end of that in which the fire burned. I could scarcely see for the smoke; but I began to make my way towards the noise, feeling along the sides of rock. Then a second gleam of light seemed to rise before me, and I came to an aperture in the wall which gave entrance to another room.

This in turn was full of smoke and glow – a murky orange glow, as if from some strange flame of roots. There were the squat moving figures, running in wild antics round the fire. I crouched in the entrance, terrified and yet curious, till I saw something beyond the blaze which held me dumb. Apart from the others and tied to some stake in the wall was a woman's figure, and the face was the face of the shepherd's sister.

My first impulse was flight. I must get away and think – plan how to achieve some desperate way of escape. I sped back to the silent chamber as if the gang were at my heels. It was still empty, and I stood helplessly in the centre, looking at the impassable walls of rock as a wearied beast may look at the walls of its cage. I bethought me of the way I had escaped before and rushed thither, only to find it blocked by a huge contrivance of stone. Yards and yards of solid rock were between me and the upper air, and yet through it all came the crash and whistle of the storm. If I were at my wits' end in this inner darkness, there was also high commotion among the powers of the air in that upper world.

As I stood I heard the soft steps of my tormentors. They seemed to think I was meditating escape, for they flung themselves on me and bore me to the ground. I did not struggle, and when they saw me quiet, they squatted round and began to speak. They told me of the holy season and its sacrifices. At first I could not follow them; then when I caught familiar words I found some clue, and they became intelligible. They spoke of a woman, and I asked, 'What woman?' With all frankness they told me of the custom which prevailed – how every twentieth summer a woman was sacrificed to some devilish god, and by the hand of one of the stranger race. I said nothing, but my whitening face must have told them a tale, though I strove hard to keep my composure. I asked if they had found the victims. 'She is in this place,' they said; 'and as for the man, thou art he.' And with this they left me.

I had still some hours; so much I gathered from their talk, for the sacrifice was at sunset. Escape was cut off for ever. I have always been something of a fatalist, and at the prospect of the irrevocable end my cheerfulness returned. I had my pistol, for they had taken nothing from me. I took out the little weapon and fingered it lovingly. Hope of the lost, refuge of the vanquished, ease to the coward – blessed be he who first conceived it!

The time dragged on, the minutes grew to hours, and still I was left solitary. Only the mad violence of the storm broke the quiet. It had increased in fury, for the stones at the mouth of the exit by which I had formerly escaped seemed to rock with some external pressure, and cutting shafts of wind slipped past and cleft the heat of the passage. What a sight the ravine outside must be, I thought, set in the forehead of a great hill, and swept clean by every breeze! Then came a crashing, and the long hollow echo of a fall. The rocks are splitting, said I, the road down the corrie will be impassable now and for evermore.

I began to grow weak with the nervousness of the waiting, and by and by I lay down and fell into a sort of doze. When I next knew consciousness I was being roused by two of the folk, and bidden get ready. I stumbled to my feet, felt for the pistol in the hollow of my sleeve, and prepared to follow.

When we came out into the wider chamber the noise of the storm was deafening. The roof rang like a shield which has been struck. I noticed, perturbed as I was, that my guards cast anxious eyes around them, alarmed, like myself, at the murderous din. Nor was the world quieter when we entered the last chamber, where the fire burned and the remnant of the folk waited. Wind had found an entrance from somewhere or other, and the flames blew here and there, and the smoke gyrated in odd circles. At the back, and apart from the rest, I saw the dazed eyes and the white and drawn old face of the woman.

They led me up beside her to a place where there was a rude flat stone, hollowed in the centre, and on it a rusty iron knife, which seemed once to have formed part of a scythe-blade. Then I saw the ceremonial which was marked out for me. It was the very rite which I had dimly figured as current among a rude people, and even in that moment of horror I had something of the scholar's satisfaction.

The oldest of the folk, who seemed to be a sort of priest, came to my side and mumbled a form of words. His fetid breath sickened me; his dull eyes, glassy like a brute's with age, brought my knees knocking together. He put the knife in my hands, dragged the terror-stricken woman forward to the altar, and bade me begin.

I began by sawing her bonds through. When she felt herself free she would have fled back, but stopped when I bade her. At that moment there came a noise of rending and crashing as if the hills were falling, and for one second the eyes of the folk were averted from the frustrated sacrifice.

Only for a moment. The next they saw what I had done, and with one impulse rushed towards me. Then began the last scene in the play. I sent a bullet through the right eye of the first thing that came on. The second shot went wide; but the third shattered the hand of an elderly ruffian with a club. Never for an instant did they stop, and now they were clutching at me. I pushed the woman behind me, and fired three rapid shots in blind panic, and then, clutching the scythe, I struck right and left like a madman.

Suddenly I saw the foreground sink before my eyes. The roof sloped down, and with a sickening hiss a mountain of rock and earth seemed to precipitate itself on the foremost of my assailants. One, nipped in the middle by a rock, caught my eye by his hideous writhings. Two only remained in what was now a little suffocating chamber, with embers from the fire still smoking on the floor.

The woman caught me by the hand and drew me with her, while the two seemed mute with fear. 'There's a road at the back,' she screamed. 'I ken it. I fand it out.' And she pulled me up a narrow hole in the rock.

How long we climbed I do not know. We were both fighting for air, with the tightness of throat and chest and the craziness of limb which mean suffocation. I cannot tell when we first came to the surface, but I remember the woman, who seemed to have the strength of extreme terror, pulling me from the edge of a crevasse and laying me on a flat rock. It seemed to be the depth of winter, with sheer-falling rain and a wind that shook the hills.

Then I was once more myself and could look about me. From my feet yawned a sheer abyss, where once had been a hill-shoulder. Some great mass of rock on the brow of the mountain had been loosened by the storm, and in its fall had caught the lips of the ravine and blocked the upper outlet from the nest of dwellings. For a moment I feared that all had been destroyed.

My feeling – heaven help me! – was not thankfulness for God's mercy and my escape, but a bitter mad regret. I rushed frantically to the edge, and when I saw only the blackness of darkness I wept weak tears. All the time the storm was tearing at my body, and I had to grip hard by hand and foot to keep my place.

Suddenly on the brink of the ravine I saw a third figure. We two were not the only fugitives. One of the folk had escaped.

I ran to it, and to my surprise the thing as soon as it saw me rushed to meet me. At first I thought it was with some instinct of self-preservation, but when I saw its eyes I knew it meant to fight. Clearly one or other should go no more from the place.

We were some ten yards from the brink when I grappled with it. Dimly I heard the woman scream with fright, and saw her scramble across the hillside. Then we were tugging in a death-throe, the hideous smell of the thing in my face, its red eyes burning into mine, and its hoarse voice muttering. Its strength seemed incredible; but I, too, am no weakling. We tugged and strained, its nails biting into my flesh, while I choked its throat unsparingly. Every second I dreaded lest we should plunge together over the ledge, for it was thither my adversary tried to draw me. I caught my heel in a nick of rock, and pulled madly against it.

And then, while I was beginning to glory with the pride of conquest, my hope was dashed in pieces. The thing seemed to break from my arms, and, as if in despair, cast itself headlong into the impenetrable darkness. I stumbled blindly after it, saved myself on the brink, and fell back, sick and ill, into a merciful swoon.

8

NOTE IN CONCLUSION BY THE EDITOR

At this point the narrative of my unfortunate friend, Mr Graves of St Chad's, breaks off abruptly. He wrote it shortly before his death, and was prevented from completing it by the attack of heart failure which carried him off. In accordance with the instructions in his will, I have prepared it for publication, and now in much fear and hesitation give it to the world. First, however, I must supplement it by such facts as fall within my knowledge.

The shepherd seems to have gone to Allemuir and by the help of the letter convinced the inhabitants. A body of men was collected under the landlord, and during the afternoon set out for the hills. But unfortunately the great midsummer storm – the most terrible of recent climatic disturbances – had filled the mosses and streams, and they found themselves unable to proceed by any direct road. Ultimately, late in the evening, they arrived at the cottage of Farawa, only to find there a raving woman, the shepherd's sister, who seemed crazy with brain-fever. She told some rambling story about her escape, but her narrative said nothing of Mr Graves. So they treated her with what skill they possessed, and sheltered for the night in and around the cottage. Next morning the storm had abated a little, and the woman had recovered something of her wits. From her they learned that Mr Graves was lying in a ravine on the side of the Muneraw in imminent danger of his life. A body set out to find him, but so immense was the landslip, and so dangerous the whole mountain, that it was nearly evening when they recovered him from the ledge of rock. He was alive, but unconscious, and when brought back to the cottage it was clear that he was, indeed, very ill. There he lay for three months, while the best skill that could be got was procured for him. By dint of an uncommon toughness of constitution he survived, but it was an old and feeble man who returned to Oxford in the early winter.

The shepherd and his sister immediately left the countryside, and were never more heard of, unless they are the pair of unfortunates who are at present in a Scottish pauper asylum, incapable of remembering even their names. The people who last spoke with them declared that their minds seemed weakened by a great shock, and that it was hopeless to try to get any connected or rational statement.

The career of my poor friend from that hour was little short of a tragedy. He awoke from his illness to find the world incredulous; even the country-folk of Allermuir set down the story to the shepherd's craziness and my friend's credulity. In Oxford his argument was received with polite scorn. An account of his experiences which he drew up for *The Times* was refused by the editor; and an article on 'Primitive Peoples of the North', embodying what he believed to be the result of his discoveries, was unanimously rejected by every responsible journal in Europe. At first he bore the treatment bravely. Reflection convinced him that the colony had not been destroyed. Proofs were still awaiting his hand, and with courage and caution he might yet triumph over his enemies. But unfortunately, though the ardour of the scholar burned more fiercely than ever and all fear seemed to have been purged from his soul, the last adventure had grievously sapped his bodily strength. In the spring following his accident he made an effort to reach the spot – alone, for no one could be persuaded to follow him in what was regarded as a childish madness. He slept at the now deserted cottage of Farawa, but in the morning found himself unable to continue, and with difficulty struggled back to the shepherd's cottage at Allercleuch, where he was confined to bed for a fortnight. Then it became necessary for him to seek health abroad, and it was not till the following autumn that he attempted the journey again. He fell sick a second time at the inn of Allermuir, and during his convalescence had himself carried to a knoll in the inn garden, whence a glimpse can be obtained of the shoulder of the Muneraw. There he would sit for hours with his eyes fixed on the horizon, and at times he would be found weeping with weakness and vexation. The last attempt was made but two months before his last illness. On this occasion he got no farther than Carlisle, where he was taken ill with what proved to be a premonition of death. After that he shut his lips tightly, as though recognising the futility of his hopes. Whether he had been soured by the treatment he received, or whether his brain had already been weakened, he had become a morose silent man, and for the two years before his death had few friends and no society. From the obituary notice in *The Times*, I take the following paragraph, which shows in what light the world had come to look upon him:

At the outset of his career he was regarded as a rising scholar in one department of archaeology, and his Taffert lectures were a real contribution to an obscure subject. But in afterlife he was led into fantastic speculations; and when he found himself unable to convince his colleagues, he gradually retired into himself, and lived practically a hermit's life till his death. His career, thus broken short, is a sad instance of the fascination which the recondite and the quack can exercise even over men of approved ability.

And now his own narrative is published, and the world can judge as it pleases about the amazing romance. The view which will doubtless find general acceptance is that the whole is a figment of the brain, begotten of some harmless moorland adventure and the company of such religious maniacs as the shepherd and his sister. But some who knew the former sobriety and calmness of my friend's mind may be disposed timorously and with deep hesitation to another verdict. They may accept the narrative, and believe that somewhere in those moorlands he met with a horrible primitive survival, passed through the strangest adventure, and had his fingers on an epoch-making discovery. In this case they will be inclined to sympathise with the loneliness and misunderstanding of his latter days. It is not for me to decide the question. Though a fellow-historian, the Picts are outside my period, and I dare not advance an opinion on a matter with which I am not fully familiar. But I would point out that the means of settling the question are still extant, and I would call upon some young archaeologist, with a reputation to make, to seize upon the chance of the century. Most of the expresses for the North stop at Allerfoot, a ten-miles' drive will bring him to Allermuir; and then with a fifteen-miles' walk he is at Farawa and on the threshold of discovery. Let him follow the burn and cross the ridge and ascend the Scarts of the Muneraw, and, if he return at all, it may be with a more charitable judgement of my unfortunate friend.

Summer Weather

John Buchan

In a certain year the prices of sheep at Gledsmuir sank so low that the hearts of the farmers were troubled; and one – he of Clachlands – sought at once to retrieve his fortunes and accepted an understudy. This was the son of a neighbouring laird, a certain John Anthony Dean, who by way of preparing himself for the possession of a great moorland estate thought it well to learn something of the life of the place. He was an amiable and idyllic young man, whom I once had the pleasure of knowing well. His interest was centred upon the composition of elegant verses, and all that savoured of the poetic was endeared to his soul. Therefore he had long admired the shepherd's life from afar; the word 'pastoral' conjured up a fragrant old-time world; so in a mood pleasantly sentimental he embarked upon the unknown. I need not describe his attainments as sheep-farmer or shepherd, he scarcely learned the barest rudiments; and the sage master of Clachlands trusted him only when he wrought under his own vigilant eye. Most of his friends had already labelled him a good-natured fool, and on the whole I do not feel ready to dispute the verdict. But that on one occasion he was not a fool, that once at least Mr John Anthony Dean rose out of his little world into the air of the heroic, this tale is written to show.

It was a warm afternoon in late June and, his dog running at heel, he went leisurely forth to the long brown ridges of moor. The whole valley lay sweltering in torrid heat; even there, on the crest of a ridge, there was little coolness. The hills shimmered blue and indeterminate through the haze, and the waters of a little loch not a mile away seemed part of the colourless benty upland. He was dressed in light flannels and reasonable shoes – vastly unlike the professional homespuns and hobnailed boots; but even he felt the airless drought and the flinty, dusty earth underfoot, and moderated his pace accordingly.

He was in a highly cheerful frame of mind, and tranquil enjoyment shone in his guileless face. On this afternoon certain cousins were walking over from his father's lodge to visit him at his labours. He contemplated gaily the prospect of showing them this upland Arcady, himself its high-priest and guardian. Of all times afternoon was the season when its charm was most dominant, when the mellow light lay on the far lines of mountain, and the streams were golden and russet in the pools. Then was the hour when ancient peace filled all the land, and the bleat of sheep and the calling of birds were but parts of a primeval silence. Even this dried-up noonday moor had the charm of an elder poetry. The hot smell of earth, the glare of the sun from the rocks, were all incidents in pastoral. Even thus, he mused, must the shepherds of Theocritus have lived in that land of downs where the sunburnt cicala hummed under the brown grass.

Some two miles from home he came to the edge of a shallow dale in whose midst a line of baked pebbles and tepid pools broke the monotonous grey. The heat was overpowering, and a vague longing for cool woods and waters stole into his mind. But the thought that this would but add to the tan of his complexion gave him comfort. He pictured the scene of his meeting with his friends; how he would confront them as the bronzed and seasoned uplander with an indescribable glamour of the poetic in his air. He was the man who lived with nature amid the endless moors, who carried always with him the romance of the inexplicable and the remote.

Such pleasing thoughts were roughly broken in on by the sight of his dog. It was a finely-bred sheep-collie, a prize-taker, and not the least costly part of his equipment. Already once in that burning summer the animal had gone into convulsions and come out of them weak and foolish. Now it lay stiffened in exactly the same way, its tongue lolling feebly, and flecks of white on its parched jaw. His sensibilities were affected, and he turned from the pitiable sight.

When he looked again it was creeping after him with tail between legs and its coat damp with sweat. Then at the crossing of a gate he missed the sound of it and looked back. There it lay again, this time more rigid than before, apparently not far from the extremities of death. His face grew grave, for he had come to like the creature and he would regret its loss.

But even as he looked the scene changed utterly. The stiffness relaxed, and before he knew the dog was on its feet and coming towards him. He rubbed his eyes with sheer amazement; for the thing looked like an incarnate devil. Its eyes glowered like coals, and its red cavern of a mouth was lined with a sickening froth. Twice its teeth met with a horrid snap as it rushed straight for him at an incredible swiftness. His mind was all but numbed, but some instinct warned him against suffering the beast to cut him off from home. The far dyke was the nearer, but he chose to make rather for the one he had already crossed. By a hairbreadth he managed to elude the rush and let the thing pass – then with a very white face and a beating heart he ran for his life.

By a kind chance the thing had run many yards ere it saw his flight. Then it turned and with great leaps like a greyhound made after him. He heard it turn, heard every bound, with the distinctness of uttermost fear. His terror was lest it should gain on him unknown, and overpower him before he had chance to strike. Now he was almost at the dyke; he glanced round, saw the thing not five yards from him, and waited. The great scarlet jaws seemed to rise in the air before him, and with all his power he brought his thick crook down full athwart them. There was something dead and unearthly about these mad jaws; he seemed to be striking lifeless yet murderous flesh, and even as his stick crashed on the teeth his heart was sick with loathing. But he had won his end; for a second the brute fell back, and he leaped on the dyke.

It was a place built of loose moor stones, and on one larger than the rest he took his stand. He dare not trust a further chase; here he must weary the thing out, or miserably perish. Meantime it was rising again, its eyes two blazing pools of fire. Two yards forward it dragged itself, then sprang clear at his throat. He struck with all his might, but the blow missed its forehead, and, hitting the gums, sufficed only to turn it slightly aside, so that it fell on the wall two feet on his left. He lashed at it with frenzied strength, till groaning miserably it rolled off and lay panting on the turf.

The sun blazed straight on his bare head (for he had lost his cap in the chase), and sweat blinded his eyes. He felt ill, giddy and hopelessly sick of heart. He had seen nothing of madness before in man or animal; the thing was an awful mystery, a voiceless, incredible horror. What not two hours before had been a friendly, sensible collie now lay blinking at him with devouring eyes and jaws where foam was beginning to be dyed with blood. He calculated mechanically on each jump, and as the beast neared him his stick fell with stiff, nerveless force. To tell the truth, the man was numb with terror; his impulse was to sink to the ground; had death faced him in any form less repulsive than this assuredly he would not have striven against it.

It is a weak figure of speech to say that to him each minute seemed of an hour's length. He had no clear sense of time at all. His one sensation was an overmastering horror which directed his aim almost without his knowledge. Three times the thing leaped on him; three times he struck, and it slipped with claws grating on the stone. Then it turned and raced round a circle of heather, with its head between its forepaws like a runaway horse. The man dropped on his knees to rest, looking intently at the circling speck, now far away, now not a dozen yards distant. He vainly hoped that it would tire or leave him – vainly, for of a sudden it made for the wall and he had barely time to get to his feet before it was upon him. This time he struck it down without difficulty, for it was somewhat exhausted; but he noted with new terror that instead of leaping and falling back with open jaws, its teeth had shut with a snap as it neared him. Henceforth he must ward more closely, or the teeth might graze his flesh.

But his strength was failing, and the accursed brute seemed to grow more active and incessant. His knees ached with the attitude, and his arm still trembled with utter fear. From what he told me himself, and from the known hours of his starting and returning, he must have remained not less than two hours perched on that scorching dyke. It is probable that the heat made him somewhat light-headed and that his feet shuffled on the granite. At any rate as the thing came on him with new force he felt the whole fabric crumble beneath him, and the next second was sprawling on his back amid a ruin of stones.

He was aware of a black body hurling on the top of him as he struck feebly in the air. For a moment of agony he waited to be torn, feeling himself beyond resistance. But no savage teeth touched him, and slowly and painfully he raised his head. To his amazement he saw the dog tearing across the moorland in the direction of home.

He was conscious at once of relief, safety, a sort of weak, hysterical joy. Then his delight ceased abruptly, and he scrambled to his feet with all haste. The thing was clearly running for the farm-town, and there in the stack-yard labourers were busied with building hay-ricks – the result of a premature summer. In the yard women would be going to and fro, and some of the Clachlands children playing. What if the mad brute should find its way thither! There could be no issue but the most dismal tragedy.

Now Mr John Anthony Dean was, speaking generally, a fool, but for one short afternoon he proved himself something more. For he turned and ran at his utmost speed after the fleeing dog. His legs were cramped and tottering, he was weak with fear, and his head was giddy with the sun; but he strained every muscle as if he ran for his own life and not for the life of others. His wind was poor at the best, and soon he was panting miserably, with a parched throat and aching chest; but with set teeth he kept up the chase, seeing only a black dot vanishing across the green moorland.

By some strange freak of madness the brute stopped for a second, looked round and waited. Its pursuer was all but helpless, labouring many yards behind; and had it attacked, it could have met little resistance. The man's heart leaped to his mouth, but – and to his glory I tell it – he never slackened pace. The thing suffered him to approach it, he had already conjured up the awful prospect of that final struggle, when by another freak it turned and set off once more for home.

To me it seems a miracle that under that blazing sun he ever reached the farm; but the fact remains that when the dog three minutes later dashed into an empty yard, the man followed some seconds behind it. By the grace of God the place was void; only a stray hen cackled in the summer stillness. Without swerving an inch it ran for the stable and entered the open door. With a last effort the man came up on its heels, shut the bolt, and left it secure.

He scarcely felt that his toil was ended, so painful was his bodily exhaustion. He had never been a strong man in the common sense, and now his heart seemed bursting, his temples throbbed with pain, and all the earth seemed to dance topsy-turvy. But an unknown hardiness of will seemed to drive him on to see this tragic business to an end. It was his part to shoot the dog there and then, to put himself out of anxiety and the world out of danger. So he staggered to the house, found it deserted – one and all being busy in the stack-yard – took down the gun from above the mantelpiece, and slipping a cartridge in each barrel, hurried out with shambling legs.

He looked in through the stable-window, but no dog was there. Cautiously he opened the door, and peered into the blackness of the stalls, but he could see nothing; then, lifting his eyes by chance to the other window, he saw a sash in fragments and the marks of a sudden leap. With a wild horror he realised that the dog was gone.

He rushed to the hill-road, but the place was vacant of life. Then with a desperate surmise he ran to the path which led to the highway. At first he saw nothing, so unsettled was his vision; then something grew upon his sight – a black object moving swiftly amid the white dust.

There was but one course for him. He summoned his strength for a hopeless effort, and set off down the long dazzling roadway in mad pursuit. By this path his cousins were coming; even now the brute might be on them, and in one moment of horror he saw the lady to whom he was devoted the prey of this nameless thing of dread. At this point he lost all control of his nerves; tears of weakness and terror ran over his face; but still he ran as fast as his failing strength suffered – faster, for an overmastering fear put a false speed into his limbs and a deceptive ease in his breast. He cried aloud that the beast might turn on him, for he felt that in any case his duration was but a thing of seconds. But he cried in vain, for the thing heeded him not but vanished into the wood, as he rounded the turn of the hill.

Halfway down the descent is a place shaded with thick trees, cool, green and mossy, a hermitage from the fiercest sun. The grass is like a shorn lawn, and a little stream tinkles in a bed of grey stones. Into this cold dell the man passed from the glare without, and the shock refreshed him. This, as it chanced, was his salvation. He increased his speed, still crying hoarsely the animal's name. When he came once more into the white dust the brute was not fifty yards from him, and as he yelled more desperately, it stopped, turned, saw him, and rushed back to the attack.

He fell on his knees from extreme weakness, and waited with his gun quivering at his shoulder. Now it raked the high heavens, now it was pointed to the distant hills. His hand shook like a child's, and in his blindness he crushed the stock almost against his throat. Up the highway meantime came those ravening jaws, nearer and ever nearer. Like a flash the whole picture of the future lay before him – himself torn and dying, the wild thing leaving him and keeping its old course till it met his friends, and then – more horror and death. And all hung on two cartridges and his uncertain aim.

His nervousness made him draw the trigger when the brute was still many yards away. The shot went clear over its head to spend itself in the empty air. In desperation he nuzzled the stock below his chin, holding it tight till he was all but choked, and waited blindly. The thing loomed up before him in proportions almost gigantic; it seemed to leap to and fro and blot out the summer heavens. He knew he was crazy; he knew, too, that life was in the balance, and that a random aim would mean a short passage to another world. Two glaring eyes shone out of the black mass, the centre, as it were, of its revolutions. With all his strength he drew the point to them and fired. Suddenly the fire seemed to go out, and the twin lights were darkened.

When the party of pretty young women in summer raiment came up the path a minute later, they saw something dark in the mid-road, and on coming nearer found that it was their cousin. But he presented a strange appearance, for in place of the elegant, bronzed young man they knew, they found a broken-down creature with a bleeding throat and a ghastly face, sitting clutching a gun and weeping hysterically beside a hideous, eyeless dog with a shattered jaw which lay dead on the ground.

Such is the tale of Mr John Anthony Dean and his doings on that afternoon of summer. Yet it must be told – and for human nature's sake I regret it – that his sudden flash into the heroic worked no appreciable difference on his ways. He fled the hill country that very month, and during the next winter published a book of very minor poetry (dedicated to his cousin, Miss Phyllis), which contained an execrable rondeau on his adventure, with the refrain – 'From Canine Jaws', wherein the author likened the dog to Cerberus, himself to 'strong Amphitryon's son', and wound up with grateful thanksgiving to the 'Muse' for his rescue. As I said before, it is not my business to apologise for Mr Dean, but it is my privilege to note this proof of the heroic inconsistency of man.

The Oasis in the Snow

John Buchan

This tale was told to me by the shepherd of Callowa, when I sheltered once in his house against an April snowstorm – for he who would fish Gled in spring must fear neither wind nor weather. The shepherd was a man of great height, with the slow, swinging gait, the bent carriage, the honest eyes and the weather-tanned face which are the marks of his class. He talked little, for life is too lonely or too serious in these uplands for idle conversation, but when once his tongue was loosened, under the influence of friendship or drink, he could speak as I have heard few men ever talk, for his mind was a storehouse of forty years' experience, the harvest of an eye shrewd and observant. This story he told me as we sat by the fire, and looked forth every now and then drearily on the weather.

They crack about snaw-storms nowadays, and ken naucht about them. Maybe there's a wee pickle driftin' and a road blockit, and there's a great cry about the terrible storm. But, lord, if they had kenned o' the storms I've kenned o' they would speak a wee thing mair serious and respectfu'. And bodies come here i' the simmer and gang daft about the bonny green hills, as they ca' them, and think life here sae quate and peacefu', as if the folk here had nocht to dae but daunder roond their hills and follow their wark as trig and easy as if they were i' the holms o' Clyde and no i' the muirs o' Gled. But they dinna ken, and weel for them, how cauld and hungry and cruel are the hills, how easy a man gangs to his death i' thae braw glens, how the wind stings i' the morn and the frost bites at nicht, o' the bogs and sklidders and dreich hillsides, where there's life neither for man nor beast.

Weel, about this story, it was yince in a Februar' mony year syne that it a' happened, when I was younger and lichter on my feet and mair gleg i' the seein'.

Ye mind Dr Crichton – he's deid thae ten 'ear, but he was a braw doctor in his time. He could cure when anither was helpless, and the man didna leeve whae wad ride further on less errand.

Now the doctor was terrible keen on fishin' and shootin' and a' manner o' sport. I've heard him say that there were three things he likit weel abune ithers. Yin was the back o' a guid horse, anither a guid water and a clear wast wind, and the third a snawy day and a shot at the white hares. He had been crakin' on me for mony a day to gang wi' him, but I was thrang that 'ear wi' cairtin' up hay for the sheep frae lower doon the glens and couldna dae't. But this day I had trystit to gang wi' him, for there had been a hard frost a' the week, and the hares on the hills wad be in graund fettle. Ye ken the way o' the thing. Yae man keeps yae side o' the hill and the ither the ither, and the beasts gang atween them, back and forrit. Whiles ye'll see them pop round the back o' a dyke and aff again afore ye can get a shot. It's no easy wark, for the skins o' the craturs are ill to tell frae the snawy grund, and a man taks to hae a gleg ee afore he can pick them oot, and a quick hand ere he can shoot. But the doctor was rale skilfu' at it and verra proud, so we set aff brisk-like wi' our guns.

It was snawin' lichtly when we startit, and ere we had gone far it begood to snaw mair. And the air was terrible keen, and cut like a scythe-blade. We were weel wrappit up and walkit a' our pith, but our fingers were soon like to come off, and it was nane sae easy to handle the gun. We tried the Wildshaw Hichts first, and got nane there, though we beat up and doon, and were near smoored wi' snaw i' the gullies. I didna half like the look o' things, for it wasna canny that there should be nae hares and, forbye, the air was getrin' like a rusty saw to the face. But the doctor wad hear naething o' turnin' back, for he had plenty o' speerit, had the man, and said if we didna get hares on yae hill we wad get them on the ither.

At that time ye'll mind that I had twae dowgs, baith guid but verra contrar' in natur'. There was yin ca'ed Tweed, a fine, canty sort o' beast, very freendly to the bairns and gien to followin' me to kirk and things o' that sort. But he was nae guid for the shootin', for he was mortal feared at the sound o' a gun, and wad rin hame as he were shot. The ither I ca'ed Voltaire, because he was terrible against releegion. On Sabbath day about kirk-time he gaed aff to the hills, and never lookit near the hoose till I cam back. But he was a guid sheep dowg and, forbye, he was broken till the gun, and verra near as guid as a retriever. He wadna miss a day's shootin' for the warld, and mony a day he's gane wi'oot his meat ower the heid o't. Weel, on this day he had startit wi' us and said nae words about it, but noo he began to fa' ahint, and I saw fine he didna like the business. I kenned the dowg never did onything wi'oot a guid reason, and that he was no easy to fricht, so I began to feel uneasy. I stopped for a meenute to try him, and pretended I was gaun to turn hame. He cam rinnin' up and barkit about my legs as pleased as ye like, and when I turned again he looked awfu' dowie.

I pointed this oot to the doctor, but he paid nae attention. 'Tut, tut,' says he, 'if ye're gaun to heed a dowg's havers, we micht gie a' thing up at yince.'

'It's nae havers,' I said, hot-like, for I didna like to hear my dowg misca'ed. 'There's mair sense in that beast than what's in a heap o' men's heids.'

'Weel, weel,' he says, 'sae let it be. But I'm gaun on, and ye can come or no, just as ye like.'

'Doctor,' says I again, 'ye dinna ken the risk ye're rinnin'. I'm a better juidge o' the wather than you, and I tell ye that I'm feared at this day. Ye see that the air is as cauld's steel, and yet there's mist a' in front o' ye and ahint. Ye ken the auld owercome, "Rouk is snaw's wraith," and if we dinna see a fearsome snaw afore this day's dune, I'll own my time's been wastit.'

But naething wad move him, and I had to follow him for fair shame. Sune after, too, we startit some hares, and though we didna get ony, it set the excitement o' the sport on us. I sune got as keen as himsel', and sae we trampit on, gettin' farther intil the hills wi' every step, and thinkin' naething about the snaw.

We tried the Gledscleuch and got naething, and syne we gaed on to the Allercleuch, and no anither beast did we see. Then we struck straucht for the Cauldhope Loch, which lies weel hoddit in hills miles frae ony man. But there we cam nae better speed, for a' we saw was the frozen loch and the dowie threshes and snaw, snaw everywhere, lyin' and fa'in'. The day had grown waur, and still that dour man wadna turn back. 'Come on,' says he, 'the drift's clearin', and in a wee we'll be on clear grund,' and he steppit oot as he were on the laigh road. The air wasna half as cauld, but thick just like a nicht in hairst; and though there wasna muckle snaw fa'in' yet, it felt as though there were miles o' 't abune in the cluds and pressin' doun to the yirth. Forbye, it was terrible sair walkin', for though the snaw on the grund wasna deep, it was thick and cloggin'. So on we gaed, the yin o' us in high fettle, the ither no verra carin', till we cam to the herd's shielin' o' the Lanely Bield, whilk lies in the very centre o' the hills, whaur I had never been afore.

We chappit at the door and they took us in. The herd was a dacent man, yin Simon Trumbull, and I had seen him aften at kirk and market. So he bade us welcome, and telled us to get our claes dried, for we wadna gang anither step that nicht. Syne his wife made us tea, and it helpit us michtily, for we had drank a' our whisky lang syne. They had a great fire roarin' up the lum, and I was sweired, I can tell ye, to gang oot o' the warm place again into the ill wather.

But I must needs be aff if I was to be hame that nicht, and keep my wife from gaun oot o' her mind. So I gets up and buttons to my coat.

'Losh, man,' says the herd, 'ye're never thinkin' o' leavin'. It'll be the awfu'est nicht that ever man heard tell o'. I've herdit thae hills this mony 'ear, and I never saw sic tokens o' death i' the air. I've my sheep fauldit lang syne, and my hoose weel stockit, or I wadna bide here wi' an easy hert.'

'A' the mair need that I should gang,' says I, 'me that has naething dune. Ye ken fine my wife. She wad die wi' fricht if I didna come hame.'

Simon went to the door and opened it. It blew back on the wa', and a solid mass o' snaw fell on the floor. 'See that,' he says. 'If ye dinna believe me, believe your ain een. Ye need never think o' seein' Callowa the nicht.'

'See it or no,' said I, 'I'll hae to try 't. Ye'd better bide, doctor; there's nae cause for you to come wi' me.'

'I'll gang wi' you,' he said. 'I brocht ye intil this, and I'll see ye oot o't.' And I never liked the man sae weel as at the word.

When the twae o' us walkit frae that hoose it was like walkin' intil a drift o' snaw. The air was sae thick that we couldna richt see the separate flakes. It was just a great solid mass sinkin' ever doun, and as heavy as a thousand ton o' leid. The breath went frae me at the verra outset. Something clappit on my chest, and I had nocht to dae but warstle on wi' nae mair fushion than a kittlin'. I had a grip o' the doctor's hand, and muckle we needit it, for we wad sune hae been separate and never mair heard o'. My dowg Voltaire, whae was gien for ordinar' to rinnin' wide and playin' himsel', kept close rubbin' against my heels. We were miles frae hame, and unless the thing cleared there was sma' chance o' us winnin' there. Yae guid thing, there was little wind, but just a saft, even fa'; so it wasna so bad as though it had been a fierce driftin'. I had a general kind o' glimmer o' the road, though I had never been in thae hills afore. If we held doun by the Lanely Bield Burn we wad come to the tap o' the Stark Water, whilk cam into Gled no a mile abune Callowa. So on we warstled, prayin' and greetin' like bairns, wi' scarce a thocht o' what we were daein'.

'Whaur are we?' says the doctor in a wee, and his voice sounded as though he had a naipkin roond his mouth.

I think we should be somewhere near the Stark heid,' said I. 'We're gaun doun, and there's nae burn hereaways but it.'

'But I aye thocht the Stark Glen was a' sklidders at the heid,' said he; 'and this is as saft a slope as a hoose riggin'.'

'I canna help that,' says I. 'It maun e'en be it, or we've clean missed the airt.'

So on we gaed again, and the snaw aye got deeper. It wasna awfu' saft, so we didna sink far as we walkit, but it was terrible wearin'. I sune was sae tired that I could scarce drag mysel', forbye being frichtit oot o' my senses. But the doctor was still stoot and hopefu', and I just followed him.

Suddenly, ere ever we kenned, the slope ceased, and we were walkin' on flat grund. I could scarce believe my een, but there it was at my feet, as laigh as a kitchen floor. But the queer thing was that while a' around was deep snaw, this place was a' but bare, and here and there rigs o' green land stuck oot.

'What in the warld's this?' says I, as I steppit oot boldly, and I turned to my companion. When I saw him I was fair astonished. For his face was white as the snaw, and he was tremblin' to his fingers.

'Ye're no feared, are ye?' I asked. 'D' ye no ken guid land when ye see 't?'

His teeth were chattering in his heid. 'You hae na sense to be feared. The Almichty help us, but I believe we're daein' what nae man ever did afore.'

I never saw sae queer a place. The great wecht o' snaw was still fa'in' on us, but it seemed to disappear when it cam to the grund. And our feet when we steppit aye sank a wee bit, but no in snaw. The feel i' the air wasna cauld, but if onything 't was het and damp. The sweat began to rin doon aff my broo, and I could hear the man ahint me pantin' like a broken-winded horse. I lookit roond me for the dowg, but nae dowg was to be seen; for at the first step we took on the queer land he had ta'en himsel' aff. I didna like the look o't, for it wad hae ta'en muckle to drive the beast frae my side.

Every now and then we cam on a wee hillock whaur the snaw lay deeper, but the spaces atween were black and saft, and crunkled aneath the feet. Ye ken i' the spring about the burn-heids how the water rins oot o' the grund, and a' the colour o' the place is a sodden grey. Weel, 't was the same here. There was a seepin', dreepin' feel i' the grund whilk made it awesome to the eye. Had I been i' my clear senses, I wad hae been rale puzzled about the maitter, but I was donnered wi' the drifts and the weariness, and thocht only o' gettin' by 't. But sune a kind o' terror o' the thing took me. Every time my feet touched the grund, as I walkit, a groo gae'd through my body. I grat wi' the fair hate o' the place, and when I lookit at my neebor it didna mak me better. For there he was gaun along shakin' like a tree-tap, and as white 's a clout. It made it waur that the snaw was sae thick i' the air that we couldna see a foot in front. It was like walkin' blindfold roond the tap o' a linn.

Then a' of a sudden the bare grund stopped, and we were flounderin' among deep drifts up to the middle. And yet it was a relief, and my hert was strengthened. By this time I had clean lost coont o' the road, but we keepit aye to the laigh land, whiles dippin' intil a glen and whiles warstlin' up a brae face. I had learned frae mony days in hill mists to keep frae gaun roond about. We focht our way like fair deevils, for the terror o' the place ahint had grippit us like a vice. We ne'er spak a word, but wrocht till our herts were like to burst and our een felt fou o' bluid. It got caulder and caulder, and thicker and ever thicker. Hope had lang syne gane frae us, and fricht had ta'en its place. It was just a maitter o' keepin' up till we fell down, and then . . .

It wasna lang ere they fund us, for find us they did, by God's grace and the help o' the dowg. For the beast went hame and made sic a steer that my wife roused the nearest neebor and got folk startit oot to seek us. And wad ye believe it, the dowg took them to the verra bit. They fund the doctor last, and he lay in his bed for a month and mair wi' the effects. But for mysel', I was nane the waur. When they took me hame, I was put to bed, and sleepit on for twenty hoor, as if I had been streikit oot. They waukened me every six hoor, and put a spoonfu' o' brandy doon my throat, and when a' was feenished, I rase as weel as ever.

It was about fower months after that I had to gang ower to Annandale wi' sheep, and cam back by the hills. It was a road I had never been afore, and I think it was the wildest that ever man trod. I mind it was a warm, bricht day, verra het and wearisome for the walkin'. By and by I cam to a place I seemed to ken, though I had never been there to my mind, and I thocht hoo I could hae seen it afore. Then I mindit that it was abune the heid o' the Stark, and though the snaw had been in my een when I last saw it, I minded the lie o' the land and the saft slope. I turned verra keen to ken what the place was whaur me and the doctor had had sic a fricht. So I went oot o' my way, and climbed yae hill and gaed doun anither, till I cam to a wee rig, and lookit doun on the verra bit.

I just lookit yince, and then turned awa' wi' my hen i' my mooth.

For there below was a great green bog, oozing and blinking in the sun.

The Far Islands

John Buchan

Lady Alice, Lady Louise,
Between the wash of the tumbling seas –

I

When Bran the Blessed, as the story goes, followed the white bird on the Last Questing, knowing that return was not for him, he gave gifts to his followers. To Heliodorus he gave the gift of winning speech, and straightaway the man went south to the Italian seas, and, becoming a scholar, left many descendants who sat in the high places of the Church. To Raymond he gave his steel battle-axe, and bade him go out to the warrior's path and hew his way to a throne, which the man forthwith accomplished, and became an ancestor in the fourth degree of the first king of Scots. But to Colin, the youngest and the dearest, he gave no gift, whispering only a word in his ear and laying a finger on his eyelids. Yet Colin was satisfied, and he alone of the three, after their master's going, remained on that coast of rock and heather.

In the third generation from Colin, as our elders counted years, came one Colin the Red, who built his keep on the cliffs of Acharra and was a mighty sea-rover in his day. Five times he sailed to the rich parts of France, and a good score of times he carried his flag of three stars against the easterly Vikings. A mere name in story, but a sounding piece of nomenclature well garnished with tales. A master-mind by all accounts, but cursed with a habit of fantasy; for, hearing in his old age of a land to the westward, he forthwith sailed into the sunset, but three days later was washed up, a twisted body, on one of the outer isles.

So far it is but legend, but with his grandson Colin the Red, we fall into the safer hands of the chroniclers. To him God gave the unnumbered sorrows of storytelling, for he was a bard, cursed with a bard's fervours, and none the less a mighty warrior among his own folk. He it was who wrote the lament called 'The White Waters of Usna', and the exquisite chain of romances, 'Glede-Red Gold and Grey Silver'. His tales were told by many fires, down to our grandfathers' time, and you will find them still pounded at by the folklorists. But his airs – they are eternal. On harp and pipe they have lived through the centuries; twisted and tortured, they survive in many song-books; and I declare that the other day I heard the most beautiful of them all murdered by a band at a German watering-place. This Colin led the wanderer's life, for he disappeared at middle-age, no one knew whither, and his return was long looked for by his people. Some thought that he became a Christian monk, the holy man living in the seagirt isle of Cuna, who was found dead in extreme old age, kneeling on the beach, with his arms, contrary to the fashion of the Church, stretched to the westward.

As history narrowed into bonds and forms the descendants of Colin took Raden for their surname, and settled more firmly on their lands in the long peninsula of crag and inlets which runs west to the Atlantic. Under Donald of the Isles they harried the Kings of Scots, or, on their own authority, made war on Macleans and Macranalds, till their flag of the three stars, their badge of the grey-goose feather and their on-cry of 'Cuna' were feared from Lochalsh to Cantire. Later they made a truce with the king, and entered into the royal councils. For years they warded the western coast, and as king's lieutenants smoked out the inferior pirates of Eigg and Torosay. A Raden was made a Lord of Sleat, another was given lands in the low country and the name Baron of Strathyre, but their honours were transitory and short as their lives. Rarely one of the house saw middle-age. A bold, handsome and stirring race, it was their fate to be cut off in the rude warfare of the times, or, if peace had them in its clutches, to man vessel and set off once more on those mad western voyages which were the weird of the family. Three of the name were found drowned on the far shore of Cuna, more than one sailed straight out of the ken of mortals. One rode with the Good Lord James on the pilgrimage of the Heart of Bruce, and died by his leader's side in the Saracen battle. Long afterwards a Raden led the western men against the Cheshire archers at Flodden, and was slain himself in the steel circle around the king.

But the years brought peace and a greater wealth, and soon the cold stone tower was left solitary on the headland, and the new house of Kinlochuna rose by the green links of the stream. The family changed its faith, and an Episcopal chaplain took the place of the old mass-priest in the tutoring of the sons. Radens were in the '15 and the '45. They rose with Bute to power, and they long disputed the pride of Dundas in the northern capital. They intermarried with great English houses till the sons of the family were Scots only in name, living much abroad or in London, many of them English landowners by virtue of a mother's blood. Soon the race was of the common over-civilised type, graceful, well-mannered, with abundant good looks, but only once in a generation reverting to the rugged northern strength. Eton and Oxford had in turn displaced the family chaplain, and the house by the windy headland grew emptier and emptier save when grouse and deer brought home its fickle masters.

2

A childish illness brought Colin to Kinlochuna when he had reached the mature age of five, and delicate health kept him there for the greater part of the next six years. During the winter he lived in London, but from the late northern spring, through all the long bright summers, he lived in the great tenantless place without company – for he was an only child. A French nurse had the charge of his doings, and when he had passed through the formality of lessons there were the long pine woods at his disposal, the rough moor, the wonderful black holes with the rich black mud in them, and best of all the bay of Acharra, below the headland, with Cuna lying in the waves a mile to the west. At such times his father was busy elsewhere; his mother was dead; the family had few near relatives; so he passed a solitary childhood in the company of seagulls and the birds of the moor.

His time for the beach was the afternoon. On the left as you go down through the woods from the house there runs out the great headland of Acharra, red and grey with mosses, and with a nimbus always of screaming sea-fowl. To the right runs a low beach of sand, passing into rough limestone boulders and then into the heather of the wood. This in turn is bounded by a reef of low rocks falling by gentle breaks to the water's edge. It is crowned with a tangle of heath and fern, bright at most seasons with flowers, and dwarf pine trees straggle on its crest till one sees the meaning of its Gaelic name, 'The Ragged Cock's-Comb'. This place was Colin's playground in fine weather. When it blew rain or snow from the north he dwelt indoors among dogs and books, puzzling his way through great volumes from his father's shelves. But when the mild west-wind weather fell on the sea, then he would lie on the hot sand – Amelie the nurse reading a novel on the nearest rock – and kick his small heels as he followed his fancy. He built great sandcastles to the shape of Acharra old tower, and peopled them with preposterous knights and ladies; he drew great moats and rivers for the tide to fill; he fought battles innumerable with crackling seaweed, till Amelie, with her sharp cry of, 'Colin, Colin,' would carry him houseward for tea.

Two fancies remained in his mind through those boyish years. One was about the mysterious shining sea before him. In certain weathers it seemed to him a solid pathway. Cuna, the little ragged isle, ceased to block the horizon, and his own white road ran away down into the west, till suddenly it stopped and he saw no farther. He knew he ought to see more, but always at one place, just when his thoughts were pacing the white road most gallantly, there came a baffling mist to his sight, and he found himself looking at a commonplace sea with Cuna lying very real and palpable in the offing. It was a vexatious limitation, for all his dreams were about this pathway. One day in June, when the waters slept in a deep heat, he came down the sands barefoot, and lo! there was his pathway. For one moment things seemed clear, the mist had not gathered on the road, and with a cry he ran down to the tide's edge and waded in. The touch of water dispelled the illusion, and almost in tears he saw the cruel back of Cuna blotting out his own magic way.

The other fancy was about the low ridge of rocks which bounded the bay on the right. His walks had never extended beyond it, either on the sands or inland, for that way lay a steep hillside and a perilous bog. But often on the sands he had come to its foot and wondered what country lay beyond. He made many efforts to explore it, difficult efforts, for the vigilant Amelie had first to be avoided. Once he was almost at the top when some seaweed to which he clung gave way, and he rolled back again to the soft warm sand. By and by he found that he knew what was beyond. A clear picture had built itself up in his brain of a mile of reefs, with sand in bars between them, and beyond all a sea-wood of alders slipping from the hill's skirts to the water's edge. This was not what he wanted in his explorations, so he stopped, till one day it struck him that the westward view might reveal something beyond the hog-backed Cuna. One day, pioneering alone, he scaled the steepest heights of the seaweed and pulled his chin over the crest of the ridge. There, sure enough, was his picture – a mile of reefs and the tattered sea-wood. He turned eagerly seawards. Cuna still lay humped on the waters, but beyond it he seemed to see his shining pathway running far to a speck which might be an island. Crazy with pleasure he stared at the vision till slowly it melted into the waves, and Cuna the inexorable once more blocked the skyline. He climbed down, his heart in a doubt between despondency and hope.

It was the last day of such fancies, for on the morrow he had to face the new world of school.

At Cecil's Colin found a new life and a thousand new interests. His early delicacy had been driven away by the sea-winds of Acharra, and he was rapidly growing up a tall, strong child, straight of limb like all his house, but sinewy and alert beyond his years. He learned new games with astonishing facility, became a fast bowler with a genius for twists, and a Rugby three-quarters full of pluck and cunning. He soon attained to the modified popularity of a private school, and, being essentially clean, strong and healthy, found himself a mark for his juniors' worship and a favourite with masters. The homage did not spoil him, for no boy was ever less self-possessed. On the cricket-ground and the football-field he was a leader, but in private he had the nervous, sensitive manners of the would-be recluse. No one ever accused him of 'side' – his polite, halting address was the same to junior and senior, and the result was that wild affection which simplicity in the great is wont to inspire. He spoke with a pure accent, in which lurked no northern trace; in a little he had forgotten all about his birthplace and his origin. His name had at first acquired for him the sobriquet of 'Scottie', but the title was soon dropped from its manifest inaptness.

In his second year at Cecil's he caught a prevalent fever, and for days lay very near the brink of death. At his worst he was wildly delirious, crying ceaselessly for Acharra and the beach at Kinlochuna. But as he grew convalescent the absorption remained, and for the moment he seemed to have forgotten his southern life. He found himself playing on the sands, always with the boundary ridge before him, and the hump of Cuna rising in the sea. When dragged back to his environment by the inquiries of Bellew, his special friend, who came to sit with him, he was so abstracted and forgetful that the good Bellew was seriously grieved. 'The chap's a bit cracked, you know,' he announced in hall. 'Didn't know me. Asked me what "footer" meant when I told him about the Bayswick match, and talked about nothing but a lot of heathen Scotch names.'

One dream haunted Colin throughout the days of his recovery. He was tormented with a furious thirst, poorly assuaged at long intervals by watered milk. So when he crossed the borders of dreamland his first search was always for a well. He tried the brushwood inland from the beach, but it was dry as stone. Then he climbed with difficulty the boundary ridge, and found little pools of salt water, while far on the other side gleamed the dark black bog-holes. Here was not what he sought, and he was in deep despair, till suddenly over the sea he caught a glimpse of his old path running beyond Cuna to a bank of mist. He rushed down to the tide's edge, and to his amazement found solid ground. Now was the chance for which he had long looked, and he ran happily westwards, till of a sudden the solid earth seemed to sink with him, and he was in the waters struggling. But two curious things he noted. One was that the far bank of mist seemed to open for a pinpoint of time, and he had a gleam of land. He saw nothing distinctly, only a line which was not mist and was not water. The second was that the water was fresh, and as he was drinking from this curious new fresh sea he awoke. The dream was repeated three times before he left the sickroom. Always he wakened at the same place, always he quenched his thirst in the fresh sea, but never again did the mist open for him and show him the strange country.

From Cecil's he went to the famous school which was the tradition in his family. The head spoke to his housemaster of his coming. 'We are to have another Raden here,' he said, 'and I am glad of it, if the young one turns out to be anything like the others. There's a good deal of dry-rot among the boys just now. They are all too old for their years and too wise in the wrong way. They haven't anything like the enthusiasm in games they had twenty years ago when I first came here. I hope this young Raden will stir them up.' The housemaster agreed, and when he first caught sight of Colin's slim, well-knit figure, looked into the handsome kindly eyes, and heard his curiously diffident speech, his doubts vanished. 'We have got the right stuff now,' he told himself, and the senior for whom the new boy fagged made the same comment.

From the anomalous insignificance of fagdom Colin climbed up the school, leaving everywhere a record of honest good-nature. He was allowed to forget his cricket and football, but in return he was initiated into the mysteries of the river. Water had always been his delight, so he went through the dreary preliminaries of being coached in a tub-pair till he learned to swing steadily and get his arms quickly forward. Then came the stages of scratch fours and scratch eights, till after a long apprenticeship he was promoted to the dignity of a thwart in the Eight itself. In his last year he was captain of boats, a position which joins the responsibility of a cabinet minister to the rapturous popular applause of a successful warrior. Nor was he the least distinguished of a great band. With Colin at seven the school won the Ladies' after the closest race on record.

The head's prophecy fell true, for Colin was a born leader. For all his good-humour and diffidence of speech, he had a trick of shutting his teeth which all respected. As captain he was the idol of the school, and he ruled it well and justly. For the rest, he was a curious boy with none of the ordinary young enthusiasms, reserved for all his kindliness. At house 'shouters' his was not the voice which led the stirring strains of 'Stroke out all you know', though his position demanded it. He cared little about work, and the Schoolhouse scholar, who fancied him from his manner a devotee of things intellectual, found in Colin but an affected interest. He read a certain amount of modern poetry with considerable boredom, fiction he never opened. The truth was that he had a romance in his own brain which, willy-nilly, would play itself out, and which left him small relish for the pale second-hand inanities of art. Often, when with others he would lie in the deep meadows by the river on some hot summer's day, his fancies would take a curious colour. He adored the soft English landscape, the lush grasses, the slow streams, the ancient secular trees. But as he looked into the hazy green distance a colder air would blow on his cheek, a pungent smell of salt and pines would be for a moment in his nostrils, and he would be gazing at a line of waves on a beach, a ridge of low rocks, and a shining sea-path running out to – ah, that he could not tell! The envious Cuna would suddenly block all the vistas. He had constantly the vision before his eyes, and he strove to strain into the distance before Cuna should intervene. Once or twice he seemed almost to achieve it. He found that by keeping on the top of the low rock-ridge he could cheat Cuna by a second or two, and get a glimpse of a misty something out in the west. The vision took odd times for recurring – once or twice in a lecture, once on the cricket-ground, many times in the fields of a Sunday, and once while he paddled down to the start in a Trials race. It gave him a keen pleasure: it was his private domain, where at any moment he might make some enchanting discovery.

At this time he began to spend his vacations at Kinlochuna. His father, an elderly ex-diplomat, had permanently taken up his abode there, and was rapidly settling into the easy life of the Scots laird. Colin returned to his native place without enthusiasm. His childhood there had been full of lonely hours, and he had come to like the warm south country. He found the house full of people, for his father entertained hugely, and the talk was of sport and sport alone. As a rule, your very great athlete is bored by Scots shooting. Long hours of tramping and crouching among heather cramp without fully exercising the body, and unless he has the love of the thing ingrained in him, the odds are that he will wish himself home. The father, in his new-found admiration for his lot, was content to face all weathers; the son found it an effort to keep pace with such vigour. He thought upon the sunlit fields and reedy watercourses with regret, and saw little in the hills but a rough waste scarred with rock and sour with mosses.

He read widely throughout these days, for his father had a taste for modern letters, and new books lay littered about the rooms. He read queer Celtic tales which he thought 'sickening rot', and mild Celtic poetry which he failed to understand. Among the guests was a noted manufacturer of fiction, whom the elder Raden had met somewhere and bidden to Kinlochuna. He had heard the tale of Colin's ancestors and the sea headland of Acharra, and one day he asked the boy to show him the place, as he wished to make a story of it. Colin assented unwillingly, for he had been slow to visit this place of memories, and he did not care to make his first experiment in such company. But the gentleman would not be gainsaid, so the two scrambled through the sea-wood and climbed the low ridge which looked over the bay. The weather was mist and drizzle; Cuna had wholly hidden herself, and the bluff Acharra loomed hazy and far. Colin was oddly disappointed: this reality was a poor place compared with his fancies. His companion stroked his peaked beard, talked nonsense about Colin the Red and rhetoric about 'the spirit of the misty grey weather having entered into the old tale'. 'Think,' he cried, 'to those old warriors beyond that bank of mist was the whole desire of life, the Golden City, the Far Islands, whatever you care to call it.' Colin shivered, as if his holy places had been profaned, set down the man in his mind most unjustly as an 'awful little cad', and hurried him back to the house.

Oxford received the boy with open arms, for his reputation had long preceded him. To the majority of men he was the one freshman of his year, and gossip was busy with his prospects. Nor was gossip disappointed. In his first year he rowed seven in the Eight. The next year he was captain of his college boats, and a year later the OUBC made him its president. For three years he rowed in the winning Eight, and old coaches agreed that in him the perfect seven had been found. It was he who in the famous race of 18— caught up in the last three hundred yards the quickened stroke which gave Oxford victory. As he grew to his full strength he became a splendid figure of a man – tall, supple, deep-chested for all his elegance. His quick dark eyes and his kindly hesitating manners made people think his face extraordinarily handsome, when really it was in no way above the common. But his whole figure, as he stood in his shorts and sweater on the raft at Putney, was so full of youth and strength that people involuntarily smiled when they saw him – a smile of pleasure in so proper a piece of manhood.

Colin enjoyed life hugely at Oxford, for to one so frank and well equipped the place gave of its best. He was the most distinguished personage of his day there, but, save to school friends and the men he met officially on the river, he was little known. His diffidence and his very real exclusiveness kept him from being the centre of a host of friends. His own countrymen in the place were utterly nonplussed by him. They claimed him eagerly as a fellow, but he had none of the ordinary characteristics of the race. There were Scots of every description around him – pale-faced Scots who worked incessantly, metaphysical Scots who talked in the Union, robustious Scots who played football. They were all men of hearty manners and many enthusiasms – who quoted Burns and dined to the immortal bard's honour every 25th of January; who told interminable Scotch stories, and fell into fervours over national sports, dishes, drinks and religions. To the poor Colin it was all inexplicable. At the remote house of Kinlochuna he had never heard of a Free Kirk or a haggis. He had never read a line of Burns, Scott bored him exceedingly, and in all honesty he thought Scots games inferior to southern sports. He had no great love for the bleak country, he cared nothing for the traditions of his house, so he was promptly set down by his compatriots as 'denationalised and degenerate'.

He was idle, too, during these years as far as his 'schools' were concerned, but he was always very intent upon his own private business. Whenever he sat down to read, when he sprawled on the grass at river picnics, in chapel, at lectures – in short, at any moment when his body was at rest and his mind at leisure – his fancies were off on the same old path. Things had changed, however, in that country. The boyish device of a hard road running over the waters had gone, and now it was invariably a boat which he saw beached on the shingle. It differed in shape. At first it was an ugly salmon-coble, such as the fishermen used for the nets at Kinlochuna. Then it passed, by rapid transitions, through a canvas skiff which it took good watermanship to sit, a whiff and an ordinary dinghy, till at last it settled itself into a long rough boat, pointed at both ends, with oar-holes in the sides instead of rowlocks. It was the devil's own business to launch it, and launch it anew he was compelled to for every journey, for though he left it bound in a little rock hollow below the ridge after landing, yet when he returned, lo! there was the clumsy thing high and dry upon the beach.

The odd point about the new venture was that Cuna had ceased to trouble him. As soon as he had pulled his first stroke the island disappeared, and nothing lay before him but the sea-fog. Yet, try as he might, he could come little nearer. The shores behind him might sink and lessen, but the impenetrable mist was still miles to the westward. Sometimes he rowed so far that the shore was a thin line upon the horizon, but when he turned the boat it seemed to ground in a second on the beach. The long laboured journey out and the instantaneous return puzzled him at first, but soon he became used to them. His one grief was the mist, which seemed to grow denser as he neared it. The sudden glimpse of land which he had got from the ridge of rock in the old boyish days was now denied him, and with the denial came a keener exultation in the quest. Somewhere in the west, he knew, must be land, and in this land a well of sweet water – for so he had interpreted his feverish dream. Sometimes, when the wind blew against him, he caught scents from it – generally the scent of pines, as on the little ridge on the shore behind him.

One day on his college barge, while he was waiting for a picnic party to start, he seemed to get nearer than before. Out on that western sea, as he saw it, it was fresh, blowing weather, with a clear hot sky above. It was hard work rowing, for the wind was against him, and the sun scorched his forehead. The air seemed full of scents – and sounds, too, sounds of faraway surf and wind in trees. He rested for a moment on his oars and turned his head. His heart beat quickly, for there was a rift in the mist, and far through a line of sand ringed with snow-white foam.

Somebody shook him roughly; 'Come on, Colin, old man. They're all waiting for you. Do you know you've been half asleep?'

Colin rose and followed silently, with drowsy eyes. His mind was curiously excited. He had looked inside the veil of mist. Now he knew what was the land he sought.

He made the voyage often, now that the spell was broken. It was short work to launch the boat, and, whereas it had been a long pull formerly, now it needed only a few strokes to bring him to the rim of the mist. There was no chance of getting farther, and he scarcely tried. He was content to rest there, in a world of curious scents and sounds, till the mist drew down and he was driven back to shore.

The change in his environment troubled him little. For a man who has been an idol at the University to fall suddenly into the comparative insignificance of Town is often a bitter experience; but Colin, whose thoughts were not ambitious, scarcely noticed it. He found that he was less his own master than before, but he humbled himself to his new duties without complaint. Many of his old friends were about him; he had plenty of acquaintances; and, being 'sufficient unto himself, he was unaccustomed to ennui. Invitations showered upon him thick and fast. Matchmaking mothers, knowing his birth and his father's income, and reflecting that he was the only child of his house, desired him as a son-in-law. He was bidden welcome everywhere, and the young girls, for whose sake he was thus courted, found in him an attractive mystery. The tall good-looking athlete, with the kind eyes and the preposterously nervous manner, wakened their maidenly sympathies. As they danced with him or sat next to him at dinner, they talked fervently of Oxford, of the north, of the army, of his friends. 'Stupid, but nice, my dear,' was Lady Afflint's comment; and Miss Clara Etheridge, the beauty of the year, declared to her friends that he was a 'dear boy, but so awkward'. He was always forgetful, and ever apologetic; and when he forgot the Shandwicks' theatre-party, the Herapaths' dance, and at least a dozen minor matters, he began to acquire the reputation of a cynic and a recluse.

'You're a queer chap, Col,' Lieutenant Bellew said in expostulation. Colin shrugged his shoulders; he was used to the description.

'Do you know that Clara Etheridge was trying all she knew to please you this afternoon, and you looked as if you weren't listening? Most men would have given their ears to be in your place.'

'I'm awfully sorry, but I thought I was very polite to her.'

'And why weren't you at the Marshams' show?'

'Oh, I went to polo with Collinson and another man. And, I say, old chap, I'm not coming to the Logans tomorrow. I've got a fence on with Adair at the school.'

Little Bellew, who was a tremendous mirror of fashion and chevalier in general, looked up curiously at his tall friend.

'Why don't you like the women. Col, when they're so fond of you?'

'They aren't,' said Colin hotly, 'and I don't dislike 'em. But, Lord! they bore me. I might be doing twenty things when I talk nonsense to one of 'em for an hour. I come back as stupid as an owl, and besides there's heaps of things better sport.'

The truth was that, while among men he was a leader and at his ease, among women his psychic balance was so oddly upset that he grew nervous and returned unhappy. The boat on the beach, ready in general to appear at the slightest call, would delay long after such experiences, and its place would be taken by some woman's face for which he cared not a straw. For the boat, on the other hand, he cared a very great deal. In all his frank wholesome existence there was this enchanting background, this pleasure-garden which he cherished more than anything in life. He had come of late to look at it with somewhat different eyes. The eager desire to search behind the mist was ever with him, but now he had also some curiosity about the details of the picture. As he pulled out to the rim of the mist sounds seemed to shape themselves on his lips, which by and by grew into actual words in his memory. He wrote them down in scraps, and after some sorting they seemed to him a kind of Latin. He remembered a college friend of his, one Medway, now reading for the Bar, who had been the foremost scholar of his acquaintance; so with the scrap of paper in his pocket he climbed one evening to Medway's rooms in the Temple.

The man read the words curiously, and puzzled for a bit. 'What's made you take to Latin comps so late in life, Colin? It's baddish, you know, even for you. I thought they'd have licked more into you at Eton.'

Colin grinned with amusement. 'I'll tell you about it later,' he said. 'Can you make out what it means?'

'It seems to be a kind of dog-Latin or monkish Latin or something of the sort,' said Medway. 'It reads like this: *Soles occidere solent* (that's cribbed from Catullus, and besides it's the regular monkish pun) . . . *qua* . . . then *blandula* something. Then there's a lot of Choctaw, and then *ilice insulae dilectae in quas festinant somnia ammulae gaudia*. That's pretty fair rot. Hullo, by George! here's something better – *Insula pomorum insula vitae*. That's Geoffrey of Monmouth.'

He made a dive to a bookcase and pulled out a battered little calf-bound duodecimo. 'Here's all about your Isle of Apple Trees. Listen.

"Situate far out in the Western ocean, beyond the Utmost Islands, beyond even the little Isle of Sheep where the cairns of dead men are, lies the Island of Apple Trees where the heroes and princes of the nations live their second life." ' He closed the book and put it back. 'It's the old ancient story, the Greek Hesperides, the British Avalon, and this Apple Tree Island is the northern equivalent.'

Colin sat entranced, his memory busy with a problem. Could he distinguish the scent of apple trees among the perfumes of the rim of the mist. For the moment he thought he could. He was roused by Medway's voice asking the story of the writing.

'Oh, it's just some nonsense that was running in my head, so I wrote it down to see what it was.'

'But you must have been reading. A new exercise for you, Colin!'

'No, I wasn't reading. Look here. You know the sort of pictures you make for yourself of places you like.'

'Rather! Mine is a Yorkshire moor with a little red shooting-box in the heart of it.'

'Well, mine is different. Mine is a sort of beach with a sea and a lot of islands somewhere far out. It is a jolly place, fresh, you know, and blowing, and smells good. 'Pon my word, now I think of it, there's always been a scent of apples.'

'Sort of cider-press? Well, I must be off. You'd better come round to the club and see the telegrams about the war. *You* should be keen about it.'

One evening, a week later, Medway met a friend called Tillotson at the club, and, being lonely, they dined together. Tillotson was a man of some note in science, a dabbler in psychology, an amateur historian, a ripe genealogist. They talked of politics and the war, of a new book, of Mrs Runnymede, and finally of their hobbies.

'I am writing an article,' said Tillotson. 'Craikes asked me to do it for the *Monthly*. It's on a nice point in psychics. I call it "The Transmission of Fallacies", but I do not mean the logical kind. The question is. Can a particular form of hallucination run in a family for generations? The proof must, of course, come from my genealogical studies. I maintain it can. I instance the Douglas-Emotts, not one of whom can see straight with the left eye. That is one side. In another class of examples I take the Drapiers, who hate salt water and never go on board ship if they can help it. Then you remember the Durwards? Old Lady Balcrynie used to tell me that no one of the lot could ever stand the sight of a green frock. There's a chance for the romancer. The Manorwaters have the same madness, only their colour is red.'

A vague remembrance haunted Medway's brain.

'I know a man who might give you points from his own case. Did you ever meet a chap named Raden – Colin Raden?'

Tillotson nodded. 'Long chap – in the Guards? 'Varsity oar, and used to be a crack bowler? No, I don't know him. I know him well by sight, and I should like to meet him tremendously – as a genealogist, of course.'

'Why?' asked Medway.

'Why? Because the man's family is unique. You never hear much about them nowadays, but away up in that north-west corner of Scotland they have ruled since the days of Noah. Why, man, they were aristocrats when our Howards and Nevilles were greengrocers. I wish you would get this Raden to meet me some night.'

'I am afraid there's no chance of it just at present,' said Medway, taking up an evening paper. 'I see that his regiment has gone to the front. But remind me when he comes back, and I'll be delighted.'

3

And now there began for Colin a curious divided life: without, a constant shifting of scene, days of heat and bustle and toil; within, a slow, tantalising, yet exquisite adventure. The rim of the mist was now no more the goal of his journeys, but the starting-point. Lying there, amid cool, fragrant sea-winds, his fanciful ear was subtly alert for the sounds of the dim land before him. Sleeping and waking the quest haunted him. As he flung himself on his bed the kerosene-filled air would change to an ocean freshness, the old boat would rock beneath him, and with clear eye and a boyish hope he would be waiting and watching. And then suddenly he would be back on shore, Cuna and the Acharra headland shining grey in the morning light, and with gritty mouth and sand-filled eyes he would awaken to the heat of the desert camp.

He was kept busy, for his good-humour and energy made him a willing slave, and he was ready enough for volunteer work when others were weak with heat and despair. A thirty-mile ride left him untired; more, he followed the campaign with a sharp intelligence and found a new enthusiasm for his profession. Discomforts there might be, but the days were happy, and then – the cool land, the bright land, which was his for the thinking of it.

Soon they gave him reconnoitring work to do, and his wits were put to the trial. He came well out of the thing, and earned golden praise from the silent colonel in command. He enjoyed it as he had enjoyed a hard race on the river or a good cricket match, and when his worried companions marvelled at his zeal he stammered and grew uncomfortable.

'How the deuce do you keep it up, Colin?' the major asked him. 'I'm an old hand at the job, and yet I've got a temper like devilled bones. You seem as chirpy as if you were going out to fish a chalk stream on a June morning.'

'Well, the fact is – ' and Colin pulled himself up short, knowing that he could never explain. He felt miserably that he had an unfair advantage over the others. Poor Bellew, who groaned and swore in the heat at his side, knew nothing of the rim of the mist. It was really rough luck on the poor beggars, and who but himself was the fortunate man?

As the days passed a curious thing happened. He found fragments of the other world straying into his common life. The barriers of the two domains were falling, and more than once he caught himself looking at a steel-blue sea when his eyes should have found a mustard-coloured desert. One day, on a reconnoitring expedition, they stopped for a little on a hillock above a jungle of scrub, and, being hot and tired, scanned listlessly the endless yellow distances.

'I suppose yon hill is about ten miles off,' said Bellew with dry lips. Colin looked vaguely. 'I should say five.'

'And what's that below it – the black patch? Stones or scrub?'

Colin was in a daydream. 'Why do you call it black? It's blue, quite blue.'

'Rot,' said the other. 'It's grey-black.'

'No, it's water with the sun shining on it. It's blue, but just at the edges it's very near sea-green.'

Bellew rose excitedly. 'Hullo, Col, you're seeing the mirage! And you the fittest of the lot of us! You've got the sun in your head, old man!'

'Mirage!' Colin cried in contempt. He was awake now, but the thought of confusing his own bright western sea with a mirage gave him a curious pain. For a moment he felt the gulf of separation between his two worlds, but only for a moment. As the party remounted he gave his fancies the rein, and ere he reached camp he had felt the oars in his hand and sniffed the apple-tree blossom from the distant beaches.

The major came to him after supper.

'Bellew told me you were a bit odd today, Colin,' he said. 'I expect your eyes are getting baddish. Better get your sand-spectacles out.'

Colin laughed. 'Thanks. It's awfully good of you to bother, but I think Bellew took me up wrong. I never was fitter in my life.'

By and by the turn came for pride to be humbled. A low desert fever took him, and though he went through the day as usual, it was with dreary lassitude; and at night, with hot hands clasped above his damp hair, he found sleep a hard goddess to conquer.

It was the normal condition of the others, so he had small cause to complain, but it worked havoc with his fancies. He had never been ill since his childish days, and this little fever meant much to one whose nature was poised on a needlepoint. He found himself confronted with a hard bare world, with the gilt rubbed from its corners. The rim of the mist seemed a place of vague horrors; when he reached it his soul was consumed with terror; he struggled impotently to advance; behind him Cuna and the Acharra coast seemed a place of evil dreams. Again, as in his old fever, he was tormented with a devouring thirst, but the sea beside him was not fresh, but brackish as a rock-pool. He yearned for the apple-tree beaches in front; there, he knew, were cold springs of water; the fresh smell of it was blown towards him in his nightmare.

But as the days passed and the misery for all grew more intense, an odd hope began to rise in his mind. It could not last, coolness and health were waiting near, and his reason for the hope came from the odd events at the rim of the mist. The haze was clearing from the foreground, the surf-lined coast seemed nearer, and though all was obscure save the milk-white sand and the foam, yet here was earnest enough for him. Once more he became cheerful; weak and light-headed he rode out again; and the major, who was recovering from sunstroke, found envy take the place of pity in his soul.

The hope was near fulfilment. One evening when the heat was changing into the cooler twilight, Colin and Bellew were sent with a small picked body to scour the foothills above the river in case of a flank attack during the night-march. It was work they had done regularly for weeks, and it is possible that precautions were relaxed. At any rate, as they turned a corner of hill, in a sandy pass where barren rocks looked down on more barren thorn thickets, a couple of rifle-shots rang out from the scarp, and above them appeared a line of dark faces and white steel. A mere handful, taken at a disadvantage, they could not hope to disperse numbers, so Colin gave the word to wheel about and return. Again shots rang out, and little Bellew had only time to catch at his friend's arm to save him from falling from the saddle.

The word of command had scarcely left Colin's mouth when a sharp pain went through his chest, and his breath seemed to catch and stop. He felt as in a condensed moment of time the heat, the desert smell, the dust in his eyes and throat, while he leaned helplessly forward on his horse's mane. Then the world vanished for him . . . The boat was rocking under him, the oars in his hand. He pulled and it moved, straight, arrow-like towards the forbidden shore. As if under a great wind the mist furled up and fled. Scents of pines, of apple trees, of great fields of thyme and heather, hung about him; the sound of wind in a forest, of cool waters falling in showers, of old moorland music, came thin and faint with an exquisite clearness. A second and the boat was among the surf, its gunwale ringed with white foam as it leaped to the still waters beyond. Clear and deep and still the water lay, and then the white beaches shelved downward, and the boat grated on the sand. He turned, every limb alert with a strange new life, crying out words which had shaped themselves on his lips and which an echo seemed to catch and answer. There was the green forest before him, the hills of peace, the cold white waters. With a passionate joy he leaped on the beach, his arms outstretched to this new earth, this light of the world, this old desire of the heart – youth, rapture, immortality.

Bellew brought the body back to camp, himself half-dead with fatigue and whimpering like a child. He almost fell from his horse, and when others took his burden from him and laid it reverently in his tent, he stood beside it, rubbing sand and sweat from his poor purblind eyes, his teeth chattering with fever. He was given something to drink, but he swallowed barely a mouthful.

'It was some d–d–damned sharpshooter,' he said. 'Right through the breast, and he never spoke to me again. My poor old Col! He was the best chap God ever created, and I do–don't care a dash what becomes of me now. I was at school with him, you know, you men.'

'Was he killed outright?' asked the major hoarsely.

'N–no. He lived for about five minutes. But I think the sun had got into his head or he was mad with pain, for he d–d–didn't know where he was. He kept crying out about the smell of pine trees and heather and a lot of pure nonsense about water.'

'*Et dulces reminiscitur Argos*,' somebody quoted mournfully, as they went out into the desert evening.

A Cry across the Black Water

S. R. Crockett

With Rosemary for remembrance,
And Rue, sweet Rue, for you.

It was at the waterfoot of the Ken, and the time of the year was June.

'Boat ahoy!'

The loud, bold cry carried far through the still morning air. The rain had washed down all that was in the sky during the night, so that the hail echoed through a world blue and empty.

Gregory Jeffray, a noble figure of a youth, stood leaning on the arch of his mare's neck, quieting the nervous tremors of Eulalie, that very dainty lady. His tall, alert figure, tight-reined and manly, was brought out by his riding-dress. His pose against the neck of the beautiful beast, from which a moment before he had swung himself, was that of Hadrian's young Antinous.

'Boat ahoy!'

Gregory Jeffray, growing a little impatient, made a trumpet of his hands, and sent the powerful voice, with which one day he meant to thrill listening senates, sounding athwart the dancing ripples of the loch.

On the farther shore was a flat white ferryboat, looking, as it lay motionless in the river, like a white table chained in the water with its legs in the air. The chain along which it moved plunged into the shallows beside him, and he could see it descending till he lost it in the dusky pool across which the ferry plied. To the north, Loch Ken ran in glistening levels and island-studded reaches to the base of Cairnsmuir.

'Boat ahoy!'

A figure, like a white mark of exclamation moving over green paper, came out of the little low whitewashed cottage opposite and stood a moment looking across the ferry, with one hand resting on its side and the other held level with its eyes. Then the observer disappeared behind a hedge, to be seen immediately coming down the narrow, deep-rutted lane towards the ferryboat. When the figure came again in sight of Gregory Jeffray, he had no difficulty in distinguishing a slim girl, clad in white, who came sedately towards him.

When she arrived at the white boat which floated so stilly on the morning glitter of the water, only just stirred by a breeze from the south, she stepped at once on board. Gregory could see her as she took from the corner of the flat, where it stood erect along with other boating gear, something which looked like a short iron hoe. With this she walked to the end of the boat nearest him. She laid the hoe end of the instrument against a chain that ran breast-high along one side of the boat and at the stern plunged diagonally into the water. His mare lifted her feet impatiently, as though the shoreward end of the chain had brought a thrill across the loch from the moving ferryboat. Turning her back to him, the girl bent her slim young body without an effort; and, as though by the gentlest magic, the ferryboat drew nearer to him. It did not seem to move; yet gradually the space of blue water between it and the shore on which the whitewashed cottage stood spread and widened. He could hear the gentle clatter of the wavelets against the lip of the landing-drop as the boat came nearer. His mare tossed her head and snuffed at this strange four-footed thing that glided towards them.

Gregory, who loved all women, watched with natural interest the sway and poise of the girlish figure. He heard the click and rattle of the chain as she deftly disengaged her gripper-iron at the farther end, and, turning, walked the deck's length towards him.

She seemed but a young thing to move so large a boat. He forgot to be angry at being kept so long waiting, for of all women, he told himself, he most admired tall girls in simple dresses. His exceptional interest arose from the fact that he had never before seen one manage a ferryboat.

As he stood on the shore, and the great flat boat moved towards him, he saw that the end of it nearest him was pulled up a couple of feet clear of the water. Still the boat moved noiselessly forward, till he heard it first grate and then ground gently, as the graceful pilot bore her weight upon the iron bar to stay its progress. Gregory specially admired the flex of her arms bent outwardly as she did so. Then she went to the end of the boat, and let down the tilted gangway upon the pebbles at his feet.

Gregory Jeffray instinctively took off his hat as he said to this girl, 'Good-morning! Can I get to the village of Dullarg by this ferry?'

'This is the way to the Dullarg,' said the girl, simply and naturally, leaning as she spoke upon her dripping gripper-iron.

Her eyes did not refuse to take in the goodliness of the youth while his attention was for the moment given to his mare.

'Gently, gently, lass!' he said, patting the neck which arched impatiently as she felt the boards hollow beneath her feet. Yet she came obediently enough on deck, arching her forefeet high and throwing them out in an uncertain and tentative manner.

Then the girl, with a quiet and matter-of-fact acceptance of her duties, placed her iron once more upon the chain, and bent herself to the task with well-accustomed effort of her slender body.

The heart of the young man was stirred within him. True, he might have beheld fifty field-wenches breaking their backs among the harvest sheaves without a pang. This, however, was very different.

'Let me help you,' he said.

'It is better that you stand by your horse,' she said.

Gregory Jeffray looked disappointed.

'Is it not too hard work for you?' he queried, humbly and with abased eyes.

'No,' said the girl. 'Ye see, sir, I live with my mother's two sisters at the boathouse. They are very kind to me. They brought me up, though I had neither father nor mother. And what signifies bringing the boat across the water a time or two?'

Her ready and easy movements told the tale for her. She needed no pity. She asked for none, for which Gregory was rather sorry. He liked to pity people, and then to right their grievances, if it were not very difficult. Of what use otherwise was it to be, what he was called in Galloway, the 'boy sheriff'? Besides, he was taking a morning ride from the great house of the Barr, and upon his return to breakfast he desired to have a tale to tell which would rivet attention upon himself.

'And do you do nothing all day, but only take the boat to and fro across the loch?' he asked.

He saw the way clear now, he thought, to matter for an interesting episode – the basis of which should be the delight of a beautiful girl in spending her life in the carrying of desirable young men, riding upon horses, over the shining morning waters of the Ken. They should all look with eyes of wonder upon her; but she, the cold Dian of the lochside, would never return look for look to any of them, save perhaps to Gregory Jeffray. Gregory went about the world finding pictures and making romances for himself. He meant to be a statesman; and, with this purpose in view, it was wholly necessary for him to study the people, and especially, he might have added, the young women of the people. Hitherto he had done this chiefly in his imagination, but here certainly was material attractive to his hand.

'Do you work at nothing else?' he repeated, for the girl was uncomplimentarily intent upon her gripper-iron. How deftly she lifted it just at the right moment, when it was in danger of being caught upon the revolving wheel! How exactly she exerted just the right amount of strength to keep the chain running sweetly upon its cogs! How daintily she stepped back, avoiding the dripping of the water from the linked iron which rose from the bed of the loch, passed under her hand, and dipped diagonally down again into the deeps! Gregory had never seen anything like it, so he told himself.

It was not until he had put his question the third time that the girl answered, 'Whiles I take the boat over to the waterfoot when there's a cry across the Black Water.'

The young man was mystified.

' "A cry across the Black Water"! What may that be?' he said.

The girl looked at him directly almost for the first time. Was he making fun of her? She wondered. His face seemed earnest enough, and handsome. It was not possible, she concluded.

'Ye'll be a stranger in these parts?' she answered interrogatively, because she was a Scottish girl, and one question for another is good national barter and exchange.

Gregory Jeffray was about to declare his names, titles and expectations; but he looked at the girl again, and saw something that withheld him.

'Yes,' he said, 'I am staying for a week or two over at the Barr.'

The boat grounded on the pebbles, and the girl went to let down the hinged end. It had seemed a very brief passage to Gregory Jeffray. He stood still by his mare, as though he had much more to say.

The girl placed her cleek in the corner, and moved to leave the boat. It piqued the young man to find her so unresponsive. 'Tell me what you mean by "a cry across the Black Water",' he said.

The girl pointed to the strip of sullen blackness that lay under the willows upon the southern shore.

'That is the Black Water of Dee,' she said simply, 'and the green point among the trees is the Rhonefoot. Whiles there's a cry from there. Then I go over in the boat, and set them across.'

'Not in this boat?' he said, looking at the upturned deal table swinging upon its iron chain.

She smiled at his ignorance.

'That is the boat that goes across the Black Water of Dee,' she said, pointing to a small boat which lay under the bank on the left.

'And do you never go anywhere else?' he asked, wondering how she came by her beauty and her manners.

'Only to the kirk on the Sabbaths,' she said, 'when I can get someone to watch the boat for me.'

'I will watch the boat for you!' he said impulsively.

The girl looked distressed. This gay gentleman was making fun of her, assuredly. She did not answer. Would he never go away?

'That is your way,' she said, pointing along the track in front. Indeed, there was but one way, and the information was superfluous.

The end of the white, rose-smothered boathouse was towards them. A tall, bowed woman's figure passed quickly round the gable.

'Is that your aunt?' he asked.

'That is my Aunt Annie,' said the girl; 'my Aunt Barbara is confined to her bed.'

'And what is your name, if I may ask?'

The girl glanced at him. He was certainly not making fun of her now.

'My name is Grace Allen,' she said.

They paced together up the path. The bridle rein slipped from his arm, but his hand instinctively caught it, and Eulalie cropped crisply at the grasses on the bank, unregarded by her master.

They did not shake hands when they parted, but their eyes followed each other a long way.

'Where is the money?' said Aunt Barbara from her bed as Grace Allen came in at the open door.

'Dear me!' said the girl, frightened: 'I have forgotten to ask him for it!'

'Did I ever see sic a lassie! Rin after him an' get it; haste ye fast.'

But Gregory was far out of reach by the time Grace got to the door. The sound of hoofs came from high up the wooded heights.

Gregory Jeffray reached the Barr in time for late breakfast. There was a large house company. The men were prowling discontentedly about, looking under covers or cutting slices from dishes on the sideboard; but the ladies were brightly curious, and eagerly welcomed Gregory. He at least did not rise with a headache and a bad temper every morning. They desired an account of his morning's ride. But on the way home he had changed his mind about telling of his adventure. He said that he had had a pleasant ride. It had been a beautiful morning.

'But have you nothing whatever to tell us?' they asked; for, indeed, they had a right to expect something.

Gregory said nothing. This was not usual, for at other times when he had nothing to tell, it did not cost him much to invent something interesting.

'You are very dull this morning, sheriff,' said the youngest daughter of the house, who, being the baby and pretty, had grown pettishly privileged in speech.

But deep within him Gregory was saying, 'What a blessing that I forgot to pay the ferry!'

When he got outside he said to his host, 'Is there such a place hereabouts as the Rhonefoot?'

'Why, yes, there is,' said Laird Cunningham of Barr. 'But why do you ask? I thought a sheriff would know everything without asking – even an ornamental one on his way to the premiership.'

'Oh, I heard the name,' said Gregory. 'It struck me as a curious one.'

So that evening there came over the river from the waterfoot of the Rhone the sound of a voice calling. Grace Allen sat thoughtfully looking out of the rose-hung window of the boathouse. Her face was an oval of perfect curve, crowned with a mass of light brown hair, in which were red lights when the sun shone directly upon it. Her skin was clear, pale as ivory, and even exertion hardly brought the latent under-flush of red to the surface.

'There's somebody at the waterfit. Gang, lassie, an' dinna be lettin' them aff withoot their siller this time!' said her Aunt Barbara from her bed. Annie Allen was accustomed to say nothing, and she did it now.

The boat to the Rhonefoot was seldom needed, and the oars were not kept in it. They leaned against the end of the cottage, and Grace Allen took them on her shoulder as she went down. She carried them as easily as another girl might carry a parasol.

Again there came the cry from the Rhonefoot, echoing joyously across the river.

Standing well back in the boat, so as to throw up the bow, she pushed off. The water was deep where the boat lay, and it had been drawn half up on the bank. Where Grace dipped her oars into the silent water, the pool was so black that the blade of the oar was lost in the gloom before it got halfway down. Above there was a light wind moaning and rustling in the trees, but it did not stir even a ripple on the dark surface of the pool where the Black Water of Dee meets the brighter Ken.

Grace bent to her oars with a springing verve and force which made the tubby little boat draw towards the shore, the whispering water gliding under its sides all the while. Three lines of wake were marked behind – a vague white turbulence in the middle and two lines of bubbles on either side where the oars had dipped, which flashed a moment and then winked themselves out.

When she reached the waterfoot, and the boat touched the shore, Grace Allen looked up to see Gregory Jeffray standing alone on the little copse-enclosed triangle of grass. He smiled pleasantly. She had not time to be surprised.

'What did you think of me this morning, running away without paying my fare?' he asked.

It seemed very natural now that he should come. She was glad that he had not brought his horse.

'I thought you would come by again,' said Grace Allen, standing up, with one oar over the side ready to pull in or push off.

Gregory extended his hand as though to ask for hers to steady him as he came into the boat. Grace was surprised. No one ever did that at the Rhonefoot, but she thought it might be that he was a stranger and did not understand about boats. She held out her hand. Gregory leapt in beside her in a moment, but did not at once release the hand. She tried to pull it away.

'It is too little a hand to do so much hard work,' he said.

Instantly Grace became conscious that it was rough and hard with rowing. She had not thought of this before. He stooped and kissed it.

'Now,' he said, 'let me row across for you, and sit in front of me where I can see you. You made me forget all about everything else this morning, and now I must make up for it.'

It was a long way across, and evidently Gregory Jeffray was not a good oarsman, for it was dark when Grace Allen went indoors to her aunts. Her heart was bounding within her. Her bosom rose and fell as she breathed quickly and silently through her parted red lips. There was a new thing in her eye.

Every evening thereafter, through all that glorious height of midsummer, there came a crying at the Waterfoot; and every evening Grace Allen went over to the edge of the Rhone wood to answer it. There the boat lay moored to a stone upon the turf, while Gregory and she walked upon the flowery forest carpet, and the dry leaves watched and clashed and muttered above them as the gloaming fell. These were days of rapture, each a doorway into yet fuller and more perfect joy.

Over at the waterfoot the copses grew close. The green turf was velvet underfoot. The blackbirds fluted in the hazels there. None of them listened to the voice of Gregory Jeffray, or cared for what he said to Grace Allen when she went nightly to meet him over the Black Water.

She rowed back alone, the simple soul that was in her forwandered and mazed with excess of joy. As she set the boat to the shore and came up the bank bearing the oars which were her wings into the world of love under the green alders, the light in the west, lingering clear and pure and cold, shone upon her and added radiance to her eyes.

But Aunt Annie watched her with silent pain. Barbara from her bed spoke sharp and cruel words which Grace Allen listened to not at all.

For as soon as the morning shone bright over the hills and ran on tiptoe up the sparkling ripples of the loch, she looked across the Black Water to the hidden ways where in the evening her love should meet her.

As she went her daily rounds, and the gripper-iron slipped on the wet chain or grew hot in the sun, as she heard the clack of the wheel and the soft slow grind of the boat's broad lip on the pebbles, Grace Allen said over and over to herself, 'It is so long, only so long, till he will come.'

So all the days she waited in a sweet content. Barbara reproached her; Aunt Annie perilled her soul by lying to shield her; but Grace herself was shut out from shame or fear, from things past or things to come, by faith and joy that at last she had found one whom her soul loved.

And overhead the dry poplar leaves clashed and rustled, telling out to one another that love was a vain thing, and the thrush cried thrice, 'Beware.' But Grace Allen would not have believed had one risen to her from the dead.

So the great wasteful summer days went by, the glory of the passionate nights of July, the crisper blonde luxuriance of August. Every night there was the calling from the green plot across the Black Water. Every night Aunt Annie wandered, a withered grey ghost, along the hither side of the inky pool, looking for what she could not see and listening for that which she could not hear. Then she would go in to lie gratuitously to Barbara, who told her to her face that she did not believe her.

But in the first chill of mid-September, swift as the dividing of the blue-black thundercloud by the winking flame, fell the sword of God, smiting and shattering. It seemed hard that it should fall on the weaker and the more innocent. But then God has plenty of time.

One chilly gloaming there was no calling at the Rhonefoot. Nevertheless Grace rowed over and waited, imagining that all evil had befallen her lover. Within, her Aunt Barbara fretted and murmured at her absence, driving her silent sister into involved refuges of lies to shield young Grace Allen, whom her soul loved.

The next day went by as the night had passed, with an awful constriction about her heart, a numbness over all her body; yet Grace did her work as one who dares not stop.

Two serving-men crossed in the ferryboat, unconcernedly talking over the country news as men do when they meet.

'Did ye hear aboot young Jeffray?' asked the herd from the Mains.

'Whatna Jeffray?' asked, without much show of interest, the ploughman from Drumglass.

'Wi', man, the young lad that the daft folk in Enbra sent here for sheriff.'

'I didna ken he was hereawa',' said the ploughman, with a purely perfunctory surprise.

'Ou ay, he has been a feck ower by at the Barr. They say he's gaun to get marriet to the youngest dochter. She's hae a gye fat stockin'-fit, I'se warrant.'

'Ye may say sae, or a lawyer wadna come speerin' her,' returned him from Drumglass as the boat reached the farther side.

'Guid-e'en to ye, Grace,' said they both as they put their pennies down on the little tin plate in the corner.

'She's an awesome still lassie, that,' said the Mains, as he took the road down to Parton Raw, where he had trysted with a maid of another sort. 'Did ye notice she never said a word to us, neyther Thank ye nor yet Guid-day? Her een were fair stelled in her head.'

'Na, I didna observe,' said the Drumglass cotman indifferently.

'Some fowk are like swine. They notice nocht that's no pitten intil the trough afore them!' said the Mains indignantly.

So they parted, each to his own errand.

Day swayed and swirled into a strange night of shooting stars and intensest darkness. The soul of Grace Allen wandered in blackest night. Sometimes the earth appeared ready to open and swallow her up. Sometimes she seemed to be wandering by the side of the great pool of the Black Water with her hands full of flowers. There were roses blush-red, like what he had said her cheeks were sometimes. There were velvety pansies, and flowers of strange intoxicating perfume, the like of which she had never seen. But at every few yards she felt that she must fling them all into the black water and fare forth into the darkness to gather more.

Then in her bed she would start up, hearing the hail of a dear voice calling to her from the Rhonefoot. Once she put on her clothes in haste and would have gone forth; but her Aunt Annie, waking and startled, a tall, gaunt apparition, came to her.

'Grace Allen,' she said, 'where are you gangin' at this time o' the nicht?'

'There's somebody at the boat,' she said, 'waiting. Let me gang, Aunt Annie: they want me; I hear them cry. Oh, Annie, I hear them crying as a bairn cries!'

'Lie doon on yer bed like a clever lass,' said her aunt gently. 'There's naebody there.'

'Or gin there be,' said Aunt Barbara from her bed, 'e'en let them cry. Is this a time for decent fowk to be gaun play-actin' aboot?'

So the daylight came, and the evening and the morning of the second day. And Grace Allen went about her work with clack of gripper-iron and dip of oar.

Late on in the gloaming of the third day following, Aunt Annie went down to the broad flat boat that lay so still at the water's edge. Something black was knocking dully against it.

Grace had been gone four hours, and it was weary work watching along the shore or going within out of the chill wind to endure Barbara's bitter tongue.

The black thing that knocked was the small boat, broken loose from her moorings and floating helplessly. Annie Allen took a boathook and pulled it to the shore. Except that the boat was half full of flowers, there was nothing and no one inside.

But the world span round and the stars went out when the finder saw the flowers.

When Aunt Annie Allen came to herself, she found the water was rising rapidly. It was up to her ankles. She went indoors and asked for Grace.

'Save us, Ann!' said Barbara; 'I thocht she was wi' you. Where hae ye been till this time o' nicht? An' your feet's dreepin' wat. Haud aff the clean floor!'

'But Gracie! Oor lassie Grace! What's come o' Gracie?' wailed the elder woman.

At that instant there came so thrilling a cry from over the dark waters out of the night that the women turned to one another and instinctively caught at each other's hands.

'Leave me, I maun gang,' said Aunt Annie. 'That's surely Grace.'

Her sister gripped her tight.

'Let me gang – let me gang. She's my ain lassie, no yours!' Annie said fiercely, endeavouring to thrust off Barbara's hands as they clutched her like birds' talons from the bed.

'Help me to get up,' said Barbara; 'I canna be left here. I'll come wi' ye.'

So she that had been sick for twelve years arose, like a ghost from the tomb, and with her sister went out to seek for the girl they had lost. They found their way to the boat, reeling together like drunken men. Annie almost lifted her sister in, and then fell herself among the drenched and waterlogged flowers.

With the instinct of old habitude they fell to the oars, Barbara rowing the better and the stronger. They felt the oily swirl of the Dee rising beneath them, and knew that there had been a mighty rain upon the hills.

'The Lord save us!' cried Barbara suddenly. 'Look!'

She pointed up the long pool of the Black Water. What she saw no man knows, for Aunt Annie had fainted, and Barbara was never herself after that hour.

Aunt Annie lay like a log across her thwart. But, with the strength of another world, Barbara unshipped the oar of her sister and slipped it upon the thole-pin opposite to her own. Then she turned the head of the boat up the pool of the Black Water. Something white floated dancingly alongside, upborne for a moment on the boiling swirls of the rising water. Barbara dropped her oars, and snatched at it. She held on to some light wet fabric by one hand; with the other she shook her sister.

'Here's oor wee Gracie,' she said. 'Ann, help me hame wi' her!'

So they brought her home, and laid her all in dripping white upon her white bed. Barbara sat at the bed-head and crooned, having lost her wits. Aunt Annie moved all in a piece, as though she were about to fall headlong.

'White floo'ers for the angels, where Gracie's ga'en to! Annie, woman, dinna ye see them by her body – four great angels, at ilka corner yin?'

Barbara's voice rose and fell, wayward and querulous. There was no other sound in the house, only the water sobbing against the edge of the ferryboat.

'And the first is like a lion,' she went on, in a more even recitative, 'and the second is like an ox, and the third has a face like a man, and the fourth is like a flying eagle. An' they're sittin' on ilka bedpost; and they hae sax wings, that meet owre my Gracie, an' they cry withoot ceasing, 'Holy! holy! holy! Woe unto him that causeth one of these little ones to perish! It were better for him that a millstone were hanged about his neck and he were cast into the deeps o' the Black Water!'

But the neighbours paid no attention to her – for, of course, she was mad.

Then the wise folk came and explained how it had all happened. Here she had been gathering flowers; here she had slipped; and here, again, she had fallen. Nothing could be clearer. There were the flowers. There was the dangerous pool on the Black Water. And there was the body of Grace Allen, a young thing dead in the flower of her days.

'I see them! I see them!' cried Barbara, fixing her eyes on the bed, her voice like a shriek; 'they are full of eyes, behind and before, and they see into the heart of man. Their faces are full of anger, and their mouths are open to devour – '

'Wheesh, wheesh, woman! Here's the young sheriff come doon frae the Barr wi' the fiscal to tak' evidence.'

And Barbara Allen was silent as Gregory Jeffray came in.

To do him justice, when he wrote her the letter that killed – concerning the necessities of his position and career – he had tried to break the parting gently. How should he know all that she knew? It was clearly an ill turn that fate had played him. Indeed, he felt ill-used. So he listened to the fiscal taking evidence, and in due course departed.

But within an inner pocket he had a letter that was not filed with the documents, but which might have shed clearer light upon when and how Grace Allen slipped and fell, gathering flowers at night above the great pool of the Black Water.

'There is set up a throne in the heavens,' chanted mad Barbara Allen as Gregory went out; 'and One sits upon it – and my Gracie's there, clothed in white robes, an' a palm in her hand. And you'll be there, young man,' she cried after him, 'and I'll be there. There's a cry comin' owre the Black Water for you, like the cry that raised me oot o' my bed yestreen. An' ye'll hear it – ye'll hear it, braw young man; ay – and rise up and answer, too!'

But they paid no heed to her – for, of course, she was mad. Neither did Gregory Jeffray hear aught as he went out, but the water lapping against the little boat that was still half full of flowers.

The days went by, and being added together one at a time, they made the years. And the years grew into one decade, and lengthened out towards another.

Aunt Annie was long dead, a white stone over her; but there was no stone over Grace Allen – only a green mound where daisies grew.

Sir Gregory Jeffray came that way. He was a great law-officer of the Crown, and first heir to the next vacant judgeship. This, however, he was thinking of refusing because of the greatness of his private practice.

He had come to shoot at the Barr, and his baggage was at Barrmark Station. How strange it would be to see the old places again in the gloom of a September evening!

Gregory still loved a new sensation. All was so long past – the bitterness clean gone out of it. The old boathouse had fallen into other hands, and railways had come to carry the traffic beyond the ferry.

As Sir Gregory Jeffray walked from the late train which set him down at the station, he felt curiously at peace. The times of the Long Ago came back not ungratefully to his mind. There had been much pleasure in them. He even thought kindly of the girl with whom he had walked in the glory of a forgotten summer along the hidden ways of the woods. Her last letter, long since destroyed, was not disagreeable to him when he thought of the secret which had been laid to rest so quietly in the pool of the Black Water.

He came to the water's edge. He sent his voice, stronger now than of yore, but without the old ring of boyish hopefulness, across the loch. A moment's silence, the whisper of the night wind, and then from the gloom of the farther side an answering hail – low, clear, and penetrating.

'I am in luck to find them out of bed,' said Gregory Jeffray to himself.

He waited and listened. The wind blew chill from the south athwart the ferry. He shivered, and drew his fur-lined travelling-coat about him. He could hear the water lapping against the mighty piers of the railway viaduct above, which, with its gaunt iron spans, like bows bent to send arrows into the heavens, dimly towered between him and the skies.

Now, this is all that men definitely know of the fate of Sir Gregory Jeffray. A surfaceman who lived in the new houses above the landing-place saw him standing there, heard him hailing the waterfoot of the

Dee, to which no boat had plied for years. Maliciously he let the stranger call, and abode to see what should happen.

Yet astonishment held him dumb when again across the dark stream came the crying, thrilling him with an unknown terror, till he clutched the door to make sure of his retreat within. Mastering his fear, he stole nearer till he could hear the oars planted in the iron pins, the push off the shore, and then the measured dip of oars coming towards the stranger across the pool of the Black Water.

'How do they know, I wonder, that I want to be taken to the Rhonefoot? They are bringing the small boat,' he heard him say.

A skiff shot out of the gloom. It was a woman who was rowing. The boat grounded stern on. The watcher saw the man step in and settle himself on the seat.

'What rubbish is this?' Gregory Jeffray cried angrily as he cleared a great armful of flowers off the seat and threw them among his feet.

The oars dipped, and without sound the boat glided out upon the waves of the loch towards the Black Water, into whose oily depths the blades fall silently, and where the water does not lap about the prow. The night grew suddenly very cold. Somewhere in the darkness over the Black Water the watching surfaceman heard someone call three times the name of Gregory Jeffray. It sounded like a young child's voice. And for very fear he ran in and shut the door, well knowing that for twenty years no boat had plied there.

It was noted as a strange thing that, on the same night on which Sir Gregory Jeffray was lost, the last of the Allens of the old ferry-house died in the Crichton Asylum. Barbara Allen was, without doubt, mad to the end, for the burden of her latest cry was, 'He kens noo! he kens noo! The Lord our God is a jealous God! Now let Thy servant depart in peace!'

But Gregory Jeffray was never seen again by water or on shore. He had heard the cry across the Black Water.

The Story of Euphemia Hewit

JAMES HOGG

Mr David Hunter, only son to the farmer of Clunkeigh, once told me one of the strangest stories I ever heard, though many I have dragged together. He said that he went to court a very dear and lovely girl, Phemie Hewit, and spent about three hours with her in the fondest endearment; kissed her, shook hands and left her about two o'clock on a winter morning. He said he was sometimes whistling a tune to himself – for, like me, he sawed a good deal on the fiddle; but he was all the way thinking and thinking of Phemie and whether he would take her home to his father's house or get a cottage of his own built on the farm; when, behold! after he was almost close to his father's house and had walked about three miles and a half, he met with Phemie coming leisurely to meet him, with her gown-skirt drawn over her lovely chestnut locks, as she always had when she went out to the courting.

'Mercy on us, Phemie!' exclaimed he, 'but ye surely are keen o' the courting the night, when ye're come a' the gate here for another brash at it.'

'I forgot two things,' said she; 'and as I kenned we were never to meet again, I coudna part wi' you without telling you: in the first place, you are never to gang back to Auchenvew again to the courting; for things are no a' right there.'

'What's wrang about Auchenvew, Phemie?'

'Oh, your Margaret's no just as she should be, poor woman; an' I'm very sorry for her; but ye maunna gang back again, else ye're sure to get o'er the fingers' ends.'

'Now, Phemie, that's sheer jealousy, for which I am sure you have little reason.'

'Oh, I dare say you gaed for her for an hour or twa's diversion; but you *did* gang; and mind you're no to do it again.'

'Weel, my dear woman, I gie you my word o' honour that I never shall gang back to the courting again. But, Phemie, what was it you said about us never meeting again?'

'Oh, yes, we'll meet again; but I'll be dead before then! and my principal errand here this morning was to get your blessing; for when you kissed me and parted with me, you did not say, "God bless you, Phemie!" which you never neglected before since ever we met. Now, I could not part with you without your blessing.'

'I dinna understand you this morning, Phemie. We are never to meet again? And you are to be dead before we meet again? What is the meaning of all this? Remember you are engaged to meet me on the 7th of next month at the easternmost tree of the Grennan Wood.'

'Well, I'll meet you there.'

'Well, God bless you, my dear girl; and I'm sure I give that blessing with all my heart and soul.'

David stretched out his hand to seize hers, to draw her to him and kiss her. There was no hand and no Phemie there! He wheeled round and round and called her name. 'Phemie! Phemie Hewit! My dear woman, what's come o' you or where are ye?' But he ran with all his speed and called in vain; there was no Phemie to be seen nor heard. He stood in breathless astonishment, recommending himself to all the Blessed Trinity and then saying audibly, 'The mercy and grace of heaven be around me! Is it possible that I have seen my dear Phemie's wraith? No, it is impossible; for it looked and spoke so like her sweet self – it could not be a spirit. But there was something very mysterious about her this morning, in following me so far; nay, in outwalking me, meeting me and uttering the words she did. But it was herself, there is no doubt of it; and she has given me the slip in a most unaccountable manner.'

David went home, and awakened his youngest sister, Mary, who gave him something to drink; but he could not speak an intelligible sentence to her and she thought he was either drunk or very ill and sat up with him till day. He slept none, but sighed, moaned and turned himself in the bed; and he continued thoughtful and ill for several days; but at length he arose and went about his father's business. This visionary courting night was on the 28th of January or February. I have forgot which; and the lovers were engaged to meet on the 7th of the next month at their trysting tree.

Now the families of the two lovers were not on very good terms; they were, I believe, rather adverse to one another. They were of different tenets in religion and never met either at church or in society. But the only son of the one family fell in love with the youngest daughter of the other at a Thornhill fair, trysted her to meet him, courted her and won her affections and they engaged themselves to one another. They were a very amiable pair and I knew them both very well, David was a handsome, stout fellow, upwards of six feet high, and Phemie a gentle, mild-looking creature, with a face something what one would suppose an angel's to be, but rather pale-looking and apparently not long for this world. She was, nevertheless, lively, witty and good-humoured and had a most affectionate and benevolent heart.

Well, the 7th of the month came and David attended punctually at the hour. He had not sat a minute and a half until Phemie came, with the skirt of her frock round her head, as usual.

'Come away, Phemie! you are true to your word as ever,' said he.

'Yes, you see I have come as I promised; for I would not break my tryst with you; but I have very short time to stay.'

'Well, come and sit under my plaid, for the time that you have to stay, my dear lassie, and let me caress you; for I have had heavy thoughts and sad misgivings about you since I last saw you.'

'No, I cannot come under your plaid, nor court tonight, for reasons that you will soon come to know. But I came principally to inform you that you are not to come back to court me till I send you word or come and tell you myself: yes, I think I'll come and tell you myself and then you are safe to come.'

'You cannot come under my plaid? I must not come to court you again until you come and tell me to do so? Will you really come and tell me that I must come and woo you, Phemie? Phemie, my dear! there is a mystery about you of late which I cannot comprehend.'

David was looking down to the ground at this moment, pondering on the words of his beloved; and when he looked up again he saw Phemie gliding away from him. He sprang to his feet and pursued her, calling her name in a sort of loud whisper; but she continued to fly on; and, though very near, he could not overtake her till she entered the minister's house by the back gate that led through the kirkyard. David's eyes were opened; he saw at once that the elegant and genteel minister had seduced his sweetheart's affections; and he now conceived that he understood all her demeanour and everything she had said to him. So he rushed into the kitchen: there were two servant-girls in it and he asked them, with a voice of fury, where Phemie was.

Now, I must tell that this parson had got a bad name with some young ladies, both married and unmarried; and though for my part I never believed a word of it, yet the report spread, which weaned the parson's congregation from him, all save a few gentlemen who came to dine at the manse every Sunday. David was perfectly enraged; for he perceived his road straight before him.

'Where is Phemie?' cried he.

'What Phemie?' said the one girl; 'What Phemie?' said the other.

'Why Phemie Hewit,' cried he fiercely. 'I know how matters are going on, so you need not make any of your confounded pretences of ignorance to me! I followed her in here this minute; so tell me instantly where she is or bring your master to answer to me.'

'Phemie Hewit!' said the one girl; 'Phemie Hewit!' said the other. And with that one of them (Sarah Robson) ran to the minister and said, 'For God's sake, sir, come an' speak to Mr David Hunter; he is come in raving mad and asking for Phemie Hewit and seems to think that you have her concealed in the house.'

Mr Nevison, with all his usual suavity of manners, came into the kitchen, asked Mr Hunter how he was and how his father and sisters were.

'I'm no that ill, sir; I hae nae grit reason to complain o' onything or onybody excepting you. Where is my sweetheart, sir? I followed her in here this minute and if ye dinna gie her up to me I'll burn the house aboot your head!'

'Your sweetheart, Mr David? Whom do you mean. Is it one of my servant-girls? for there is no other woman in the house, to my knowledge.'

'No, sir, it is Phemie Hewit that I want – my own Phemie Hewit – my betrothed! I followed her in here at your back gate this instant and I insist on seeing her.'

'Phemie Hewit!' exclaimed the two servant-girls; 'Phemie Hewit!' exclaimed the minister. 'My dear sir, you are raving and out of your senses; there was but one Phemie Hewit whom I knew in all this country, the merchant's daughter of Thornhill, and she is dead and was buried here, within six paces of the back of my house, the day before yesterday.'

'Come now, sir, that is a hoax to get me off,' cried David, in a loud tone, betwixt laughing and crying. 'That winna do; tell me the truth at aince. That is ower serious a matter to joke on; therefore, for the sake of heaven and this poor heart, tell me the real truth.'

'I tell you the real truth, Mr Hunter. I was at her funeral myself and laid her left shoulder into the grave and saw engraved in gold letters on the coffin-lid, "Euphemia Hewit, aged 22".'

David's whole frame grew rigid, his hands and his eyes turned up convulsively; and, after uttering a few internal groans, or rather shrieks, he fell backward in a swoon. They carried him to bed and he soon came again to his senses; but the distress of his mind was deplorable. He lay at the manse for nearly three weeks; and though the minister administered every anodyne to him that he possessed or could procure, his patient remained in a very precarious and unsettled state and continued to exclaim, every day, 'Oh, had I been but warned of it! to have watched by her dying bed and received her parting blessing and her parting breath between my lips and to have laid her head in an honoured grave, I would have been satisfied! But to be parted thus! Oh, my beloved Phemie, would to God I had died for thee! Oh my Phemie, my Phemie!'

We had some fine curling on the ice after this, therefore I think it must have been about the end of February; and we were all astonished to find that our friend David, one of the best and strongest curlers of us all, never appeared on the ice. So one evening I went that way to take my tea with the family and see what was the matter; for he and I were great cronies and talked much about religion and the Scriptures and sometimes about the lasses, but not often. But he had a strong attachment to me and said one day, before all the club, that there was nothing in the world he would court independence so much for as to keep me independent.

I found him pale and emaciated, sitting in the kitchen, with his plaid about him. He took no tea; he ate not a bite of bread; he spoke not a word. My blood ran chill to my heart; for he was a good lad and I loved him.

As we were going into the parlour for our tea, his sister Margaret took me aside and said, 'I am very glad that you have come tonight; for we are perplexed about Davie. Something extraordinary seems to have happened to him; but we know nothing and he is continually speaking about you. See if you can find out what it is that distresses him.'

'He is sadly changed, indeed, for the worse,' said I; 'and I am very much alarmed about him. He is too retired and too thoughtful. Could you not persuade Jane Wilson or Nancy McTurk or Jane Armstrong to come over and stay with you awhile? I have seen each of these put him into high glee and good humour.'

'He would not once look or speak to any of them,' said she. 'His spirits are broken and I am afraid he is not long for this world.'

'For God's sake, do not say so, Miss Margaret,' said I. 'But I am sure he will open his mind to me.'

He set me on my way as far as the limits of his father's farm that night and related the above narrative, adding, 'She has, you see, promised to call on me again and inform me when I am to meet her; and do you not think that when that happens it will be a warning for me to prepare for leaving this world?'

'Yes I do, David,' said I. 'After what has already happened, in such a mysterious way, between you and your beloved, I believe that when your Phemie comes and gives you this intimation, even in a dream, it will be a death-warning to you and that you must prepare to meet her in another and a better world.'

'Oh no, no, not in a dream,' said he; 'she is with me in every dream, evening, midnight and morning. I see her, I caress her, kiss her and bless her, without ever once recollecting that the grave separates us. Oh no, not in a dream! I shall see her face to face and speak to her as a man speaketh to his friend; and when that happens, if it should ever happen, I shall send you word.'

This was at the laight gate. So we shook hands and parted; for I durst not let him stand longer in the cold. But he continued to grow worse and worse, until one morning, about the beginning of May, a servant came posting me on horseback and requested me to go and see Mr David Hunter, who was very poorly and wished particularly to see me. I obeyed the summons with alacrity and found him in bed, very low indeed.

He desired his two sisters to go out and then, taking my hand, he said, 'Now, my dear friend, my time is come – the time which I have long desired. I have seen my Phemie again today.'

'But only in a dream, David, I am sure. Consider yourself; only in a dream.'

'No, I was wide awake and sensible as at this moment while speaking to you. The door was standing open, to give me air. I was all alone, which you know I choose mostly to be, for prayer and meditation, when in glided my Phemie, with the train of her grey frock drawn over her lovely locks. I had no thought, no remembrance that she was dead. It was impossible to think so; for her smile was so sweet, so heavenly, even more beatific than I had ever seen it and her complexion was that of the pale rose. She threw her locks back from each cheek with her left hand and said, 'You see I have come to invite you as I promised, David. Are you ready to meet me tonight at our trysting tree and at the usual hour.'

' "I am afraid, my beloved Phemie, that I shall scarcely be able to attend," said I.

' "Yes, but you will," said she, "and you must not disappoint me, for

I will await your arrival." And with a graceful curtsy and a smile she retired, saying, as she left the room, "God be with you till then, David." '

This narrative quite confounded me. It was a long time before I could either act or think. At length I sat down on his bedside and took his hand in mine; it was worn to the hand of a skeleton. I felt his pulse; that strong and manly pulse had dwindled into a mere shiver, with an interval every seven or eight strokes. I easily perceived that it was all over with him.

'How do you think my pulse is?' said he.

'The pulse is not amiss,' said I; 'but you may depend on Phemie's word. You will meet her tonight at the trysting-hour, I have no doubt of it. When is your trysting-hour? for I think you may rely on Phemie's word.'

'Oh yes, Oh yes!' said he. 'Phemie never told a lie in her life and it would be absurd to think she would do it now. Let me have your prayers, my dear friend, let me have your prayers to take with me and I will trust my Redeemer for the rest!'

These were the last words he uttered in this life and he uttered them with a creaking voice perfectly sepulchral. I called in his father and his two sisters and told them that David was dying; and that I wished, by his own desire, to pray with him before parting with him for ever. His sisters were like to burst their hearts with crying; but the old father seemed perfectly resigned. I sung the fifth verse of the thirty-first psalm – I remember it well; and read about the latter half of the fifteenth chapter of the first book of Corinthians; and if I did not pray eloquently, I am sure I did fervently. When I had done, he seized my hand feebly and held it, until death loosed his grasp; for the trysting-hour was fast approaching; and whether he longed for it or wished to remain a little longer in this to him miserable state of existence, I cannot tell; but he turned his eye frequently to the clock that stood right opposite to his bed and exactly at the trysting-hour he expired. The two young lovers were virtuous and lovely in their lives and in their deaths they were but shortly divided.

The Brownie of the Black Haggs

James Hogg

When the Sprots were lairds of Wheelhope, which is now a long time ago, there was one of the ladies who was very badly spoken of in the country. People did not just openly assert that Lady Wheelhope was a witch, but everyone had an aversion even at hearing her named; and when by chance she happened to be mentioned, old men would shake their heads and say, 'Ah! let us alane o' her! The less ye meddle wi' her the better.' Auld wives would give over spinning, and, as a pretence for hearing what might be said about her, poke in the fire with the tongs, cocking up their ears all the while; and then, after some meaning coughs, hems and haws, would haply say, 'Hech-wow, sirs! An a' be true that's said!' or something equally wise and decisive as that.

In short, Lady Wheelhope was accounted a very bad woman. She was an inexorable tyrant in her family, quarrelled with her servants, often cursing them, striking them, and turning them away; especially if they were religious, for these she could not endure, but suspected them of everything bad. Whenever she found out any of the servant men of the laird's establishment for religious characters, she soon gave them up to the military, and got them shot; and several girls that were regular in their devotions, she was supposed to have popped off with poison. She was certainly a wicked woman, else many good people were mistaken in her character, and the poor persecuted Covenanters were obliged to unite in their prayers against her.

As for the laird, he was a stump. A big, dun-faced, pluffy body, that cared neither for good nor evil, and did not well know the one from the other. He laughed at his lady's tantrums and barley-hoods; and the greater the rage that she got into, the laird thought it the better sport. One day, when two servant maids came running to him, in great agitation, and told him that his lady had felled one of their companions, the laird laughed heartily at them, and said he did not doubt it.

'Why, sir, how can you laugh?' said they. 'The poor girl is killed.'

'Very likely, very likely,' said the laird. 'Well, it will teach her to take care who she angers again.'

'And, sir, your lady will be hanged.'

'Very likely; well, it will teach her not to strike so rashly again – Ha, ha, ha! Will it not, Jessy?'

But when this same Jessy died suddenly one morning, the laird was greatly confounded, and seemed dimly to comprehend that there had been unfair play going. There was little doubt that she was taken off by poison; but whether the lady did it through jealousy or not, was never divulged; but it greatly bamboozled and astonished the poor laird, for his nerves failed him, and his whole frame became paralytic. He seems to have been exactly in the same state of mind as a collie that I once had. He was extremely fond of the gun as long as I did not kill anything with it (there being no game laws in Ettrick Forest in those days) and he got a grand chase after the hares when I missed them. But there was one day that I chanced for a marvel to shoot one dead, a few paces before his nose. I'll never forget the astonishment that the poor beast manifested. He stared one while at the gun, and another while at the dead hare, and seemed to be drawing the conclusion that if the case stood thus there was no creature sure of its life. Finally, he took his tail between his legs, and ran away home, and never would face a gun all his life again.

So was it precisely with Laird Sprot of Wheelhope. As long as his lady's wrath produced only noise and splutter among the servants, he thought it fine sport; but when he saw what he believed the dreadful effects of it, he became like a barrel organ out of tune, and could only discourse one note, which he did to everyone he met: 'I wish she maunna hae gotten something she has been the waur of.' This note he repeated early and late, night and day, sleeping and waking, alone and in company, from the moment that Jessy died till she was buried, and on going to the churchyard as chief mourner, he whispered it to her relations by the way. When they came to the grave, he took his stand at the head, nor would he give place to the girl's father, but there he stood, like a huge post, as though he neither saw nor heard; and when he had lowered her late comely head into the grave, and dropped the cord, he slowly lifted his hat with one hand, wiped his dim eyes with the back of the other, and said, in a deep tremulous tone, 'Poor lassie! I wish she didna get something she had been the waur of.'

This death made a great noise among the common people, but there was no protection for the life of the subject in those days; and provided a man or woman was a true loyal subject, and a real Anti-Covenanter, any of them might kill as many as they liked. So there was no one to take cognisance of the circumstances relating to the death of poor Jessy.

After this, the lady walked softly for the space of two or three years. She saw that she had rendered herself odious, and had entirely lost her husband's countenance, which she liked worst of all. But the evil propensity could not be overcome; and a poor boy, whom the laird, out of sheer compassion, had taken into his service, being found dead one morning, the country people could no longer be restrained; so they went in a body to the sheriff, and insisted on an investigation. It was proved that she detested the boy, had often threatened him, and had given him brose and butter the afternoon before he died; but the cause was ultimately dismissed, and the pursuers fined.

No one can tell to what height of wickedness she might now have proceeded, had not a check of a very singular kind been laid upon her. Among the servants that came home at the next term, was one who called himself Merodach; and a strange person he was. He had the form of a boy, but the features of one a hundred years old, save that his eyes had a brilliancy and restlessness, which was very extra-ordinary, bearing a strong resemblance to the eyes of a well-known species of monkey. He was froward and perverse in all his actions, and disregarded the pleasure or displeasure of any person; but he performed his work well, and with apparent ease. From the moment that he entered the house, the lady conceived a mortal antipathy against him, and besought the laird to turn him away. But the laird, of himself, never turned away anybody, and moreover he had hired him for a trivial wage, and the fellow neither wanted activity nor perseverance. The natural consequence of this arrangement was that the lady instantly set herself to make Merodach's life as bitter as it was possible, in order to get early quit of a domestic every way so disgusting. Her hatred of him was not like a common antipathy entertained by one human being against another – she hated him as one might hate a toad or an adder; and his occupation of jotteryman (as the laird termed his servant of all work) keeping him always about her hand, it must have proved highly disagreeable.

She scolded him, she raged at him, but he only mocked her wrath, and giggled and laughed at her, with the most provoking derision. She tried to fell him again and again, but never, with all her address, could she hit him; and never did she make a blow at him that she did not repent it. She was heavy and unwieldy, and he as quick in his motions as a monkey; besides, he generally had her in such an ungovernable rage that when she flew at him she hardly knew what she was doing. At one time she guided her blow towards him and he at the same instant avoided it with such dexterity that she knocked down the chief hind or foresman; and then Merodach giggled so heartily that, lifting the kitchen poker, she threw it at him with a full design of knocking out his brains; but the missile only broke every plate and ashet on the kitchen dresser.

She then hasted to the laird, crying bitterly, and telling him she would not suffer that wretch Merodach, as she called him, to stay another night in the family. 'Why, then, put him away, and trouble me no more about him,' said the laird.

'Put him away!' exclaimed she; 'I have already ordered him away a hundred times, and charged him never to let me see his horrible face again; but he only flouts me, and tells me he'll see me at the devil first.'

The pertinacity of the fellow amused the laird exceedingly; his dim eyes turned upwards into his head with delight; he then looked two ways at once, turned round his back, and laughed till the tears ran down his dun cheeks, but he could only articulate 'You're fitted now.'

The lady's agony of rage still increasing from this derision, she flew on the laird, and said he was not worthy the name of a man if he did not turn away that pestilence after the way he had abused her.

'Why, Shusy, my dear, what has he done to you?'

'What done to me! has he not caused me to knock down John Thomson, and I do not know if ever he will come to life again?'

'Have you felled your favourite John Thomson?' said the laird, laughing more heartily than before; 'you might have done a worse deed than that. But what evil has John done?'

'And has he not broke every plate and dish on the whole dresser?' continued the lady, disregarding the laird's question; 'and for all this devastation, he only mocks at my displeasure – absolutely mocks me – and if you do not have him turned away, and hanged or shot for his deeds, you are not worthy the name of man.'

'Oh alack! What a devastation among the china metal!' said the laird; and calling on Merodach, he said, 'Tell me, thou evil Merodach of Babylon, how thou dared'st knock down thy lady's favourite servant, John Thomson?'

'Not I, your honour. It was my lady herself, who got into such a furious rage at me that she mistook her man and felled Mr Thomson; and the good man's skull is fractured.'

'That was very odd,' said the laird, chuckling; 'I do not comprehend it. But then, what the devil set you on smashing all my lady's delft and china ware? That was a most infamous and provoking action.'

'It was she herself, your honour. Sorry would I have been to have broken one dish belonging to the house. I take all the house-servants to witness that my lady smashed all the dishes with a poker, and now lays the blame on me.'

The laird turned his dim and delighted eyes on his lady, who was crying with vexation and rage, and seemed meditating another personal attack on the culprit, which he did not at all appear to shun, but rather encourage. She, however, vented her wrath in threatenings of the most deep and desperate revenge, the creature all the while assuring her that she would be foiled, and that in all her encounters and contests with him, she would uniformly come to the worst. He was resolved to do his duty, and there before his master he defied her.

The laird thought more than he considered it prudent to reveal; but he had little doubt that his wife would wreak that vengeance on his jotteryman which she avowed, and as little of her capability. He almost shuddered when he recollected one who had taken *something that she had been the waur of.*

In a word, the Lady of Wheelhope's inveterate malignity against this one object was like the rod of Moses that swallowed up the rest of the serpents. All her wicked and evil propensities seemed to be superseded by it, if not utterly absorbed in its virtues. The rest of the family now lived in comparative peace and quietness; for early and late her malevolence was venting itself against the jotteryman, and him alone. It was a delirium of hatred and vengeance, on which the whole bent and bias of her inclination was set. She could not stay from the creature's presence, for in the intervals when absent from him she spent her breath in curses and execrations, and then not able to rest, she ran again to seek him, her eyes gleaming with the anticipated delights of vengeance, while, ever and anon, all the scaith, the ridicule and the harm redounded on herself.

Was it not strange that she could not get quit of this sole annoyance of her life? One would have thought she easily might. But by this time there was nothing farther from her intention; she wanted vengeance, full, adequate and delicious vengeance, on her audacious opponent. But he was a strange and terrible creature, and the means of retaliation came always, as it were, to his hand.

Bread and sweet milk was the only fare that Merodach cared for, and he having bargained for that, was wont to receive it, though he often got it with a curse and with ill will. The lady having intentionally kept back his wonted allowance for some days, on the Sabbath morning following she set him down a bowl of rich sweet milk, well drugged with a deadly poison, and then she lingered in a little anteroom to watch the success of her grand plot, and prevent any other creature from tasting of the potion. Merodach came in, and the housemaid says to him, 'There is your breakfast, creature.'

'Oho! my lady has been liberal this morning,' said he; 'but I am beforehand with her. Here, little Missie, you seem very hungry today – take you my breakfast.' And with that he set the beverage down to the lady's little favourite spaniel. It so happened that the lady's only son came at that instant into the anteroom, seeking her and teasing his mamma about something which took her attention from the hall-table for a space. When she looked again, and saw Missie lapping up the sweet milk, she burst from her lobby like a dragon, screaming as if her head had been on fire, kicked the bowl and the remainder of its contents against the wall, and lifting Missie in her bosom, she retreated hastily, crying all the way.

'Ha, ha, ha – I have you now!' cried Merodach, as she vanished from the hall.

Poor Missie died immediately, and very privately; indeed, she would have died and been buried, and never one have seen her, save her mistress, had not Merodach, by a luck that never failed him, popped his nose over the flower-garden wall, just as his lady was laying her favourite in a grave of her own digging. She, not perceiving her tormentor, plied on at her task, apostrophising the insensate little carcass – 'Ah! poor dear little creature, thou hast had a hard fortune and hast drank of the bitter potion that was not intended for thee; but he shall drink it three times double, for thy sake!'

'Is that little Missie?' said the eldrich voice of the jotteryman, close at the lady's ear. She uttered a loud scream, and sank down on the bank. 'Alack for poor little Missie!' continued the creature in a tone of mockery. 'My heart is sorry for Missie. What has befallen her – whose breakfast cup did she drink?'

'Hence with thee, thou fiend!' cried the lady; 'what right hast thou to intrude on thy mistress's privacy? Thy turn is coming yet, or may the nature of woman change within me.'

'It is changed already,' said the creature, grinning with delight; 'I have thee now, I have thee now! And were it not to show my superiority over thee, which I do every hour, I should soon see thee strapped like a mad cat or a worrying bratch. What wilt thou try next?'

'I will cut thy throat, and if I die for it, will rejoice in the deed; a deed of charity to all that dwell on the face of the earth. Go about thy business.'

'I have warned thee before, dame, and I now warn thee again, that all thy mischief meditated against me will fall double on thine own head.'

'I want none of your warning, and none of your instructions, fiendish cur. Hence with your elvish face, and take care of yourself.'

It would be too disgusting and horrible to relate or read all the incidents that fell out between this unaccountable couple. Their enmity against each other had no end, and no mitigation; and scarcely a single day passed over on which her acts of malevolent ingenuity did not terminate fatally for some favourite thing of the lady's, while all these doings never failed to appear as her own act. Scarcely was there a thing, animate or inanimate, on which she set a value, left to her, that was not destroyed, and yet scarcely one hour or minute could she remain absent from her tormentor, and all the while, it seems, solely for the purpose of tormenting him.

But while all the rest of the establishment enjoyed peace and quietness from the fury of their termagant dame, matters still grew worse and worse between the fascinated pair. The lady haunted the menial, in the same manner as the raven haunts the eagle, for a perpetual quarrel, though the former knows that in every encounter she is to come off the loser. But now noises were heard on the stairs by night, and it was whispered among the menials that the lady had been seeking Merodach's bed by night, on some horrible intent. Several of them would have sworn that they had seen her passing and repassing on the stair after midnight, when all was quiet; but then it was likewise well known that Merodach slept with well-fastened doors, and a companion in another bed in the same room, whose bed, too, was nearest the door. Nobody cared much what became of the jottery-man, for he was an unsocial and disagreeable person; but someone told him what they had seen, and hinted a suspicion of the lady's intent. But the creature only bit his upper lip, winked with his eyes, and said, 'She had better let alone; she will be the first to rue that.'

Not long after this, to the horror of the family and the whole countryside, the laird's only son was found murdered in his bed one morning, under circumstances that manifested the most fiendish cruelty and inveteracy on the part of his destroyer. As soon as the atrocious act was divulged, the lady fell into convulsions, and lost her reason; and happy had it been for her had she never recovered either the use of reason, or her corporeal functions any more, for there was blood upon her hand, which she took no care to conceal, and there was too little doubt that it was the blood of her own innocent and beloved boy, the sole heir and hope of the family.

This blow deprived the laird of all power of action; but the lady had a brother, a man of the law, who came and instantly proceeded to an investigation of this unaccountable murder; but before the sheriff arrived, the housekeeper took the lady's brother aside, and told him he had better not go on with the scrutiny, for she was sure the crime would be brought home to her unfortunate mistress; and after examining into several corroborative circumstances, and viewing the state of the raving maniac, with the blood on her hand and arm, he made the investigation a very short one, declaring the domestics all exculpated.

The laird attended his boy's funeral, and laid his head in the grave, but appeared exactly like a man walking in a trance, an automaton, without feelings or sensations, oftentimes gazing at the funeral procession as on something he could not comprehend. And when the death-bell of the parish church fell a-tolling as the corpse approached the kirk-stile, he cast a dim eye up towards the belfry, and said hastily, 'What, what's that? Och ay, we're just in time, just in time.' And often was he hammering over the name of 'Evil Merodach, King of Babylon', to himself. He seemed to have some far-fetched conception that his unaccountable jotteryman had a hand in the death of his only son, and other lesser calamities, although the evidence in favour of Merodach's innocence was as usual quite decisive.

This grievous mistake of Lady Wheelhope (for every landward laird's wife was then styled Lady) can only be accounted for by supposing her in a state of derangement, or rather under some evil influence, over which she had no control; and to a person in such a state, the mistake was not so very unnatural. The mansion house of Wheelhope was old and irregular. The stair had four acute turns, all the same, and four landing-places, all the same. In the uppermost chamber slept the two domestics, Merodach in the bed farthest in, and in the chamber immediately below that, which was exactly similar, slept the young laird and his tutor, the former in the bed farthest in; and thus, in the turmoil of raging passions, her own hand made herself childless.

Merodach was expelled the family forthwith, but refused to accept of his wages, which the man of law pressed upon him, for fear of further mischief; but he went away in apparent sullenness and discontent, no one knowing whither.

When his dismissal was announced to the lady, who was watched day and night in her chamber, the news had such an effect on her that her whole frame seemed electrified; the horrors of remorse vanished, and another passion, which I neither can comprehend nor define, took the sole possession of her distempered spirit. 'He *must* not go! He *shall* not go!' she exclaimed. 'No, no, no he shall not – he shall not – he shall not!' and then she instantly set herself about making ready to follow him, uttering all the while the most diabolical expressions, indicative of anticipated vengeance. 'Oh, could I but snap his nerves one by one, and birl among his vitals! Could I but slice his heart off piecemeal in small messes, and see his blood lopper and bubble, and spin away in purple slays; and then to see him grin, and grin, and grin, and grin! Oh – oh – oh! How beautiful and grand a sight it would be to see him grin, and grin, and grin!' And in such a style would she run on for hours together.

She thought of nothing, she spake of nothing, but the discarded jotteryman, whom most people now began to regard as a creature that was not canny. They had seen him eat, and drink, and work like other people, still he had that about him that was not like other men. He was a boy in form, and an antediluvian in feature. Some thought he was a mule, between a Jew and an ape; some a wizard, some a kelpie or a fairy, but most of all, that he was really and truly a brownie. What he was I do not know, and therefore will not pretend to say; but be that as it may, in spite of locks and keys, watching and waking, the Lady of Wheelhope soon made her escape and eloped after him. The attendants, indeed, would have made oath that she was carried away by some invisible hand, for that it was impossible she could have escaped on foot like other people, and this edition of the story took in the country; but sensible people viewed the matter in another light.

As for instance, when Wattie Blythe, the laird's old shepherd, came in from the hill one morning, his wife Bessie thus accosted him: 'His presence be about us, Wattie Blythe! have ye heard what has happened at the ha'? Things are aye turning waur and waur there, and it looks like as if Providence had gi'en up our laird's house to destruction. This grand estate maun now gang frae the Sprots, for it has finished them.'

'Na, na, Bessie, it isna the estate that has finished the Sprots, but the Sprots that hae finished it, an' themsells into the boot. They hae been a wicked and degenerate race, an' aye the langer the waur, till they hae reached the utmost bounds o' earthly wickedness; an' it's time the deil were looking after his ain.'

'Ah, Wattie Blythe, ye never said a truer say. An' that's just the very point where your story ends, and mine commences; for hasna the deil, or the fairies, or the brownies, ta'en away our lady bodily, an' the haill country is running and riding in search o' her; and there is twenty hunder merks offered to the first that can find her, an' bring her safe back. They hae ta'en her away, skin an' bane, body an' soul, an' a', Wattie!'

'Hech-wow! but that is awsome! And where is it thought they have ta'en her to, Bessie?'

'Oh, they hae some guess at that frae her ain hints afore. It is thought they hae carried her after that Satan of a creature wha wrought sae muckle wae about the house. It is for him they are a-looking, for they ken weel that where they get the tane they will get the tither.'

'Whew! Is that the gate o't, Bessie? Why, then, the awfu' story is nouther mair nor less than this, that the leddy has made a lopment, as they ca't, and run away after a blackgaird jotteryman. Hech-wow! wae's me for human frailty! But that's just the gate! When aince the deil gets in the point o' his finger, he will soon have in his haill hand. Ay, he wants but a hair to make a tether of, ony day. I hae seen her a braw sonsy lass, but even then I feared she was devoted to destruction, for she aye mockit at religion, Bessie, an' that's no a good mark of a young body. An' she made a' its servants her enemies; an' think you these good men's prayers were a' to blaw away i' the wind, and be nae mair regarded? Na, na, Bessie, my woman, take ye this mark baith o' our ain bairns and ither folk's – if ever ye see a young body that disregards the Sabbath, and makes a mock at the ordinances o' religion, ye will never see that body come to muckle good. A braw hand she has made o' her gibes an' jeers at religion, an' her mockeries o' the poor persecuted hill-folk! – sunk down by degrees into the very dregs o' sin and misery! Run away after a scullion!'

'Fy, fy, Wattie, how can ye say sae? It was weel kenn'd that she hatit him wi' a perfect an' mortal hatred, an' tried to make away wi' him mae ways nor ane.'

'Aha, Bessie; but nipping an' scarting are Scots folk's wooing; an' though it is but right that we suspend our judgements, there will naebody persuade me, if she be found alang wi' the creature, but that she has run away after him in the natural way, on her twa shanks, without help either frae fairy or brownie.'

'I'll never believe sic a thing of any woman born, let be a lady weel up in years.'

''Od help ye, Bessie! ye dinna ken the stretch o' corrupt nature. The best o' us, when left to oursells, are nae better than strayed sheep that will never find the way back to their ain pastures; an' of a' things made o' mortal flesh, a wicked woman is the warst.'

'Alack-a-day! we get the blame o' muckle that we little deserve. But, Wattie, keep ye a gayan sharp lookout about the cleuchs and the caves o' our glen, or hope, as ye ca't; for the lady kens them a' gayan weel; and gin the twenty hunder merks wad come our way, it might gang a waur gate. It wad tocher a' our bonny lasses.'

'Ay, weel I wat, Bessie, that's nae lee. And now, when ye bring me amind o't, the Lord forgie me gin I didna hear a creature up in the Brock-holes this morning, skirling as if something war cutting its throat. It gars a' the hairs stand on my head when I think it may hae been our leddy, an' the droich of a creature murdering her. I took it for a battle of wulcats, and wished they might pu' out ane anither's thrapples; but when I think on it again, they war unco like some o' our leddy's unearthly screams.'

'His presence be about us, Wattie! Haste ye. Pit on your bonnet – take your staff in your hand, and gang an' see what it is.'

'Shame fa' me, if I daur gang, Bessie.'

'Hout, Wattie, trust in the Lord.'

'Aweel, sae I do. But ane's no to throw himself ower a linn, an' trust that the Lord's to kep him in a blanket; nor hing himsell up in a raip, an' expect the Lord to come and cut him down. An' it's nae muckle safer for an auld stiff man to gang away out to a wild remote place, where there is ae body murdering another – What is that I hear, Bessie? Haud the lang tongue o' you, and rin to the door, an' see what noise that is.'

Bessie ran to the door, but soon returned an altered creature, with her mouth wide open and her eyes set in her head.

'It is them, Wattie! it is them! His presence be about us! What will we do?'

'Them? whaten them?'

'Why, that blackguard creature, coming here, leading our leddy be the hair o' the head, an' yerking her wi' a stick. I am terrified out o' my wits. What will we do?'

'We'll *see* what they *say*,' said Wattie, manifestly in as great terror as his wife; and by a natural impulse, or as a last resource, he opened the Bible, not knowing what he did, and then hurried on his spectacles; but before he got two leaves turned over, the two entered, a frightful looking couple indeed. Merodach, with his old withered face and ferret eyes, leading the Lady of Wheelhope by the long hair, which was mixed with grey, and whose face was all bloated with wounds and bruises, and having stripes of blood on her garments.

'How's this! How's this, sirs?' said Wattie Blythe.

'Close that book, and I will tell you, goodman,' said Merodach.

'I can hear what you hae to say wi' the beuk open, sir,' said Wattie, turning over the leaves, as if looking for some particular passage, but apparently not knowing what he was doing. 'It is a shamefu' business this, but some will hae to answer for't. My leddy, I am unco grieved to see you in sic a plight. Ye hae surely been dooms sair left to yoursell.'

The lady shook her head, uttered a feeble hollow laugh, and fixed her eyes on Merodach. But such a look! It almost frightened the simple aged couple out of their senses. It was not a look of love nor of hatred exclusively; neither was it of desire or disgust, but it was a combination of them all. It was such a look as one fiend would cast on another, in whose everlasting destruction he rejoiced. Wattie was glad to take his eyes from such countenances and look into the Bible, that firm foundation of all his hopes and all his joy.

'I request that you will shut that book, sir,' said the horrible creature; 'or if you do not, I will shut it for you with a vengeance;' and with that he seized it, and flung it against the wall. Bessie uttered a scream, and Wattie was quite paralysed; and although he seemed disposed to run after his best friend, as he called it, the hellish looks of the brownie interposed, and glued him to his seat.

'Hear what I have to say first,' said the creature, 'and then pore your fill on that precious book of yours. One concern at a time is enough. I came to do you a service. Here, take this cursed, wretched woman, whom you style your lady, and deliver her up to the lawful authorities, to be restored to her husband and her place in society. She is come upon one that hates her, and never said one kind word to her in his life, and though I have beat her like a dog, still she clings to me, and will not depart, so enchanted is she with the laudable purpose of cutting my throat. Tell your master and her brother, that I am not to be burdened with their maniac. I have scourged, I have spurned and kicked her, afflicting her night and day, and yet from my side she will not depart. Take her. Claim the reward in full, and your fortune is made, and so farewell.'

The creature bowed and went away, but the moment his back was turned the lady fell a-screaming and struggling like one in an agony, and, in spite of all the old couple's exertions, she forced herself out of their hands and ran after the retreating Merodach. When he saw better would not be, he turned upon her, and, by one blow with his stick, struck her down; and, not content with that, he continued to kick and baste her in such a manner as to all appearance would have killed twenty ordinary persons. The poor devoted dame could do nothing, but now and then utter a squeak like a half-worried cat, and writhe and grovel on the sward, till Wattie and his wife came up and withheld her tormentor from further violence. He then bound her hands behind her back with a strong cord, and delivered her once more to the charge of the old couple, who contrived to hold her by that means and take her home.

Wattie had not the face to take her into the hall, but into one of the outhouses, where he brought her brother to receive her. The man of the law was manifestly vexed at her reappearance, and scrupled not to testify his dissatisfaction; for when Wattie told him how the wretch had abused his sister, and that, had it not been for Bessie's interference and his own, the lady would have been killed outright, 'Why, Walter, it is a great pity that he did not kill her outright,' said he. 'What good can her life now do to her, or of what value is her life to any creature living? After one has lived to disgrace all connected with them, the sooner they are taken off the better.'

The man, however, paid old Walter down his two thousand merks, a great fortune for one like him in those days; and not to dwell longer on this unnatural story, I shall only add, very shortly, that the Lady of Wheelhope soon made her escape once more, and flew, as by an irresistible charm, to her tormentor. Her friends looked no more after her; and the last time she was seen alive, it was following the uncouth creature up the water of Daur, weary, wounded and lame, while he was all the way beating her, as a piece of excellent amusement. A few days after that, her body was found among some wild haggs, in a place called Crookburn, by a party of the persecuted Covenanters that were in hiding there, some of the very men whom she had exerted herself to destroy, and who had been driven, like David of old, to pray for a curse and earthly punishment upon her. They buried her like a dog at the Yetts of Keppel, and rolled three huge stones upon her grave, which are lying there to this day. When they found her corpse, it was mangled and wounded in a most shocking manner, the fiendish creature having manifestly tormented her to death. He was never more seen or heard of in this kingdom, though all that countryside was kept in terror of him many years afterwards; and to this day, they will tell you of the Brownie of the Black Haggs, which title he seems to have acquired after his disappearance.

This story was told to me by an old man named Adam Halliday, whose great grandfather, Thomas Halliday, was one of those that found the body and buried it. It is many years since I heard it; but, however ridiculous it may appear, I remember it made a dreadful impression on my young mind. I never heard any story like it, save one of an old foxhound that pursued a fox through the Grampians for a fortnight, and when at last discovered by the Duke of Athole's people, neither of them could run, but the hound was still continuing to walk after the fox, and when the latter lay down the other lay down beside him, and looked at him steadily all the while; though unable to do him the least harm. The passion of inveterate malice seems to have influenced these two exactly alike. But, upon the whole, I scarcely believe the tale can be true.

The Mysterious Bride

James Hogg

A great number of people nowadays are beginning broadly to insinuate that there are no such things as ghosts, or spiritual beings visible to mortal sight. Even Sir Walter Scott is turned renegade, and, with his stories made up of half-and-half, like Nathaniel Gow's toddy, is trying to throw cold water on the most certain, though most impalpable, phenomena of human nature. The bodies are daft. Heaven mend their wits! Before they had ventured to assert such things, I wish they had been where I have often been; or, in particular, where the Laird of Birkendelly was on St Lawrence's Eve, in the year 1777, and sundry times subsequent to that.

Be it known, then, to every reader of this relation of facts that happened in my own remembrance, that the road from Birkendelly to the great muckle village of Balmawhapple (commonly called the muckle town, in opposition to the little town that stood on the other side of the burn) – that road, I say, lay between two thorn-hedges, so well kept by the laird's hedger, so close, and so high, that a rabbit could not have escaped from the highway into any of the adjoining fields. Along this road was the laird riding on the Eve of St Lawrence, in a careless, indifferent manner, with his hat to one side and his cane dancing a hornpipe before him. He was, moreover, chanting a song to himself, and I have heard people tell what song it was too. There was once a certain, or rather uncertain, bard, ycleped Robert Burns, who made a number of good songs; but this that the laird sang was an amorous song of great antiquity, which, like all the said bard's best songs, was sung one hundred and fifty years before he was born. It began thus:

> I am the Laird of Windy-wa's,
> I cam nae here without a cause,
> An' I hae gotten forty fa's
> In coming o'er the knowe, Joe.
> The night it is baith wind and weet;

> The morn it will be snaw and sleet;
> My shoon are frozen to my feet;
> Oh, rise an' let me in, Joe!
> Let me in this ae night . . .

This song was the laird singing, while, at the same time, he was smudging and laughing at the catastrophe, when, ere ever aware, he beheld, a short way before him, an uncommonly elegant and beautiful girl walking in the same direction with him. 'Aye,' said the laird to himself, 'here is something very attractive indeed! Where the deuce can she have sprung from? She must have risen out of the earth, for I never saw her till this breath. Well, I declare I have not seen such a female figure – I wish I had such an assignation with her as the Laird of Windy-wa's had with his sweetheart.'

As the laird was half-thinking, half-speaking this to himself, the enchanting creature looked back at him with a motion of intelligence that she knew what he was half-saying, half-thinking, and then vanished over the summit of the rising ground before him, called the Birky Brow. 'Aye, go your ways!' said the laird; 'I see by you, you'll not be very hard to overtake. You cannot get off the road, and I'll have a chat with you before you make the Deer's Den.'

The laird jogged on. He did not sing 'The Laird of Windy-wa's' any more, for he felt a stifling about his heart; but he often repeated to himself, 'She's a very fine woman! – a very fine woman indeed! – and to be walking here by herself! I cannot comprehend it.'

When he reached the summit of the Birky Brow he did not see her, although he had a longer view of the road than before. He thought this very singular, and began to suspect that she wanted to escape him, although apparently rather lingering on him before. 'I shall have another look at her, however,' thought the laird, and off he set at a flying trot. No. He came first to one turn, then another. There was nothing of the young lady to be seen. 'Unless she take wings and fly away, I shall be up with her,' quoth the laird, and off he set at the full gallop.

In the middle of his career he met with Mr McMurdie, of Aulton, who hailed him with, 'Hilloa, Birkendelly! Where the deuce are you flying at that rate?'

'I was riding after a woman,' said the laird, with great simplicity, reining in his steed.

'Then I am sure no woman on earth can long escape you, unless she be in an air balloon.'

'I don't know that. Is she far gone?'

'In which way do you mean?'

'In this.'

'Aha ha ha! Hee hee hee!' nichered McMurdie, misconstruing the laird's meaning.

'What do you laugh at, my dear sir? Do you know her, then?'

'Ho ho ho! Hee hee hee! How should I, or how can I, know her, Birkendelly, unless you inform me who she is?'

'Why, that is the very thing I want to know of you. I mean the young lady whom you met just now.'

'You are raving, Birkendelly. I met no young lady, nor is there a single person on the road I have come by, while you know that for a mile and a half forward your way she could not get out of it.'

'I know that,' said the laird, biting his lip and looking greatly puzzled; 'but confound me if I understand this; for I was within speech of her just now on the top of the Birky Brow there, and, when I think of it, she could not have been even thus far as yet. She had on a pure white gauze frock, a small green bonnet and feathers, and a green veil, which, flung back over her left shoulder, hung below her waist, and was altogether such an engaging figure that no man could have passed her on the road without taking some note of her. Are you not making game of me? Did you not really meet with her?'

'On my word of truth and honour, I did not. Come, ride back with me, and we shall meet her still, depend on it. She has given you the go-by on the road. Let us go; I am only to call at the mill about some barley for the distillery, and will return with you to the big town.'

Birkendelly returned with his friend. The sun was not yet set, yet McMurdie could not help observing that the laird looked thoughtful and confused, and not a word could he speak about anything save this lovely apparition with the white frock and the green veil; and lo! when they reached the top of Birky Brow there was the maiden again before them, and exactly at the same spot where the Laird first saw her before, only walking in the contrary direction.

'Well, this is the most extraordinary thing that I ever knew!' exclaimed the laird.

'What is it, sir?' said McMurdie.

'How that young lady could have eluded me,' returned the laird. 'See, here she is still!'

'I beg your pardon, sir, I don't see her. Where is she?'

'There, on the other side of the angle; but you are short sighted.

See, there she is ascending the other eminence in her white frock and green veil, as I told you. What a lovely creature!'

'Well, well, we have her fairly before us now, and shall see what she is like at all events,' said McMurdie.

Between the Birky Brow and this other slight eminence there is an obtuse angle of the road at the part where it is lowest, and, in passing this, the two friends necessarily lost sight of the object of their curiosity. They pushed on at a quick pace, cleared the low angle – the maiden was not there! They rode full speed to the top of the eminence from whence a long extent of road was visible before them – there was no human creature in view. McMurdie laughed aloud, but the laird turned pale as death and bit his lip. His friend asked him good-humouredly why he was so much affected. He said, because he could not comprehend the meaning of this singular apparition or illusion, and it troubled him the more as he now remembered a dream of the same nature which he had, and which terminated in a dreadful manner.

'Why, man, you are dreaming still,' said McMurdie. 'But never mind; it is quite common for men of your complexion to dream of beautiful maidens with white frocks and green veils, bonnets, feathers and slender waists. It is a lovely image, the creation of your own sanguine imagination, and you may worship it without any blame. Were her shoes black or green? And her stockings – did you note them? The symmetry of the limbs? I am sure you did! Goodbye; I see you are not disposed to leave the spot. Perhaps she will appear to you again.'

So saying, McMurdie rode on toward the mill, and Birkendelly, after musing for some time, turned his beast's head slowly round, and began to move toward the great muckle village.

The laird's feelings were now in terrible commotion. He was taken beyond measure with the beauty and elegance of the figure he had seen, but he remembered, with a mixture of admiration and horror, that a dream of the same enchanting object had haunted his slumbers all the days of his life; yet, how singular that he should never have recollected the circumstance till now! But further, with the dream there were connected some painful circumstances which, though terrible in their issue, he could not recollect so as to form them into any degree of arrangement.

As he was considering deeply of these things and riding slowly down the declivity, neither dancing his cane nor singing 'The Laird of Windy-wa's', he lifted up his eyes, and there was the girl on the same spot where he saw her first, walking deliberately up the Birky Brow. The sun was down, but it was the month of August and a fine evening, and the Laird, seized with an unconquerable desire to see and speak with that incomparable creature, could restrain himself no longer, but shouted out to her to stop till he came up. She beckoned acquiescence, and slackened her pace into a slow movement. The laird turned the corner quickly, and when he had rounded it the maiden was still there, though on the summit of the brow. She turned round, and, with an ineffable smile and curtsy, saluted him, and again moved slowly on. She vanished gradually beyond the summit, and while the green feathers were still nodding in view, and so nigh that the laird could have touched them with a fishing-rod, he reached the top of the brow himself. There was no living soul there, nor onward, as far as his view reached. He now trembled in every limb, and, without knowing what he did, rode straight on to the big town, not daring well to return and see what he had seen for three several times; and certain he would see it again when the shades of evening were deepening, he deemed it proper and prudent to decline the pursuit of such a phantom any further.

He alighted at the Queen's Head, called for some brandy and water, and quite forgot what was his errand to the great muckle town that afternoon, there being nothing visible to his mental sight but lovely images, with white gauze frocks and green veils. His friend McMurdie joined him; they drank deep, bantered, reasoned, got angry, reasoned themselves calm again, and still all would not do. The laird was conscious that he had seen the beautiful apparition, and, moreover, that she was the very maiden, or the resemblance of her, who, in the irrevocable decrees of Providence, was destined to be his. It was in vain that McMurdie reasoned of impressions on the imagination, and

> Of fancy moulding in the mind,
> Light visions on the passing wind.

Vain also was a story that he told him of a relation of his own, who was greatly harassed by the apparition of an officer in a red uniform that haunted him day and night, and had very nigh put him quite distracted several times, till at length his physician found out the nature of this illusion so well that he knew, from the state of his pulse, to an hour when the ghost of the officer would appear, and by bleeding, low diet and emollients contrived to keep the apparition away altogether.

The laird admitted the singularity of this incident, but not that it was one in point; for the one, he said, was imaginary, the other real, and that no conclusions could convince him in opposition to the authority of his own senses. He accepted of an invitation to spend a few days with McMurdie and his family, but they all acknowledged afterward that the laird was very much like one bewitched.

As soon as he reached home he went straight to the Birky Brow, certain of seeing once more the angelic phantom, but she was not there. He took each of his former positions again and again, but the desired vision would in no wise make its appearance. He tried every day and every hour of the day, all with the same effect, till he grew absolutely desperate, and had the audacity to kneel on the spot and entreat of heaven to see her. Yes, he called on heaven to see her once more, whatever she was, whether a being of earth, heaven or hell.

He was now in such a state of excitement that he could not exist; he grew listless, impatient and sickly, took to his bed and sent for McMurdie and the doctor; and the issue of the consultation was that Birkendelly consented to leave the country for a season, on a visit to his only sister in Ireland, whither we must accompany him for a short space.

His sister was married to Captain Bryan the younger, of Scoresby, and they two lived in a cottage on the estate, and the captain's parents and sisters at Scoresby Hall. Great was the stir and preparation when the gallant young Laird of Birkendelly arrived at the cottage, it never being doubted that he came to forward a second bond of connection with the family, which still contained seven dashing sisters, all unmarried, and all alike willing to change that solitary and helpless state for the envied one of matrimony – a state highly popular among the young women of Ireland. Some of the Misses Bryan had now reached the years of womanhood, several of them scarcely, but these small disqualifications made no difference in the estimation of the young ladies themselves; each and all of them brushed up for the competition with high hopes and unflinching resolutions. True, the elder ones tried to check the younger in their good-natured, forthright Irish way; but they retorted, and persisted in their superior pretensions. Then there was such shopping in the county town! It was so boundless that the credit of the Hall was finally exhausted, and the old squire was driven to remark that, 'Och, and to be sure it was a dreadful and tirrabell concussion, to be put upon the equipment of seven daughters all at the same moment, as if the young gentleman could marry them all! Och, then, even should he choose, he would be after finding that one was sufficient, if not one too many. And therefore there was no occasion, none at all, at all, and that there was not, for him to have to rig out more than one.'

It was hinted that the squire had some reason for complaint at this time, but as the lady sided with her daughters, he had no chance. One of the items of his account was thirty-seven buckling-combs, then greatly in vogue. There were black combs, pale combs, yellow combs and gilt ones, all to suit or set off various complexions; and if other articles bore any proportion at all to these, it had been better for the squire and all his family that Birkendelly had never set foot in Ireland.

The plan was all concocted. There was to be a grand dinner at the Hall, at which the damsels were to appear in all their finery. A ball was to follow, and note be taken which of the young ladies was their guest's choice, and measures taken accordingly. The dinner and the ball took place; and what a pity I may not describe that entertainment, the dresses and the dancers, for they were all exquisite in their way, and *outré* beyond measure. But such details only serve to derange a winter evening's tale such as this.

Birkendelly having at this time but one model for his choice among womankind, all that ever he did while in the presence of ladies was to look out for some resemblance to her, the angel of his fancy; and it so happened that in one of old Bryan's daughters named Luna, or, more familiarly, Loony, he perceived, or thought he perceived, some imaginary similarity in form and air to the lovely apparition. This was the sole reason why he was incapable of taking his eyes off from her the whole of that night; and this incident settled the point, not only with the old people, but even the young ladies were forced, after every exertion on their own parts, to 'yild the p'int to their sister Loony, who certainly was not the mist genteelest nor mist handsomest of that guid-lucking fimily'.

The next day Lady Luna was dispatched off to the cottage in grand style, there to live hand in glove with her supposed lover. There was no standing all this. There were the two parrocked together, like a ewe and a lamb, early and late; and though the laird really appeared to have, and probably had, some delight in her company, it was only in contemplating that certain indefinable air of resemblance which she bore to the sole image impressed on his heart. He bought her a white gauze frock, a green bonnet and feather, with a veil, which she was obliged to wear thrown over her left shoulder, and every day after, six times a day, was she obliged to walk over a certain eminence at a certain distance before her lover. She was delighted to oblige him; but still, when he came up, he looked disappointed, and never said, 'Luna, I love you; when are we to be married?' No, he never said any such thing, for all her looks and expressions of fondest love; for, alas! in all this dalliance he was only feeding a mysterious flame that preyed upon his vitals, and proved too severe for the powers either of reason or religion to extinguish. Still, time flew lighter and lighter by, his health was restored, the bloom of his cheek returned, and the frank and simple confidence of Luna had a certain charm with it that reconciled him to his sister's Irish economy. But a strange incident now happened to him which deranged all his immediate plans.

He was returning from angling one evening, a little before sunset, when he saw Lady Luna awaiting him on his way home. But instead of rushing up to meet him as usual, she turned, and walked up the rising ground before him. 'Poor sweet girl! how condescending she is,' said he to himself, 'and how like she is in reality to the angelic being whose form and features are so deeply impressed on my heart! I now see it is no fond or fancied resemblance. It is real! real! real! How I long to clasp her in my arms, and tell her how I love her; for, after all, that is the girl that is to be mine, and the former a vision to impress this the more on my heart.'

He posted up the ascent to overtake her. When at the top she turned, smiled and curtsied. Good heavens! it was the identical lady of his fondest adoration herself, but lovelier, far lovelier, than ever. He expected every moment that she would vanish, as was her wont; but she did not – she awaited him, and received his embraces with open arms. She was a being of real flesh and blood, courteous, elegant and affectionate. He kissed her hand, he kissed her glowing cheek, and blessed all the powers of love who had thus restored her to him again, after undergoing pangs of love such as man never suffered.

'But, dearest heart, here we are standing in the middle of the highway,' said he; 'suffer me to conduct you to my sister's house, where you shall have an apartment with a child of nature having some slight resemblance to yourself.' She smiled, and said, 'No, I will not sleep with Lady Luna tonight. Will you please to look round you, and see where you are.' He did so, and behold they were standing on the Birky Brow, on the only spot where he had ever seen her. She smiled at his embarrassed look, and asked if he did not remember aught of his coming over from Ireland. He said he thought he did remember something of it, but love with him had long absorbed every other sense. He then asked her to his own house, which she declined, saying she could only meet him on that spot till after their marriage, which could not be before St Lawrence's Eve come three years. 'And now,' said she, 'we must part. My name is Jane Ogilvie, and you were betrothed to me before you were born. But I am come to release you this evening, if you have the slightest objection.'

He declared he had none; and kneeling, swore the most solemn oath to be hers for ever, and to meet her there on St Lawrence's Eve next, and every St Lawrence's Eve until that blessed day on which she had consented to make him happy by becoming his own for ever. She then asked him affectionately to change rings with her, in pledge of their faith and troth, in which he joyfully acquiesced; for she could not have then asked any conditions which, in the fullness of his heart's love, he would not have granted; and after one fond and affectionate kiss, and repeating all their engagements over again, they parted.

Birkendelly's heart was now melted within him, and all his senses overpowered by one overwhelming passion. On leaving his fair and kind one, he got bewildered, and could not find the road to his own house, believing sometimes that he was going there, and sometimes to his sister's, till at length he came, as he thought, upon the Liffey, at its junction with Loch Allan; and there, in attempting to call for a boat, he awoke from a profound sleep, and found himself lying in his bed within his sister's house, and the day sky just breaking.

If he was puzzled to account for some things in the course of his dream, he was much more puzzled to account for them now that he was wide awake. He was sensible that he had met his love, had embraced, kissed and exchanged vows and rings with her, and, in token of the truth and reality of all these, her emerald ring was on his finger, and his own away; so there was no doubt that they had met – by what means it was beyond the power of man to calculate.

There was then living with Mrs Bryan an old Scotswoman, commonly styled Lucky Black. She had nursed Birkendelly's mother, and been dry-nurse to himself and sister; and having more than a mother's attachment for the latter, when she was married, old Lucky left her country to spend the last of her days in the house of her beloved young lady. When the laird entered the breakfast-parlour that morning she was sitting in her black velvet hood, as usual, reading *The Fourfold State of Man*, and, being paralytic and somewhat deaf, she seldom regarded those who went or came. But chancing to hear him say something about the 9th of August, she quitted reading, turned round her head to listen, and then asked, in a hoarse, tremulous voice: 'What's that he's saying? What's the unlucky callant saying about the 9th of August? Aih? To be sure it is St

Lawrence's Eve, although the 10th be his day. It's ower true, ower true, ower true for him an' a' his kin, poor man! Aih? What was he saying then?'

The men smiled at her incoherent earnestness, but the lady, with true feminine condescension, informed her, in a loud voice, that Allan had an engagement in Scotland on St Lawrence's Eve. She then started up, extended her shrivelled hands, that shook like the aspen, and panted out: 'Aih, aih? Lord preserve us! Whaten an engagement has he on St Lawrence's Eve? Bind him! bind him! Shackle him wi' bands of steel, and of brass, and of iron! Oh may He whose blessed will was pleased to leave him an orphan sae soon, preserve him from the fate which I tremble to think on!'

She then tottered round the table, as with supernatural energy, and seizing the laird's right hand, she drew it close to her unstable eyes, and then perceiving the emerald ring chased in blood, she threw up her arms with a jerk, opened her skinny jaws with a fearful gape, and uttering a shriek that made all the house yell, and everyone within it to tremble, she fell back lifeless and rigid on the floor. The gentlemen both fled, out of sheer terror; but a woman never deserts her friends in extremity. The lady called her maids about her and had her old nurse conveyed to bed, where every means were used to restore animation. But, alas, life was extinct! The vital spark had fled for ever, which filled all their hearts with grief, disappointment and horror, as some dreadful tale of mystery was now sealed up from their knowledge which, in all likelihood, no other could reveal. But to say the truth, the laird did not seem greatly disposed to probe it to the bottom.

Not all the arguments of Captain Bryan and his lady, nor the simple entreaties of Lady Luna, could induce Birkendelly to put off his engagement to meet his love on the Birky Brow on the evening of the 9th of August; but he promised soon to return, pretending that some business of the utmost importance called him away. Before he went, however, he asked his sister if ever she had heard of such a lady in Scotland as Jane Ogilvie. Mrs Bryan repeated the name many times to herself, and said that name undoubtedly was once familiar to her, although she thought not for good, but at that moment she did not recollect one single individual of the name. He then showed her the emerald ring that had been the death of Lucky Black, and the moment the lady looked at it, she made a grasp at it to take it off by force, which she very nearly effected. 'Oh, burn it! burn it!' cried she; 'it is not a right ring! Burn it!'

'My dear sister, what fault is in the ring?' said he. 'It is a very pretty ring, and one that I set great value by.'

'Oh, for heaven's sake, burn it, and renounce the giver!' cried she. 'If you have any regard for your peace here or your soul's welfare hereafter, burn that ring! If you saw with your own eyes, you would easily perceive that that is not a ring befitting a Christian to wear.'

This speech confounded Birkendelly a good deal. He retired by himself and examined the ring, and could see nothing in it unbecoming a Christian to wear. It was a chased gold ring, with a bright emerald, which last had a red foil, in some lights giving it a purple gleam, and inside was engraven *Elegit*, much defaced, but that his sister could not see; therefore he could not comprehend her vehement injunctions concerning it. But that it might no more give her offence, or any other, he sewed it within his vest, opposite his heart, judging that there was something in it which his eyes were withholden from discerning.

Thus he left Ireland with his mind in great confusion, groping his way, as it were, in a hole of mystery, yet with the passion that preyed on his heart and vitals more intense than ever. He seems to have had an impression all his life that some mysterious fate awaited him, which the correspondence of his dreams and day visions tended to confirm. And though he gave himself wholly up to the sway of one overpowering passion, it was not without some yearnings of soul, manifestations of terror and so much earthly shame that he never more mentioned his love, or his engagements, to any human being, not even to his friend McMurdie, whose company he forthwith shunned.

It is on this account that I am unable to relate what passed between the lovers thenceforward. It is certain they met at the Birky Brow that St Lawrence's Eve, for they were seen in company together; but of the engagements, vows or dalliance that passed between them I can say nothing; nor of all their future meetings, until the beginning of August 1781, when the laird began decidedly to make preparations for his approaching marriage; yet not as if he and his betrothed intended to reside at Birkendelly, all his provisions rather bespeaking a meditated journey.

On the morning of the 9th he wrote to his sister, and then arraying himself in his new wedding suit, and putting the emerald ring on his finger, he appeared all impatience until toward evening, when he sallied out on horseback to his appointment. It seems that his mysterious inamorata had met him, for he was seen riding through the big town before sunset, with a young lady behind him, dressed in white and green, and the villagers affirmed that they were riding at the rate of fifty miles an hour! They were seen to pass a cottage called Mosskilt, ten miles farther on, where there was no highway, at the same tremendous speed; and I could never hear that they were any more seen, until the following morning, when Birkendelly's fine bay horse was found lying dead at his own stable door; and shortly after his master was likewise discovered lying, a blackened corpse, on the Birky Brow at the very spot where the mysterious but lovely dame had always appeared to him. There was neither wound, bruise nor dislocation in his whole frame; but his skin was of a livid colour, and his features terribly distorted.

This woeful catastrophe struck the neighbourhood with great consternation, so that nothing else was talked of. Every ancient tradition and modern incident were raked together, compared and combined; and certainly a most rare concatenation of misfortunes was elicited. It was authenticated that his father had died on the same spot that day twenty years, and his grandfather that day forty years, the former, as was supposed, by a fall from his horse when in liquor, and the latter, nobody knew how; and now this Allan was the last of his race, for Mrs Bryan had no children.

It was, moreover, now remembered by many, and among the rest by the Revd Joseph Taylor, that he had frequently observed a young lady, in white and green, sauntering about the spot on a St Lawrence's Eve.

When Captain Bryan and his lady arrived to take possession of the premises, they instituted a strict enquiry into every circumstance; but nothing further than what was related to them by Mr McMurdie could be learned of this mysterious bride, besides what the laird's own letter bore. It ran thus:

DEAREST SISTER – I shall before this time tomorrow be the most happy, or most miserable, of mankind, having solemnly engaged myself this night to wed a young and beautiful lady, named Jane Ogilvie, to whom it seems I was betrothed before I was born. Our correspondence has been of a most private and mysterious nature; but my troth is pledged and my resolution fixed. We set out on a far journey to the place of her abode on the nuptial eve, so that it will be long before I see you again.
Yours till death,

ALLAN GEORGE SANDISON
Birkendelly, August 8, 1781

That very same year, an old woman, named Marion Haw, was returned upon that, her native parish, from Glasgow. She had led a migratory life with her son – who was what he called a bell-hanger, but in fact a tinker of the worst grade – for many years, and was at last returned to the muckle town in a state of great destitution. She gave the parishioners the history of the Mysterious Bride, so plausibly correct, but withal so romantic, that everybody said of it (as is often said of my narratives, with the same narrow-minded prejudice and injustice) that it was a *made story*. There were, however, some strong testimonies of its veracity.

She said the first Allan Sandison, who married the great heiress of Birkendelly, was previously engaged to a beautiful young lady named Jane Ogilvie, to whom he gave anything but fair play; and, as she believed, either murdered her, or caused her to be murdered, in the midst of a thicket of birch and broom, at a spot which she mentioned; and she had good reason for believing so, as she had seen the red blood and the new grave when she was a little girl, and ran home and mentioned it to her grandfather, who charged her as she valued her life never to mention that again, as it was only the nombles and hide of a deer which he himself had buried there. But when, twenty years subsequent to that, the wicked and unhappy Allan Sandison was found dead on that very spot, and lying across the green mound, then nearly level with the surface, which she had once seen a new grave, she then for the first time ever thought of a Divine Providence; and she added, 'For my grandfather, Neddy Haw, he dee'd too; there's naebody kens how, nor ever shall.'

As they were quite incapable of conceiving from Marion's description anything of the spot, Mr McMurdie caused her to be taken out to the Birky Brow in a cart, accompanied by Mr Taylor and some hundreds of the town's folks; but whenever she saw it, she said, 'Aha, birkies! the haill kintra's altered now. There was nae road here then; it gaed straight ower the tap o' the hill. An' let me see – there's the thorn where the cushats biggit; an' there's the auld birk that I ance fell aff an' left my shoe sticking i' the cleft. I can tell ye, birkies, either the deer's grave or bonny Jane Ogilvie's is no twa yards aff the place where that horse's hind-feet are standin'; sae ye may howk, an' see if there be ony remains.'

The minister and McMurdie and all the people stared at one another, for they had purposely caused the horse to stand still on the very spot where both the father and son had been found dead.

They digged, and deep, deep below the road they found part of the slender bones and skull of a young female, which they deposited decently in the churchyard. The family of the Sandisons is extinct, the Mysterious Bride appears no more on the Eve of St Lawrence, and the wicked people of the great muckle village have got a lesson on divine justice written to them in lines of blood.

Mary Burnet

JAMES HOGG

The following incidents are related as having occurred at a shepherd's house, not a hundred miles from St Mary's Loch; but, as the descendants of one of the families still reside in the vicinity, I deem it requisite to use names which cannot be recognised, save by those who have heard the story.

John Allanson, the farmer's son of Inverlawn, was a handsome, roving and incautious young man, enthusiastic, amorous and fond of adventure, and one who could hardly be said to fear the face of either man, woman or spirit. Among other love adventures, he fell a-courting Mary Burnet, of Kirkstyle, a most beautiful and innocent maiden, and one who had been bred up in rural simplicity. She loved him, but yet she was afraid of him; and though she had no objection to meeting with him among others, yet she carefully avoided meeting him alone, though often and earnestly urged to it. One day, the young man, finding an opportunity, at Our Lady's Chapel, after mass, urged his suit for a private meeting so ardently, and with so many vows of love and sacred esteem, that Mary was so far won as to promise that perhaps she would come and meet him.

The trysting place was a little green sequestered spot, on the very verge of the lake, well known to many an angler, and to none better than the writer of this old tale; and the hour appointed, the time when the King's Elwand (now foolishly termed the Belt of Orion) set his first golden knob above the hill. Allanson came too early; and he watched the sky with such eagerness and devotion that he thought every little star that arose in the south-east the top knob of the King's Elwand. At last the Elwand did arise in good earnest, and then the youth, with a heart palpitating with agitation, had nothing for it but to watch the heathery brow by which bonny Mary Burnet was to descend. No Mary Burnet made her appearance, even although the King's Elwand had now measured its own equivocal length five or six times up the lift.

Young Allanson now felt all the most poignant miseries of

disappointment; and, as the story goes, uttered in his heart an unhallowed wish – he wished that some witch or fairy would influence his Mary to come to him in spite of her maidenly scruples. This wish was thrice repeated with all the energy of disappointed love. It was thrice repeated, and no more, when, behold, Mary appeared on the brae, with wild and eccentric motions, speeding to the appointed place. Allanson's excitement seems to have been more than he was able to bear, as he instantly became delirious with joy, and always professed that he could remember nothing of their first meeting, save that Mary remained silent, and spoke not a word, either good or bad. In a short time she fell a-sobbing and weeping, refusing to be comforted, and then, uttering a piercing shriek, sprang up, and ran from him with amazing speed.

At this part of the loch, which, as I said, is well known to many, the shore is overhung by a precipitous cliff, of no great height, but still inaccessible, either from above or below. Save in a great drought, the water comes to within a yard of the bottom of this cliff, and the intermediate space is filled with rough unshapely pieces of rock fallen from above. Along this narrow and rude space, hardly passable by the angler at noon, did Mary bound with the swiftness of a kid, although surrounded with darkness. Her lover, pursuing with all his energy, called out, 'Mary! Mary! my dear Mary, stop and speak with me. I'll conduct you home, or anywhere you please, but do not run from me. Stop, my dearest Mary – stop!'

Mary would not stop; but ran on, till, coming to a little cliff that jutted into the lake, round which there was no passage, and perceiving that her lover would there overtake her, she uttered another shriek and plunged into the lake. The loud sound of her fall into the still water rang in the young man's ears like the knell of death and if before he was crazed with love, he was now as much so with despair. He saw her floating lightly away from the shore towards the deepest part of the loch but, in a short time, she began to sink, and gradually disappeared, without uttering a throb or a cry. A good while previous to this, Allanson had flung off his bonnet, shoes and coat, and plunged in. He swam to the place where Mary disappeared but there was neither boil nor gurgle on the water, nor even a bell of departing breath, to mark the place where his beloved had sunk. Being strangely impressed, at that trying moment, with a determination to live or die with her, he tried to dive, in hopes either to bring her up or to die in her arms; and he thought of their being so found on the shore of the lake, with a melancholy satisfaction; but by no effort of his could he reach the bottom, nor knew he what distance he was still from it. With an exhausted frame, and a despairing heart, he was obliged again to seek the shore, and, dripping wet as he was, and half-naked, he ran to her father's house with the woeful tidings. Everything there was quiet. The old shepherd's family, of whom Mary was the youngest, and sole daughter, were all sunk in silent repose; and oh, how the distracted lover wept at the thoughts of wakening them to hear the doleful tidings! But waken them he must; so, going to the little window close by the goodman's bed, he called, in a melancholy tone, 'Andrew! Andrew Burnet, are you waking?'

'Troth, man, I think I be; or, at least, I'm half-and-half. What hast thou to say to auld Andrew Burnet at this time o' night?'

'Are you waking, I say?'

'Gudewife, am I waking? Because if I be, tell that stravaiger sae. He'll maybe tak' your word for it, for mine he winna tak'.'

'Oh, Andrew, none of your humour tonight; I bring you tidings the most woeful, the most dismal, the most heart-rending, that ever were brought to an honest man's door.'

'To his window, you mean,' cried Andrew, bolting out of bed, and proceeding to the door. 'Gude sauff us, man, come in, whatever you be, and tell us your tidings face to face; and then we'll can better judge of the truth of them. If they be in concord wi' your voice, they are melancholy indeed. Have the reavers come, and are our kye driven?'

'Oh, alas! waur than that – a thousand times waur than that! Your daughter – your dear beloved and only daughter, Mary – '

'What of Mary?' cried the goodman. 'What of Mary?' cried her mother, shuddering and groaning with terror; and at the same time she kindled a light.

The sight of their neighbour, half-naked, and dripping with wet, and madness and despair in his looks, sent a chillness to their hearts that held them in silence, and they were unable to utter a word, till he went on thus, 'Mary is gone; your darling and mine is lost, and sleeps this night in a watery grave – and I have been her destroyer!'

'Thou art mad, John Allanson,' said the old man, vehemently, 'raving mad; at least I hope so. Wicked as thou art, thou hadst not the heart to kill my dear child. Oh yes, you are mad – God be thankful, you are mad. I see it in your looks and demeanour. Heaven be praised, you are mad You are mad; but you'll get better again. But what do I say?' continued he, as recollecting himself. 'We can soon convince our own senses. Wife, lead the way to our daughter's bed.'

With a heart throbbing with terror and dismay, old Jean Linton led the way to Mary's chamber, followed by the two men, who were eagerly gazing, one over each of her shoulders. Mary's little apartment was in the farther end of the long narrow cottage; and as soon as they entered it, they perceived a form lying on the bed, with the bedclothes drawn over its head; and on the lid of Mary's little chest, that stood at the bedside, her clothes were lying neatly folded, as they were wont to be. Hope seemed to dawn on the faces of the two old people when they beheld this, but the lover's heart sank still deeper in despair. The father called her name, but the form on the bed returned no answer; however, they all heard distinctly sobs, as of one weeping. The old man then ventured to pull down the clothes from her face; and, strange to say, there indeed lay Mary Burnet, drowned in tears, yet apparently nowise surprised at the ghastly appearance of the three naked figures. Allanson gasped for breath, for he remained still incredulous. He touched her clothes – he lifted her robes one by one – and all of them were dry, neat and clean, and had no appearance of having sunk in the lake.

There can be no doubt that Allanson was confounded by the strange event that had befallen him, and felt like one struggling with a frightful vision, or some energy beyond the power of man to comprehend. Nevertheless the assurance that Mary was there in life, weeping although she was, put him once more beside himself with joy; and he kneeled at her bedside, beseeching permission but to kiss her hand. She, however, repulsed him with disdain, saying with great emphasis, 'You are a bad man, John Allanson, and I entreat you to go out of my sight. The sufferings that I have undergone this night have been beyond the power of flesh and blood to endure; and by some cursed agency of yours have these sufferings been brought about. I therefore pray you, in his name, whose law you have transgressed, to depart out of my sight.'

Wholly overcome by conflicting passions, by circumstances so contrary to one another and so discordant with everything either in the works of nature or providence, the young man could do nothing but stand like a rigid statue, with his hands lifted up, and his visage like that of a corpse, until led away by the two old people from their daughter's apartment. Then they lighted up a fire to dry him, and began to question him with the most intense curiosity; but they could elicit nothing from him but the most disjointed exclamations – such as, 'Lord in heaven, what can be the meaning of this?' And at other times: 'It is all the enchantment of the devil; the evil spirits have got dominion over me!'

Finding they could make nothing or him, they began to form conjectures of their own. Jean affirmed that it had been the mermaid of the loch that had come to him in Mary's shape, to allure him to his destruction; but Andrew Burnet, setting his bonnet to one side, and raising his left hand to a level with it, so that he might have full scope to motion and flourish, suiting his action to his words, thus began, with a face of sapience never to be excelled: 'Gudewife, it doth strike me that thou art very wide of the mark. It must have been a spirit of a great deal higher quality than a mere-maiden who played this extraordinary prank. The mere-maiden is not a spirit, but a beastly sensitive creature, with a malicious spirit within it. Now, what influence could a cauld clatch of a creature like that, wi' a tail like a great saumont-fish, hae ower our bairn, either to make her happy or unhappy? Or where could it borrow her claes, Jean? Tell me that. Na, na, Jean Linton, depend on it, the spirit that courtit wi' poor sinfu' Jock there has been a fairy; but whether a good ane or an ill ane, it is hard to determine.'

Andrew's disquisition was interrupted by the young man falling into a fit of trembling that was fearful to look at, and threatened soon to terminate his existence. Jean ran for the family cordial, observing by the way, that 'though he was a wicked person, he was still a fellow-creature, and might live to repent'; and influenced by this spark of genuine humanity, she made him swallow two horn-spoonfuls of strong aqua vitae. Andrew then put a piece of scarlet thread round each wrist, and taking a strong rowan-tree staff in his hand, he conveyed his trembling and astonished guest home, giving him at parting this sage advice: 'I'll tell you what it is, Jock Allanson – ye hae run a near risk o' perdition, and, escaping that for the present, o' losing your right reason. But take an auld man's advice – never gang again out by night to beguile ony honest man's daughter, lest a worse thing befall thee.'

Next morning Mary dressed herself more neatly than usual, but there was manifestly a deep melancholy settled on her lovely face, and at times the unbidden tear would start into her eye. She spoke no word, either good or bad, that ever her mother could recollect, that whole morning, but she once or twice observed her daughter gazing at her, as with an intense and melancholy interest. About nine o'clock in the morning, Mary took a hay-rake over her shoulder, and went down to a meadow at the east end of the loch to coil a part of her father's hay, her father and brother engaging to join her about noon, when they came from the sheepfold. As soon as old Andrew came home, his wife and he, as was natural, instantly began to converse on the events of the preceding night; and in the course of their conversation Andrew said, 'Gudeness be about us, Jean, was not yon an awfu' speech o' our bairn's to young Jock Allanson last night?'

'Ay, it was a downsetter, gudeman, and spoken like a good Christian lass.'

'I'm no sae sure o' that, Jean Linton. My good woman, Jean Linton, I'm no sae sure o' that. Yon speech has gi'en me a great deal o' trouble o' heart; for d'ye ken, an' take my life – ay, an' take your life, Jean – nane o' us can tell whether it was in the Almighty's name or the devil's that she discharged her lover.'

'Oh fy, Andrew, how can ye say sae? How can ye doubt that it was in the Almighty's name?'

'Couldna she have said sae then, and that wad hae put it beyond a' doubt? And that wad hae been the natural way too; but instead of that she says, 'I pray you, in the name of him whose law you have transgressed, to depart out o' my sight.' I confess I'm terrified when I think about yon speech, Jean Linton. Didna she say too that 'her sufferings had been beyond what flesh and blood could have endured'? What was she but flesh and blood. Didna that remark infer that she was something mair than a mortal creature? Jean Linton, Jean Linton! what will you say if it should turn out that our daughter *is* drowned, and that yon was the fairy we had in the house a' the night and this morning?'

'Oh, haud your tongue, Andrew Burnet, and dinna make my heart cauld within me. We hae aye trusted in the Lord yet, and he has never forsaken us, nor will he yet gie the Wicked One power ower us or ours.'

'Ye say very well, Jean, and we maun e'en hope for the best,' quoth old Andrew; and away he went, accompanied by his son Alexander, to assist their beloved Mary on the meadow.

No sooner had Andrew set his head over the bents, and come in view of the meadow, than he said to his son, 'I wish Jock Allanson maunna hae been east the loch fishing for geds the day, for I think my Mary has made very little progress in the meadow.'

'She's ower muckle ta'en up about other things this while to mind her wark,' said Alexander; 'I wadna wonder, father, if that lassie gangs a black gate yet.'

Andrew uttered a long and a deep sigh, that seemed to ruffle the very fountains of life, and, without speaking another word, walked on to the hayfield. It was three hours since Mary had left home, and she ought at least to have put up a dozen coils of hay each hour. But, in place of that, she had put up only seven altogether, and the last was unfinished. Her own hay-rake, that had an M and a B neatly cut on the head of it, was leaning on the unfinished coil, and Mary was wanting. Her brother, thinking she had hid herself from them in sport, ran from one coil to another, calling her many bad names, playfully; but after he had turned them all up, and several deep swathes besides, she was not to be found. This young man, who slept in the byre, knew nothing of the events of the foregoing night, the old people and Allanson having mutually engaged to keep them a profound secret, and he had therefore less reason than his father to be seriously alarmed. When they began to work at the hay Andrew could work none; he looked this way and that way, but in no way could he see Mary approaching; so he put on his coat and went away home, to pour his sorrows into the bosom of his wife; and, in the meantime, he desired his son to run to all the neighbouring farming-houses and cots, every one, and make enquiries if anybody had seen Mary.

When Andrew went home and informed his wife that their darling was missing, the grief and astonishment of the aged couple knew no bounds. They sat down and wept together, and declared over and over that this act of providence was too strong for them, and too high to be understood. Jean besought her husband to kneel instantly, and pray urgently to God to restore their child to them; but he declined it, on account of the wrong frame of his mind, for he declared that his rage against John Allanson was so extreme as to unfit him for approaching the throne of his Maker. 'But if the profligate refuses to listen to the entreaties of an injured parent,' added he, 'he shall feel the weight of an injured father's arm.'

Andrew went straight away to Inverlawn, though without the least hope of finding young Allanson at home; but, on reaching the place, to his amazement, he found the young man lying ill of a burning fever, raving incessantly of witches, spirits and Mary Burnet. To such a height had his frenzy arrived, that when Andrew went there, it required three men to hold him in the bed. Both his parents testified their opinions openly, that their son was bewitched, or possessed of a demon, and the whole family was thrown into the greatest consternation. The good old shepherd, finding enough of grief there already, was obliged to confine his to his own bosom, and return disconsolate to his little family circle, in which there was a woeful blank that night.

His son returned also from a fruitless search. No one had seen any traces of his sister, but an old crazy woman, at a place called Oxcleuch, said that she had seen her go by in a grand chariot with young Jock Allanson, toward the Birkhill Path, and by that time they were at the Cross of Dumgree. The young man said he asked her what sort of a chariot it was, as there was never such a thing in that country as a chariot, nor yet a road for one. But she replied that he was widely mistaken, for that a great number of chariots sometimes passed that way, though never any of them returned. Those words appearing to be merely the ravings of superannuation, they were not regarded; but when no other traces of Mary could be found, old Andrew went up to consult this crazy dame once more, but he was not able to bring any such thing to her recollection. She spoke only in parables, which to him were incomprehensible.

Bonny Mary Burnet was lost. She left her father's house at nine o'clock on a Wednesday morning, 17th of September, neatly dressed in a white jerkin and green bonnet, with her hay-rake over her shoulder; and that was the last sight she was doomed ever to see of her native cottage. She seemed to have had some presentiment of this, as appeared from her demeanour that morning before she left it. Mary Burnet of Kirkstyle was lost, and great was the sensation produced over the whole country by the mysterious event. There was a long ballad extant at one period on the melancholy catastrophe, which was supposed to have been composed by the chaplain of St Mary's; but I have only heard tell of it, without ever hearing it sung or recited. Many of the verses concluded thus:

> But Bonny Mary Burnet
> We will never see again.

The story soon got abroad, with all its horrid circumstances (and there is little doubt that it was grievously exaggerated), and there was no obloquy that was not thrown on the survivor, who certainly in some degree deserved it, for, instead of growing better, he grew ten times more wicked than he was before. In one thing the whole country agreed, that it had been the real Mary Burnet who was drowned in the loch, and that the being which was found in her bed, lying weeping and complaining of suffering, and which vanished the next day, had been a fairy, an evil spirit or a changeling of some sort, for that it never spoke save once, and that in a mysterious manner;

nor did it partake of any food with the rest of the family. Her father and mother knew not what to say or what to think, but they wandered through this weary world like people wandering in a dream. Everything that belonged to Mary Burnet was kept by her parents as the most sacred relics, and many a tear did her aged mother shed over them. Every article of her dress brought the once comely wearer to mind. Andrew often said, 'That to have lost the darling child of their old age in any way would have been a great trial, but to lose her in the way that they had done, was really mair than human frailty could endure.'

Many a weary day did he walk by the shores of the loch, looking eagerly for some vestige of her garments, and though he trembled at every appearance, yet did he continue to search on. He had a number of small bones collected, that had belonged to lambs and other minor animals, and, haply, some of them to fishes, from a fond supposition that they might once have formed joints of her toes or fingers. These he kept concealed in a little bag, in order, as he said, 'to let the doctors see them'. But no relic, besides these, could he ever discover of Mary's body.

Young Allanson recovered from his raging fever scarcely in the manner of other men, for he recovered all at once, after a few days' raving and madness. Mary Burnet, it appeared, was by him no more remembered. He grew ten times more wicked than before, and hesitated at no means of accomplishing his unhallowed purposes. The devout shepherds and cottagers around detested him; and, both in their families and in the wild, when there was no ear to hear but that of heaven, they prayed protection from his devices, as if he had been the Wicked One; and they all prophesied that he would make a bad end.

One fine day about the middle of October, when the days begin to get very short, and the nights long and dark, on a Friday morning, the next year but one after Mary Burnet was lost, a memorable day in the fairy annals, John Allanson, younger of Inverlawn, went to a great hiring fair at a village called Moffat, in Annandale, in order to hire a housemaid. His character was so notorious that not one young woman in the district would serve in his father's house; so away he went to the fair at Moffat, to hire the prettiest and loveliest girl he could there find, with the intention of ruining her as soon as she came home. This is no suppositious accusation, for he acknowledged his plan to Mr David Welch of Cariferan, who rode down to the market with him, and seemed to boast of it and dwell on it with delight. But the maidens of Annandale had a guardian angel in the fair that day, of which neither he nor they were aware.

Allanson looked through the hiring-market, and through the hiring-market, and at length fixed on one young woman, which indeed was not difficult to do, for there was no such form there for elegance and beauty. Mr Welch stood still and eyed him. He took the beauty aside. She was clothed in green, and as lovely as a new-blown rose.

'Are you to hire, pretty maiden?'

'Yes, sir.'

'Will you hire with me?'

'I care not though I do. But if I hire with you, it must be for a long term.'

'Certainly. The longer the better. What are your wages to be?'

'You know, if I hire, I must be paid in kind. I must have the first living creature that I see about Inverlawn to myself.'

'I wish it may be me, then. But what do you know about Inverlawn?'

'I think I *should* know about it.'

'Bless me! I know the face as well as I know my own, and better. But the name has somehow escaped me. Pray, may I ask your name?'

'Hush! hush!' said she solemnly, and holding up her hand at the same time. 'Hush, hush, you had better say nothing about that here.'

'I am in utter amazement!' he exclaimed. 'What is the meaning of this? I conjure you to tell me your name!'

'It is Mary Burnet,' said she, in a soft whisper; and at the same time she let down a green veil over her face.

If Allanson's death-warrant had been announced to him at that moment, it could not have deprived him so completely of sense and motion. His visage changed into that of a corpse, his jaws fell down, and his eyes became glazed, so as apparently to throw no reflections inwardly. Mr Welch, who had kept his eye steadily on them all the while, perceived his comrade's dilemma, and went up to him. 'Allanson? Mr Allanson? What is the matter with you, man?' said he. 'Why, the girl has bewitched you, and turned you into a statue!'

Allanson made some sound in his throat, as if attempting to speak, but his tongue refused its office, and he only jabbered. Mr Welch, conceiving that he was seized with some fit, or about to faint, supported him into the Johnston Arms; but he either could not, or would not grant him any explanation. Welch being, however, resolved to see the maiden in green once more, persuaded Allanson, after causing him to drink a good deal, to go out into the hiring-market again, in search of her. They ranged the market through and through, but the maiden in green was gone, and not to be found. She had vanished in the crowd the moment she divulged her name, and even though Welch had his eye fixed on her, he could not discover which way she went. Allanson appeared to be in a kind of stupor as well as terror, but when he found that she had left the market, he began to recover himself, and to look out again for the top of the market.

He soon found one more beautiful than the last. She was like a sylph, clothed in robes of pure snowy white, with green ribands. Again he pointed this new flower out to Mr David Welch, who declared that such a perfect model of beauty he had never in his life seen. Allanson, being resolved to have this one at any wages, took her aside, and put the usual question: 'Do you wish to hire, pretty maiden?'

'Yes, sir.'

'Will you hire with me?'

'I care not though I do.'

'What, then, are your wages to be? Come – say? And be reasonable; I am determined not to part with you for a trifle.'

'My wages must be in kind; I work on no other conditions. Pray, how are all the good people about Inverlawn?'

Allanson's breath began to cut, and a chillness to creep through his whole frame, and he answered, with a faltering tongue: 'I thank you – much in their ordinary way.'

'And your aged neighbours,' rejoined she, 'are they still alive and well?'

'I – I – I think they are,' said he, panting for breath. 'But I am at a loss to know whom I am indebted to for these kind recollections.'

'What,' said she, 'have you so soon forgot Mary Burnet of Kirkstyle?'

Allanson started as if a bullet had gone through his heart. The lovely sylphlike form glided into the crowd, and left the astounded libertine once more standing like a rigid statue, until aroused by his friend, Mr Welch. He tried a third fair one, and got the same answers, and the same name given. Indeed, the first time ever I heard the tale, it bore that he tried *seven*, who all turned out to be Mary Burnets of Kirkstyle; but I think it unlikely that he would try so many, as he must long ere that time have been sensible that he laboured under some power of enchantment. However, when nothing else would do, he helped himself to a good proportion of strong drink. While he was thus engaged, a phenomenon of beauty and grandeur came into the fair that caught the sole attention of all present. This was a lovely dame, riding in a gilded chariot, with two liverymen before, and two behind, clothed in green and gold; and never sure was there so splendid a meteor seen in a Moffat fair. The word instantly circulated in the market that this was the Lady Elizabeth Douglas, eldest daughter to the Earl of Morton, who then sojourned at Auchincastle, in the vicinity of Moffat, and which lady at that time was celebrated as a great beauty all over Scotland. She was afterwards Lady Keith; and the mention of this name in the tale, as it were by mere accident, fixes the era of it in the reign of James IV, at the very time that fairies, brownies and witches were at the rifest in Scotland.

Everyone in the market believed the lady to be the daughter of the Earl of Morton; and when she came to the Johnston Arms, a gentleman in green came out bareheaded, and received her out of the carriage. All the crowd gazed at such unparalleled beauty and grandeur, but none was half so much overcome as Allanson. He had never conceived aught half so lovely either in earth, or heaven, or fairyland; and while he stood in a burning fever of admiration, think of his astonishment, and the astonishment of the countless crowd that looked on, when this brilliant and matchless beauty beckoned him towards her! He could not believe his senses, but looked this way and that way to see how others regarded the affair; but she beckoned him a second time, with such a winning courtesy and smile, that immediately he pulled off his beaver cap and hasted up to her; and without more ado she gave him her arm, and the two walked into the hostel.

Allanson conceived that he was thus distinguished by Lady Elizabeth Douglas, the flower of the land, and so did all the people of the market; and greatly they wondered who the young farmer could be that was thus particularly favoured; for it ought to have been mentioned that he had not one personal acquaintance in the fair save Mr David Welch of Cariferan. The first thing the lady did was to enquire kindly after his health. Allanson thanked her ladyship with all the courtesy he was master of; and being by this time persuaded that she was in love with him, he became as light as if treading on the air. She next enquired after his father and mother. Oho! thought he to himself, poor creature, she is terribly in for it! but her love *shall not* be thrown away upon a backward or ungrateful object. He answered her with great politeness, and at length began to talk of her noble father and young Lord William, but she cut him short by asking if he did not recognise her.

'Oh, yes! He knew who her ladyship was, and remembered that he had seen her comely face often before, although he could not, at that particular moment, recall to his memory the precise times or places of their meeting.'

She next asked for his old neighbours of Kirkstyle, and if they were still in life and health. Allanson felt as if his heart were a piece of ice. A chillness spread over his whole frame; he sank back on a seat, and remained motionless; but the beautiful and adorable creature soothed him with kind words, till he again gathered courage to speak.

'What!' said he; 'and has it been your own lovely self who has been playing tricks on me this whole day?'

'A first love is not easily extinguished, Mr Allanson,' said she. 'You may guess from my appearance, that I have been fortunate in life; but, for all that, my first love for you has continued the same, unaltered and unchanged, and you must forgive the little freedoms I used today to try your affections, and the effects my appearance would have on you.'

'It argues something for my good taste, however, that I never pitched on any face for beauty today but your own,' said he. 'But now that we have met once more, we shall not so easily part again. I will devote the rest of my life to you, only let me know the place of your abode.'

'It is hard by,' said she, 'only a very little space from this; and happy, happy, would I be to see you there tonight, were it proper or convenient. But my lord is at present from home and in a distant country.'

'I should not conceive that any particular hindrance to my visit,' said he.

With great apparent reluctance she at length consented to admit of his visit, and offered to leave one of her gentlemen, whom she could trust, to be his conductor; but this he positively refused. It was his desire, he said, that no eye of man should see him enter or leave her happy dwelling. She said he was a self-willed man, but should have his own way; and after giving him such directions as would infallibly lead him to her mansion, she mounted her chariot and was driven away.

Allanson was uplifted above every sublunary concern. Seeking out his friend, David Welch, he imparted to him his extraordinary good fortune, but he did not tell him that she was not the Lady Elizabeth Douglas. Welch insisted on accompanying him on the way, and refused to turn back till he came to the very point of the road next to the lady's splendid mansion; and in spite of all that Allanson could say, Welch remained there till he saw his comrade enter the court gate, which glowed with lights as innumerable as the stars of the firmament.

Allanson had promised his father and mother to be home on the morning after the fair to breakfast. He came not either that day or the next; and the third day the old man mounted his white pony, and rode away towards Moffat in search of his son. He called at Cariferan on his way, and made enquiries of Mr Welch. The latter manifested some astonishment that the young man had not returned; nevertheless he assured his father of his safety, and desired him to return home; and then with reluctance confessed that the young man was engaged in an amour with the Earl of Morton's beautiful daughter; that he had gone to the castle by appointment, and that he, David Welch, had accompanied him to the gate, and seen him enter, and it was apparent that his reception had been a kind one, since he had tarried so long.

Mr Welch, seeing the old man greatly distressed, was persuaded to accompany him on his journey, as the last who had seen his son and seen him enter the castle. On reaching Moffat they found his steed standing at the hostel, whither it had returned on the night of the fair, before the company broke up; but the owner had not been heard of since seen in company with Lady Elizabeth Douglas. The old man set out for Auchincastle, taking Mr David Welch along with him; but long ere they reached the place, Mr Welch assured him he would not find his son there, as it was nearly in a different direction that they rode on the evening of the fair. However, to the castle they went, and were admitted to the earl, who, after hearing the old man's tale, seemed to consider him in a state of derangement. He sent for his daughter Elizabeth, and questioned her concerning her meeting with the son of the old respectable countryman – of her appointment with him on the night of the preceding Friday, and concluded by saying he hoped she had him still in safe concealment about the castle.

The lady, hearing her father talk in this manner, and seeing the serious and dejected looks of the old man, knew not what to say, and asked an explanation. But Mr Welch put a stop to it by declaring to old Allanson that the Lady Elizabeth was not the lady with whom his son made the appointment, for he had seen her, and would engage to know her again among ten thousand; nor was that the castle towards which he had accompanied his son, nor anything like it. 'But go with me,' continued he, 'and, though I am a stranger in this district, I think I can take you to the very place.'

They set out again; and Mr Welch traced the road from Moffat, by which young Allanson and he had gone, until, after travelling several miles, they came to a place where a road struck off to the right at an angle. 'Now I know we are right,' said Welch; 'for here we stopped, and your son entreated me to return, which I refused, and accompanied him to yon large tree, and a little way beyond it, from whence I saw him received in at the splendid gate. We shall be in sight of the mansion in three minutes.'

They passed on to the tree, and a space beyond it; but then Mr Welch lost the use of his speech, as he perceived that there was neither palace nor gate there, but a tremendous gulf, fifty fathoms deep, and a dark stream foaming and boiling below.

'How is this?' said old Allanson. 'There is neither mansion nor habitation of man here!' Welch's tongue for a long time refused its office, and he stood like a statue, gazing on the altered and awful scene. 'He only, who made the spirits of men,' said he, at last, 'and all the spirits that sojourn in the earth and air, can tell how this is. We are wandering in a world of enchantment, and have been influenced by some agencies above human nature, or without its pale; for here of a certainty did I take leave of your son – and there, in that direction, and apparently either on the verge of that gulf, or the space above it, did I see him received in at the court gate of a mansion, splendid beyond all conception. How can human comprehension make anything of this?'

They went forward to the verge, Mr Welch leading the way to the very spot on which he saw the gate opened, and there they found marks where a horse had been plunging. Its feet had been over the brink, but it seemed to have recovered itself, and deep, deep down, and far within, lay the mangled corpse of John Allanson; and in this manner, mysterious beyond all example, terminated the career of that wicked and flagitious young man. What a beautiful moral may be extracted from this fairy tale!

But among all these turnings and windings, there is no account given, you will say, of the fate of Mary Burnet; for this last appearance of hers at Moffat seems to have been altogether a phantom or illusion. Gentle and kind reader, I can give you no account of the fate of that maiden; for though the ancient fairy tale proceeds, it seems to me to involve her fate in ten times more mystery than what we have hitherto seen of it.

The yearly return of the day on which Mary was lost was observed as a day of mourning by her aged and disconsolate parents – a day of sorrow, of fasting and humiliation. Seven years came and passed away, and the seventh returning day of fasting and prayer was at hand. On the evening previous to it, old Andrew was moving along the sands of the loch, still looking for some relic of his beloved Mary, when he was aware of a little shrivelled old man, who came posting towards him. The creature was not above five spans in height, and had a face scarcely like that of a human creature; but he was, nevertheless, civil in his deportment and sensible in speech. He bade Andrew a good-evening, and asked him what he was looking for. Andrew answered that he was looking for that which he should never find.

'Pray, what is your name, ancient shepherd?' said the stranger; 'for methinks I should know something of you, and perhaps have a commission to you.'

'Alas! why should you ask after my name?' said Andrew. 'My name is now nothing to anyone.'

'Had not you once a beautiful daughter, named Mary?' said the stranger.

'It is a heart-rending question, man,' said Andrew; 'but certes, I had once a beloved daughter named Mary.'

'What became or her?' asked the stranger.

Andrew shook his head, turned round, and began to move away; it was a theme that his heart could not brook. He sauntered along the loch sands, his dim eye scanning every white pebble as he passed along. There was a hopelessness in his stooping form, his gait, his eye, his feature – in every step that he took there was a hopeless apathy. The dwarf followed him, and began to expostulate with him. 'Old man, I see you are pining under some real or fancied affliction,' said he. 'But in continuing to do so, you are neither acting according to the dictates of reason nor true religion. What is man that he should fret, or the son of man that he should repine, under the chastening hand of his Maker?'

'I am far frae justifying myself,' returned Andrew, surveying his shrivelled monitor with some degree of astonishment. 'But there are some feelings that neither reason nor religion can o'er-master; and there are some that a parent may cherish without sin.'

'I deny the position,' said the stranger, 'taken either absolutely or relatively. All repining under the Supreme decree is leavened with unrighteousness. But, subtleties aside, I ask you, as I did before, What became of your daughter?'

'Ask the Father of her spirit, and the framer of her body,' said Andrew solemnly; 'ask Him into whose hands I committed her from childhood. He alone knows what became of her, but I do not.'

'How long is it since you lost her?'

'It is seven years tomorrow!'

'Ay! you remember the time well. And you have mourned for her all that while?'

'Yes; and I will go down to the grave mourning for my only daughter, the child of my old age, and of all my affection. Oh, thou unearthly-looking monitor, knowest thou aught of my darling child? for if thou dost, thou wilt know that she was not like other women. There was a simplicity and a purity about my Mary that was hardly consistent with our frail nature.'

'Wouldst thou like to see her again?' said the dwarf.

Andrew turned round, his whole frame shaking as with a palsy, and gazed on the audacious imp. 'See her again, creature!' cried he vehemently. 'Would I like to see her again, sayest thou?'

'I said so,' said the dwarf, 'and I say further, Dost thou know this token? Look, and see if thou dost!'

Andrew took the token, and looked at it, then at the shrivelled stranger, and then at the token again; and at length he burst into tears, and wept aloud; but they were tears of joy, and his weeping seemed to have some breathings of laughter intermingled in it. And still as he kissed the token, he called out in broken and convulsive sentences, 'Yes, auld body, I *do* know it! – I *do* know it – I *do* know it! It is indeed the same golden Edward, with three holes in it, with which I presented my Mary on her birthday, in her eighteenth year, to buy a new suit for the holidays. But when she took it she said – ay, I mind weel what my bonny woman said – "It is sae bonny and sae kenspeckle," said she, "that I think I'll keep it for the sake of the giver." Oh dear, dear! Blessed little creature, tell me how she is, and where she is? Is she living, or is she dead?'

'She is living, and in good health,' said the dwarf; 'and better, and braver, and happier, and lovelier than ever; and if you make haste, you will see her and her family at Moffat tomorrow afternoon. They are to pass there on a journey, but it is an express one, and I am sent to you with that token, to inform you of the circumstance, that you may have it in your power to see and embrace your beloved daughter once before you die.'

'And am I to meet my Mary at Moffat? Come away, little, dear, welcome body, thou blessed of heaven, come away, and taste of an auld shepherd's best cheer, and I'll gang foot for foot with you to Moffat, and my auld wife shall gang foot for foot with us too. I tell you, little, blessed and welcome crile, come along with me.'

'I may not tarry to enter your house, or taste of your cheer, good shepherd,' said the being. 'May plenty still be within your walls, and a thankful heart to enjoy it! But my directions are neither to taste meat nor drink in this country, but to haste back to her that sent me. Go – haste, and make ready, for you have no time to lose.'

'At what time will she be there?' cried Andrew, flinging the plaid from him to run home with the tidings.

'Precisely when the shadow of the Holy Cross fails due east,' cried the dwarf; and turning round, he hasted on his way.

When old Jean Linton saw her husband coming hobbling and running home without his plaid, and having his doublet flying wide open, she had no doubt that he had lost his wits; and, full of anxiety, she met him at the side of the kail-yard. 'Gudeness preserve us a' in our right senses, Andrew Burnet, what's the matter wi' you?'

'Stand out o' my gate, wife, for, d'ye see, I am rather in a haste, Jean Linton.'

'I see that indeed, gudeman; but stand still, and tell me what has putten you in sic a haste. Ir ye dementit?'

'Na, na, gudewife, Jean Linton, I'm no dementit – I'm only gaun away till Moffat.'

'O gudeness, pity the poor auld body! How can ye gang to Moffat, man? Or what have ye to do at Moffat? Dinna ye mind that the morn is the day o' our solemnity?'

'Haud out o' my gate, auld wife, and dinna speak o' solemnities to me. I'll keep it at Moffat the morn. Ay, gudewife, and ye shall keep it at Moffat, too. What d'ye think o' that, woman? Too-whoo! ye dinna ken the mettle that's in an auld body till it be tried.'

'Andrew – Andrew Burnet!'

'Get awa' wi' your frightened looks, woman; and haste ye, gang and fling me out my Sabbath-day claes. And, Jean Linton, my woman, d'ye hear, gang and pit on your bridal gown, and your silk hood, for ye maun be at Moffat the morn too; and it is mair nor time we were awa'. Dinna look sae surprised, woman, till I tell ye that our ain Mary is to meet us at Moffat the morn.'

'Oh, Andrew! dinna sport wi' the feelings of an auld forsaken heart.'

'Gude forbid, my auld wife, that I should ever sport wi' feelings o' yours,' cried Andrew, bursting into tears; ' they are a' as sacred to me as breathings frae the Throne o' Grace. But it is true that I tell ye; our dear bairn is to meet us at Moffat the morn, wi' a son in every hand; and we maun e'en gang and see her aince again, and kiss her and bless her afore we dee.'

The tears now rushed from the old woman's eyes like fountains, and dropped from her sorrow-worn cheeks to the earth; and then, as with a spontaneous movement, she threw her skirt over her head, kneeled down at her husband's feet and poured out her soul in thanksgiving to her Maker. She then rose up, quite deprived of her senses through joy, and ran crouching away on the road, towards Moffat, as if hasting beyond her power to be at it. But Andrew brought her back; and they prepared themselves for their journey.

Kirkstyle being twenty miles from Moffat, they set out on the afternoon of Tuesday, the 16th of September; slept that night at a place called Turnbery Shiel, and were in Moffat next day by noon. Wearisome was the remainder of the day to that aged couple; they wandered about conjecturing by what road their daughter would come, and how she would come attended. 'I have made up my mind on baith these matters,' said Andrew; 'at first I thought it was likely that she would come out of the east, because a' our blessings come frae that airt; but finding now that would be o'er near to the very road we hae come oursells, I now take it for granted she'll come frae the south; and I just think I see her leading a bonny boy in every hand, and a servant lass carrying a bit bundle ahint her.'

The two now walked out on all the southern roads, in hopes to meet their Mary, but always returned to watch the shadow of the Holy Cross; and, by the time it fell due east, they could do nothing but stand in the middle of the street, and look round them in all directions. At length, about half a mile out on the Dumfries road, they perceived a poor beggar woman approaching with two children following close to her, and another beggar a good way behind. Their eyes were instantly riveted on these objects; for Andrew thought he perceived his friend the dwarf in the one that was behind; and now all other earthly objects were to them nothing, save these approaching beggars. At that moment a gilded chariot entered the village from the south, and drove by them at full speed, having two liverymen before, and two behind, clothed in green and gold. 'Ach-wow! the vanity of worldly grandeur!' ejaculated Andrew, as the splendid vehicle went thundering by; but neither he nor his wife deigned to look at it further, their whole attention being fixed on the group of beggars.

'Ay, it is just my woman,' said Andrew, 'it is just herself: I ken her gang yet, sair pressed down wi' poortith although she be. But I dinna care how poor she be, for baith her and hers sall be welcome to my fireside as lang as I hae ane.'

While their eyes were thus strained, and their hearts melting with tenderness and pity, Andrew felt something embracing his knees, and, on looking down, there was his Mary, blooming in splendour and beauty, kneeling at his feet. Andrew uttered a loud hysterical scream of joy, and clasped her to his bosom; and old Jean Linton stood trembling, with her arms spread, but durst not close them on so splendid a creature till her daughter first enfolded her in a fond embrace, and then she hung upon her and wept. It was a wonderful event – a restoration without a parallel. They indeed beheld their Mary, their long-lost darling; they held her in their embraces, believed in her identity, and were satisfied. Satisfied, did I say? They were happy beyond the lot of mortals. She had just alighted from her chariot; and, perceiving her aged parents standing together, she ran and kneeled at their feet They now retired into the hostel, where Mary presented her two sons to her father and mother. They spent the evening in every social endearment; and Mary loaded the good old couple with rich presents, watched over them till midnight, when they both fell into a deep and happy sleep, and then she remounted her chariot, and was driven away. If she was any more seen in Scotland, I never heard of it; but her parents rejoiced in the thoughts of her happiness till the day of their death.

Ticonderoga

ANDREW LANG

The ghost in the following famous tale had a purpose. He was a
Highland ghost, a Campbell, and desired vengeance on a Macniven,
who murdered him. The ghost, practically, 'cried Cruachan', and
tried to rouse the clan. Failing in this, owing to Inverawe's loyalty to
his oath, the ghost uttered a prophecy.

The tale is given in the words of Miss Elspeth Campbell, who
collected it at Inverawe from a Highland narrator. [Robert Louis
Stevenson's version of the legend appears on pages 502–10.]

Ticonderoga

It was one evening in the summer of the year 1755 that Campbell of
Inverawe was on Cruachan hillside. He was startled by seeing a man
coming towards him at full speed; a man ragged, bleeding, and
evidently suffering agonies of terror. 'The avengers of blood are on
my track, Oh, save me!' the poor wretch managed to gasp out.

Inverawe, filled with pity for the miserable man, swore 'by the word
of an Inverawe which never failed friend or foe yet' to save him.
Inverawe then led the stranger to the secret cave on Cruachan hillside.

None knew of this cave but the laird of Inverawe himself, as the
secret was most carefully kept and had been handed down from
father to son for many generations. The entrance was small, and no
one passing would for an instant suspect it to be other than a tod's
hole, but within were fair-sized rooms, one containing a well of the
purest spring water. It is said that Wallace and Bruce had made use of
this cave in earlier days.

Here Inverawe left his guest. The man was so overcome by terror
that he clung on to Inverawe's plaid, imploring him not to leave him
alone. Inverawe was filled with disgust at this cowardly conduct, and
already almost repented having plighted his word to save such a
worthless creature.

On Inverawe's return home he found a man in a state of great excitement waiting to see him. This man informed him of the murder of his (Inverawe's) foster-brother by one Macniven. 'We have,' said he, 'tracked the murderer to within a short distance of this place, and I am here to warn you in case he should seek your protection.' Inverawe turned pale and remained silent, not knowing what answer to give. The man, knowing the love that subsisted between the foster-brothers, thought this silence arose from grief alone, and left the house to pursue the search for Macniven further.

The compassion Inverawe felt for the trembling man he had left in the cave turned to hate when he thought of his beloved foster-brother murdered; but as he had plighted his word to save him, save him he must and would. As soon, therefore, as night fell he went to the cave with food, and promised to return with more the next day.

Thoroughly worn out, as soon as he reached home he retired to rest, but sleep he could not. So taking up a book he began to read. A shadow fell across the page. He looked up and saw his foster-brother standing by the bedside. But, oh, how changed! His fair hair clotted with blood; his face pale and drawn, and his garments all gory. He uttered the following words: 'Inverawe, shield not the murderer; blood must flow for blood,' and then faded away out of sight.

In spite of the spirit's commands, Inverawe remained true to his promise, and returned next day to Macniven with fresh provisions. That night his foster-brother again appeared to him uttering the same warning: 'Inverawe, Inverawe, shield not the murderer; blood must flow for blood.' At daybreak Inverawe hurried off to the cave, and said to Macniven: 'I can shield you no longer; you must escape as best you can.' Inverawe now hoped to receive no further visit from the vengeful spirit. In this he was disappointed, for at the usual hour the ghost appeared, and in anger said, 'I have warned you once, I have warned you twice; it is too late now. We shall meet again at Ticonderoga.'

Inverawe rose before dawn and went straight to the cave. Macniven was gone!

Inverawe saw no more of the ghost, but the adventure left him a gloomy, melancholy man. Many a time he would wander on Cruachan hillside, brooding over his vision, and people passing him would see the faraway look in his eyes, and would say one to the other: 'The puir laird, he is aye thinking on him that is gone.' Only his dearest friends knew the cause of his melancholy.

In 1756 the war between the English and French in America broke out. The 42nd regiment embarked, and landed at New York in June of that year. Campbell of Inverawe was a major in the regiment. The lieutenant-colonel was Francis Grant. From New York the 42nd proceeded to Albany, where the regiment remained inactive till the spring of 1757. One evening when the 42nd were still quartered at this place, Inverawe asked the colonel 'if he had ever heard of a place called Ticonderoga'. Colonel Grant replied he had never heard the name before. Inverawe then told his story. Most of the officers were present at the time; some were impressed, others were inclined to look upon the whole thing as a joke, but seeing how very much disturbed Inverawe was about it all, even the most unbelieving refrained from bantering him.

In 1758 an expedition was to be directed against Ticonderoga, on Lake George, a fort erected by the French. The Highlanders were to form part of this expedition. The force was under Major-General Abercromby.

Ticonderoga was called by the French St Louis [really 'Fort Carillon'], and Inverawe knew it by no other name. One of the officers told Colonel Grant that the Indian name of the place was Ticonderoga. Grant, remembering Campbell's story, said: 'For God's sake don't let Campbell know this, or harm will come of it.'

The troops embarked on Lake George and landed without opposition near the extremity of the lake early in July. They marched from there, through woods, upon Ticonderoga, having had one successful skirmish with the enemy, driving them back with considerable loss. Lord Howe was killed in this engagement.

On the 10th of July the assault was directed to be commenced by the picquets. The Grenadiers were to follow, supported by the battalions and reserves. The Highlanders and 55th regiment formed the reserve.

In vain the troops attempted to force their way through the abatis, they themselves being exposed to heavy artillery and musket fire from an enemy well under cover. The Highlanders could no longer be restrained, and rushed forward from the reserve, cutting and carving their way through trees and other obstacles with their claymores. The deadly fire still continued from the fort. As no ladders had been provided for scaling the breastwork, the soldiers climbed on to one another's shoulders, and made holes for their feet in the face of the work with their swords and bayonets, but as soon as a man reached the top he was thrown down. Captain John Campbell and a few men succeeded at last in forcing their way over the breastworks, but were immediately cut down.

After a long and desperate struggle, lasting in fact nearly four hours, General Abercromby gave orders for a retreat. The troops could hardly be prevailed upon to retire, and it was not till the order had been given for the third time that the Highlanders withdrew from the hopeless encounter. The loss sustained by the regiment was as follows: eight officers, nine sergeants and 297 men killed; seventeen officers, ten sergeants and 306 men wounded.

Inverawe, after having fought with the greatest courage, received at length his death wound. Colonel Grant hastened to the dying man's side, who looked reproachfully at him, and said: 'You deceived me; this is Ticonderoga, for I have seen him.' Inverawe never spoke again. Inverawe's son, an officer in the same regiment, also lost his life at Ticonderoga.

On the very day that these events were happening in faraway America, two ladies, Miss Campbell of Ederein and her sister, were walking from Kilmalieu to Inveraray, and had reached the then new bridge over the Aray. One of them happened to look up at the sky. She gave a call to her sister to look also. They both of them saw in the sky what looked like a siege going on. They saw the different regiments with their colours, and recognised many of their friends among the Highlanders. They saw Inverawe and his son fall, and other men whom they knew. When they reached Inveraray they told all their friends of the vision they had just seen. They also took down the names of those they had seen fall, and the time and date of the occurrence. The well-known Danish physician, Sir William Hart, was, together with an Englishman and a servant, walking round the Castle of Inveraray. These men saw the same phenomena, and confirmed the statements made by the two ladies. Weeks after the gazette corroborated their statements in its account of the attempt made on Ticonderoga. Every detail was correct in the vision, down to the actual number of the killed and wounded.

But there was sorrow throughout Argyll long before the gazette appeared.

The Old Nurse's Story

George MacDonald

I set out one evening for the cottage of my old nurse, to bid her goodbye for many months, probably years. I was to leave the next day for Edinburgh, on my way to London, whence I had to repair by coach to my new abode – almost to me like the land beyond the grave, so little did I know about it, and so wide was the separation between it and my home. The evening was sultry when I began my walk, and before I arrived at its end, the clouds rising from all quarters of the horizon, and especially gathering around the peaks of the mountain, betokened the near approach of a thunderstorm. This was a great delight to me. Gladly would I take leave of my home with the memory of a last night of tumultuous magnificence; followed, probably, by a day of weeping rain, well suited to the mood of my own heart in bidding farewell to the best of parents and the dearest of homes. Besides, in common with most Scotchmen who are young and hardy enough to be unable to realise the existence of coughs and rheumatic fevers, it was a positive pleasure to me to be out in rain, hail or snow.

'I am come to bid you goodbye, Margaret, and to hear the story which you promised to tell me before I left home: I go tomorrow.'

'Do you go so soon, my darling? Well, it will be an awful night to tell it in; but, as I promised, I suppose I must.'

At the moment, two or three great drops of rain, the first of the storm, fell down the wide chimney, exploding in the clear turf-fire.

'Yes, indeed you must,' I replied.

After a short pause, she commenced. Of course she spoke in Gaelic; and I translate from my recollection of the Gaelic; but rather from the impression left upon my mind, than from any recollection of words. She drew her chair near the fire, which we had reason to fear would soon be put out by the falling rain, and began.

'How old the story is, I do not know. It has come down through many generations. My grandmother told it to me as I tell it to you; and her mother and my mother sat beside, never interrupting, but nodding their heads at every turn. Almost it ought to begin like the fairy tales, *Once upon a time* – it took place so long ago; but it is too dreadful and too true to tell like a fairy tale.

'There were two brothers, sons of the chief of our clan, but as different in appearance and disposition as two men could be. The elder was fair-haired and strong, much given to hunting and fishing; fighting too, upon occasion, I dare say, when they made a foray upon the Saxon, to get back a mouthful of their own. But he was gentleness itself to everyone about him, and the very soul of honour in all his doings. The younger was very dark in complexion, and tall and slender compared to his brother. He was very fond of book-learning, which, they say, was an uncommon taste in those times. He did not care for any sports or bodily exercises but one; and that, too, was unusual in these parts. It was horsemanship. He was a fierce rider, and as much at home in the saddle as in his study-chair. You may think that, so long ago, there was not much fit room for riding hereabouts; but, fit or not fit, he rode. From his reading and riding, the neighbours looked doubtfully upon him, and whispered about the black art. He usually bestrode a great powerful black horse, without a white hair on him; and people said it was either the devil himself or a demon-horse from the devil's own stud. What favoured this notion was that in or out of the stable, the brute would let no other than his master go near him. Indeed, no one would venture, after he had killed two men, and grievously maimed a third, tearing him with his teeth and hoofs like a wild beast. But to his master he was obedient as a hound, and would even tremble in his presence sometimes.

'The youth's temper corresponded to his habits. He was both gloomy and passionate. Prone to anger, he had never been known to forgive. Debarred from anything on which he had set his heart, he would have gone mad with longing if he had not gone mad with rage. His soul was like the night around us now, dark and sultry, and silent, but lighted up by the red levin of wrath, and torn by the bellowings of thunder-passion. He must have his will; hell might have his soul. Imagine, then, the rage and malice in his heart, when he suddenly became aware that an orphan girl, distantly related to them, who had lived with them for nearly two years, and whom he had loved for almost all that period, was loved by his elder brother and loved him in return. He flung his right hand above his head and swore a terrible oath that if he might not, his brother should not, rushed out of the house and galloped off among the hills.

'The orphan was a beautiful girl, tall, pale and slender, with plentiful dark hair, which, when released from the snood, rippled down below her knees. Her appearance formed a strong contrast with that of her favoured lover, while there was some resemblance between her and the younger brother. This fact seemed, to his fierce selfishness, ground for a prior claim.

'It may appear strange that a man like him should not have had instant recourse to his superior and hidden knowledge, by means of which he might have got rid of his rival with far more of certainty and less of risk; but I presume that, for the moment, his passion overwhelmed his consciousness of skill. Yet I do not suppose that he foresaw the mode in which his hatred was about to operate. At the moment when he learned of their mutual attachment, probably through a domestic, the lady was on her way to meet her lover as he returned from the day's sport. The appointed place was on the edge of a deep, rocky ravine, down in whose dark bosom brawled and foamed a little mountain torrent. You know the place, Duncan, my dear, I dare say.'

(Here she gave me a minute description of the spot, with directions how to find it.)

'Whether anyone saw what I am about to relate, or whether it was put together afterwards, I cannot tell. The story is like an old tree – so old that it has lost the marks of its growth. But this is how my grandmother told it to me. An evil chance led him in the right direction. The lovers, startled by the sound of the approaching horse, parted in opposite directions along a narrow mountain-path on the edge of the ravine. Into this path he struck at a point near where the lovers had met, but to opposite sides of which they had now receded; so that he was between them on the path. Turning his horse up the course of the stream, he soon came in sight of his brother on the ledge before him. With a suppressed scream of rage, he rode headlong at him, and, ere he had time to make the least defence, hurled him over the precipice. The helplessness of the strong man was uttered in one single despairing cry as he shot into the abyss. Then all was still. The sound of his fall could not reach the edge of the gulf. Divining in a moment that the lady, whose name was Elsie, must have fled in the opposite direction, he reined his steed on his haunches. He could touch the precipice with his bridle-hand half outstretched; his sword-hand half outstretched would have dropped a stone to the bottom of the ravine. There was no room to wheel. One desperate practibility alone remained. Turning his horse's head towards the edge, he compelled him, by means of the powerful bit, to rear till he stood almost erect; and so, his body swaying over the gulf, with quivering and straining muscles, to turn on his hind legs. Having completed the half-circle, he let him drop, and urged him furiously in the opposite direction. It must have been by the devil's own care that he was able to continue his gallop along that ledge of rock.

'He soon caught sight of the maiden. She was leaning, half fainting, against the precipice. She had heard her lover's last cry, and, although it had conveyed no suggestion of his voice to her ear, she trembled from head to foot, and her limbs would bear her no farther. He checked his speed, rode gently up to her, lifted her unresisting, laid her across the shoulders of his horse, and, riding carefully till he reached a more open path, dashed again wildly along the mountain side. The lady's long hair was shaken loose, and dropped, trailing on the ground. The horse trampled upon it, and stumbled, half dragging her from the saddle-bow. He caught her, lifted her up, and looked at her face. She was dead. I suppose he went mad. He laid her again across the saddle before him, and rode on, reckless whither. Horse and man and maiden were found the next day, lying at the foot of a cliff, dashed to pieces. It was observed that a hind shoe of the horse was loose and broken. Whether this had been the cause of his fall, could not be told; but ever when he races, as race he will, till the day of doom, along that mountainside, his gallop is mingled with the clank of the loose and broken shoe. For, like the sin, the punishment is awful; he shall carry about for ages the phantom-body of the girl, knowing that her soul is away, sitting with the soul of his brother down in the deep ravine or scaling with him the topmost crags of the towering mountain peaks. There are some who, from time to time, see the doomed man careering along the face of the mountain, with the lady hanging across the steed; and they say it always betokens a storm, such as this which is now raving about us.'

I had not noticed till now, so absorbed had I been in her tale, that the storm had risen to a very ecstasy of fury.

'They say, likewise, that the lady's hair is still growing; for, every time they see her, it is longer than before; and that now such is its length and the headlong speed of the horse, that it floats and streams out behind, like one of those curved clouds, like a comet's tail, far up in the sky; only the cloud is white, and the hair dark as night. And they say it will go on growing until the Last Day, when the horse will falter, and her hair will gather in; and the horse will fall, and the hair will twist, and twine, and wreathe itself like a mist of threads about the rider, and blind him to everything but her. Then the body will rise up within it, face to face with him, animated by a fiend, who, twining *her* arms around him, will drag him down to the bottomless pit.'

I may mention something which now occurred, and which had a strange effect on my old nurse. It illustrates the assertion that we see around us only what is within us; marvellous things enough will show themselves to the marvellous mood. During a short lull in the storm, just as she had finished her story, we heard the sound of iron-shod hoofs approaching the cottage. There was no bridleway into the glen. A knock came to the door, and, on opening it, we saw an old man seated on a horse, with a long, slenderly-filled sack lying across the saddle before him. He said he had lost the path in the storm, and, seeing the light, had scrambled down to enquire his way. I perceived at once, from the scared and mysterious look of the old woman's eyes, that she was persuaded that this appearance had more than a little to do with the awful rider, the terrific storm and myself, who had heard the sound of the phantom hoofs. As he ascended the hill, she looked after him, with wide and pale but unshrinking eyes; then turning in, shut and locked the door behind her, as by a natural instinct.

After two or three of her significant nods, accompanied by the compression of her lips, she said: 'He need not think to take me in, wizard as he is, with his disguises. I can see him through them all. Duncan, my dear, when you suspect anything, do not be too incredulous. This human demon is, of course, a wizard still, and knows how to make himself, as well as anything he touches, take a quite different appearance from the real one; only every appearance must bear some resemblance, however distant, to the natural form. That man you saw at the door was the phantom of which I have been telling you. What he is after now, of course, I cannot tell; but you must keep a bold heart, and a firm and wary foot, as you go home tonight.'

I showed some surprise, I do not doubt, and, perhaps, some fear as well; but I only said: 'How do you know him, Margaret?'

'I can hardly tell you,' she replied; 'but I do know him. I think he hates me. Often, of a wild night, when there is moonlight enough by fits, I see him tearing round this little valley, just on the top edge – all round; the lady's hair and the horse's mane and tail driving far behind, and mingling, vaporous, with the stormy clouds. About he goes, in wild careering gallop; now lost as the moon goes in, then visible far round when she looks out again – an airy, pale-grey spectre, which few eyes but mine could see; for, as far as I am aware, no one of the family but myself has ever possessed the double gift of

seeing and hearing both. In this case I hear no sound, except now and
then a clank from the broken shoe. But I did not mean to tell you that
I had ever seen him. I am not a bit afraid of him. He cannot do more
than he may. His power is limited; else ill enough would he work, the
miscreant.'

'But,' said I, 'what has all this, terrible as it is, to do with the fright
you took at my telling you that I had heard the sound of the broken
shoe? Surely you are not afraid of only a storm?'

'No, my boy; I fear no storm. But the fact is that that sound is
seldom heard, and never, as far as I know, by any of the blood of that
wicked man, without betokening some ill to one of the family, and
most probably to the one who hears it – but I am not quite sure about
that. Only some evil it does portend, although a long time may elapse
before it shows itself; and I have a hope it may mean someone else
than you.'

'Do not wish that,' I replied. 'I know no one better able to bear it
than I am; and I hope, whatever it may be, that I only shall have to
meet it. It must surely be something serious to be so foretold – it can
hardly be connected with my disappointment in being compelled to
be a pedagogue instead of a soldier.'

'Do not trouble yourself about that, Duncan,' replied she. 'A
soldier you must be. The same day you told me of the clank of the
broken horseshoe, I saw you return wounded from battle, and fall
fainting from your horse in the street of a great city – only fainting,
thank God. But I have particular reasons for being uneasy at *your*
hearing that boding sound. Can you tell me the day and hour of your
birth?'

'No,' I replied. 'It seems very odd when I think of it, but I really do
not know even the day.'

'Nor anyone else, which is stranger still,' she answered.

'How does that happen, nurse?'

'We were in terrible anxiety about your mother at the time. So ill
was she, after you were just born, in a strange, unaccountable way,
that you lay almost neglected for more than an hour. In the very act
of giving birth to you, she seemed to the rest around her to be out of
her mind, so wildly did she talk; but I knew better. I knew that she
was fighting some evil power; and what power it was, I knew full well;
for twice, during her pains, I heard the click of the horseshoe. But no
one could help her. After her delivery, she lay as if in a trance, neither
dead, nor at rest, but as if frozen to ice, and conscious of it all the
while. Once more I heard the terrible sound of iron, and, at that

moment, your mother started from her trance, screaming, 'My child! my child!' We suddenly became aware that no one had attended to the child, and rushed to the place where he lay wrapped in a blanket. Uncovering him, we found him black in the face, and spotted with dark spots upon the throat. I thought he was dead; but, with great and almost hopeless pains, we succeeded in making him breathe, and he gradually recovered. But his mother continued dreadfully exhausted. It seemed as if she had spent her life for her child's defence and birth. That was you, Duncan, my dear.

'I was in constant attendance upon her. About a week after your birth, as near as I can guess, just in the gloaming, I heard yet again the awful clank – only once. Nothing followed till about midnight. Your mother slept, and you lay asleep beside her. I sat by the bedside. A horror fell upon me suddenly, though I neither saw nor heard anything. Your mother started from her sleep with a cry, which sounded as if it came from far away, out of a dream, and did not belong to this world. My blood curdled with fear. She sat up in bed, with wide staring eyes, and half-open rigid lips, and, feeble as she was, thrust her arms straight out before her with great force, her hands open and lifted up, with the palms outwards. The whole action was of one violently repelling another. She began to talk wildly as she had done before you were born, but, though I seemed to hear and understand it all at the time, I could not recall a word of it afterwards. It was as if I had listened to it when half asleep. I attempted to soothe her, putting my arms round her, but she seemed quite unconscious of my presence, and my arms seemed powerless upon the fixed muscles of hers. Not that I tried to constrain her, for I knew that a battle was going on of some kind or other, and my interference might do awful mischief. I only tried to comfort and encourage her. All the time, I was in a state of indescribable cold and suffering, whether more bodily or mental I could not tell. But at length I heard yet again the clank of the shoe. A sudden peace seemed to fall upon my mind – or was it a warm, odorous wind that filled the room? Your mother dropped her arms, and turned feebly towards her baby. She saw that he slept a blessed sleep. She smiled like a glorified spirit, and fell back exhausted on the pillow. I went to the other side of the room to get a cordial. When I returned to the bedside, I saw at once that she was dead. Her face smiled still, with an expression of the uttermost bliss.'

Nurse ceased, trembling as overcome by the recollection; and I was too much moved and awed to speak. At length, resuming the conversation, she said: 'You see it is no wonder, Duncan, my dear, if, after all this, I should find, when I wanted to fix the date of your birth, that I could not determine the day or the hour when it took place. All was confusion in my poor brain. But it was strange that no one else could, any more than I. One thing only I can tell you about it. As I carried you across the room to lay you down – for I assisted at your birth – I happened to look up to the window. Then I saw what I did not forget, although I did not think of it again till many days after – a bright star was shining on the very tip of the thin crescent moon.'

'Oh, then,' said I, 'it is possible to determine the day and the very hour when my birth took place.'

'See the good of book-learning!' replied she. 'When you work it out, just let me know, my dear, that I may remember it.'

'That I will.'

A silence of some moments followed. Margaret resumed: 'I am afraid you will laugh at my foolish fancies, Duncan; but in thinking over all these things, as you may suppose I often do, lying awake in my lonely bed, the notion sometimes comes to me: What if my Duncan be the youth whom his wicked brother hurled into the ravine, come again in a new body, to live out his life, cut short by his brother's hatred? If so, his persecution of you, and of your mother for your sake, is easy to understand. And if so, you will never be able to rest till you find your fere, wherever she may have been born on the face of the earth. For born she must be, long ere now, for you to find. I misdoubt me much, however, if you will find her without great conflict and suffering between, for the Powers of Darkness will be against you; though I have good hope that you will overcome at last. You must forgive the fancies of a foolish old woman, my dear.'

I will not try to describe the strange feelings, almost sensations, that arose in me while listening to these extraordinary utterances, lest it should be supposed I was ready to believe all that Margaret narrated or concluded. I could not help doubting her sanity; but no more could I help feeling peculiarly moved by her narrative.

Few more words were spoken on either side, but, after receiving renewed exhortations to carefulness on the way home, I said goodbye to dear old nurse, considerably comforted, I must confess, that I was not doomed to be a tutor all my days; for I never questioned the truth of that vision and its consequent prophecy.

I went out into the midst of the storm, into the alternating throbs of blackness and radiance; now the possessor of no more room than what my body filled, and now isolated in world-wide space. And the thunder seemed to follow me, bellowing after me as I went.

Absorbed in the story I had heard, I took my way, as I thought, homewards. The whole country was well known to me. I should have said, before that night, that I could have gone home blindfold. Whether the lightning bewildered me and made me take a false turn, I cannot tell, for the hardest thing to understand, in intellectual as well as moral mistakes, is how we came to go wrong. But after wandering for some time, plunged in meditation, and with no warning whatever of the presence of inimical powers, a brilliant lightning-flash showed me that at least I was not near home. The light was prolonged for a second or two by a slight electric pulsation, and by that I distinguished a wide space of blackness on the ground in front of me. Once more wrapped in the folds of a thick darkness, I dared not move. Suddenly it occurred to me what the blackness was, and whither I had wandered. It was a huge quarry, of great depth, long disused and half filled with water. I knew the place perfectly. A few more steps would have carried me over the brink. I stood still, waiting for the next flash, that I might be quite sure of the way I was about to take before I ventured to move. While I stood, I fancied I heard a single hollow plunge in the black water far below. When the lightning came, I turned, and took my path in another direction. After walking for some time across the heath, I fell. The fall became a roll, and down a steep declivity I went, over and over, arriving at the bottom uninjured.

Another flash soon showed me where I was – in the hollow valley, within a couple of hundred yards of nurse's cottage. I made my way towards it. There was no light in it, except the feeblest glow from the embers of her peat fire. 'She is in bed,' I said to myself, 'and I will not disturb her.' Yet something drew me towards the little window. I looked in. At first I could see nothing. At length, as I kept gazing, I saw something, indistinct in the darkness, like an outstretched human form.

By this time the storm had lulled. The moon had been up for some time, but had been quite concealed by tempestuous clouds. Now, however, these had begun to break up; and, while I stood looking into the cottage, they scattered away from the face of the moon, and a faint, vapoury gleam of her light, entering the cottage through a window opposite that at which I stood, fell directly on the face of my old nurse, as she lay on her back outstretched upon chairs, pale as death, and with her eyes closed. The light fell nowhere but on her face. A stranger to her habits would have thought that she was dead; but she had so much of the appearance she had had on a former occasion, that I concluded at once she was in one of her trances. But having often heard that persons in such a condition ought not to be disturbed, and feeling quite sure she knew best how to manage herself, I turned, though reluctantly, and left the lone cottage behind me in the night, with the deathlike woman lying motionless in the midst of it.

I found my way home without any further difficulty, and went to bed, where I soon fell asleep, thoroughly wearied, more by the mental excitement I had been experiencing than by the amount of bodily exercise I had gone through.

My sleep was tormented with awful dreams; yet, strange to say, I awoke in the morning refreshed and fearless. The sun was shining through the chinks in my shutters, which had been closed because of the storm, and was making streaks and bands of golden brilliancy upon the wall. I had dressed and completed my preparations long before I heard the steps of the servant who came to call me.

What a wonderful thing waking is! The time of the ghostly moonshine passes by, and the great positive sunlight comes. A man who dreams, and knows that he is dreaming, thinks he knows what waking is; but knows it so little that he mistakes, one after another, many a vague and dim change in his dream for an awaking. When the true waking comes at last, he is filled and overflowed with the power of its reality. So, likewise, one who, in the darkness, lies waiting for the light about to be struck, and trying to conceive, with all the force of his imagination, what the light will be like, is yet, when the reality flames up before him, seized as by a new and unexpected thing, different from and beyond all his imagining. He feels as if the darkness were cast to an infinite distance behind him. So shall it be with us when we wake from this dream of life into the truer life beyond, and find all our present notions of being thrown back as into a dim vapoury region of dreamland, where yet we thought we knew, and whence we looked forward into the present. This must be what Novalis means when he says: 'Our life is not a dream; but it may become a dream, and perhaps ought to become one.'

And so I look back upon the strange history of my past, sometimes asking myself: 'Can it be that all this has really happened to the same *me*, who am now thinking about it in doubt and wonderment?'

The Haunted Major

Robert Marshall

I

About Myself

I am a popular man and withal I am not vain. To the people who know me I am an acquaintance of importance. This is due to a combination of circumstances.

First of all, I am a youthful (aged thirty-five) major in that smart cavalry regiment, the 1st Royal Light Hussars, commonly called the 'Chestnuts'. Secondly, I am an excellent polo player, standing practically at the top of that particular tree of sport; and again, I am a quite unusually brilliant cricketer. That I do not play in first-class cricket is due to long service abroad with my regiment; but now that we are at last quartered in England, I daily expect to be approached by the committee of my county eleven.

I considered myself, not before taking the opinion of my warmest friends, the best racquet player of my day in India; and I have rarely played football (Rugby) without knowing by a strange instinct (born, I feel sure, of truth) that I was the best man on the ground.

In the hunting field I am well known as one of the hardest riders across country living; and this statement, so far from being my own, emanates from my father's land agent, a poor relative of ours, and himself a fair performer in the saddle. As a shot, I will only refer you to my own game-book; and if, after examining the records contained therein, you can show me an equally proficient man in that special line, well – I'll take off my hat to him.

The trophies of head, horn and skin at Castle Goreby, our family's country seat, are sufficient guarantees of my prowess with big game in all parts of the world; and when I mention that I have been one of an Arctic Expedition, have climbed to the highest mountain peaks explored by man, voyaged for days in a balloon, dived to a wreck in the complete modern outfit of a professional diver, am as useful on a yacht as any man of my acquaintance, think nothing of scoring a hundred break at billiards, and rarely meet my match at whist, piquet or poker, it will be admitted that I have not confined my talents, such as they are, to any one particular branch of sport.

In fact, I am Jacky Gore, and although the War Office addresses me officially as 'Major the Honourable John William Wentworth Gore, 1st Royal Light Hussars', nothing is sweeter to my ear than to hear, as I often do, a passing remark such as, 'There goes good old Jacky Gore, the finest sportsman living!'

I take it for granted that the reader will accept this candour as to my performances in the spirit which inspires it, and not as a stupid form of self-conceit. I desire to be absolutely confidential and unreserved with those who peruse these pages, and a false modesty would be as misleading as it would be untrue to my nature.

For true modesty, as I conceive it, consists in an accurate valuation of one's own worth; an estimate of one's self that is conceived, not for purposes of advertisement, but rather to foster one's own self-respect. Thus, were these pages designed only for the eyes of sportsmen, there would appear no other description of myself than the laconic intimation, 'I am Jacky Gore.'

That, I know, would be sufficient to arrest electrically the ears of the sporting world. But as I desire my singular story to interest the whole range of human beings, from the Psychical Research Society down to the merest schoolboy who vaguely wonders if he will ever see a ghost, I must perforce be explicit, even to the extent of expounding my personal character as well as enumerating my achievements.

First, then, I am not a snob; I have no occasion to be one. I am the younger son of one of England's oldest earls, Lord Goresby, and my mother is the daughter of one of our newest marquises, Lord Dundrum. My friends are all of the very best, socially and otherwise. Indeed, I have established myself on a plane from which all acquaintances who have been financially unfortunate, or have otherwise become socially undesirable, must inevitably drop. For I hold that true friends are those whose position, affluence and affection for one may be of material assistance in the race towards the goal of one's personal ambition.

If there is one thing that jars on me more than another, it is when a person of lower social status than my own presumes to associate with me in a style and with a manner that imply equality. I can readily, and I believe gracefully, meet people of higher rank than mine on their own platform, but the converse is, at least to me, odious.

Lest, from these candid statements, the reader might be inclined to consider me a trifle exclusive, I will frankly own that I often shoot, fish or yacht with those *nouveaux riches* whose lacquer of gold so ineffectually conceals the real underlying metal. Still, a breadth of view of life, which has always been one of my characteristics, inspires me with the hope that the association of such people with one of my own type may in the process of time tend to the refining of the class from which they spring. Besides, one need not know people all one's life.

A keen eye for the artistic, a considerable talent for painting, a delicate and highly trained ear for music, and a quick perception as to what is of value in literature, have led me to frequent at times the houses where one meets the best class of so-called Bohemians. They are interesting people whom one may cultivate or drop according to social convenience, and useful as living dictionaries of the intellectual fashions of the moment. Sometimes I have thought that their interest in my experiences (as related in conversation by myself) has been strangely apathetic, not to say inattentive, due perhaps (as indeed I have been told) to the admiration of my physical points. In explanation I may point out that I have been modelled in marble as

Hercules. It was a birthday gift I devised for my second cousin (by marriage) the Duke of Haredale, and I gave the commission to that admirable French sculptor, Moreau.

My means, viewed in proportion to those of my friends, are at least sufficient. For, although my allowance is nominally but £2,000 a year, my father has such a morbid sense of the family honour that he is always ready to pay up the casual debts that spring from daily intercourse with the best of everything. And as he enjoys an income of quite £150,000 a year, mainly derived from coal mines in Wales, there really seems no reason why I should not occasionally, indeed frequently, furnish him with an opportunity for indulging in his harmless hobby of keeping the family escutcheon clean.

I endeavour to keep in touch with society journalism, and frequently entertain the editors of the more responsible sporting and smart papers. The Press being one of the glories of the age, I am ever ready to foster it; and though I care not one straw for the personal puffs of which I myself am so often the subject, still I know that they give pleasure to my friends, both at home and abroad.

As regards the literary style of these pages, I desire to point out that its agreeable flavour has been purveyed by a friend of mine, an eminent critic who writes for all the best daily and weekly papers both in London and the provinces. I have merely supplied the facts with such reflections and embroideries thereon as seemed to me both necessary and graceful. He has done the rest. Thus, if any adverse criticisms of my book should appear – an idea which I do not seriously entertain – the reader will understand that they are prompted either by professional jealousy or unfair rivalry, motives which, I am happy to think, have no place in the advanced and altruistic journalism of today.

And now, my reader, just before we plunge *in medias res*, I approach a subject which, if treated with candour, must also be handled with delicacy.

I desire to marry.

I desire to marry Katherine Clavering Gunter.

She is an American and a widow.

She is an enthusiastic golfer.

She is quite beautiful, especially in her photographs.

Since the day Carmody said, in the billiard-room at White's, that she reminded him of a blush rose whose outer petals were becoming touched with the tint of biscuits, I have cut him dead. Her beauty is to me full of freshness, especially at night.

She has a fortune of £2,000,000 sterling, and I love her with a very true and real love. That is to say, I love her with a perfectly balanced affection; an affection based impartially on an estimate of her personal worth, an admiration for her physical charms, and an appreciation of her comfortable circumstances. I perceive that our union would further our respective interests in providing each of us with certain extensions of our present modes of living. I have long desired a place of my own in the country; and Katherine, I know, wishes to move freely in smart circles without having to employ the services of impoverished dowagers. In many other ways I could be of assistance to Katherine. I could tell her how to wear her diamonds, for instance, a difficult art she has not yet acquired. She is inclined on the slightest provocation to decorate herself in exuberant imitation of a cut-crystal chandelier.

There are, however, difficulties.

Prominent among these is the fact, already mentioned, that she is an ardent golfer. Except during the season in town, she spends her year in golfing, either at St Magnus or Pau, for, like all good Americans, she has long since abjured her native soil.

Now golf is a game that presents no attractions to me. I have never tried it, nor even held a golf-stick in my hand. A really good game, to my mind, must have an element, however slight, of physical danger to the player. This is the great whet to skilled performance. It is the condition that fosters pluck and self-reliance and develops our perception of the value of scientific play. It breeds a certain fearlessness that stimulates us not merely during the actual progress of the game, but unconsciously in the greater world where we play at Life with alert and daring opponents.

Now golf presents no such condition, and I despise it.

Once, by means of jocular query (a useful method of extracting such information as may not always be asked for bluntly), I gathered from Katherine that marriage with a keen golfer would probably be her future state; and this admission, I confess, was extremely galling to me, the more so as I had just been entertaining her with a long summary of my own achievements in other games.

I little thought at the time that before many weeks had passed I should be playing golf as heaven knows it was never played before. And this is how it happened.

2

I Dine at Lowchester House

One warm, delicious evening late in July I was dining at Lowchester House. It was almost my last dinner engagement of the season, as all the world and his wife had suddenly got sick of the baking pavements and dusty trees of the great city, and were making in shoals for green fields or briny sea.

The ladies had just left us, and we men were preparing to enjoy the heavenly hour that brings cigarettes, coffee and liqueurs in its wake. Through the wide-open French windows of the dining-room (which look out over St James's Park) came softened sounds of busy traffic; a ravishing odour of sweet peas stole in from the garden, and the moon gave to the trees and shrubs without those strange, grave tints that are her wonderful gifts to the night.

As a rule such an environment impresses and invigorates me pleasurably. I enjoy the journeys of the eye as it travels lightly over polished mahogany, glittering silver and gleaming glass, noting here the deep red of the wine and roses, there the sunset-like effulgence of the hanging lamps, the vague outlines of the pictured oak walls and the clearer groups of well-groomed men that sit in easy comfort under a blue canopy of lazily curling smoke. Or, as the glance passes to the scented garden without, noting the blue-green and silver wonderlands that the moon creates in the most commonplace and probably grimy of trees, and the quiver that the soft July wind gives to branch, leaf and flower.

But tonight, somehow, such things had no charm for me.

And yet Lady Lowchester's dinner had been good. The cutlets, perhaps, a trifle uninteresting and the wine somewhat over-iced; but, on the whole, distinctly good.

How, then, account for my mood?

Katherine was of the party, but at the other end of the table from mine. A tall, well-built, massive man, good-looking and possessed of an attractive smile, had taken her into dinner, and I have rarely seen two people so completely absorbed in each other.

Therein lay the sting of the evening.

I had eaten and drunk mechanically with eyes riveted, as far as good breeding would permit, on Katherine and her neighbour.

Who was he?

I know everybody that one meets in London, either personally or by sight, yet I had never before come across this good-looking Hercules. I must find out.

He was talking to Lowchester as, leaving my chair, I carelessly joined the group at the other end of the table.

'Yes, I first held the open championship five years ago,' I heard him say.

I pricked my ears. Of what championship was he speaking?

'And again last year, I think?' asked Lowchester.

'Yes,' replied Hercules.

I quickly enquired of my neighbour as to what championship was under discussion.

'Why golf, of course,' was the response. 'That's Jim Lindsay, the finest player living.'

So that was it. No wonder Katherine was so deeply absorbed during dinner.

I hated the man at once. I lost not a moment. I darted my eyes across the table, caught his, and stabbed him with one of those withering knifelike glances that only the descendants of the great can inflict.

Then I discovered that he wasn't looking at me at all, but at one of my shirt studs which had escaped from its buttonhole. He drew my attention to it. I grunted out an ungrateful 'Thanks!' and hated him the more.

Now, as a rule, after dinner – wherever I may be – I manage to hold the conversation. So much a habit has this become with me that I can scarcely endure to hear another man similarly exploiting himself. Not, I am bound to say, that Lindsay was belauding his own prowess.

But, what was worse, he appeared a centre of enormous interest to the men around him. They drew him out. They hung on his words. They gaped at him with reverential admiration. Truly golf must have made many converts during the last three years I had been in India. Bah! And I knew it to be such a childish game.

'I've taken a house close to the links at St Magnus for the summer, Lindsay,' Lowchester presently observed. 'And as you tell me you're going there next month, you must let me put you up. There's lots of room, and Mrs Gunter will be with us during August and September.'

'I shall be delighted; it will suit me exactly,' replied Lindsay.

So Lowchester too had become a golfer! Lowchester – who used to live for hunting and cricket! Lowchester – the President of the Board of Education! Good heavens!

Presently we were all in the hideous gilded and damasked drawing-room; for Lowchester House is a sort of museum of the tawdry vulgarities of the early fifties.

The rooms were hot. That no doubt was the reason why presently Mrs Gunter and the champion were to be seen hanging over the railing of a flower-laden balcony; but the heat could in no way account for their gazing into each other's eyes so frequently, or so raptly.

I seized on a slip of a girl in pink, led her close to the window, and in tones that I knew must be overheard by the occupants of the balcony, began to relate how I won the Lahore Polo Cup for my team in '92.

I was well under weigh and just reaching a stirring description of the magnificent goal I scored by taking the ball the whole length of the ground on a pony that had suddenly gone lame, when Katherine and the champion pointedly left the window and proceeded to another and more distant one.

So! My reminiscences bored them! Polo was nothing if golf were in the air!

It was enough. I could stand no more. I peevishly bade my hostess good-night, and passed through the rooms.

As I entered the great hall, which was but dimly lit, my eyes encountered a portrait of the famous (or infamous) Cardinal Smeaton, one of Lowchester's proudest pictorial possessions. The great Scotch prelate, I could have sworn, winked at me.

I was moving on, when suddenly, close to my shoulder, I heard the words, 'I will meet ye at St Magnus!'

I started and turned. There was no one near. I gazed fixedly at the portrait, but never was marble more immovable. I was about to investigate a recess and some pillars, near me, when I observed a footman at the hall door eyeing me with mild but interested scrutiny. He came forward with my coat and hat, and putting them on I passed listlessly into the courtyard and thence to St James's Street, where I mechanically entered the doors of the Racing Club.

I rang the bell and ordered a brandy-and-soda.

3

The Challenge

The Racing Club, as the reader knows, is the smartest sporting club in London, and the Inner Temple of the popular game of bridge. But tonight cards held no temptation for me; and I sat alone in the reading-room, chewing the cud of a humiliation that was quite novel to my experience.

The incident of the cardinal's wink and the unknown voice had already escaped my memory, and I was rapt in rankling memories of the unsatisfactory evening I had spent.

To me, it was inconceivable that even the finest exponent of a wretched game like golf could oust an all-round sportsman like myself from the circle of interest at a dinner table. It was not so much that I had not been afforded an opportunity to talk, as that when I did I was listened to with a wandering and simulated attention, suggesting that the listeners were only waiting for me to stop. The moment I paused between two anecdotes, someone precipitately led the conversation away to a channel that had no possible interest for me.

Then Katherine had indubitably avoided and ignored me.

It has always been understood between us that if I am in a room with her, mine is the first claim on her attention. Yet, tonight, there was, if not an open rebellion, at least a new departure.

It was extremely galling, and I ordered a second brandy-and-soda.

Must I, then, take to golf in self-defence?

Of course I could pick it up easily. There is no minor game that I have not mastered with ease, after about a week's hard application; and to acquire the art of striking a ball from a certain distance into a hole presents no alarming difficulties to the adroit cricketer and

practised polo player. Still, to go over, as it were, to the camp of the
enemy, to apply myself to a game that I have openly and avowedly
sneered at, was not altogether a pleasing prospect.

How it would tickle my pals at Hurlingham, Ranelagh, the Oval
and Lord's!

I took from the bookshelves the Badminton volume on Golf, and
with a third brandy-and-soda applied myself to a rapid study of its
contents. I admit that I was somewhat dismayed at the mass of
printed matter and numerous diagrams that confronted me, but
reflecting that I had often seen voluminous books on such trivial
games as croquet or tennis, I concluded that the principle of sporting
journalism is to make the maximum of bricks out of the minimum of
straw.

I had not read more than three chapters when half a dozen men,
including Lowchester and Lindsay, entered the room.

'My dear Jacky,' said the former, 'you left us very early tonight.'

'Yes,' I replied. 'I found the atmosphere indoors a bit oppressive;
and I'm not as yet a convert to golf, your sole topic of discussion
during the evening.'

'You ought to try the game,' said Lindsay. 'There's more in it than
outsiders imagine.'

' "Outsiders" in what sense?' I enquired, with an obvious courtship
of a wordy wrangle.

'Oh! only as regards golf, of course. For aught I know you may be
a celebrity in many other branches of sport.'

'I am,' was on the tip of my tongue, but I repressed it.

I felt strangely antagonistic towards this man. A sort of magnetic
antipathy (if I may be allowed such a seeming contradiction in terms)
warned me that we should influence each other's lives in the future,
and that to the detriment of one, if not both of us. In fact, I felt myself
being drawn irresistibly towards the vulgar vortex of a 'row' with
him.

'Golf,' I suddenly found myself asserting after one of those deadly
pauses that give an altogether exaggerated significance to any casual
remark that may break the silence, 'Golf is a game for one's dotage.'

'A period that sets in quite early in the lives of many of us,' retorted
Lindsay.

There was another pause. Lowchester was chuckling quietly. A
club waiter with thin lips was grinning faintly.

'Which means?' I asked, with an affectation of bored inattention.

'Well, it means,' was the reply, 'that to stigmatise as only suitable for one's dotage, a fine, healthy, outdoor sport, that employs skill and science, and exercises one's patience and temper as few other games do, suggests to my mind incipient dotage in common perception.'

I did not understand this at first, so merely remarked, 'Really,' an ambiguous and useful word, which commits one to nothing.

But as I reflected on Lindsay's words, I perceived a deadly stab at my authority as a judge of sport. My blood tingled. I seized a fourth brandy-and-soda and drank it. It was Lowchester's, but I was only aware of this when the glass was empty. My lips compressed themselves. I recalled Katherine and the champion hanging over the balcony. The thin-lipped club waiter was loitering with an evident desire to overhear what else was to be said. Lowchester looked at me with gently humorous enquiry in his eyes. The others regarded me with the sphinx-like calm that is the ordinary expression of the average Englishman when he is thinking hard but not lucidly. I had, in fact, an audience, always to me an overpowering temptation.

'I'll tell you what I'll do,' I said, in the calm, deep tones born of a great determination. 'After one week's practice on the St Magnus links I'll play you a match on even terms, and I dare to hope, lick your head off at your own game.'

There was a pause of a moment. Then, as if to clear the oppressive air, a chorus of, 'Bravo, old Jacky!' broke out from the bystanders.

Only Lindsay was silent, barring, of course, the waiters.

'Well?' I asked him.

'I accept, of course,' said he; 'you leave me no alternative. But the whole scheme is absolutely childish, and, as I fear you will find, quite futile.'

'I'll take my chance of that,' I replied. 'I can reach St Magnus by August 8th, and on the 15th I'll play you.'

'It's a match,' cried Lowchester, and proceeded to enter it in a notebook. 'Any stakes?'

'I will privately suggest to Mr Lindsay the stakes to be played for,' I answered. 'May I ask you to come with me for a moment?'

Lindsay assented, and I led him to an adjoining room that was empty.

'The stake I suggest – and it must be known to none but ourselves – is this. The winner of the match shall have the first right to propose matrimony to a certain lady. I mention no names. It is enough if we agree that neither of us shall propose to any lady whatsoever on or before August 15th, and that the loser shall further abstain from any such proposal till August 22nd. This will give the winner a clear week's start, which really constitutes the stake. The subject is a delicate one,' I hastily added, as I saw his surprise and evident desire to go further into the matter, 'and I shall be obliged if you merely signify your assent or dissent, as the case may be.'

With a certain bewildered yet half-amused air he replied, 'I assent, of course, but – '

'There is nothing more that need be said,' I hurriedly interrupted, 'except that I shall be glad if you will join me at supper.'

For at one of my own clubs, when a stranger is introduced, even by another member, I trust I can ever play the host with tact and grace. I asked Lowchester and Grimsby to join us, and during supper I was able to recount the chief exploits of my life to the attentive audience that a host can always rely on.

4

St Magnus

I left London on August 6th, travelling by night to Edinburgh, and leaving the latter city at 9 a.m. on the 7th, reached St Magnus a few minutes before noon. I had been recommended to try the Metropole Hotel, and accordingly took up my quarters there. It is quite near the St Magnus Golf Club (for which I was put up at once as a temporary member), and is equally convenient to the links. Lord and Lady Lowchester were in their house, a stone's-throw from the hotel, and amongst their guests were Mr Lindsay and Mrs Gunter.

St Magnus, as the golfing world knows, is situated on the east coast of Scotland, and is second only in importance as a golfing centre to St Andrews, which, indeed, it closely resembles. It is a grim, grey old town, standing on bleak, precipitous cliffs that court every passing hurricane, and possessed in addition of a respectable perennial gale of its own. It is always blowing there. Indeed, I think a fair description of normal weather of St Magnus would be 'wind with gales'.

The ancient town boasts many ruins of once noble buildings. Cathedrals, castles, monasteries, colleges and priories, that formed strongholds of Roman Catholicism before the Reformation, are now outlined only by picturesque and crumbling walls, held in a green embrace by the ever-sympathetic ivy, and preserved mainly to please the antiquarian or artistic eye.

And many are the tales that are told of the ghostly occupants of these dead strongholds.

The hotel was tolerably comfortable, although under any conditions hotel life is, to me, a hateful business. The constant traversing of passages that lead chiefly to other people's rooms; the garrulous noisiness of the guests, the forced yet blasé alacrity of the waiters, the commercial suavity and professional geniality of the proprietor, the absolute lack of originality in the cook, the fact that one becomes merely an easily forgotten number, these and a thousand other trivial humiliations combine to render residence in an hotel a source of irritation to the nerves.

The clubhouse, however, was airy and comfortably managed; and the older frequenters appeared to me to be good types of Scotch county gentlemen or courteous members of the learned professions. Some of the younger men I met I did not quite understand. They had, to begin with, quite extraordinary accents. If you can imagine a native and strong Scotch accent asserting itself in defiance of a recently acquired cockney twang, you have some idea of the strange sounds these youths emitted. They were, however, quite harmless; and there really seemed no reason why, if it pleased them, they should not garnish their Caledonian and somewhat bucolic dialogue with misplaced 'Don't-you-knows', or denude it, in accordance with a long defunct phonetic fashion, of the letter 'g'. They were quite charmed with my prefix 'Honourable', and duly acquainted me of such people of title as they had either seen at a distance or once spoken to at a railway station.

The general society of the place was considered 'mixed' by the younger bloods of the town; though, to my mind, these latter formed the most unpalatable part of the mixture. It numbered, to my surprise, half a dozen socially well-known people whom I frequently met in London. True, they kept pretty much to themselves and were not to be seen at the numerous tea-parties, female putting tournaments, badly cooked but pretentious dinners, and other social barbarities that were – heaven help us! – considered *de rigueur* in this fresh seaside country town.

I, too, avoided all such festivities; though from the moment I set foot in the club, with name and condition advertised on the notice board, I was inundated with invitations; one of the many penalties, I suppose, of being more or less of a sporting celebrity. I felt, indeed, much as a great actor must when he goes 'starring' in the provinces.

There was, however, one charming section of society in the grey old town, comprising mainly those learned and cultured people who owned the city as their home. Mingling with these, some modern *littérateurs* in search of bracing health gave a vivacity to the free exchange of ideas; whilst one or two staid but intelligent clergymen formed a sort of moral anchor that held cultured thought to the needs of the world rather than let it drift to the summer seas of imagination. In such society I should have been, of course, a welcome recruit; but I was in St Magnus for one purpose only, and that was golf.

I have been writing calmly, but during the days that followed my challenge to Lindsay my brain was in a fever. I had stipulated but one week's practice, and, consequently, though dying to handle the sticks (or 'clubs' as I find I ought to call them), I had been debarred from more than a study of the game, as set forth in the various published works on the subject.

I had taken a suite of four rooms in the hotel. One was my sitting-room, another my bedroom, a third my servant's room and the fourth I had fitted up as a golf studio. The latter is entirely my own invention, and I make no doubt that, after the publication of this volume, similar studios will become quite common institutions.

By arrangement with the proprietor, I had the room denuded of all furniture; and it was understood between us that during my residence no one, not even a housemaid, should be permitted to enter the chamber, with, of course, the exception of myself and my servant. I had no desire that St Magnus should know the extent to which I was laying myself out to defeat my opponent.

A strip of coconut matting, lightly strewn with sand, represented a teeing ground, whilst a number of padded targets, designed to receive the balls as I drove them, almost entirely covered the walls. A fourth of the floor was boarded in with sand, eighteen inches deep, to represent a bunker. The remainder I turfed to represent a putting green. I constructed a small movable grassy hillock which could be placed in the centre of the room for practice in 'hanging' or 'uphill' lies, and I imported whin bushes, sods of long grass, etc., to represent the assorted difficulties that beset the golfer. By day, and until I was finished with the studio for the night, the windows were removed in case of accidents; and altogether nothing was left undone that would conduce to complete and unobserved practice of the game.

In addition to this indoor preparation, I decided to do at least two rounds daily, starting at daybreak. Allowing two hours for each round, this could easily be accomplished before 9 a.m., and St Magnus would be little the wiser. Then, if my progress should prove unsatisfactory, starting out about 5 p.m., I could edge in a third almost unnoticed round.

I had six volumes by different writers on the game, and from these I gathered that instruction from a first-class professional was practically indispensable to the beginner. By dint of offering extremely liberal terms, I secured the services of the well-known professional Kirkintulloch, it being understood that he was to coach me more or less *sub rosa*, and that in any case he was not to talk promiscuously of the extent to which I practised. I exhorted him to spare no expense – an arrangement he accepted with evident and spontaneous alacrity, selling me a number of his own unrivalled clubs at what I have since learnt were exorbitant prices. He also made a selection of other implements of the game, from the best makers, that included fifteen beautifully balanced and polished clubs, four dozen balls and several minor appliances, such as artificial tees, sponges, etc., to say nothing of a seven-and-sixpenny and pagoda-like umbrella. All these preparations were completed on the day of my arrival, and it was arranged that I should begin practice in deadly earnest at 4.30 on the following morning.

5

I Begin to Golf

The morning of the 8th dawned with a warm flush of saffron, rose and gold, behind which the faint purple of the night that was gone died into the mists of early morning. The pure, sweet air was delicious as the sparkling vapour that rises from a newly opened bottle of invigorating wine. The incoming tide plashed on the beach with lazy and musical kisses, and a soft, melodious wind was stirring the bending grasses that crowned the sand dunes on the outskirts of the links.

I inhaled the glorious air with the rapture of the warrior who sniffs the battle from afar.

[The literary grace of my esteemed journalistic colleague will be observed in the foregoing lines. 'It was a ripping morning' was all I actually said to him. J. W. W. G.]

Kirkintulloch was waiting for me at the first putting green.

I may say at once that during my entire stay in St Magnus I never quite mastered this man's name. It became confused in my mind with other curious-sounding names of Scotch towns, and I addressed him promiscuously as Tullochgorum, Tillicoutry, Auchtermuchty and the like. To his credit, be it said that, after one or two attempts to put me right, he suppressed any claim to nominal individuality and adapted himself philosophically to my weakness; answering cheerfully to any name that greeted his surprised but resigned ears.

He was the brawny son of honest fisherfolk. Of middle height, he was sturdily yet flexibly built. His hands were large and horny; his feet, I have no doubt, the same. At all events his boots were of ample proportions. He had blue eyes, with that alert, steady and far-seeing gaze that is the birthright of folk born to look out over the sea, sandy hair and moustache, and a ruddy colour that suggested equally sunshine, salt winds and whisky. His natural expression was inclined to be sour, but on occasion this was dissipated by a quite genial smile. His manner and address had the odd deferential familiarity that belongs exclusively to the old-fashioned Scotch peasantry. His face I soon found to be a sort of barometer of my progress, for every time I struck a ball I could see exactly the value of the stroke recorded in the grim lines of his weather-beaten features. In movement he was clumsy, except, indeed, when golfing, for then his body and limbs became possessed of that faultless grace which only proficiency in a given line can impart.

'It's a fine moarn fur goalf,' was his greeting.

'So I suppose,' said I. 'Where do we go?'

'We'll gang ower here,' he replied, as, tucking my clubs under his arm, he led me in the direction of a comparatively remote part of the links.

As we went I thought it advisable to let him know that, although not yet a golfer, I could more than hold my own in far higher branches of sport. I told him that I was one of the best-known polo players of the day.

There was a considerable pause, but we tramped steadily on.

'Whaat's polo?' said he, at length.

I gave him a brief description of the game.

'Aweel, ye'll no hae a hoarse to help ye at goalf.'

'But don't you see, Tullochgorum – '

'Kirkintulloch, sir.'

'Kirkintulloch, that the fact of playing a game on ponies makes it much more difficult?'

'Then whaat fur d'ye hae them?'

'Well, it's the game, that's all.'

'M'hm,' was his sphinx-like response.

I felt that I had not convinced him.

I next hinted that I was a prominent cricketer, and, as a rule, went in first wicket down when playing for my regiment.

'Ay; it's a fine ploy fur laddies.'

'It's a game that can only properly be played by men,' I replied, with indignant warmth.

'Is't?'

'Yes, is't – I mean it is.' He had certain phrases that I often unconsciously and involuntarily repeated, generally with ludicrous effect.

The reader, of course, understands that I was not in any sense guilty of such gross taste as to imitate the man to his own ears. I simply could not help pronouncing certain words as he did.

'Aweel, in goalf ye'll no hae a man to birstle the ba' to yer bat; ye'll just hae to play it as it lies.'

'But, man alive,' I cried, 'don't you see that to hit a moving object must be infinitely more difficult than to strike a ball that is stationary?'

'Ye've no bunkers at cricket,' he replied, with irrelevant but disconcerting conviction, adding, with an indescribable and prophetic relish, 'No, nor yet whins.'

I could make no impression on this man, and it worried me.

'I take it,' I resumed presently, 'that what is mainly of importance at golf is a good eye.'

'That's ae thing.'

'What's ae thing?'

'Yer e'e. The thing is, can ye keep it on the ba'?'

'Of course I can keep it on the ba' – ball.'

'We'll see in a meenit,' he answered, and stopped. We had reached a large field enclosed by a wall, and here Kirkintulloch dropped the clubs and proceeded to arrange a little heap of damp sand, on which he eventually poised a golf ball.

'Noo, tak' yer driver. Here,' and he handed me a beautifully varnished implement decorated with sunk lead, inlaid bone and resined cord. 'Try a swing' – he said, 'a swing like this,' and, standing in position before the ball, he proceeded to wave a club of his own in semicircular sweeps as if defying the world in general and myself in particular, till suddenly and rapidly descending on the ball, he struck it with such force and accuracy that it shot out into the faint morning mist and disappeared. It was really a remarkably fine shot. I began to feel quite keen.

'Noo it's your turn,' said he, as he teed a second ball, 'but hae a wheen practice at the swung first.'

So I began 'addressing' an imaginary ball.

We wrestled with the peculiar flourishes that are technically known as 'addressing the ball' for some minutes, at the end of which my movements resembled those of a man who, having been given a club, was undecided in his mind as to whether he should keep hold of it or throw it away. I wiggled first in one direction, then in another. I described eights and threes, double circles, triangles and parallelograms in the air, only to be assailed with, 'Na, na!' from Kirkintulloch.

'See here, dea it like this,' he cried; and again he flourished his driver with the easy grace of a lifetime's practice.

'I'll tell you what, Kirkcudbright – '

'Kirkintulloch, sir.'

'Kirkintulloch, just you let me have a smack at the ball.'

'Gang on then, sir. Hae a smack.'

I took up position. I got my eye on the ball. I wiggled for all I was worth, I swung a mighty swing, I swooped with terrific force down on the ball, and behold, when all was over, there it was still poised on the tee, insolently unmoved, and Kirkintulloch sniffing in the direction of the sea.

'Ye've missed the globe,' was his comment. 'An' it's a black disgrace to a gowfer.'

I settled to the ball again – and with a running accompaniment from Kirkintulloch of, 'Keep yer eye on the ba'; up wi' yer richt fut; tak' plenty time; dinna swee ower fast,' I let drive a second time, with the result that the ball took a series of trifling hops and skips like a startled hare, and deposited itself in rough ground some thirty yards off, at an angle of forty-five degrees from the line I had anxiously hoped to take.

'Ye topped it, sir,' was Kirkintulloch's view of the performance.

'I moved it, anyhow,' I muttered moodily.

'Ay, ye did that,' was the response; 'and ye'll never move that ba' again, fur it's doon a rabbit hole and oot o' sicht.'

Nevertheless, I went steadily on, ball after ball. They took many and devious routes, and entirely different methods of reaching their destinations. Some leapt into the air with half-hearted and affrighted purpose; others shot along the ground with strange irregularity of direction and distance; a number went off at right or left angles with the pleasing uncertainty that only a beginner can command; whilst not a few merely trickled off the tee in sickly obedience to my misdirected energy. At length I struck one magnificent shot. The ball soared straight and sure from the club just as Kirkintulloch's had, and I felt for the first time the delicious thrill that tingles through the arms right to the very brain, as the clean-struck ball leaves the driver's head. I looked at Kirkintulloch with a proud and gleaming eye.

'No bad,' said he, 'but ye'll no do that again in a hurry. It was guy like an accident.'

'Look here, Kirkincoutry,' I said, nettled at last, 'it's your business to encourage me, not to throw cold water; and you ought to know it.'

'Ma name's Kirkintulloch,' he answered phlegmatically; 'but it doesna' maitter.' (And this was the last time he corrected my errors as to his name.) 'An' I can tell ye this, that cauld watter keeps the heed cool at goalf, and praise is a snare and a deloosion.' Then with the ghost of a smile he added, 'Gang on, ye're daein' fine.'

The field was now dotted with some fifteen balls at such alarmingly varied distances and angles from the tee that they formed an irregular semicircle in front of us (one ball had even succeeded in travelling backwards); and as I reflected that my original and sustained purpose had been to strike them all in one particular line, I began to perceive undreamt-of difficulties in this royal and ancient game.

But I struggled on, and Kirkintulloch himself admitted that I showed signs of distinct, if spasmodic, improvement. At seven o'clock the driver was temporarily laid aside, and I was introduced in turn to the brassey, the iron, the cleek, the putter and the niblick, the latter a curious implement not unlike a dentist's reflector of magnified proportions. The brassey much resembled the driver, but the iron opened out quite a new field of practice; and my first attempts with it were rather in the nature of sod-cutting with a spade, varied at intervals by deadly strokes that left deep incisions on the ball.

As the clock of the parish church tolled the hour of 8.30, I returned to the hotel with an enormous appetite and a thoughtful mind.

6

I Continue Practice

My practice in the studio was not attended with that measure of success I had anticipated. The turf got dry and lumpy, and when, by my instructions, my servant watered it liberally, an old lady occupying the room immediately below intimated to the proprietor that her ceiling had unaccountably begun to drip, and that strange noises from the floor above deprived her of that tranquil rest for which she had sought the salubrious breezes of St Magnus. A gouty dean, whose room adjoined the studio, also complained that sudden bangs and rattles on the walls, intermittent and varied but on the whole continuous, had so completely got on his nerves that residence in that quarter of the hotel had become an impossibility; whilst a number of other guests pointed out that to walk beneath my window was an extremely dangerous proceeding, as golf balls and even broken clubs flew out on them with alarming frequency and exciting results. I admit that I had a thoughtless habit of throwing offending clubs from the window in moments of extreme exasperation, but I exonerate myself of any intentional bombarding of my fellow-lodgers.

I myself suffered from this indoor zeal, for if a ball failed to strike one of the padded targets, and came in contact with the wall (as often happened), it would fly back boomerang-like to where I stood, not infrequently striking me so hard as to raise grisly lumps on various parts of my body. Once I invited Wetherby, my servant, to witness my progress, and during the few minutes of his incarceration with me he was driven to execute a series of leaps and springs to avoid the rapidly travelling and seemingly malignant ball. It struck him, I believe, three times, which somewhat militated against his evident desire to pay me encouraging compliments, for these latter he condensed into a meagre and breathless, 'Wonderful, sir!' as he dashed from the studio with an alacrity that was by no means constitutional with him.

The miniature bunker also gave rise to a certain amount of speculation on the part of inmates of the hotel, for as I generally practised on it facing the window, casual loiterers below experienced brief but disconcerting sandstorms, and the porters and hall boys were kept busily occupied in sweeping the unaccountably sanded pavement.

I will not weary the reader with a description of my progress on the links from day to day. Suffice it to say that whilst I really made wonderful strides, it became borne in upon me, after five days' practice, that under no possible conditions could I hope to win the match I had set myself to play. For although I made many excellent, and even brilliant, strokes, I would constantly 'foozle' others, with the result that I never got round the links under 100, whereas Lindsay, I knew, seldom if ever exceeded 90, and averaged, I suppose, something like 86.

What, then, was I to do? Give in?

No.

I would play the match, and be beaten like a man. There was a remote chance that fortune might favour me. Lindsay might be seedy – I knew he suffered at times from the effects of malarial fever – or I might by some unlooked-for providence suddenly develop a slashing game.

At all events I felt I must confide in Kirkintulloch's ears the task I had set myself.

Accordingly, on the morning of Saturday the 13th, I intimated to him, as we started on our first round, that I had to play my first match on the Monday.

'Ay,' said he quite imperturbably.

'Yes,' I resumed, 'and rather an important one.'

'Weel, I'll cairry for ye. Whaat time?'

'Eleven o'clock,' I replied; and then, plunging *in medias res*, I added, 'I'm playing a single against Mr Lindsay, Mr James Lindsay.'

Kirkintulloch stopped dead, and gazed at me with blue-eyed and unceremonious incredulity.

'Jim Lindsay!' he cried.

'Yes,' I growled doggedly.

We proceeded to walk on, but, despite his impenetrable expression, I knew that Kirkintulloch was charged with violent emotion of some sort.

'What's he giein' ye?' he asked presently.

'What?'

'What's yer hondicop?'

'None. I'm playing him level.'

'Weel, of a' the pairfect noansense – '

'Eh?' I interrupted, with a certain dignity that was not lost on

Kirkintulloch. But he again stopped dead, and for once in a way betrayed signs of some excitement.

'See here whaat I'm tellin' ye. He'll lay ye oot like a corp! D'ye ken thaat? Forbye ye'll be the laughin'-stock o' the links. Ay, and *me* cairryin' for ye! I've pit up wi' a' the names ye've ca'd me – Tullochgorum, Tillicoutry, ay, and Auchtermuchty tae – but I'd hae ye mind I'm Wully Kirkintulloch, the professional. I've been in the mileeshy, an' I've done ma fowerteen days in the clink, but I'm no for ony black disgrace like cairryin' in a maatch the tail end o' which'll be Jim Lindsay scorin' nineteen up an' seventeen tae play.'

I am not vain, but I confess that this speech, the longest oratorical effort that I remember Kirkintulloch to have indulged in, wounded my *amour propre*.

'If you don't wish to cairry – I mean carry – for me on Monday,' I said, 'there is no occasion for you to do so. I can easily get another caddie, and whoever does undertake the job will be paid one guinea.'

I watched his features keenly as I said this, and though he in no wise betrayed himself by look or gesture, there was an alteration in his tone when next he addressed me.

'It's like this, ye see,' said he. 'I ken ma business fine, and I ken a reel gentleman when I see yin, even when he's no whaat ye might ca' profeecient as a goalfer, an' I'm no sayin' I'll no cairry fur ye; a' I say is that ye're no tae blame me if Jim Lindsay wuns by three or fower holes.'

With this change of professional attitude we proceeded on our way, and were soon absorbed in the intricacies of the game.

That morning – how well I remember it! – I was pounding away in one of the deepest bunkers, filling my eyes, ears, hair and clothes with sand, exhausting my vocabulary of language and yet not appreciably moving the ball. I had played seven strokes with ever-increasing frenzy. With the eighth, to my momentary relief, the ball soared from the sand to the grassy slope above, only – oh, maddening game! – to trickle slowly back and nest itself in one of my deepest heel-marks. Under the impression that I was alone, I was engaging in a one-sided, but ornate, conversation with the ball – for it is quite extraordinary how illogically angry one gets with inanimate objects – when, suddenly, from behind me came the clear ring of a woman's laughter.

I turned and beheld Mrs Gunter.

She was dressed in a tailor-made coat and skirt of butcher blue, and wore a Tam o' Shanter of the same colour. A white collar and bright red sailor knot, adorable white spats, and a white waistcoat completed the costume. Over her shoulder she carried a cleek, and by her side was a caddie bearing her other clubs. Her eyes were sparkling with humour and enjoyment of life, her cheeks glowed with the bright fresh red that comes of sea air and healthy exercise. Her enemies used to say she was an adept at suitable complexions, but, personally, I give the credit to the salubrious breezes of St Magnus.

I turned and beheld Mrs Gunter

'Well?' she cried, lustily (and she did *not* pronounce it 'wal'). 'How goes it?'

'Tolerably,' I replied, as I mopped my perspiring brow. 'You see me at present at my worst.'

'Anna Lowchester is going to ask you to dinner on Monday to celebrate the great match. Mind you come. Say now, what are the stakes? You know it's all over the town you're playing for something colossal. You'll have quite a crowd at your heels. And tell me why you avoid us all?'

'I am here simply and solely to golf,' I replied, with as much dignity as is possible for the occupant of a bunker that the merest novice could have avoided.

'Ye're keepin' the green waitin', sir,' cried Kirkintulloch, as he appeared on the grassy slope in front of me.

'Then will you excuse me?' I asked Mrs Gunter, and settling down again I proceeded patiently to manoeuvre under and round my ball. As I played the 'eleven more', it rose in the air, and I left the bunker with a dignified bow to Katherine.

She passed on with a merry laugh and a wave of the hand, crying out as she watched the destination of my gutta-percha, 'You poor soul! You're bang into another.'

And so I was. For a passing moment I almost hated Katherine.

It was quite true that I had avoided the Lowchesters. I was in no mood for society, still less did I care to meet Mr Lindsay. True, I stumbled across him frequently in the club, but we instinctively limited our intercourse to a distant 'Good-morning', or a perfunctory 'Good-night'.

Moreover, I was becoming extremely depressed.

Katherine's flippant and unsympathetic bearing during my vicissitudes in the bunker; the certainty that for the first time in my life I was about to be made a fool of; the extraordinary difficulty I experienced in attaining to anything like an even sample of play; and the half-pitiful, half-fearful regard in which I was held by the guests at the hotel, combined to rob life of the exhilaration that I had hitherto never failed to enjoy.

7

I Meet the Cardinal

The morning of Sunday the 14th broke with a dark and stormy scowl. The sea was lashed to a foaming lather by frantic gusts of easterly wind, and great black masses of clouds sped landward and piled themselves in an ominous canopy over the grey and bleak-looking city. A seething and swirling mist all but enveloped the links, and the bending grasses of the dunes swayed and swished with every scourge of the salt-laden gale. Hard-driven and drenching rain swept in furious torrents across land and sea. The ground was as a swamp; the wet rocks, cold and streaming, stood as black targets for the fury of the mighty and resounding breakers that, spent in impotent attack, rose in vast clouds of spray.

Not a soul was to be seen out of doors. The church bells, faintly and fitfully heard, clanged their invitation to an irresponsive town; indoors, fires were already crackling, pipes were lighted, magazines unearthed, and soon St Magnus was courting the drowsy comfort that snug shelter from a raging storm ever induces.

I passed the time till luncheon in the golf studio, but, out of consideration for such Sabbatarian scruples as might possibly be entertained by the adjoining dean, I merely trifled with a putter, and indeed I had little heart even for that. The clamour of the gong for the midday meal was a welcome break to the black monotony of the morning, and, descending to the dining-room, I partook freely of such northern delicacies as haggis (a really excellent if stodgy dish), crab pies and oat cakes.

I then devoted a couple of hours to the perusal of my books on golf and copied out, on a scale sufficiently small to be easily carried in the pocket, a map of the St Magnus links for use on the morrow. A glance at this before each stroke would show me all the concealed hazards with which this admirably-laid-out course abounds. The idea is, I believe, a new one, and I present it gratuitously to all golfers who peruse this veracious history.

Dinner at the Metropole on Sundays is a more pretentious meal than on weekdays. Game, cooked to a rag, figures on the menu, as also a profuse dessert of the cheaper and not quite ripe fruits of the season. Why this should be is not quite clear, as the golfer is robbed of his wonted exercise on a Sunday, and therefore should be lightly fed. It may be that in view of the spiritual rations dealt out to the immortal part of man that day, the hotel proprietor, in the spirit of competition which becomes his second nature, feels it incumbent on him to provide for the mortal interior with a prodigality that will bear comparison. Be that as it may, I did full justice to my host's catering, seeing it out to the bitter end, and banishing my depression with a bottle of the 'Boy' and a few glasses of a port which was officially dated '64. It may have been that this wine had reached the sober age claimed for it, but to my palate, at least, it seemed to retain all the juvenile vigour and rough precocity of a wine still in its infancy.

About 10 p.m. I proceeded to the smoking-room and stretched myself luxuriously on a couch in front of a blazing fire, only to find that rest was not possible, and that I was the victim of what Scotch folk so aptly term the 'fidgets'. First, it appeared that I had been wrong to cross the right leg over the left, and I accordingly reversed the position. The momentary ease secured by this change was succeeded by a numbness in the right elbow which demanded that I should turn over on my left side. But this movement led to a stiffening of the neck, unaccountable yet unmistakable, and I turned for relief to the broad of my back, only to start a sudden and most irritating tickling in the sole of my right foot. I endured these tortures in silence for a time, attributing them, rightly, I imagine, to the fact that I had had no exercise during the day. The culminating point, however, was reached when the tickling sensation incontinently transferred itself to the back, suggesting to my now maddened imagination two prickly-footed scorpions golfing between my shoulder blades. I scraped myself, after the manner of cattle, against the wooden arms of the couch without obtaining appreciable relief, and finally sprang to my feet with a bound that startled a number of somnolent old gentlemen into wide-awake and indignant observation.

I must have exercise.

I drew aside one of the curtains and looked out on the night. The storm had somewhat abated, and the moon sailed brilliantly at intervals through the black and scudding clouds.

I decided on a walk, despite the weather and the lateness of the hour. I made for my room, arrayed myself, with Wetherby's assistance, in top-boots, mackintosh and sou'-wester, and thus armoured against the elements I sallied forth into the wild and eerie night.

As I left the doors of the hotel eleven solemn clangs from the parish church warned me of the approaching 'witching hour of night'.

The town, despite the fact that most of the town councillors are interested in the local gas company, is extremely badly lighted; and by the time I had passed the hospitable and inviting rays that streamed from the doors and lamps of the clubhouse, I was practically in the dark.

I took the road that extends along the cliffs to the harbour, at times compelled to probe for and feel my way, at times guided by fitful splashes of moonlight. And the scene when the moon chose to break through her pall-like veil was superb. Before me, in cold and inky outline, stood the ruined towers and windows of cathedral and castle; to the left the sea, in a riot of black and white, still hurled itself with unabated fury against the adamant rocks and along the unresisting beach. The sky was an ever-changing canopy of black and sullen grey, sparsely streaked with rifts of gleaming silver. Great trees bent and creaked on my right, flinging, as in a perspiration of midnight fear, great drops on the roadway below, sighing and screaming as if the horrid winds were whispering ghastly tales to their sobbing and tear-stained leaves, tales not to be breathed in the light of day.

A profound sense of awe stole over me as, riveted by the scene each passing glimpse of the moon revealed, I stood my ground from time to time, and held my breath in a frame of mind quite foreign to my experience.

[Here again will be observed the literary elegance of my gifted colleague. The preceding paragraphs have been evolved from my simple statement, 'It was a beastly wet night.' J. W. W. G.]

So slow had been my progress that almost an hour must have passed before I reached the gates of the ruined castle. As I stood gazing up at the weather-beaten heights, faintly limned against the flying clouds, I became conscious of a sudden and strange atmospheric change. The gale inexplicably died; the trees hushed themselves into a startling silence; the moon crept behind an enormous overhanging mountain of clouds; and warm, humid and oppressive air replaced the sea-blown easterly winds. A great and portentous stillness prevailed around me, broken only by a dull moaning – as of a soul in agony – from the sea.

The effect was awful.

I strained eyes and ears in an ecstasy of anxiety. I knew not what was awaiting me, and yet knew of a certainty that I was about to face some strange revelation of the night.

Above all a great and overpowering horror of the dead was in me.

I tried to retrace my steps and found myself immovable, a living and breathing statue clutching the iron bars of the castle gate, waiting – waiting for what?

Could it be that I, this quivering, powerless, quaking creature, was indeed John William Wentworth G –

Crash! – Crash!!

Within, as it seemed to me, a few feet of where I stood, a mighty blue and blinding flame shot out from the massive pile of clouds, firing sea and land with livid and fearsome light. Crash upon crash, roar upon roar of such thunder as I pray I may never hear again, struck up into the heights of the heavens and down again to the resounding rocks and ruins that fronted me. They broke in deafening awful blows upon my ear and stunned me. In a moment of utter collapse I fell through the gate, and lay with closed eyes on the soaking turf within. But closed eyes had no power to keep out such burning fire, and each blue flash came piercing through the eyelids.

Gasping, and with a supreme and almost superhuman effort, I staggered to my feet and opened my eyes in bewildered and fearful expectation.

And what was the wild, weird thing I saw?

At the entrance to the castle, just beyond the drawbridge, holding aloft a wrought-iron lamp of ecclesiastical design that burnt with a sputtering and spectral flame, stood the red-robed figure of a ghostly cardinal!

With a wildly beating heart I recognised at a glance the face of the long dead Cardinal Smeaton, the cardinal whose portrait had arrested my eyes at Lowchester House!

8

The Cardinal's Chamber

I shivered in every limb, and a cold beady dew sprang out on my temples as I stood with eyes riveted on the spectral figure before me. The light from the lamp fell on the left side of the cardinal's head with a weird and Rembrandt-like effect, revealing a face with the tightly stretched grey-blue skin of the dead, and a fiercely flashing eye that seemed to divine the fear and horror that possessed me. Never to my dying day shall I forget that awful burning eye, glowing in what seemed to be the face of a corpse. I saw in its depths a grim triumph, a sardonic rapture, and a hideous relish of the blind horror betrayed in my blanched and streaming face.

The faded *vieux-rose* robes of the cardinal (through which, as it seemed to me, I could faintly see the grey walls of the castle) only served to heighten the unearthly pallor of the face.

I swayed to and fro in the weakness of a sudden fever. My dry lips bit the air. I raised a hand to my eyes to shut out the appalling sight; but of strength I had none, and my arm dropped nervelessly to my side. Presently – and I almost shrieked aloud as I saw it – his thin but redly gleaming lips moved, displaying a set of yellow and wolfish teeth.

'Come,' he said, in hollow yet imperious tones; 'it's a sair nicht, and there is shelter within.'

I swayed to and fro in the weakness of a sudden fever

'No! no!' I cried, in an agony of fearful apprehension. But even as I spoke I moved mechanically towards him, and no words can convey the horror with which I realised my unconscious advance.

The wind shrieked out anew, and a deluge of sudden rain beat down from the clouds above.

Nearer and nearer I drew, with staring eyes and parted lips, until, as I found myself within a few feet of the ghastly thing, I stretched out my hands towards it in mute and awestricken appeal.

In a moment the cardinal's right hand shot out and fixed an icy grasp on my left wrist. I shivered violently to the very marrow, stricken powerless as a little child. The calm of despair came to me. I moved as in a dream. I was conscious that I was absolutely in the power of a spirit of the dead.

A flash of lightning and a crash of thunder heralded our entrance beneath the portcullis gate of the ruins.

I dared not look at the cardinal's face. My eyes I kept on the ground, and I noted in a dreamily unconscious way the yellow pointed shoes of my ghostly guide as they slipped noiselessly from beneath the flowing draperies. At times, through his robes, I seemed to see glimpses of a white skeleton, and my teeth chattered loudly at the fearsome sight.

We had passed into the shelter of the archway that led to the open courtyard of the castle, and on our right was a doorway that opened into a dark and damp recess.

Into this I was dragged, the bony fingers of His Eminence still eating into my throbbing wrist. At the distant end of the recess the cardinal pressed with the open palm of his disengaged hand (for he had set down the lamp) a keystone that stood out an inch or so from the dripping and moss-grown wall. In immediate answer to the pressure a great block in the wall moved slowly inwards, revealing a faintly lit staircase with a spiral descent, evidently cut through solid rock. This we descended, I half slipping, half dragged, until at length we reached a chamber lighted almost brilliantly with flickering tapers, and furnished in what had once no doubt been sumptuous fashion.

Here the cardinal closed the old oak and iron-studded door with a clang that resounded eerily behind me, and releasing my almost frozen wrist, seated himself with grave dignity in a carved chair of ancient and pontifical design.

I looked around me.

The chamber, some sixteen feet square, was vaulted in the manner of a crypt, and the roofing stones were painted in frescoes, each panel representing the coat-of-arms of some old Catholic family. The walls were hung with faded and moth-eaten tapestry, depicting scenes of wild carousal, wherein nymphs, satyrs and bacchantes disported themselves with cup and vine leaf to the piping of a figure that closely resembled his satanic majesty. In one corner of the room stood a prie-dieu, and above it a broken and almost shapeless crucifix, overgrown with a dry, lichen-like moss and shrouded in cobwebs. In front of this, depending from the roof, swung an incense burner that emitted a faint green light and an overpowering and sickly aromatic vapour.

The floor was of plain, dull granite in smooth slabs, from which a cold sweat seemed to exude. The four chairs were of carved oak, with the high pointed backs of the cathedral stall, and on either side of each tall candles burned with sepulchral flames of yellow and purple.

In the centre was a small square table of oak, the legs of which were carved to represent hideous and snakelike monsters, and on it stood a skull, a book and an hour-glass.

A sense of disconcerting creepiness was diffused throughout the chamber by the fact that it was overrun by numerous immense spiders, some red, some yellow and others black. Indeed, so ubiquitous were these horrid creatures that once or twice I fancied I saw them running up and down the faint white lines of His Eminence's skeleton. But as the cardinal himself evinced no signs of inconvenience from these intimate and presumably tickling recreations, I concluded that they were the fevered creations of my own heated imagination.

Another strange thing was that through the apparently material appointments of the chamber, I could dimly, yet undoubtedly, see the rough, dripping walls of the solid rock; and when, by the cardinal's invitation, I seated myself on one of the chairs facing him, I was conscious that I passed, as it were, through it, and actually sat on a wet stone, of which the chair was seemingly but a ghostly and ineffective covering.

There was a certain sense of relief in this, for I argued that if my surroundings had no substance, no more probably had the cardinal or the spiders. And yet a glance at my wrist showed me the livid imprints of His Eminence's bony fingers.

Presently I ventured to let my gaze fall on the cardinal, and was somewhat relieved to note in his otherwise inscrutable face a distinct twinkle of amusement. The corners of his lips suggested an appreciation of humour; and his eyes betrayed an ill-concealed merriment as, from time to time, I shifted uneasily on my seat in an endeavour to find the driest part of it.

I was reflecting on the strange calm that was gradually coming to me – for, oddly enough, I began to lose the overwhelming sense of terror that a few minutes before had possessed me – when my ghostly companion broke the silence, speaking in profound and dignified tones.

'When the moon is at the full, gude sir, and eke the tide is low, a body that speirs within the castle gates maun e'en be guest o' mine.'

I did not quite understand this, but feeling it to be an announcement that demanded a response of some sort, I replied respectfully, if somewhat feebly, 'Quite so.'

That my answer did not altogether satisfy His Eminence seemed apparent, for after regarding me in contemplative silence for a moment he uttered the portentous words, 'I'm tellin' ye!'

I quite felt that it was my turn to say something, but for the life of me I could not focus my ideas. At length, with much diffidence, and with a distinct tremor in my voice, I murmured, 'I fear I'm inconveniencing Your Eminence by calling at so late an hour.'

At this the cardinal lay back in his chair and laughed consumedly for the space of at least a minute.

'Gude sake!' cried he at last. 'The Sassenach is glib eneuch tae jest; wi' deeficulty nae doot, as indeed befits the occasion!'

It will be observed that my ghostly prelate spoke in broad Scotch, much as Kirkintulloch did, with, however, the difference that is lent to speech by cultured cadences and a comparatively exhaustive vocabulary. From the unexpected laughter with which my diffident remark had been received, I instinctively derived a cue. It seemed to me that the cardinal appreciated the subdued effrontery that I now perceived in my words, though at the moment of their utterance, heaven knows, I only intended to convey extreme humility and deference. So I hazarded a question.

'May I ask,' I ventured, with deferential gravity, 'what keeps Your Eminence up so late?'

'Hech! sir,' was the reply. 'That's what liteegious folk would ca' a leadin' question. Forbye, I'm no just at leeberty tae tell ye. Ye see, folk maun work oot their ain salvation, and it's no permitted to the likes o' me, a wanderer in the speerit, to acquaint mortal man wi' information as to the existence of heaven, hell, purgatory, or – or otherwise.'

'Then,' I timidly pursued, with a good deal of hesitation, and

beating about the bush to find appropriate terms, 'I presume I have
the – the – honour of addressing a – a spirit?'

'Jist that,' responded the cardinal, with a sort of jocose cordiality
that was very reassuring and comforting.

His whole manner had incredibly changed, and was now calculated
to set one at ease, at least as far as might be between one
representative of the quick and another of the dead. So conspicuously
was this the case that I soon found the fear and horror that at first had
so completely overwhelmed me replaced by an absorbing and
inquisitive interest.

9

His Eminence and I

'From the exalted ecclesiastical position held in life by Your
Eminence,' I presently found myself saying, 'I feel justified in
assuming that you are now enjoying the well-merited reward of
residence in heaven.'

The cardinal eyed me shrewdly for a moment, and eventually
replied in diplomatic but evasive terms, 'I'm obleeged for the
coampliment, be it merited or otherwise; but I'm na' disposed tae
enter into ony personal exposeetion of my speeritual career. This,
however, I'm constrained to tell ye, that nine-tenths o' the clergy and
pious laity of a' creeds, at present in the enjoyment o' life, will be fair
dumbfounded when they shuffle off this moartal coil, and tak'
possession of the immortal lodgin' provided for them – lodgin's that
hae scant resemblance to the tangible Canaans of their quasi-
releegious but businesslike imaginations. Catholic and Protestant
alike, they're a' under the impression that releegion is a profession
for the lips and no' for the lives. As for Presbyterians, aweel! they'll
find oot in guid time the value o' their dour pride in hard and
heartless piety. They ken fine hoo tae mak' a bargain in siller wi' their
neebors, but the same perspicacity 'll no' avail them when it comes
tae – but Hoots! It's nae business o' mine.' Then, as if to change the
subject, he added, 'I suppose ye've read a' aboot me in the histories of
Scotland?'

'Well,' I replied, 'I've read a good deal about Your Eminence. I've
often pictured you sitting at a window of the castle, watching with
grim enjoyment young Dishart burning at the stake.'

It was an unwise remark to make, and I saw the cardinal's eye flash balefully.

'Yer speech,' he answered slowly and with dignity, 'is no' in the best of taste, but it affords me an opportunity of explaining that misrepresented circumstance. Ye see, from a lad upwards, I was aye fond of a bonfire, and what for was I no' to watch the bonny red flames loupin' up forenenst the curlin' smoke? Was that pleasure tae be denied me, a' because a dwaibly manbody ca'd Dishart was frizzlin' on the toap? Na, na, guid sir, I was glowering at the bonny flames, no' at Dishart. I saw Dishart, nae doot; still, and there had no' been a fire, I wouldna hae lookit.'

During this speech my attention had been somewhat distracted by the creepy spectacle of two spiders, one red, one black, fighting viciously on one of His Eminence's white ribs. The sight affected me so disagreeably that I felt constrained to inform the cardinal of the unpleasant incident.

'Your Eminence will excuse me,' I said respectfully, 'but I see two poisonous-looking spiders diverting themselves on one of your ribs, the lowest but one on the left side.'

The cardinal smiled, but made no movement. 'I'm much obleeged,' he responded, with grave amusement. 'Nae doot ye're ruminatin' that sich internal gambols are no' compatible wi' the residence in heaven ye were guid eneuch to credit me wi'.' Then, with a certain air of resigned weariness, he added, 'Dinna mind them, they're daein' nae herm; ye canna kittle a speerit, ye ken.'

My seat was so extremely wet, and the damp was now penetrating my clothes in such an uncomfortable manner, that I resolved to assume an erect position at any cost. I may mention that we have rheumatism in our family. I cast about in my mind for a suitable reason for rising, and after some hesitation rose, remarking, 'Your Eminence will excuse me, but I feel it fitting that I should stand whilst a prelate of your exalted rank and undying celebrity' (this last, I thought, under the circumstances, a particularly happy inspiration) 'is good enough to condescend to hold intercourse with me.'

'Ay! Ye're guy wet,' replied the undying celebrity, with a grasp of the situation that I had not looked for.

I stood shifting about on my feet, conscious of a rather painful stiffness in my joints, and wondering when and how this extra-ordinary séance would draw to a close, when the cardinal, who had been lost for a time in the silence of a brown study, suddenly leaned forward in his chair and addressed me with an eager intensity that he had not displayed before.

'I'm gaun tae tell 'ee,' said he, 'what for I summoned ye here this nicht. Here!' he exclaimed, and rising he indicated the vaulted chamber with an imposing sweep of his gaunt arms and bony fingers, 'Here! In this ma *sanctum sanctorum*.'

He paused and eyed me steadily.

'I'm delighted, Your Eminence,' I murmured feebly.

'Ye'll be mair than delighted, I'm thinkin',' he continued, 'when ye ken ma purpose; the whilk is this. The moarn's moarn ye're playin', an I'm no mistaken, a match at goalf agin a callant ca'd Jim Lindsay?'

'That is so,' I answered, in vague bewilderment at this sudden reference to a standing engagement in real life. For a moment a wild doubt swept over me. Was I living or dead? The dampness of my trousers gave a silent answer in favour of the former condition.

'Aweel!' resumed the cardinal, 'I'd have 'ee ken that he's a descendant in the straight line o' ane o' my maist determined foes – ye'll understand I'm referrin' tae sich time as I was Cardinal

I stood shifting about on my feet

Airchbishop o' St Magnus in the flesh – and ony blow that I can deal tae ane o' his kith is a solace to ma hameless and disjasket speerit. Noo, in ma day, I was unrivalled as a gowfer; there wasna ma equal in the land. Nane o' the coortiers frae Holyrood were fit tae tee a ba' tae me. It's a fac'. And here – here ma gentleman!' (and the cardinal sank his voice to the low tremulous wail of a sepulchral but operatic spectre, and his eyes gleamed with the sudden and baleful light that had first so riveted my gaze), 'ahint the arras in this verra chamber is concealed ma ain bonny set of clubs!'

He paused and scrutinised

my face to observe the effect of this announcement. I accordingly assumed an expression of intense interest.

'Noo,' he continued, his eyes blazing with vindictive triumph, 'I'm gaun tae lend ye this verra set o' clubs, an' I guarantee that an ye play wi' them ye'll win the day. D'ye hear that?'

'It is extremely good of you,' I murmured hurriedly.

'Hoots! It's mair for ma ain gratification than for yours. In addeetion I'll be wi' ye on the links, but veesible to nane but yersel. Ye'll wun the day, and fair humeeliate the varmint spawn o' my ancient foe; and, eh! guid sir, but these auld bones will fair rattle wi' the pleesure o't! Will 'ee dae't?'

'I will,' I solemnly replied. What else could I have said?

'Then hud yer wheest whiles I fetch the clubs.'

With this His Eminence turned to the tapestry behind him, and, drawing it aside, disclosed a deep and narrow cavity in the rock. From this he extracted, one by one, a set of seven such extraordinarily unwieldy-looking golf clubs that I felt it in me to laugh aloud. Needless to say I indulged in no such folly. I examined them one by one with apparent interest and simulated appreciation, as, fondling them lovingly, my companion expatiated on their obviously obsolete beauties. A strange and almost pathetic enthusiasm shone in his eyes.

'Nane o' yer new-fangled clubs for me,' cried the cardinal; 'they auld things canna be bate. Tak' them wi' ye back tae whaur ye bide; bring them to the links the moarn's moarn, and as sure as we stand here this nicht – or moarn, fur the brak o' day is close at haun' – I'll be wi' ye at the first tee, tae witness sic a game o' gowf as never mortal played before. But eh! guid sir, as ye'd conserve yer body and soul frae destruction and damnation, breathe nae word o' this queer compact tae man, wumman or bairn. Sweer it, man, sweer it on this skull!'

His bloodless hands extended the grinning skull towards me, and I, repressing an involuntary shudder, stooped and kissed it.

A gleam of malignant triumph again lit up his face as I took the oath. Then he seized the weird-looking clubs, and, caressing them with loving care, muttered to himself reminiscences of bygone years.

'Ay, fine I mind it,' he cried, 'when young Ruthven came gallivantin' tae St Magnus, and thocht his match was naewhere tae be foond. We had but five holes in thae days, ye ken, and ilka yin a mile in length. Hech, sir! what a match was that! I dinged him doon wi' three up and twa tae play. Ye'll no be disposed to gie me credence, but it's a fact that I did yin hole in seventeen!'

'That was unfortunate,' I replied, mistaking his meaning.

'Ay, for Ruthven,' was his quick and peevish rejoinder. 'For he took thirty-seven and lost the hole.'

I had not grasped that he considered his own score extremely good.

'Of course I meant for Ruthven,' I stammered, with the vague and silly smile of clumsy apology.

'Ye didna,' replied His Eminence; 'but I'm no mindin'. Ruthven, wi' a' his roughness, was an affectit callant in thae days, and rode his horse atween ilka shot. He moonted and dismoonted seeventy-fower times in three holes that day.' And the cardinal chuckled loud and long.

He related many other tales of his prowess with great gusto and enjoyment. We were now on such unaccountably familiar terms that I ventured to tell him of the marvellous goal I had won, playing for the Lahore Polo Cup in '62, when, of a sudden, he interrupted me, crying out, 'The oor is late! Ye maun hae a sleep. Awa! man, awa! For ony sake, tak' the set and awa!'

And indeed I needed no second invitation; so, seizing the seven weird clubs, I made a low obeisance to His Eminence, and turning, found the door behind me open. I fled up the stone-cut staircase, passed like a flash through the recess to the archway, and, with a cry of such delight as surely never greeted mortal ears, I hailed the faintly dawning day. With the joy of a captive set free, or the rapture of one who has returned from a living tomb to bustling life, I inhaled the precious air in deep lung-filling draughts.

The storm had passed, the sea was calm, birds twittered in the gently whispering trees, the world was waking, and I was on its broad earth again.

But my thoughts were chaos. My brain refused to work. I had but one desire, and that was to sleep. In wretched plight I reached the doors of the hotel, where the astounded night porter eyed me, and more particularly the hockey-stick-like clubs, with a questioning surprise and bated breath.

I made him bring me a stiff glass of hot whisky and water. This revived me somewhat, and telling him to warn my servant not to call me before 10 a.m., I staggered to my room, flung the clubs with a sudden, if scarcely surprising, abhorrence into a wardrobe, got out of my dripping clothes into welcome pyjamas, and, pulling the bed-clothes up to my chin, was soon at rest in a dreamless sleep.

10

The Fateful Morning

I woke to find sunshine streaming in at the windows, a cloudless sky without, and my servant Wetherby busily occupied over his customary matutinal duties.

With a sudden flash of memory I recalled the weird scene of the night that was gone, only, however, to dismiss it as an unusually vivid dream. For a time I felt quite sure it was nothing more. But presently, as my eye fell on the empty glass that had held the hot whisky and water, I began to experience an uneasy doubt.

Ah! Now I remembered!

If it were a dream, there would be no clubs in the wardrobe.

I lit a cigarette, and asked Wetherby the time.

'Ten o'clock, sir,' was the reply; 'and you've no time to lose, sir. The match is at eleven.'

I sprang from bed, and casually opened the wardrobe.

Good heavens! It was no dream! There they were! Seven of the queerest clubs that antiquarian imagination could conceive.

So it had actually happened! I had been the guest of cardinal Smeaton's ghost, and had entered into a compact with him to use his ridiculous clubs in order that he might revel in a trumpery revenge on the house of Lindsay.

Be hanged if I would! I remembered vaguely that in law an oath exacted from a party by threat or terror was not held to be binding, and I determined to ignore my unholy bond with the shadowy prelate. I would play with my own clubs and be defeated like a man.

I jumped into my bath. The pure morning air swept through the open window, the sunlight streamed in on the carpet and danced in circles of glancing gold in the clear cold water of the bath, and a glow of health and vigour (despite the late hours I had kept) sent the blood tingling through my veins. Indeed, what with the ordinary routine of dressing, my servant's presence, the hum of life that came from the links, the footsteps of housemaid and boots hurrying past my door, and generally my accustomed surroundings, I found it all but impossible to believe that I had really gone through the strange experiences of a few hours ago.

Yet, undoubtedly, there stood the clubs. Curious and perplexing ideas flashed through my mind as I dressed, ideas that clashed against or displaced each other with kaleidoscopic rapidity.

Was such an oath binding? Was the whole incident a dream, and the presence of the clubs an unexplainable mystery? Was there mental eccentricity on either side of my family? Had my father, the son of a hundred earls (or, more correctly, of as many as can be conveniently crowded into a period of a hundred years), transmitted to me some disconcerting strain in the blue blood that filled my veins; or, had my mother, with her less important but more richly gilt lineage, dowered me with a plebeian taint of which absurd superstition was the outcome? Or had the combination of both produced in myself a decadent creature abashed at his first intro-duction to the supernatural? How could I tell? Was there really a spectral world, and I its victim? Was I reaping the harvest of years of cynical unbelief? Was I myself? And, if not, who was I?

I gave it up.

I determined to ignore and if possible to forget entirely my creepy adventure in the vaults of the ruined castle. In this endeavour I was assisted by the pangs of healthy hunger. There is something so homely, so accustomed, so matter-of-fact in a good appetite, that I felt less awed by the unwilling oath I had taken when Wetherby announced that an omelette and a broiled sole were awaiting me in the next room.

I was endeavouring to force into my tie and collar one of those aggravating pins that bend but never break, and alternately wounding my neck and forefinger in the process, when, through the open window, my eye fell on a dense and apparently increasing crowd that surged on the links behind the first teeing ground. A dozen men held a rope that must have measured close on a hundred yards, and behind it the entire population of the town seemed to be gathering.

What could it be? Possibly a popular excursion, a public holiday or a big professional match.

I asked Wetherby.

'I understand, sir,' replied that phlegmatic youth, 'the crowd is gatherin' in anticipation of your match with Mr Lindsay, sir.'

'Oh! Is it?' I murmured vaguely.

'It's been talked about considerable, sir.'

'Has it?' was all the comment I could muster.

I was appalled at the sight. There was a horribly expectant air in the crowd. Their faces had that deadly going-to-be-amused expression that I have seen in the spectators at a bull fight in Spain. Many eager faces were turned in the direction of my windows, and I shrank instinctively into the seclusion that a muslin curtain affords.

That dim recollection of the bull fight I had seen in Cadiz haunted me. Was I to be a golfing bull?

Or was Lindsay?

Was I to be the golfing equivalent of the wretched horse that eventually is gored to death, to the huge delight of thousands of butcher-souled brutes?

Well, if so, they would see a bold front. I'd show no craven spirit.

I began to wonder if the seven queer clubs had the properties that the cardinal claimed for them. And then an idea seized me. I would have them near me on the links, and if the game went desperately against me I'd put them to the test.

'Wetherby,' I said, as I put the finishing twist to my moustache, 'I should like you to carry these odd-looking clubs round the links in case I want them. I don't propose to use them, but it is just possible that I might.'

'Yes, sir.'

I handed him a capacious canvas bag. I had purchased three similar bags from Kirkintulloch by his advice: one for fine weather, a second for wet and the third (which I now gave Wetherby), an immense one for travelling. Kirkintulloch had informed me that without these my equipment as a golfer was incomplete.

'I don't wish them to be seen, unless it happens that I decide to use them, so you needn't follow me too closely,' I added.

'I understand, sir.'

'But you'll be at hand should occasion arise?'

'Certainly, sir.'

And shouldering the seven unwieldy weapons, Wetherby left the room with a twinkle in his eye that I had never remarked before.

I took another furtive glance at the crowd, and my heart gave a leap as I saw way being made for a party that included Mrs Gunter and Lord and Lady Lowchester.

I passed mechanically to my sitting-room and sat down to breakfast.

I began to eat.

Thanks to the discipline of daily habit, my hands and jaws performed their accustomed tasks, but my mind was in a condition alternately comatose and chaotic, so much so that it was a matter of surprise to me when I found my eyes resting on the bones of my sole and the sloppery trail of a departed omelette.

I drained my coffee to the dregs and lit a cigarette.

I began to feel a sense of importance. The knowledge that one's personality is of interest to a crowd is always stimulating, but I was haunted with the uncomfortable reflection that sometimes a crowd is bent on jeering, not to say jostling. Ah! if only I could manage that those who came to laugh remained to – well to laugh at the other man.

Presently the door opened and Wetherby presented himself, with the smug deference for which I paid wages at the rate of sixty pounds a year.

'Mr Lindsay's compliments, sir, and if you are ready, sir, he is.'

'I am coming,' I replied, as, passing a napkin across my lips, I pulled myself together for the impending ordeal.

As I walked through the hall of the hotel I saw that the entire domestic staff had gathered together to witness my exit. There was an uncomfortable sort of suppressed merriment in their faces that was not encouraging. The waiter who attended me at meals had the refined impertinence to blush as I passed. The boots seized his lips with two blacking-black hands, as if to deny his face the satisfaction of an insubordinate smile. A beast of a boy in buttons winked, and the general manager bowed to me with a deference so absurdly overdone as to be extremely unconvincing.

I passed through the folding doors; and stood on the steps of the hotel facing the crowd.

A tremendous cheer greeted me. When I say 'cheer', possibly I don't quite convey what I mean. It was more of a roar. It was a blend of delight, expectation, amusement, derision and exhilaration. Every face was smiling, every mouth open, every eye glistening. As the first hoarse echoes died a sound of gratified mumbling succeeded, as when the lions at the zoo, having bellowed at the first glimpse of their food, merely pant and lick their lips till the raw meat is flung to them.

Kirkintulloch was waiting for me at the foot of the steps. He looked a trifle shamefaced, I thought, and I fancied I heard him say to a bystander as I went towards him, 'Aweel, it's nae business o' mine!'

Presently it pleased the mob to adopt a facetious tone, and as Kirkintulloch elbowed a passage for me through the crowd, I heard on all sides cries of, 'Here comes the champion!' 'He's guy jaunty-like!' 'Eh! but he looks awfy fierce!' 'Gude luck ti ye, ma man!' 'He's a born gowfer!' 'Gude sakes! He's a braw opeenion o' himsel'!' 'The puir lamb's awa tae the slaughter!' 'It's an ill day this for Jim Lindsay!' (this with a blatant laugh intended to convey irony). 'Ay! His pride'll hae a fa', nae doot!' and the like.

11

An Expectant Crowd

Of a sudden my heart stood still, and for a moment I stopped dead. There in front of me, and approaching by a series of jinks and dives amid the crowd, was the ghostly figure of the cardinal. Faint and ill-defined as the apparition seemed in the brilliant sunshine, there was no mistaking the cadaverous features or the flowing robes. In less time than it takes to tell, he had reached my side and was whispering into my ear.

'Dinna mind thae folk,' he said, 'they'll sing anither tune afore the day's dune. And dinna mind me. I'm no veesible to livin' soul but yersell, and nane but yer ain ears can hear what I'm sayin'. But if ye've a mind tae speak tae me, a' ye've got tae dae is to *thenk*; tae speak in-tae yersel, as it were; for I can thole the jist o' yer thochts, wi' no sae muckle as a soond frae yer lips.'

I was flabbergasted.

'Sic a clanjamfray o' vermin!' he added, as he swept a contemptuous glance over the noisy mob.

But his presence exasperated me beyond endurance. My nerves were strung to all but the breaking strain, and I found a relief in venting my spleen on this self-appointed colleague of mine.

'Look here,' I said, and I was at no pains to conceal my ill-humour, 'I'm fed up with you! You understand, I'm sick of you and your devilish wiles. I'm no longer in your power, and I snap my fingers at you. Get out!'

I had neglected His Eminence's instructions only to *think* when I addressed him, and the crowd naturally regarded my words as a sally in reply to its own ponderous wit.

The result was a babel of words, furious, jocular, jeering.

'Did ye ever hear the like?' 'Ay! Did ye hear him say "deevilish wiles"? An' this a Presbyterian toon forbye!' 'Mercy on us! An' ma man an elder in Dr MacBide's kirk!' 'Awa wi' the bairns; a'll no hae their ears contaaminated,' and so on.

'Hoots toots!' was the cardinal's response, 'and you a gentleman! I'm fair ashamed o' ye. But ye canna win awa' frae yer oath, ye ken. It wad mean perdeetion to yer soul an ye did, though I'm far frae assertin' that ye'll no receive that guerdon as it is.'

I stopped again, with the intention of arguing out the point once and for all, when I realised that if I went on addressing this invisible spectre, I might possibly be mistaken for a madman. I therefore contented myself with a withering glance of abhorrence at the prelate, and a few unspoken words to the effect that nothing in heaven or earth would induce me to have further truck with him. I then walked calmly on, but I was conscious of the ghostly presence dogging my steps with grim persistence, and several times I heard the never-to-be-forgotten voice mutter, 'Ay! We'll jist see,' or 'M'hm! Is he daft, I wonder?'

At last I reached the inner circle of the crowd, and at the teeing ground Lindsay came forward, looking, I am bound to admit, the picture of manly health and vigour.

He held out his hand.

I accepted it with dignity, then looked about me, bowing here and there as I recognised acquaintances. This section of the crowd showed signs of better breeding. There was neither vulgar laughter nor insolent jeering. On the contrary, its demeanour was so extremely grave as to suggest to my sensitive imagination a suspicion of covert irony. I recognised many celebrities of the golfing world. There was Grayson, who wept if he missed a put, and spent his evenings in chewing the cud of his daily strokes to the ears of his depressed but resigned family. There too was Twinkle, the founder of the Oxbridge Golf Club, whose 'style' was as remarkable as his mastery of the technical 'language' of the game. Near him was General Simpkins, who, having had a vast experience of fighting on the sandy plains of the Sahara, now employed his old age in exploring the sandy tracts of the St Magnus bunkers so assiduously that he seldom, if ever, played a stroke on the grass. He was one of the many golfers who find a difficulty in getting up a 'foursome'. Not far off was Sir William Wilkins, another notable enthusiast, whose scores when playing alone are remarkably low, though he seldom does a hole in less than eight strokes if playing in a game or under the scrutiny of a casual onlooker. I nodded to Mr Henry Grove, the celebrated actor-manager, and a keen golfer. I didn't know that he was celebrated when first I met him, but I gathered it from the few minutes' conversation that passed between us.

Standing near the Lowchesters was Mrs Gunter, in a heavenly confection of shell-pink and daffodil-yellow, a sort of holiday frock, delicate in tint and diaphanous as a sufficiently modest spider's web. She greeted me with the brightest of smiles, and laughingly kissed her fingertips to me. Certainly she was the most charming woman present. Her bright colour and gleaming hair seemed to defy the wind and sunshine, though I fancy that rain might have proved a trifle inconvenient. There was no manner of doubt that I loved her. She represented to me a sort of allegorical figurehead symbolising affluence, luxury and independence. That is, assuming that she would consent to occupy the central niche in my own ambitious temple of matrimony.

Even the University of St Magnus was represented in the gathering by a group of its professors, rusty-looking gentlemen who betrayed no indication of anything so trivial as a bygone youth; but, on the contrary, closely resembled a number of chief mourners at the funeral of their own intellects. A notable figure was the genial and cultured Dr MacBide, one of the ablest and most popular divines that Scotland has given to the world, one in whom is to be found the rare combination of an aesthetic soul allied to a fearless character, a man who, keeping one eye on heaven and the other on earth, has used both to the benefit of the world in general and St Magnus in particular.

Mr Monktown, the more or less distinguished politician, was also in the crowd. His eyes had the faraway look of a minor celebrity on whom has been forced the conviction that due recognition of his talents will never be found this side of the grave. On the other hand, his charming and brilliant wife conveys the impression that she will continue lustily to insist on the aforesaid recognition until a peerage or some such badge of notoriety is administered as a narcotic by a peace-at-any-price premier.

But to enumerate all the interesting people in the dense crowd is an impossible task. Suffice it to say that such a constellation of golfing stars could be seen only on the links of St Magnus, with perhaps the single exception of those of St Andrews.

How little did the crowd guess that, unruffled and confident as I seemed, I yet knew that I was destined for a humiliating defeat; and how much less did I know what a bitter thing is defeat to a man of my sanguine temperament and former achievements!

The Match Begins

I was startled from a brief brown study by the sound of Lindsay's voice.

'Shall we toss for the honour?'

'As you please,' I replied.

He spun a coin.

'Head or tail?'

I chose the head.

'It's a tail,' he said, as, pocketing the coin, he took the driver that his caddie handed.

Then he drove. It was a magnificent shot, straight and sure, and the ball landed halfway between the public road and the stream that bounds the first putting green. A murmur of approval rose from the crowd.

Then I took up position.

Again a murmur arose from the crowd, but not a reassuring one.

Kirkintulloch endeavoured to inspire me with confidence as he handed me my driver by whispering in a hoarse, spirituous undertone that must have been audible to everyone near, 'Dinna mind the crowd, sir. Just pretend that ye *caan goalf*.'

I was about to address the ball when my eye caught sight of the cardinal. His face was livid with rage, and I could barely repress a chuckle as he shrieked in a voice that apparently only reached my ears (for the crowd never budged), 'Tak' the auld clubs, I tell 'ee!'

Afraid of betraying myself by vacant look or startled mien, I ignored His Eminence's fury, and precipitately drove the ball.

I topped it.

It shot along the ground, hurling itself against casual stones, as if under the impression that I was a billiard player desirous of making a break in cannons.

Then we moved on.

As we walked over the hundred yards that my ball had travelled, the cardinal sidled up to me, and thrusting his face (through which I could clearly see a view of beach and sea) close to mine, exclaimed, 'Ye're a fule!'

I took no notice. I was beginning to enjoy the discomfiture of one who had caused me such acute sufferings a few hours before.

'D'ye hear?' he persisted. 'Wi' yer ain clubs ye're no match for a callant like Lindsay! For ony sake, tak' mine. Are ye feared the folk'll laugh at sic antediluvian implements? Ye needna mind the mob, I assure ye. If ye win hole after hole, ye'll turn the laugh on Lindsay, nae maitter what the clubs be like. Forbye, there's yer oath.'

I still ignored him, and I saw the yellow teeth grind in silent fury.

Meantime, behind us plodded the crowd, the dull thud of their steps on the spongy grass almost drowned by their voluble and exasperating chatter.

There are no words in my vocabulary to express the humiliation that I felt as I played. I was at my worst. My second shot landed me about a hundred yards further; Lindsay dropped his on to the putting green. With my third the ball travelled to the burn and stopped there, embedding itself in the soft black mud. This incident afforded unbounded delight to the mob, and I fancied that I heard Mrs Gunter's silvery laugh. The only satisfaction that I experienced was in the uncontrollable rage of the cardinal. He danced and leapt about me, gesticulating wildly, alternately pouring sixteenth-century vituperation into my ears, and imploring me to use his accursed clubs. He even indulged in weeping on the off-chance of softening my heart, but I saw no pathos in the tears that flowed down his spectral cheek from eyes that never lost their vindictive glare.

Lindsay behaved extremely well. He showed no sign of triumph as he won hole after hole, and several times he turned upon the crowd and upbraided them roundly for the howls of laughter with which they received my miserable efforts. Kirkintulloch became gradually more and more depressed, and eventually took the line of a Job's comforter.

'It's jist as I tell't ye. He's layin' ye oot like a corp,' said he.

'Well, let him,' I growled.

'It's mesel' I'm thinkin' o'. Ye see I've a poseetion tae keep up. They a' ken I've been learnin' ye the game, forbye I'm the professional champion. I'll be fair howled at when I gang in tae the public hoose the nicht.'

'Then the simple remedy is not to go there,' I argued.

'Whaat? No gang tae the public hoose?'

I had apparently propounded a quite unheard-of course of action, but I stuck to it, and said, 'No.'

'Aweel,' he resumed, 'a' I can say is ye dinna ken oor faimily' (which was true). 'Ma faither never missed a nicht but what he was half-seas over in the Gowfer's Arms, an' it's no in my blood to forget the words, "Honour yer faither and mither," an' a' the rest o' it. So I just dae the same, and it's a grand tribute to the memory o' my kith and kin. Forbye – I like it. I canna sleep if I'm ower sober.'

I leave the reader to imagine my feelings as Kirkintulloch thus unfolded the hereditary tendencies of his family to one ear, and the cardinal poured violent anathemas into the other. The crowd was convulsed in spasms of derisive delight at each of my futile strokes, and certainly Mrs Gunter seemed furtively amused when I ventured to glance in her direction. Only Wetherby was unmoved. Bearing the cardinal's clubs, he followed me at a discreet distance, with an inscrutable expression that would have done credit to a priest of the Delphic Oracle.

I got into every possible bunker, to the noisy gratification of the mob which, despite the frequent remonstrances of the better class of people present, had now abandoned itself to the wildest hilarity. The match was, in fact, a harlequinade, with Lindsay as the clever clown and myself as the idiotic pantaloon.

I seemed to tread on air, with only a vague idea of what was going on. By a lucky fluke I won the short hole, albeit in a rather undignified manner. Mr Lindsay's caddie, though some distance off, was nevertheless slightly in front of me as I drove, and my ball (which I topped so that it shot away at right angles) struck his boot, on which Kirkintulloch loudly claimed the hole.

At the 'turn' (i.e. the end of the first nine holes) I was seven down; and at the end of the eighteen – let me confess it at once – Lindsay was sixteen up.

The first round over, the garrulous crowd dispersed in various directions, gabbling, cackling, laughing and howling with an absence of breeding truly astounding.

Even the 'society' section no longer concealed its amusement. I have never understood the limitations of that word 'society'. It seems to me such an elastic term nowadays that if a person says he is in it, then *ipso facto* he is. Formerly it applied exclusively to my own class, i.e. the aristocracy; but since we latter have taken to emulating the peculiarities and tendencies of the criminal classes we are possibly excluded.

An interval of an hour and a half was allowed for luncheon, and it was arranged that we should meet for the final round at 2.30 p.m.

I refused all invitations to lunch at the club or at private houses, and retired to a solitary meal in my own room.

But it was only solitary in a sense.

I had just begun to tackle a mutton cutlet and tomato sauce when, raising my eyes for a moment to look for the salt, I beheld my ubiquitous cardinal seated opposite me.

This was a little too much, and seizing a decanter of claret I hurled it in his face. His shadowy features offered so little resistance that the wine eventually distributed itself over Wetherby, who seemed for once mildly surprised.

I muttered an apology to that irreproachable domestic, explaining that the liquor was corked, and then I desired him to leave the room.

I was alone with my tormentor, and I determined to have it out with him. But His Eminence anticipated me, for whilst I was framing in my mind a declamatory and indignant exordium, he leaned across the table, and with a singularly suave voice and subdued manner addressed me as follows: 'I apologise, young sir, if I have caused you ony inconvenience on this momentous occasion. I was ower keen, an' I tak a' the blame o' yer ill fortune on ma ain shoulders. Just eat your denner like a man, and dinna fash yersel' wi' me; but when ye've feenished, an ye'll be sae gude as to hear me for the space of five meenits, I'll be obleeged. Mair than that, I'll undertake that ye'll no' be worrit by me again.'

This was an important offer, and a certain unexpected charm in my unbidden guest's suavity turned the balance in his favour.

'Do you mean,' I asked, 'that if I grant you a short interview when I have finished luncheon, you will undertake to cease annoying me with your enervating companionship and intemperate language?'

'That's it,' replied the prelate.

'Very good,' said I; 'I agree.'

I continued the meal. Wetherby returned with a fresh bottle of wine and a custard pudding, brought me cigarettes, coffee and Cognac in due course, and though in the discharge of his duties he frequently walked through the dim anatomy of my ecclesiastical patron, his doing so seemed to afford no inconvenience whatever to that perplexing prelate.

As I ate and drank in silence my red-robed friend paced the room with bent head and thoughtful mien, in the manner adopted by every Richelieu that I have seen on the stage. I fancied that I detected a wistful glance in his eyes as from time to time I raised a glass of wine to my lips, but I may have been mistaken.

It must seem odd to the matter-of-fact reader that I could golf, talk, eat, drink and generally comport myself as an ordinary mortal whilst haunted by this remarkable spectre; but the fact is, I had no choice in the matter. Suppose I had drawn the attention of my neighbours to the fact that I was pursued by a shadowy cardinal! It was abundantly clear that none but I could see him, and I should only have been laughed at. And, after all, a man of my varied experiences and quick intelligence adapts himself, through sheer force of habit, to any situation, though at the time he may utterly fail to comprehend its *raison d'être* or significance.

At one period of the meal I was on the point of asking Wetherby if he saw no faintly defined figure, robed in red and standing near him. But just as I was about to speak to him he advanced with the coffee, and in setting down the tray actually stood within the same cubic space that the cardinal occupied. That is to say, I distinctly saw them mixed up with each other, Wetherby passing in and out of the prelate's robes quite unconsciously. Nor did His Eminence seem to mind, for not only did the coffee and Cognac pass through the region of his stomach, but also the tray, cups, saucers and cigarettes.

13

I Test the Clubs

My luncheon over, I pushed back the plates, drank a glass of Cognac, poured out a cup of coffee and lit a cigarette.

The combined effects of the fresh air of the links and the moderately good wine I had drunk during lunch had braced me up, and as the first puff of pale blue smoke left my lips, I leaned back in my chair and contemplated my guest. 'Well, old man,' said I, with perhaps undue familiarity, 'out with it!'

He turned and swept me such a graceful bow that I felt a sheepish shame at the flippant and vulgar tone I had adopted.

'I will noo mak' ye a final proposal, young sir,' he said. 'Ahint the hotel is a secluded field, and if ye'll tak' ma clubs there and try a shot or two, I ask nae mair. If so be ye find a speecial virtue in them, gude and weel; if no', then a' thing is ower atween us, and the even tenour o' yer way'll no be interfered wi' by me.'

I saw what he meant. I was to try the clubs and test the marvellous qualities that he insisted on.

Well, there was no harm in that.

I rang the bell, and told Wetherby to carry the clubs to the field indicated by my ghostly counsellor.

It was a good grass meadow of some ten acres, and not a soul was near, with, of course, the exception of the cardinal. I teed a ball, and selecting a club that most resembled a driver (though it was more like a gigantic putter than anything else), I began to address the ball.

As I did so I experienced a curious sensation.

I suddenly felt as if I had been a golfer all my life. There was no longer any hesitation as to where my hands or feet should be. Instinctively I fell into the right attitude.

I was no longer self-conscious. I found myself addressing the ball with the same easy grace I had observed in Kirkintulloch. A sense of extraordinary power came over me. My legs and arms tingled as if some strong stimulant were flowing in my veins. The club had taken a mastery over me. I swung it almost involuntarily, and the first shot was by far the finest drive I had ever made. I tried again and yet again, six shots in all, and each was as straight and sure as the very best of Lindsay's.

I was amazed and dumbfounded.

'Weel! Did I no' tell ye?' cried the cardinal, as he hopped about in a grotesque and undignified ecstasy. 'Try the putter noo!'

Harry Furniss

I took the putter. It was something like a flat-headed croquet mallet, and very heavy. Then I threw a silver matchbox on the ground to represent a hole and began to putt.

I simply couldn't miss it. A sense of awe came over me.

No matter from what distance I played, nor how rough the ground was, the ball went straight to the box, as a needle to a magnet. I even tried to miss it and failed in the attempt.

I looked at His Eminence, and words fail me to describe the childish yet passionate exultation that shone in his face.

'I can dae nae mair!' he cried. 'Ye see what they're like. Play wi' them, and ye'll win as sure as my name's Alexander Smeaton! It's a fact. Ay! And ye've time to wander into the clubhoose and lay yer wagers, if ye're minded to mak' a wheen siller. For the love o' ma auld bones, dae as I tell ye, man!'

I didn't at all love his old bones, but my mind was made up.

'I'll play with the clubs,' I said, and the old man staggered in an intensity of delight.

'Hech! sir,' he cried, 'this'll be a grand day for Sandy Smeaton! When the match is ower I'll be there to compliment ye, and then – aweel, then I'll no fash ye till ye "shuffle off yer mortal coil", as auld Bacon has it. When ye're like myself – a speerit, ye ken – ye may be glad tae hae a freend at court, an' I'll dae what I can for ye. I can introduce ye to a' the canonised saints. They're a wheen ponderous in conversation and awfy orthodox in doctrine, but on the whole verra respectable. Hooever, that'll no' be for a while. Meantime, young sir, win yer match and humeeliate this varmint spawn o' the hoose o' Lindsay. So – *Buon giorno* – as we used to say in the auld Vatican days – *Arivederci!*'

With these valedictory remarks the cardinal left me, and returning the clubs to Wetherby, who had been standing some hundred yards off, I returned to the hotel.

It was two o'clock.

How shall I describe what I felt? I could win this match – of that I felt absolutely sure. I cannot explain this curious sense of certainty as to the issue of the game, but I knew by a sort of prophetic inspiration that I could not lose.

The cardinal had hinted at wagers. Well, why not?

I could turn the tables on some of the crowd who had smiled in pity at my efforts of the morning, and there is no revenge so sweet as that of scoring off men who have laughed at one. I decided to get a little money on the event, if possible.

I strolled leisurely over to the club and entered the smoking-room, an immense room with bay windows that opened on to the links. It was crowded. The members had finished luncheon and were discussing the afternoon's prospects over coffee, liqueurs, cigars and cigarettes, amid a noisy jingle of laughter, clinking of glasses, tinkling of cups, hurrying footsteps of waiters and general hubbub.

My entrance had something of the effect that oil has on troubled waters. Everybody near me ceased laughing. No doubt I had been the bull's-eye for their hilarious shafts of wit. They hummed and hawed as if I had detected them in some nefarious plot. A few bowed to me, and one or two invited me to have a drink. But I was bent on business, so, joining a group in which I saw a few acquaintances, I asked casually if any bets had been made on the match.

'Not one, don't you know!' replied O'Hagan, a Scotch youth of Irish name, who cultivated a highly ornate English accent with intermittent success.

'Anybody want a bet?' I asked, adding, 'Of course I should want very heavy odds.'

There was a general movement on this.

Members gathered round me, some laughing, some chaffing, some whispering. Lowchester came up to me, and growled in an under-tone, 'Don't make a fool of yourself, my dear chap; you can't possibly win.'

'Still, I don't mind making a bet or two,' I persisted. 'Will anyone lay me fifty to one?'

'I'll lay you forty to one in fivers,' said Mr Grove, the actor, no doubt considering the publicity of the offer as a good advertisement.

'Done!' I replied, and took a note of it.

'So will I!' 'And I!' 'Put me down for the same.' 'In sovereigns?' 'Yes.' 'Tenners if you like!' 'Done!'

These and other cries now sounded all round the room till the babel reminded me of the Stock Exchange, and I think quite two-thirds of the men present laid me the odds at forty to one in sovereigns, fivers or tenners.

I suppose they considered me a madman, or at least an intolerably vain and eccentric person who deserved a 'dressing down'. A hurried adding up of my bets showed me that I stood to lose about £250, or win £10,000.

It was now close on two-thirty, and we moved off to the links. The crowd was not quite so dense. Evidently many people considered the match as good as over, and the interest of those who remained was almost apathetic. The heavy midday meal that is eaten in St Magnus may account to some extent for this lethargy.

I found the faithful Wetherby waiting for me, at a discreetly remote distance, and telling him that I meant to play with the clubs he was carrying, I walked up to Kirkintulloch. The latter had all the air of a martyr. His head was thrown back, as if in the act of challenging the world in general to laugh at him. He glared suspiciously at everyone near him, and with difficulty brought himself to touch his hat at my approach.

I chuckled inwardly.

'Whaat's this I hear, sir?' he said. 'Ye've been wagerin', they tell me.'

'I've made a few bets, if that's what you mean,' I answered.

'Weel, sir, as man tae man, if ye'll excuse the leeberty, ye're fair demented. It's no' possible to win. A'body kens that. As for mesel', I'm the laughin'-stock o' the toon. I huvna had sae muckle as time for ma denner – '

'Why not?' I asked.

'I've been busy blackin' the een and spleetin' the nebs o' yer traducers. I've been fechtin' seeven men. It's a caddie's beesiness to stand up for his maister, nae maitter what kind o' a gowfer he is.'

'Ah, well!' I answered, 'you'll make them sing to another tune tonight. I am going to play with these.'

And uncovering the canvas flap that concealed them, I exposed the weird-looking clubs to his gaze.

I think he thought I was joking. He looked first at the clubs, and then at me, with a half-questioning, half-stupid twinkle in his hard, blue eyes. Then he spat.

I apologise to the reader for mentioning anything so unpleasant, but it is an uncomfortable habit that certain classes indulge in when they desire to punctuate or emphasise their views. Amongst themselves, I believe, it is considered highly expressive, if employed at the true psychological moment.

'What kin' o' things are they?' he asked, after a portentous pause.

'The clubs I mean to play with,' I replied.

'Aweel!' he answered, 'that concludes a' relations atween us. I may be daft, but I'm no' a fule, an' I'm seek of the hale stramash. Ye mun get another caddie, I'll no cairry the likes o' thae things.'

'My servant is going to carry them,' I answered quickly; and I fancied Kirkintulloch looked a trifle crestfallen at such an unexpected exhibition of independence.

'I'll be glad, however,' I added, 'if you'll accompany me round the links, and I promise you the pleasing sensation of astonishment if you do.'

With this I left him, but I could hear fragments of a voluble explanation that he apparently deemed it necessary to make to the bystanders.

'There are leemits, ye ken – it's no' for the likes o' me to say – I've been a caddie twenty-fower year – the man's no' richt in the heed – no' but what he's free with his siller an' a born gentleman – I wouldna say he wasna – but ma name's Kirkintulloch, an' I've a poseetion tae keep up.'

The clock of the parish church boomed out the half-hour, and I advanced to the teeing ground, with Wetherby at my heels. The flap had been replaced over the heads of the clubs, and the bag looked ordinary enough, though my new 'caddie' was so faultlessly attired in his well-cut grey suit as to be a target for the derision of a number of Kirkintulloch's professional friends.

14

The Second Round

The 'honour' being Lindsay's, the first drive was his. It was a clean-hit ball, but a wind had arisen that carried it a trifle out of the course.

Then I took my stand, and received from Wetherby the cardinal's driver.

Of all hearty laughter that my ears have ever listened to, none could equal that of the bystanders who were near enough to see the club. If I had made the most witty joke that mind can conceive, it could not have elicited more spontaneous, prolonged or uproarious appreciation. Mrs Gunter's mezzo-soprano rang out in a paroxysm of musical hysterics. Even Lindsay edged behind me that I might not see the smile he found it impossible to repress. Members of the club and their friends, who had behaved with decorous gravity during the morning, now abandoned themselves frankly to unrestrained laughter. The infection spread to the masses of the crowd who were not near enough to see my curious club, and they gradually pressed closer and closer, anxious to share and enjoy any new source of merriment, so that it took the men with the rope all their time to maintain the semicircle that divided the spectators from the players.

Under ordinary circumstances I should have resented such

behaviour, but somehow it didn't seem to affect me. I even felt inclined to join in the general hilarity. I certainly felt the humour of the situation. As it was, I approached the ball with perfect composure and the ghost of a sardonic smile.

And then I drove it.

Away it winged, hard-hit and fast, travelling straight in the line of the hole. I had never, of course, played such a magnificent shot, and the effect on the crowd was electrical. Laughter died of a sudden, as if choked in a thousand throats. Broad grins seemed frozen on the upraised faces round me. Mouths opened unconsciously, eyes stared vacantly at the flying ball. For the moment I was surrounded by so many living statues, transfixed in mute amazement.

I think it was Lowchester who first spoke. 'A fine shot,' I fancied I heard him say mechanically.

We moved on, and the act of walking loosened the tongues around me. A confused murmuring ensued, gradually increasing in volume till everybody seemed to be talking and arguing, agreeing with or contradicting each other at the pitch of the voice.

I caught stray phrases from time to time.

'I never seed the likes o' that.' 'Man, it was a braw drive!' 'He'll no' dae it again, I'm thinkin'.' 'By Jove! that was a flyer – but what an extraordinary club!' and so on.

I had outdriven Lindsay by about sixty yards – no small feat when one bore in mind that he had the reputation of being the longest driver living.

His second shot was a good one, landing him some thirty yards short of the burn. As we reached my ball, I selected the cardinal's ponderous and much-corroded cleek. There were faint indications of amusement at the sight of it, but a nervous curiosity as to my next shot was the predominating note.

I played the shot quite easily. As before, the ball flew straight as a bird in the line of the hole, crossed the burn and dropped dead within a few feet of the flag. An unwilling murmur of admiration rose from the crowd, and Lindsay, no longer smiling, said very frankly that he had never seen two finer strokes in his life.

I think it only right to admit that he is a sensible, manly and modest fellow.

He took his lofting iron and with a very neat wrist shot dropped the ball dead, within a foot of the hole.

A hearty cheer greeted the stroke. It was quite evident that he was the popular favourite. Well, I could wait, and I meant to.

Arrived on the putting-green, I advanced with the odd-looking putter. One or two of the spectators indulged in a cynical, though somewhat half-hearted, snigger at its curious lines, but for the most part the crowd was quite silent, and one could almost feel in the air the nervous tension of the onlookers. My ball was about seven feet from the hole. With complete self-possession I went up to it and glanced almost carelessly at the ground.

There was a dead silence.

I played, and the ball dropped lightly into the hole. I was one up on the second round. I had holed out in three.

I half expected a murmur of applause for the putt, but a bewildered stupor was the actual effect produced. In all that concourse of people only two appeared to be quite calm and collected, namely, Wetherby and myself. I caught a glimpse of Kirkintulloch's face. The features were there, but all expression had departed.

For myself, I walked on air. The outward calm of my demeanour gave no index to the wild exultation that I felt. Truly there is no more satisfying or stimulating anticipation than that of a coming revenge. The sentiment, I am aware, is not a Christian one, but at least it is eminently human. I felt no desire to be revenged on Lindsay. Any hostile feeling that I had entertained towards him had passed away. But I did desire to score off the crowd. More, I desired to humiliate Mrs Gunter. Her callous treatment of me, her silvery but malicious laughter, her avowed admiration of Lindsay, had galled me to an extent the expression of which I have carefully kept from these pages. *Noblesse oblige!* One cannot be rude. But I wanted to annoy her – a very common phase of love.

As the match proceeded I won hole after hole, often in the most astonishing manner. Twice I landed in bunkers close to the greens (the result of exceptionally long shots), and in each case the cardinal's iron lifted the ball from the sand and deposited it in the hole. I cannot take credit to myself for such prodigious feats; they were undoubtedly the work of the clubs.

At the eighth hole, however, I experienced an important reverse. It is, as everybody who knows the St Magnus links is aware, the short hole. I took the iron and dropped the ball within a yard of the hole. Lindsay followed, and landed some twenty yards off; and then, by a splendid putt, he holed out in two. I, of course, had no difficulty in doing likewise, and we halved the hole; but the awkward fact remained that I must now gain every hole to win the match, for my opponent's score was 'nine up', and there only remained ten holes to play.

If the match was intensely exciting – and to me it was more than that – the demeanour of the crowd was no less psychologically interesting. The ragtag and bobtail, with the fickleness that has ever characterised the emotions of the unwashed, and even of the occasionally clean, now began to acclaim me as their chosen champion, and each brilliant shot I made was hailed with a vociferous delight that might have turned a less steadily balanced head than my own. The reason of this is, of course, more or less obvious. There is more pleasurable excitement to be derived from making a god of the man whose star is in the ascendant than in continuing allegiance with falling crest to one whom we have placed on a pinnacle by an error of judgement, to which we are loath to attract attention.

But if the crowd was a source of ever-increasing interest, what shall I say of the demeanour of the men who had made heavy bets with me?

It is not strictly true that Scotchmen are mean in money matters, any more than it is to say that they can't see a joke. As regards the latter point, it is my experience that a Scot won't laugh at the average jest that amuses an Englishman, simply because it isn't good enough. And since he doesn't laugh he is supposed to have missed the point. In support of my theory is the fact that there is an established vein of Scotch wit and humour, but I have yet to learn that England has evolved anything of the sort. True, England has many comic papers, and Scotland has none. But it must be borne in mind that the statements announcing such periodicals to be 'comic' emanate solely from the proprietors.

There is, however, a substratum – or rather a perversion – of truth in the aphorism that deals with the Scotch and their money. And I take it the real truth is that a Scot cannot bear to part with money for which he gets no return of any sort – a very natural and proper feeling. Again, he dislikes any extra or unusual call on his purse. For the rest he is generous, hospitable and public-spirited to a degree. It may be argued that if this be the case the Scot ought never to make a bet; the answer to which is that as a rule he doesn't, unless something almost in the nature of a certainty presents itself. Then he forgets his nationality and becomes merely human. And that is precisely what happened to my Caledonian friends in the smoking-room of the club. An apparently unprecedented opportunity of making a little money had presented itself, and they had accepted its conditions with a noisy humour intended to lacquer their inbred acquisitive propensities.

And now, as I casually watched their faces, I saw an interesting awakening. Their faces were as those of infants who, having been roused from a long and profound sleep, gaze about with enquiring but stupefied wonder. They were quite silent for the most part, as with every shot I played they seemed to feel the sovereigns melting in their pockets. Ah! this unhappy craze for gold! I have seen the same set faces at Monte Carlo, when, as the croupier cries out, '*Rouge, Pair et Passe!*' the bulk of the money is staked on '*Noir, Impair et Manque*'. How deplorable it all is! And I stood to win £10,000 – a most exhilarating prospect.

15

In the Throes

As the match progressed I continued playing an absolutely faultless game, and there was no manner of doubt that Lindsay had become more or less demoralised. At the end of the fifteenth hole his score was reduced to two up, with three more holes to play. That is to say, so far I had won every hole of the second round, with the exception of the short one which we had halved. I had only to win the last three holes to gain the match, nay more, to break the record score of the links!

A curious change in the crowd's bearing was now apparent. They preserved a complete silence. Each shot, whether my own or Lindsay's, was played in a profound stillness. An intense suppressed excitement seemed to consume every soul present. Even during the marches from shot to shot scarcely a word was spoken; only the dull thud of thousands of feet gave audible token of their presence.

The news of the sudden and extraordinary change in the fortunes of the game had evidently travelled backwards to St Magnus, for as we worked homewards the mob was increased at every hole by such vast numbers that it seemed impossible for the men with the rope to control so great a concourse.

Once or twice I glanced in Mrs Gunter's direction, and I should have thought her face was pale but for two vivid splashes of a most exquisite carmine that glowed, or at all events dwelt, on her cheeks. Her jet-black eyebrows formed two thoughtful lines below the golden cloud of her beautiful hair. How resplendent she was! I have never seen a complexion at all like hers except on the stage. What wonder that Lindsay should be demoralised, with the prospect of being forestalled hanging over him like the sword of Damocles?

Only once did I catch sight of the shadowy cardinal, and that was at the end of the sixteenth hole, which I had won easily. As we walked towards the teeing ground of the seventeenth I chanced to let my eyes fall on the railway shed built against the wall bounding the links, and there – executing the most extraordinary and grotesque fandango of delight – was His Eminence. He was evidently in a rapture of delirious intoxication, for, in the passing glimpse I had, I saw him standing on his head, so that the ghostly robes fell downward to the roof of the shed, leaving his white skeleton immodestly bare and feet upwards in the air. It was not a pleasing exhibition, and very nearly unnerved me; but the mere handling of my marvellous driver seemed to steady me in a moment. And fortunately none but I could see the antics of my ecclesiastical patron.

Reader, do you know what it is to be outwardly as calm as a blasé policeman, and all the time quivering with inward excitement? If I could have yelled once or twice it would have been an immense relief, but I had a part to play, and I meant to play it. As it was, I puffed carelessly at a cigarette, professed to admire the view, glanced carelessly at my watch, and generally indulged in such little bits of byplay as were calculated to indicate extreme sang-froid. (I ought to mention that I am a very capable amateur actor, and at our annual Thespian Club theatricals always take the leading part. I founded the club and manage it.)

That I played my new role of champion golfer with credit was evident. The seething crowd had originally assembled to jeer, but it remained to accept me at my own valuation – always a pleasing change to find registered in the barometer of public opinion.

My drive at the seventeenth hole (the last but one to be played) was a perfect shot, whilst Lindsay's was comparatively feeble. He was now but one up, and at the end of the hole we ought to be 'all square and one to play'. But the strain on my nerves was beginning to tell. I felt like Hood's Eugene Aram –

> Merrily rose the lark, and shook
>   The dewdrop from its wing;
> But I never marked its morning flight,
>   I never heard it sing;
> For I was stooping once again
>   Beneath the horrid thing!

I was conscious in a vague somnambulistic fashion of the green links, the blue sky, the purple crowd, splashed here and there with the bright colours of frock and parasol. My eyes took in mechanically the onward movement of the people, the rosy light that caught the spires of the old grey town, the shrieking railway train, the red blaze of the sun in the windows of St Magnus, and a hundred other ocular impressions. Yet all these things seemed unreal; the dream background in a land whereof the cardinal, Lindsay and I formed the sole population.

Moreover, pressing as it seemed on my very brain, came the humiliating conviction that I was nothing short of a fraud, a charlatan, a ghostly conjurer's accomplice.

Was it an honourable game that I was playing? Would I be justified in taking the money I stood to win? Was it fair to usurp the throne of champion by the aid of a supernatural agency, whose purpose I could not even pretend to fathom? Could I look Mrs Gunter in the face if, crowned with a stolen golfing halo, I asked her to be my wife? And if I couldn't, what more deplorable type of lover was possible? Ought I to burden myself with a secret that I should have to carry with me in silence to the grave? Was the nominal prefix 'Honourable', with which my parents had dowered me without either warrant on my part or enquiry on their own, to be a prefix only? These and many other thoughts flashed through my mind as we played the seventeenth hole.

I got on the green in three, Lindsay in four. He then played the 'two more', and by a remarkably good putt holed out in five.

I took the putter, and in a profound and most impressive silence holed out in four. A stifled gasp rose from the crowd.

The score was now, 'All square, and one to play.'

I stood on the teeing ground of the eighteenth hole. The landscape in front of me was blurred and blotted; the dense crowds on either side of me were as mere inky blotches. The ground at my feet seemed miles away. Only the teed ball was in focus. That I saw clearly.

It was a test moment in my life. I could lose the match if I chose, and keep a clean conscience.

I could play the last hole with my own clubs!

And if I did – well, I'd lose; but, by heaven! I'd still be an honourable gentleman.

I caught sight of Lindsay's face. It was white and set, but he looked a manly fellow for all that. It was a cowardly trick to tear the laurels from his brow as I was doing. He had won them after a lifetime's devotion to the game.

And I – ?

Faugh! I would not touch the accursed clubs again. For aught I knew, to win was to sell my soul, and become a servile creature doomed to the tender mercies of a phantom's patronage.

*　*　*

'Ye fushiomless eediot!' I suddenly heard the words ring in my ears, and at the same moment I saw the cardinal's deadly face peering into my eyes as if to read my very soul. 'What's come ower ye? Are ye daft? Nane o' yer pauky humour at this time o' day. Tak' ma driver an' catch the ba' the bonniest skite of a'! Whaat?' – and his voice rose in indescribable fury – 'Ye'll no do sic a thing? Ye lily-livered loon, if ye dinna dae as I tell ye I'll hae ye back in the castle vaults and wring the neck o' yer soul wi' ma ain bony fingers! Ay, an' haunt ye till the day ye're deid!' (What good purpose could be served by haunting me till the day of death, after wringing the neck of my soul, was not quite clear.) 'Mind that!' he continued, 'I'm no' to be trifled wi'!'

I turned on him and answered deliberately, 'You fiend!'

'Beg pardon, sir?' said Wetherby. I had forgotten for the moment, and spoken aloud.

'Give me the driver from Kirkintulloch's bag,' I replied.

Kirkintulloch heard me, and elbowed his way to my side. He was shaking with excitement. I feel certain he had never been so sober for years.

'Will 'ee no jist gang on wi' the one ye've been playin' wi'?' he urged. 'Ye're daein' fine!'

'Give me the driver with which I played the first round this morning,' I persisted.

During all this the cardinal was moving and shrieking round me in a whirlwind of red draperies and white corroded bones.

Reluctantly Kirkintulloch drew the driver from his bag, and handed it to me.

'I think ye're wrong, sir,' he whispered very earnestly in my ear, mixing himself up with the demented prelate in doing so.

'For heaven's sake let no one speak to me!' I cried. 'Get out of my way!' I added fiercely – really to the cardinal, though Kirkintulloch, Wetherby, and everyone near seemed to take it to themselves, and drew back hastily. Then I gave a vicious kick at His Eminence's shins. Lowchester has since told me the action appeared most inexplicable and uncalled for, inasmuch as I apparently kicked at space.

I addressed the ball.

His Eminence promptly sat on it. Then, stretching his arms in front of me, he cursed me wildly and volubly in Latin. What the exact words were I cannot tell, and could not have translated had I known, but the general effect was awful.

Crash through his bones – not that such a trifle could inconvenience my intangible enemy – went the club.

The ball, feebly struck on the top, shot along the grass, and dropped into the burn!

The match was as good as lost.

A shriek, whether of delight, dismay, relief or anxiety, I know not, rose from the mob. I believe everyone in that crowd was suffering from the same nervous strain that affected me.

Then Lindsay stepped to the front.

He drove a magnificent ball, and, strange as it may seem, the mere sight wrought a complete upheaval of the altruistic pedestal on which

I had perched myself. I was suddenly conscious of a wild exasperation at having thrown my chances to the winds. For, after all, my objections to winning had been purely sentimental, not to say childish. It is marvellous how the realisation of our best intentions very frequently betrays the insincerity of the moral mood that inspired them. It is easy to be magnanimous if we don't foresee the unhappy but common result of poignant regret.

The vision of a heavenly and luxurious life with Mrs Gunter seemed to fade. I turned and looked at her. She was as white as a sheet, save for the faithful discs of carmine. Ah, what a fool I had been!

But the game was not yet over; and even as the thought flashed across me, Lindsay made his first serious mistake. It was a mistake of judgement.

'Thank Heaven,' he exclaimed, with an ill-bred grunt of relief, 'I've cooked your goose for you at last!'

I have no doubt this thoughtless and ill-timed speech was the result of the strain he had been put to. Perhaps I ought to have made allowance for it. In point of fact, it reawakened in me the most consuming desire to win, and I cursed my extravagant magnanimity.

Meantime a rapt and beautiful change had come over the faces of the men with whom I had made bets. Frowns were dissipated as by a ray of beatific sunshine, and lively smiles and chuckles were the order of the moment. There was even a touch of insolence in their sidelong glances. They began to chatter volubly. I could hear the drift of their sudden recall to speech.

'I knew he was bound to break down in the long run,' said somebody.

'Undoubtedly; still he's played a remarkable game.' 'I win ten pounds' – 'and I a fiver', and so forth. My miserable drive had acted on their tongues as the first round of champagne does at dinner.

We were walking towards the burn as Lindsay spoke, and I was about to answer when – springing apparently from nowhere – the cardinal again appeared, or rather shot up before me, in a state of incontinent frenzy. None the less, he seemed to divine the thoughts that were chasing each other through my mind, for, bending towards me, he whispered in hoarse, trembling tones, and with the utmost intensity –

'Tak' ma club! Tak' ma club!! Tak' ma clubs – ye eediot!!! He's dealt ye a black affront; but, by a' the buried bones o' the Smeatons he hasna yet won the day!'

'You think I still may win?' I silently asked him, albeit in a state of incredulous stupefaction.

'Try, man – try!' he shrieked in reply 'I'll see what I can dae!'

And with that he caught up his skirts and flew off in a series of amazing leaps and bounds in the direction of the last hole. What this change in his tactics meant I was at a loss to conjecture.

I wish I could adequately describe the extraordinary flight of the prelate across the green turf of the links. He seemed to be borne on the wings of the wind, and each leap he took must have covered at least twenty yards. He gave me the impression of a grotesque competitor in an unearthly game of 'Hop, skip, and leap'. At length, after an elapse of perhaps fifteen seconds, I saw him halt in the distance about twenty yards from the red flag of the hole. Then he turned and faced us, as if patiently awaiting the next shot. I little guessed what his purpose was. His figure was clearly outlined against a distant crowd of some two or three hundred assembled behind the final hole to witness the end of this unprecedented struggle.

16

An Exciting Finish

My ball was duly fished out of the burn and dropped behind my shoulder. I returned my own faithless driver to Kirkintulloch, and once again took hold of the cardinal's. As I did so a telepathic throb of excitement passed through the bystanders.

I played the shot.

It eclipsed all my former efforts. I never have seen, nor shall I ever see again, such a hard-hit ball. With a trajectory scarcely higher than that of a rifle bullet at a medium range, it winged its way straight to the hole, dropping eventually within a yard or so of His Eminence. And then, straining my eyes, I saw a sight that startled me into a sudden realisation of the latter's purpose. He had, so to speak, fielded the ball – that is to say, he had dashed towards it as it fell; and now, by a series of nervous but skilful kicks, he was directing its course straight to the hole! The red skirts were held high in his hands, and the white bony legs flashed to and fro as he sped in the wake of the running globe. I could not, of course, actually see the ball, but, by an intuition that admitted of no doubt whatever, I knew what he was up to. I held my breath in an agony of suspense as nearer and nearer to the red flag flew the gaunt figure of the cardinal. I swear my heart stopped beating, and the paralysed crowd seemed similarly affected, though the sight that I saw was mercifully denied to its eyes. There was no doubt about it. The cardinal had so manipulated the ball that I had holed out in three.

But the match was not yet over.

What Lindsay's feelings at the moment were I know not, but he managed to play a clever second stroke that landed him on the green, some seven feet from the hole.

And now came the supreme moment.

If Lindsay holed his putt we halved the match, if he failed I won the day.

Such was the pressure of the excited crowd that only the most strenuous efforts enabled the rope holders to maintain a clear circular space round the hole. It measured about fifteen yards in diameter, and within this charmed circle stood Lindsay and his caddie, Wetherby and Kirkintulloch, old Jock Johnson (the keeper of the green), Hanbury-Smith (the captain of the golf club) and myself. All other spectators were without the pale, with the important exception of the cardinal.

I looked about me. My part in the game was over. I had but to watch and wait. I was thankful the final shot was Lindsay's and not mine.

The faces of my betting friends had changed again in expression, and become drawn and strained. The unfortunate gentlemen no longer chattered and chuckled. The magnet of luck was again slowly but surely attracting golden coins from the depths of their purses, and such pangs could only be borne with dumb fortitude.

The crowd were so terribly congested that two women fainted. I looked anxiously at Mrs Gunter, but – thank Heaven! – the rich carmine still glowed on her cheeks.

At length, putter in hand, Lindsay approached his ball, and even the breathing of the crowd seemed to be suspended.

I moved to a spot some six feet from the hole, on the opposite side to Lindsay. As I did so my eyes fell on the ground, and I saw a startling and curious sight.

My terrible ally, the cardinal, had stretched himself at full length, face downward, on the turf, so that his ghastly head was directly over the hole and his shadowy feet close to mine.

A sense of faintness crept over me.

As in a red mist I saw Lindsay strike the ball. I saw it travelling straight and sure to the hole!

And then – heavens above us! – I saw the cardinal take a quick and gulping breath, and blow with might and main against the skilfully directed ball! It reached the edge of the hole, trembled a moment on the brink, and then ran off at an angle and lay still on the turf a couple of inches from the hole!

I had won the match.

A tumult sounded in my ears, the sky turned a blazing scarlet, the crowd swam before my eyes, and of a sudden I fell prone on the turf with my nose plunged in the fateful hole!

* * *

When I came to myself I found kind friends grouped about me, and my head resting luxuriously in Mrs Gunter's lap. I think I should have been perfectly happy and content with this state of things, had I not unfortunately just at that moment caught a glimpse of the ubiquitous cardinal standing ridiculously on his head and kicking his heels in mid-air in an ecstasy of frenzied glee.

The sight so upset me that I went off a second time into a dead faint.

17

And Last

Again I was myself, and this time I felt revived and strong. I rose to my feet. Immediately the crowd closed round me and acclaimed me with cheers and yells. Presently I found myself being carried shoulder-high by a dozen lusty caddies, Kirkintulloch heading their progress with proud bearing and gleaming eye.

A thousand voices were howling, 'See, the conquering hero comes!' A thousand hats and handkerchiefs were waving in the air. A thousand smiling faces beamed up into mine.

Mrs Gunter cried out to me, as I passed her in triumphal procession, 'You'll dine with the Lowchesters tonight, won't you?'

And turning a smiling and radiant face to her, I answered, 'I will.'

I was the idol of the hour, not – I may add – an altogether new experience.

At length, after what seemed an eternity of acclamation and adulation, I was set down in the great bay window of the club, and immediately surrounded by all members who had *not* made bets with me. Fulsome flattery, genuine congratulation and general admiration were showered on me. At writing-tables in distant corners of the room I saw my betting friends busily writing out cheques. They did not seem inclined to participate in the enthusiastic ovation. But what did I care?

Surfeited with the overwhelming tributes to my achievement (and, I fancy, to my personality), I broke away from my friends, only to be seized again by my escort of caddies and carried shoulder-high in the direction of the Metropole. The sturdy fellows finally deposited me on the top step of the main entrance to the hotel, and I stood facing the seething crowd.

Here a fresh outburst of applause greeted me from my fellow-guests and the domestic staff.

I bowed incessantly right and left.

'Speech! Speech!' now rang out on every side from a thousand throats, and I felt that if only to get rid of them, I must say something. So holding aloft my right hand as a token that I accepted the invitation, and in the profound silence instantly produced by my action, I said: 'My friends, I thank you. I have excelled in all other games, and why not in golf? Again I thank you.'

The simple words completely captivated them, and I retired indoors to a volley of tumultuous and long-continued cheers.

As an example of how trivial things often imprint themselves on our dazed memories during crises in our lives, I remember noting, as I passed through the hall to my suite of rooms, an immense pile of luggage, evidently just arrived, and labelled 'The Prince Vladimir Demidoff'. I had not heard of his intention to visit St Magnus. In fact, I don't think I'd ever heard of the man at all.

Reaching my room, I stretched myself on a couch, lit a cigarette and got Wetherby to bring me a stiff brandy-and-soda. At last, thought I, I had breathing space. Imagine, then, my consternation and irritation when, on opening my eyes – I had closed them for a moment as I revelled in the first deep draught of my 'peg' – I beheld, seated opposite me, His Eminence!

'Upon my soul!' I cried, 'this is too bad. You swore – '

'Hud yer wheesht!' interrupted the cardinal. 'I'm here to thank ye and bid ye gudebye.'

'I'm glad to hear it,' I muttered, sulkily.

'Ye've focht a grand fecht,' he proceeded, 'an' I'm much obleeged tae ye. But, man, there's ae thing that worrits me extraordinar'. Ye ken, I had tae cheat! I aye played fair in the auld days, and it gaed agin' the grain tae blaw on Lindsay's ba' at the last putt, but what could I dae? Hooever, it canna be helpit. The queer thing is that noo that my revenge is complete, it doesna seem to gratify me muckle. Hech, sir! – life, moartal or speeritual, is guy disappointin'. For a' that I'm much obleeged, an' ye'll never see me mair. Gudebye!'

And with that he faded into space, and, truth to tell, he has honourably abstained from haunting me since.

Sheer physical fatigue precluded the possibility of anything in the nature of psychical research, or even of attempting to think out the weird supernatural experiences I had gone through.

I was dozing off into a gentle sleep when Wetherby opened the door and informed me that Kirkintulloch was waiting below, and would be proud if I could grant him a short interview.

I consented, and presently Kirkintulloch appeared.

'It's no' for the guinea I've come, sir,' he began (I've no doubt, by way of a gentle reminder); 'I thocht ye'd be glad o' a card wi' yer score, an' I've had it made oot.'

He handed me a card, and on it I read the score:

Out	3	3	4	3	4	5	3	2	3	– 30
In	3	2	3	4	5	3	3	4	3	– 30

Total   60

'Ye're a credit to my teachin', sir,' he continued, 'an' I'm real prood o' ye. The record for thae links is seventy-twa, and ye're jist a clean dozen below that. The likes o' it was never seen. It's a fact. Ay! an' long after a'body here's dead ye'll still hud the record. I little thocht I had pit ma ain style sae coampletely into ye! Ye're a pairfect marvel!'

'Thank you,' I muttered wearily.

'I see ye're tired, sir, an' I'll no keep ye, but jist afore I gang, wad ye mind showin' me thae queer-like clubs ye played wi'?'

'By all means,' said I. 'Weatherby, where are the clubs?'

'Ain't you got 'em, sir?' asked the latter, with some surprise.

'Not I!' I answered. 'You had them.'

'Well, sir, I can't quite tell 'ow it is, but in the crowd I suddenly felt 'em slip out from under my arm, and look as I would I couldn't lay eyes on 'em after that. I supposed some friend of yours had taken them out of curiosity, and meant to bring 'em to you, sir.'

'Dinna fash yersel',' broke in Kirkintulloch; 'if they're in St Magnus I'll lay hands on them, never fear. Gude nicht, sir!'

And so that admirable caddie passed out of my life. I tipped him well (and I've since been told he paid me the high – if deplorable – compliment of a week's continuous intoxication), but from that day to this no mortal eye has seen the bewitched clubs of the ghostly Cardinal Archbishop of St Magnus.

Much revived by two hours' sound and dreamless sleep, I dressed at half-past seven, and a few minutes before eight I started for the Lowchesters' house.

It had somehow got abroad that I was dining there, and a large crowd had assembled in front of the hotel. I was again received with an outburst of cheers, and subsequently escorted to my destination to a lustily sung chorus of 'For he's a jolly good fellow!'

Arrived at the Lowchesters' gates, I bade the kindly crowd good-night, and retired from their sight to a final volley of echoing cheers.

I need not describe the welcome I received from my host and hostess, Mrs Gunter and the other guests. Even Lindsay spoke to me tactfully on the subject of our match, expressing genuine admiration of my performance, though I was slightly startled when he said, 'In fact, I consider your play today nothing short of supernatural.'

So did I, but I didn't venture to say so.

The dinner was delightful. Excellent food, perfect wine, charming people, and myself the centre of interest. I ask no more at such a function.

I took my hostess in to dinner of course but on my other side was Mrs Gunter, exquisitely dressed in a Parisian triumph of eau-de-Nil velvet with groups of mauve and purple pansies. Her wonderful complexion was more ravishing than ever in the soft lamplight. Indeed it seemed to have specially adapted itself to the requirements of her delicately tinted gown. Her hands and arms had the bloom of peaches, and her luxuriant hair, dark underneath, was a mist of everchanging gold on the top.

Several times during dinner I saw the jet-black lashes raised and felt her glorious eyes regarding me with the rapt gaze of hero-worship.

Well, tonight I should know, for weal or woe, what fortune the Fates held in store for me.

When the ladies had left us I drew Lindsay aside on the pretence of examining some engravings in the hall, and as soon as we were alone I touched on the subject uppermost in my mind.

'I think it only right to tell you, my dear Lindsay,' I began, 'that tonight I shall propose to Mrs Gunter, and if by any chance she should dismiss me, then I leave the field clear for you. I have to thank you for all the courtesy you have shown during my visit to St Magnus, and I sincerely trust that whatever may happen we shall always remain friends.'

'As far as I'm concerned you may be sure of that,' replied Lindsay. 'But it does seem to me that you've been labouring under a delusion. I've never desired to propose to Mrs Gunter. And even if I wanted to, I couldn't. I'm a married man, with three of a family. More than that, I'm very deeply in love with my wife, and not at all with Mrs Gunter.'

'But – good heavens!' I exclaimed, 'surely we agreed – '

'If you remember,' he interrupted, 'that night in the Racing Club, I wanted to explain these things and you simply wouldn't hear me.'

'Then,' I continued blankly, as in a sudden flash of memory I recalled the fact he alluded to, 'we've been fighting for nothing?'

'Exactly,' he replied.

In silence we shook hands, and the matter dropped.

Presently we joined the ladies in the drawing-room, and after a decent interval I drew Mrs Gunter aside. We sat by each other on a couch concealed from view by a group of palms. A pretty girl in white was playing the 'Moonlight Sonata'.

I admit it at once – my heart was beating. I wished I had rehearsed the role I was about to play. Then I reflected that I had often witnessed proposals on the stage, so taking a leaf from that reliable book I cleared my throat.

'Mrs Gunter,' I began, 'may I say Katherine?'

'Ah! So it has come to this!' she murmured, lowering her eyes with the most captivating grace.

'Yes, this,' I whispered passionately. 'This, that I love you and only you! This, that I am here to ask you to be my wife!'

'It can never be!' she murmured conventionally, and a low cry, half sob, half sigh, escaped her.

'Katherine!' I cried, 'why not?'

'Because,' she answered slowly, and as if the words were dragged from her, 'I have lost every penny of my fortune. And a penniless woman I cannot, will not come to you. Unless – ' and her voice trembled into silence.

She was wearing several thousand pounds' worth of diamonds at the time, but somehow I didn't grasp the sparkling contradiction.

Now I am a man of quick resolution. I can grasp a situation in a moment. In a flash I realised that I alone could never afford to keep this beautiful creature in surroundings worthy of her, at least not without such personal sacrifice as at my time of life would be extremely inconvenient. I am but a younger son. To force her then to marry me under such circumstances would be a cruelty to her and an injustice to myself.

Afraid, therefore, that the murmured word 'Unless – ' was about to open up possibilities not altogether desirable, I broke the silence with: 'And so you dismiss me?'

She looked at me for a moment in blank surprise.

Then the ghost of a faint smile flickered over her face as she answered, 'Yes, *so I dismiss you!*'

I gave a suitable sigh.

The 'Moonlight Sonata' was over, and poor Katherine rose.

I followed her to a group of guests in the centre of the room, and as I did so she turned and said: 'I was going to say, "*Unless* you can induce my future husband to give me up," when you interrupted me.'

'Your future husband!' I exclaimed aghast.

'Yes,' she answered serenely; 'let me introduce you to him.'

And touching the sleeve of the good-looking foreigner who had taken her in to dinner, she said: 'Vladimir, let me present Major Gore,' adding to me, 'Prince Vladimir Demidoff. Didn't you know that we are to be married next week?'

I murmured confused words of congratulation, and escaped to Lady Lowchester's side.

'Are they really going to be married?' I asked her.

'Of course they are!' replied my hostess. 'Why shouldn't they?'

'But – but,' I stammered, 'she's lost every penny of her fortune!'

'Not she!' replied Lady Lowchester, with a merry ringing laugh. 'That's what she tells every man who proposes to her. She says she finds it an excellent gauge of devotion.'

'I see,' I answered.

I stood still for a moment. Then I walked over to Lowchester and asked him which was the best morning train from St Magnus to London.

* * *

I did not feel justified in keeping for my own use the £10,000 I had won, but it may interest the reader to know that with it I founded the now flourishing and largely patronised Home for Inebriate Caddies.

Old Lady Mary

MARGARET OLIPHANT

I

She was very old, and therefore it was very hard for her to make up her mind to die. I am aware that this is not at all the general view, but that it is believed, as old age must be near death, that it prepares the soul for that inevitable event. It is not so, however, in many cases. In youth we are still so near the unseen out of which we came, that death is rather pathetic than tragic – a thing that touches all hearts, but to which, in many cases, the young hero accommodates himself sweetly and courageously. And amid the storms and burdens of middle life there are many times when we would fain push open the door that stands ajar, and behind which there is ease for all our pains, or at least rest, if nothing more. But age, which has gone through both these phases, is apt, out of long custom and habit, to regard the matter from a different view. All things that are violent have passed out of its life – no more strong emotions, such as rend the heart; no great labours, bringing after them the weariness which is unto death; but the calm of an existence which is enough for its needs, which affords the moderate amount of comfort and pleasure for which its being is now adapted, and of which there seems no reason that there should ever be any end. To passion, to joy, to anguish, an end must come; but mere gentle living, determined by a framework of gentle rules and habits – why should that ever be ended? When a soul has got to this retirement and is content in it, it becomes very hard to die; hard to accept the necessity of dying, and to accustom oneself to the idea, and still harder to consent to carry it out.

The woman who is the subject of the following narrative was in this position. She had lived through almost everything that is to be found in life. She had been beautiful in her youth, and had enjoyed all the triumphs of beauty; had been intoxicated with flattery, and triumphant in conquest, and mad with jealousy and the bitterness of defeat when it became evident that her day was over. She had never been a bad woman, or false, or unkind; but she had thrown herself with all her heart into those different stages of being, and had suffered as much as she enjoyed, according to the unfailing usage of life. Many a day during these storms and victories, when things went against her, when delights did not satisfy her, she had thrown out a cry into the wide air of the universe and wished to die. And then she had come to the higher tableland of life, and had borne all the spites of fortune – had been poor and rich, and happy and sorrowful; had lost and won a hundred times over; had sat at feasts, and kneeled by deathbeds, and followed her best-beloved to the grave, often, often crying out to God above to liberate her, to make an end of her anguish, for that her strength was exhausted and she could bear no more. But she had borne it and lived through all; and now had arrived at a time when all strong sensations are over, when the soul is no longer either triumphant or miserable, and when life itself, and comfort and ease, and the warmth of the sun, and of the fireside, and the mild beauty of home were enough for her, and she required no more. That is, she required very little more, a useful routine of hours and rules, a play of reflected emotion, a pleasant exercise of faculty, making her feel herself still capable of the best things in life – of interest in her fellow-creatures, kindness to them, and a little gentle intellectual occupation, with books and men around. She had not forgotten anything in her life – not the excitements and delights of her beauty, nor love, nor grief, nor the higher levels she had touched in her day. She did not forget the dark day when her first-born was laid in the grave, nor that triumphant and brilliant climax of her life when everyone pointed to her as the mother of a hero. All these things were like pictures hung in the secret chambers of her mind, to which she could go back in silent moments, in the twilight seated by the fire, or in the balmy afternoon, when languor and sweet thoughts are over the world. Sometimes at such moments there would be heard from her a faint sob, called forth, it was quite as likely, by the recollection of the triumph as by that of the deathbed. With these pictures to go back upon at her will she was never dull, but saw herself moving through the various scenes of her life with a continual sympathy, feeling for herself in all her troubles – sometimes approving, sometimes judging that woman who had been so pretty, so happy, so miserable, and had gone through everything that life can go through. How much that is, looking back upon it! – passages so hard that the wonder was how she could survive them; pangs so terrible that the heart would seem at its last gasp, but yet would revive and go on.

Besides these, however, she had many mild pleasures. She had a pretty house full of things which formed a graceful *entourage* suitable, as she felt, for such a woman as she was, and in which she took pleasure for their own beauty – soft chairs and couches, a fireplace and lights which were the perfection of tempered warmth and illumination. She had a carriage, very comfortable and easy, in which, when the weather was suitable, she went out; and a pretty garden and lawns, in which, when she preferred staying at home, she could have her little walk or sit out under the trees. She had books in plenty, and all the newspapers, and everything that was needful to keep her within the reflection of the busy life which she no longer cared to encounter in her own person. The post rarely brought her painful letters; for all those impassioned interests which bring pain had died out, and the sorrows of others, when they were communicated to her, gave her a luxurious sense of sympathy, yet exemption. She was sorry for them, but such catastrophes could touch her no more; and often she had pleasant letters, which afforded her something to talk and think about, and discuss as if it concerned her – and yet did not concern her – business which could not hurt her if it failed, which would please her if it succeeded. Her letters, her papers, her books, each coming at its appointed hour, were all instruments of pleasure. She came downstairs at a certain hour, which she kept to as if it had been of the utmost importance, although it was of no importance at all; she took just so much good wine, so many cups of tea. Her repasts were as regular as clockwork – never too late, never too early. Her whole life went on velvet, rolling smoothly along, without jar or interruption, blameless, pleasant, kind. People talked of her old age as a model of old age, with no bitterness or sourness in it. And, indeed, why should she have been sour or bitter? It suited her far better to be kind. She was in reality kind to everybody, liking to see pleasant faces about her. The poor had no reason to complain of her; her servants were very comfortable; and the one person in her house who was nearer to her own level, who was her companion and most important minister, was very comfortable too. This was a young woman about twenty, a very distant relation, with 'no claim', everybody said, upon her kind mistress and friend – the daughter of a distant cousin. How very few think anything at all of such a tie! but Lady Mary had taken her young namesake when she was a child, and she had grown up as it were at her godmother's footstool, in the conviction that the measured existence of the old was the rule of life, and that her own trifling personality counted for nothing, or next to nothing, in its steady progress. Her name was Mary too – always called 'little Mary' as having once been little, and not yet very much in the matter of size. She was one of the pleasantest things to look at of all the pretty things in Lady Mary's rooms, and she had the most sheltered, peaceful and pleasant life that could be conceived. The only little thorn in her pillow was that whereas in the novels, of which she read a great many, the heroines all go and pay visits and have adventures, she had none, but lived constantly at home. There was something much more serious in her life, had she known, which was that she had nothing, and no power of doing anything for herself; that she had all her life been accustomed to a modest luxury which would make poverty very hard to her; and that Lady Mary was over eighty, and had made no will. If she did not make any will, her property would all go to her grandson, who was so rich already that her fortune would be but as a drop in the ocean to him; or to some great-grandchildren of whom she knew very little – the descendants of a daughter long ago dead who had married an Austrian, and who were therefore foreigners both in birth and name. That she should provide for little Mary was therefore a thing which nature demanded, and which would hurt nobody. She had said so often; but she deferred the doing of it as a thing for which there was no hurry. For why should she die? There seemed no reason or need for it. So long as she lived, nothing could be more sure, more happy and serene, than little Mary's life; and why should she die? She did not perhaps put this into words; but the meaning of her smile, and the manner in which she put aside every suggestion about the chances of the hereafter away from her, said it more clearly than words. It was not that she had any superstitious fear about the making of a will. When the doctor or the vicar or her man of business, the only persons who ever talked to her on the subject, ventured periodically to refer to it, she assented pleasantly – yes, certainly, she must do it – sometime or other.

'It is a very simple thing to do,' the lawyer said. 'I will save you all trouble; nothing but your signature will be wanted – and that you give every day.'

'Oh, I should think nothing of the trouble!' she said.

'And it would liberate your mind from all care, and leave you free to think of things more important still,' said the clergyman.

'I think I am very free of care,' she replied.

Then the doctor added bluntly, 'And you will not die an hour the sooner for having made your will.'

'Die!' said Lady Mary, surprised. And then she added, with a smile, 'I hope you don't think so little of me as to believe I would be kept back by that?'

These gentlemen all consulted together in despair, and asked each other what should be done. They thought her an egotist – a cold-hearted old woman, holding at arm's length any idea of the inevitable. And so she did; but not because she was cold-hearted – because she was so accustomed to living, and had survived so many calamities, and gone on so long – so long; and because everything was so comfortably arranged about her – all her little habits so firmly established, as if nothing could interfere with them. To think of the day arriving which should begin with some other formula than that of her maid's entrance drawing aside the curtains, lighting the cheerful fire, bringing her a report of the weather; and then the little tray, resplendent with snowy linen and shining silver and china, with its bouquet of violets or a rose in the season, the newspaper carefully dried and cut, the letters – every detail was so perfect, so unchanging, regular as the morning. It seemed impossible that it should come to an end. And then when she came downstairs, there were all the little articles upon her table always ready to her hand; a certain number of things to do, each at the appointed hour; the slender refreshments it was necessary for her to take, in which there was a little exquisite variety – but never any change in the fact that at eleven and at three and so forth something had to be taken. Had a woman wanted to abandon the peaceful life which was thus supported and carried on, the very framework itself would have resisted. It was impossible (almost) to contemplate the idea that at a given moment the whole machinery must stop. She was neither without heart nor without religion, but on the contrary a good woman, to whom many gentle thoughts had been given at various portions of her career. But the occasion seemed to have passed for that as well as other kinds of emotion. The mere fact of living was enough for her. The little exertion which it was well she was required to make produced a pleasant weariness. It was a duty much enforced upon her by all around her, that she should do nothing which would exhaust or fatigue. 'I don't want you to think,' even the doctor would say; 'you have done enough of thinking in your time.' And this she accepted with great composure of spirit. She had thought and felt and done much in her day; but now everything of the kind was over. There was no need for her to fatigue herself; and day followed day, all warm and sheltered and pleasant. People died, it is true, now and then, out of doors; but they were mostly young people, whose death might have been prevented had proper care been taken – who were seized with violent maladies, or caught sudden infections, or were cut down by accident; all which things seemed natural. Her own contemporaries were very few, and they were like herself – living on in something of the same way. At eighty-five all people under seventy are young; and one's contemporaries are very, very few.

Nevertheless these men did disturb her a little about her will. She had made more than one will in the former days during her active life; but all those to whom she had bequeathed her possessions were dead. She had survived them all, and inherited from many of them; which had been a hard thing in its time. One day the lawyer had been more than ordinarily pressing. He had told her stories of men who had died intestate, and left trouble and penury behind them to those whom they would have most wished to preserve from all trouble. It would not have become Mr Furnival to say brutally to Lady Mary, 'This is how you will leave your godchild when you die.' But he told her story after story, many of them piteous enough.

'People think it is so troublesome a business,' he said, 'when it is nothing at all – the most easy matter in the world. We are getting so much less particular nowadays about formalities. So long as the testator's intentions are made quite apparent – that is the chief matter, and a very bad thing for us lawyers.'

'I dare say,' said Lady Mary, 'it is unpleasant for a man to think of himself as "the testator". It is a very abstract title, when you come to think of it.'

'Pooh,' said Mr Furnival, who had no sense of humour.

'But if this great business is so very simple,' she went on, 'one could do it, no doubt, for oneself?'

'Many people do, but it is never advisable,' said the lawyer. 'You will say it is natural for me to tell you that. When they do, it should be as simple as possible. I give all my real property, or my personal property, or my share in so-and-so, or my jewels, or so forth, to – whoever it may be. The fewer words the better – so that nobody may be able to read between the lines, you know – and the signature attested by two witnesses; but they must not be witnesses that have any interest; that is, that have anything left to them by the document they witness.'

Lady Mary put up her hand defensively, with a laugh. It was still a most delicate hand, like ivory, a little yellowed with age, but fine, the veins standing out a little upon it, the fingertips still pink. 'You speak,' she said, 'as if you expected me to take the law in my own hands. No, no, my old friend; never fear, you shall have the doing of it.'

'Whenever you please, my dear lady – whenever you please. Such a thing cannot be done an hour too soon. Shall I take your instructions now?'

Lady Mary laughed, and said, 'You were always a very keen man for business. I remember your father used to say, Robert would never neglect an opening.'

'No,' he said, with a peculiar look. 'I have always looked after my six-and-eightpences; and in that case it is true, the pounds take care of themselves.'

'Very good care,' said Lady Mary; and then she bade her young companion bring that book she had been reading, where there was something she wanted to show Mr Furnival. 'It is only a case in a novel, but I am sure it is bad law; give me your opinion,' she said.

He was obliged to be civil, very civil. Nobody is rude to the Lady Marys of life; and besides, she was old enough to have an additional right to every courtesy. But while he sat over the novel, and tried with unnecessary vehemence to make her see what very bad law it was, and glanced from her smiling attention to the innocent sweetness of the girl beside her, who was her loving attendant, the good man's heart was sore. He said many hard things of her in his own mind as he went away.

'She will die,' he said bitterly. 'She will go off in a moment when nobody is looking for it, and that poor child will be left destitute.'

It was all he could do not to go back and take her by her fragile old shoulders and force her to sign and seal at once. But then he knew very well that as soon as he found himself in her presence, he would of necessity be obliged to subdue his impatience, and be once more civil, very civil, and try to suggest and insinuate the duty which he dared not force upon her. And it was very clear that till she pleased she would take no hint. He supposed it must be that strange reluctance to part with their power which is said to be common to old people, or else that horror of death, and determination to keep it at arm's length, which is also common. Thus he did as spectators are so apt to do, he forced a meaning and motive into what had no motive at all, and imagined Lady Mary, the kindest of women, to be of purpose and intention risking the future of the girl whom she had brought up, and whom she loved – not with passion, indeed, or anxiety, but with tender benevolence; a theory which was as false as anything could be.

That evening in her room, Lady Mary, in a very cheerful mood, sat by a little bright unnecessary fire, with her writing-book before her, waiting till she should be sleepy. It was the only point in which she was a little hard upon her maid, who in every other respect was the best-treated of servants. Lady Mary, as it happened, had often no inclination for bed till the night was far advanced. She slept little, as is common enough at her age. She was in her warm wadded dressing-gown, an article in which she still showed certain traces (which were indeed visible in all she wore) of her ancient beauty, with her white hair becomingly arranged under a cap of cambric and lace. At the last moment, when she had been ready to step into bed, she had changed her mind, and told Jervis that she would write a letter or two first. And she had written her letters, but still felt no inclination to sleep. Then there fluttered across her memory somehow the conversation she had held with Mr Furnival in the morning. It would be amusing, she thought, to cheat him out of some of those six-and-eightpences he pretended to think so much of. It would be still more amusing, next time the subject of her will was recurred to, to give his arm a little tap with her fan, and say, 'Oh, that is all settled, months ago.' She laughed to herself at this, and took out a fresh sheet of paper. It was a little jest that pleased her.

'Do you think there is anyone up yet, Jervis, except you and me?' she said to the maid. Jervis hesitated a little, and then said that she believed Mr Brown had not gone to bed yet; for he had been going over the cellar, and was making up his accounts. Jervis was so explanatory that her mistress divined what was meant. 'I suppose I have been spoiling sport, keeping you here,' she said good-humouredly; for it was well known that Miss Jervis and Mr Brown were engaged, and that they were only waiting (everybody knew but Lady Mary, who never suspected it) the death of their mistress, to set up a lodging-house in Jermyn Street, where they fully intended to make their fortune. 'Then go,' Lady Mary said, 'and call Brown. I have a little business paper to write, and you must both witness my signature.' She laughed to herself a little as she said this, thinking how she would steal a march on Mr Furnival. 'I give, and bequeath,' she said to herself playfully, after Jervis had hurried away. She fully intended to leave both of these good servants something, but then she recollected that people who are interested in a will cannot sign as witnesses. 'What does it matter?' she said to herself gayly; 'If it ever should be wanted, Mary would see to that.' Accordingly she dashed off, in her pretty, old-fashioned handwriting, which was very angular and pointed, as was the fashion in her day, and still very clear, though slightly tremulous, a few lines, in which, remembering playfully Mr Furnival's recommendation of 'few words', she left to little Mary all she possessed, adding, by the prompting of that recollection about the witnesses, 'She will take care of the servants.' It filled one side only of the large sheet of notepaper, which was what Lady Mary habitually used. Brown, introduced timidly by Jervis, and a little overawed by the solemnity of the bedchamber, came in and painted solidly his large signature after the spidery lines of his mistress. She had folded down the paper, so that neither saw what it was.

'Now I will go to bed,' Lady Mary said, when Brown had left the room. 'And Jervis, you must go to bed too.'

'Yes, my lady,' said Jervis.

'I don't approve of courtship at this hour.'

'No, my lady,' Jervis replied, deprecating and disappointed.

'Why cannot he tell his tale in daylight?'

'Oh, my lady, there's no tale to tell,' cried the maid. 'We are not of the gossiping sort, my lady, neither me nor Mr Brown.' Lady Mary laughed, and watched while the candles were put out, the fire made a pleasant flicker in the room – it was autumn and still warm, and it was 'for company' and cheerfulness that the little fire was lit; she liked to see it dancing and flickering upon the walls – and then closed her eyes amid an exquisite softness of comfort and luxury, life itself bearing her up as softly, filling up all the crevices as warmly as the downy pillow upon which she rested her still beautiful old head.

If she had died that night! The little sheet of paper that meant so much lay openly, innocently, in her writing-book, along with the letters she had written, and looking of as little importance as they. There was nobody in the world who grudged old Lady Mary one of those pretty placid days of hers. Brown and Jervis, if they were sometimes a little impatient, consoled each other that they were both sure of something in her will, and that in the meantime it was a very good place. And all the rest would have been very well content that Lady Mary should live for ever. But how wonderfully it would have simplified everything, and how much trouble and pain it would have saved everybody, herself included, could she have died that night!

But naturally, there was no question of dying on that night. When she was about to go downstairs, next day, Lady Mary, giving her letters to be posted, saw the paper she had forgotten lying beside them. She had forgotten all about it, but the sight of it made her smile. She folded it up and put it in an envelope while Jervis went downstairs with the letters; and then, to carry out her joke, she looked round her to see where she would put it. There was an old Italian cabinet in the room, with a secret drawer, which it was a little difficult to open – almost impossible for anyone who did not know the secret. Lady Mary looked round her, smiled, hesitated a little, and then walked across the room and put the envelope in the secret drawer. She was still fumbling with it when Jervis came back; but there was no connection in Jervis's mind, then or ever after, between the paper she had signed and this old cabinet, which was one of the old lady's toys. She arranged Lady Mary's shawl, which had dropped off her shoulders a little in her unusual activity, and took up her book and her favourite cushion, and all the little paraphernalia that moved with her, and gave her lady her arm to go downstairs; where little Mary had placed her chair just at the right angle, and arranged the little table, on which there were so many little necessaries and conveniences, and was standing smiling, the prettiest object of all, the climax of the gentle luxury and pleasantness, to receive her godmother, who had been her providence all her life.

But what a pity! oh, what a pity, that she had not died that night!

2

Life went on after this without any change. There was never any change in that delightful house; and if it was years, or months, or even days, the youngest of its inhabitants could scarcely tell, and Lady Mary could not tell at all. This was one of her little imperfections – a little mist which hung, like the lace about her head, over her memory. She could not remember how time went, or that there was any difference between one day and another. There were Sundays, it was true, which made a kind of gentle measure of the progress of time; but she said, with a smile, that she thought it was always Sunday – they came so close upon each other. And time flew on gentle wings that made no sound and left no reminders. She had her little ailments like anybody, but in reality less than anybody, seeing there was nothing to fret her, nothing to disturb the even tenor of her days. Still there were times when she took a little cold, or got a chill, in spite of all precautions, as she went from one room to another. She came to be one of the marvels of the time – an old lady who had seen everybody worth seeing for generations back; who remembered as distinctly as if they had happened yesterday, great events that had taken place before the present age began at all, before the great statesmen of our time were born; and in full possession of all her faculties, as everybody said, her mind as clear as ever, her intelligence as active, reading everything, interested in everything, and still beautiful, in extreme old age. Everybody about her, and in particular all the people who helped to keep the thorns from her path, and felt themselves to have a hand in her preservation, were proud of Lady Mary and she was perhaps a little, a very little, delightfully, charmingly, proud of herself. The doctor, beguiled by professional vanity, feeling what a feather she was in his cap, quite confident that she would reach her hundredth birthday, and with an ecstatic hope that even, by grace of his admirable treatment and her own beautiful constitution, she might (almost) solve the problem and live for ever, gave up troubling about the will which at a former period he had taken so much interest in. 'What is the use?' he said; 'she will see us all out.' And the vicar, though he did not give in to this, was overawed by the old lady, who knew everything that could be taught her, and to whom it seemed an impertinence to utter commonplaces about duty, or even to suggest subjects of thought. Mr Furnival was the only man who did not cease his representations, and whose anxiety about the young Mary, who was so blooming and sweet in the shadow of the old, did not decrease. But the recollection of the bit of paper in the secret drawer of the cabinet, fortified his old client against all his attacks. She had intended it only as a jest, with which someday or other to confound him, and show how much wiser she was than he supposed. It became quite a pleasant subject of thought to her, at which she laughed to herself. Someday, when she had a suitable moment, she would order him to come with all his formalities, and then produce her bit of paper, and turn the laugh against him. But oddly, the very existence of that little document kept her indifferent even to the laugh. It was too much trouble; she only smiled at him, and took no more notice, amused to think how astonished he would be – when, if ever, he found it out.

It happened, however, that one day in the early winter the wind changed when Lady Mary was out for her drive; at least they all vowed the wind changed. It was in the south, that genial quarter, when she set out, but turned about in some uncomfortable way, and was a keen northeaster when she came back. And in the moment of stepping from the carriage, she caught a chill. It was the coachman's fault, Jervis said, who allowed the horses to make a step forward when Lady Mary was getting out, and kept her exposed, standing on the step of the carriage, while he pulled them up; and it was Jervis's fault, the footman said, who was not clever enough to get her lady out, or even to throw a shawl round her when she perceived how the weather had changed. It is always someone's fault, or some unforeseen, unprecedented change, that does it at the last. Lady Mary was not accustomed to be ill, and did not bear it with her usual grace. She was a little impatient at first, and thought they were making an unnecessary fuss. But then there passed a few uncomfortable feverish days, when she began to look forward to the doctor's visit as the only thing there was any comfort in. Afterwards she passed a night of a very agitating kind. She dozed and dreamed, and awoke and dreamed again. Her life seemed all to run into dreams – a strange confusion was about her, through which she could define nothing. Once waking up, as she supposed, she saw a group round her bed, the doctor – with a candle in his hand (how should the doctor be there in the middle of the night?), holding her hand or feeling her pulse; little Mary at one side, crying – why should the child cry? – and Jervis, very anxious, pouring something into a glass. There were other faces there which she was sure must have come out of a dream – so unlikely was it that they should be collected in her bedchamber – and all with a sort of halo of feverish light about them; a magnified and mysterious importance. This strange scene, which she did not understand, seemed to make itself visible all in a moment out of the darkness, and then disappeared again as suddenly as it came.

3

When she woke again, it was morning; and her first waking consciousness was that she must be much better. The choking sensation in her throat was altogether gone. She had no desire to cough – no difficulty in breathing. She had a fancy, however, that she must be still dreaming, for she felt sure that someone had called her by her name, 'Mary.' Now all who could call her by her Christian name were dead years ago; therefore it must be a dream. However, in a short time it was repeated – 'Mary, Mary! get up; there is a great deal to do.' This voice confused her greatly. Was it possible that all that was past had been mere fancy, that she had but dreamed those long, long years – maturity and motherhood, and trouble and triumph, and old age at the end of all? It seemed to her possible that she might have dreamed the rest – for she had been a girl much given to visions – but she said to herself that she never could have dreamed old age. And then with a smile she mused, and thought that it must be the voice that was a dream; for how could she get up without Jervis, who had never appeared yet to draw the curtains or make the fire? Jervis perhaps had sat up late. She remembered now to have seen her that time in the middle of the night by her bedside; so that it was natural enough, poor thing, that she should be late. Get up! who was it that was calling to her so? She had not been so called to, she who had always been a great lady, since she was a girl by her mother's side. 'Mary, Mary!' It was a very curious dream. And what was more curious still was that by and by she could not keep still any longer, but got up without thinking any more of Jervis, and going out of her room came all at once into the midst of a company of people, all very busy; whom she was much surprised to find, at first, but whom she soon accustomed herself to, finding the greatest interest in their proceedings, and curious to know what they were doing. They, for their part, did not seem at all surprised by her appearance, nor did anyone stop to explain, as would have been natural; but she took this with great composure, somewhat astonished, perhaps, being used, wherever she went, to a great many observances and much respect, but soon, very soon, becoming used to it. Then someone repeated what she had heard before. 'It is time you got up – for there is a great deal to do.'

'To do,' she said, 'for me?' and then she looked round upon them with that charming smile which had subjugated so many. 'I am afraid,' she said, 'you will find me of very little use. I am too old now, if ever I could have done much, for work.'

'Oh no, you are not old – you will do very well,' someone said.

'Not old!' – Lady Mary felt a little offended in spite of herself. 'Perhaps I like flattery as well as my neighbours,' she said with dignity, 'but then it must be reasonable. To say I am anything but a very old woman – '

Here she paused a little, perceiving for the first time, with surprise, that she was standing and walking without her stick or the help of anyone's arm, quite freely and at her ease, and that the place in which she was had expanded into a great place like a gallery in a palace, instead of the room next her own into which she had walked a few minutes ago; but this discovery did not at all affect her mind, or occupy her except with the most passing momentary surprise.

'The fact is, I feel a great deal better and stronger,' she said.

'Quite well, Mary, and stronger than ever you were before?'

'Who is it that calls me Mary? I have had nobody for a long time to call me Mary; the friends of my youth are all dead. I think that you must be right, although the doctor, I feel sure, thought me very bad last night. I should have got alarmed if I had not fallen asleep again.'

'And then woke up well?'

'Quite well: it is wonderful, but quite true. You seem to know a great deal about me.'

'I know everything about you. You have had a very pleasant life, and do you think you have made the best of it? Your old age has been very pleasant.'

'Ah! you acknowledge that I am old, then?' cried Lady Mary with a smile.

'You are old no longer, and you are a great lady no longer. Don't you see that something has happened to you? It is seldom that such a great change happens without being found out.'

'Yes; it is true I have got better all at once. I feel an extraordinary renewal of strength. I seem to have left home without knowing it; none of my people seem near me. I feel very much as if I had just awakened from a long dream. Is it possible,' she said, with a wondering look, 'that I have dreamed all my life, and after all am just a girl at home?' The idea was ludicrous, and she laughed. 'You see I am very much improved indeed,' she said.

She was still so far from perceiving the real situation, that someone came towards her out of the group of people about – someone whom she recognised – with the evident intention of explaining to her how it was. She started a little at the sight of him, and held out her hand, and cried: 'You here! I am very glad to see you – doubly glad, since I was told a few days ago that you had – died.'

There was something in this word as she herself pronounced it that troubled her a little. She had never been one of those who are afraid of death. On the contrary, she had always taken a great interest in it, and liked to hear everything that could be told her on the subject. It gave her now, however, a curious little thrill of sensation, which she did not understand: she hoped it was not superstition.

'You have guessed rightly,' he said, 'quite right. That is one of the words with a false meaning, which is to us a mere symbol of something we cannot understand. But you see what it means now.'

It was a great shock, it need not be concealed. Otherwise, she had been quite pleasantly occupied with the interest of something new, into which she had walked so easily out of her own bedchamber, without any trouble, and with the delightful new sensation of health and strength. But when it flashed upon her that she was not to go

back to her bedroom again, nor have any of those cares and
attentions which had seemed necessary to existence, she was very
much startled and shaken. Died? Was it possible that she personally
had died? She had known it was a thing that happened to everybody;
but yet – And it was a solemn matter, to be prepared for, and looked
forward to, whereas – 'If you mean that I too – ' she said, faltering a
little; and then she added, 'it is very surprising,' with a trouble in
her mind which yet was not all trouble. 'If that is so, it is a thing well
over. And it is very wonderful how much disturbance people give
themselves about it – if this is all.'

'This is not all, however,' her friend said; 'you have an ordeal
before you which you will not find pleasant. You are going to think
about your life, and all that was imperfect in it, and which might have
been done better.'

'We are none of us perfect,' said Lady Mary, with a little of that
natural resentment with which one hears oneself accused – however
ready one may be to accuse oneself.

'Permit me,' said he, and took her hand and led her away without
further explanation. The people about were so busy with their own
occupations that they took very little notice; neither did she pay
much attention to the manner in which they were engaged. Their
looks were friendly when they met her eye, and she too felt friendly,
with a sense of brotherhood. But she had always been a kind
woman. She wanted to step aside and help, on more than one
occasion, when it seemed to her that some people in her way had a
task above their powers; but this her conductor would not permit.
And she endeavoured to put some questions to him as they went
along, with still less success.

'The change is very confusing,' she said; 'one has no standard to
judge by. I should like to know something about – the kind of
people – and the – manner of life.'

'For a time,' he said, 'you will have enough to do, without troubling
yourself about that.'

This naturally produced an uneasy sensation in her mind. 'I
suppose,' she said, rather timidly, 'that we are not in – what we have
been accustomed to call heaven?'

'That is a word,' he said, 'which expresses rather a condition than a
place.'

'But there must be a place – in which that condition can exist.' She
had always been fond of discussions of this kind, and felt encouraged
to find that they were still practicable. 'It cannot be the – Inferno;

that is clear, at least,' she added, with the sprightliness which was one of her characteristics; 'perhaps – Purgatory? since you infer I have something to endure.'

'Words are interchangeable,' he said: 'that means one thing to one of us which to another has a totally different signification.' There was something so like his old self in this, that she laughed with an irresistible sense of amusement.

'You were always fond of the oracular,' she said. She was conscious that on former occasions, if he made such a speech to her, though she would have felt the same amusement, she would not have expressed it so frankly. But he did not take it at all amiss. And her thoughts went on in other directions. She felt herself saying over to herself the words of the old north-country dirge, which came to her recollection she knew not how – 'If hosen and shoon thou gavest nane, The whins shall prick thee intil the bane.'

When she saw that her companion heard her, she asked, 'Is that true?'

He shook his head a little. 'It is too matter of fact,' he said, 'as I need hardly tell you. Hosen and shoon are good, but they do not always sufficiently indicate the state of the heart.'

Lady Mary had a consciousness, which was pleasant to her, that so far as the hosen and shoon went, she had abundant means of preparing herself for the pricks of any road, however rough; but she had no time to indulge this pleasing reflection, for she was shortly introduced into a great building, full of innumerable rooms, in one of which her companion left her.

4

The door opened, and she felt herself free to come out. How long she had been there, or what passed there, is not for anyone to say. She came out tingling and smarting – if such words can be used – with an intolerable recollection of the last act of her life. So intolerable was it that all that had gone before, and all the risings up of old errors and visions long dead, were forgotten in the sharp and keen prick of this, which was not over and done like the rest. No one had accused her, or brought before her judge the things that were against her. She it was who had done it all – she, whose memory did not spare her one fault, who remembered everything. But when she came to that last frivolity of her old age, and saw for the first time how she had played with the future of the child whom she had brought up, and abandoned to the hardest fate – for nothing, for folly, for a jest – the horror and bitterness of the thought filled her mind to overflowing. In the first anguish of that recollection she had to go forth, receiving no word of comfort in respect to it, meeting only with a look of sadness and compassion, which went to her very heart. She came forth as if she had been driven away, but not by any outward influence, by the force of her own miserable sensations. 'I will write,' she said to herself, 'and tell them; I will go – ' And then she stopped short, remembering that she could neither go nor write – that all communication with the world she had left was closed. Was it all closed? Was there no way in which a message could reach those who remained behind? She caught the first passer-by whom she passed, and addressed him piteously. 'Oh, tell me – you have been longer here than I – cannot one send a letter, a message, if it were only a single word?'

'Where?' he said, stopping and listening; so that it began to seem possible to her that some such expedient might still be within her reach.

'It is to England,' she said, thinking he meant to ask as to which quarter of the world.

'Ah,' he said, shaking his head, 'I fear that it is impossible.'

'But it is to set something right, which out of mere inadvertence, with no ill meaning,' – No, no (she repeated to herself), no ill-meaning – none! 'Oh sir, for charity! tell me how I can find a way. There must – there must be some way.'

He was greatly moved by the sight of her distress. 'I am but a stranger here,' he said; 'I may be wrong. There are others who can tell you better; but' – and he shook his head sadly – 'most of us would be so thankful, if we could, to send a word, if it were only a single word, to those we have left behind, that I fear, I fear – '

'Ah!' cried Lady Mary, 'but that would be only for the tenderness; whereas this is for justice and for pity, and to do away with a great wrong which I did before I came here.'

'I am very sorry for you,' he said; but shook his head once more as he went away. She was more careful next time, and chose one who had the look of much experience and knowledge of the place. He listened to her very gravely, and answered yes, that he was one of the officers, and could tell her whatever she wanted to know; but when she told him what she wanted, he too shook his head. 'I do not say it cannot be done,' he said. 'There are some cases in which it has been successful, but very few. It has often been attempted. There is no law against it. Those who do it do it at their own risk. They suffer much, and almost always they fail.'

'No, oh no! You said there were some who succeeded. No one can be more anxious than I. I will give – anything – everything I have in the world!'

He gave her a smile, which was very grave nevertheless, and full of pity. 'You forget,' he said, 'that you have nothing to give; and if you had, that there is no one here to whom it would be of any value.'

Though she was no longer old and weak, yet she was still a woman, and she began to weep, in the terrible failure and contrariety of all things; but yet she would not yield. She cried: 'There must be someone here who would do it for love. I have had people who loved me in my time. I must have some here who have not forgotten me. Ah! I know what you would say. I lived so long I forgot them all, and why should they remember me?'

Here she was touched on the arm, and looking round, saw close to her the face of one whom, it was very true, she had forgotten. She remembered him but dimly after she had looked long at him. A little group had gathered about her, with grieved looks, to see her distress. He who had touched her was the spokesman of them all.

'There is nothing I would not do,' he said, 'for you and for love.' And then they all sighed, surrounding her, and added, 'But it is impossible – impossible!'

She stood and gazed at them, recognising by degrees faces that she knew, and seeing in all that look of grief and sympathy which makes all human souls brothers. Impossible was not a word that had been often said to be in her life; and to come out of a world in which everything could be changed, everything communicated in the twinkling of an eye, and find a dead blank before her and around her, through which not a word could go, was more terrible than can be said in words. She looked piteously upon them, with that anguish of helplessness which goes to every heart, and cried, 'What is impossible? To send a word – only a word – to set right what is wrong? Oh, I understand,' she said, lifting up her hands. 'I understand that to send messages of comfort must not be; that the people who love you must bear it, as we all have done in our time, and trust to God for consolation. But I have done a wrong! Oh, listen, listen to me, my friends. I have left a child, a young creature, unprovided for – without anyone to help her. And must that be? Must she bear it, and I bear it, for ever, and no means, no way of setting it right? Listen to me! I was there last night – in the middle of the night I was still there – and here this morning. So it must be easy to come – only a short way; and two words would be enough – only two words!'

They gathered closer and closer round her, full of compassion. 'It is easy to come,' they said, 'but not to go.'

And one added, 'It will not be for ever; comfort yourself. When she comes here, or to a better place, that will seem to you only as a day.

'But to her,' cried Lady Mary – 'to her it will be long years – it will be trouble and sorrow; and she will think I took no thought for her; and she will be right,' the penitent said with a great and bitter cry.

It was so terrible that they were all silent, and said not a word – except the man who had loved her, who put his hand upon her arm, and said, 'We are here for that; this is the fire that purges us – to see at last what we have done, and the true aspect of it, and to know the cruel wrong, yet never be able to make amends.'

She remembered then that this was a man who had neglected all lawful affections, and broken the hearts of those who trusted him for her sake; and for a moment she forgot her own burden in sorrow for his.

It was now that he who had called himself one of the officers came forward again; for the little crowd had gathered round her so closely that he had been shut out. He said, 'No one can carry your message for you; that is not permitted. But there is still a possibility. You may have permission to go yourself. Such things have been done, though they have not often been successful. But if you will – '

She shivered when she heard him; and it became apparent to her why no one could be found to go – for all her nature revolted from that step, which it was evident must be the most terrible which could be thought of. She looked at him with troubled, beseeching eyes, and the rest all looked at her, pitying and trying to soothe her.

'Permission will not be refused,' he said, 'for a worthy cause.'

Upon which the others all spoke together, entreating her. 'Already,' they cried, 'they have forgotten you living. You are to them one who is dead. They will be afraid of you if they can see you. Oh, go not back! Be content to wait – to wait; it is only a little while. The life of man is nothing; it appears for a little time, and then it vanishes away. And when she comes here she will know – or in a better place.' They sighed as they named the better place; though some smiled too, feeling perhaps more near to it.

Lady Mary listened to them all, but she kept her eyes upon the face of him who offered her this possibility. There passed through her mind a hundred stories she had heard of those who had *gone back*. But not one that spoke of them as welcome, as received with joy, as comforting those they loved. Ah no! was it not rather a curse upon the house to which they came? The rooms were shut up, the houses abandoned, where they were supposed to appear. Those whom they had loved best feared and fled them. They were a vulgar wonder – a thing that the poorest laughed at, yet feared. Poor, banished souls! it was because no one would listen to them that they had to linger and wait, and come and go. She shivered, and in spite of her longing and her repentance, a cold dread and horror took possession of her. She looked round upon her companions for comfort, and found none.

'Do not go,' they said; 'do not go. We have endured like you. We wait till all things are made clear.'

And another said, 'All will be made clear. It is but for a time.'

She turned from one to another, and back again to the first speaker – he who had authority.

He said, 'It is very rarely successful; it retards the course of your penitence. It is an indulgence, and it may bring harm and not good but if the meaning is generous and just, permission will be given, and you may go.'

Then all the strength of her nature rose in her. She thought of the child forsaken, and of the dark world round her, where she would find so few friends; and of the home shut up in which she had lived her young and pleasant life; and of the thoughts that must rise in her heart, as though she were forsaken and abandoned of God and man. Then Lady Mary turned to the man who had authority. She said, 'If he whom I saw today will give me his blessing, I will go – ' and they all pressed round her, weeping and kissing her hands.

'He will not refuse his blessing,' they said; 'but the way is terrible, and you are still weak. How can you encounter all the misery of it? He commends no one to try that dark and dreadful way.'

'I will try,' Lady Mary said.

5

The night which Lady Mary had been conscious of, in a momentary glimpse full of the exaggeration of fever, had not indeed been so expeditious as she believed. The doctor, it is true, had been pronouncing her death-warrant when she saw him holding her wrist, and wondered what he did there in the middle of the night; but she had been very ill before this, and the conclusion of her life had been watched with many tears. Then there had risen up a wonderful commotion in the house, of which little Mary, her godchild, was very little sensible. Had she left any will, any instructions, the slightest indication of what she wished to be done after her death? Mr Furnival, who had been very anxious to be allowed to see her, even in the last days of her illness, said emphatically, no. She had never executed any will, never made any disposition of her affairs, he said, almost with bitterness, in the tone of one who is ready to weep with vexation and distress. The vicar took a more hopeful view. He said it was impossible that so considerate a person could have done this, and that there must, he was sure, be found somewhere, if close examination was made, a memorandum, a letter – something which should show what she wished; for she must have known very well, notwithstanding all flatteries and compliments upon her good looks, that from day to day her existence was never to be calculated upon. The doctor did not share this last opinion. He said that there was no fathoming the extraordinary views that people took of their own case; and that it was quite possible, though it seemed incredible, that Lady Mary might really be as little expectant of death, on the way to ninety, as a girl of seventeen; but still he was of opinion that she might have left a memorandum somewhere.

These three gentlemen were in the foreground of affairs; because she had no relations to step in and take the management. The earl, her grandson, was abroad, and there were only his solicitors to interfere on his behalf, men to whom Lady Mary's fortune was quite unimportant, although it was against their principles to let anything slip out of their hands that could aggrandise their client; but who knew nothing about the circumstances – about little Mary, about the old lady's peculiarities – in any way. Therefore the persons who had surrounded her in her life, and Mr Furnival, her man of business, were the persons who really had the management of everything. Their wives interfered a little too, or rather the one wife who only could do so – the wife of the vicar, who came in beneficently at once, and took poor little Mary, in her first desolation, out of the melancholy house. Mrs Vicar did this without any hesitation, knowing very well that, in all probability, Lady Mary had made no will, and consequently that the poor girl was destitute. A great deal is said about the hardness of the world, and the small consideration that is shown for a destitute dependent in such circumstances. But this is not true; and, as a matter of fact, there is never, or very rarely, such profound need in the world, without a great deal of kindness and much pity. The three gentlemen all along had been entirely in Mary's interest. They had not expected legacies from the old lady, or any advantage to themselves. It was of the girl that they had thought. And when now they examined everything and enquired into all her ways and what she had done, it was of Mary they were thinking. But Mr Furnival was very certain of his point. He knew that Lady Mary had made no will; time after time he had pressed it upon her. He was very sure, even while he examined her writing-table, and turned out all the drawers, that nothing would be found. The little Italian cabinet had chiffons in its drawers, fragments of old lace, pieces of ribbon, little nothings of all sorts. Nobody thought of the secret drawer; and if they had thought of it, where could a place have been found less likely? If she had ever made a will, she could have had no reason for concealing it. To be sure, they did not reason in this way, being simply unaware of any place of concealment at all. And Mary knew nothing about this search they were making. She did not know how she was herself 'left'. When the first misery of grief was exhausted, she began, indeed, to have troubled thoughts in her own mind – to expect that the vicar would speak to her, or Mr Furnival send for her and tell her what she was to do. But nothing was said to her. The vicar's wife had asked her to come for a long visit; and the anxious people, who were forever talking over this subject and consulting what was best for her, had come to no decision as yet, as to what must be said to the person chiefly concerned. It was too heart-rending to have to put the real state of affairs before her.

The doctor had no wife; but he had an anxious mother, who, though she would not for the world have been unkind to the poor girl, yet was very anxious that she should be disposed of and out of her son's way. It is true that the doctor was forty and Mary only eighteen – but what then? Matches of that kind were seen every day; and his heart was so soft to the child that his mother never knew from one day to another what might happen. She had naturally no doubt at all that Mary would seize the first hand held out to her; and as time went on, held many an anxious consultation with the vicar's wife on the subject. 'You cannot have her with you for ever,' she said. 'She must know one time or another how she is left, and that she must learn to do something for herself.'

'Oh,' said the vicar's wife, 'how is she to be told? It is heart-rending to look at her and to think – nothing but luxury all her life, and now, in a moment, destitution. I am very glad to have her with me: she is a dear little thing, and so nice with the children. And if some good man would only step in – '

The doctor's mother trembled; for that a good man should step in was exactly what she feared. 'That is a thing that can never be depended upon,' she said; 'and marriages made out of compassion are just as bad as mercenary marriages. Oh no, my dear Mrs Bowyer, Mary has a great deal of character. You should put more confidence in her than that. No doubt she will be much cast down at first, but when she knows, she will rise to the occasion and show what is in her.'

'Poor little thing! what is in a girl of eighteen, and one that has lain on the roses and fed on the lilies all her life? Oh, I could find it in my heart to say a great deal about old Lady Mary that would not be pleasant! Why did she bring her up so if she did not mean to provide for her? I think she must have been at heart a wicked old woman.'

'Oh no! we must not say that. I dare say, as my son says, she always meant to do it sometime – '

'Sometime! how long did she expect to live, I wonder?'

'Well,' said the doctor's mother, 'it is wonderful how little old one feels sometimes within oneself, even when one is well up in years.' She was of the faction of the old, instead of being like Mrs Bowyer, who was not much over thirty, of the faction of the young. She could make excuses for Lady Mary; but she thought that it was unkind to bring the poor little girl here in ignorance of her real position, and in the way of men who, though old enough to know better, were still capable of folly – as what man is not, when a girl of eighteen is concerned? 'I hope,' she added, 'that the earl will do something for her. Certainly he ought to, when he knows all that his grandmother did, and what her intentions must have been. He ought to make her a little allowance; that is the least he can do – not, to be sure, such a provision as we all hoped Lady Mary was going to make for her, but enough to live upon. Mr Furnival, I believe, has written to him to that effect.'

'Hush!' cried the vicar's wife; indeed she had been making signs to the other lady, who stood with her back to the door, for some moments. Mary had come in while this conversation was going on. She had not paid any attention to it; and yet her ear had been caught by the names of Lady Mary, and the earl, and Mr Furnival. For whom was it that the earl should make an allowance enough to live upon? whom Lady Mary had not provided for, and whom Mr Furnival had written about? When she sat down to the needlework in which she was helping Mrs Vicar, it was not to be supposed that she should not ponder these words – for some time very vaguely, not perceiving the meaning of them; and then with a start she woke up to perceive that there must be something meant, someone – even someone she knew. And then the needle dropped out of the girl's hand, and the pinafore she was making fell on the floor. Someone! it must be herself they meant! Who but she could be the subject of that earnest conversation? She began to remember a great many conversations as earnest, which had been stopped when she came into the room, and the looks of pity which had been bent upon her. She had thought in her innocence that this was because she had lost her godmother, her protectress – and had been very grateful for the kindness of her friends. But now another meaning came into everything. Mrs Bowyer had accompanied her visitor to the door, still talking, and when she returned her face was very grave. But she smiled when she met Mary's look, and said cheerfully, 'How kind of you, my dear, to make all those pinafores for me! The little ones will not know themselves. They never were so fine before.'

'Oh, Mrs Bowyer,' cried the girl, 'I have guessed something! and I want you to tell me! Are you keeping me for charity, and is it I that am left – without any provision, and that Mr Furnival has written – '

She could not finish her sentence, for it was very bitter to her, as may be supposed.

'I don't know what you mean, my dear,' cried the vicar's wife. 'Charity – well, I suppose that is the same as love – at least it is so in the 13th chapter of 1st Corinthians. You are staying with us, I hope, for love, if that is what you mean.'

Upon which she took the girl in her arms and kissed her, and cried, as women must. 'My dearest,' she said, 'as you have guessed the worst, it is better to tell you. Lady Mary – I don't know why; oh, I don't wish to blame her – has left no will; and, my dear, my dear, you who have been brought up in luxury, you have not a penny.' Here the vicar's wife gave Mary a closer hug, and kissed her once more. 'We love you all the better – if that was possible,' she said.

How many thoughts will fly through a girl's mind while her head rests on some kind shoulder, and she is being consoled for the first calamity that has touched her life! She was neither ungrateful nor unresponsive; but as Mrs Bowyer pressed her close to her kind breast and cried over her, Mary did not cry, but thought – seeing in a moment a succession of scenes, and realising in a moment so complete a new world that all her pain was quelled by the hurry and rush in her brain as her forces rallied to sustain her. She withdrew from her kind support after a moment, with eyes tearless and shining, the colour mounting to her face, and not a sign of discouragement in her, nor yet of sentiment, though she grasped her kind friend's hands with a pressure which her innocent small fingers seemed incapable of giving. 'One has read of such things – in books,' she said, with a faint courageous smile; 'and I suppose they happen – in life.'

'Oh, my dear, too often in life. Though how people can be so cruel, so indifferent, so careless of the happiness of those they love – '

Here Mary pressed her friend's hands till they hurt, and cried, 'Not cruel, not indifferent. I cannot hear a word – '

'Well, dear, it is like you to feel so – I knew you would; and I will not say a word. Oh, Mary, if she ever thinks of such things now – '

'I hope she will not – I hope she cannot!' cried the girl, with once more a vehement pressure of her friend's hands.

'What is that?' Mrs Bowyer said, looking round. 'It is somebody in the next room, I suppose. No, dear, I hope so too, for she would not be happy if she remembered. Mary, dry your eyes, my dear. Try not to think of this. I am sure there is someone in the next room. And you must try not to look wretched, for all our sakes – '

'Wretched!' cried Mary, springing up. 'I am not wretched.' And she turned with a countenance glowing and full of courage to the door. But there was no one there – no visitor lingering in the smaller room as sometimes happened.

'I thought I heard someone come in,' said the vicar's wife. 'Didn't you hear something, Mary? I suppose it is because I am so agitated with all this, but I could have sworn I heard someone come in.'

'There is nobody,' said Mary, who, in the shock of the calamity which had so suddenly changed the world to her, was perfectly calm. She did not feel at all disposed to cry or 'give way'. It went to her head with a thrill of pain, which was excitement as well, like a strong stimulant suddenly applied; and she added, 'I should like to go out a little, if you don't mind, just to get used to the idea.'

'My dear, I will get my hat in a moment – '

'No, please. It is not unkindness; but I must think it over by myself – by myself,' Mary cried. She hurried away, while Mrs Bowyer took another survey of the outer room, and called the servant to know who had been calling. Nobody had been calling, the maid said; but her mistress still shook her head.

'It must have been someone who does not ring, who just opens the door,' she said to herself. 'That is the worst of the country. It might be Mrs Blunt, or Sophia Blackburn, or the curate, or half a dozen people – and they have just gone away when they heard me crying. How could I help crying? But I wonder how much they heard, whoever it was.'

6

It was winter, and snow was on the ground.

Lady Mary found herself on the road that led through her own village, going home. It was like a picture of a wintry night – like one of those pictures that please the children at Christmas. A little snow sprinkled on the roofs, just enough to define them, and on the edges of the roads; every cottage window showing a ruddy glimmer in the twilight; the men coming home from their work; the children, tied up in comforters and caps, stealing in from the slides, and from the pond, where they were forbidden to go; and, in the distance, the trees of the great House standing up dark, turning the twilight into night. She had a curious enjoyment in it, simple like that of a child, and a wish to talk to someone out of the fullness of her heart. She overtook, her step being far lighter than his, one of the men going home from his work, and spoke to him, telling him with a smile not to be afraid; but he never so much as raised his head, and went plodding on with his heavy step, not knowing that she had spoken to him. She was startled by this; but said to herself that the men were dull, that their perceptions were confused, and that it was getting dark; and went on, passing him quickly. His breath made a cloud in the air as he walked, and his heavy plodding steps sounded into the frosty night. She perceived that her own were invisible and inaudible, with a curious momentary sensation, half of pleasure, half of pain. She felt no cold, and she saw through the twilight as clearly as if it had been day. There was no fatigue or sense of weakness in her; but she had the strange, wistful feeling of an exile returning after long years, not knowing how he may find those he had left. At one of the first houses in the village there was a woman standing at her door, looking out for her children; one who knew Lady Mary well. She stopped quite cheerfully to bid her good-evening, as she had done in her vigorous days, before she grew old. It was a little experiment, too. She thought it possible that Catherine would scream out, and perhaps fly from her; but surely would be easily reassured when she heard the voice she knew, and saw by her one who was no ghost, but her own kind mistress. But Catherine took no notice when she spoke; she did not so much as turn her head. Lady Mary stood by her patiently, with more and more of that wistful desire to be recognised. She put her hand timidly upon the woman's arm, who was thinking of nothing but her boys, and calling to them, straining her eyes in the fading light. 'Don't be afraid, they are coming, they are safe,' she said, pressing Catherine's arm. But the woman never moved. She took no notice. She called to a neighbour who was passing, to ask if she had seen the children, and the two stood and talked in the dim air, not conscious of the third who stood between them, looking from one to another, astonished, paralysed. Lady Mary had not been prepared for this; she could not believe it even now. She repeated their names more and more anxiously, and even plucked at their sleeves to call their attention. She stood as a poor dependent sometimes stands, wistful, civil, trying to say something that will please, while they talked and took no notice; and then the neighbour passed on, and Catherine went into her house. It is hard to be left out in the cold when others go into their cheerful houses; but to be thus left outside of life, to speak and not be heard, to stand unseen, astounded, unable to secure any attention! She had thought they would be frightened, but it was not they who were frightened. A great panic seized the woman who was no more of this world. She had almost rejoiced to find herself back walking so lightly, so strongly, finding everything easy that had been so hard; and yet but a few minutes had passed, and she knew, never more to be deceived, that she was no longer of this world. What if she should be condemned to wander for ever among familiar places that knew her no more, appealing for a look, a word, to those who could no longer see her, or hear her cry, or know of her presence? Terror seized upon her, a chill and pang of fear beyond description. She felt an impulse to fly wildly into the dark, into the night, like a lost creature; to find again somehow, she could not tell how, the door out of which she had come, and beat upon it wildly with her hands, and implore to be taken home. For a moment she stood looking round her, lost and alone in the wide universe; no one to speak to her, no one to comfort her; outside of life altogether. Other rustic figures, slow-stepping, leisurely, at their ease, went and came, one at a time; but in this place, where every stranger was an object of curiosity, no one cast a glance at her. She was as if she had never been.

Presently she found herself entering her own house. It was all shut and silent – not a window lighted along the whole front of the house which used to twinkle and glitter with lights. It soothed her somewhat to see this, as if in evidence that the place had changed with her. She went in silently, and the darkness was as day to her. Her own rooms were all shut up, yet were open to her steps, which no external obstacle could limit. There was still the sound of life below stairs, and in the housekeeper's room a cheerful party gathered round the fire. It was then that she turned first, with some wistful human attraction, towards the warmth and light rather than to the still places in which her own life had been passed. Mrs Prentiss, the house-keeper, had her daughter with her on a visit, and the daughter's baby lay asleep in a cradle placed upon two chairs, outside the little circle of women round the table, one of whom was Jervis, Lady Mary's maid. Jervis sat and worked and cried, and mixed her words with little sobs. 'I never thought as I should have had to take another place,' she said. 'Brown and me, we made sure of a little something to start upon. He's been here for twenty years, and so have you, Mrs Prentiss; and me, as nobody can say I wasn't faithful night and day.'

'I never had that confidence in my lady to expect anything,' Prentiss said.

'Oh, mother, don't say that: many and many a day you've said, "When my lady dies – " '

'And we've all said it,' said Jervis. 'I can't think how she did it, nor why she did it; for she was a kind lady, though appearances is against her.'

'She was one of them, and I've known a many, as could not abide to see a gloomy face,' said the housekeeper. 'She kept us all comfortable for the sake of being comfortable herself, but no more.'

'Oh, you are hard upon my lady!' cried Jervis, 'and I can't bear to hear a word against her, though it's been an awful disappointment to me.'

'What's you or me or anyone,' cried Mrs Prentiss, 'in comparison of that poor little thing that can't work for her living like we can; that is left on the charity of folks she don't belong to? I'd have forgiven my lady anything, if she'd done what was right by Miss Mary. You'll get a place, and a good place; and me, they'll leave me here when the new folks come as have taken the house. But what will become of her, the darling? and not a penny, nor a friend, nor one to look to her? Oh, you selfish old woman! oh, you heart of stone! I just hope you are feeling it where you're gone,' the housekeeper cried.

But as she said this, the woman did not know who was looking at her with wide, wistful eyes, holding out her hands in appeal, receiving every word as if it had been a blow – though she knew it was useless. Lady Mary could not help it. She cried out to them, 'Have pity upon me! Have pity upon me! I am not cruel, as you think,' with a keen anguish in her voice, which seemed to be sharp enough to pierce the very air and go up to the skies. And so, perhaps, it did; but never touched the human atmosphere in which she stood a stranger. Jervis was threading her needle when her mistress uttered that cry; but her hand did not tremble, nor did the thread deflect a hair's-breadth from the straight line. The young mother alone seemed to be moved by some faint disturbance. 'Hush!' she said, 'is he waking?' – looking towards the cradle. But as the baby made no further sound, she too, returned to her sewing; and they sat bending their heads over their work round the table, and continued their talk. The room was very comfortable, bright and warm, as Lady Mary had liked all her rooms to be. The warm firelight danced upon the walls; the women talked in cheerful tones. She stood outside their circle, and looked at them with a wistful face. Their notice would have been more sweet to her, as she stood in that great humiliation, than in other times the look of a queen.

'But what is the matter with baby?' the mother said, rising hastily.

It was with no servile intention of securing a look from that little prince of life that she who was not of this world had stepped aside forlorn, and looked at him in his cradle. Though she was not of this world, she was still a woman, and had nursed her children in her arms. She bent over the infant by the soft impulse of nature, tenderly, with no interested thought. But the child saw her; was it possible? He turned his head towards her, and flickered his baby hands, and cooed with that indescribable voice that goes to every woman's heart. Lady Mary felt such a thrill of pleasure go through her, as no incident had given her for long years. She put out her arms to him as his mother snatched him from his little bed; and he, which was more wonderful, stretched towards her in his innocence, turning away from them all.

'He wants to go to someone,' cried the mother. 'Oh look, look, for God's sake! Who is there that the child sees?'

'There's no one there – not a soul. Now dearie, dearie, be reasonable. You can see for yourself there's not a creature,' said the grandmother.

'Oh, my baby, my baby! He sees something we can't see,' the young woman cried. 'Something has happened to his father, or he's going to be taken from me!' she said, holding the child to her in a sudden passion. The other women rushed to her to console her – the mother with reason, and Jervis with poetry. 'It's the angels whispering, like the song says.' Oh, the pang that was in the heart of the other whom they could not hear! She stood wondering how it could be – wondering with an amazement beyond words, how all that was in her heart, the love and the pain, and the sweetness and bitterness, could all be hidden – all hidden by that air in which the women stood so clear! She held out her hands, she spoke to them, telling who she was, but no one paid any attention; only the little dog Fido, who had been basking by the fire, sprang up, looked at her, and retreating slowly backwards till he reached the wall, sat down there and looked at her again, with now and then a little bark of enquiry. The dog saw her. This gave her a curious pang of humiliation, yet pleasure. She went away out of that little centre of human life in a great excitement and thrill of her whole being. The child had seen her, and the dog; but, oh heavens! how was she to work out her purpose by such auxiliaries as these?

She went up to her old bedchamber with unshed tears heavy about her eyes, and a pathetic smile quivering on her mouth. It touched her beyond measure that the child should have that confidence in her. 'Then God is still with me,' she said to herself. Her room, which had been so warm and bright, lay desolate in the stillness of the night; but she wanted no light, for the darkness was no darkness to her. She looked round her for a little, wondering to think how far away from her now was this scene of her old life, but feeling no pain in the sight of it – only a kind indulgence for the foolish simplicity which had taken so much pride in all these infantile elements of living. She went to the little Italian cabinet which stood against the wall, feeling now at least that she could do as she would – that here there was no blank of human unconsciousness to stand in her way. But she was met by something that baffled and vexed her once more. She felt the polished surface of the wood under her hand, and saw all the pretty ornamentation, the inlaid-work, the delicate carvings, which she knew so well; they swam in her eyes a little, as if they were part of some phantasmagoria about her, existing only in her vision. Yet the smooth surface resisted her touch; and when she withdrew a step from it, it stood before her solidly and square, as it had stood always – a glory to the place. She put forth her hands upon it, and could have traced the waving lines of the exquisite work, in which some artist soul had worked itself out in the old times; but though she thus saw it and felt, she could not with all her endeavours find the handle of the drawer, the richly-wrought knob of ivory, the little door that opened into the secret place. How long she stood by it, attempting again and

again to find what was as familiar to her as her own hand, what was
before her, visible in every line, what she felt with fingers which
began to tremble, she could not tell. Time did not count with her as
with common men. She did not grow weary, or require refreshment
or rest, like those who were still of this world. But at length her head
grew giddy and her heart failed. A cold despair took possession of her
soul. She could do nothing, then – nothing; neither by help of man,
neither by use of her own faculties, which were greater and clearer
than ever before. She sank down upon the floor at the foot of that old
toy, which had pleased her in the softness of her old age, to which she
had trusted the fortunes of another; by which, in wantonness and
folly she had sinned, she had sinned! And she thought she saw
standing round her companions in the land she had left, saying, 'It is
impossible, impossible!' with infinite pity in their eyes; and the face
of him who had given her permission to come, yet who had said no
word to her to encourage her in what was against nature. And there
came into her heart a longing to fly, to get home, to be back in the
land where her fellows were, and her appointed place. A child lost,
how pitiful that is! without power to reason and divine how help will
come; but a soul lost, outside of one method of existence, withdrawn
from the other, knowing no way to retrace its steps, nor how help can
come! There had been no bitterness in passing from earth to the land
where she had gone; but now there came upon her soul, in all the
power of her new faculties, the bitterness of death. The place which
was hers she had forsaken and left, and the place that had been hers
knew her no more.

7

Mary, when she left her kind friend in the vicarage, went out and
took a long walk. She had received a shock so great that it took all
sensation from her, and threw her into the seething and surging of an
excitement altogether beyond her control. She could not think until
she had got familiar with the idea, which indeed had been vaguely
shaping itself in her mind ever since she had emerged from the first
profound gloom and prostration of the shadow of death. She had
never definitely thought of her position before – never even asked
herself what was to become of her when Lady Mary died. She did not
see, any more than Lady Mary did, why she should ever die; and girls
who have never wanted anything in their lives, who have had no

sharp experience to enlighten them, are slow to think upon such subjects. She had not expected anything; her mind had not formed any idea of inheritance; and it had not surprised her to hear of the earl, who was Lady Mary's natural heir, nor to feel herself separated from the house in which all her previous life had been passed. But there had been gradually dawning upon her a sense that she had come to a crisis in her life, and that she must soon be told what was to become of her. It was not so urgent as that she should ask any questions; but it began to appear very clearly in her mind that things were not to be with her as they had been. She had heard the complaints and astonishment of the servants, to whom Lady Mary had left nothing, with resentment – Jervis, who could not marry and take her lodging-house, but must wait until she had saved more money, and wept to think, after all her devotion, of having to take another place; and Mrs Prentiss, the housekeeper, who was cynical, and expounded Lady Mary's kindness to her servants to be the issue of a refined selfishness; and Brown, who had sworn subdued oaths, and had taken the liberty of representing himself to Mary as 'in the same box' with herself. Mary had been angry, very angry at all this; and she had not by word or look given anyone to understand that she felt herself 'in the same box'. But yet she had been vaguely anxious, curious, desiring to know. And she had not even begun to think what she should do. That seemed a sort of affront to her godmother's memory, at all events, until someone had made it clear to her. But now, in a moment, with her first consciousness of the importance of this matter in the sight of others, a consciousness of what it was to herself, came into her mind. A change of everything – a new life – a new world; and not only so, but a severance from the old world – a giving up of everything that had been most near and pleasant to her.

These thoughts were driven through her mind like the snowflakes in a storm. The year had slid on since Lady Mary's death. Winter was beginning to yield to spring; the snow was over, and the great cold. And other changes had taken place. The great house had been let, and the family who had taken it had been about a week in possession. Their coming had inflicted a wound upon Mary's heart; but everybody had urged upon her the idea that it was much better the house should be let for a time, 'till everything was settled'. When all was settled, things would be different. Mrs Vicar did not say, 'You can then do what you please,' but she did convey to Mary's mind somehow a sort of inference that she would have something to do it with. And when Mary had protested, 'It shall never be let again with

my will,' the kind woman had said tremulously, 'Well, my dear!' and
had changed the subject. All these things now came to Mary's mind.
They had been afraid to tell her; they had thought it would be so
much to her – so important, such a crushing blow. To have nothing –
to be destitute; to be written about by Mr Furnival to the earl; to have
her case represented – Mary felt herself stung by such unendurable
suggestions into an energy – a determination – of which her soft
young life had known nothing. No one should write about her, or ask
charity for her, she said to herself. She had gone through the woods
and round the park, which was not large, and now she could not leave
these beloved precincts without going to look at the house. Up to this
time she had not had the courage to go near the house; but to the
commotion and fever of her mind every violent sensation was
congenial, and she went up the avenue now almost gladly, with a little
demonstration to herself of energy and courage. Why not that as well
as all the rest?

It was once more twilight, and the dimness favoured her design.
She wanted to go there unseen, to look up at the windows with their
alien lights, and to think of the time when Lady Mary sat behind the
curtains, and there was nothing but tenderness and peace throughout
the house. There was a light in every window along the entire front,
a lavishness of firelight and lamplight which told of a household in
which there were many inhabitants. Mary's mind was so deeply
absorbed, and perhaps her eyes so dim with tears, that she could
scarcely see what was before her, when the door opened suddenly and
a lady came out. 'I will go myself,' she said in an agitated tone to
someone behind her. 'Don't get yourself laughed at,' said a voice
from within. The sound of the voices roused the young spectator.
She looked with a little curiosity, mixed with anxiety, at the lady who
had come out of the house, and who started, too, with a gesture of
alarm, when she saw Mary move in the dark. 'Who are you?' she
cried out in a trembling voice, 'and what do you want here?'

Then Mary made a step or two forward and said, 'I must ask your
pardon if I am trespassing. I did not know there was any objection – '
This stranger to make an objection! It brought something like a
tremulous laugh to Mary's lips.

'Oh, there is no objection,' said the lady, 'only we have been a little
put out. I see now; you are the young lady who – you are the young
lady that – you are the one that – suffered most.'

'I am Lady Mary's goddaughter,' said the girl. 'I have lived here all
my life.'

'Oh, my dear, I have heard all about you,' the lady cried. The people who had taken the house were merely rich people; they had no other characteristic; and in the vicarage, as well as in the other houses about, it was said, when they were spoken of, that it was a good thing they were not people to be visited, since nobody could have had the heart to visit strangers in Lady Mary's house. And Mary could not but feel a keen resentment to think that her story, such as it was, the story which she had only now heard in her own person, should be discussed by such people. But the speaker had a look of kindness, and, so far as could be seen, of perplexity and fretted anxiety in her face, and had been in a hurry, but stopped herself in order to show her interest. 'I wonder,' she said impulsively, 'that you can come here and look at the place again, after all that has passed.'

'I never thought,' said Mary, 'that there could be – any objection.'

'Oh, how can you think I mean that? – how can you pretend to think so?' cried the other, impatiently. 'But after you have been treated so heartlessly, so unkindly – and left, poor thing! they tell me, without a penny, without any provision – '

'I don't know you,' cried Mary, breathless with quick rising passion. 'I don't know what right you can have to meddle with my affairs.'

The lady stared at her for a moment without speaking, and then she said, all at once, 'That is quite true – but it is rude as well; for though I have no right to meddle with your affairs, I did it in kindness, because I took an interest in you from all I have heard.'

Mary was very accessible to such a reproach and argument. Her face flushed with a sense of her own churlishness. 'I beg your pardon,' she said; 'I am sure you mean to be kind.'

'Well,' said the stranger, 'that is perhaps going too far on the other side, for you can't even see my face, to know what I mean. But I do mean to be kind, and I am very sorry for you. And though I think you've been treated abominably, all the same I like you better for not allowing anyone to say so. And now, do you know where I was going? I was going to the vicarage – where you are living, I believe – to see if the vicar, or his wife, or you, or all of you together, could do a thing for me.'

'Oh, I am sure Mrs Bowyer – ' said Mary, with a voice much less assured than her words.

'You must not be too sure, my dear. I know she doesn't mean to call upon me, because my husband is a city man. That is just as she pleases. I am not very fond of city men myself. But there's no reason why I should stand on ceremony when I want something, is there? Now, my dear, I want to know – Don't laugh at me. I am not superstitious, so far as I am aware; but – Tell me, in your time was there ever any disturbance, any appearance you couldn't understand, any – Well, I don't like the word ghost. It's disrespectful, if there's anything of the sort; and it's vulgar if there isn't. But you know what I mean. Was there anything – of that sort – in your time?'

In your time! Poor Mary had scarcely realised yet that her time was over. Her heart refused to allow it when it was thus so abruptly brought before her, but she obliged herself to subdue these rising rebellions, and to answer, though with some *hauteur*, 'There is nothing of the kind that I ever heard of. There is no superstition or ghost in our house.'

She thought it was the vulgar desire of new people to find a conventional mystery, and it seemed to Mary that this was a desecration of her home. Mrs Turner, however (for that was her name), did not receive the intimation as the girl expected, but looked at her very gravely, and said, 'That makes it a great deal more serious,' as if to herself. She paused and then added, 'You see, the case is this. I have a little girl who is our youngest, who is just my husband's idol. She is a sweet little thing, though perhaps I should not say it. Are you fond of children? Then I almost feel sure you would think so too. Not a moping child at all, or too clever, or anything to alarm one. Well, you know, little Connie, since ever we came in, has seen an old lady walking about the house.'

'An old lady!' said Mary, with an involuntary smile.

'Oh, yes. I laughed too, the first time. I said it would be old Mrs Prentiss, or perhaps the charwoman, or some old lady from the village that had been in the habit of coming in the former people's time. But the child got very angry. She said it was a real lady. She would not allow me to speak. Then we thought perhaps it was someone who did not know the house was let, and had walked in to look at it; but nobody would go on coming like that with all the signs of a large family in the house. And now the doctor says the child must be low, that the place perhaps doesn't agree with her, and that we must send her away. Now I ask you, how could I send little Connie away, the apple of her father's eye? I should have to go with her, of course, and how could the house get on without me? Naturally we are very anxious. And this afternoon she has seen her again, and sits there crying because she says the dear old lady looks so sad. I just seized my hat, and walked out, to come to you and your friends at the vicarage, to see if you could help me. Mrs Bowyer may look down upon a city person – I don't mind that; but she is a mother, and surely she would feel for a mother,' cried the poor lady vehemently, putting up her hands to her wet eyes.

'Oh, indeed, indeed she would! I am sure now that she will call directly. We did not know what a – ' Mary stopped herself in saying, 'what a nice woman you are,' which she thought would be rude, though poor Mrs Turner would have liked it. But then she shook her head and added, 'What could any of us do to help you? I have never heard of any old lady. There never was anything – I know all about the house, everything that has ever happened, and Prentiss will tell you. There is nothing of that kind – indeed, there is nothing. You must have – ' But here Mary stopped again; for to suggest that a new family, a city family, should have brought an apparition of their own with them, was too ridiculous an idea to be entertained.

'Miss Vivian,' said Mrs Turner, 'will you come back with me and speak to the child?'

At this Mary faltered a little. 'I have never been there – since the – funeral,' she said.

The good woman laid a kind hand upon her shoulder, caressing and soothing. 'You were very fond of her – in spite of the way she has used you?'

'Oh, how dare you, or anyone, to speak of her so! She used me as if I had been her dearest child. She was more kind to me than a mother. There is no one in the world like her!' Mary cried.

'And yet she left you without a penny. Oh, you must be a good girl to feel for her like that. She left you without – What are you going to do, my dear? I feel like a friend. I feel like a mother to you, though you don't know me. You mustn't think it is only curiosity. You can't stay with your friends for ever – and what are you going to do?'

There are some cases in which it is more easy to speak to a stranger than to one's dearest and oldest friend. Mary had felt this when she rushed out, not knowing how to tell the vicar's wife that she must leave her, and find some independence for herself. It was, however, strange to rush into such a discussion with so little warning, and Mary's pride was very sensitive. She said, 'I am not going to burden my friends,' with a little indignation; but then she remembered how forlorn she was, and her voice softened. 'I must do something – but I don't know what I am good for,' she said, trembling, and on the verge of tears.

'My dear, I have heard a great deal about you,' said the stranger; 'it is not rash, though it may look so. Come back with me directly, and see Connie. She is a very interesting little thing, though I say it; it is wonderful sometimes to hear her talk. You shall be her governess, my dear. Oh, you need not teach her anything – that is not what I mean. I think, I am sure, you will be the saving of her, Miss Vivian; and such a lady as you are, it will be everything for the other girls to live with you. Don't stop to think, but just come with me. You shall have whatever you please, and always be treated like a lady. Oh, my dear, consider my feelings as a mother, and come; oh, come to Connie! I know you will save her; it is an inspiration. Come back! Come back with me!'

It seemed to Mary too like an inspiration. What it cost her to cross that threshold and walk in a stranger, to the house which had been all her life as her own, she never said to anyone. But it was independence; it was deliverance from entreaties and remonstrances without end. It was a kind of setting right, so far as could be, of the balance which had got so terribly wrong. No writing to the earl now; no appeal to friends; anything in all the world – much more, honest service and kindness – must be better than that.

8

'Tell the young lady all about it, Connie,' said her mother.

But Connie was very reluctant to tell. She was very shy, and clung to her mother, and hid her face in her ample dress; and though presently she was beguiled by Mary's voice, and in a short time came to her side, and clung to her as she had clung to Mrs Turner, she still kept her secret to herself. They were all very kind to Mary, the elder girls standing round in a respectful circle looking at her, while their mother exhorted them to 'take a pattern' by Miss Vivian. The novelty, the awe which she inspired, the real kindness about her, ended in overcoming in Mary's young mind the first miserable impression of such a return to her home. It gave her a kind of pleasure to write to Mrs Bowyer that she had found employment, and had thought it better to accept it at once. 'Don't be angry with me; and I think you will understand me,' she said. And then she gave herself up to the strange new scene.

The 'ways' of the large simple-minded family, homely, yet kindly, so transformed Lady Mary's graceful old rooms that they no longer looked the same place. And when Mary sat down with them at the big heavy-laden table, surrounded with the hum of so large a party, it was impossible for her to believe that everything was not new about her. In no way could the saddening recollections of a home from which the chief figure had disappeared, have been more completely broken up. Afterwards Mrs Turner took her aside, and begged to know which was Mary's old room, 'for I should like to put you there, as if nothing had happened.' 'Oh, do not put me there!' Mary cried, 'so much has happened.' But this seemed a refinement to the kind woman, which it was far better for her young guest not to 'yield' to. The room Mary had occupied had been next to her godmother's, with a door between, and when it turned out that Connie, with an elder sister, was in Lady Mary's room, everything seemed perfectly arranged in Mrs Turner's eyes. She thought it was providential – with a simple belief in Mary's powers that in other circumstances would have been amusing. But there was no amusement in Mary's mind when she took possession of the old room 'as if nothing had happened'. She sat by the fire for half the night, in an agony of silent recollection and thought, going over the last days of her godmother's life, calling up everything before her, and realising as she had never realised till now, the lonely career on which she was setting out, the subjection to the will and convenience of strangers in which henceforth her life must be passed. This was a kind woman who had opened her doors to the destitute girl; but notwithstanding, however great the torture to Mary, there was no escaping this room which was haunted by the saddest recollections of her life. Of such things she must no longer complain – nay, she must think of nothing but thanking the mistress of the house for her thoughtfulness, for the wish to be kind, which so often exceeds the performance.

The room was warm and well lighted; the night was very calm and sweet outside, nothing had been touched or changed of all her little decorations, the ornaments which had been so delightful to her girlhood. A large photograph of Lady Mary held the chief place over the mantelpiece, representing her in the fullness of her beauty – a photograph which had been taken from the picture painted ages ago by a Royal Academician. It fortunately was so little like Lady Mary in her old age that, save as a thing which had always hung there, and belonged to her happier life, it did not affect the girl; but no picture was necessary to bring before her the well-remembered figure. She could not realise that the little movements she heard on the other side of the door were any other than those of her mistress, her friend, her mother; for all these names Mary lavished upon her in the fullness of her heart. The blame that was being cast upon Lady Mary from all sides made this child of her bounty but more deeply her partisan, more warm in her adoration. She would not, for all the inheritances of the world, have acknowledged even to herself that Lady Mary was in fault. Mary felt that she would rather a thousand times be poor and have to gain her daily bread, than that she who had nourished and cherished her should have been forced in her cheerful old age to think, before she chose to do so, of parting and farewell and the inevitable end.

She thought, like every young creature in strange and painful circumstances, that she would be unable to sleep, and did indeed lie awake and weep for an hour or more, thinking of all the changes that had happened; but sleep overtook her before she knew, while her mind was still full of these thoughts; and her dreams were endless, confused, full of misery and longing. She dreamed a dozen times over that she heard Lady Mary's soft call through the open door – which was not open, but shut closely and locked by the sisters who now inhabited the next room; and once she dreamed that Lady Mary came to her bedside and stood there looking at her earnestly, with the tears flowing from her eyes. Mary struggled in her sleep to tell her benefactress how she loved her, and approved of all she had done, and wanted nothing – but felt herself bound as by a nightmare, so that she could not move or speak, or even put out a hand to dry those tears which it was intolerable to her to see; and woke with the struggle, and the miserable sensation of seeing her dearest friend weep and being unable to comfort her. The moon was shining into the room, throwing part of it into a cold, full light, while blackness lay in all corners. The impression of her dream was so strong that Mary's eyes turned instantly to the spot where in her dream her godmother had stood. To be sure, there was nobody there; but as her consciousness returned, and with it the sweep of painful recollection, the sense of change, the miserable contrast between the present and the past – sleep fled from her eyes. She fell into the vividly awake condition which is the alternative of broken sleep, and gradually, as she lay, there came upon her that mysterious sense of another presence in the room which is so subtle and indescribable. She neither saw anything nor heard anything, and yet she felt that someone was there.

She lay still for some time and held her breath, listening for a movement, even for the sound of breathing – scarcely alarmed, yet sure that she was not alone. After a while she raised herself on her pillow, and in a low voice asked, 'Who is there? is anyone there?' There was no reply, no sound of any description, and yet the conviction grew upon her. Her heart began to beat, and the blood to mount to her head. Her own being made so much sound, so much commotion, that it seemed to her she could not hear anything save those beatings and pulsings. Yet she was not afraid. After a time, however, the oppression became more than she could bear. She got up and lit her candle, and searched through the familiar room; but she found no trace that anyone had been there. The furniture was all in its usual order. There was no hiding-place where any human thing could find refuge. When she had satisfied herself, and was about to return to bed, suppressing a sensation which must, she said to herself, be altogether fantastic, she was startled by a low knocking at the door of communication. Then she heard the voice of the elder girl. 'Oh, Miss Vivian, what is it? Have you seen anything?' A new sense of anger, disdain, humiliation, swept through Mary's mind. And if she had seen anything, she said to herself, what was that to those strangers? She replied, 'No, nothing; what should I see?' in a tone which was almost haughty, in spite of herself.

'I thought it might be – the ghost. Oh, please, don't be angry. I thought I heard this door open, but it is locked. Oh! perhaps it is very silly, but I am so frightened, Miss Vivian.'

'Go back to bed,' said Mary; 'there is no – ghost. I am going to sit up and write some – letters. You will see my light under the door.'

'Oh, thank you,' cried the girl.

Mary remembered what a consolation and strength in all wakefulness had been the glimmer of the light under her godmother's door. She smiled to think that she herself, so desolate as she was, was able to afford this innocent comfort to another girl, and then sat down and wept quietly, feeling her solitude and the chill about her, and the dark and the silence. The moon had gone behind a cloud. There seemed no light but her small miserable candle in earth and heaven. And yet that poor little speck of light kept up the heart of another – which made her smile again in the middle of her tears. And by and by the commotion in her head and heart calmed down, and she too fell asleep.

Next day she heard all the floating legends that were beginning to rise in the house. They all arose from Connie's questions about the old lady whom she had seen going upstairs before her, the first evening after the new family's arrival. It was in the presence of the doctor – who had come to see the child, and whose surprise at finding

Mary there was almost ludicrous – that she heard the story, though much against his will.

'There can be no need for troubling Miss Vivian about it,' he said, in a tone which was almost rude. But Mrs Turner was not sensitive.

'When Miss Vivian has just come like a dear, to help us with Connie!' the good woman cried. 'Of course she must hear it, doctor, for otherwise, how could she know what to do?'

'Is it true that you have come here – *here*? to help – Good heavens, Miss Mary, *here*? '

'Why not here?' Mary said, smiling as but she could. 'I am Connie's governess, doctor.'

He burst out into that suppressed roar which serves a man instead of tears, and jumped up from his seat, clenching his fist. The clenched fist was to the intention of the dead woman whose fault this was; and if it had ever entered the doctor's mind, as his mother supposed, to marry this forlorn child, and thus bestow a home upon her whether she would or no, no doubt he would now have attempted to carry out that plan. But as no such thing had occurred to him, the doctor only showed his sense of the intolerable by look and gesture. 'I must speak to the vicar. I must see Furnival. It can't be permitted,' he cried.

'Do you think I shall not be kind to her, doctor?' cried Mrs Turner. 'Oh, ask her! she is one that understands. She knows far better than that. We're not fine people, doctor, but we're kind people. I can say that for myself. There is nobody in this house but will be good to her, and admire her, and take an example by her. To have a real lady with the girls, that is what I would give anything for; and as she wants taking care of, poor dear, and petting, and an 'ome – ' Mary, who would not hear any more, got up hastily, and took the hand of her new protectress, and kissed her, partly out of gratitude and kindness, partly to stop her mouth, and prevent the saying of something which it might have been still more difficult to support. 'You are a real lady yourself, dear Mrs Turner,' she cried. (And this notwithstanding the one deficient letter: but many people who are much more dignified than Mrs Turner – people who behave themselves very well in every other respect – say ' 'ome'.)

'Oh, my dear, I don't make any pretensions,' the good woman cried, but with a little shock of pleasure which brought the tears to her eyes.

And then the story was told. Connie had seen the lady walk upstairs, and had thought no harm. The child supposed it was someone belonging to the house. She had gone into the room which was now Connie's room; but as that had a second door, there was no suspicion caused by the fact that she was not found there a little time after, when the child told her mother what she had seen. After this, Connie had seen the same lady several times, and once had met her face to face. The child declared that she was not at all afraid. She was a pretty old lady, with white hair and dark eyes. She looked a little sad, but smiled when Connie stopped and stared at her – not angry at all, but rather pleased – and looked for a moment as if she would speak. That was all. Not a word about a ghost was said in Connie's hearing. She had already told it all to the doctor, and he had pretended to consider which of the old ladies in the neighbourhood this could be. In Mary's mind, occupied as it was by so many important matters, there had been up to this time no great question about Connie's apparition; now she began to listen closely, not so much from real interest as from a perception that the doctor, who was her friend, did not want her to hear. This naturally aroused her attention at once. She listened to the child's description with growing eagerness, all the more because the doctor opposed. 'Now that will do, Miss Connie,' he said; 'it is one of the old Miss Murchisons, who are always so fond of finding out about their neighbours. I have no doubt at all on that subject. She wants to find you out in your pet naughtiness, whatever it is, and tell me.'

'I am sure it is not for that,' cried Connie. 'Oh, how can you be so disagreeable? I know she is not a lady who would tell. Besides, she is not thinking at all about me. She was either looking for something she had lost, or – oh, I don't know what it was! – and when she saw me she just smiled. She is not dressed like any of the people here. She had got no cloak on, or bonnet, or anything that is common, but a beautiful white shawl and a long dress, and it gives a little sweep when she walks – oh no! not like your rustling, mamma; but all soft, like water – and it looks like lace upon her head, tied here,' said Connie, putting her hands to her chin, 'in such a pretty, large, soft knot.' Mary had gradually risen as this description went on, starting a little at first, looking up, getting upon her feet. The colour went altogether out of her face – her eyes grew to twice their natural size. The doctor put out his hand without looking at her, and laid it on her arm with a strong, emphatic pressure. 'Just like someone you have seen a picture of,' he said.

'Oh no. I never saw a picture that was so pretty,' said the child.

'Doctor, why do you ask her any more? don't you see, don't you see, the child has seen – '

'Miss Mary, for God's sake, hold your tongue; it is folly, you know. Now, my little girl, tell me. I know this old lady is the very image of that pretty old lady with the toys for good children, who was in the last Christmas number?'

'Oh!' said Connie, pausing a little. 'Yes, I remember; it was a very pretty picture – mamma put it up in the nursery. No, she is not like that, not at all, much prettier; and then *my* lady is sorry about something – except when she smiles at me. She has her hair put up like this, and this,' the child went on, twisting her own bright locks.

'Doctor, I can't bear any more.'

'My dear, you are mistaken, it is all a delusion. She has seen a picture. I think now, Mrs Turner, that my little patient had better run away and play. Take a good run through the woods, Miss Connie, with your brother, and I will send you some physic which will not be at all nasty, and we shall hear no more of your old lady. My dear Miss Vivian, if you will but hear reason! I have known such cases a hundred times. The child has seen a picture, and it has taken possession of her imagination. She is a little below par, and she has a lively imagination; and she has learned something from Prentiss, though probably she does not remember that. And there it is! a few doses of quinine, and she will see visions no more.'

'Doctor,' cried Mary, 'how can you speak so to me? You dare not look me in the face. You know you dare not: as if you did not know as well as I do! Oh, why does that child see her, and not me?'

'There it is,' he said, with a broken laugh. 'Could anything show better that it is a mere delusion? Why, in the name of all that is reasonable, should this stranger child see her, if it was anything, and not you?'

Mrs Turner looked from one to another with wondering eyes. 'You know what it is?' she said. 'Oh, you know what it is? Doctor, doctor, is it because my Connie is so delicate? Is it a warning? Is it – '

'Oh, for heaven's sake! You will drive me mad, you ladies. Is it this, and is it that? It is nothing, I tell you. The child is out of sorts, and she has seen some picture that has caught her fancy – and she thinks she sees – I'll send her a bottle,' he cried, jumping up, 'that will put an end to all that.'

'Doctor, don't go away, tell me rather what I must do – if she is looking for something! Oh, doctor, think if she were unhappy, if she were kept out of her sweet rest!'

'Miss Mary, for God's sake, be reasonable. You ought never to have heard a word.'

'Doctor, think! if it should be anything we can do. Oh, tell me, tell me! Don't go away and leave me; perhaps we can find out what it is.'

'I will have nothing to do with your findings out. It is mere delusion. Put them both to bed, Mrs Turner; put them all to bed! – as if there was not trouble enough!'

'What is it?' cried Connie's mother; 'is it a warning! Oh, for the love of God, tell me, is that what comes before a death?'

When they were all in this state of agitation, the vicar and his wife were suddenly shown into the room. Mrs Bowyer's eyes flew to Mary, but she was too well bred a woman not to pay her respects first to the lady of the house, and there were a number of politenesses exchanged, very breathlessly on Mrs Turner's part, before the newcomers were free to show the real occasion of their visit. 'Oh, Mary, what did you mean by taking such a step all in a moment? How could you come here, of all places in the world? And how could you leave me without a word?' the vicar's wife said, with her lips against Mary's cheek. She had already perceived, without dwelling upon it, the excitement in which all the party were. This was said while the vicar was still making his bow to his new parishioner, who knew very well that her visitors had not intended to call; for the Turners were dissenters, to crown all their misdemeanours, beside being city people and *nouveaux riches*.

'Don't ask me any questions just now,' said Mary, clasping almost hysterically her friend's hand.

'It was providential. Come and hear what the child has seen.' Mrs Turner, though she was so anxious, was too polite not to make a fuss about getting chairs for all her visitors. She postponed her own trouble to this necessity, and trembling, sought the most comfortable seat for Mrs Bowyer, the largest and most imposing for the vicar himself. When she had established them in a little circle, and done her best to draw Mary, too, into a chair, she sat down quietly, her mind divided between the cares of courtesy and the alarms of an anxious mother. Mary stood at the table and waited till the commotion was over. The newcomers thought she was going to explain her conduct in leaving them; and Mrs Bowyer, at least, who was critical in point of manners, shivered a little, wondering if perhaps (though she could not find it in her heart to blame Mary) her proceedings were in perfect taste.

'The little girl,' Mary said, beginning abruptly. She had been standing by the table, her lips apart, her countenance utterly pale, her mind evidently too much absorbed to notice anything. 'The little girl has seen several times a lady going upstairs. Once she met her and saw her face, and the lady smiled at her; but her face was sorrowful, and the child thought she was looking for something. The lady was old, with white hair done up upon her forehead, and lace upon her head. She was dressed – ' here Mary's voice began to be interrupted from time to time by a brief sob – 'in a long dress that made a soft sound when she walked, and a white shawl, and the lace tied under her chin in a large soft knot – '

'Mary, Mary!' Mrs Bowyer had risen and stood behind the girl, in whose slender throat the climbing sorrow was almost visible, supporting her, trying to stop her. 'Mary, Mary!' she cried; 'oh, my darling, what are you thinking of? Francis! doctor! make her stop, make her stop.'

'Why should she stop?' said Mrs Turner, rising, too, in her agitation. 'Oh, is it a warning, is it a warning? for my child has seen it – Connie has seen it.'

'Listen to me, all of you,' said Mary, with an effort. 'You all know – who that is. And she has seen her – the little girl – '

Now the others looked at each other, exchanging a startled look.

'My dear people,' cried the doctor, 'the case is not the least unusual. No, no, Mrs Turner, it is no warning – it is nothing of the sort. Look here, Bowyer; you'll believe me. The child is very nervous and sensitive. She has evidently seen a picture somewhere of our dear old friend. She has heard the story somehow – oh, perhaps in some garbled version from Prentiss, or – of course they've all been talking of it. And the child is one of those creatures with its nerves all on the surface – and a little below par in health, in need of iron and quinine, and all that sort of thing. I've seen a hundred such cases,' cried the doctor, ' – a thousand such; but now, of course, we'll have a fine story made of it, now that it's come into the ladies' hands.'

He was much excited with this long speech; but it cannot be said that anyone paid much attention to him. Mrs Bowyer was holding Mary in her arms, uttering little cries and sobs over her, and looking anxiously at her husband. The vicar sat down suddenly in his chair, with the air of a man who has judgement to deliver without the least idea what to say; while Mary, freeing herself unconsciously from her friend's restraining embrace, stood facing them all with a sort of trembling defiance; and Mrs Turner kept on explaining nervously that – 'no, no, her Connie was not excitable, was not oversensitive, had never known what a delusion was.'

'This is very strange,' the vicar said.

'Oh, Mr Bowyer,' cried Mary, 'tell me what I am to do! – think if she cannot rest, if she is not happy, she that was so good to everybody, that never could bear to see anyone in trouble. Oh, tell me, tell me what I am to do! It is you that have disturbed her with all you have been saying. Oh, what can I do, what can I do to give her rest?'

'My dear Mary! my dear Mary!' they all cried, in different tones of consternation; and for a few minutes no one could speak. Mrs Bowyer, as was natural, said something, being unable to endure the silence; but neither she nor any of the others knew what it was she said. When it was evident that the vicar must speak, all were silent, waiting for him; and though it now became imperative that something in the shape of a judgement must be delivered, yet he was as far as ever from knowing what to say.

'Mary,' he said, with a little tremulousness of voice, 'it is quite natural that you should ask me; but, my dear, I am not at all prepared to answer. I think you know that the doctor, who ought to know best about such matters – '

'Nay, not I. I only know about the physical; the other – if there is another – that's your concern.'

'Who ought to know best,' repeated Mr Bowyer; 'for everybody will tell you, my dear, that the mind is so dependent upon the body. I suppose he must be right. I suppose it is just the imagination of a nervous child working upon the data which have been given – the picture; and then, as you justly remind me, all we have been saying – '

'How could the child know what we have been saying, Francis?'

'Connie has heard nothing that anyone has been saying; and there is no picture.'

'My dear lady, you hear what the doctor says. If there is no picture, and she has heard nothing, I suppose, then, your premises are gone, and the conclusion falls to the ground.'

'What does it matter about premises?' cried the vicar's wife; 'here is something dreadful that has happened. Oh, what nonsense that is about imagination; children have no imagination. A dreadful thing has happened. In heaven's name, Francis, tell this poor child what she is to do.'

'My dear,' said the vicar again, 'you are asking me to believe in purgatory – nothing less. You are asking me to contradict the church's teaching. Mary, you must compose yourself. You must wait till this excitement has passed away.'

'I can see by her eyes that she did not sleep last night,' the doctor said, relieved. 'We shall have her seeing visions too, if we don't take care.'

'And, my dear Mary,' said the vicar, 'if you will think of it, it is derogatory to the dignity of – of our dear friends who have passed away. How can we suppose that one of the blessed would come down from heaven, and walk about her own house, which she had just left, and show herself to a – to a – little child who had never seen her before.'

'Impossible,' said the doctor. 'I told you so; a stranger – that had no connection with her, knew nothing about her – '

'Instead of,' said the vicar, with a slight tremor, 'making herself known, if that was permitted, to – to me, for example, or our friend here.'

'That sounds reasonable, Mary,' said Mrs Bowyer; 'don't you think so, my dear? If she had come to one of us, or to yourself, my darling, I should never have wondered, after all that has happened. But to this little child – '

'Whereas there is nothing more likely – more consonant with all the teachings of science – than that the little thing should have this hallucination, of which you ought never to have heard a word. You are the very last person – '

'That is true,' said the vicar, 'and all the associations of the place must be overwhelming. My dear, we must take her away with us. Mrs Turner, I am sure, is very kind, but it cannot be good for Mary to be here.'

'No, no! I never thought so,' said Mrs Bowyer. 'I never intended – dear Mrs Turner, we all appreciate your motives. I hope you will let us see much of you, and that we may become very good friends. But Mary – it is her first grief, don't you know?' said the vicar's wife, with the tears in her eyes; 'she has always been so much cared for, so much thought of all her life – and then all at once! You will not think that we misunderstand your kind motives; but it is more than she can bear. She made up her mind in a hurry, without thinking. You must not be annoyed if we take her away.'

Mrs Turner had been looking from one to another while this dialogue went on. She said now, a little wounded, 'I wished only to do what was kind; but, perhaps I was thinking most of my own child. Miss Vivian must do what she thinks best.'

'You are all kind – too kind,' Mary cried; 'but no one must say another word, please. Unless Mrs Turner should send me away, until I know what this all means, it is my place to stay here.'

9

It was Lady Mary who had come into the vicarage that afternoon when Mrs Bowyer supposed someone had called. She wandered about to a great many places in these days, but always returned to the scenes in which her life had been passed, and where alone her work could be done, if it could be done at all. She came in and listened while the tale of her own carelessness and heedlessness was told, and stood by while her favourite was taken to another woman's bosom for comfort, and heard everything and saw everything. She was used to it by this time; but to be nothing is hard, even when you are accustomed to it; and though she knew that they would not hear her, what could she do but cry out to them as she stood there unregarded? 'Oh, have pity upon me!' Lady Mary said; and the pang in her heart was so great that the very atmosphere was stirred, and the air could scarcely contain her and the passion of her endeavour to make herself known, but thrilled like a harp-string to her cry. Mrs Bowyer heard the jar and tingle in the inanimate world, but she thought only that it was some charitable visitor who had come in, and gone softly away again at the sound of tears.

And if Lady Mary could not make herself known to the poor cottagers who had loved her, or to the women who wept for her loss while they blamed her, how was she to reveal herself and her secret to the men who, if they had seen her, would have thought her an hallucination? Yes, she tried all, and even went a long journey over land and sea to visit the earl, who was her heir, and awake in him an interest in her child. And she lingered about all these people in the silence of the night, and tried to move them in dreams, since she could not move them waking. It is more easy for one who is no more of this world, to be seen and heard in sleep; for then those who are still in the flesh stand on the borders of the unseen, and see and hear things which, waking, they do not understand. But, alas! when they woke, this poor wanderer discovered that her friends remembered no more what she had said to them in their dreams.

Presently, however, when she found Mary established in her old home, in her old room, there came to her a new hope. For there is nothing in the world so hard to believe, or to be convinced of, as that no effort, no device, will ever make you known and visible to those you love. Lady Mary being little altered in her character, though so much in her being, still believed that if she could but find the way, in a moment – in the twinkling of an eye, all would be revealed and understood. She went to Mary's room with this new hope strong in her heart. When they were alone together in that nest of comfort which she had herself made beautiful for her child – two hearts so full of thought for each other – what was there in earthly bonds which could prevent them from meeting? She went into the silent room, which was so familiar and dear, and waited like a mother long separated from her child, with a faint doubt trembling on the surface of her mind, yet a quaint, joyful confidence underneath in the force of nature. A few words would be enough – a moment, and all would be right. And then she pleased herself with fancies of how, when that was done, she would whisper to her darling what has never been told to flesh and blood; and so go home proud, and satisfied, and happy in the accomplishment of all she had hoped.

Mary came in with her candle in her hand, and closed the door between her and all external things. She looked round wistful with that strange consciousness which she had already experienced, that someone was there. The other stood so close to her that the girl could not move without touching her. She held up her hands, imploring, to the child of her love. She called to her, 'Mary, Mary!' putting her hands upon her, and gazed into her face with an intensity and anguish of eagerness which might have drawn the stars out of the sky. And a strange tumult was in Mary's bosom. She stood looking blankly round her, like one who is blind with open eyes, and saw nothing; and strained her ears like a deaf man, but heard nothing. All was silence, vacancy, an empty world about her. She sat down at her little table, with a heavy sigh. 'The child can see her, but she will not come to me,' Mary said, and wept.

Then Lady Mary turned away with a heart full of despair. She went quickly from the house, out into the night. The pang of her disappointment was so keen, that she could not endure it. She remembered what had been said to her in the place from whence she came, and how she had been entreated to be patient and wait. Oh, had she but waited and been patient! She sat down upon the ground, a soul forlorn, outside of life, outside of all things, lost in a world which had no place for her. The moon shone, but she made no shadow in it; the rain fell upon her, but did not hurt her; the little night breeze blew without finding any resistance in her. She said to herself, 'I have failed. What am I, that I should do what they all said was impossible? It was my pride, because I have had my own way all my life. But now I have no way and no place on earth, and what I have to tell them will never, never be known. Oh, my little Mary, a servant in her own house! And a word would make it right! – but never, never can she hear that word. I am wrong to say never; she will know when she is in heaven. She will not live to be old and foolish, like me. She will go up there early, and then she will know. But I, what will become of me? – for I am nothing here, I cannot go back to my own place.'

A little moaning wind rose up suddenly in the middle of the dark night, and carried a faint wail, like the voice of someone lost, to the windows of the great house. It woke the children and Mary, who opened her eyes quickly in the dark, wondering if perhaps now the vision might come to her. But the vision had come when she could not see it, and now returned no more.

10

On the other side, however, visions which had nothing sacred in them began to be heard of, and 'Connie's ghost', as it was called in the house, had various vulgar effects. A housemaid became hysterical, and announced that she too had seen the lady, of whom she gave a description, exaggerated from Connie's, which all the household were ready to swear she had never heard. The lady, whom Connie had only seen passing, went to Betsey's room in the middle of the night, and told her, in a hollow and terrible voice, that she could not rest, opening a series of communications by which it was evident all the secrets of the unseen world would soon be disclosed. And following upon this, there came a sort of panic in the house; noises were heard in various places, sounds of footsteps pacing, and of a long robe sweeping about the passages; and Lady Mary's costumes, and the headdress which was so peculiar, which all her friends had recognised in Connie's description, grew into something portentous under the heavier hand of the foot-boy and the kitchen-maid. Mrs Prentiss, who had remained, as a special favour to the new people, was deeply indignant and outraged by this treatment of her mistress. She appealed to Mary with mingled anger and tears.

'I would have sent the hussy away at an hour's notice, if I had the power in my hands,' she cried, 'but, Miss Mary, it's easily seen who is a real lady and who is not. Mrs Turner interferes herself in everything, though she likes it to be supposed that she has a housekeeper.'

'Dear Prentiss, you must not say Mrs Turner is not a lady. She has far more delicacy of feeling than many ladies,' cried Mary.

'Yes, Miss Mary, dear, I allow that she is very nice to you; but who could help that? and to hear my lady's name – that might have had her faults, but who was far above anything of the sort – in every mouth, and her costume, that they don't know how to describe, and to think that *she* would go and talk to the like of Betsy Barnes about what is on her mind! I think sometimes I shall break my heart, or else throw up my place, Miss Mary,' Prentiss said, with tears.

'Oh, don't do that; oh, don't leave me, Prentiss!' Mary said, with an involuntary cry of dismay.

'Not if you mind, not if you mind, dear,' the housekeeper cried. And then she drew close to the young lady with an anxious look. 'You haven't seen anything?' she said. 'That would be only natural, Miss Mary. I could well understand she couldn't rest in her grave – if she came and told it all to you.'

'Prentiss, be silent,' cried Mary; 'that ends everything between you and me, if you say such a word. There has been too much said already – oh, far too much! as if I only loved her for what she was to leave me.'

'I did not mean that, dear,' said Prentiss; 'but – '

'There is no but; and everything she did was right,' the girl cried with vehemence. She shed hot and bitter tears over this wrong which all her friends did to Lady Mary's memory. 'I am glad it was so,' she said to herself when she was alone, with youthful extravagance. 'I am glad it was so; for now no one can think that I loved her for anything but herself.'

The household, however, was agitated by all these rumours and inventions. Alice, Connie's elder sister, declined to sleep any longer in that which began to be called the haunted room. She, too, began to think she saw something, she could not tell what, gliding out of the room as it began to get dark, and to hear sighs and moans in the corridors. The servants, who all wanted to leave, and the villagers, who avoided the grounds after nightfall, spread the rumour far and near that the house was haunted.

11

In the meantime, Connie herself was silent, and saw no more of the lady. Her attachment to Mary grew into one of those visionary passions which little girls so often form for young women. She followed her so-called governess wherever she went, hanging upon her arm when she could, holding her dress when no other hold was possible – following her everywhere, like her shadow. The vicarage, jealous and annoyed at first, and all the neighbours indignant too, to see Mary transformed into a dependent of the city family, held out as long as possible against the good-nature of Mrs Turner, and were revolted by the spectacle of this child claiming poor Mary's attention wherever she moved. But by and by all these strong sentiments softened, as was natural. The only real drawback was that amid all these agitations Mary lost her bloom. She began to droop and grow pale under the observation of the watchful doctor, who had never been otherwise than dissatisfied with the new position of affairs, and betook himself to Mrs Bowyer for sympathy and information. 'Did you ever see a girl so fallen off?' he said. 'Fallen off, doctor! I think she is prettier and prettier every day.' 'Oh,' the poor man cried, with a strong breathing of impatience, 'you ladies think of nothing, but prettiness! – was I talking of prettiness? She must have lost a stone since she went back there. It is all very well to laugh,' the doctor added, growing red with suppressed anger, 'but I can tell you that is the true test. That little Connie Turner is as well as possible; she has handed over her nerves to Mary Vivian. I wonder now if she ever talks to you on that subject.'

'Who? little Connie?'

'Of course I mean Miss Vivian, Mrs Bowyer. Don't you know the village is all in a tremble about the ghost at the Great House?'

'Oh yes, I know, and it is very strange. I can't help thinking, doctor – '

'We had better not discuss that subject. Of course I don't put a moment's faith in any such nonsense. But girls are full of fancies. I want you to find out for me whether she has begun to think she sees anything. She looks like it; and if something isn't done she will soon do so, if not now.'

'Then you do think there is something to see,' said Mrs Bowyer, clasping her hands; 'that has always been my opinion: what so natural as that – ?'

'As that Lady Mary, the greatest old aristocrat in the world, should come and make private revelations to Betsey Barnes, the under housemaid – ?' said the doctor, with a sardonic grin.

'I don't mean that, doctor; but if she could not rest in her grave, poor old lady – '

'You think, then, my dear,' said the vicar, 'that Lady Mary, an old friend, who was as young in her mind as any of us, lies body and soul in that old dark hole of a vault?'

'How you talk, Francis! what can a woman say between you horrid men? I say if she couldn't rest – wherever she is – because of leaving Mary destitute, it would be only natural – and I should think the more of her for it,' Mrs Bowyer cried.

The vicar had a gentle professional laugh over the confusion of his wife's mind. But the doctor took the matter more seriously. 'Lady Mary is safely buried and done with, I am not thinking of her,' he said; 'but I am thinking of Mary Vivian's senses, which will not stand this much longer. Try and find out from her if she sees anything: if she has come to that, whatever she says we must have her out of there.'

But Mrs Bowyer had nothing to report when this conclave of friends met again. Mary would not allow that she had seen anything. She grew paler every day, her eyes grew larger, but she made no confession; and Connie bloomed and grew, and met no more old ladies upon the stairs.

12

The days passed on, and no new event occurred in this little history. It came to be summer – balmy and green – and everything around the old house was delightful, and its beautiful rooms became more pleasant than ever in the long days and soft brief nights. Fears of the earl's return and of the possible end of the Turners' tenancy began to disturb the household, but no one so much as Mary, who felt herself to cling as she had never done before to the old house. She had never got over the impression that a secret presence, revealed to no one else, was continually near her, though she saw no one. And her health was greatly affected by this visionary double life.

This was the state of affairs on a certain soft wet day when the family were all within doors. Connie had exhausted all her means of amusement in the morning. When the afternoon came, with its long, dull, uneventful hours, she had nothing better to do than to fling herself upon Miss Vivian, upon whom she had a special claim. She came to Mary's room, disturbing the strange quietude of that place, and amused herself looking over all the trinkets and ornaments that were to be found there, all of which were associated to Mary with her godmother. Connie tried on the bracelets and brooches which Mary in her deep mourning had not worn, and asked a hundred questions. The answer which had to be so often repeated, 'That was given to me by my godmother,' at last called forth the child's remark, 'How fond your godmother must have been of you, Miss Vivian! She seems to have given you everything – '

'Everything!' cried Mary, with a full heart.

'And yet they all say she was not kind enough,' said little Connie – 'what do they mean by that? for you seem to love her very much still, though she is dead. Can one go on loving people when they are dead?'

'Oh yes, and better than ever,' said Mary; 'for often you do not know how you loved them, or what they were to you, till they are gone away.'

Connie gave her governess a hug and said, 'Why did not she leave you all her money, Miss Vivian? everybody says she was wicked and unkind to die without – '

'My dear,' cried Mary, 'do not repeat what ignorant people say, because it is not true.'

'But mamma said it, Miss Vivian.'

'She does not know, Connie – you must not say it. I will tell your mamma she must not say it; for nobody can know so well as I do – and it is not true – '

'But they say,' cried Connie, 'that that is why she can't rest in her grave. You must have heard. Poor old lady, they say she cannot rest in her grave, because – '

Mary seized the child in her arms with a pressure that hurt Connie. 'You must not! You must not!' she cried, in a sort of panic. Was she afraid that someone might hear? She gave Connie a hurried kiss, and turned her face away, looking out into the vacant room. 'It is not true! it is not true!' she cried, with a great excitement and horror, as if to stay a wound. 'She was always good, and like an angel to me. She is with the angels. She is with God. She cannot be disturbed by anything – anything! Oh, let us never say, or think, or imagine – ' Mary cried. Her cheeks burned, her eyes were full of tears. It seemed to her that something of wonder and anguish and dismay was in the room round her – as if someone unseen had heard a bitter reproach, an accusation undeserved, which must wound to the very heart.

Connie struggled a little in that too tight hold. 'Are you frightened, Miss Vivian? What are you frightened for? No one can hear; and if you mind it so much, I will never say it again.'

'You must never, never say it again. There is nothing I mind so much,' Mary said.

'Oh,' said Connie, with mild surprise. Then, as Mary's hold relaxed, she put her arms round her beloved companion's neck. 'I will tell them all you don't like it. I will tell them they must not – oh!' cried Connie again, in a quick astonished voice. She clutched Mary round the neck, returning the violence of the grasp which had hurt her, and with the other hand pointed to the door. 'The lady! the lady! oh, come and see where she is going!' Connie cried.

Mary felt as if the child in her vehemence lifted her from her seat. She had no sense that her own limbs or her own will carried her, in the impetuous rush with which Connie flew. The blood mounted to her head. She felt a heat and throbbing as if her spine were on fire. Connie holding by her skirts, pushing her on, went along the corridor to the other door, now deserted, of Lady Mary's room. 'There, there! don't you see her? She is going in!' the child cried, and rushed on, clinging to Mary, dragging her on, her light hair streaming, her little white dress waving.

Lady Mary's room was unoccupied and cold – cold, though it was summer, with the chill that rests in uninhabited apartments. The blinds were drawn down over the windows; a sort of blank whiteness, greyness, was in the place, which no one ever entered. The child rushed on with eager gestures, crying, 'Look! look!' turning her lively head from side to side. Mary, in a still and passive expectation, seeing nothing, looking mechanically to where Connie told her to look, moving like a creature in a dream, against her will, followed. There was nothing to be seen. The blank, the vacancy, went to her heart. She no longer thought of Connie or her vision. She felt the emptiness with a desolation such as she had never felt before. She loosed her arm with something like impatience from the child's close clasp. For months she had not entered the room which was associated with so much of her life. Connie and her cries and warnings passed from her mind like the stir of a bird or a fly. Mary felt herself alone with her dead, alone with her life, with all that had been and that never could be again. Slowly, without knowing what she did, she sank upon her knees. She raised her face in the blank of desolation about her to the unseen heaven. Unseen! unseen! whatever we may do. God above us, and those who have gone from us, and He who has taken them, who has redeemed them, who is ours and theirs, our only hope – but all unseen, unseen, concealed as much by the blue skies as by the dull blank of that roof. Her heart ached and cried into the unknown. 'O God,' she cried, 'I do not know where she is, but Thou art everywhere. O God, let her know that I have never blamed her, never wished it otherwise, never ceased to love her, and thank her, and bless her. God! God!' cried Mary, with a great and urgent cry, as if it were a man's name. She knelt there for a moment before her senses failed her, her eyes shining as if they would burst from their sockets, her lips dropping apart, her countenance like marble.

13

'And *she* was standing there all the time,' said Connie, crying and telling her little tale after Mary had been carried away – 'standing with her hand upon that cabinet, looking and looking, oh, as if she wanted to say something and couldn't. Why couldn't she, mamma? Oh, Mr Bowyer, why couldn't she, if she wanted so much? Why wouldn't God let her speak?'

14

Mary had a long illness, and hovered on the verge of death. She said a great deal in her wanderings about someone who had looked at her. 'For a moment, a moment,' she would cry; 'only a moment! and I had so much to say.' But as she got better, nothing was said to her about this face she had seen. And perhaps it was only the suggestion of some feverish dream. She was taken away, and was a long time getting up her strength; and in the meantime the Turners insisted that the chains should be thoroughly seen to, which were not all in a perfect state. And the earl coming to see the place, took a fancy to it, and determined to keep it in his own hands. He was a friendly person, and his ideas of decoration were quite different from those of his grandmother. He gave away a great deal of her old furniture, and sold the rest.

Among the articles given away was the Italian cabinet, which the vicar had always had a fancy for; and naturally it had not been in the vicarage a day, before the boys insisted on finding out the way of opening the secret drawer. And there the paper was found, in the most natural way, without any trouble or mystery at all.

15

They all gathered to see the wanderer coming back. She was not as she had been when she went away. Her face, which had been so easy, was worn with trouble; her eyes were deep with things unspeakable. Pity and knowledge were in the lines, which time had not made. It was a great event in that place to see one come back who did not come by the common way. She was received by the great officer who had given her permission to go, and her companions who had received her at the first all came forward, wondering, to hear what she had to say; because it only occurs to those wanderers who have gone back to earth of their own will, to return when they have accomplished what they wished, or it is judged above that there is nothing possible more. Accordingly, the question was on all their lips, 'You have set the wrong right – you have done what you desired?'

'Oh,' she said, stretching out her hands, 'how well one is in one's own place! how blessed to be at home! I have seen the trouble and sorrow in the earth till my heart is sore, and sometimes I have been near to die.'

'But that is impossible,' said the man who had loved her.

'If it had not been impossible, I should have died,' she said. 'I have stood among people who loved me, and they have not seen me, nor known me, nor heard my cry. I have been outcast from all life, for I belonged to none. I have longed for you all, and my heart has failed me. Oh how lonely it is in the world, when you are a wanderer, and can be known of none – '

'You were warned,' said he who was in authority, 'that it was more bitter than death.' 'What is death?' she said; and no one made any reply. Neither did anyone venture to ask her again whether she had been successful in her mission. But at last, when the warmth of her appointed home had melted the ice about her heart, she smiled once more and spoke.

'The little children knew me. They were not afraid of me; they held out their arms. And God's dear and innocent creatures – ' She wept a few tears, which were sweet after the ice tears she had shed upon the earth. And then someone, more bold than the rest, asked again, 'And did you accomplish what you wished?'

She had come to herself by this time, and the dark lines were melting from her face. 'I am forgiven,' she said, with a low cry of happiness. 'She whom I wronged, loves me and blessed me; and we saw each other face to face. I know nothing more.'

'There is no more,' said all together. For everything is included in pardon and love.

The Open Door

Margaret Oliphant

I

I took the house of Brentwood on my return from India in 18 – , for the temporary accommodation of my family, until I could find a permanent home for them. It had many advantages which made it peculiarly appropriate. It was within reach of Edinburgh; and my boy Roland, whose education had been considerably neglected, could go in and out to school; which was thought to be better for him than either leaving home altogether or staying there always with a tutor. The first of these expedients would have seemed preferable to me; the second commended itself to his mother. The doctor, like a judicious man, took the midway between. 'Put him on his pony, and let him ride into the High School every morning; it will do him all the good in the world,' Dr Simson said; 'and when it is bad weather, there is the train.' His mother accepted this solution of the difficulty more easily than I could have hoped; and our pale-faced boy, who had never known anything more invigorating than Simla, began to encounter the brisk breezes of the North in the subdued severity of the month of May. Before the time of the vacation in July we had the satisfaction of seeing him begin to acquire something of the brown and ruddy complexion of his schoolfellows. The English system did not commend itself to Scotland in these days. There was no little Eton at Fettes; nor do I think, if there had been, that a genteel exotic of that class would have tempted either my wife or me. The lad was doubly precious to us, being the only one left us of many; and he was fragile in body, we believed, and deeply sensitive in mind. To keep him at home, and yet to send him to school – to combine the advantages of the two systems – seemed to be everything that could be desired. The two girls also found at Brentwood everything they wanted. They were near enough to Edinburgh to have masters and lessons as many as they required for completing that never-ending education which the young people seem to require nowadays. Their mother married me when she was younger than Agatha; and I should like to see them improve upon their mother! I myself was then no more than twenty-five – an age at which I see the young fellows now groping about them, with no notion what they are going to do with their lives. However, I suppose every generation has a conceit of itself which elevates it, in its own opinion, above that which comes after it.

Brentwood stands on that fine and wealthy slope of country – one of the richest in Scotland – which lies between the Pentland Hills and the Firth. In clear weather you could see the blue gleam – like a bent bow, embracing the wealthy fields and scattered houses – of the great estuary on one side of you, and on the other the blue heights, not gigantic like those we had been used to, but just high enough for all the glories of the atmosphere, the play of clouds, and sweet reflections, which give to a hilly country an interest and a charm which nothing else can emulate. Edinburgh – with its two lesser heights, the Castle and the Calton Hill, its spires and towers piercing through the smoke, and Arthur's Seat lying crouched behind, like a guardian no longer very needful, taking his repose beside the well-beloved charge, which is now, so to speak, able to take care of itself without him – lay at our right hand. From the lawn and drawing-room windows we could see all these varieties of landscape. The colour was sometimes a little chilly, but sometimes, also, as animated and full of vicissitude as a drama. I was never tired of it. Its colour and freshness revived the eyes which had grown weary of arid plains and blazing skies. It was always cheery, and fresh, and full of repose.

The village of Brentwood lay almost under the house, on the other side of the deep little ravine, down which a stream – which ought to have been a lovely, wild and frolicsome little river – flowed between its rocks and trees. The river, like so many in that district, had, however, in its earlier life been sacrificed to trade, and was grimy with paper-making. But this did not affect our pleasure in it so much as I have known it to affect other streams. Perhaps our water was more rapid; perhaps less clogged with dirt and refuse. Our side of the dell was charmingly *accidenté*, and clothed with fine trees, through which various paths wound down to the riverside and to the village bridge which crossed the stream. The village lay in the hollow, and climbed, with very prosaic houses, the other side. Village architecture does not flourish in Scotland. The blue slates and the grey stone are sworn foes to the picturesque; and though I do not, for my own part, dislike the interior of an old-fashioned hewed and galleried church, with its little family settlements on all sides, the square box outside, with its bit of a spire like a handle to lift it by, is not an improvement to the landscape. Still a cluster of houses on differing elevations, with scraps of garden coming in between, a hedgerow with clothes laid out to dry, the opening of a street with its rural sociability, the women at their doors, the slow wagon lumbering along, gives a centre to the landscape. It was cheerful to look at, and convenient in a hundred ways. Within ourselves we had walks in plenty, the glen being always beautiful in all its phases, whether the woods were green in the spring or ruddy in the autumn. In the park which surrounded the house were the ruins of the former mansion of Brentwood – a much smaller and less important house than the solid Georgian edifice which we inhabited. The ruins were picturesque, however, and gave importance to the place. Even we, who were but temporary tenants, felt a vague pride in them, as if they somehow reflected a certain consequence upon ourselves. The old building had the remains of a tower – an indistinguishable mass of mason-work, over-grown with ivy; and the shells of walls attached to this were half filled up with soil. I had never examined it closely, I am ashamed to say. There was a large room, or what had been a large room, with the lower part of the windows still existing, on the principal floor, and underneath other windows, which were perfect, though half filled up with fallen soil, and waving with a wild growth of brambles and chance growths of all kinds. This was the oldest part of all. At a little distance were some very commonplace and disjointed fragments of building, one of them suggesting a certain pathos by its very commonness and the complete wreck which it showed. This was the end of a low gable, a bit of grey wall, all incrusted with lichens, in which was a common doorway. Probably it had been a servants' entrance, a backdoor or opening into what are called 'the offices' in Scotland. No offices remained to be entered – pantry and kitchen had all been swept out of being; but there stood the doorway open and vacant, free to all the winds, to the rabbits and every wild creature. It struck my eye, the first time I went to Brentwood, like a melancholy comment upon a life that was over. A door that led to nothing – closed once, perhaps, with anxious care, bolted and guarded, now void of any meaning. It impressed me, I remember, from the first; so perhaps it may be said that my mind was prepared to attach to it an importance which nothing justified.

The summer was a very happy period of repose for us all. The warmth of Indian suns was still in our veins. It seemed to us that we could never have enough of the greenness, the dewiness, the freshness of the northern landscape. Even its mists were pleasant to us, taking all the fever out of us, and pouring in vigour and refreshment. In autumn we followed the fashion of the time, and went away for change which we did not in the least require. It was when the family had settled down for the winter, when the days were short and dark, and the rigorous reign of frost upon us, that the incidents occurred which alone could justify me in intruding upon the world my private affairs. These incidents were, however, of so curious a character that I hope my inevitable references to my own family and pressing personal interests will meet with a general pardon.

I was absent in London when these events began. In London an old Indian plunges back into the interests with which all his previous life has been associated, and meets old friends at every step. I had been circulating among some half-dozen of these – enjoying the return to my former life in shadow, though I had been so thankful in substance to throw it aside – and had missed some of my home letters, what with going down from Friday to Monday to old Benbow's place in the country, and stopping on the way back to dine and sleep at Sellar's and to take a look into Cross's stables, which occupied another day. It is never safe to miss one's letters. In this transitory life, as the Prayer-book says, how can one ever be certain what is going to happen? All was well at home. I knew exactly (I thought) what they would have to say to me: 'The weather has been so fine that Roland has not once gone by train, and he enjoys the ride beyond anything.' 'Dear papa, be sure that you don't forget anything, but bring us so-and-so, and so-and-so' – a list as long as my arm. Dear girls and dearer mother! I would not for the world have forgotten their commissions, or lost their little letters, for all the Benbows and Crosses in the world.

But I was confident in my home-comfort and peacefulness. When I got back to my club, however, three or four letters were lying for one, upon some of which I noticed the words 'immediate' and 'urgent', which old-fashioned people and anxious people still believe will influence the post-office and quicken the speed of the mails. I was about to open one of these, when the club porter brought me two telegrams, one of which, he said, had arrived the night before. I opened, as was to be expected, the last first, and this was what I read: 'Why don't you come or answer? For God's sake, come. He is much worse.' This was a thunderbolt to fall upon a man's head who had one only son, and he the light of his eyes! The other telegram, which I opened with hands trembling so much that I lost time by my haste, was to much the same purport: 'No better; doctor afraid of brain-fever. Calls for you day and night. Let nothing detain you.' The first thing I did was to look up the timetables to see if there was any way of getting off sooner than by the night-train, though I knew well enough there was not; and then I read the letters, which furnished, alas! too clearly, all the details. They told me that the boy had been pale for some time, with a scared look. His mother had noticed it before I left home, but would not say anything to alarm me. This look had increased day by day, and soon it was observed that Roland came home at a wild gallop through the park, his pony panting and in foam, himself 'as white as a sheet', but with the perspiration streaming from his forehead. For a long time he had resisted all questioning, but at length had developed such strange changes of mood, showing a reluctance to go to school, a desire to be fetched in the carriage at night – which was a ridiculous piece of luxury – an unwillingness to go out into the grounds, and nervous starts at every sound, that his mother had insisted upon an explanation. When the boy – our boy Roland, who had never known what fear was – began to talk to her of voices he had heard in the park, and shadows that had appeared to him among the ruins, my wife promptly put him to bed and sent for Dr Simson, which, of course, was the only thing to do.

I hurried off that evening, as may be supposed, with an anxious heart. How I got through the hours before the starting of the train, I cannot tell. We must all be thankful for the quickness of the railway when in anxiety; but to have thrown myself into a post-chaise as soon as horses could be put to, would have been a relief. I got to Edinburgh very early in the blackness of the winter morning, and scarcely dared look the man in the face, at whom I gasped, 'What news?' My wife had sent the brougham for me, which I concluded, before the man spoke, was a bad sign. His answer was that stereotyped answer which leaves the imagination so wildly free – 'Just the same.' Just the same! What might that mean? The horses seemed to me to creep along the long dark country road. As we dashed through the park, I thought I heard someone moaning among the trees, and clenched my fist at him (whoever he might be) with fury. Why had the fool of a woman at the gate allowed anyone to come in to disturb the quiet of the place? If I had not been in such hot haste to get home, I think I should have stopped the carriage and got out to see what tramp it was that had made an entrance, and chosen my grounds, of all places in the world – when my boy was ill! – to grumble and groan in. But I had no reason to complain of our slow pace here. The horses flew like lightning along the intervening path, and drew up at the door all panting, as if they had run a race. My wife stood waiting to receive me, with a pale face, and a candle in her hand, which made her look paler still as the wind blew the flame about. 'He is sleeping,' she said in a whisper, as if her voice might wake him. And I replied, when I could find my voice, also in a whisper, as though the jingling of the horses' furniture and the sound of their hoofs must not have been more dangerous. I stood on the steps with her a moment, almost afraid to go in, now that I was here; and it seemed to me that I saw without observing, if I may say so, that the horses were unwilling to turn round, though their stables lay that way, or that the men were unwilling. These things occurred to me afterwards, though at the moment I was not capable of anything but to ask questions and to hear of the condition of the boy.

I looked at him from the door of his room, for we were afraid to go near, lest we should disturb that blessed sleep. It looked like actual sleep, not the lethargy into which my wife told me he would sometimes fall. She told me everything in the next room, which communicated with his, rising now and then and going to the door of communication; and in this there was much that was very startling and confusing to the mind. It appeared that ever since the winter began – since it was early dark, and night had fallen before his return from school – he had been hearing voices among the ruins: at first only a groaning, he said, at which his pony was as much alarmed as he was, but by degrees a voice. The tears ran down my wife's cheeks as she described to me how he would start up in the night and cry out, 'Oh, mother, let me in! oh, mother, let me in!' with a pathos which rent her heart. And she sitting there all the time, only longing to do everything his heart could desire! But though she would try to soothe him, crying, 'You are at home, my darling. I am here. Don't you know me? Your mother is here!' he would only stare at her, and after a while spring up again with the same cry. At other times he would be quite reasonable, she said, asking eagerly when I was coming, but declaring that he must go with me as soon as I did so, 'to let them in'. 'The doctor thinks his nervous system must have received a shock,' my wife said. 'Oh, Henry, can it be that we have pushed him on too much with his work – a delicate boy like Roland? And what is his work in comparison with his health? Even you would think little of honours or prizes if it hurt the boy's health.' Even I! – as if I were an inhuman father sacrificing my child to my ambition. But I would not increase her trouble by taking any notice. After awhile they persuaded me to lie down, to rest, and to eat, none of which things had been possible since I received their letters. The mere fact of being on the spot, of course, in itself was a great thing; and when I knew that I could be called in a moment, as soon as he was awake and wanted me, I felt able, even in the dark, chill morning twilight, to snatch an hour or two's sleep. As it happened, I was so worn out with the strain of anxiety, and he so quieted and consoled by knowing I had come, that I was not disturbed till the afternoon, when the twilight had again settled down. There was just daylight enough to see his face when I went to him; and what a change in a fortnight! He was paler and more worn, I thought, than even in those dreadful days in the plains before we left India. His hair seemed to me to have grown long and lank; his eyes were like blazing lights projecting out of his white face. He got hold of my hand in a cold and tremulous clutch, and waved to everybody to go away. 'Go away – even mother,' he said; 'go away.' This went to her heart; for she did not like that even I should have more of the boy's confidence than herself; but my wife has never been a woman to think of herself, and she left us alone. 'Are they all gone?' he said eagerly. 'They would not let me speak. The doctor treated me as if I were a fool. You know I am not a fool, papa.'

'Yes, yes, my boy, I know. But you are ill, and quiet is so necessary. You are not only not a fool, Roland, but you are reasonable and understand. When you are ill you must deny yourself; you must not do everything that you might do being well.'

He waved his thin hand with a sort of indignation. 'Then, father, I am not ill,' he cried. 'Oh, I thought when you came you would not stop me – you would see the sense of it! What do you think is the matter with me, all of you? Simson is well enough; but he is only a doctor. What do you think is the matter with me? I am no more ill than you are. A doctor, of course, he thinks you are ill the moment he looks at you – that's what he's there for – and claps you into bed.'

'Which is the best place for you at present, my dear boy.'

'I made up my mind,' cried the little fellow, 'that I would stand it till you came home. I said to myself, I won't frighten mother and the girls. But now, father,' he cried, half jumping out of bed, 'it's not illness: it's a secret.'

His eyes shone so wildly, his face was so swept with strong feeling, that my heart sank within me. It could be nothing but fever that did it, and fever had been so fatal. I got him into my arms to put him back into bed. 'Roland,' I said, humouring the poor child, which I knew was the only way, 'if you are going to tell me this secret to do any good, you know you must be quite quiet, and not excite yourself. If you excite yourself, I must not let you speak.'

'Yes, father,' said the boy. He was quiet directly, like a man, as if he quite understood. When I had laid him back on his pillow, he looked up at me with that grateful, sweet look with which children, when they are ill, break one's heart, the water coming into his eyes in his weakness. 'I was sure as soon as you were here you would know what to do,' he said.

'To be sure, my boy. Now keep quiet, and tell it all out like a man.' To think I was telling lies to my own child! for I did it only to humour him, thinking, poor little fellow, his brain was wrong.

'Yes, father. Father, there is someone in the park – someone that has been badly used.'

'Hush, my dear; you remember there is to be no excitement. Well, who is this somebody, and who has been ill-using him? We will soon put a stop to that.'

'Ah,' cried Roland, 'but it is not so easy as you think. I don't know who it is. It is just a cry. Oh, if you could hear it! It gets into my head in my sleep. I heard it as clear – as clear; and they think that I am dreaming, or raving perhaps,' the boy said, with a sort of disdainful smile.

This look of his perplexed me; it was less like fever than I thought. 'Are you quite sure you have not dreamed it, Roland?' I said.

'Dreamed? – that!' He was springing up again when he suddenly bethought himself, and lay down flat, with the same sort of smile on his face. 'The pony heard it, too,' he said. 'She jumped as if she had been shot. If I had not grasped at the reins – for I was frightened, father –'

'No shame to you, my boy,' said I, though I scarcely knew why.

'If I hadn't held to her like a leech, she'd have pitched me over her head, and she never drew breath till we were at the door. Did the pony dream it?' he said, with a soft disdain, yet indulgence for my foolishness. Then he added slowly, 'It was only a cry the first time, and all the time before you went away. I wouldn't tell you, for it was so wretched to be frightened. I thought it might be a hare or a rabbit snared, and I went in the morning and looked; but there was nothing. It was after you went I heard it really first; and this is what he says.' He raised himself on his elbow close to me, and looked me in the face: ' "Oh, mother, let me in! oh, mother, let me in!" ' As he said the words a mist came over his face, the mouth quivered, the soft features all melted and changed, and when he had ended these pitiful words, dissolved in a shower of heavy tears.

Was it a hallucination? Was it the fever of the brain? Was it the disordered fancy caused by great bodily weakness? How could I tell? I thought it wisest to accept it as if it were all true.

'This is very touching, Roland,' I said.

'Oh, if you had just heard it, father! I said to myself, if father heard it he would do something; but mamma, you know, she's given over to Simson, and that fellow's a doctor, and never thinks of anything but clapping you into bed.'

'We must not blame Simson for being a doctor, Roland.'

'No, no,' said my boy, with delightful toleration and indulgence; 'oh, no; that's the good of him; that's what he's for; I know that. But you – you are different; you are just father; and you'll do something – directly, papa, directly; this very night.'

'Surely,' I said. 'No doubt it is some little lost child.'

He gave me a sudden, swift look, investigating my face as though to see whether, after all, this was everything my eminence as 'father' came to – no more than that. Then he got hold of my shoulder, clutching it with his thin hand. 'Look here,' he said, with a quiver in his voice; 'suppose it wasn't – living at all!'

'My dear boy, how then could you have heard it?' I said.

He turned away from me with a pettish exclamation – 'As if you didn't know better than that!'

'Do you want to tell me it is a ghost?' I said.

Roland withdrew his hand; his countenance assumed an aspect of great dignity and gravity; a slight quiver remained about his lips. 'Whatever it was – you always said we were not to call names. It was something – in trouble. Oh, father, in terrible trouble!'

'But, my boy,' I said (I was at my wits' end), 'if it was a child that was lost, or any poor human creature – but, Roland, what do you want me to do?'

'I should know if I was you,' said the child eagerly. 'That is what I always said to myself – Father will know. Oh, papa, papa, to have to face it night after night, in such terrible, terrible trouble, and never to be able to do it any good! I don't want to cry; it's like a baby, I know; but what can I do else? Out there all by itself in the ruin, and nobody to help it! I can't bear it! I can't bear it!' cried my generous boy. And in his weakness he burst out, after many attempts to restrain it, into a great childish fit of sobbing and tears.

I do not know that I ever was in a greater perplexity, in my life; and afterwards, when I thought of it, there was something comic in it too. It is bad enough to find your child's mind possessed with the conviction that he has seen, or heard, a ghost; but that he should require you to go instantly and help that ghost was the most bewildering experience that had ever come my way. I am a sober man myself, and not superstitious – at least any more than everybody is superstitious. Of course I do not believe in ghosts; but I don't deny, any more than other people, that there are stories which I cannot pretend to understand. My blood got a sort of chill in my veins at the idea that Roland should be a ghost-seer; for that generally means a hysterical temperament and weak health, and all that men most hate and fear for their children. But that I should take up his ghost and right its wrongs, and save it from its trouble, was such a mission as was enough to confuse any man. I did my best to console my boy without giving any promise of this astonishing kind; but he was too sharp for me: he would have none of my caresses. With sobs breaking in at intervals upon his voice, and the raindrops hanging on his eyelids, he yet returned to the charge.

'It will be there now! – it will be there all the night! Oh, think, papa – think if it was me! I can't rest for thinking of it. Don't!' he cried, putting away my hand – 'don't! You go and help it, and mother can take care of me.'

'But, Roland, what can I do?'

My boy opened his eyes, which were large with weakness and fever, and gave me a smile such, I think, as sick children only know the secret of. 'I was sure you would know as soon as you came. I always said, Father will know. And mother,' he cried, with a softening of repose upon his face, his limbs relaxing, his form sinking with a luxurious ease in his bed – 'mother can come and take care of me.'

I called her, and saw him turn to her with the complete dependence of a child; and then I went away and left them, as perplexed a man as any in Scotland. I must say, however, I had this consolation, that my mind was greatly eased about Roland. He might be under a hallucination; but his head was clear enough, and I did not think him so ill as everybody else did. The girls were astonished even at the ease with which I took it. 'How do you think he is?' they said in a breath, coming round me, laying hold of me. 'Not half so ill as I expected,' I said; 'not very bad at all.' 'Oh, papa, you are a darling!' cried Agatha, kissing me, and crying upon my shoulder; while little Jeanie, who was as pale as Roland, clasped both her arms round mine, and could not speak at all. I knew nothing about it, not half so much as Simson; but they believed in me: they had a feeling that all would go right now. God is very good to you when your children look to you like that. It makes one humble, not proud. I was not worthy of it; and then I recollected that I had to act the part of a father to Roland's ghost – which made me almost laugh, though I might just as well have cried. It was the strangest mission that ever was entrusted to mortal man.

It was then I remembered suddenly the looks of the men when they turned to take the brougham to the stables in the dark that morning. They had not liked it, and the horses had not liked it. I remembered that even in my anxiety about Roland I had heard them tearing along the avenue back to the stables, and had made a memorandum mentally that I must speak of it. It seemed to me that the best thing I could do was to go to the stables now and make a few enquiries. It is impossible to fathom the minds of rustics; there might be some devilry of practical joking, for anything I knew; or they might have some interest in getting up a bad reputation for the Brentwood avenue. It was getting dark by the time I went out, and nobody who knows the country will need to be told how black is the darkness of a November night under high laurel bushes and yew trees. I walked into the heart of the shrubberies two or three times, not seeing a step before me, till I came out upon the broader carriage-road, where the trees opened a little, and there was a faint grey glimmer of sky visible, under which the great limes and elms stood darkling like ghosts; but it grew black again as I approached the corner where the ruins lay. Both eyes and ears were on the alert, as may be supposed; but I could see nothing in the absolute gloom, and, so far as I can recollect, I heard nothing. Nevertheless there came a strong impression upon me that somebody was there. It is a sensation which most people have felt. I have seen when it has been strong enough to awake me out of sleep, the sense of someone looking at me. I suppose my imagination had been affected by Roland's story; and the mystery of the darkness is always full of suggestions. I stamped my feet violently on the gravel to rouse myself, and called out sharply, 'Who's there?' Nobody answered, nor did I expect anyone to answer, but the impression had been made. I was so foolish that I did not like to look back, but went sideways, keeping an eye on the gloom behind. It was with great relief that I spied the light in the stables, making a sort of oasis in the darkness. I walked very quickly into the midst of that lighted and cheerful place, and thought the clank of the groom's pail one of the pleasantest sounds I had ever heard. The coachman was the head of this little colony, and it was to his house I went to pursue my investigations. He was a native of the district, and had taken care of the place in the absence of the family for years; it was impossible but that he must know everything that was going on, and all the traditions of the place. The men, I could see, eyed me anxiously when I thus appeared at such an hour among them, and followed me with their eyes to Jarvis's house, where he lived alone with his old wife, their children being all married and out in the world. Mrs Jarvis met me with anxious questions. How was the poor young gentleman? But the others knew, I could see by their faces, that not even this was the foremost thing in my mind.

*   *   *

'Noises? – ou ay, there'll be noises – the wind in the trees, and the water soughing down the glen. As for tramps, Cornel, no, there's little o' that kind o' cattle about here; and Merran at the gate's a careful body.' Jarvis moved about with some embarrassment from one leg to another as he spoke. He kept in the shade, and did not look at me more than he could help. Evidently his mind was perturbed, and he had reasons for keeping his own counsel. His wife sat by, giving him a quick look now and then, but saying nothing. The kitchen was very snug and warm and bright – as different as could be from the chill and mystery of the night outside.

'I think you are trifling with me, Jarvis,' I said.

'Triflin', Cornel? No me. What would I trifle for? If the deevil himsel was in the auld hoose, I have no interest in 't one way or another – '

'Sandy, hold your peace!' cried his wife imperatively.

'And what am I to hold my peace for, wi' the cornel standing there asking a' thae questions? I'm saying, if the deevil himsel – '

'And I'm telling ye hold your peace!' cried the woman, in great excitement. 'Dark November weather and lang nichts, and us that ken a' we ken. How daur ye name – a name that shouldna be spoken?' She threw down her stocking and got up, also in great agitation. 'I tellt ye you never could keep it. It's no a thing that will hide, and the haill toun kens as weel as you or me. Tell the cornel straight out – or see, I'll do it. I dinna hold wi' your secrets, and a secret that the haill toun kens!' She snapped her fingers with an air of large disdain. As for Jarvis, ruddy and big as he was, he shrank to nothing before this decided woman. He repeated to her two or three times her own adjuration, 'Hold your peace!' then, suddenly changing his tone, cried out, 'Tell him then, confound ye! I'll wash my hands o't. If a' the ghosts in Scotland were in the auld hoose, is that ony concern o' mine?'

After this I elicited without much difficulty the whole story. In the opinion of the Jarvises, and of everybody about, the certainty that the place was haunted was beyond all doubt. As Sandy and his wife warmed to the tale, one tripping up another in their eagerness to tell everything, it gradually developed as distinct a superstition as I ever heard, and not without poetry and pathos. How long it was since the voice had been heard first, nobody could tell with certainty. Jarvis's opinion was that his father, who had been coachman at Brentwood before him, had never heard anything about it, and that the whole thing had arisen within the last ten years, since the complete dismantling of the old house; which was a wonderfully modern date for a tale so well authenticated. According to these witnesses, and to several whom I questioned afterwards, and who were all in perfect agreement, it was only in the months of November and December that 'the visitation' occurred. During these months, the darkest of the year, scarcely a night passed without the recurrence of these inexplicable cries. Nothing, it was said, had ever been seen – at least, nothing that could be identified. Some people, bolder or more imaginative than the others, had seen the darkness moving, Mrs Jarvis said, with unconscious poetry. It began when night fell, and continued, at intervals, till day broke. Very often it was only an inarticulate cry and moaning, but sometimes the words which had taken possession of my poor boy's fancy had been distinctly audible – 'Oh, mother, let me in!' The Jarvises were not aware that there had ever been any investigation into it. The estate of Brentwood had lapsed into the hands of a distant branch of the family, who had lived but little there; and of the many people who had taken it, as I had done, few had remained through two Decembers. And nobody had taken the trouble to make a very close examination into the facts. 'No, no,' Jarvis said, shaking his head. 'No, no, Cornel. Wha wad set themsels up for a laughin'-stock to a' the countryside, making a wark about a ghost? Naebody believes in ghosts. It bid to be the wind in the trees, the last gentleman said, or some effec' o' the water wrastlin' among the rocks. He said it was a' quite easy explained; but he gave up the hoose. And when you cam, Cornel, we were awfu' anxious you should never hear. What for should I have spoiled the bargain and hairmed the property for nothing?'

'Do you call my child's life nothing?' I said in the trouble of the moment, unable to restrain myself. 'And instead of telling this all to me, you have told it to him – to a delicate boy, a child unable to sift evidence or judge for himself, a tender-hearted young creature – '

I was walking about the room with an anger all the hotter that I felt it to be most likely quite unjust. My heart was full of bitterness against the stolid retainers of a family who were content to risk other people's children and comfort rather than let a house be empty. If I had been warned I might have taken precautions, or left the place, or sent Roland away, a hundred things which now I could not do; and here I was with my boy in a brain-fever, and his life, the most precious life on earth, hanging in the balance, dependent on whether or not I could get to the reason of a commonplace ghost-story! I paced about in high wrath, not seeing what I was to do; for to take Roland away, even if he were able to travel, would not settle his agitated mind; and I feared even that a scientific explanation of refracted sound or reverberation, or any other of the easy certainties with which we elder men are silenced, would have very little effect upon the boy.

'Cornel,' said Jarvis solemnly, 'and *she'll* bear me witness – the young gentleman never heard a word from me – no, nor from either groom or gardener; I'll gie ye my word for that. In the first place, he's no a lad that invites ye to talk. There are some that are, and some that arena. Some will draw ye on, till ye've tellt them a' the clatter of the toun, and a' ye ken, and whiles mair. But Maister Roland, his mind's fu' of his books. He's aye civil and kind, and a fine lad; but no that sort. And ye see it's for a' our interest, Cornel, that you should stay at Brentwood. I took it upon me mysel to pass the word – 'No a syllable to Maister Roland, nor to the young leddies – no a syllable.' The women-servants, that have little reason to be out at night, ken little or nothing about it. And some think it grand to have a ghost so long as they're no in the way of coming across it. If you had been tellt the story to begin with, maybe ye would have thought so yourself.'

This was true enough, though it did not throw any light upon my perplexity. If we had heard of it to start with, it is possible that all the family would have considered the possession of a ghost a distinct advantage. It is the fashion of the times. We never think what a risk it is to play with young imaginations, but cry out, in the fashionable jargon, 'A ghost! – nothing else was wanted to make it perfect.' I should not have been above this myself. I should have smiled, of course, at the idea of the ghost at all, but then to feel that it was mine would have pleased my vanity. Oh, yes, I claim no exemption. The girls would have been delighted. I could fancy their eagerness, their interest and excitement. No; if we had been told, it would have done no good – we should have made the bargain all the more eagerly, the fools that we are. 'And there has been no attempt to investigate it,' I said, 'to see what it really is?'

'Eh, Cornel,' said the coachman's wife, 'wha would investigate, as ye call it, a thing that nobody believes in? Ye would be the laughin'-stock of a' the countryside, as my man says.'

'But you believe in it,' I said, turning upon her hastily. The woman was taken by surprise. She made a step backward out of my way.

'Lord, Cornel, how ye frichten a body! Me! – there's awfu' strange things in this world. An unlearned person doesna ken what to think. But the minister and the gentry they just laugh in your face. Enquire into the thing that is not! Na, na, we just let it be.'

'Come with me, Jarvis,' I said hastily, 'and we'll make an attempt at least. Say nothing to the men or to anybody. I'll come back after dinner, and we'll make a serious attempt to see what it is, if it is anything. If I hear it – which I doubt – you may be sure I shall never rest till I make it out. Be ready for me about ten o'clock.'

'Me, Cornel!' Jarvis said, in a faint voice. I had not been looking at him in my own preoccupation, but when I did so, I found that the greatest change had come over the fat and ruddy coachman. 'Me, Cornel!' he repeated, wiping the perspiration from his brow. His ruddy face hung in flabby folds, his knees knocked together, his voice seemed half extinguished in his throat. Then he began to rub his hands and smile upon me in a deprecating, imbecile way. 'There's nothing I wouldna do to pleasure ye, Cornel,' taking a step farther back. 'I'm sure *she* kens I've aye said I never had to do with a mair fair, weel-spoken gentleman – ' Here Jarvis came to a pause, again looking at me, rubbing his hands.

'Well?' I said.

'But eh, sir!' he went on, with the same imbecile yet insinuating smile, 'if ye'll reflect that I am no used to my feet. With a horse atween my legs, or the reins in my hand, I'm maybe nae worse than other men; but on fit, Cornel – It's no the – bogles – but I've been cavalry, ye see,' with a little hoarse laugh, 'a' my life. To face a thing ye dinna understan' – on your feet, Cornel.'

'Well, sir, if *I* do it,' said I tartly, 'why shouldn't you?'

'Eh, Cornel, there's an awfu' difference. In the first place, ye tramp about the haill countryside, and think naething of it; but a walk tires me mair than a hunard miles' drive; and then ye're a gentleman, and do your ain pleasure; and you're no so auld as me; and it's for your ain bairn, ye see, Cornel; and then – '

'He believes in it, Cornel, and you dinna believe in it,' the woman said.

'Will you come with me?' I said, turning to her.

She jumped back, upsetting her chair in her bewilderment. 'Me!' with a scream, and then fell into a sort of hysterical laugh. 'I wouldna say but what I would go; but what would the folk say to hear of Cornel Mortimer with an auld silly woman at his heels?'

The suggestion made me laugh too, though I had little inclination for it. 'I'm sorry you have so little spirit, Jarvis,' I said. 'I must find someone else, I suppose.'

Jarvis, touched by this, began to remonstrate, but I cut him short. My butler was a soldier who had been with me in India, and was not supposed to fear anything – man or devil – certainly not the former; and I felt that I was losing time. The Jarvises were too thankful to get rid of me. They attended me to the door with the most anxious courtesies. Outside, the two grooms stood close by, a little confused by my sudden exit. I don't know if perhaps they had been listening – as least standing as near as possible, to catch any scrap of the conversation. I waved my hand to them as I went past, in answer to their salutations, and it was very apparent to me that they also were glad to see me go.

And it will be thought very strange, but it would be weak not to add, that I myself, though bent on the investigation I have spoken of, pledged to Roland to carry it out, and feeling that my boy's health, perhaps his life, depended on the result of my enquiry – I felt the most unaccountable reluctance to pass these ruins on my way home. My curiosity was intense; and yet it was all my mind could do to pull my body along. I dare say the scientific people would describe it the other way, and attribute my cowardice to the state of my stomach. I went on; but if I had followed my impulse, I should have turned and bolted. Everything in me seemed to cry out against it: my heart thumped, my pulses all began, like sledgehammers, beating against my ears and every sensitive part. It was very dark, as I have said; the old house, with its shapeless tower, loomed a heavy mass through the darkness, which was only not entirely so solid as itself. On the other hand, the great dark cedars of which we were so proud seemed to fill up the night. My foot strayed out of the path in my confusion and the gloom together, and I brought myself up with a cry as I felt myself knock against something solid. What was it? The contact with hard stone and lime and prickly bramble bushes restored me a little to myself. 'Oh, it's only the old gable,' I said aloud, with a little laugh to reassure myself. The rough feeling of the stones reconciled me. As I groped about thus, I shook off my visionary folly. What so easily explained as that I should have strayed from the path in the darkness? This brought me back to common existence, as if I had been shaken by a wise hand out of all the silliness of superstition. How silly it was, after all! What did it matter which path I took? I laughed again, this time with better heart, when suddenly, in a moment, the blood was chilled in my veins, a shiver stole along my spine, my faculties seemed to forsake me. Close by me, at my side, at my feet, there was a sigh. No, not a groan, not a moaning, not anything so tangible – a perfectly soft, faint, inarticulate sigh. I sprang back, and my heart stopped beating. Mistaken! no, mistake was impossible. I heard it as clearly as I hear myself speak; a long, soft, weary sigh, as if drawn to the utmost, and emptying out a load of sadness that filled the breast. To hear this in the solitude, in the dark, in the night (though it was still early), had an effect which I cannot describe. I feel it now – something cold creeping over me, up into my hair and down to my feet, which refused to move. I cried out, with a trembling voice, 'Who is there?' as I had done before; but there was no reply.

I got home I don't quite know how; but in my mind there was no longer any indifference as to the thing, whatever it was, that haunted these ruins. My scepticism disappeared like a mist. I was as firmly determined that there was something as Roland was. I did not for a moment pretend to myself that it was possible I could be deceived; there were movements and noises which I understood all about – cracklings of small branches in the frost, and little rolls of gravel on the path, such as have a very eerie sound sometimes, and perplex you with wonder as to who has done it, *when there is no real mystery*; but I assure you all these little movements of nature don't affect you one bit *when there is something*. I understood *them*. I did not understand the sigh. That was not simple nature; there was meaning in it, feeling, the soul of a creature invisible. This is the thing that human nature trembles at – a creature invisible, yet with sensations, feelings, a power somehow of expressing itself. I had not the same sense of unwillingness to turn my back upon the scene of the mystery which I had experienced in going to the stables; but I almost ran home, impelled by eagerness to get everything done that had to be done, in order to apply myself to finding it out. Bagley was in the hall as usual when I went in. He was always there in the afternoon, always with the appearance of perfect occupation, yet, so far as I know, never doing anything. The door was open, so that I hurried in without any pause, breathless; but the sight of his calm regard, as he came to help me off with my overcoat, subdued me in a moment. Anything out of the way, anything incomprehensible, faded to nothing in the presence of Bagley. You saw and wondered how *he* was made: the parting of his hair, the tie of his white neckcloth, the fit of his trousers, all perfect as works of art; but you could see how they were done, which makes all the difference. I flung myself upon him, so to speak, without waiting to note the extreme unlikeness of the man to anything of the kind I meant. 'Bagley,' I said, 'I want you to come out with me tonight to watch for – '

'Poachers, Colonel?' he said, a gleam of pleasure running all over him.

'No, Bagley; a great deal worse,' I cried.

'Yes, Colonel; at what hour, sir?' the man said; but then I had not told him what it was.

It was ten o'clock when we set out. All was perfectly quiet indoors. My wife was with Roland, who had been quite calm, she said, and who (though, no doubt, the fever must run its course) had been better ever since I came. I told Bagley to put on a thick greatcoat over his evening coat, and did the same myself, with strong boots; for the soil was like a sponge, or worse. Talking to him, I almost forgot what we were going to do. It was darker even than it had been before, and Bagley kept very close to me as we went along. I had a small lantern in my hand, which gave us a partial guidance. We had come to the corner where the path turns. On one side was the bowling-green, which the girls had taken possession of for their croquet-ground – a wonderful enclosure surrounded by high hedges of holly, three hundred years old and more; on the other, the ruins. Both were black as night; but before we got so far, there was a little opening in which we could just discern the trees and the lighter line of the road. I thought it best to pause there and take breath. 'Bagley,' I said, 'there is something about these ruins I don't understand. It is there I am going. Keep your eyes open and your wits about you. Be ready to pounce upon any stranger you see – anything, man or woman. Don't hurt, but seize anything you see.' 'Colonel,' said Bagley, with a little tremor in his breath, 'they do say there's things there – as is neither man nor woman.' There was no time for words. 'Are you game to follow me, my man? that's the question,' I said. Bagley fell in without a word, and saluted. I knew then I had nothing to fear.

We went, so far as I could guess, exactly as I had come; when I heard that sigh. The darkness, however, was so complete that all marks, as of trees or paths, disappeared. One moment we felt our feet on the gravel, another sinking noiselessly into the slippery grass, that was all. I had shut up my lantern, not wishing to scare anyone, whoever it might be. Bagley followed, it seemed to me, exactly in my footsteps as I made my way, as I supposed, towards the mass of the ruined house. We seemed to take a long time groping along seeking this; the squash of the wet soil under our feet was the only thing that marked our progress. After a while I stood still to see, or rather feel, where we were. The darkness was very still, but no stiller than is usual in a winter's night. The sounds I have mentioned – the crackling of twigs, the roll of a pebble, the sound of some rustle in the dead leaves or creeping creature on the grass – were audible when you listened, all mysterious enough when your mind is disengaged, but to me cheering now as signs of the livingness of nature, even in the death of the frost. As we stood still there came up from the trees in the glen the prolonged hoot of an owl. Bagley started with alarm, being in a state of general nervousness, and not knowing what he was afraid of. But to me the sound was encouraging and pleasant, being so comprehensible.

'An owl,' I said, under my breath. 'Y–es, Colonel,' said Bagley, his teeth chattering. We stood still about five minutes, while it broke into the still brooding of the air, the sound widening out in circles, dying upon the darkness. This sound, which is not a cheerful one, made me almost gay. It was natural, and relieved the tension of the mind. I moved on with new courage, my nervous excitement calming down.

When all at once, quite suddenly, close to us, at our feet, there broke out a cry. I made a spring backwards in the first moment of surprise and horror, and in doing so came sharply against the same rough masonry and brambles that had struck me before. This new sound came upwards from the ground – a low, moaning, wailing voice, full of suffering and pain. The contrast between it and the hoot of the owl was indescribable – the one with a wholesome wildness and naturalness that hurt nobody; the other, a sound that made one's blood curdle, full of human misery. With a great deal of fumbling – for in spite of everything I could do to keep up my courage my hands shook – I managed to remove the slide of my lantern. The light leaped out like something living, and made the place visible in a moment. We were what would have been inside the ruined building had anything remained but the gable-wall which I have described. It was close to us, the vacant doorway in it going out straight into the blackness outside. The light showed the bit of wall, the ivy glistening upon it in clouds of dark green, the bramble-branches waving, and below, the open door – a door that led to nothing. It was from this the voice came which died out just as the light flashed upon this strange scene. There was a moment's silence, and then it broke forth again. The sound was so near, so penetrating, so pitiful, that, in the nervous start I gave, the light fell out of my hand. As I groped for it in the dark my hand was clutched by Bagley, who, I think, must have dropped upon his knees; but I was too much perturbed myself to think much of this. He clutched at me in the confusion of his terror, forgetting all his usual decorum. 'For God's sake, what is it, sir?' he gasped. If I yielded, there was evidently an end of both of us. 'I can't tell,' I said, 'any more than you; that's what we've got to find out. Up, man, up!' I pulled him to his feet. 'Will you go round and examine the other side, or will you stay here with the lantern?' Bagley gasped at me with a face of horror. 'Can't we stay together, Colonel?' he said; his knees were trembling under him. I pushed him against the corner of the wall, and put the light into his hands. 'Stand fast till I come back; shake yourself together, man; let nothing pass you,' I said. The voice was within two or three feet of us; of that there could be no doubt.

I went myself to the other side of the wall, keeping close to it. The light shook in Bagley's hand, but, tremulous though it was, shone out through the vacant door, one oblong block of light marking all the crumbling corners and hanging masses of foliage. Was that something dark huddled in a heap by the side of it? I pushed forward across the light in the doorway, and fell upon it with my hands; but it was only a juniper bush growing close against the wall. Meanwhile, the sight of my figure crossing the doorway had brought Bagley's nervous excitement to a height: he flew at me, gripping my shoulder. 'I've got him, Colonel! I've got him!' he cried, with a voice of sudden exultation. He thought it was a man, and was at once relieved. But at that moment the voice burst forth again between us, at our feet – more close to us than any separate being could be. He dropped off from me, and fell against the wall, his jaw dropping as if he were dying. I suppose, at the same moment, he saw that it was me whom he had clutched. I, for my part, had scarcely more command of myself. I snatched the light out of his hand, and flashed it all about me wildly. Nothing – the juniper bush which I thought I had never seen before, the heavy growth of the glistening ivy, the brambles waving. It was close to my ears now, crying, crying, pleading as if for life. Either I heard the same words Roland had heard, or else, in my excitement, his imagination got possession of mine. The voice went on, growing into distinct articulation, but wavering about, now from one point, now from another, as if the owner of it were moving slowly back and forward. 'Mother! mother!' and then an outburst of wailing. As my mind steadied, getting accustomed (as one's mind gets accustomed to anything), it seemed to me as if some uneasy, miserable creature was pacing up and down before a closed door. Sometimes – but that must have been excitement – I thought I heard a sound like knocking, and then another burst, 'Oh, mother! mother!' All this close, close to the space where I was standing with my lantern, now before me, now behind me: a creature restless, unhappy, moaning, crying before the vacant doorway, which no one could either shut or open more.

'Do you hear it, Bagley? do you hear what it is saying?' I cried, stepping in through the doorway. He was lying against the wall, his eyes glazed, half dead with terror. He made a motion of his lips as if to answer me, but no sounds came; then lifted his hand with a curious imperative movement as if ordering me to be silent and listen. And how long I did so I cannot tell. It began to have an interest, an exciting hold upon me, which I could not describe. It seemed to call up visibly a scene anyone could understand – a something shut out, restlessly wandering to and fro; sometimes the voice dropped, as if throwing itself down, sometimes wandered off a few paces, growing sharp and clear. 'Oh, mother, let me in! oh, mother, mother, let me in! oh, let me in!' Every word was clear to me. No wonder the boy had gone wild with pity. I tried to steady my mind upon Roland, upon his conviction that I could do something, but my head swam with the excitement, even when I partially overcame the terror. At last the words died away, and there was a sound of sobs and moaning. I cried out, 'In the name of God, who are you?' with a kind of feeling in my mind that to use the name of God was profane, seeing that I did not believe in ghosts or anything supernatural; but I did it all the same, and waited, my heart giving a leap of terror lest there should be a reply. Why this should have been I cannot tell, but I had a feeling that if there was an answer it would be more than I could bear. But there was no answer; the moaning went on, and then, as if it had been real, the voice rose a little higher again, the words recommenced, 'Oh, mother, let me in! oh, mother, let me in!' with an expression that was heart-breaking to hear.

As if it had been real! What do I mean by that? I suppose I got less alarmed as the thing went on. I began to recover the use of my senses – I seemed to explain it all to myself by saying that this had once happened, that it was a recollection of a real scene. Why there should have seemed something quite satisfactory and composing in this explanation I cannot tell, but so it was. I began to listen almost as if it had been a play, forgetting Bagley, who, I almost think, had fainted, leaning against the wall. I was startled out of this strange spectatorship that had fallen upon me by the sudden rush of something which made my heart jump once more, a large black figure in the doorway waving its arms. 'Come in! come in! come in!' it shouted out hoarsely at the top of a deep bass voice, and then poor Bagley fell down senseless across the threshold. He was less sophisticated than I – he had not been able to bear it any longer. I took him for something supernatural, as he took me, and it was some time before I awoke to the necessities of the moment. I remembered only after, that from the time I began to give my attention to the man, I heard the other voice no more. It was some time before I brought him to. It must have been a strange scene: the lantern making a luminous spot in the darkness, the man's white face lying on the black earth, I over him, doing what I could for him; probably I should have been thought to be murdering him had anyone seen us. When at last I succeeded in pouring a little brandy down his throat, he sat up and looked about him wildly. 'What's up?' he said; then recognising me, tried to struggle to his feet with a faint, 'Beg your pardon, Colonel.' I got him home as best I could, making him lean upon my arm. The great fellow was as weak as a child. Fortunately he did not for some time remember what had happened. From the time Bagley fell the voice had stopped, and all was still.

*   *   *

'You've got an epidemic in your house, Colonel,' Simson said to me next morning. 'What's the meaning of it all? Here's your butler raving about a voice. This will never do, you know; and so far as I can make out, you are in it too.'

'Yes, I am in it, doctor. I thought I had better speak to you. Of course you are treating Roland all right, but the boy is not raving, he is as sane as you or me. It's all true.'

'As sane as – I – or you. I never thought the boy insane. He's got cerebral excitement, fever. I don't know what you've got. There's something very queer about the look of your eyes.'

'Come,' said I, 'you can't put us all to bed, you know. You had better listen and hear the symptoms in full.'

The doctor shrugged his shoulders, but he listened to me patiently. He did not believe a word of the story, that was clear; but he heard it all from beginning to end. 'My dear fellow,' he said, 'the boy told me just the same. It's an epidemic. When one person falls a victim to this sort of thing, it's as safe as can be – there's always two or three.'

'Then how do you account for it?' I said.

'Oh, account for it! – that's a different matter; there's no accounting for the freaks our brains are subject to. If it's delusion, if it's some trick of the echoes or the winds – some phonetic disturbance or other – '

'Come with me tonight, and judge for yourself,' I said.

Upon this he laughed aloud, then said, 'That's not such a bad idea; but it would ruin me for ever if it were known that John Simson was ghost-hunting.'

'There it is,' said I; 'you dart down on us who are unlearned with your phonetic disturbances, but you daren't examine what the thing really is for fear of being laughed at. That's science!'

'It's not science – it's common-sense,' said the doctor. 'The thing has delusion on the front of it. It is encouraging an unwholesome tendency even to examine. What good could come of it? Even if I am convinced, I shouldn't believe.'

'I should have said so yesterday; and I don't want you to be convinced or to believe,' said I. 'If you prove it to be a delusion, I shall be very much obliged to you for one. Come; somebody must go with me.'

'You are cool,' said the doctor. 'You've disabled this poor fellow of yours, and made him – on that point – a lunatic for life; and now you want to disable me. But, for once, I'll do it. To save appearance, if you'll give me a bed, I'll come over after my last rounds.'

It was agreed that I should meet him at the gate, and that we should visit the scene of last night's occurrences before we came to the house, so that nobody might be the wiser. It was scarcely possible to hope that the cause of Bagley's sudden illness should not somehow steal into the knowledge of the servants at least, and it was better that all should be done as quietly as possible. The day seemed to me a very long one. I had to spend a certain part of it with Roland, which was a terrible ordeal for me, for what could I say to the boy? The improvement continued, but he was still in a very precarious state, and the trembling vehemence with which he turned to me when his mother left the room filled me with alarm. 'Father?' he said quietly. 'Yes, my boy, I am giving my best attention to it; all is being done that I can do. I have not come to any conclusion – yet. I am neglecting nothing you said,' I cried. What I could not do was to give his active mind any encouragement to dwell upon the mystery. It was a hard predicament, for some satisfaction had to be given him. He looked at me very wistfully, with the great blue eyes which shone so large and brilliant out of his white and worn face. 'You must trust me,' I said. 'Yes, father. Father understands,' he said to himself, as if to soothe some inward doubt. I left him as soon as I could. He was about the most precious thing I had on earth, and his health my first thought; but yet somehow, in the excitement of this other subject, I put that aside, and preferred not to dwell upon Roland, which was the most curious part of it all.

That night at eleven I met Simson at the gate. He had come by train, and I let him in gently myself. I had been so much absorbed in the coming experiment that I passed the ruins in going to meet him, almost without thought, if you can understand that. I had my lantern; and he showed me a coil of taper which he had ready for use. 'There is nothing like light,' he said, in his scoffing tone. It was a very still night, scarcely a sound, but not so dark. We could keep the path without difficulty as we went along. As we approached the spot we could hear a low moaning, broken occasionally by a bitter cry. 'Perhaps that is your voice,' said the doctor; 'I thought it must be something of the kind. That's a poor brute caught in some of these infernal traps of yours; you'll find it among the bushes somewhere.' I said nothing. I felt no particular fear, but a triumphant satisfaction in what was to follow. I led him to the spot where Bagley and I had stood on the previous night. All was silent as a winter night could be – so silent that we heard far off the sound of the horses in the stables, the shutting of a window at the house. Simson lighted his taper and went peering about, poking into all the corners. We looked like two conspirators lying in wait for some unfortunate traveller; but not a sound broke the quiet. The moaning had stopped before we came up; a star or two shone over us in the sky, looking down as if surprised at our strange proceedings. Dr Simson did nothing but utter subdued laughs under his breath. 'I thought as much,' he said. 'It is just the same with tables and all other kinds of ghostly apparatus; a sceptic's presence stops everything. When I am present nothing ever comes off. How long do you think it will be necessary to stay here? Oh, I don't complain; only when *you* are satisfied, *I* am – quite.'

I will not deny that I was disappointed beyond measure by this result. It made me look like a credulous fool. It gave the doctor such a pull over me as nothing else could. I should point all his morals for years to come; and his materialism, his scepticism, would be increased beyond endurance. 'It seems, indeed,' I said, 'that there is to be no – ' 'Manifestation,' he said, laughing; 'that is what all the mediums say. No manifestations, in consequence of the presence of an unbeliever.' His laugh sounded very uncomfortable to me in the silence; and it was now near midnight. But that laugh seemed the signal; before it died away the moaning we had heard before was resumed. It started from some distance off, and came towards us, nearer and nearer, like someone walking along and moaning to himself. There could be no idea now that it was a hare caught in a trap. The approach was slow, like that of a weak person, with little halts and pauses. We heard it coming along the grass straight towards the vacant doorway. Simson had been a little startled by the first sound. He said hastily, 'That child has no business to be out so late.' But he felt, as well as I, that this was no child's voice. As it came nearer, he grew silent, and, going to the doorway with his taper, stood looking out towards the sound. The taper being unprotected blew about in the night air, though there was scarcely any wind. I threw the light of my lantern steady and white across the same space. It was in a blaze of light in the midst of the blackness. A little icy thrill had gone over me at the first sound, but as it came close, I confess that my only feeling was satisfaction. The scoffer could scoff no more. The light touched his own face, and showed a very perplexed countenance. If he was afraid, he concealed it with great success, but he was perplexed. And then all that had happened on the previous night was enacted once more. It fell strangely upon me with a sense of repetition. Every cry, every sob seemed the same as before. I listened almost without any emotion at all in my own person, thinking of its effect upon Simson. He maintained a very bold front, on the whole. All that coming and going of the voice was, if our ears could be trusted, exactly in front of the vacant, blank doorway, blazing full of light, which caught and shone in the glistening leaves of the great hollies at a little distance. Not a rabbit could have crossed the turf without being seen; but there was nothing. After a time, Simson, with a certain caution and bodily reluctance, as it seemed to me, went out with his roll of taper into this space. His figure showed against the holly in full outline. Just at this moment the voice sank, as was its custom, and seemed to fling itself down at the door. Simson recoiled violently, as if someone had come up against him, then turned, and held his taper low, as if examining something. 'Do you see anybody?' I cried in a whisper, feeling the chill of nervous panic steal over me at this action. 'It's nothing but a – confounded juniper bush,' he said. This I knew very well to be nonsense, for the juniper bush was on the other side. He went about after this round and round, poking his taper everywhere, then returned to me on the inner side of the wall. He scoffed no longer; his face was contracted and pale. 'How long does this go on?' he whispered to me, like a man who does not wish to interrupt someone who is speaking. I had become too much perturbed myself to remark whether the successions and changes of the voice were the same as last night. It suddenly went out in the air almost as he was speaking, with a soft reiterated sob dying away. If there had been anything to be seen, I should have said that the person was at that moment crouching on the ground close to the door.

We walked home very silent afterwards. It was only when we were in sight of the house that I said, 'What do you think of it?' 'I can't tell what to think of it,' he said quickly. He took – though he was a very temperate man – not the claret I was going to offer him, but some brandy from the tray, and swallowed it almost undiluted. 'Mind you, I don't believe a word of it,' he said, when he had lighted his candle; 'but I can't tell what to think,' he turned round to add, when he was halfway upstairs.

All of this, however, did me no good with the solution of my problem. I was to help this weeping, sobbing thing, which was already to me as distinct a personality as anything I knew; or what should I say to Roland? It was on my heart that my boy would die if I could not find some way of helping this creature. You may be surprised that I should speak of it in this way. I did not know if it was man or woman; but I no more doubted that it was a soul in pain than I doubted my own being; and it was my business to soothe this pain – to deliver it, if that was possible. Was ever such a task given to an anxious father trembling for his only boy? I felt in my heart, fantastic as it may appear, that I must fulfil this somehow, or part with my child; and you may conceive that rather than do that I was ready to die. But even my dying would not have advanced me, unless by bringing me into the same world with that seeker at the door.

*   *   *

Next morning Simson was out before breakfast, and came in with evident signs of the damp grass on his boots, and a look of worry and weariness, which did not say much for the night he had passed. He improved a little after breakfast, and visited his two patients – for Bagley was still an invalid. I went out with him on his way to the train, to hear what he had to say about the boy. 'He is going on very well,' he said; 'there are no complications as yet. But mind you, that's not a boy to be trifled with, Mortimer. Not a word to him about last night.' I had to tell him then of my last interview with Roland, and of the impossible demand he had made upon me, by which, though he tried to laugh, he was much discomposed, as I could see. 'We must just perjure ourselves all round,' he said, 'and swear you exorcised it;' but the man was too kind-hearted to be satisfied with that. 'It's frightfully serious for you, Mortimer. I can't laugh as I should like to. I wish I saw a way out of it, for your sake. By the way,' he added shortly, 'didn't you notice that juniper bush on the left-hand side?' 'There was one on the right hand of the door. I noticed you made that mistake last night.' 'Mistake!' he cried, with a curious low laugh, pulling up the collar of his coat as though he felt the cold – 'there's no juniper there this morning, left or right. Just go and see.' As he stepped into the train a few minutes after, he looked back upon me and beckoned me for a parting word. 'I'm coming back tonight,' he said.

I don't think I had any feeling about this as I turned away from that common bustle of the railway which made my private pre-occupations feel so strangely out of date. There had been a distinct satisfaction in my mind before, that his scepticism had been so entirely defeated. But the more serious part of the matter pressed upon me now. I went straight from the railway to the manse, which stood on a little plateau on the side of the river opposite to the woods of Brentwood. The minister was one of a class which is not so common in Scotland as it used to be. He was a man of good family, well educated in the Scotch way, strong in philosophy, not so strong in Greek, strongest of all in experience – a man who had 'come across', in the course of his life, most people of note that had ever been in Scotland, and who was said to be very sound in doctrine, without infringing the toleration with which old men, who are good men, are generally endowed. He was old-fashioned; perhaps he did not think so much about the troublous problems of theology as many of the young men, nor ask himself any hard questions about the Confession of Faith; but he understood human nature, which is perhaps better. He received me with a cordial welcome.

'Come away, Colonel Mortimer,' he said; 'I'm all the more glad to see you, that I feel it's a good sign for the boy. He's doing well? – God be praised – and the Lord bless him and keep him. He has many a poor body's prayers, and that can do nobody harm.'

'He will need them all, Dr Moncrieff,' I said, 'and your counsel too.' And I told him the story – more than I had told Simson. The old clergyman listened to me with many suppressed exclamations, and at the end the water stood in his eyes.

'That's just beautiful,' he said. 'I do not mind to have heard anything like it; it's as fine as Burns when he wished deliverance to one – that is prayed for in no kirk. Ay, ay! so he would have you console the poor lost spirit? God bless the boy! There's something more than common in that, Colonel Mortimer. And also the faith of him in his father! – I would like to put that into a sermon.' Then the old gentleman gave me an alarmed look, and said, 'No, no; I was not meaning a sermon; but I must write it down for the *Children's Record*.' I saw the thought that passed through his mind. Either he thought, or he feared I would think, of a funeral sermon. You may believe this did not make me more cheerful.

I can scarcely say that Dr Moncrieff gave me any advice. How could anyone advise on such a subject? But he said, 'I think I'll come too. I'm an old man; I'm less liable to be frightened than those that are further off the world unseen. It behooves me to think of my own journey there. I've no cut-and-dry beliefs on the subject. I'll come too; and maybe at the moment the Lord will put into our heads what to do.'

This gave me a little comfort – more than Simson had given me. To be clear about the cause of it was not my grand desire. It was another thing that was in my mind – my boy. As for the poor soul at the open door, I had no more doubt, as I have said, of its existence than I had of my own. It was no ghost to me. I knew the creature, and it was in trouble. That was my feeling about it, as it was Roland's. To hear it first was a great shock to my nerves, but not now; a man will get accustomed to anything. But to do something for it was the great problem; how was I to be serviceable to a being that was invisible, that was mortal no longer? 'Maybe at the moment the Lord will put it into our heads.' This is very old-fashioned phraseology, and a week before, most likely, I should have smiled (though always with kindness) at Dr Moncrieff's credulity; but there was a great comfort, whether rational or otherwise I cannot say, in the mere sound of the words.

The road to the station and the village lay through the glen, not by the ruins; but though the sunshine and the fresh air, and the beauty of the trees, and the sound of the water were all very soothing to the spirits, my mind was so full of my own subject that I could not refrain from turning to the right hand as I got to the top of the glen, and going straight to the place which I may call the scene of all my thoughts. It was lying full in the sunshine, like all the rest of the world. The ruined gable looked due east, and in the present aspect of the sun the light streamed down through the doorway as our lantern had done, throwing a flood of light upon the damp grass beyond. There was a strange suggestion in the open door – so futile, a kind of emblem of vanity: all free around, so that you could go where you pleased, and yet that semblance of an enclosure – that way of entrance, unnecessary, leading to nothing. And why any creature should pray and weep to get in – to nothing, or be kept out – by nothing, you could not dwell upon it, or it made your brain go round. I remembered, however, what Simson said about the juniper, with a little smile on my own mind as to the inaccuracy of recollection which even a scientific man will be guilty of. I could see now the light of my lantern gleaming upon the wet glistening surface of the spiky leaves at the right hand – and he ready to go to the stake for it that it was the left! I went round to make sure. And then I saw what he had said. Right or left there was no juniper at all! I was confounded by this, though it was entirely a matter of detail; nothing at all – a bush of brambles waving, the grass growing up to the very walls. But after all, though it gave me a shock for a moment, what did that matter? There were marks as if a number of footsteps had been up and down in front of the door, but these might have been our steps; and all was bright and peaceful and still. I poked about the other ruin – the larger ruins of the old house – for some time, as I had done before. There were marks upon the grass here and there – I could not call them footsteps – all about; but that told for nothing one way or another. I had examined the ruined rooms closely the first day. They were half filled up with soil and debris, withered brackens and bramble – no refuge for anyone there. It vexed me that Jarvis should see me coming from that spot when he came up to me for his orders. I don't know whether my nocturnal expeditions had got wind among the servants, but there was a significant look in his face. Something in it I felt was like my own sensation when Simson in the midst of his scepticism was struck dumb. Jarvis felt satisfied that his veracity had been put beyond question. I never spoke to a servant of mine in such a peremptory tone before. I sent him away 'with a flea in his lug', as the man described it afterwards. Interference of any kind was intolerable to me at such a moment.

But what was strangest of all was that I could not face Roland. I did not go up to his room, as I would have naturally done, at once. This the girls could not understand. They saw there was some mystery in it. 'Mother has gone to lie down,' Agatha said; 'he has had such a good-night.' 'But he wants you so, papa!' cried little Jeanie, always with her two arms embracing mine in a pretty way she had. I was obliged to go at last, but what could I say? I could only kiss him, and tell him to keep still – that I was doing all I could. There is something mystical about the patience of a child. 'It will come all right, won't it, father?' he said. 'God grant it may! I hope so, Roland.' 'Oh, yes, it will come all right.' Perhaps he understood that in the midst of my anxiety I could not stay with him as I should have done otherwise. But the girls were more surprised than it is possible to describe. They looked at me with wondering eyes. 'If I were ill, papa, and you only stayed with me a moment, I should break my heart,' said Agatha. But the boy had a sympathetic feeling. He knew that of my own will I would not have done it. I shut myself up in the library, where I could not rest, but kept pacing up and down like a caged beast. What could I do? and if I could do nothing, what would become of my boy? These were the questions that, without ceasing, pursued each other through my mind.

Simson came out to dinner, and when the house was all still, and most of the servants in bed, we went out and met Dr Moncrieff, as we had appointed, at the head of the glen. Simson, for his part, was disposed to scoff at the minister. 'If there are to be any spells, you know, I'll cut the whole concern,' he said. I did not make him any reply. I had not invited him; he could go or come as he pleased. He was very talkative, far more so than suited my humour, as we went on. 'One thing is certain, you know; there must be some human agency,' he said. 'It is all bosh about apparitions. I never have investigated the laws of sound to any great extent, and there's a great deal in ventriloquism that we don't know much about.' 'If it's the same to you,' I said, 'I wish you'd keep all that to yourself, Simson. It doesn't suit my state of mind.' 'Oh, I hope I know how to respect idiosyncrasy,' he said. The very tone of his voice irritated me beyond measure. These scientific fellows, I wonder people put up with them as they do, when you have no mind for their cold-blooded confidence. Dr Moncrieff met us about eleven o'clock, the same time as on the previous night. He was a large man, with a venerable countenance and white hair – old, but in full vigour, and thinking less of a cold night walk than many a younger man. He had his lantern, as I had. We were fully provided with means of lighting the place, and we were all of us resolute men. We had a rapid consultation as we went up, and the result was that we divided to different posts. Dr Moncrieff remained inside the wall – if you can call that inside where there was no wall but one. Simson placed himself on the side next the ruins, so as to intercept any communication with the old house, which was what his mind was fixed upon. I was posted on the other side. To say that nothing could come near without being seen was self-evident. It had been so also on the previous night. Now, with our three lights in the midst of the darkness, the whole place seemed illuminated. Dr Moncrieff's lantern, which was a large one, without any means of shutting up – an old-fashioned lantern with a pierced and ornamental top – shone steadily, the rays shooting out of it upward into the gloom. He placed it on the grass, where the middle of the room, if this had been a room, would have been. The usual effect of the light streaming out of the doorway was prevented by the illumination which Simson and I on either side supplied. With these differences, everything seemed as on the previous night.

And what occurred was exactly the same, with the same air of repetition, point for point, as I had formerly remarked. I declare that it seemed to me as if I were pushed against, put aside, by the owner of the voice as he paced up and down in his trouble – though these are perfectly futile words, seeing that the stream of light from my lantern, and that from Simson's taper, lay broad and clear, without a shadow, without the smallest break, across the entire breadth of the grass. I had ceased even to be alarmed, for my part. My heart was rent with pity and trouble – pity for the poor suffering human creature that moaned and pleaded so, and trouble for myself and my boy. God! if I could not find any help – and what help could I find? – Roland would die.

We were all perfectly still till the first outburst was exhausted, as I knew, by experience, it would be. Dr Moncrieff, to whom it was new, was quite motionless on the other side of the wall, as we were in our places. My heart had remained almost at its usual beating during the voice. I was used to it; it did not rouse all my pulses as it did at first. But just as it threw itself sobbing at the door (I cannot use other words), there suddenly came something which sent the blood coursing through my veins, and my heart into my mouth. It was a voice inside the wall – the minister's well-known voice. I would have been prepared for it in any kind of adjuration, but I was not prepared for what I heard. It came out with a sort of stammering, as if too much moved for utterance. 'Willie, Willie! Oh, God preserve us! is it you?'

These simple words had an effect upon me that the voice of the invisible creature had ceased to have. I thought the old man, whom I had brought into this danger, had gone mad with terror. I made a dash round to the other side of the wall, half crazed myself with the thought. He was standing where I had left him, his shadow thrown vague and large upon the grass by the lantern which stood at his feet. I lifted my own light to see his face as I rushed forward. He was very pale, his eyes wet and glistening, his mouth quivering with parted lips. He neither saw nor heard me. We that had gone through this experience before, had crouched towards each other to get a little strength to bear it. But he was not even aware that I was there. His whole being seemed absorbed in anxiety and tenderness. He held out his hands, which trembled, but it seemed to me with eagerness, not fear. He went on speaking all the time. 'Willie, if it is you – and it's you, if it is not a delusion of Satan – Willie, lad! why come ye here frighting them that know you not? Why came ye not to me?'

He seemed to wait for an answer. When his voice ceased, his countenance, every line moving, continued to speak. Simson gave me another terrible shock, stealing into the open doorway with his light, as much awe-stricken, as wildly curious, as I.

But the minister resumed, without seeing Simson, speaking to someone else. His voice took a tone of expostulation: 'Is this right to come here? Your mother's gone with your name on her lips. Do you think she would ever close her door on her own lad? Do ye think the Lord will close the door, ye faint-hearted creature? No! – I forbid ye! I forbid ye!' cried the old man. The sobbing voice had begun to resume its cries. He made a step forward, calling out the last words in a voice of command. 'I forbid ye! Cry out no more to man. Go home, ye wandering spirit! go home! Do you hear me? – me that christened ye, that have struggled with ye, that have wrestled for ye with the Lord!' Here the loud tones of his voice sank into tenderness. 'And her too, poor woman! poor woman! her you are calling upon. She's not here. You'll find her with the Lord. Go there and seek her, not here. Do you hear me, lad? go after her there. He'll let you in, though it's late. Man, take heart! if you will lie and sob and greet, let it be at heaven's gate, and not your poor mother's ruined door.'

He stopped to get his breath; and the voice had stopped, not as it had done before, when its time was exhausted and all its repetitions said, but with a sobbing catch in the breath as if overruled. Then the minister spoke again, 'Are you hearing me, Will? Oh, laddie, you've liked the beggarly elements all your days. Be done with them now. Go home to the Father – the Father! Are you hearing me?' Here the old man sank down upon his knees, his face raised upwards, his hands held up with a tremble in them, all white in the light in the midst of the darkness. I resisted as long as I could, though I cannot tell why; then I, too, dropped upon my knees. Simson all the time stood in the doorway, with an expression in his face such as words could not tell, his underlip dropped, his eyes wild, staring. It seemed to be to him, that image of blank ignorance and wonder, that we were praying. All the time the voice, with a low arrested sobbing, lay just where he was standing, as I thought.

'Lord,' the minister said – 'Lord, take him into Thy everlasting habitations. The mother he cries to is with Thee. Who can open to him but Thee? Lord, when is it too late for Thee, or what is too hard for Thee? Lord, let that woman there draw him inower! Let her draw him inower!'

I sprang forward to catch something in my arms that flung itself wildly within the door. The illusion was so strong, that I never paused till I felt my forehead graze against the wall and my hands clutch the ground – for there was nobody there to save from falling, as in my foolishness I thought. Simson held out his hand to me to help me up. He was trembling and cold, his lower lip hanging, his speech almost inarticulate. 'It's gone,' he said, stammering – 'it's gone!' We leaned upon each other for a moment, trembling so much, both of us, that the whole scene trembled as if it were going to dissolve and disappear; and yet as long as I live I will never forget it – the shining of the strange lights, the blackness all round, the kneeling figure with all the whiteness of the light concentrated on its white venerable head and uplifted hands. A strange solemn stillness seemed to close all round us. By intervals a single syllable, 'Lord! Lord!' came from the old minister's lips. He saw none of us, nor thought of us. I never knew how long we stood, like sentinels guarding him at his prayers, holding our lights in a confused dazed way, not knowing what we did. But at last he rose from his knees, and standing up at his full height, raised his arms, as the Scotch manner is at the end of a religious service, and solemnly gave the apostolical benediction – to what? to the silent earth, the dark woods, the wide breathing atmosphere; for we were but spectators gasping an Amen!

It seemed to me that it must be the middle of the night, as we all walked back. It was in reality very late. Dr Moncrieff put his arm into mine. He walked slowly, with an air of exhaustion. It was as if we were coming from a deathbed. Something hushed and solemnised the very air. There was that sense of relief in it which there always is at the end of a death-struggle. And nature, persistent, never daunted, came back in all of us, as we returned into the ways of life. We said nothing to each other, indeed, for a time; but when we got clear of the trees and reached the opening near the house, where we could see the sky, Dr Moncrieff himself was the first to speak. 'I must be going,' he said; 'it's very late, I'm afraid. I will go down the glen, as I came.'

'But not alone. I am going with you, Doctor.'

'Well, I will not oppose it. I am an old man, and agitation wearies more than work. Yes; I'll be thankful of your arm. Tonight, Colonel, you've done me more good turns than one.'

I pressed his hand on my arm, not feeling able to speak. But Simson, who turned with us, and who had gone along all this time with his taper flaring, in entire unconsciousness, came to himself, apparently at the sound of our voices, and put out that wild little torch with a quick movement, as if of shame. 'Let me carry your lantern,' he said; 'it is heavy.' He recovered with a spring; and in a moment, from the awe-stricken spectator he had been, became himself, sceptical and cynical. 'I should like to ask you a question,' he said. 'Do you believe in Purgatory, Doctor? It's not in the tenets of the Church, so far as I know.'

'Sir,' said Dr Moncrieff, 'an old man like me is sometimes not very sure what he believes. There is just one thing I am certain of – and that is the loving kindness of God.'

'But I thought that was in this life. I am no theologian – '

'Sir,' said the old man again, with a tremor in him which I could feel going over all his frame, 'if I saw a friend of mine within the gates of hell, I would not despair but his Father would take him by the hand still, if he cried like *you*.'

'I allow it is very strange, very strange. I cannot see through it. That there must be human agency, I feel sure. Doctor, what made you decide upon the person and the name?'

The minister put out his hand with the impatience which a man might show if he were asked how he recognised his brother. 'Tuts!' he said, in familiar speech; then more solemnly, 'How should I not recognise a person that I know better – far better – than I know you?'

'Then you saw the man?'

Dr Moncrieff made no reply. He moved his hand again with a little impatient movement, and walked on, leaning heavily on my arm. And we went on for a long time without another word, threading the dark paths, which were steep and slippery with the damp of the winter. The air was very still – not more than enough to make a faint sighing in the branches, which mingled with the sound of the water to which we were descending. When we spoke again, it was about indifferent matters – about the height of the river, and the recent rains. We parted with the minister at his own door, where his old housekeeper appeared in great perturbation, waiting for him. 'Eh, me, minister! the young gentleman will be worse?' she cried.

'Far from that – better. God bless him!' Dr Moncrieff said.

I think if Simson had begun again to me with his questions, I should have pitched him over the rocks as we returned up the glen; but he was silent, by a good inspiration. And the sky was clearer than it had been for many nights, shining high over the trees, with here and there a star faintly gleaming through the wilderness of dark and bare branches. The air, as I have said, was very soft in them, with a subdued and peaceful cadence. It was real, like every natural sound, and came to us like a hush of peace and relief. I thought there was a sound in it as of the breath of a sleeper, and it seemed clear to me that Roland must be sleeping, satisfied and calm. We went up to his room when we went in. There we found the complete hush of rest. My wife looked up out of a doze, and gave me a smile: 'I think he is a great deal better; but you are very late,' she said in a whisper, shading the light with her hand that the doctor might see his patient. The boy had got back something like his own colour. He woke as we stood all round his bed. His eyes had the happy, half-awakened look of childhood, glad to shut again, yet pleased with the interruption and glimmer of the light. I stooped over him and kissed his forehead, which was moist and cool. 'All is well, Roland,' I said. He looked up at me with a glance of pleasure, and took my hand and laid his cheek upon it, and so went to sleep.

*   *   *

For some nights after, I watched among the ruins, spending all the dark hours up to midnight patrolling about the bit of wall which was associated with so many emotions; but I heard nothing, and saw nothing beyond the quiet course of nature; nor, so far as I am aware, has anything been heard again. Dr Moncrieff gave me the history of the youth, whom he never hesitated to name. I did not ask, as Simson did, how he recognised him. He had been a prodigal – weak, foolish, easily imposed upon, and 'led away', as people say. All that we had heard had passed actually in life, the minister said. The young man had come home thus a day or two after his mother died – who was no more than the housekeeper in the old house – and distracted with the news, had thrown himself down at the door and called upon her to let him in. The old man could scarcely speak of it for tears. To me it seemed as if – heaven help us, how little do we know about anything! – a scene like that might impress itself somehow upon the hidden heart of nature. I do not pretend to know how, but the repetition had struck me at the time as, in its terrible strangeness and incomprehensibility, almost mechanical – as if the unseen actor could not exceed or vary, but was bound to re-enact the whole. One thing that struck me, however, greatly, was the likeness between the old minister and my boy in the manner of regarding these strange phenomena. Dr Moncrieff was not terrified, as I had been myself, and all the rest of us. It was no 'ghost', as I fear we all vulgarly considered it, to him – but a poor creature whom he knew under these conditions, just as he had known him in the flesh, having no doubt of his identity. And to Roland it was the same. This spirit in pain – if it was a spirit – this voice out of the unseen – was a poor fellow-creature in misery, to be succoured and helped out of his trouble, to my boy. He spoke to me quite frankly about it when he got better. 'I knew father would find out some way,' he said. And this was when he was strong and well, and all idea that he would turn hysterical or become a seer of visions had happily passed away.

*   *   *

I must add one curious fact, which does not seem to me to have any relation to the above, but which Simson made great use of, as the human agency which he was determined to find somehow. We had examined the ruins very closely at the time of these occurrences; but afterwards, when all was over, as we went casually about them one Sunday afternoon in the idleness of that unemployed day, Simson with his stick penetrated an old window which had been entirely blocked up with fallen soil. He jumped down into it in great excitement, and called me to follow. There we found a little hole – for it was more a hole than a room – entirely hidden under the ivy and ruins, in which there was a quantity of straw laid in a corner, as if someone had made a bed there, and some remains of crusts about the floor. Someone had lodged there, and not very long before, he made out; and that this unknown being was the author of all the mysterious sounds we heard he is convinced. 'I told you it was human agency,' he said triumphantly. He forgets, I suppose, how he and I stood with our lights, seeing nothing, while the space between us was audibly traversed by something that could speak, and sob, and suffer. There is no argument with men of this kind. He is ready to get up a laugh against me on this slender ground. 'I was puzzled myself – I could not make it out – but I always felt convinced human agency was at the bottom of it. And here it is – and a clever fellow he must have been,' the doctor says.

Bagley left my service as soon as he got well. He assured me it was no want of respect, but he could not stand 'them kind of things'; and the man was so shaken and ghastly that I was glad to give him a present and let him go. For my own part, I made a point of staying out the time – two years – for which I had taken Brentwood; but I did not renew my tenancy. By that time we had settled, and found for ourselves a pleasant home of our own.

I must add that when the doctor defies me, I can always bring back gravity to his countenance, and a pause in his railing, when I remind him of the juniper bush. To me that was a matter of little importance. I could believe I was mistaken. I did not care about it one way or another; but on his mind the effect was different. The miserable voice, the spirit in pain, he could think of as the result of ventriloquism, or reverberation, or – anything you please: an elaborate prolonged hoax, executed somehow by the tramp that had found a lodging in the old tower; but the juniper bush staggered him. Things have effects so different on the minds of different men.

The Library Window

Margaret Oliphant

I

I was not aware at first of the many discussions which had gone on about that window. It was almost opposite one of the windows of the large old-fashioned drawing-room of the house in which I spent that summer, which was of so much importance in my life. Our house and the library were on opposite sides of the broad High Street of St Rule's, which is a fine street, wide and ample, and very quiet, as strangers think who come from noisier places; but in a summer evening there is much coming and going, and the stillness is full of sound – the sound of footsteps and pleasant voices, softened by the summer air. There are even exceptional moments when it is noisy: the time of the fair, and on Saturday nights sometimes, and when there are excursion trains. Then even the softest sunny air of the evening will not smooth the harsh tones and the stumbling steps; but at these unlovely moments we shut the windows, and even I, who am so fond of that deep recess where I can take refuge from all that is going on inside, and make myself a spectator of all the varied story out of doors, withdraw from my watchtower. To tell the truth, there never was very much going on inside. The house belonged to my aunt, to whom (she says, 'Thank God!') nothing ever happens. I believe that many things have happened to her in her time; but that was all over at the period of which I am speaking, and she was old, and very quiet. Her life went on in a routine never broken. She got up at the same hour every day, and did the same things in the same rotation, day by day the same. She said that this was the greatest support in the world, and that routine is a kind of salvation. It may be so; but it is a very dull salvation, and I used to feel that I would rather have incident, whatever kind of incident it might be. But then at that time I was not old, which makes all the difference. At the time of which I speak the deep recess of the drawing-room window was a great comfort to me. Though she was an old lady (perhaps because she was so old) she was very tolerant, and had a kind of feeling for me. She never said a word, but often gave me a smile when she saw how I had built myself up, with my books and my basket of work. I did very little work, I fear – now and then a few stitches when the spirit moved me, or when I had got well afloat in a dream, and was more tempted to follow it out than to read my book, as sometimes happened. At other times, and if the book were interesting, I used to get through volume after volume sitting there, paying no attention to anybody. And yet I did pay a kind of attention. Aunt Mary's old ladies came in to call, and I heard them talk, though I very seldom listened; but for all that, if they had anything to say that was interesting, it is curious how I found it in my mind afterwards, as if the air had blown it to me. They came and went, and I had the sensation of their old bonnets gliding out and in, and their dresses rustling, and now and then had to jump up and shake hands with someone who knew me and asked after my papa and mamma. Then Aunt Mary would give me a little smile again, and I slipped back to my window. She never seemed to mind. My mother would not have let me do it, I know. She would have remembered dozens of things there were to do. She would have sent me upstairs to fetch something which I was quite sure she did not want, or downstairs to carry some quite unnecessary message to the housemaid. She liked to keep me running about. Perhaps that was one reason why I was so fond of Aunt Mary's drawing-room, and the deep recess of the window, and the curtain that fell half over it, and the broad window-seat where one could collect so many things without being found fault with for untidiness. Whenever we had anything the matter with us in these days, we were sent to St Rule's to get up our strength. And this was my case at the time of which I am going to speak.

Everybody had said, since ever I learned to speak, that I was fantastic and fanciful and dreamy, and all the other words with which a girl who may happen to like poetry, and to be fond of thinking, is so often made uncomfortable. People don't know what they mean when they say fantastic. It sounds like Madge Wildfire or something of that sort. My mother thought I should always be busy, to keep nonsense out of my head. But really I was not at all fond of nonsense. I was rather serious than otherwise. I would have been no trouble to anybody if I had been left to myself. It was only that I had a sort of second-sight, and was conscious of things to which I paid no attention. Even when reading the most interesting book, the things that were being talked about blew in to me; and I heard what the people were saying in the streets as they passed under the window. Aunt Mary always said I could do two or indeed three things at once – both read and listen and see. I am sure that I did not listen much, and seldom looked out, of set purpose – as some people do who notice what bonnets the ladies in the street have on; but I did hear what I couldn't help hearing, even when I was reading my book, and I did see all sorts of things, though often for a whole half-hour I might never lift my eyes.

This does not explain what I said at the beginning, that there were many discussions about that window. It was, and still is, the last window in the row, of the College Library, which is opposite my aunt's house in the High Street. Yet it is not exactly opposite, but a little to the west, so that I could see it best from the left side of my recess. I took it calmly for granted that it was a window like any other till I first heard the talk about it which was going on in the drawing-room. 'Have you never made up your mind, Mrs Balcarres,' said old Mr Pitmilly, 'whether that window opposite is a window or no?' He said Mistress Balcarres – and he was always called Mr Pitmilly, Morton: which was the name of his place.

'I am never sure of it, to tell the truth,' said Aunt Mary, 'all these years.'

'Bless me!' said one of the old ladies, 'and what window may that be?'

Mr Pitmilly had a way of laughing as he spoke, which did not please me; but it was true that he was not perhaps desirous of pleasing me. He said, 'Oh, just the window opposite,' with his laugh running through his words; 'our friend can never make up her mind about it, though she has been living opposite it since – '

'You need never mind the date,' said another; 'the Leebrary window! Dear me, what should it be but a window? up at that height it could not be a door.'

'The question is,' said my aunt, 'if it is a real window with glass in it, or if it is merely painted, or if it once was a window, and has been built up. And the oftener people look at it, the less they are able to say.'

'Let me see this window,' said old Lady Carnbee, who was very active and strong-minded; and then they all came crowding upon me – three or four old ladies, very eager, and Mr Pitmilly's white hair appearing over their heads, and my aunt sitting quiet and smiling behind.

'I mind the window very well,' said Lady Carnbee; 'ay: and so do more than me. But in its present appearance it is just like any other window; but has not been cleaned, I should say, in the memory of man.'

'I see what ye mean,' said one of the others. 'It is just a very dead thing without any reflection in it; but I've seen as bad before.'

'Ay, it's dead enough,' said another, 'but that's no rule; for these hizzies of women-servants in this ill age – '

'Nay, the women are well enough,' said the softest voice of all, which was Aunt Mary's. 'I will never let them risk their lives cleaning the outside of mine. And there are no women-servants in the Old Library: there is maybe something more in it than that.'

They were all pressing into my recess, pressing upon me, a row of old faces, peering into something they could not understand. I had a sense in my mind of how curious it was, the wall of old ladies in their old satin gowns all glazed with age, Lady Carnbee with her lace about her head. Nobody was looking at me or thinking of me; but I felt unconsciously the contrast of my youngness to their oldness, and stared at them as they stared over my head at the Library window. I had given it no attention up to this time. I was more taken up with the old ladies than with the thing they were looking at.

'The framework is all right at least, I can see that, and pented black – '

'And the panes are pented black too. It's no window, Mrs Balcarres. It has been filled in, in the days of the window duties: you will mind, Leddy Carnbee.'

'Mind!' said that oldest lady. 'I mind when your mother was marriet, Jeanie: and that's neither the day nor yesterday. But as for the window, it's just a delusion: and that is my opinion of the matter, if you ask me.'

'There's a great want of light in that muckle room at the college,' said another. 'If it was a window, the Leebrary would have more light.'

'One thing is clear,' said one of the younger ones, 'it cannot be a window to see through. It may be filled in or it may be built up, but it is not a window to give light.'

'And who ever heard of a window that was no to see through?' Lady Carnbee said. I was fascinated by the look on her face, which was a curious scornful look as of one who knew more than she chose to say: and then my wandering fancy was caught by her hand as she held it up, throwing back the lace that dropped over it. Lady Carnbee's lace was the chief thing about her – heavy black Spanish lace with large flowers.

Everything she wore was trimmed with it. A large veil of it hung over her old bonnet. But her hand coming out of this heavy lace was a curious thing to see. She had very long fingers, very taper, which had been much admired in her youth; and her hand was very white, or rather more than white, pale, bleached and bloodless, with large blue veins standing up upon the back; and she wore some fine rings, among others a big diamond in an ugly old claw setting. They were too big for her, and were wound round and round with yellow silk to make them keep on: and this little cushion of silk, turned brown with long wearing, had twisted round so that it was more conspicuous than the jewels; while the big diamond blazed underneath in the hollow of her hand, like some dangerous thing hiding and sending out darts of light. The hand, which seemed to come almost to a point, with this strange ornament underneath, clutched at my half-terrified imagination. It too seemed to mean far more than was said. I felt as if it might clutch me with sharp claws, and the lurking, dazzling creature bite – with a sting that would go to the heart.

Presently, however, the circle of the old faces broke up, the old ladies returned to their seats, and Mr Pitmilly, small but very erect, stood up in the midst of them, talking with mild authority like a little oracle among the ladies. Only Lady Carnbee always contradicted the neat little old gentleman. She gesticulated, when she talked, like a Frenchwoman, and darted forth that hand of hers with the lace hanging over it, so that I always caught a glimpse of the lurking diamond. I thought she looked like a witch among the comfortable little group which gave such attention to everything Mr Pitmilly said.

'For my part, it is my opinion there is no window there at all,' he said. 'It's very like the thing that's called in scientific language an optical illusion. It arises generally, if I may use such a word in the presence of ladies, from a liver that is not just in the perfitt order and balance that organ demands – and then you will see things – a blue dog, I remember, was the thing in one case, and in another – '

'The man has gane gyte,' said Lady Carnbee; 'I mind the windows in the Auld Leebrary as long as I mind anything. Is the Leebrary itself an optical illusion too?'

'Na, na,' and 'No, no,' said the old ladies; 'a blue dogue would be a strange vagary: but the Library we have all kent from our youth,' said one. 'And I mind when the Assemblies were held there one year when the Town Hall was building,' another said.

'It is just a great divert to me,' said Aunt Mary; but what was strange was that she paused there, and said in a low tone, 'now'; and then went on again, 'for whoever comes to my house, there are aye discussions about that window. I have never just made up my mind about it myself. Sometimes I think it's a case of these wicked window duties, as you said, Miss Jeanie, when half the windows in our houses were blocked up to save the tax. And then, I think, it may be due to that blank kind of building like the great new buildings on the Earthen Mound in Edinburgh, where the windows are just ornaments. And then whiles I am sure I can see the glass shining when the sun catches it in the afternoon.'

'You could so easily satisfy yourself, Mrs Balcarres, if you were – '

'Give a laddie a penny to cast a stone, and see what happens,' said Lady Carnbee.

'But I am not sure that I have any desire to satisfy myself,' Aunt Mary said. And then there was a stir in the room, and I had to come out from my recess and open the door for the old ladies and see them downstairs, as they all went away following one another. Mr Pitmilly gave his arm to Lady Carnbee, though she was always contradicting him; and so the tea-party dispersed. Aunt Mary came to the head of the stairs with her guests in an old-fashioned gracious way, while I went down with them to see that the maid was ready at the door. When I came back Aunt Mary was still standing in the recess looking out. Returning to her seat, she said, with a kind of wistful look, 'Well, honey: and what is your opinion?'

'I have no opinion. I was reading my book all the time,' I said.

'And so you were, honey, and no' very civil; but all the same I ken well you heard every word we said.'

2

It was a night in June; dinner was long over, and had it been winter the maids would have been shutting up the house, and my Aunt Mary preparing to go upstairs to her room. But it was still clear daylight, that daylight out of which the sun has been long gone, and which has no longer any rose reflections, but all has sunk into a pearly neutral tint – a light which is daylight yet is not day. We had taken a turn in the garden after dinner, and now we had returned to what we called our usual occupations. My aunt was reading. The English post had come in, and she had got her *Times*, which was her great diversion. The *Scotsman* was her morning reading, but she liked her *Times* at night.

As for me, I too was at my usual occupation, which at that time was doing nothing. I had a book as usual, and was absorbed in it: but I was conscious of all that was going on all the same. The people strolled along the broad pavement, making remarks as they passed under the open window which came up into my story or my dream, and sometimes made me laugh. The tone and the faint sing-song, or rather chant, of the accent, which was 'a wee Fifish', was novel to me, and associated with holiday, and pleasant; and sometimes they said to each other something that was amusing, and often something that suggested a whole story; but presently they began to drop off, the footsteps slackened, the voices died away. It was getting late, though the clear soft daylight went on and on. All through the lingering evening, which seemed to consist of interminable hours, long but not weary, drawn out as if the spell of the light and the outdoor life might never end, I had now and then, quite unawares, cast a glance at the mysterious window which my aunt and her friends had discussed, as I felt, though I dared not say it even to myself, rather foolishly. It caught my eye without any intention on my part, as I paused, as it were, to take breath, in the flowing and current of undistinguishable thoughts and things from without and within which carried me along. First it occurred to me, with a little sensation of discovery, how absurd to say it was not a window, a living window, one to see through! Why, then, had they never *seen* it, these old folk? I saw as I looked up suddenly the faint greyness as of visible space within – a room behind, certainly dim, as it was natural a room should be on the other side of the street – quite indefinite: yet so clear that if someone were to come to the window there would be nothing surprising in it. For certainly there was a feeling of space behind the panes which these old half-blind ladies had disputed about – whether they were glass or only fictitious panes marked on the wall. How silly! when eyes that could see could make it out in a minute. It was only a greyness at present, but it was unmistakable, a space that went back into gloom, as every room does when you look into it across a street. There were no curtains to show whether it was inhabited or not; but a room – oh, as distinctly as ever room was! I was pleased with myself, but said nothing, while Aunt Mary rustled her paper, waiting for a favourable moment to announce a discovery which settled her problem at once. Then I was carried away upon the stream again, and forgot the window, till somebody threw unawares a word from the outer world, 'I'm goin' hame; it'll soon be dark.' Dark! what was the fool thinking of? it never would be dark if one waited out, wandering

in the soft air for hours longer; and then my eyes, acquiring easily
that new habit, looked across the way again.

Ah, now! nobody indeed had come to the window; and no light had
been lighted, seeing it was still beautiful to read by – a still, clear,
colourless light; but the room inside had certainly widened. I could
see the grey space and air a little deeper, and a sort of vision, very
dim, of a wall, and something against it; something dark, with the
blackness that a solid article, however indistinctly seen, takes in the
lighter darkness that is only space – a large, black, dark thing coming
out into the grey. I looked more intently, and made sure it was a piece
of furniture, either a writing-table or perhaps a large bookcase. No
doubt it must be the last, since this was part of the old library. I never
visited the old College Library, but I had seen such places before, and
I could well imagine it to myself. How curious that for all the time
these old people had looked at it, they had never seen this before!

It was more silent now, and my eyes, I suppose, had grown dim
with gazing, doing my best to make it out, when suddenly Aunt Mary
said, 'Will you ring the bell, my dear? I must have my lamp.'

'Your lamp?' I cried, 'when it is still daylight.' But then I gave
another look at my window, and perceived with a start that the light
had indeed changed: for now I saw nothing. It was still light, but
there was so much change in the light that my room, with the grey
space and the large shadowy bookcase, had gone out, and I saw them
no more: for even a Scotch night in June, though it looks as if it
would never end, does darken at the last. I had almost cried out, but
checked myself, and rang the bell for Aunt Mary, and made up my
mind I would say nothing till next morning, when to be sure naturally
it would be more clear.

Next morning I rather think I forgot all about it – or was busy: or
was more idle than usual; the two things meant nearly the same. At all
events I thought no more of the window, though I still sat in my own,
opposite to it, but occupied with some other fancy. Aunt Mary's
visitors came as usual in the afternoon; but their talk was of other
things, and for a day or two nothing at all happened to bring back my
thoughts into this channel. It might be nearly a week before the
subject came back, and once more it was old Lady Carnbee who set
me thinking; not that she said anything upon that particular theme.
But she was the last of my aunt's afternoon guests to go away, and
when she rose to leave she threw up her hands, with those lively
gesticulations which so many old Scotch ladies have. 'My faith!' said
she, 'there is that bairn there still like a dream. Is the creature

bewitched, Mary Balcarres? and is she bound to sit there by night and by day for the rest of her days? You should mind that there's things about, uncanny for women of our blood.'

I was too much startled at first to recognise that it was of me she was speaking. She was like a figure in a picture, with her pale face the colour of ashes, and the big pattern of the Spanish lace hanging half over it, and her hand held up, with the big diamond blazing at me from the inside of her uplifted palm. It was held up in surprise, but it looked as if it were raised in malediction; and the diamond threw out darts of light and glared and twinkled at me. If it had been in its right place it would not have mattered; but there, in the open of the hand! I started up, half in terror, half in wrath. And then the old lady laughed, and her hand dropped. 'I've wakened you to life, and broke the spell,' she said, nodding her old head at me, while the large black silk flowers of the lace waved and threatened. And she took my arm to go downstairs, laughing and bidding me be steady, and no' tremble and shake like a broken reed. 'You should be as steady as a rock at your age. I was like a young tree,' she said, leaning so heavily that my willowy girlish frame quivered – 'I was a support to virtue, like Pamela, in my time.'

'Aunt Mary, Lady Carnbee is a witch!' I cried, when I came back.

'Is that what you think, honey? well: maybe she once was,' said Aunt Mary, whom nothing surprised.

And it was that night once more after dinner, and after the post came in, and *The Times*, that I suddenly saw the Library window again. I had seen it every day and noticed nothing; but tonight, still in a little tumult of mind over Lady Carnbee and her wicked diamond which wished me harm, and her lace which waved threats and warnings at me, I looked across the street, and there I saw quite plainly the room opposite, far more clear than before. I saw dimly that it must be a large room, and that the big piece of furniture against the wall was a writing-desk. That in a moment, when first my eyes rested upon it, was quite clear: a large old-fashioned escritoire, standing out into the room; and I knew by the shape of it that it had a great many pigeon-holes and little drawers in the back, and a large table for writing. There was one just like it in my father's library at home. It was such a surprise to see it all so clearly that I closed my eyes, for the moment almost giddy, wondering how papa's desk could have come here – and then when I reminded myself that this was nonsense, and that there were many such writing-tables besides papa's, and looked again – lo! it had all become quite vague and indistinct as it was at first; and I saw nothing but the blank window, of which the old ladies could never be certain whether it was filled up to avoid the window-tax, or whether it had ever been a window at all.

This occupied my mind very much, and yet I did not say anything to Aunt Mary. For one thing, I rarely saw anything at all in the early part of the day; but then that is natural: you can never see into a place from outside, whether it is an empty room or a looking-glass, or people's eyes, or anything else that is mysterious, in the day. It has, I suppose, something to do with the light. But in the evening in June in Scotland – then is the time to see. For it is daylight, yet it is not day, and there is a quality in it which I cannot describe, it is so clear, as if every object was a reflection of itself.

I used to see more and more of the room as the days went on. The large escritoire stood out more and more into the space, with sometimes white glimmering things, which looked like papers, lying on it; and once or twice I was sure I saw a pile of books on the floor close to the writing-table, as if they had gilding upon them in broken specks, like old books. It was always about the time when the lads in the street began to call to each other that they were going home, and sometimes a shriller voice would come from one of the doors, bidding somebody to 'cry upon the laddies' to come back to their suppers. That was always the time I saw best, though it was close upon the moment when the veil seemed to fall and the clear radiance became less living, and all the sounds died out of the street, and Aunt Mary said in her soft voice, 'Honey! will you ring for the lamp?' She said honey as people say darling, and I think it is a prettier word.

Then finally, while I sat one evening with my book in my hand, looking straight across the street, not distracted by anything, I saw a little movement within. It was not anyone visible – but everybody must know what it is to see the stir in the air, the little disturbance – you cannot tell what it is, but that it indicates someone there, even though you can see no one. Perhaps it is a shadow making just one flicker in the still place. You may look at an empty room and the furniture in it for hours, and then suddenly there will be the flicker, and you know that something has come into it. It might only be a dog or a cat; it might be, if that were possible, a bird flying across; but it is someone, something living, which is so different, so completely different, in a moment from the things that are not living. It seemed to strike quite through me, and I gave a little cry. Then Aunt Mary stirred a little, and put down the huge newspaper that almost covered her from sight, and said, 'What is it, honey?' I cried, 'Nothing,' with a little gasp, quickly, for I did not want to be disturbed just at this moment when somebody was coming! But I suppose she was not satisfied, for she got up and stood behind to see what it was, putting her hand on my shoulder. It was the softest touch in the world, but I could have flung it off angrily: for that moment everything was still again, and the place grew grey and I saw no more.

'Nothing,' I repeated, but I was so vexed I could have cried. 'I told you it was nothing, Aunt Mary. Don't you believe me, that you come to look – and spoil it all!'

I did not mean of course to say these last words; they were forced out of me. I was so much annoyed to see it all melt away like a dream: for it was no dream, but as real as – as real as – myself or anything I ever saw.

She gave my shoulder a little pat with her hand. 'Honey,' she said, 'were you looking at something? Is't that? is't that?' 'Is it what?' I wanted to say, shaking off her hand, but something in me stopped me: for I said nothing at all, and she went quietly back to her place. I suppose she must have rung the bell herself, for immediately I felt the soft flood of the light behind me, and the evening outside dimmed down, as it did every night, and I saw nothing more.

It was next day, I think, in the afternoon that I spoke. It was brought on by something she said about her fine work. 'I get a mist before my eyes,' she said; 'you will have to learn my old lace stitches, honey – for I soon will not see to draw the threads.'

'Oh, I hope you will keep your sight,' I cried, without thinking what I was saying. I was then young and very matter-of-fact. I had not found out that one may mean something, yet not half or a hundredth part of what one seems to mean: and even then probably hoping to be contradicted if it is anyhow against oneself.

'My sight!' she said, looking up at me with a look that was almost angry; 'there is no question of losing my sight – on the contrary, my eyes are very strong. I may not see to draw fine threads, but I see at a distance as well as ever I did – as well as you do.'

'I did not mean any harm, Aunt Mary,' I said. 'I thought you said . . . But how can your sight be as good as ever when you are in doubt about that window? I can see into the room as clear as – ' My voice wavered, for I had just looked up and across the street, and I could have sworn that there was no window at all, but only a false image of one painted on the wall.

'Ah!' she said, with a little tone of keenness and of surprise; and she half rose up, throwing down her work hastily, as if she meant to come to me: then, perhaps seeing the bewildered look on my face, she paused and hesitated – 'Ay, honey!' she said, 'have you got so far ben as that?'

What did she mean? Of course I knew all the old Scotch phrases as well as I knew myself; but it is a comfort to take refuge in a little ignorance, and I know I pretended not to understand whenever I was put out. 'I don't know what you mean by "far ben",' I cried out, very impatient. I don't know what might have followed, but someone just then came to call, and she could only give me a look before she went forward, putting out her hand to her visitor. It was a very soft look, but anxious, and as if she did not know what to do: and she shook her head a very little, and I thought, though there was a smile on her face, there was something wet about her eyes. I retired into my recess, and nothing more was said.

But it was very tantalising that it should fluctuate so; for sometimes I saw that room quite plain and clear – quite as clear as I could see papa's library, for example, when I shut my eyes. I compared it naturally to my father's study, because of the shape of the writing-table, which, as I tell you, was the same as his. At times I saw the papers on the table quite plain, just as I had seen his papers many a day. And the little pile of books on the floor at the foot – not ranged regularly in order, but put down one above the other, with all their angles going different ways, and a speck of the old gilding shining here and there. And then again at other times I saw nothing, absolutely nothing, and was no better than the old ladies who had peered over my head, drawing their eyelids together, and arguing that the window had been shut up because of the old long-abolished window tax, or else that it had never been a window at all. It annoyed me very much at those dull moments to feel that I too puckered up my eyelids and saw no better than they.

Aunt Mary's old ladies came and went day after day while June went on. I was to go back in July, and I felt that I should be very unwilling indeed to leave until I had quite cleared up – as I was indeed in the way of doing – the mystery of that window which changed so strangely and appeared quite a different thing, not only to different people, but to the same eyes at different times. Of course I said to myself it must simply be an effect of the light. And yet I did not quite like that explanation either, but would have been better pleased to make out to myself that it was some superiority in me which made it so clear to me, if it were only the great superiority of young eyes over old – though that was not quite enough to satisfy me, seeing it was a superiority which I shared with every little lass and lad in the street. I rather wanted, I believe, to think that there was some particular insight in me which gave clearness to my sight – which was a most impertinent assumption, but really did not mean half the harm it seems to mean when it is put down here in black and white. I had several times again, however, seen the room quite plain, and made out that it was a large room, with a great picture in a dim gilded frame hanging on the farther wall, and many other pieces of solid furniture making a blackness here and there, besides the great escritoire against the wall, which had evidently been placed near the window for the sake of the light. One thing became visible to me after another, till I almost thought I should end by being able to read the old lettering on one of the big volumes which projected from the others and caught the light; but this was all preliminary to the great event which happened about Midsummer Day – the day of St John, which was once so much thought of as a festival, but now means nothing at all in Scotland any more than any other of the saints' days: which I shall always think a great pity and loss to Scotland, whatever Aunt Mary may say.

3

It was about midsummer, I cannot say exactly to a day when, but near that time, when the great event happened. I had grown very well acquainted by this time with that large dim room. Not only the escritoire, which was very plain to me now, with the papers upon it, and the books at its foot, but the great picture that hung against the farther wall, and various other shadowy pieces of furniture, especially a chair which one evening I saw had been moved into the space before the escritoire – a little change which made my heart beat, for it spoke so distinctly of someone who must have been there, the someone who had already made me start, two or three times before, by some vague shadow of him or thrill of him which made a sort of movement in the silent space: a movement which made me sure that next minute I must see something or hear something which would explain the whole – if it were not that something always happened outside to stop it, at the very moment of its accomplishment. I had no warning this time of movement or shadow. I had been looking into the room very attentively a little while before, and had made out everything almost clearer than ever; and then had bent my attention again on my book, and read a chapter or two at a most exciting period of the story: and consequently had quite left St Rule's, and the High Street, and the College Library, and was really in a South American forest, almost throttled by the flowery creepers, and treading softly lest I should put my foot on a scorpion or a dangerous snake. At this moment something suddenly calling my attention to the outside, I looked across, and then, with a start, sprang up, for I could not contain myself. I don't know what I said, but enough to startle the people in the room, one of whom was old Mr Pitmilly. They all looked round upon me to ask what was the matter. And when I gave my usual answer of, 'Nothing,' sitting down again shamefaced but very much excited, Mr Pitmilly got up and came forward, and looked out, apparently to see what was the cause. He saw nothing, for he went back again, and I could hear him telling Aunt Mary not to be alarmed, for Missy had fallen into a doze with the heat, and had startled herself waking up, at which they all laughed; another time I could have killed him for his impertinence, but my mind was too much taken up now to pay any attention. My head was throbbing and my heart beating. I was in such high excitement, however, that to restrain myself completely, to be perfectly silent, was more easy to me then than at any other time of my life. I waited until the old gentleman had taken his seat again, and then I looked back. Yes, there he was! I had not been deceived. I knew then, when I looked across, that this was what I had been looking for all the time – that I had known he was there, and had been waiting for him, every time there was that flicker of movement in the room – him and no one else. And there at last, just as I had expected, he was. I don't know that in reality I ever had expected him, or anyone: but this was what I felt when, suddenly looking into that curious dim room, I saw him there.

He was sitting in the chair, which he must have placed for himself, or which someone else in the dead of night when nobody was looking must have set for him, in front of the escritoire – with the back of his head towards me, writing. The light fell upon him from the left hand, and therefore upon his shoulders and the side of his head, which, however, was too much turned away to show anything of his face. Oh, how strange that there should be someone staring at him as I was doing, and he never to turn his head, to make a movement! If anyone stood and looked at me, were I in the soundest sleep that ever was, I would wake, I would jump up, I would feel it through everything. But there he sat and never moved. You are not to suppose, though I said the light fell upon him from the left hand, that there was very much light. There never is in a room you are looking into like that across the street; but there was enough to see him by – the outline of his figure dark and solid, seated in the chair, and the fairness of his head visible faintly, a clear spot against the dimness. I saw this outline against the dim gilding of the frame of the large picture which hung on the farther wall.

I sat all the time the visitors were there, in a sort of rapture, gazing at this figure. I knew no reason why I should be so much moved. In an ordinary way, to see a student at an opposite window quietly doing his work might have interested me a little, but certainly it would not have moved me in any such way. It is always interesting to have a glimpse like this of an unknown life – to see so much and yet know so little, and to wonder, perhaps, what the man is doing, and why he never turns his head. One would go to the window – but not too close, lest he should see you and think you were spying upon him – and one would ask, Is he still there? is he writing, writing always? I wonder what he is writing! And it would be a great amusement: but no more. This was not my feeling at all in the present case. It was a sort of breathless watch, an absorption. I did not feel that I had eyes for anything else, or any room in my mind for another thought. I no longer heard, as I generally did, the stories and the wise remarks (or foolish) of Aunt Mary's old ladies or Mr Pitmilly. I heard only a murmur behind me, the interchange of voices, one softer, one sharper; but it was not as in the time when I sat reading and heard every word, till the story in my book and the stories they were telling (what they said almost always shaped into stories) were all mingled into each other, and the hero in the novel became somehow the hero (or more likely heroine) of them all. But I took no notice of what they were saying now. And it was not that there was anything very interesting to look at, except the fact that he was there. He did nothing to keep up the absorption of my thoughts. He moved just so much as a man will do when he is very busily writing, thinking of nothing else. There was a faint turn of his head as he went from one side to another of the page he was writing; but it appeared to be a long long page which never wanted turning. Just a little inclination when he was at the end of the line, outward, and then a little inclination inward when he began the next. That was little enough to keep one gazing. But I suppose it was the gradual course of events leading up to this, the finding out of one thing after another as the eyes got accustomed to the vague light: first the room itself, and then the writing-table, and then the other furniture, and last of all the human inhabitant who gave it all meaning. This was all so interesting that it was like a country which one had discovered. And then the extraordinary blindness of the other people who disputed among themselves whether it was a window at all! I did not, I am sure, wish to be disrespectful, and I was very fond of my Aunt Mary, and I liked Mr Pitmilly well enough, and I was afraid of Lady Carnbee. But yet to think of the – I know I ought not to say stupidity – the blindness of them, the foolishness, the insensibility! discussing it as if a thing that your eyes could see was a thing to discuss! It would have been unkind to think it was because they were old and their faculties dimmed. It is so sad to think that the faculties grow dim, that such a woman as my Aunt Mary should fail in seeing, or hearing, or feeling, that I would not have dwelt on it for a moment, it would have seemed so cruel! And then such a clever old lady as Lady Carnbee, who could see through a millstone, people said – and Mr Pitmilly, such an old man of the world. It did indeed bring tears to my eyes to think that all those clever people, solely by reason of being no longer young as I was, should have the simplest things shut out from them; and for all their wisdom and their knowledge be unable to see what a girl like me could see so easily. I was too much grieved for them to dwell upon that thought, and half ashamed, though perhaps half proud too, to be so much better off than they.

All those thoughts flitted through my mind as I sat and gazed across the street. And I felt there was so much going on in that room across the street! He was so absorbed in his writing, never looked up, never paused for a word, never turned round in his chair, or got up and walked about the room as my father did. Papa is a great writer, everybody says: but he would have come to the window and looked out, he would have drummed with his fingers on the pane, he would have watched a fly and helped it over a difficulty, and played with the fringe of the curtain, and done a dozen other nice, pleasant, foolish things, till the next sentence took shape. 'My dear, I am waiting for a word,' he would say to my mother when she looked at him, with a question why he was so idle, in her eyes; and then he would laugh, and go back again to his writing-table. But he over there never stopped at all. It was like a fascination. I could not take my eyes from him and that little scarcely perceptible movement he made, turning his head. I trembled with impatience to see him turn the page, or perhaps throw down his finished sheet on the floor, as somebody looking into a window like me once saw Sir Walter do, sheet after sheet. I should have cried out if this Unknown had done that. I should not have been able to help myself, whoever had been present; and gradually I got into such a state of suspense waiting for it to be done that my head grew hot and my hands cold. And then, just when there was a little movement of his elbow, as if he were about to do this, to be called away by Aunt Mary to see Lady Carnbee to the door! I believe I did not hear her till she had called me three times, and then I stumbled up, all flushed and hot and nearly crying. When I came out from the recess to give the old lady my arm (Mr Pitmilly had gone away some time before), she put up her hand and stroked my cheek. 'What ails the bairn?' she said; 'she's fevered. You must not let her sit her lane in the window, Mary Balcarres. You and me know what comes of that.' Her old fingers had a strange touch, cold like something not living, and I felt that dreadful diamond sting me on the cheek.

I do not say that this was not just a part of my excitement and suspense; and I know it is enough to make anyone laugh when the excitement was all about an unknown man writing in a room on the other side of the way, and my impatience because he never came to an end of the page. If you think I was not quite as well aware of this as anyone could be! but the worst was that this dreadful old lady felt my heart beating against her arm that was within mine. 'You are just in a dream,' she said to me, with her old voice close at my ear as we went downstairs. 'I don't know who it is about, but it's bound to be some man that is not worth it. If you were wise you would think of him no more.'

'I am thinking of no man!' I said, half crying. 'It is very unkind and dreadful of you to say so, Lady Carnbee. I never thought of – any man, in all my life!' I cried in a passion of indignation. The old lady clung tighter to my arm, and pressed it to her, not unkindly.

'Poor little bird,' she said, 'how it's strugglin' and flutterin'! I'm not saying but what it's more dangerous when it's all for a dream.'

She was not at all unkind; but I was very angry and excited, and would scarcely shake that old pale hand which she put out to me from her carriage window when I had helped her in. I was angry with her, and I was afraid of the diamond, which looked up from under her finger as if it saw through and through me; and whether you believe me or not, I am certain that it stung me again – a sharp malignant prick, oh full of meaning! She never wore gloves, but only black lace mittens, through which that horrible diamond gleamed.

I ran upstairs – she had been the last to go and Aunt Mary too had gone to get ready for dinner, for it was late. I hurried to my place, and looked across, with my heart beating more than ever. I made quite sure I should see the finished sheet lying white upon the floor. But what I gazed at was only the dim blank of that window which they said was no window. The light had changed in some wonderful way during that five minutes I had been gone, and there was nothing, nothing, not a reflection, not a glimmer. It looked exactly as they all said, the blank form of a window painted on the wall. It was too much; I sat down in my excitement and cried as if my heart would break. I felt that they had done something to it, that it was not natural, that I could not bear their unkindness – even Aunt Mary. They thought it not good for me! not good for me! and they had done something – even Aunt Mary herself – and that wicked diamond that hid itself in Lady Carnbee's hand. Of course I knew all this was ridiculous as well as you could tell me; but I was exasperated by the disappointment and the sudden stop to all my excited feelings, and I could not bear it. It was more strong than I.

I was late for dinner, and naturally there were some traces in my eyes that I had been crying when I came into the full light in the dining-room, where Aunt Mary could look at me at her pleasure, and I could not run away. She said, 'Honey, you have been shedding tears. I'm loth, loth that a bairn of your mother's should be made to shed tears in my house.'

'I have not been made to shed tears,' cried I; and then, to save myself another fit of crying, I burst out laughing and said, 'I am afraid of that dreadful diamond on old Lady Carnbee's hand. It bites – I am sure it bites! Aunt Mary, look here.'

'You foolish lassie,' Aunt Mary said; but she looked at my cheek under the light of the lamp, and then she gave it a little pat with her soft hand. 'Go away with you, you silly bairn. There is no bite; but a flushed cheek, my honey, and a wet eye. You must just read out my paper to me after dinner when the post is in: and we'll have no more thinking and no more dreaming for tonight.'

'Yes, Aunt Mary,' said I. But I knew what would happen; for when she opens up her *Times*, all full of the news of the world, and the speeches and things which she takes an interest in, though I cannot tell why – she forgets. And as I kept very quiet and made not a sound, she forgot tonight what she had said, and the curtain hung a little more over me than usual, and I sat down in my recess as if I had been a hundred miles away. And my heart gave a great jump, as if it would have come out of my breast; for he was there. But not as he had been earlier – I suppose the light, perhaps, was not good enough to go on with his work without a lamp or candles – for he had turned away from the table and was fronting the window, sitting leaning back in his chair, and turning his head to me. Not to me – he knew nothing about me. I thought he was not looking at anything; but with his face turned my way. My heart was in my mouth: it was so unexpected, so strange! though why it should have seemed strange I know not, for there was no communication between him and me that it should have moved me; and what could be more natural than that a man, wearied of his work, and feeling the want perhaps of more light, and yet that it was not dark enough to light a lamp, should turn round in his own chair, and rest a little, and think – perhaps of nothing at all? Papa always says he is thinking of nothing at all. He says things blow through his mind as if the doors were open, and he has no responsibility. What sort of things were blowing through this man's mind? or was he thinking, still thinking, of what he had been writing and going on with it still? The thing that troubled me most was that I could not make out his face. It is very difficult to do so when you see a person only through two windows, your own and his. I wanted very much to recognise him afterwards if I should chance to meet him in the street. If he had only stood up and moved about the room, I should have made out the rest of his figure, and then I should have known him again; or if he had only come to the window (as papa always did), then I should have seen his face clearly enough to have recognised him. But, to be sure, he did not see any need to do anything in order that I might recognise him, for he did not know I existed; and probably if he had known I was watching him, he would have been annoyed and gone away.

But he was as immovable there facing the window as he had been seated at the desk. Sometimes he made a little faint stir with a hand or a foot, and I held my breath, hoping he was about to rise from his chair – but he never did it. And with all the efforts I made I could not be sure of his face. I puckered my eyelids together as old Miss Jeanie did who was shortsighted, and I put my hands on each side of my face to concentrate the light on him: but it was all in vain. Either the face changed as I sat staring, or else it was the light that was not good enough, or I don't know what it was. His hair seemed to me light – certainly there was no dark line about his head, as there would have been had it been very dark – and I saw, where it came across the old gilt frame on the wall behind, that it must be fair: and I am almost sure he had no beard. Indeed I am sure that he had no beard, for the outline of his face was distinct enough; and the daylight was still quite clear out of doors, so that I recognised perfectly a baker's boy who was on the pavement opposite, and whom I should have known again whenever I had met him: as if it was of the least importance to recognise a baker's boy! There was one thing, however, rather curious about this boy. He had been throwing stones at something or somebody. In St Rule's they have a great way of throwing stones at each other, and I suppose there had been a battle. I suppose also that he had one stone in his hand left over from the battle, and his roving eye took in all the incidents of the street to judge where he could throw it with most effect and mischief. But apparently he found nothing worthy of it in the street, for he suddenly turned round with a flick under his leg to show his cleverness, and aimed it straight at the window. I remarked without remarking that it struck with a hard sound and without any breaking of glass, and fell straight down on the pavement. But I took no notice of this even in my mind, so intently was I watching the figure within, which moved not nor took the slightest notice, and remained just as dimly clear, as perfectly seen, yet as indistinguishable, as before. And then the light began to fail a little, not diminishing the prospect within, but making it still less distinct than it had been.

Then I jumped up, feeling Aunt Mary's hand upon my shoulder. 'Honey,' she said, 'I asked you twice to ring the bell; but you did not hear me.'

'Oh, Aunt Mary!' I cried in great penitence, but turning again to the window in spite of myself.

'You must come away from there; you must come away from there,' she said, almost as if she were angry; and then her soft voice grew softer, and she gave me a kiss: 'never mind about the lamp, honey; I have rung myself, and it is coming; but, silly bairn, you must not aye be dreaming – your little head will turn.'

All the answer I made, for I could scarcely speak, was to give a little wave with my hand to the window on the other side of the street.

She stood there patting me softly on the shoulder for a whole minute or more, murmuring something that sounded like, 'She must go away, she must go away.' Then she said, always with her hand soft on my shoulder, 'Like a dream when one awaketh.' And when I looked again, I saw the blank of an opaque surface and nothing more.

Aunt Mary asked me no more questions. She made me come into the room and sit in the light and read something to her. But I did not know what I was reading, for there suddenly came into my mind and took possession of it, the thud of the stone upon the window, and its descent straight down, as if from some hard substance that threw it off: though I had myself seen it strike upon the glass of the panes across the way.

4

I am afraid I continued in a state of great exaltation and commotion of mind for some time. I used to hurry through the day till the evening came, when I could watch my neighbour through the window opposite. I did not talk much to anyone, and I never said a word about my own questions and wonderings. I wondered who he was, what he was doing, and why he never came till the evening (or very rarely); and I also wondered much to what house the room belonged in which he sat. It seemed to form a portion of the old College Library, as I have often said. The window was one of the line of windows which I understood lighted the large hall; but whether this room belonged to the library itself, or how its occupant gained access to it, I could not tell. I made up my mind that it must open out of the hall, and that the gentleman must be the Librarian or one of his assistants, perhaps kept busy all the day in his official duties, and only able to get to his desk and do his own private work in the evening. One has heard of so many things like that – a man who had to take up some other kind of work for his living, and then when his leisure-time came, gave it all up to something he really loved – some study or some book he was writing. My father himself at one time had been like that. He had been in the Treasury all day, and then in the evening wrote his books, which made him famous. His daughter, however little she might know of other things, could not but know that! But it discouraged me very much when somebody pointed out to me one day in the street an old gentleman who wore a wig and took a great deal of snuff, and said, 'That's the Librarian of the old College.' It gave me a great shock for a moment; but then I remembered that an old gentleman has generally assistants, and that it must be one of them.

Gradually I became quite sure of this. There was another small window above, which twinkled very much when the sun shone, and looked a very kindly bright little window, above that dullness of the other which hid so much. I made up my mind this was the window of his other room, and that these two chambers at the end of the beautiful hall were really beautiful for him to live in, so near all the books, and so retired and quiet that nobody knew of them. What a

fine thing for him! and you could see what use he made of his good
fortune as he sat there, so constant at his writing for hours together.
Was it a book he was writing, or could it be perhaps poems? This was
a thought which made my heart beat; but I concluded with much
regret that it could not be poems, because no one could possibly
write poems like that, straight off, without pausing for a word or a
rhyme. Had they been poems he must have risen up, he must have
paced about the room or come to the window as papa did – not that
papa wrote poems: he always said, 'I am not worthy even to speak of
such prevailing mysteries,' shaking his head – which gave me a
wonderful admiration and almost awe of a poet, who was thus much
greater even than papa. But I could not believe that a poet could have
kept still for hours and hours like that. What could it be then?
perhaps it was history; that is a great thing to work at, but you would
not perhaps need to move nor to stride up and down, or look out
upon the sky and the wonderful light.

He did move now and then, however, though he never came to the
window. Sometimes, as I have said, he would turn round in his chair
and turn his face towards it, and sit there for a long time musing when
the light had begun to fail, and the world was full of that strange day
which was night, that light without colour, in which everything was
so clearly visible, and there were no shadows. 'It was between the
night and the day, when the fairy folk have power.' This was the
after-light of the wonderful, long, long summer evening, the light
without shadows. It had a spell in it, and sometimes it made me
afraid; and all manner of strange thoughts seemed to come in, and I
always felt that if only we had a little more vision in our eyes we might
see beautiful folk walking about in it, who were not of our world. I
thought most likely he saw them, from the way he sat there looking
out: and this made my heart expand with the most curious sensation,
as if of pride that, though I could not see, he did, and did not even
require to come to the window, as I did, sitting close in the depth of
the recess, with my eyes upon him, and almost seeing things through
his eyes.

I was so much absorbed in these thoughts and in watching him
every evening – for now he never missed an evening, but was always
there – that people began to remark that I was looking pale and that
I could not be well, for I paid no attention when they talked to me,
and did not care to go out, nor to join the other girls for their tennis,
nor to do anything that others did; and some said to Aunt Mary that
I was quickly losing all the ground I had gained, and that she could

never send me back to my mother with a white face like that. Aunt Mary had begun to look at me anxiously for some time before that, and, I am sure, held secret consultations over me, sometimes with the doctor, and sometimes with her old ladies, who thought they knew more about young girls than even the doctors. And I could hear them saying to her that I wanted diversion, that I must be diverted, and that she must take me out more, and give a party, and that when the summer visitors began to come there would perhaps be a ball or two, or Lady Carnbee would get up a picnic. 'And there's my young lord coming home,' said the old lady whom they called Miss Jeanie, 'and I never knew the young lassie yet that would not cock up her bonnet at the sight of a young lord.'

But Aunt Mary shook her head. 'I would not lippen much to the young lord,' she said. 'His mother is sore set upon siller for him; and my poor bit honey has no fortune to speak of. No, we must not fly so high as the young lord; but I will gladly take her about the country to see the old castles and towers. It will perhaps rouse her up a little.'

'And if that does not answer we must think of something else,' the old lady said.

I heard them perhaps that day because they were talking of me, which is always so effective a way of making you hear – for latterly I had not been paying any attention to what they were saying; and I thought to myself how little they knew, and how little I cared about even the old castles and curious houses, having something else in my mind. But just about that time Mr Pitmilly came in, who was always a friend to me, and, when he heard them talking, he managed to stop them and turn the conversation into another channel. And after a while, when the ladies were gone away, he came up to my recess, and gave a glance right over my head. And then he asked my Aunt Mary if ever she had settled her question about the window opposite, 'that you thought was a window sometimes, and then not a window, and many curious things,' the old gentleman said.

My Aunt Mary gave me another very wistful look; and then she said, 'Indeed, Mr Pitmilly, we are just where we were, and I am quite as unsettled as ever; and I think my niece has taken up my views, for I see her many a time looking across and wondering, and I am not clear now what her opinion is.'

'My opinion, Aunt Mary!' I said. I could not help being a little scornful, as one is when one is very young. 'I have no opinion. There is not only a window but there is a room, and I could show you – ' I was going to say, 'show you the gentleman who sits and writes in it,' but I stopped, not knowing what they might say, and looked from one to another. 'I could tell you – all the furniture that is in it,' I said. And then I felt something like a flame that went over my face, and that all at once my cheeks were burning. I thought they gave a little glance at each other, but that may have been folly. 'There is a great picture, in a big dim frame,' I said, feeling a little breathless, 'on the wall opposite the window.'

'Is there so?' said Mr Pitmilly, with a little laugh. And he said, 'Now I will tell you what we'll do. You know that there is a conversation party, or whatever they call it, in the big room tonight, and it will be all open and lighted up. And it is a handsome room, and two-three things well worth looking at. I will just step along after we have all got our dinner, and take you over to the pairty, madam – missy and you – '

'Dear me!' said Aunt Mary. 'I have not gone to a pairty for more years than I would like to say – and never once to the Library Hall.' Then she gave a little shiver, and said quite low, 'I could not go there.'

'Then you will just begin again tonight, madam,' said Mr Pitmilly, taking no notice of this, 'and a proud man will I be leading in Mistress Balcarres that was once the pride of the ball!'

'Ah, once!' said Aunt Mary, with a low little laugh and then a sigh. 'And we'll not say how long ago;' and after that she made a pause, looking always at me; and then she said, 'I accept your offer, and we'll put on our braws; and I hope you will have no occasion to think shame of us. But why not take your dinner here?'

That was how it was settled, and the old gentleman went away to dress, looking quite pleased. But I came to Aunt Mary as soon as he was gone, and besought her not to make me go. 'I like the long bonnie night and the light that lasts so long. And I cannot bear to dress up and go out, wasting it all in a stupid party. I hate parties, Aunt Mary!' I cried, 'and I would far rather stay here.'

'My honey,' she said, taking both my hands, 'I know it will maybe be a blow to you, but it's better so.'

'How could it be a blow to me?' I cried; 'but I would far rather not go.'

'You'll just go with me, honey, just this once: it is not often I go out. You will go with me this one night, just this one night, my honey sweet.'

I am sure there were tears in Aunt Mary's eyes, and she kissed me between the words. There was nothing more that I could say; but how I grudged the evening! A mere party, a conversazione (when all

the College was away, too, and nobody to make conversation!),
instead of my enchanted hour at my window and the soft strange
light, and the dim face looking out, which kept me wondering and
wondering what was he thinking of, what was he looking for, who
was he? all one wonder and mystery and question, through the long,
long, slowly fading night!

It occurred to me, however, when I was dressing – though I was so
sure that he would prefer his solitude to everything – that he might
perhaps, it was just possible, be there. And when I thought of that, I
took out my white frock though Janet had laid out my blue one – and
my little pearl necklace which I had thought was too good to wear.
They were not very large pearls, but they were real pearls, and very
even and lustrous though they were small; and though I did not think
much of my appearance then, there must have been something about
me – pale as I was but apt to colour in a moment, with my dress so
white, and my pearls so white, and my hair all shadowy perhaps, that
was pleasant to look at: for even old Mr Pitmilly had a strange look in
his eyes, as if he was not only pleased but sorry too, perhaps thinking
me a creature that would have troubles in this life, though I was so
young and knew them not. And when Aunt Mary looked at me, there
was a little quiver about her mouth. She herself had on her pretty lace
and her white hair very nicely done, and looking her best. As for Mr
Pitmilly, he had a beautiful fine French cambric frill to his shirt,
pleated in the most minute pleats, and with a diamond pin in it which
sparkled as much as Lady Carnbee's ring; but this was a fine frank
kindly stone, that looked you straight in the face and sparkled, with
the light dancing in it as if it were pleased to see you and to be shining
on that old gentleman's honest and faithful breast: for he had been
one of Aunt Mary's lovers in their early days, and still thought there
was nobody like her in the world.

I had got into quite a happy commotion of mind by the time we set
out across the street in the soft light of the evening to the Library Hall.
Perhaps, after all, I should see him, and see the room which I was so
well acquainted with, and find out why he sat there so constantly and
never was seen abroad. I thought I might even hear what he was
working at, which would be such a pleasant thing to tell papa when I
went home. A friend of mine at St Rule's – oh, far, far more busy than
you ever were, papa! – and then my father would laugh as he always
did, and say he was but an idler and never busy at all.

The room was all light and bright, flowers wherever flowers could
be, and the long lines of the books that went along the walls on each

side, lighting up, wherever there was a line of gilding or an ornament, with a little response. It dazzled me at first all that light: but I was very eager, though I kept very quiet, looking round to see if perhaps in any corner, in the middle of any group, he would be there. I did not expect to see him among the ladies. He would not be with them – he was too studious, too silent; but, perhaps among that circle of grey heads at the upper end of the room – perhaps –

No: I am not sure that it was not half a pleasure to me to make quite sure that there was not one whom I could take for him, who was at all like my vague image of him. No: it was absurd to think that he would be here, amid all that sound of voices, under the glare of that light. I felt a little proud to think that he was in his room as usual, doing his work, or thinking so deeply over it, as when he turned round in his chair with his face to the light.

I was thus getting a little composed and quiet in my mind, for now that the expectation of seeing him was over, though it was a disappointment, it was a satisfaction too – when Mr Pitmilly came up to me, holding out his arm. 'Now,' he said, 'I am going to take you to see the curiosities.' I thought to myself that after I had seen them and spoken to everybody I knew, Aunt Mary would let me go home, so I went very willingly, though I did not care for the curiosities. Something, however, struck me strangely as we walked up the room. It was the air, rather fresh and strong, from an open window at the east end of the hall. How should there be a window there? I hardly saw what it meant for the first moment, but it blew in my face as if there was some meaning in it, and I felt very uneasy without seeing why.

Then there was another thing that startled me. On that side of the wall which was to the street there seemed no windows at all. A long line of bookcases filled it from end to end. I could not see what that meant either, but it confused me. I was altogether confused. I felt as if I was in a strange country, not knowing where I was going, not knowing what I might find out next. If there were no windows on the wall to the street, where was my window? My heart, which had been jumping up and calming down again all this time, gave a great leap at this, as if it would have come out of me – but I did not know what it could mean.

Then we stopped before a glass case, and Mr Pitmilly showed me some things in it. I could not pay much attention to them. My head was going round and round. I heard his voice going on, and then myself speaking with a queer sound that was hollow in my ears; but I did not know what I was saying or what he was saying. Then he took me to the very end of the room, the east end, saying something that I caught – that I was pale, that the air would do me good. The air was blowing full on me, lifting the lace of my dress, lifting my hair, almost chilly. The window opened into the pale daylight, into the little lane that ran by the end of the building. Mr Pitmilly went on talking, but I could not make out a word he said. Then I heard my own voice, speaking through it, though I did not seem to be aware that I was speaking. 'Where is my window? – where, then, is my window?' I seemed to be saying, and I turned right round, dragging him with me, still holding his arm. As I did this my eye fell upon something at last which I knew. It was a large picture in a broad frame, hanging against the farther wall.

What did it mean? Oh, what did it mean? I turned round again to the open window at the east end, and to the daylight, the strange light without any shadow, that was all round about this lighted hall, holding it like a bubble that would burst, like something that was not real. The real place was the room I knew, in which that picture was hanging, where the writing-table was, and where he sat with his face to the light. But where was the light and the window through which it came? I think my senses must have left me. I went up to the picture which I knew, and then I walked straight across the room, always dragging Mr Pitmilly, whose face was pale, but who did not struggle but allowed me to lead him, straight across to where the window was – where the window was not; – where there was no sign of it. 'Where is my window? – where is my window?' I said. And all the time I was sure that I was in a dream, and these lights were all some theatrical illusion, and the people talking; and nothing real but the pale, pale, watching, lingering day standing by to wait until that foolish bubble should burst.

'My dear,' said Mr Pitmilly, 'my dear! Mind that you are in public. Mind where you are. You must not make an outcry and frighten your Aunt Mary. Come away with me. Come away, my dear young lady! and you'll take a seat for a minute or two and compose yourself; and I'll get you an ice or a little wine.' He kept patting my hand, which was on his arm, and looking at me very anxiously. 'Bless me! bless me! I never thought it would have this effect,' he said.

But I would not allow him to take me away in that direction. I went to the picture again and looked at it without seeing it; and then I went across the room again, with some kind of wild thought that if I insisted I should find it. 'My window – my window!' I said.

There was one of the professors standing there, and he heard me. 'The window!' said he. 'Ah, you've been taken in with what appears outside. It was put there to be in uniformity with the window on the stair. But it never was a real window. It is just behind that bookcase. Many people are taken in by it,' he said.

His voice seemed to sound from somewhere far away, and as if it would go on for ever; and the hall swam in a dazzle of shining and of noises round me; and the daylight through the open window grew greyer, waiting till it should be over, and the bubble burst.

5

It was Mr Pitmilly who took me home; or rather it was I who took him, pushing him on a little in front of me, holding fast by his arm, not waiting for Aunt Mary or anyone. We came out into the daylight again outside, I, without even a cloak or a shawl, with my bare arms, and uncovered head, and the pearls round my neck. There was a rush of the people about, and a baker's boy, that baker's boy, stood right in my way and cried, 'Here's a braw ane!' shouting to the others: the words struck me somehow, as his stone had struck the window, without any reason. But I did not mind the people staring, and hurried across the street, with Mr Pitmilly half a step in advance. The door was open, and Janet standing at it, looking out to see what she could see of the ladies in their grand dresses. She gave a shriek when she saw me hurrying across the street; but I brushed past her, and pushed Mr Pitmilly up the stairs, and took him breathless to the recess, where I threw myself down on the seat, feeling as if I could not have gone another step farther, and waved my hand across to the window. 'There! there!' I cried. Ah! there it was – not that senseless mob – not the theatre and the gas, and the people all in a murmur and clang of talking. Never in all these days had I seen that room so clearly. There was a faint tone of light behind, as if it might have been a reflection from some of those vulgar lights in the hall, and he sat against it, calm, wrapped in his thoughts, with his face turned to the window. Nobody but must have seen him. Janet could have seen him had I called her upstairs. It was like a picture, all the things I knew, and the same attitude, and the atmosphere, full of quietness, not disturbed by anything. I pulled Mr Pitmilly's arm before I let him go – 'You see, you see!' I cried. He gave me the most bewildered look, as if he would have liked to cry. He saw nothing! I was sure of that from his eyes. He was an old man, and there was no vision in him. If I had called up Janet, she would have seen it all. 'My dear!' he said. 'My dear!' waving his hands in a helpless way. 'He has been there all these nights,' I cried, 'and I thought you could tell me who he was and what he was doing; and that he might have taken me in to that room, and showed me, that I might tell papa. Papa would understand, he would like to hear. Oh, can't you tell me what work he is doing, Mr Pitmilly? He never lifts his head as long as the light throws a shadow, and then when it is like this he turns round and thinks, and takes a rest!'

Mr Pitmilly was trembling, whether it was with cold or I know not what. He said, with a shake in his voice, 'My dear young lady – my dear – ' and then stopped and looked at me as if he were going to cry. 'It's peetiful, it's peetiful,' he said; and then in another voice, 'I am going across there again to bring your Aunt Mary home; do you understand, my poor little thing, I am going to bring her home – you will be better when she is here.' I was glad when he went away, as he could not see anything: and I sat alone in the dark which was not dark, but quite clear light – a light like nothing I ever saw. How clear it was in that room! not glaring like the gas and the voices, but so quiet, everything so visible, as if it were in another world. I heard a little rustle behind me, and there was Janet, standing staring at me with two big eyes wide open. She was only a little older than I was. I called to her, 'Janet, come here, come here, and you will see him – come here and see him!' impatient that she should be so shy and keep behind. 'Oh, my bonnie young leddy!' she said, and burst out crying. I stamped my foot at her, in my indignation that she would not come, and she fled before me with a rustle and swing of haste, as if she were afraid. None of them, none of them! not even a girl like myself, with the sight in her eyes, would understand. I turned back again, and held out my hands to him sitting there, who was the only one that knew. 'Oh,' I said, 'say something to me! I don't know who you are, or what you are: but you're lonely and so am I; and I only – feel for you. Say something to me!' I neither hoped that he would hear, nor expected any answer. How could he hear, with the street between us, and his window shut, and all the murmuring of the voices and the people standing about? But for one moment it seemed to me that there was only him and me in the whole world.

But I gasped with my breath, that had almost gone from me, when I saw him move in his chair! He had heard me, though I knew not how. He rose up, and I rose too, speechless, incapable of anything but this mechanical movement. He seemed to draw me as if I were a puppet moved by his will. He came forward to the window, and stood looking across at me. I was sure that he looked at me. At last he had seen me: at last he had found out that somebody, though only a girl, was watching him, looking for him, believing in him. I was in such trouble and commotion of mind and trembling that I could not keep on my feet, but dropped kneeling on the window-seat, supporting myself against the window, feeling as if my heart were being drawn out of me. I cannot describe his face. It was all dim, yet there was a light on it: I think it must have been a smile; and as closely as I looked at him he looked at me. His hair was fair, and there was a little quiver about his lips. Then he put his hands upon the window to open it. It was stiff and hard to move; but at last he forced it open with a sound that echoed all along the street. I saw that the people heard it, and several looked up. As for me, I put my hands together, leaning with my face against the glass, drawn to him as if I could have gone out of myself, my heart out of my bosom, my eyes out of my head. He opened the window with a noise that was heard from the West Port to the Abbey. Could anyone doubt that?

And then he leaned forward out of the window, looking out. There was not one in the street but must have seen him. He looked at me first, with a little wave of his hand, as if it were a salutation – yet not exactly that either, for I thought he waved me away; and then he looked up and down in the dim shining of the ending day, first to the east, to the old Abbey towers, and then to the west, along the broad line of the street where so many people were coming and going, but with so little noise, all like enchanted folk in an enchanted place. I watched him with such a melting heart, with such a deep satisfaction as words could not say; for nobody could tell me now that he was not there – nobody could say I was dreaming any more. I watched him as if I could not breathe – my heart in my throat, my eyes upon him. He looked up and down, and then he looked back to me. I was the first, and I was the last, though it was not for long: he did know, he did see, who it was that had recognised him and sympathised with him all the time. I was in a kind of rapture, yet stupor too; my look went with his look, following it as if I were his shadow; and then suddenly he was gone, and I saw him no more.

I dropped back again upon my seat, seeking something to support me, something to lean upon. He had lifted his hand and waved it once again to me. How he went I cannot tell, nor where he went I cannot tell; but in a moment he was away, and the window standing open, and the room fading into stillness and dimness, yet so clear, with all its space, and the great picture in its gilded frame upon the wall. It gave me no pain to see him go away. My heart was so content, and I was so worn out and satisfied – for what doubt or question could there be about him now? As I was lying back as weak as water, Aunt Mary came in behind me, and flew to me with a little rustle as if she had come on wings, and put her arms round me, and drew my head on to her breast. I had begun to cry a little, with sobs like a child. 'You saw him, you saw him!' I said. To lean upon her, and feel her so soft, so kind, gave me a pleasure I cannot describe, and her arms round me, and her voice saying, 'Honey, my honey!' – as if she were nearly crying too. Lying there I came back to myself, quite sweetly, glad of everything. But I wanted some assurance from them that they had seen him too. I waved my hand to the window that was still standing open, and the room that was stealing away into the faint dark. 'This time you saw it all?' I said, getting more eager. 'My honey!' said Aunt Mary, giving me a kiss; and Mr Pitmilly began to walk about the room with short little steps behind, as if he were out of patience. I sat straight up and put away Aunt Mary's arms. 'You cannot be so blind, so blind!' I cried. 'Oh, not tonight, at least not tonight!' But neither the one nor the other made any reply. I shook myself quite free, and raised myself up. And there, in the middle of the street, stood the baker's boy like a statue, staring up at the open window, with his mouth open and his face full of wonder – breathless, as if he could not believe what he saw. I darted forward, calling to him, and beckoned him to come to me. 'Oh, bring him up! bring him, bring him to me!' I cried.

Mr Pitmilly went out directly, and got the boy by the shoulder. He did not want to come. It was strange to see the little old gentleman, with his beautiful frill and his diamond pin, standing out in the street, with his hand upon the boy's shoulder, and the other boys round, all in a little crowd. And presently they came towards the house, the others all following, gaping and wondering. He came in unwilling, almost resisting, looking as if we meant him some harm. 'Come away, my laddie, come and speak to the young lady,' Mr Pitmilly was saying. And Aunt Mary took my hands to keep me back. But I would not be kept back.

'Boy,' I cried, 'you saw it too: you saw it; tell them you saw it! It is that I want, and no more.'

He looked at me as they all did, as if he thought I was mad. 'What's she wantin' wi' me?' he said; and then, 'I did nae harm, even if I did throw a bit stane at it – and it's nae sin to throw a stane.'

'You rascal!' said Mr Pitmilly, giving him a shake; 'have you been throwing stones? You'll kill somebody some of these days with your stones.' The old gentleman was confused and troubled, for he did not understand what I wanted, nor anything that had happened. And then Aunt Mary, holding my hands and drawing me close to her, spoke. 'Laddie,' she said, 'answer the young lady, like a good lad. There's no intention of finding fault with you. Answer her, my man, and then Janet will give ye your supper before you go.'

'Oh speak, speak!' I cried; 'answer them and tell them! you saw that window opened, and the gentleman look out and wave his hand?'

'I saw nae gentleman,' he said, with his head down, 'except this wee gentleman here.'

'Listen, laddie,' said Aunt Mary. 'I saw ye standing in the middle of the street staring. What were ye looking at?'

'It was naething to make a wark about. It was just yon windy yonder in the Library that is nae windy. And it was open as sure's death. You may laugh if you like. Is that a' she's wantin' wi' me?'

'You are telling a pack of lies, laddie,' Mr Pitmilly said.

'I'm tellin' nae lees – it was standin' open just like ony ither windy. It's as sure's death. I couldna believe it mysel'; but it's true.'

'And there it is,' I cried, turning round and pointing it out to them with great triumph in my heart. But the light was all grey, it had faded, it had changed. The window was just as it had always been, a sombre break upon the wall.

I was treated like an invalid all that evening, and taken upstairs to bed, and Aunt Mary sat up in my room the whole night through. Whenever I opened my eyes she was always sitting there close to me, watching. And there never was in all my life so strange a night. When I would talk in my excitement, she kissed me and hushed me like a child. 'Oh, honey, you are not the only one!' she said. 'Oh whisht, whisht, bairn! I should never have let you be there!'

'Aunt Mary, Aunt Mary, you have seen him too?'

'Oh whisht, whisht, honey!' Aunt Mary said: her eyes were shining – there were tears in them. 'Oh whisht, whisht! Put it out of your mind, and try to sleep. I will not speak another word,' she cried.

But I had my arms round her, and my mouth at her ear. 'Who is he there? – tell me that and I will ask no more – '

'Oh, honey, rest, and try to sleep! It is just – how can I tell you? – a dream, a dream! Did you not hear what Lady Carnbee said? – the women of our blood – '

'What? what? Aunt Mary, oh Aunt Mary – '

'I canna tell you,' she cried in her agitation, 'I canna tell you! How can I tell you, when I know just what you know and no more? It is a longing all your life after – it is a looking – for what never comes.'

'He will come,' I cried. 'I shall see him tomorrow – that I know, I know!'

She kissed me and cried over me, her cheek hot and wet like mine. 'My honey, try if you can sleep – try if you can sleep: and we'll wait to see what tomorrow brings.'

'I have no fear,' said I; and then I suppose, though it is strange to think of, I must have fallen asleep – I was so worn-out, and young, and not used to lying in my bed awake. From time to time I opened my eyes, and sometimes jumped up remembering everything; but Aunt Mary was always there to soothe me, and I lay down again in her shelter like a bird in its nest.

But I would not let them keep me in bed next day. I was in a kind of fever, not knowing what I did. The window was quite opaque, without the least glimmer in it, flat and blank like a piece of wood. Never from the first day had I seen it so little like a window. 'It cannot be wondered at,' I said to myself, 'that seeing it like that, and with eyes that are old, not so clear as mine, they should think what they do.' And then I smiled to myself to think of the evening and the long light, and whether he would look out again, or only give me a signal with his hand. I decided I would like that best: not that he should take the trouble to come forward and open it again, but just a turn of his head and a wave of his hand. It would be more friendly and show more confidence – not as if I wanted that kind of demonstration every night.

I did not come down in the afternoon, but kept at my own window upstairs alone, till the tea-party should be over. I could hear them making a great talk; and I was sure they were all in the recess staring at the window, and laughing at the silly lassie. Let them laugh! I felt above all that now. At dinner I was very restless, hurrying to get it over; and I think Aunt Mary was restless too. I doubt whether she read her *Times* when it came; she opened it up so as to shield her, and watched from a corner. And I settled myself in the recess, with my heart full of expectation. I wanted nothing more than to see him writing at his table, and to have him turn his head and give me a little wave of his hand, just to show that he knew I was there. I sat from half-past seven o'clock to ten o'clock, and the daylight grew softer and softer, till at last it was as if it was shining through a pearl, and not a shadow to be seen. But the window all the time was as black as night, and there was nothing, nothing there.

Well: but other nights it had been like that: he would not be there every night only to please me. There are other things in a man's life, a great learned man like that. I said to myself I was not disappointed. Why should I be disappointed? There had been other nights when he was not there. Aunt Mary watched me, every movement I made, her eyes shining, often wet, with a pity in them that almost made me cry; but I felt as if I were more sorry for her than for myself. And then I flung myself upon her, and asked her, again and again, what it was, and who it was, imploring her to tell me if she knew? and when she had seen him, and what had happened? and what it meant about the women of our blood? She told me that how it was she could not tell, nor when: it was just at the time it had to be; and that we all saw him in our time – 'that is,' she said, 'the ones that are like you and me.' What was it that made her and me different from the rest? but she only shook her head and would not tell me. 'They say –' she said, and then stopped short. 'Oh, honey, try and forget all about it – if I had but known you were of that kind! They say – that once there was one that was a scholar, and liked his books more than any lady's love. Honey, do not look at me like that. To think I should have brought all this on you!'

'He was a scholar?' I cried.

'And one of us, that must have been a light woman, not like you and me – But maybe it was just in innocence; for who can tell? She waved to him and waved to him to come over; and yon ring was the token; but he would not come. But still she sat at her window and waved and waved – till at last her brothers heard of it, that were stirring men; and then – oh, my honey, let us speak of it no more!'

'They killed him!' I cried, carried away. And then I grasped her with my hands, and gave her a shake, and flung away from her. 'You tell me that to throw dust in my eyes – when I saw him only last night: and he as living as I am, and as young!'

'My honey, my honey!' Aunt Mary said.

After that I would not speak to her for a long time; but she kept close to me, never leaving me when she could help it, and always with that pity in her eyes. For the next night it was the same; and the third night. That third night I thought I could not bear it any longer. I would have to do something if only I knew what to do! If it would ever get dark, quite dark, there might be something to be done. I had wild dreams of stealing out of the house and getting a ladder, and mounting up to try if I could not open that window, in the middle of the night – if perhaps I could get the baker's boy to help me; and then my mind got into a whirl, and it was as if I had done it; and I could almost see the boy put the ladder to the window, and hear him cry out that there was nothing there. Oh, how slow it was, the night! and how light it was, and everything so clear, no darkness to cover you, no shadow, whether on one side of the street or on the other side! I could not sleep, though I was forced to go to bed. And in the deep midnight, when it is dark dark in every other place, I slipped very softly downstairs, though there was one board on the landing-place that creaked – and opened the door and stepped out. There was not a soul to be seen, up or down, from the Abbey to the West Port; and the trees stood like ghosts, and the silence was terrible, and everything as clear as day. You don't know what silence is till you find it in the light like that, not morning but night, no sunrising, no shadow, but everything as clear as the day.

It did not make any difference as the slow minutes went on: one o'clock, two o'clock. How strange it was to hear the clocks striking in that dead light when there was nobody to hear them! But it made no difference. The window was quite blank; even the marking of the panes seemed to have melted away. I stole up again after a long time, through the silent house, in the clear light, cold and trembling, with despair in my heart.

I am sure Aunt Mary must have watched and seen me coming back, for after a while I heard faint sounds in the house; and very early, when there had come a little sunshine into the air, she came to my bedside with a cup of tea in her hand; and she, too, was looking like a ghost. 'Are you warm, honey – are you comfortable?' she said. 'It doesn't matter,' said I. I did not feel as if anything mattered; unless if one could get into the dark somewhere – the soft, deep dark that would cover you over and hide you – but I could not tell from what. The dreadful thing was that there was nothing, nothing to look for, nothing to hide from – only the silence and the light.

That day my mother came and took me home. I had not heard she was coming; she arrived quite unexpectedly, and said she had no time to stay, but must start the same evening so as to be in London next day, papa having settled to go abroad. At first I had a wild thought I would not go. But how can a girl say I will not, when her mother has come for her, and there is no reason, no reason in the world, to resist, and no right! I had to go, whatever I might wish or anyone might say. Aunt Mary's dear eyes were wet; she went about the house drying them quietly with her handkerchief, but she always said, 'It is the best thing for you, honey – the best thing for you!' Oh, how I hated to hear it said that it was the best thing, as if anything mattered, one more than another! The old ladies were all there in the afternoon, Lady Carnbee looking at me from under her black lace, and the diamond lurking, sending out darts from under her finger. She patted me on the shoulder, and told me to be a good bairn. 'And never lippen to what you see from the window,' she said. 'The eye is deceitful as well as the heart.' She kept patting me on the shoulder, and I felt again as if that sharp wicked stone stung me. Was that what Aunt Mary meant when she said yon ring was the token? I thought afterwards I saw the mark on my shoulder. You will say why? How can I tell why? If I had known, I should have been contented, and it would not have mattered any more.

I never went back to St Rule's, and for years of my life I never again looked out of a window when any other window was in sight. You ask me did I ever see him again? I cannot tell: the imagination is a great deceiver, as Lady Carnbee said; and if he stayed there so long, only to punish the race that had wronged him, why should I ever have seen him again? for I had received my share. But who can tell what happens in a heart that often, often, and so long as that, comes back to do its errand? If it was he whom I have seen again, the anger is gone from him, and he means good and no longer harm to the house of the woman that loved him. I have seen his face looking at me from a crowd. There was one time when I came home a widow from India, very sad, with my little children. I am certain I saw him there among all the people coming to welcome their friends. There was nobody to welcome me – for I was not expected; and very sad was I, without a face I knew; when all at once I saw him, and he waved his hand to me. My heart leaped up again; I had forgotten who he was, but only that it was a face I knew, and I landed almost cheerfully, thinking here was someone who would help me. But he had disappeared, as he did from the window, with that one wave of his hand.

And again I was reminded of it all when old Lady Carnbee died – an old, old woman – and it was found in her will that she had left me that diamond ring. I am afraid of it still. It is locked up in an old sandalwood box in the lumber-room in the little old country-house which belongs to me, but where I never live. If anyone would steal it, it would be a relief to my mind. Yet I never knew what Aunt Mary meant when she said, 'Yon ring was the token,' nor what it could have to do with that strange window in the old College Library of St Rule's.

The Portrait

Margaret Oliphant

At the period when the following incidents occurred, I was living with my father at The Grove, a large old house in the immediate neighbourhood of a little town. This had been his home for a number of years; and I believe I was born in it. It was a kind of house which, notwithstanding all the red and white architecture known at present by the name of Queen Anne, builders nowadays have forgotten how to build. It was straggling and irregular, with wide passages, wide staircases, broad landings; the rooms large but not very lofty; the arrangements leaving much to be desired, with no economy of space; a house belonging to a period when land was cheap, and, so far as that was concerned, there was no occasion to economise. Though it was so near the town, the clump of trees in which it was environed was a veritable grove. In the grounds in spring the primroses grew as thickly as in the forest. We had a few fields for the cows, and an excellent walled garden. The place is being pulled down at this moment to make room for more streets of mean little houses – the kind of thing, and not a dull house of faded gentry, which perhaps the neighbourhood requires. The house was dull, and so were we, its last inhabitants; and the furniture was faded, even a little dingy – nothing to brag of. I do not, however, intend to convey a suggestion that we were faded gentry, for that was not the case. My father, indeed, was rich, and had no need to spare any expense in making his life and his house bright if he pleased; but he did not please, and I had not been long enough at home to exercise any special influence of my own. It was the only home I had ever known; but except in my earliest childhood, and in my holidays as a schoolboy, I had in reality known but little of it. My mother had died at my birth, or shortly after, and I had grown up in the gravity and silence of a house without women. In my infancy, I believe, a sister of my father's had lived with us, and taken charge of the household and of me; but she, too, had died long, long ago, my mourning for her being one of the first things I could recollect. And she had no successor. There were, indeed, a house-keeper and some maids – the latter of whom I only saw disappearing at the end of a passage, or whisking out of a room when one of 'the gentlemen' appeared. Mrs Weir, indeed, I saw nearly every day; but a curtsy, a smile, a pair of nice round arms which she caressed while folding them across her ample waist, and a large white apron, were all I knew of her. This was the only female influence in the house. The drawing-room I was aware of only as a place of deadly good order, into which nobody ever entered. It had three long windows opening on the lawn, and communicated at the upper end, which was rounded like a great bay, with the conservatory. Sometimes I gazed into it as a child from without, wondering at the needlework on the chairs, the screens, the looking-glasses which never reflected any living face. My father did not like the room, which probably was not wonderful, though it never occurred to me in those early days to enquire why.

I may say here, though it will probably be disappointing to those who form a sentimental idea of the capabilities of children, that it did not occur to me either, in these early days, to make any enquiry about my mother. There was no room in life, as I knew it, for any such person; nothing suggested to my mind either the fact that she must have existed, or that there was need of her in the house. I accepted, as I believe most children do, the facts of existence, on the basis with which I had first made acquaintance with them, without question or remark. As a matter of fact, I was aware that it was rather dull at home; but neither by comparison with the books I read, nor by the communications received from my school-fellows, did this seem to me anything remarkable. And I was possibly somewhat dull too by nature, for I did not mind. I was fond of reading, and for that there was unbounded opportunity. I had a little ambition in respect to work, and that too could be prosecuted undisturbed. When I went to the university, my society lay almost entirely among men; but by that time and afterwards, matters had of course greatly changed with me, and though I recognised women as part of the economy of nature, and did not indeed by any means dislike or avoid them, yet the idea of connecting them at all with my own home never entered into my head. That continued to be as it had always been, when at intervals I descended upon the cool, grave, colourless place, in the midst of my traffic with the world: always very still, well-ordered, serious – the cooking very good, the comfort perfect; old Morphew, the butler, a little older (but very little older, perhaps on the whole less old, since in my childhood I had thought him a kind of Methuselah); and Mrs Weir, less active, covering up her arms in sleeves, but folding and caressing them just as always. I remember looking in from the lawn through the windows upon that deadly-orderly drawing-room, with a humorous recollection of my childish admiration and wonder, and feeling that it must be kept so for ever and ever, and that to go into it would break some sort of amusing mock mystery, some pleasantly ridiculous spell.

But it was only at rare intervals that I went home. In the long vacation, as in my school holidays, my father often went abroad with me, so that we had gone over a great deal of the Continent together very pleasantly. He was old in proportion to the age of his son, being a man of sixty when I was twenty, but that did not disturb the pleasure of the relations between us. I don't know that they were ever very confidential. On my side there was but little to communicate, for I did not get into scrapes nor fall in love, the two predicaments which demand sympathy and confidences. And as for my father himself, I was never aware what there could be to communicate on his side. I knew his life exactly – what he did almost at every hour of the day; under what circumstances of the temperature he would ride and when walk; how often and with what guests he would indulge in the occasional break of a dinner-party, a serious pleasure – perhaps, indeed, less a pleasure than a duty. All this I knew as well as he did, and also his views on public matters, his political opinions, which naturally were different from mine. What ground, then, remained for confidence? I did not know any. We were both of us of a reserved nature, not apt to enter into our religious feelings, for instance. There are many people who think reticence on such subjects a sign of the most reverential way of contemplating them. Of this I am far from being sure; but, at all events, it was the practice most congenial to my own mind.

And then I was for a long time absent, making my own way in the world. I did not make it very successfully. I accomplished the natural fate of an Englishman, and went out to the Colonies; then to India in a semi-diplomatic position; but returned home after seven or eight years, invalided, in bad health and not much better spirits, tired and disappointed with my first trial of life. I had, as people say, 'no occasion' to insist on making my way. My father was rich, and had never given me the slightest reason to believe that he did not intend me to be his heir. His allowance to me was not illiberal, and though he did not oppose the carrying out of my own plans, he by no means urged me to exertion. When I came home he received me very affectionately, and expressed his satisfaction in my return. 'Of course,' he said, 'I am not glad that you are disappointed, Philip, or that your health is broken; but otherwise it is an ill wind, you know, that blows nobody good; and I am very glad to have you at home. I am growing an old man – '

'I don't see any difference, sir,' said I; 'everything here seems exactly the same as when I went away – '

He smiled, and shook his head. 'It is true enough,' he said; 'after we have reached a certain age we seem to go on for a long time on a plane, and feel no great difference from year to year; but it is an inclined plane, and the longer we go on the more sudden will be the fall at the end. But at all events it will be a great comfort to me to have you here.'

'If I had known that,' I said, 'and that you wanted me, I should have come in any circumstances. As there are only two of us in the world – '

'Yes,' he said, 'there are only two of us in the world; but still I should not have sent for you, Phil, to interrupt your career.'

'It is as well, then, that it has interrupted itself,' I said rather bitterly; for disappointment is hard to bear.

He patted me on the shoulder, and repeated, 'It is an ill wind that blows nobody good,' with a look of real pleasure which gave me a certain gratification too; for, after all, he was an old man, and the only one in all the world to whom I owed any duty. I had not been without dreams of warmer affections, but they had come to nothing – not tragically, but in the ordinary way. I might perhaps have had love which I did not want but not that which I did want – which was not a thing to make any unmanly moan about, but in the ordinary course of events. Such disappointments happen every day; indeed, they are more common than anything else, and sometimes it is apparent afterwards that it is better it was so.

However, here I was at thirty stranded, yet wanting for nothing – in a position to call forth rather envy than pity from the greater part of my contemporaries; for I had an assured and comfortable existence, as much money as I wanted, and the prospect of an excellent fortune for the future. On the other hand, my health was still low, and I had no occupation. The neighbourhood of the town was a drawback rather than an advantage. I felt myself tempted, instead of taking the long walk into the country which my doctor recommended, to take a much shorter one through the High Street, across the river, and back again, which was not a walk but a lounge. The country was silent and full of thoughts – thoughts not always very agreeable – whereas there were always the humours of the little urban population to glance at, the news to be heard – all those petty matters which so often make up life in a very impoverished version for the idle man. I did not like it, but I felt myself yielding to it, not having energy enough to make a stand. The rector and the leading lawyer of the place asked me to dinner. I might have glided into the society, such as it was, had I been disposed for that; everything about me began to close over me as if I had been fifty, and fully contented with my lot.

It was possibly my own want of occupation which made me observe with surprise, after a while, how much occupied my father was. He had expressed himself glad of my return; but now that I had returned, I saw very little of him. Most of his time was spent in his library, as had always been the case. But on the few visits I paid him there, I could not but perceive that the aspect of the library was much changed. It had acquired the look of a business-room, almost an office. There were large businesslike books on the table, which I could not associate with anything he could naturally have to do; and his correspondence was very large. I thought he closed one of those books hurriedly as I came in, and pushed it away, as if he did not wish me to see it. This surprised me at the moment without arousing any other feeling; but afterwards I remembered it with a clearer sense of what it meant. He was more absorbed altogether than I had been used to see him. He was visited by men sometimes not of very prepossessing appearance. Surprise grew in my mind without any very distinct idea of the reason of it; and it was not till after a chance conversation with Morphew that my vague uneasiness began to take definite shape. It was begun without any special intention on my part. Morphew had informed me that master was very busy on some occasion when I wanted to see him. And I was a little annoyed to be thus put off. 'It appears to me that my father is always busy,' I said hastily.

Morphew then began very oracularly to nod his head in assent. 'A deal too busy, sir, if you take my opinion,' he said.

This startled me much, and I asked hurriedly, 'What do you mean?' without reflecting that to ask for private information from a servant about my father's habits was as bad as investigating into a stranger's affairs. It did not strike me in the same light.

'Mr Philip,' said Morphew, 'a thing 'as 'appened as 'appens more often than it ought to. Master has got awful keen about money in his old age.'

'That's a new thing for him,' I said.

'No, sir, begging your pardon, it ain't a new thing. He was once broke of it, and that wasn't easy done; but it's come back, if you'll excuse me saying so. And I don't know as he'll ever be broke of it again at his age.'

I felt more disposed to be angry than disturbed by this. 'You must be making some ridiculous mistake,' I said. 'And if you were not so old a friend as you are, Morphew, I should not have allowed my father to be so spoken of to me.'

The old man gave me a half-astonished, half-contemptuous look. 'He's been my master a deal longer than he's been your father,' he said, turning on his heel. The assumption was so comical that my anger could not stand in face of it. I went out, having been on my way to the door when this conversation occurred, and took my usual lounge about, which was not a satisfactory sort of amusement. Its vanity and emptiness appeared to be more evident than usual today. I met half a dozen people I knew, and had as many pieces of news confided to me. I went up and down the length of the High Street. I made a small purchase or two. And then I turned homeward, despising myself, yet finding no alternative within my reach. Would a long country walk have been more virtuous? It would at least have been more wholesome; but that was all that could be said. My mind did not dwell on Morphew's communication. It seemed without sense or meaning to me; and after the excellent joke about his superior interest in his master to mine in my father was dismissed lightly enough from my mind. I tried to invent some way of telling this to my father without letting him perceive that Morphew had been finding faults in him, or I listening; for it seemed a pity to lose so good a joke. However, as I returned home, something happened which put the joke entirely out of my head. It is curious when a new subject of trouble or anxiety has been suggested to the mind in an unexpected way, how often a second advertisement follows immediately after the first, and gives to that a potency which in itself it had not possessed.

I was approaching our own door, wondering whether my father had gone, or whether, on my return, I should find him at leisure – for I had several little things to say to him – when I noticed a poor woman lingering about the closed gates. She had a baby sleeping in her arms. It was a spring night, the stars shining in the twilight, and everything soft and dim; and the woman's figure was like a shadow, flitting about, now here, now there, on one side or another of the gate. She stopped when she saw me approaching, and hesitated for a moment, then seemed to take a sudden resolution. I watched her without knowing, with a prevision that she was going to address me, though with no sort of idea as to the subject of her address. She came up to me doubtfully, it seemed, yet certainly, as I felt, and when she was close to me, dropped a sort of hesitating curtsy, and said, 'It's Mr Philip?' in a low voice.

'What do you want with me?' I said.

Then she poured forth suddenly, without warning or preparation, her long speech – a flood of words which must have been all ready and waiting at the doors of her lips for utterance. 'Oh, sir, I want to speak to you! I can't believe you'll be so hard, for you're young; and I can't believe he'll be so hard if so be as his own son, as I've always heard he had but one, 'll speak up for us. Oh, gentleman, it is easy for the likes of you that if you ain't comfortable in one room can just walk into another; but if one room is all you have, and every bit of furniture you have taken out of it, and nothing but the four walls left – not so much as the cradle for the child, or a chair for your man to sit down upon when he comes from his work, or a saucepan to cook him his supper – '

'My good woman,' I said, 'who can have taken all that from you? Surely nobody can be so cruel?'

'You say it's cruel!' she cried with a sort of triumph. 'Oh, I knowed you would, or any true gentleman that don't hold with screwing poor folks. Just go and say that to him inside there for the love of God. Tell him to think what he's doing, driving poor creatures to despair. Summer's coming, the Lord be praised, but yet it's bitter cold at night with your counterpane gone; and when you've been working hard all day, and nothing but four bare walls to come home to, and all your poor little sticks of furniture that you've saved up for, and got together one by one, all gone, and you no better than when you started, or rather worse, for then you was young. Oh, sir!' the woman's voice rose into a sort of passionate wail. And then she added, beseechingly, recovering herself, 'Oh, speak for us; he'll not refuse his own son – '

'To whom am I to speak? Who is it that has done this to you?' I said.

The woman hesitated again, looking keenly in my face, then repeated with a slight faltering, 'It's Mr Philip?' as if that made everything right.

'Yes; I am Philip Canning,' I said; 'but what have I to do with this? and to whom am I to speak?'

She began to whimper, crying and stopping herself. 'Oh, please, sir! it's Mr Canning as owns all the house property about; it's him that our court and the lane and everything belongs to. And he's taken the bed from under us, and the baby's cradle, although it's said in the Bible as you're not to take poor folks' beds.'

'My father!' I cried in spite of myself; 'then it must be some agent, someone else in his name. You may be sure he knows nothing of it. Of course I shall speak to him at once.'

'Oh, God bless you, sir,' said the woman. But then she added, in a lower tone, 'It's no agent. It's one as never knows trouble. It's him that lives in that grand house.' But this was said under her breath, evidently not for me to hear.

Morphew's words flashed through my mind as she spoke. What was this? Did it afford an explanation of the much-occupied hours, the big books, the strange visitors? I took the poor woman's name, and gave her something to procure a few comforts for the night, and went indoors disturbed and troubled. It was impossible to believe that my father himself would have acted thus; but he was not a man to brook interference, and I did not see how to introduce the subject, what to say. I could but hope that, at the moment of broaching it, words would be put into my mouth, which often happens in moments of necessity, one knows not how, even when one's theme is not so all-important as that for which such help has been promised. As usual, I did not see my father till dinner. I have said that our dinners were very good, luxurious in a simple way, everything excellent in its kind, well cooked, well served – the perfection of comfort without show – which is a combination very dear to the English heart. I said nothing till Morphew, with his solemn attention to everything that was going, had retired; and then it was with some strain of courage that I began.

'I was stopped outside the gate today by a curious sort of petitioner – a poor woman, who seems to be one of your tenants, sir, but whom your agent must have been rather too hard upon.'

'My agent? Who is that?' said my father quietly.

'I don't know his name, but I doubt his competence. The poor creature seems to have had everything taken from her – her bed, her child's cradle.'

'No doubt she was behind with her rent.'

'Very likely, sir. She seemed very poor,' said I.

'You take it coolly,' said my father, with an upward glance, half-amused, not in the least shocked by my statement. 'But when a man, or a woman either, takes a house, I suppose you will allow that they ought to pay rent for it.'

'Certainly, sir,' I replied, 'when they have got anything to pay.'

'I don't allow the reservation,' he said. But he was not angry, which I had feared he would be.

'I think,' I continued, 'that your agent must be too severe. And this emboldens me to say something which has been in my mind for some time' – (these were the words, no doubt, which I had hoped would be put into my month; they were the suggestion of the moment, and yet as I said them it was with the most complete conviction of their truth) – 'and that is this: I am doing nothing; my time hangs heavy on my hands. Make me your agent. I will see for myself, and save you from such mistakes; and it will be an occupation – '

'Mistakes? What warrant have you for saying these are mistakes?' he said testily; then after a moment: 'This is a strange proposal from you, Phil. Do you know what it is you are offering? – to be a collector of rents, going about from door to door, from week to week; to look after wretched little bits of repairs, drains, etc.; to get paid, which, after all, is the chief thing, and not to be taken in by tales of poverty.'

'Not to let you be taken in by men without pity,' I said.

He gave me a strange glance, which I did not very well understand, and said abruptly a thing which, so far as I remember, he had never in my life said before, 'You've become a little like your mother, Phil – '

'My mother!' the reference was so unusual – nay, so unprecedented – that I was greatly startled. It seemed to me like the sudden introduction of a quite new element in the stagnant atmosphere, as well as a new party to our conversation. My father looked across the table, as if with some astonishment at my tone of surprise.

'Is that so very extraordinary?' he said.

'No; of course it is not extraordinary that I should resemble my mother. Only – I have heard very little of her – almost nothing.'

'That is true.' He got up and placed himself before the fire, which was very low, as the night was not cold – had not been cold heretofore at least; but it seemed to me now that a little chill came into the dim and faded room. Perhaps it looked more dull from the suggestion of a something brighter, warmer, that might have been. 'Talking of mistakes,' he said, 'perhaps that was one: to sever you entirely from her side of the house. But I did not care for the connection. You will understand how it is that I speak of it now when I tell you – ' He stopped here, however, said nothing more for a minute or so, and then rang the bell. Morphew came, as he always did, very deliberately, so that some time elapsed in silence, during which my surprise grew.

When the old man appeared at the door – 'Have you put the lights in the drawing-room, as I told you?' my father said.

'Yes, sir; and opened the box, sir; and it's a – it's a speaking likeness – '

This the old man got out in a great hurry, as if afraid that his master would stop him. My father did so with a wave of his hand.

'That's enough. I asked no information. You can go now.'

The door closed upon us, and there was again a pause. My subject had floated away altogether like a mist, though I had been so concerned about it. I tried to resume, but could not. Something seemed to arrest my very breathing; and yet in this dull, respectable house of ours, where everything breathed good character and integrity, it was certain that there could be no shameful mystery to reveal. It was some time before my father spoke, not from any purpose that I could see, but apparently because his mind was busy with probably unaccustomed thoughts.

'You scarcely know the drawing-room, Phil,' he said at last.

'Very little. I have never seen it used. I have a little awe of it, to tell the truth.'

'That should not be. There is no reason for that. But a man by himself, as I have been for the greater part of my life, has no occasion for a drawing-room. I always, as a matter of preference, sat among my books; however, I ought to have thought of the impression on you.'

'Oh, it is not important,' I said; 'the awe was childish. I have not thought of it since I came home.'

'It never was anything very splendid at the best,' said he. He lifted the lamp from the table with a sort of abstraction, not remarking even my offer to take it from him, and led the way. He was on the verge of seventy, and looked his age; but it was a vigorous age, with no symptom of giving way. The circle of light from the lamp lit up his white hair and keen blue eyes and clear complexion; his forehead was like old ivory, his cheek warmly coloured; an old man, yet a man in full strength. He was taller than I was, and still almost as strong. As he stood for a moment with the lamp in his hand, he looked like a tower in his great height and bulk. I reflected as I looked at him that I knew him intimately, more intimately than any other creature in the world – I was familiar with every detail of his outward life; could it be that in reality I did not know him at all?

*　　*　　*

The drawing-room was already lighted with a flickering array of candles upon the mantelpiece and along the walls, producing the pretty, starry effect which candles give without very much light. As I had not the smallest idea what I was about to see, for Morphew's 'speaking likeness' was very hurriedly said, and only half comprehensible in the bewilderment of my faculties, my first glance was at this very unusual illumination, for which I could assign no reason. The next showed me a large full-length portrait, still in the box in which apparently it had travelled, placed upright, supported against a table in the centre of the room. My father walked straight up to it, motioned to me to place a smaller table close to the picture on the left side, and put his lamp upon that. Then he waved his hand towards it, and stood aside that I might see.

It was a full-length portrait of a very young woman – I might say a girl scarcely twenty – in a white dress, made in a very simple old fashion, though I was too little accustomed to female costume to be able to fix the date. It might have been a hundred years old, or twenty, for aught I knew. The face had an expression of youth, candour and simplicity more than any face I had ever seen – or so, at least in my surprise, I thought. The eyes were a little wistful, with something which was almost anxiety – which at least was not content – in them; a faint, almost imperceptible, curve in the lids. The complexion was of a dazzling fairness, the hair light, but the eyes dark, which gave individuality to the face. It would have been as lovely had the eyes been blue – probably more so – but their darkness gave a touch of character, a slight discord, which made the harmony finer. It was not, perhaps, beautiful in the highest sense of the word. The girl must have been too young, too slight, too little developed for actual beauty; but a face which so invited love and confidence I never saw. One smiled at it with instinctive affection. 'What a sweet face!' I said. 'What a lovely girl! Who is she? Is this one of the relations you were speaking of on the other side?'

My father made me no reply. He stood aside, looking at it as if he knew it too well to require to look – as if the picture was already in his eyes. 'Yes,' he said, after an interval, with a long-drawn breath, 'she was a lovely girl, as you say.'

'Was? – then she is dead. What a pity!' I said; 'what a pity! so young and so sweet!'

We stood gazing at her thus, in her beautiful stillness and calm – two men, the younger of us full-grown and conscious of many experiences, the other an old man – silent before this impersonation of tender youth. At length he said, with a slight tremulousness in his voice, 'Does nothing suggest to you who she is, Phil?'

I turned round to look at him with profound astonishment, but he turned away from my look. A sort of quiver passed over his face. 'That is your mother,' he said, and walked suddenly away, leaving me there.

My mother!

I stood for a moment in a kind of consternation before the white-robed innocent creature, to me no more than a child; then a sudden laugh broke from me, without any will of mine something ludicrous, as well as something awful, was in it. When the laugh was over, I found myself with tears in my eyes, gazing, holding my breath. The soft features seemed to melt, the lips to move, the anxiety in the eyes to become a personal enquiry. Ah, no! nothing of the kind; only because of the water in mine. My mother! oh, fair and gentle creature, scarcely woman, how could any man's voice call her by that name! I had little idea enough of what it meant – had heard it laughed at, scoffed at, reverenced, but never had learned to place it even among the ideal powers of life. Yet if it meant anything at all, what it meant was worth thinking of. What did she ask, looking at me with those eyes? What would she have said if 'those lips had language'? If I had known her only as Cowper did – with a child's recollection – there might have been some thread, some faint but comprehensible link, between us; but now all that I felt was the curious incongruity. Poor child! I said to myself; so sweet a creature: poor little tender soul! as if she had been a little sister, a child of mine – but my mother! I cannot tell how long I stood looking at her, studying the candid, sweet face, which surely had germs in it of everything that was good and beautiful; and sorry, with a profound regret, that she had died and never carried these promises to fulfilment. Poor girl! poor people who had loved her! These were my thoughts; with a curious vertigo and giddiness of my whole being in the sense of a mysterious relationship which it was beyond my power to understand.

Presently my father came back, possibly because I had been a long time unconscious of the passage of the minutes, or perhaps because he was himself restless in the strange disturbance of his habitual calm. He came in and put his arm within mine, leaning his weight partially upon me, with an affectionate suggestion which went deeper than words. I pressed his arm to my side: it was more between us two grave Englishmen than any embracing.

'I cannot understand it,' I said.

'No. I don't wonder at that; but if it is strange to you, Phil, think how much more strange to me! That is the partner of my life. I have never had another, or thought of another. That – girl! If we are to meet again, as I have always hoped we should meet again, what am I to say to her – I, an old man? Yes; I know what you mean. I am not an old man for my years; but my years are threescore and ten, and the play is nearly played out. How am I to meet that young creature? We used to say to each other that it was for ever, that we never could be but one, that it was for life and death. But what – what am I to say to her, Phil, when I meet her again, that – that angel? No, it is not her being an angel that troubles me; but she is so young! She is like my – my granddaughter,' he cried, with a burst of what was half sob, half laughter; 'and she is my wife – and I am an old man – an old man! And so much has happened that she could not understand.'

I was too much startled by this strange complaint to know what to say. It was not my own trouble, and I answered it in the conventional way.

'They are not as we are, sir,' I said; 'they look upon us with larger, other eyes than ours.'

'Ah! you don't know what I mean,' he said quickly; and in the interval he had subdued his emotion. 'At first, after she died, it was my consolation to think that I should meet her again – that we never could be really parted. But, my God, how I have changed since then! I am another man – I am a different being. I was not very young even then – twenty years older than she was; but her youth renewed mine. I was not an unfit partner; she asked no better, and knew as much more than I did in some things – being so much nearer the source – as I did in others that were of the world. But I have gone a long way since then, Phil – a long way; and there she stands, just where I left her.'

I pressed his arm again. 'Father,' I said, which was a title I seldom used, 'we are not to suppose that in a higher life the mind stands still.' I did not feel myself qualified to discuss such topics, but something one must say.

'Worse, worse!' he replied; 'then she too will be, like me, a different being, and we shall meet as what? as strangers, as people who have lost sight of each other, with a long past between us – we who parted, my God! with – with – '

His voice broke and ended for a moment, then while, surprised and almost shocked by what he said, I cast about in my mind what to reply, he withdrew his arm suddenly from mine, and said in his usual tone, 'Where shall we hang the picture, Phil? It must be here in this room. What do you think will be the best light?'

This sudden alteration took me still more by surprise, and gave me almost an additional shock; but it was evident that I must follow the changes of his mood, or at least the sudden repression of sentiment which he originated. We went into that simpler question with great seriousness, consulting which would be the best light. 'You know I can scarcely advise,' I said; 'I have never been familiar with this room. I should like to put off, if you don't mind, till daylight.'

'I think,' he said, 'that this would be the best place.' It was on the other side of the fireplace, on the wall which faced the windows – not the best light, I knew enough to be aware, for an oil-painting. When I said so, however, he answered me with a little impatience, 'It does not matter very much about the best light; there will be nobody to see it but you and me. I have my reasons – ' There was a small table standing against the wall at this spot, on which he had his hand as he spoke. Upon it stood a little basket in very fine lace-like wickerwork. His hand must have trembled, for the table shook, and the basket fell, its contents turning out upon the carpet – little bits of needlework, coloured silks, a small piece of knitting half done. He laughed as they rolled out at his feet, and tried to stoop to collect them, then tottered to a chair, and covered for a moment his face with his hands.

No need to ask what they were. No woman's work had been seen in the house since I could recollect it. I gathered them up reverently and put them back. I could see, ignorant as I was, that the bit of knitting was something for an infant. What could I do less than put it to my lips? It had been left in the doing – for me.

'Yes, I think this is the best place,' my father said a minute after, in his usual tone.

We placed it there that evening with our own hands. The picture was large, and in a heavy frame, but my father would let no one help me but himself. And then, with a superstition for which I never could give any reason even to myself, having removed the packings, we closed and locked the door, leaving the candles about the room, in their soft, strange illumination, lighting the first night of her return to her old place.

That night no more was said. My father went to his room early, which was not his habit. He had never, however, accustomed me to sit late with him in the library. I had a little study or smoking-room of my own, in which all my special treasures were – the collections of my travels and my favourite books – and where I always sat after prayers, a ceremonial which was regularly kept up in the house. I retired as usual this night to my room, and, as usual, read – but tonight somewhat vaguely, often pausing to think. When it was quite late, I went out by the glass door to the lawn, and walked round the house, with the intention of looking in at the drawing-room windows, as I had done when a child. But I had forgotten that these windows were all shuttered at night; and nothing but a faint penetration of the light within through the crevices bore witness to the instalment of the new dweller there.

In the morning my father was entirely himself again. He told me without emotion of the manner in which he had obtained the picture. It had belonged to my mother's family, and had fallen eventually into the hands of a cousin of hers, resident abroad – 'A man whom I did not like, and who did not like me,' my father said; 'there was, or had been, some rivalry, he thought: a mistake, but he was never aware of that. He refused all my requests to have a copy made. You may suppose, Phil, that I wished this very much. Had I succeeded, you would have been acquainted, at least, with your mother's appearance, and need not have sustained this shock. But he would not consent. It gave him, I think, a certain pleasure to think that he had the only picture. But now he is dead, and out of remorse, or with some other intention, has left it to me.'

'That looks like kindness,' said I.

'Yes; or something else. He might have thought that by so doing he was establishing a claim upon me,' my father said; but he did not seem disposed to add any more. On whose behalf he meant to establish a claim I did not know, nor who the man was who had laid us under so great an obligation on his deathbed. He *had* established a claim on me at least; though, as he was dead, I could not see on whose behalf it was. And my father said nothing more; he seemed to dislike the subject. When I attempted to return to it, he had recourse to his letters or his newspapers. Evidently he had made up his mind to say no more.

Afterwards I went into the drawing-room, to look at the picture once more. It seemed to me that the anxiety in her eyes was not so evident as I had thought it last night. The light possibly was more favourable. She stood just above the place where, I make no doubt, she had sat in life, where her little work-basket was – not very much above it. The picture was full-length, and we had hung it low, so that she might have been stepping into the room, and was little above my own level as I stood and looked at her again. Once more I smiled at the strange thought that this young creature – so young, almost childish – could be my mother; and once more my eyes grew wet looking at her. He was a benefactor, indeed, who had given her back to us. I said to myself that if I could ever do anything for him or his, I would certainly do it, for my – for this lovely young creature's sake. And with this in my mind, and all the thoughts that came with it, I am obliged to confess that the other matter, which I had been so full of on the previous night, went entirely out of my head.

*　　*　　*

It is rarely, however, that such matters are allowed to slip out of one's mind. When I went out in the afternoon for my usual stroll – or rather when I returned from that stroll – I saw once more before me the woman with her baby, whose story had filled me with dismay on the previous evening. She was waiting at the gate as before, and, 'Oh, gentleman, but haven't you got some news to give me?' she said.

'My good woman – I – have been greatly occupied. I have had – no time to do anything.'

'Ah!' she said, with a little cry of disappointment, 'my man said not to make too sure, and that the ways of the gentlefolks is hard to know.'

'I cannot explain to you,' I said, as gently as I could, 'what it is that has made me forget you. It was an event that can only do you good in the end. Go home now, and see the man that took your things from you, and tell him to come to me. I promise you it shall all be put right.'

The woman looked at me in astonishment, then burst forth, as it seemed, involuntarily, 'What! without asking no questions?' After this there came a storm of tears and blessings, from which I made haste to escape, but not without carrying that curious commentary on my rashness away with me – 'Without asking no questions?' It might be foolish, perhaps; but after all, how slight a matter. To make the poor creature comfortable at the cost of what – a box or two of cigars, perhaps, or some other trifle. And if it should be her own fault, or her husband's – what then? Had I been punished for all my faults, where should I have been now? And if the advantage should be only temporary, what then? To be relieved and comforted even for a day or two, was not that something to count in life? Thus I quenched the fiery dart of criticism which my *protégée* herself had thrown into the transaction, not without a certain sense of the humour of it. Its effect, however, was to make me less anxious to see my father, to repeat my proposal to him, and to call his attention to the cruelty performed in his name. This one case I had taken out of the category of wrongs to be righted, by assuming arbitrarily the position of Providence in my own person – for, of course, I had bound myself to pay the poor creature's rent as well as redeem her goods – and, whatever might happen to her in the future, had taken the past into my own hands.

The man came presently to see me, who, it seems, had acted as my father's agent in the matter. 'I don't know, sir, how Mr Canning will take it,' he said. 'He don't want none of those irregular, bad-paying ones in his property. He always says as to look over it and let the rent run on is making things worse in the end. His rule is, "Never more than a month, Stevens;" that's what Mr Canning says to me, sir. He says, "More than that they can't pay. It's no use trying." And it's a good rule; it's a very good rule. He won't hear none of their stories, sir. Bless you, you'd never get a penny of rent from them small houses if you listened to their tales. But if so be as you'll pay Mrs Jordan's rent, it's none of my business how it's paid, so long as it's paid, and I'll send her back her things. But they'll just have to be took next time,' he added composedly. 'Over and over; it's always the same story with them sort of poor folks – they're too poor for anything, that's the truth,' the man said.

Morphew came back to my room after my visitor was gone. 'Mr Philip,' he said, 'you'll excuse me, sir, but if you're going to pay all the poor folks' rent as have distresses put in, you may just go into the court at once, for it's without end – '

'I am going to be the agent myself, Morphew, and manage for my father; and we'll soon put a stop to that,' I said, more cheerfully than I felt.

'Manage for – master,' he said, with a face of consternation. 'You, Mr Philip!'

'You seem to have a great contempt for me, Morphew.'

He did not deny the fact. He said with excitement, 'Master, sir – master don't let himself be put a stop to by any man. Master's – not one to be managed. Don't you quarrel with master, Mr Philip, for the love of God.' The old man was quite pale.

'Quarrel!' I said. 'I have never quarrelled with my father, and I don't mean to begin now.'

Morphew dispelled his own excitement by making up the fire, which was dying in the grate. It was a very mild spring evening, and he made up a great blaze which would have suited December. This is one of many ways in which an old servant will relieve his mind. He muttered all the time as he threw on the coals and wood. 'He'll not like it – we all know as he'll not like it. Master won't stand no meddling, Mr Philip' – this last he discharged at me like a flying arrow as he closed the door.

I soon found there was truth in what he said. My father was not angry, he was even half amused. 'I don't think that plan of yours will hold water, Phil. I hear you have been paying rents and redeeming furniture – that's an expensive game, and a very profitless one. Of course, so long as you are a benevolent gentleman acting for your own pleasure, it makes no difference to me. I am quite content if I get my money, even out of your pockets – so long as it amuses you. But as my collector, you know, which you are good enough to propose to be – '

'Of course I should act under your orders,' I said; 'but at least you might be sure that I would not commit you to any – to any – ' I paused for a word.

'Act of oppression,' he said, with a smile – 'piece of cruelty, exaction – there are half a dozen words – '

'Sir – ' I cried.

'Stop, Phil, and let us understand each other. I hope I have always been a just man. I do my duty on my side, and I expect it from others. It is your benevolence that is cruel. I have calculated anxiously how much credit it is safe to allow; but I will allow no man, or woman either, to go beyond what he or she can make up. My law is fixed. Now you understand. My agents, as you call them, originate nothing; they execute only what I decide – '

'But then no circumstances are taken into account – no bad luck, no evil chances, no loss unexpected.'

'There are no evil chances,' he said; 'there is no bad luck; they reap as they sow. No, I don't go among them to be cheated by their stories, and spend quite unnecessary emotion in sympathising with them. You will find it much better for you that I don't. I deal with them on a general rule, made, I assure you, not without a great deal of thought.'

'And must it always be so?' I said. 'Is there no way of ameliorating or bringing in a better state of things?'

'It seems not,' he said; 'we don't get "no forrarder" in that direction so far as I can see.' And then he turned the conversation to general matters.

I retired to my room greatly discouraged that night. In former ages – or so one is led to suppose – and in the lower primitive classes who still linger near the primeval type, action of any kind was, and is, easier than amid the complication of our higher civilisation. A bad man is a distinct entity, against whom you know more or less what steps to take. A tyrant, an oppressor, a bad landlord, a man who lets miserable tenements at a rack-rent (to come down to particulars), and exposes his wretched tenants to all those abominations of which we have heard so much – well! he is more or less a satisfactory opponent. There he is, and there is nothing to be said for him – down with him! and let there be an end of his wickedness. But when, on the contrary, you have before you a good man, a just man, who has considered deeply a question which you allow to be full of difficulty; who regrets, but cannot, being human, avert the miseries which to some unhappy individuals follow from the very wisdom of his rule – what can you do? What is to be done? Individual benevolence at haphazard may balk him here and there, but what have you to put in the place of his well-considered scheme? Charity which makes paupers? or what else? I had not considered the question deeply, but it seemed to me that I now came to a blank wall, which my vague human sentiment of pity and scorn could find no way to breach. There must be wrong somewhere, but where? There must be some change for the better to be made, but how?

I was seated with a book before me on the table, with my head supported on my hands. My eyes were on the printed page, but I was not reading; my mind was full of these thoughts, my heart of great discouragement and despondency – a sense that I could do nothing, yet that there surely must and ought, if I but knew it, be something to do. The fire which Morphew had built up before dinner was dying out, the shaded lamp on my table left all the corners in a mysterious twilight. The house was perfectly still, no one moving: my father in the library, where, after the habit of many solitary years, he liked to be left alone, and I here in my retreat, preparing for the formation of similar habits. I thought all at once of the third member of the party, the newcomer, alone too in the room that had been hers; and there suddenly occurred to me a strong desire to take up my lamp and go to the drawing-room and visit her, to see whether her soft, angelic face would give any inspiration. I restrained, however, this futile impulse – for what could the picture say? – and instead wondered what might have been had she lived, had she been there, warmly enthroned beside the warm domestic centre, the hearth which would have been a common sanctuary, the true home. In that case what might have been? Alas! the question was no more simple to answer than the other: she might have been there alone too, her husband's business, her son's thoughts, as far from her as now, when her silent representative held her old place in the silence and darkness. I had known it so, often enough. Love itself does not always give comprehension and sympathy. It might be that she was more to us there, in the sweet image of her undeveloped beauty, than she might have been had she lived and grown to maturity and fading, like the rest.

I cannot be certain whether my mind was still lingering on this not very cheerful reflection, or if it had been left behind, when the strange occurrence came of which I have now to tell. Can I call it an occurrence? My eyes were on my book, when I thought I heard the sound of a door opening and shutting, but so far away and faint that if real at all it must have been in a far corner of the house. I did not move except to lift my eyes from the book as one does instinctively the better to listen; when – But I cannot tell, nor have I ever been able to describe exactly what it was. My heart made all at once a sudden leap in my breast. I am aware that this language is figurative, and that the heart cannot leap; but it is a figure so entirely justified by sensation, that no one will have any difficulty in understanding what I mean. My heart leaped up and began beating wildly in my throat, in my ears, as if my whole being had received a sudden and intolerable shock. The sound went through my head like the dizzy sound of some strange mechanism, a thousand wheels and springs circling, echoing, working in my brain. I felt the blood bound in my veins, my mouth became dry, my eyes hot; a sense of something insupportable took possession of me. I sprang to my feet, and then I sat down again. I cast a quick glance round me beyond the brief circle of the lamplight, but there was nothing there to account in any way for this sudden extraordinary rush of sensation, nor could I feel any meaning in it, any suggestion, any moral impression. I thought I must be going to be ill, and got out my watch and felt my pulse: it was beating furiously, about one hundred and twenty-five throbs in a minute. I knew of no illness that could come on like this without warning, in a moment, and I tried to subdue myself, to say to myself that it was nothing, some flutter of the nerves, some physical disturbance. I laid myself down upon my sofa to try if rest would help me, and kept still, as long as the thumping and throbbing of this wild, excited mechanism within, like a wild beast plunging and struggling, would let me. I am quite aware of the confusion of the metaphor; the reality was just so. It was like a mechanism deranged, going wildly with ever-increasing precipitation, like those horrible wheels that from time to time catch a helpless human being in them and tear him to pieces; but at the same time it was like a maddened living creature making the wildest efforts to get free.

When I could bear this no longer I got up and walked about my room; then having still a certain command of myself, though I could not master the commotion within me, I deliberately took down an exciting book from the shelf, a book of breathless adventure which had always interested me, and tried with that to break the spell. After a few minutes, however, I flung the book aside; I was gradually losing all power over myself. What I should be moved to do – to shout aloud, to struggle with I know not what; or if I was going mad altogether, and next moment must be a raving lunatic – I could not tell. I kept looking round, expecting I don't know what; several times with the corner of my eye I seemed to see a movement, as if someone was stealing out of sight; but when I looked straight, there was never anything but the plain outlines of the wall and carpet, the chairs standing in good order. At last I snatched up the lamp in my hand, and went out of the room. To look at the picture, which had been faintly showing in my imagination from time to time, the eyes, more anxious than ever, looking at me from out the silent air? But no; I passed the door of that room swiftly, moving, it seemed, without any volition of my own, and before I knew where I was going, went into my father's library with my lamp in my hand.

He was still sitting there at his writing-table; he looked up astonished to see me hurrying in with my light. 'Phil!' he said, surprised. I remember that I shut the door behind me, and came up to him, and set down the lamp on his table. My sudden appearance alarmed him. 'What is the matter?' he cried. 'Philip, what have you been doing with yourself?'

I sat down on the nearest chair and gasped, gazing at him. The wild commotion ceased; the blood subsided into its natural channels; my heart resumed its place. I use such words as mortal weakness can to express the sensations I felt. I came to myself thus, gazing at him, confounded at once by the extraordinary passion which I had gone through and its sudden cessation. 'The matter?' I cried; 'I don't know what is the matter.'

My father had pushed his spectacles up from his eyes. He appeared to me as faces appear in a fever, all glorified with light which is not in them – his eyes glowing, his white hair shining like silver; but his looks were severe. 'You are not a boy, that I should reprove you; but you ought to know better,' he said.

Then I explained to him, so far as I was able, what had happened. Had happened? Nothing had happened. He did not understand me; nor did I, now that it was over, understand myself; but he saw enough to make him aware that the disturbance in me was serious, and not caused by any folly of my own. He was very kind as soon as he had assured himself of this, and talked, taking pains to bring me back to unexciting subjects. He had a letter in his hand with a very deep border of black when I came in. I observed it, without taking any notice or associating it with anything I knew. He had many correspondents; and although we were excellent friends, we had never been on those confidential terms which warrant one man in asking another from whom a special letter has come. We were not so near to each other as this, though we were father and son. After a while I went back to my own room, and finished the evening in my usual way, without any return of the excitement which, now that it was over, looked to me like some extraordinary dream. What had it meant? Had it meant anything? I said to myself that it must be purely physical, something gone temporarily amiss, which had righted itself. It was physical; the excitement did not affect my mind. I was independent of it all the time, a spectator of my own agitation, a clear proof that, whatever it was, it had affected my bodily organisation alone.

Next day I returned to the problem which I had not been able to solve. I found out my petitioner in the back street, and that she was happy in the recovery of her possessions, which to my eyes indeed did not seem very worthy either of lamentation or delight. Nor was her house the tidy house which injured virtue should have when restored to its humble rights. She was not injured virtue, it was clear. She made me a great many curtsies, and poured forth a number of blessings. Her 'man' came in while I was there, and hoped in a gruff voice that God would reward me, and that the old gentleman'd let 'em alone. I did not like the look of the man. It seemed to me that in the dark lane behind the house of a winter's night he would not be a pleasant person to find in one's way. Nor was this all: when I went out into the little street which it appeared was all, or almost all, my father's property, a number of groups formed in my way, and at least half a dozen applicants sidled up. 'I've more claims nor Mary Jordan any day,' said one; 'I've lived on Squire Canning's property, one place and another, this twenty year.' 'And what do you say to me?' said another; 'I've six children to her two, bless you, sir, and ne'er a father to do for them.' I believed in my father's rule before I got out of the street, and approved his wisdom in keeping himself free from personal contact with his tenants. Yet when I looked back upon the swarming thoroughfare, the mean little houses, the women at their doors all so open-mouthed and eager to contend for my favour, my heart sank within me at the thought that out of their misery some portion of our wealth came, I don't care how small a portion; that I, young and strong, should be kept idle and in luxury, in some part through the money screwed out of their necessities, obtained sometimes by the sacrifice of everything they prized! Of course I know all the ordinary commonplaces of life as well as anyone – that if you build a house with your hand or your money, and let it, the rent of it is your just due; and must be paid. But yet –

'Don't you think, sir,' I said that evening at dinner, the subject being reintroduced by my father himself, 'that we have some duty towards them when we draw so much from them?'

'Certainly,' he said; 'I take as much trouble about their drains as I do about my own.'

'That is always something, I suppose.'

'Something! it is a great deal; it is more than they get anywhere else. I keep them clean, as far as that's possible. I give them at least the means of keeping clean, and thus check disease, and prolong life, which is more, I assure you, than they've any right to expect.'

I was not prepared with arguments as I ought to have been. That is all in the Gospel according to Adam Smith, which my father had been brought up in, but of which the tenets had begun to be less binding in my day. I wanted something more, or else something less; but my views were not so clear, nor my system so logical and well-built, as that upon which my father rested his conscience, and drew his percentage with a light heart.

Yet I thought there were signs in him of some perturbation. I met him one morning coming out of the room in which the portrait hung, as if he had gone to look at it stealthily. He was shaking his head, and saying, 'No, no,' to himself, not perceiving me, and I stepped aside when I saw him so absorbed. For myself, I entered that room but little. I went outside, as I had so often done when I was a child, and looked through the windows into the still and now sacred place, which had always impressed me with a certain awe. Looked at so, the slight figure in its white dress seemed to be stepping down into the room from some slight visionary altitude, looking with that which had seemed to me at first anxiety, which I sometimes represented to myself now as a wistful curiosity, as if she were looking for the life which might have been hers. Where was the existence that had belonged to her, the sweet household place, the infant she had left? She would no more recognise the man who thus came to look at her as through a veil, with a mystic reverence, than I could recognise her. I could never be her child to her, any more than she could be a mother to me.

*   *   *

Thus time passed on for several quiet days. There was nothing to make us give any special heed to the passage of time, life being very uneventful and its habits unvaried. My mind was very much preoccupied by my father's tenants. He had a great deal of property in the town which was so near us – streets of small houses, the best-paying property (I was assured) of any. I was very anxious to come to some settled conclusion: on the one hand, not to let myself be carried away by sentiment; on the other, not to allow my strongly roused feelings to fall into the blank of routine, as his had done. I was seated one evening in my own sitting-room, busy with this matter – busy with calculations as to cost and profit, with an anxious desire to convince him, either that his profits were greater than justice allowed, or that they carried with them a more urgent duty than he had conceived.

It was night, but not late, not more than ten o'clock, the household still astir. Everything was quiet – not the solemnity of midnight silence, in which there is always something of mystery, but the soft-breathing quiet of the evening, full of the faint habitual sounds of a human dwelling, a consciousness of life about. And I was very busy with my figures, interested, feeling no room in my mind for any other thought. The singular experience which had startled me so much had passed over very quickly, and there had been no return. I had ceased to think of it; indeed, I had never thought of it save for the moment, setting it down after it was over to a physical cause without much difficulty. At this time I was far too busy to have thoughts to spare for anything, or room for imagination; and when suddenly in a moment, without any warning, the first symptom returned, I started with it into determined resistance, resolute not to be fooled by any mock influence which could resolve itself into the action of nerves or ganglions. The first symptom, as before, was that my heart sprang up with a bound, as if a cannon had been fired at my ear. My whole being responded with a start. The pen fell out of my fingers, the figures went out of my head as if all faculty had departed; and yet I was conscious for a time at least of keeping my self-control. I was like the rider of a frightened horse, rendered almost wild by something which in the mystery of its voiceless being it has seen, something on the road which it will not pass, but wildly plunging, resisting every persuasion, turns from, with ever-increasing passion. The rider himself after a time becomes infected with this inexplicable desperation of terror, and I suppose I must have done so; but for a time I kept the upper hand. I would not allow myself to spring up as I wished, as my impulse was, but sat there doggedly, clinging my books, to my table, fixing myself on I did not mind what, to resist the flood of sensation, of emotion, which was sweeping through me, carrying me away. I tried to continue my calculations. I tried to stir myself up with recollections of the miserable sights I had seen, the poverty, the helplessness. I tried to work myself into indignation; but all through these efforts I felt the contagion growing upon me, my mind falling into sympathy with all those straining faculties of the body, startled, excited, driven wild by something, I knew not what. It was not fear. I was like a ship at sea straining and plunging against wind and tide, but I was not afraid. I am obliged to use these metaphors, otherwise I could give no explanation of my condition, seized upon against my will, and torn from all those moorings of reason to which I clung with desperation, as long as I had the strength.

When I got up from my chair at last, the battle was lost, so far as my powers of self-control were concerned. I got up, or rather was dragged up, from my seat, clutching at these material things round me as with a last effort to hold my own. But that was no longer possible; I was overcome. I stood for a moment looking round me feebly, feeling myself begin to babble with stammering lips, which was the alternative of shrieking, and which I seemed to choose as a lesser evil. What I said was, 'What am I to do?' and after a while, 'What do you want me to do?' although throughout I saw no one, heard no voice, and had in reality not power enough in my dizzy and confused brain to know what I myself meant. I stood thus for a moment, looking blankly round me for guidance, repeating the question, which seemed after a time to become almost mechanical, 'What do you want me to do?' though I neither knew to whom I addressed it nor why I said it. Presently – whether in answer, whether in mere yielding of nature, I cannot tell – I became aware of a difference: not a lessening of the agitation, but a softening, as if my powers of resistance being exhausted, a gentler force, a more benignant influence, had room. I felt myself consent to whatever it was. My heart melted in the midst of the tumult; I seemed to give myself up, and move as if drawn by someone whose arm was in mine, as if softly swept along, not forcibly, but with an utter consent of all my faculties to do I knew not what, for love of I knew not whom.

For love – that was how it seemed – not by force, as when I went before. But my steps took the same course: I went through the dim passages in an exaltation indescribable, and opened the door of my father's room.

He was seated there at his table as usual, the light of the lamp falling on his white hair; he looked up with some surprise at the sound of the opening door. 'Phil,' he said, and with a look of wondering apprehension on his face, watched my approach. I went straight up to him and put my hand on his shoulder. 'Phil, what is the matter? What do you want with me? What is it?' he said.

'Father, I can't tell you. I come not of myself. There must be something in it, though I don't know what it is. This is the second time I have been brought to you here.'

'Are you going – ?' He stopped himself. The exclamation had been begun with an angry intention. He stopped, looking at me with a scared look, as if perhaps it might be true.

'Do you mean mad? I don't think so. I have no delusions that I know of. Father, think – do you know any reason why I am brought here? for some cause there must be.'

I stood with my hand upon the back of his chair. His table was covered with papers, among which were several letters with the broad black border which I had before observed. I noticed this now in my excitement without any distinct association of thoughts, for that I was not capable of; but the black border caught my eye. And I was conscious that he too gave a hurried glance at them, and with one hand swept them away.

'Philip,' he said, pushing back his chair, 'you must be ill, my poor boy. Evidently we have not been treating you rightly; you have been more ill than I supposed. Let me persuade you to go to bed.'

'I am perfectly well,' I said. 'Father, don't let us deceive one another. I am neither a man to go mad nor to see ghosts. What it is that has got the command over me I can't tell; but there is some cause for it. You are doing something or planning something with which I have a right to interfere.'

He turned round squarely in his chair, with a spark in his blue eyes. He was not a man to be meddled with. 'I have yet to learn what can give my son a right to interfere. I am in possession of all my faculties, I hope.'

'Father,' I cried, 'won't you listen to me? No one can say I have been undutiful or disrespectful. I am a man, with a right to speak my mind, and I have done so; but this is different. I am not here by my own will. Something that is stronger than I has brought me. There is something in your mind which disturbs – others. I don't know what I am saying. This is not what I meant to say; but you know the meaning better than I. Someone – who can speak to you only by me – speaks to you by me; and I know that you understand.'

He gazed up at me, growing pale, and his underlip fell. I, for my part, felt that my message was delivered. My heart sank into a stillness so sudden that it made me faint. The light swam in my eyes; everything went round with me. I kept upright only by my hold upon the chair; and in the sense of utter weakness that followed, I dropped on my knees I think first, then on the nearest seat that presented itself, and, covering my face with my hands, had hard ado not to sob, in the sudden removal of that strange influence – the relaxation of the strain.

There was silence between us for some time; then he said, but with a voice slightly broken, 'I don't understand you, Phil. You must have taken some fancy into your mind which my slower intelligence – Speak out what you want to say. What do you find fault with? Is it all – all that woman Jordan?'

He gave a short, forced laugh as he broke off, and shook me almost roughly by the shoulder, saying, 'Speak out! what – what do you want to say?'

'It seems, sir, that I have said everything.' My voice trembled more than his, but not in the same way. 'I have told you that I did not come by my own will – quite otherwise. I resisted as long as I could: now all is said. It is for you to judge whether it was worth the trouble or not.'

He got up from his seat in a hurried way. 'You would have me as – mad as yourself,' he said, then sat down again as quickly. 'Come, Phil: if it will please you, not to make a breach – the first breach between us – you shall have your way. I consent to your looking into that matter about the poor tenants. Your mind shall not be upset about that, even though I don't enter into all your views.'

'Thank you,' I said; 'but, father, that is not what it is.'

'Then it is a piece of folly,' he said angrily. 'I suppose you mean – but this is a matter in which I choose to judge for myself.'

'You know what I mean,' I said, as quietly as I could, 'though I don't myself know; that proves there is good reason for it. Will you do one thing for me before I leave you? Come with me into the drawing-room – '

'What end,' he said, with again the tremble in his voice, 'is to be served by that?'

'I don't very well know; but to look at her, you and I together, will always do something for us, sir. As for breach, there can be no breach when we stand there.'

He got up, trembling like an old man, which he was, but which he never looked like save at moments of emotion like this, and told me to take the light; then stopped when he had got halfway across the room. 'This is a piece of theatrical sentimentality,' he said. 'No, Phil, I will not go. I will not bring her into any such – Put down the lamp, and, if you will take my advice, go to bed.'

'At least,' I said, 'I will trouble you no more, father, tonight. So long as you understand, there need be no more to say.'

He gave me a very curt good-night, and turned back to his papers – the letters with the black edge, either by my imagination or in reality, always keeping uppermost. I went to my own room for my lamp, and then alone proceeded to the silent shrine in which the portrait hung. I at least would look at her tonight. I don't know whether I asked myself, in so many words, if it were she who – or if it was anyone – I knew nothing; but my heart was drawn with a softness – born, perhaps, of the great weakness in which I was left after that visitation – to her, to look at her, to see, perhaps, if there was any sympathy, any approval in her face. I set down my lamp on the table where her little work-basket still was; the light threw a gleam upward upon her – she seemed more than ever to be stepping into the room, coming down towards me, coming back to her life. Ah, no! her life was lost and vanished: all mine stood between her and the days she knew. She looked at me with eyes that did not change. The anxiety I had seen at first seemed now a wistful, subdued question; but that difference was not in her look but in mine.

* * *

I need not linger on the intervening time. The doctor who attended us usually, came in next day 'by accident', and we had a long conversation. On the following day a very impressive yet genial gentleman from town lunched with us – a friend of my father's, Dr Something; but the introduction was hurried, and I did not catch his name. He, too, had a long talk with me afterwards, my father being called away to speak to someone on business. Dr — drew me out on the subject of the dwellings of the poor. He said he heard I took great interest in this question, which had come so much to the front at the present moment. He was interested in it too, and wanted to know the view I took. I explained at considerable length that my view did not concern the general subject, on which I had scarcely thought, so much as the individual mode of management of my father's estate. He was a most patient and intelligent listener, agreeing with me on some points, differing in others; and his visit was very pleasant. I had no idea until after of its special object; though a certain puzzled look and slight shake of the head when my father returned, might have thrown some light upon it. The report of the medical experts in my case must, however, have been quite satisfactory, for I heard nothing more of them. It was, I think, a fortnight later when the next and last of these strange experiences came.

This time it was morning, about noon – a wet and rather dismal spring day. The half-spread leaves seemed to tap at the window, with an appeal to be taken in; the primroses, that showed golden upon the grass at the roots of the trees, just beyond the smooth-shorn grass of the lawn, were all drooped and sodden among their sheltering leaves. The very growth seemed dreary – the sense of spring in the air making the feeling of winter a grievance, instead of the natural effect which it had conveyed a few months before. I had been writing letters, and was cheerful enough, going back among the associates of my old life, with, perhaps, a little longing for its freedom and independence, but at the same time a not ungrateful consciousness that for the moment my present tranquillity might be best.

This was my condition – a not unpleasant one – when suddenly the now well-known symptoms of the visitation to which I had become subject suddenly seized upon me – the leap of the heart; the sudden, causeless, overwhelming physical excitement, which I could neither ignore nor allay. I was terrified beyond description, beyond reason, when I became conscious that this was about to begin over again: what purpose did it answer; what good was in it? My father indeed understood the meaning of it though I did not understand; but it was little agreeable to be thus made a helpless instrument, without any will of mine, in an operation of which I knew nothing; and to enact the part of the oracle unwillingly, with suffering and such a strain as it took me days to get over. I resisted, not as before, but yet desperately, trying with better knowledge to keep down the growing passion. I hurried to my room and swallowed a dose of a sedative which had been given me to procure sleep on my first return from India. I saw Morphew in the hall, and called him to talk to him, and cheat myself, if possible, by that means. Morphew lingered, however, and, before he came, I was beyond conversation. I heard him speak, his voice coming vaguely through the turmoil which was already in my ears, but what he said I have never known. I stood staring, trying to recover my power of attention, with an aspect which ended by completely frightening the man. He cried out at last that he was sure I was ill, that he must bring me something; which words penetrated more or less into my maddened brain. It became impressed upon me that he was going to get someone – one of my father's doctors, perhaps – to prevent me from acting, to stop my interference, and that if I waited a moment longer I might be too late. A vague idea seized me at the same time of taking refuge with the portrait – going to its feet, throwing myself there, perhaps, till the paroxysm should be over. But it was not there that my footsteps were directed. I can remember making an effort to open the door of the drawing-room, and feeling myself swept past it, as if by a gale of wind. It was not there that I had to go. I knew very well where I had to go – once more on my confused and voiceless mission to my father, who understood, although I could not understand.

Yet as it was daylight, and all was clear, I could not help noting one or two circumstances on my way. I saw someone sitting in the hall as if waiting – a woman, a girl, a black-shrouded figure, with a thick veil over her face; and asked myself who she was, and what she wanted there. This question, which had nothing to do with my present condition, somehow got into my mind, and was tossed up and down upon the tumultuous tide like a stray log on the breast of a fiercely rolling stream, now submerged, now coming uppermost, at the mercy of the waters. It did not stop me for a moment, as I hurried towards my father's room, but it got upon the current of my mind. I flung open my father's door, and closed it again after me, without seeing who was there or how he was engaged. The full clearness of the daylight did not identify him as the lamp did at night. He looked up at the sound of the door, with a glance of apprehension; and rising suddenly, interrupting someone who was standing speaking to him with much earnestness and even vehemence, came forward to meet me. 'I cannot be disturbed at present,' he said quickly; 'I am busy.' Then seeing the look in my face, which by this time he knew, he too changed colour. 'Phil,' he said, in a low, imperative voice, 'wretched boy, go away – go away; don't let a stranger see you – '

'I can't go away,' I said. 'It is impossible. You know why I have come. I cannot, if I would. It is more powerful than I – '

'Go, sir,' he said; 'go at once; no more of this folly. I will not have you in this room: Go – go!'

I made no answer. I don't know that I could have done so. There had never been any struggle between us before; but I had no power to do one thing or another. The tumult within me was in full career. I heard indeed what he said, but his words were like straws tossed upon the tremendous stream. I saw now with my feverish eyes who the other person present was. It was a woman, dressed also in mourning similar to the figure in the hall; but this was a middle-aged woman, like a respectable servant. She had been crying, and in the pause caused by this encounter between my father and myself, dried her eyes with a handkerchief, which she rolled like a ball in her hand, evidently in strong emotion. She turned and looked at me as my father spoke to me, for a moment with a gleam of hope, then falling back into her former attitude.

My father returned to his seat. He was much agitated too, though doing all that was possible to conceal it. My inopportune arrival was evidently a great and unlooked-for vexation to him. He gave me the only look of passionate displeasure I have ever had from him as he sat down again; but he said nothing more.

'You must understand,' he said, addressing the woman, 'that I have said my last words on this subject. I don't choose to enter into it again in the presence of my son, who is not well enough to be made a party to any discussion. I am sorry that you should have had so much trouble in vain, but you were warned beforehand, and you have only yourself to blame. I acknowledge no claim, and nothing you can say will change my resolution. I must beg you to go away. All this is very painful and quite useless. I acknowledge no claim.'

'Oh, sir,' she cried, her eyes beginning once more to flow, her speech interrupted by little sobs. 'Maybe I did wrong to speak of a claim. I'm not educated to argue with a gentleman. Maybe we have no claim. But if it's not by right, oh, Mr Canning, won't you let your heart be touched by pity? She don't know what I'm saying, poor dear. She's not one to beg and pray for herself, as I'm doing for her. Oh, sir, she's so young! She's so lone in this world – not a friend to stand by her, nor a house to take her in! You are the nearest to her of anyone that's left in this world. She hasn't a relation – not one so near as you – oh!' she cried, with a sudden thought, turning quickly round upon me, 'this gentleman's your son! Now I think of it, it's not your relation she is, but his, through his mother! That's nearer, nearer! Oh, sir! you're young; your heart should be more tender. Here is my young lady that has no one in the world to look to her. Your own flesh and blood; your mother's cousin – your mother's – '

My father called to her to stop, with a voice of thunder. 'Philip, leave us at once. It is not a matter to be discussed with you.'

And then in a moment it became clear to me what it was. It had been with difficulty that I had kept myself still. My breast was labouring with the fever of an impulse poured into me, more than I could contain. And now for the first time I knew why. I hurried towards him, and took his hand, though he resisted, into mine. Mine were burning, but his like ice: their touch burnt me with its chill, like fire. 'This is what it is?' I cried. 'I had no knowledge before. I don't know now what is being asked of you. But, father, understand! You know, and I know now, that someone sends me – someone – who has a right to interfere.'

He pushed me away with all his might. 'You are mad,' he cried. 'What right have you to think – ? Oh, you are mad – mad! I have seen it coming on – '

The woman, the petitioner, had grown silent, watching this brief conflict with the terror and interest with which women watch a struggle between men. She started and fell back when she heard what he said, but did not take her eyes off me, following every movement I made. When I turned to go away, a cry of indescribable disappointment and remonstrance burst from her, and even my father raised himself up and stared at my withdrawal, astonished to find that he had overcome me so soon and easily. I paused for a moment, and looked back on them, seeing them large and vague through the mist of fever. 'I am not going away,' I said. 'I am going for another messenger – one you can't gainsay.'

My father rose and called to me threateningly, 'I will have nothing touched that is hers. Nothing that is hers shall be profaned – '

I waited to hear no more; I knew what I had to do. By what means it was conveyed to me I cannot tell; but the certainty of an influence which no one thought of calmed me in the midst of my fever. I went out into the hall, where I had seen the young stranger waiting. I went up to her and touched her on the shoulder. She rose at once, with a little movement of alarm, yet with docile and instant obedience, as if she had expected the summons. I made her take off her veil and her bonnet, scarcely looking at her, scarcely seeing her, knowing how it was: I took her soft, small, cool, yet trembling hand into mine; it was so soft and cool – not cold – it refreshed me with its tremulous touch. All through I moved and spoke like a man in a dream; swiftly, noiselessly, all the complications of waking life removed; without embarrassment, without reflection, without the loss of a moment. My father was still standing up, leaning a little forward as he had done when I withdrew; threatening, yet terror-stricken, not knowing what I might be about to do, when I returned with my companion. That was the one thing he had not thought of. He was entirely undecided, unprepared. He gave her one look, flung up his arms above his head, and uttered a distracted cry, so wild that it seemed the last outcry of nature – 'Agnes!' then fell back like a sudden ruin, upon himself, into his chair.

I had no leisure to think how he was, or whether he could hear what I said. I had my message to deliver. 'Father,' I said, labouring with my panting breath, 'it is for this that heaven has opened, and one whom I never saw, one whom I know not, has taken possession of me. Had we been less earthly, we should have seen her – herself, and not merely her image. I have not even known what she meant. I have been as a fool without understanding. This is the third time I have come to you with her message, without knowing what to say. But now I have found it out. This is her message. I have found it out at last.' There was an awful pause – a pause in which no one moved or breathed. Then there came a broken voice out of my father's chair. He had not understood, though I think he heard what I said. He put out two feeble hands. 'Phil – I think I am dying – has she – has she come for me?' he said.

We had to carry him to his bed. What struggles he had gone through before I cannot tell. He had stood fast, and had refused to be moved, and now he fell – like an old tower, like an old tree. The necessity there was for thinking of him saved me from the physical consequences which had prostrated me on a former occasion. I had no leisure now for any consciousness of how matters went with myself.

His delusion was not wonderful, but most natural. She was clothed in black from head to foot, instead of the white dress of the portrait. She had no knowledge of the conflict, of nothing but that she was called for, that her fate might depend on the next few minutes. In her eyes there was a pathetic question, a line of anxiety in the lids, an innocent appeal in the looks. And the face the same: the same lips, sensitive, ready to quiver; the same innocent, candid brow; the look of a common race, which is more subtle than mere resemblance. How I knew that it was so I cannot tell, nor any man. It was the other, the elder – ah, no! not elder; the ever young, the Agnes to whom age can never come, she who they say was the mother of a man who never saw her – it was she who led her kinswoman, her representative, into our hearts.

*   *   *

My father recovered after a few days: he had taken cold, it was said, the day before; and naturally, at seventy, a small matter is enough to upset the balance even of a strong man. He got quite well; but he was willing enough afterwards to leave the management of that ticklish kind of property which involves human well-being in my hands, who could move about more freely, and see with my own eyes how things were going on. He liked home better, and had more pleasure in his personal existence in the end of his life. Agnes is now my wife, as he had, of course, foreseen. It was not merely the disinclination to receive her father's daughter, or to take upon him a new responsibility, that had moved him, to do him justice; but both these motives had told strongly. I have never been told, and now will never be told, what his griefs against my mother's family, and specially against that cousin, had been; but that he had been very determined, deeply prejudiced, there can be no doubt. It turned out after, that the first occasion on which I had been mysteriously commissioned to him with a message which I did not understand, and which for that time he did not understand, was the evening of the day on which he had received the dead man's letter, appealing to him – to him, a man whom he had wronged – on behalf of the child who was about to be left friendless in the world. The second time, further letters – from the nurse who was the only guardian of the orphan, and the chaplain of the place where her father had died, taking it for granted that my father's house was her natural refuge – had been received. The third I have already described, and its results.

For a long time after, my mind was never without a lurking fear that the influence which had once taken possession of me might return again. Why should I have feared to be influenced, to be the messenger of a blessed creature, whose wishes could be nothing but heavenly? Who can say? Flesh and blood is not made for such encounters: they were more than I could bear. But nothing of the kind has ever occurred again.

Agnes had her peaceful domestic throne established under the picture. My father wished it to be so, and spent his evenings there in the warmth and light, instead of in the old library – in the narrow circle cleared by our lamp out of the darkness, as long as he lived. It is supposed by strangers that the picture on the wall is that of my wife; and I have always been glad that it should be so supposed. She who was my mother, who came back to me and became as my soul for three strange moments and no more, but with whom I can feel no credible relationship as she stands there, has retired for me into the tender regions of the unseen. She has passed once more into the secret company of those shadows, who can only become real in an atmosphere fitted to modify and harmonise all differences, and make all wonders possible – the light of the perfect day.

The Tapestried Chamber

Sir Walter Scott

About the end of the American War, when the officers of Lord Cornwallis's army, which surrendered at Yorktown, and others, who had been made prisoners during the impolitic and ill-fated controversy, were returning to their own country to relate their adventures and repose themselves after their fatigues, there was amongst them a general officer, of the name of Browne – an officer of merit, as well as a gentleman of high consideration for family and attainments.

Some business had carried General Browne upon a tour through the western counties, when, in the conclusion of a morning stage, he found himself in the vicinity of a small country town, which presented a scene of uncommon beauty and of a character peculiarly English.

The little town, with its stately old church, whose tower bore testimony to the devotion of ages long past, lay amidst pastures and cornfields of small extent, but bounded and divided with hedgerow timber of great age and size. There were few marks of modern improvement. The environs of the place intimated neither the solitude of decay nor the bustle of novelty; the houses were old, but in good repair; and the beautiful little river murmured freely on its way to the left of the town, neither restrained by a dam nor bordered by a towing-path.

Upon a gentle eminence, nearly a mile to the southward of the town, were seen, amongst many venerable oaks and tangled thickets, the turrets of a castle as old as the wars of York and Lancaster, but which seemed to have received important alterations during the age of Elizabeth and her successor. It had not been a place of great size; but whatever accommodation it formerly afforded was, it must be supposed, still to be obtained within its walls; at least, such was the inference which General Browne drew from observing the smoke arise merrily from several of the ancient wreathed and carved chimney-stalks. The wall of the park ran alongside of the highway for two or three hundred yards; and through the different points by which the eye found glimpses into the woodland scenery it seemed to be well stocked. Other points of view opened in succession – now a full one of the front of the old castle, and now a side glimpse at its particular towers, the former rich in all the bizarrerie of the Elizabethan school, while the simple and solid strength of other parts of the building seemed to show that they had been raised more for defence than ostentation.

Delighted with the partial glimpses which he obtained of the castle through the woods and glades by which this ancient feudal fortress was surrounded, our military traveller was determined to enquire whether it might not deserve a nearer view and whether it contained family pictures or other objects of curiosity worthy of a stranger's visit, when, leaving the vicinity of the park, he rolled through a clean and well-paved street and stopped at the door of a well-frequented inn.

Before ordering horses to proceed on his journey, General Browne made enquiries concerning the proprietor of the château which had so attracted his admiration and was equally surprised and pleased at hearing in reply a nobleman named whom we shall call Lord Woodville. How fortunate! Much of Browne's early recollections, both at school and at college, had been connected with young Woodville, whom, by a few questions, he now ascertained to be the same with the owner of this fair domain. He had been raised to the peerage by the decease of his father a few months before and, as the general learned from the landlord, the term of mourning being ended, was now taking possession of his paternal estate, in the jovial season of merry autumn, accompanied by a select party of friends, to enjoy the sports of a country famous for game.

This was delightful news to our traveller. Frank Woodville had been Browne's fag at Eton, and his chosen intimate at Christ Church; their pleasures and their tasks had been the same; and the honest soldier's heart warmed to find his early friend in possession of so delightful a residence, and of an estate, as the landlord assured him with a nod and a wink, fully adequate to maintain and add to his dignity. Nothing was more natural than that the traveller should suspend a journey which there was nothing to render hurried to pay a visit to an old friend under such agreeable circumstances.

The fresh horses, therefore, had only the brief task of conveying the general's travelling-carriage to Woodville Castle. A porter admitted them at a modern Gothic lodge, built in that style to correspond with the castle itself, and at the same time rang a bell to give warning of the approach of visitors. Apparently the sound of the bell had suspended the separation of the company, bent on the various amusements of the morning, so that when the carriage entered the court of the château several young men were lounging about in their sporting-dresses, looking at and criticising the dogs, which the keepers held in readiness to attend their pastime. As General Browne alighted, the young lord came to the gate of the hall, and for an instant gazed as at a stranger upon the countenance of his friend, on which war, with its fatigues and its wounds, had made a great alteration. But the uncertainty lasted no longer than till the visitor had spoken, and the hearty greeting which followed was such as can only be exchanged betwixt those who have passed together the merry days of careless boyhood or early youth.

'If I could have formed a wish, my dear Browne,' said Lord Woodville, 'it would have been to have you here, of all men, upon this occasion, which my friends are good enough to hold as a sort of holiday. Do not think you have been unwatched during the years you have been absent from us. I have traced you through your dangers, your triumphs, your misfortunes, and was delighted to see that, whether in victory or defeat, the name of my old friend was always distinguished with applause.'

The general made a suitable reply, and congratulated his friend on his new dignities, and the possession of a place and domain so beautiful.

'Nay, you have seen nothing of it as yet,' said Lord Woodville, 'and I trust you do not mean to leave us till you are better acquainted with it. It is true, I confess, that my present party is pretty large, and the old house, like other places of the kind, does not possess so much accommodation as the extent of the outward walls appears to promise. But we can give you a comfortable old-fashioned room, and I venture to suppose that your campaigns have taught you to be glad of worse quarters.'

The general shrugged his shoulders and laughed. 'I presume,' he said, 'the worst apartment in your château is considerably superior to the old tobacco-cask in which I was fain to take up my night's lodging when I was in the bush, as the Virginians call it, with the light corps. There I lay, like Diogenes himself, so delighted with my covering from the elements that I made a vain attempt to have it rolled into my next quarters; but my commander for the time would give way to no such luxurious provision, and I took farewell of my beloved cask with tears in my eyes.'

'Well, then, since you do not fear your quarters,' said Lord Woodville, 'you will stay with me a week at least. Of guns, dogs, fishing-rods, flies, and means of sport by sea and land, we have enough and to spare; you cannot pitch on an amusement, but we will find the means of pursuing it. But if you prefer the gun and pointers, I will go with you myself, and see whether you have mended your shooting since you have been amongst the Indians of the back settlements.'

The general gladly accepted his friendly host's proposal in all its points. After a morning of manly exercise, the company met at dinner, where it was the delight of Lord Woodville to conduce to the display of the high properties of his recovered friend, so as to recommend him to his guests, most of whom were persons of distinction. He led General Browne to speak of the scenes he had witnessed; and as every word marked alike the brave officer and the sensible man, who retained possession of his cool judgement under the most imminent dangers, the company looked upon the soldier with general respect, as on one who had proved himself possessed of an uncommon portion of personal courage – that attribute, of all others, of which everybody desires to be thought possessed.

The day at Woodville Castle ended as usual in such mansions. The hospitality stopped within the limits of good order; music, in which the young lord was a proficient, succeeded to the circulation of the bottle; cards and billiards, for those who preferred such amusements, were in readiness; but the exercise of the morning required early hours, and not long after eleven o'clock the guests began to retire to their several apartments.

The young lord himself conducted his friend, General Browne, to the chamber destined for him, which answered the description he had given of it, being comfortable, but old-fashioned. The bed was of the massive form used in the end of the seventeenth century, and the curtains of faded silk, heavily trimmed with tarnished gold. But then the sheets, pillows and blankets looked delightful to the campaigner, when he thought of his 'mansion, the cask'. There was an air of gloom in the tapestry hangings which, with their worn-out graces, curtained the walls of the little chamber, and gently undulated as the autumnal breeze found its way through the ancient lattice-window, which pattered and whistled as the air gained entrance. The toilet, too, with its mirror, turbaned, after the manner of the beginning of the century, with a coiffure of murrey-coloured silk, and its hundred strange-shaped boxes, providing for arrangements which had been obsolete for more than fifty years, had an antique, and in so far a melancholy aspect. But nothing could blaze more brightly and cheerfully than the two large wax candles; or if aught could rival them, it was the flaming, bickering faggots in the chimney, that sent at once their gleam and their warmth through the snug apartment, which, notwithstanding the general antiquity of its appearance, was not wanting in the least convenience that modern habits rendered either necessary or desirable.

'This is an old-fashioned sleeping-apartment, general,' said the young lord, 'but I hope you find nothing that makes you envy your old tobacco-cask.'

'I am not particular respecting my lodgings,' replied the general; 'yet were I to make any choice, I would prefer this chamber by many degrees to the gayer and more modern rooms of your family mansion. Believe me that when I unite its modern air of comfort with its venerable antiquity, and recollect that it is your lordship's property, I shall feel in better quarters here than if I were in the best hotel London could afford.'

'I trust – I have no doubt – that you will find yourself as comfortable as I wish you, my dear general,' said the young nobleman; and once more bidding his guest good-night, he shook him by the hand and withdrew.

The general once more looked round him, and internally congratulating himself on his return to peaceful life, the comforts of which were endeared by the recollection of the hardships and dangers he had lately sustained, undressed himself, and prepared for a luxurious night's rest.

Here, contrary to the custom of this species of tale, we leave the general in possession of his apartment until the next morning.

The company assembled for breakfast at an early hour, but without the appearance of General Browne, who seemed the guest that Lord Woodville was desirous of honouring above all whom his hospitality had assembled around him. He more than once expressed surprise at the general's absence, and at length sent a servant to make enquiry after him. The man brought back information that General Browne had been walking abroad since an early hour of the morning, in defiance of the weather, which was misty and ungenial.

'The custom of a solder,' said the young nobleman to his friends; 'many of them acquire habitual vigilance, and cannot sleep after the early hour at which their duty usually commands them to be alert.'

Yet the explanation which Lord Woodville thus offered to the company seemed hardly satisfactory to his own mind, and it was in a fit of silence and abstraction that he awaited the return of the general. It took place near an hour after the breakfast bell had rung. He looked fatigued and feverish. His hair, the powdering and arrangement of which was at this time one of the most important occupations of a man's whole day, and marked his fashion as much as, in the present time, the tying of a cravat or the want of one, was dishevelled, uncurled, void of powder and dank with dew. His clothes were huddled on with a careless negligence remarkable in a military man, whose real or supposed duties are usually held to include some attention to the toilet; and his looks were haggard and ghastly in a peculiar degree.

'So you have stolen a march upon us this morning, my dear general,' said Lord Woodville; 'or you have not found your bed so much to your mind as I had hoped and you seemed to expect. How did you rest last night?'

'Oh, excellently well – remarkably well – never better in my life!' said General Browne rapidly, and yet with an air of embarrassment which was obvious to his friend. He then hastily swallowed a cup of tea and, neglecting or refusing whatever else he was offered, seemed to fall into a fit of abstraction.

'You will take the gun today, general?' said his friend and host, but had to repeat the question twice ere he received the abrupt answer, 'No, my lord; I am sorry I cannot have the honour of spending another day with your lordship; my post-horses are ordered and will be here directly.'

All who were present showed surprise, and Lord Woodville immediately replied, 'Post-horses, my good friend! What can you possibly want with them, when you promised to stay with me quietly for at least a week?'

'I believe,' said the general, obviously much embarrassed, 'that I might, in the pleasure of my first meeting with your lordship, have said something about stopping here a few days; but I have since found it altogether impossible.'

'That is very extraordinary,' answered the young nobleman. 'You seemed quite disengaged yesterday, and you cannot have had a summons today, for our post has not come up from town, and therefore you cannot have received any letters.'

General Browne, without giving any further explanation, muttered something of indispensable business, and insisted on the absolute necessity of his departure in a manner which silenced all opposition on the part of his host, who saw that his resolution was taken, and forbore all further importunity.

'At least, however,' he said, 'permit me, my dear Browne, since go you will or must, to show you the view from the terrace, which the mist, that is now rising, will soon display.'

He threw open a sash-window and stepped down upon the terrace as he spoke. The general followed him mechanically, but seemed little to attend to what his host was saying, as, looking across an extended and rich prospect, he pointed out the different objects worthy of observation. Thus they moved on till Lord Woodville had attained his purpose of drawing his guest entirely apart from the rest of the company, when, turning round upon him with an air of great solemnity, he addressed him thus: 'Richard Browne, my old and very dear friend, we are now alone. Let me conjure you to answer me upon the word of a friend and the honour of a soldier. How did you in reality rest during the night?'

'Most wretchedly indeed, my lord,' answered the general, in the same tone of solemnity; 'so miserably, that I would not run the risk of such a second night, not only for all the lands belonging to this castle, but for all the country which I see from this elevated point of view.'

'This is most extraordinary,' said the young lord, as if speaking to himself; 'then there must be something in the reports concerning that apartment.' Again turning to the general, he said, 'For God's sake, my dear friend, be candid with me and let me know the disagreeable particulars which have befallen you under a roof where, with consent of the owner, you should have met nothing save comfort.'

The general seemed distressed by this appeal and paused a moment before he replied. 'My dear lord,' he at length said, 'what happened to me last night is of a nature so peculiar and so unpleasant that I could hardly bring myself to detail it even to your lordship, were it not that, independent of my wish to gratify any request of yours, I think that sincerity on my part may lead to some explanation about a circumstance equally painful and mysterious. To others, the communication I am about to make might place me in the light of a weak-minded, superstitious fool, who suffered his own imagination to delude and bewilder him; but you have known me in childhood and youth and will not suspect me of having adopted in manhood the feelings and frailties from which my early years were free.'

Here he paused, and his friend replied: 'Do not doubt my perfect confidence in the truth of your communication, however strange it may be. I know your firmness of disposition too well to suspect you could be made the object of imposition, and am aware that your honour and your friendship will equally deter you from exaggerating whatever you may have witnessed.'

'Well, then,' said the general, 'I will proceed with my story as well as I can, relying upon your candour, and yet distinctly feeling that I would rather face a battery than recall to my mind the odious recollections of last night.'

He paused a second time, and then perceiving that Lord Woodville remained silent and in an attitude of attention, he commenced, though not without obvious reluctance, the history of his night's adventures in the Tapestried Chamber.

'I undressed and went to bed so soon as your lordship left me yesterday evening; but the wood in the chimney, which nearly fronted my bed, blazed brightly and cheerfully and, aided by a hundred recollections of my childhood and youth, which had been recalled by the unexpected pleasure of meeting your lordship, prevented me from falling immediately asleep. I ought, however, to say that these reflections were all of a pleasant and agreeable kind, grounded on a sense of having for a time exchanged the labour, fatigues and dangers of my profession for the enjoyments of a peaceful life, and the reunion of those friendly and affectionate ties which I had torn asunder at the rude summons of war.

'While such pleasing reflections were stealing over my mind, and gradually lulling me to slumber, I was suddenly aroused by a sound like that of the rustling of a silken gown and the tapping of a pair of high-heeled shoes, as if a woman were walking in the apartment. Ere I could draw the curtain to see what the matter was, the figure of a little woman passed between the bed and the fire. The back of this form was turned to me, and I could observe, from the shoulders and neck, it was that of an old woman, whose dress was an old-fashioned gown, which, I think, ladies call a sacque – that is, a sort of robe completely loose in the body, but gathered into broad pleats upon the neck and shoulders which fall down to the ground and terminate in a species of train.

'I thought the intrusion singular enough, but never harboured for a moment the idea that what I saw was anything more than the mortal form of some old woman about the establishment, who had a fancy to dress like her grandmother, and who, having perhaps, as your lordship mentioned that you were rather straitened for room, been dislodged from her chamber for my accommodation, had forgotten the circumstances and returned by twelve to her old haunt. Under this persuasion I moved myself in bed and coughed a little, to make the intruder sensible of my being in possession of the premises. She turned slowly round, but, gracious heaven! my lord, what a countenance did she display to me! There was no longer any question what she was, or any thought of her being a living being. Upon a face which wore the fixed features of a corpse were imprinted the traces of the vilest and most hideous passions which had animated her while she lived. The body of some atrocious criminal seemed to have been given up from the grave, and the soul restored from the penal fire, in order to form, for a space, a union with the ancient accomplice of its guilt. I started up in bed, and sat upright, supporting myself on my palms, as I gazed on this horrible spectre. The hag made, as it seemed, a single and swift stride to the bed where I lay, and squatted herself down upon it, in precisely the same attitude which I had assumed in the extremity of horror, advancing her diabolical countenance within half a yard of mine, with a grin which seemed to intimate the malice and the derision of an incarnate fiend.'

Here General Browne stopped, and wiped from his brow the cold perspiration with which the recollection of his horrible vision had covered it.

'My lord,' he said, 'I am no coward. I have been in all the mortal dangers incidental to my profession, and I may truly boast that no man ever knew Richard Browne dishonour the sword he wears; but in these horrible circumstances, under the eyes, and, as it seemed, almost in the grasp, of an incarnation of an evil spirit, all firmness forsook me, all manhood melted from me like wax in the furnace, and I felt my hairs individually bristle. The current of my life-blood ceased to flow, and I sank back in a swoon, as very a victim to panic terror as ever was a village girl or a child of ten years old. How long I lay in this condition I cannot pretend to guess.

'But I was roused by the castle clock striking one, so loud that it seemed as if it were in the very room. It was some time before I dared open my eyes, lest they should again encounter the horrible spectacle. When, however, I summoned courage to look up, she was no longer visible. My first idea was to pull my bell, wake the servants, and remove to a garret or a hay-loft, to be ensured against a second visitation. Nay, I will confess the truth, that my resolution was altered, not by the shame of exposing myself, but by the fear that, as the bell-cord hung by the chimney, I might, in making my way to it, be again crossed by the fiendish hag, who, I figured to myself, might be still lurking about some corner of the apartment.

'I will not pretend to describe what hot and cold fever-fits tormented me for the rest of the night, through broken sleep, weary vigils, and that dubious state which forms the neutral ground between them. A hundred terrible objects appeared to haunt me; but there was the great difference betwixt the vision which I have described and those which followed – I knew the last to be deceptions of my own fancy and over-excited nerves.

'Day at last appeared, and I rose from my bed ill in health and humiliated in mind. I was ashamed of myself as a man and a soldier, and still more so at feeling my own extreme desire to escape from the haunted apartment, which, however, conquered all other considerations; so that, huddling on my clothes with the most careless haste, I made my escape from your lordship's mansion to seek in the open air some relief to my nervous system, shaken as it was by this horrible encounter with a visitant, for such I must believe her, from the other world. Your lordship has now heard the cause of my discomposure, and of my sudden desire to leave your hospitable castle. In other places I trust we may often meet; but God protect me from ever spending a second night under that roof!'

Strange as the general's tale was, he spoke with such a deep air of conviction that it cut short all the usual commentaries which are made on such stories. Lord Woodville never once asked him if he was sure he did not dream of the apparition, or suggested any of the possibilities by which it is fashionable to explain supernatural appearances, such as wild vagaries of the fancy or deceptions of the optic nerves. On the contrary, he seemed deeply impressed with the truth and reality of what he had heard; and, after a considerable pause, regretted, with much appearance of sincerity, that his early friend should in his house have suffered so severely.

'I am the more sorry for your pain, my dear Browne,' he continued, 'that it is the unhappy, though most unexpected, result of an experiment of my own. You must know that for my father and grandfather's time, at least, the apartment which was assigned to you last night had been shut on account of reports that it was disturbed by supernatural sights and noises. When I came, a few weeks since, into possession of the estate, I thought the accommodation which the castle afforded for my friends was not extensive enough to permit the inhabitants of the invisible world to retain possession of a comfortable sleeping-apartment. I therefore caused the Tapestried

Chamber, as we call it, to be opened and, without destroying its air of antiquity, I had such new articles of furniture placed in it as become the modern times. Yet, as the opinion that the room was haunted very strongly prevailed among the domestics and was also known in the neighbourhood and to many of my friends, I feared some prejudice might be entertained by the first occupant of the Tapestried Chamber, which might tend to revive the evil report which it had laboured under, and so disappoint my purpose of rendering it a useful part of the house. I must confess, my dear Browne, that your arrival yesterday, agreeable to me for a thousand reasons besides, seemed the most favourable opportunity of removing the unpleasant rumours which attached to the room, since your courage was indubitable, and your mind free of any preoccupation on the subject. I could not, therefore, have chosen a more fitting subject for my experiment.'

'Upon my life,' said General Browne, somewhat hastily, 'I am infinitely obliged to your lordship – very particularly indebted indeed. I am likely to remember for some time the consequences of the experiment, as your lordship is pleased to call it.'

'Nay, now you are unjust, my dear friend,' said Lord Woodville. 'You have only to reflect for a single moment in order to be convinced that I could not augur the possibility of the pain to which you have been so unhappily exposed. I was yesterday morning a complete sceptic on the subject of supernatural appearances. Nay, I am sure that, had I told you what was said about that room, those very reports would have induced you, by your own choice, to select it for your accommodation. It was my misfortune, perhaps my error, but really cannot be termed my fault, that you have been afflicted so strangely.'

'Strangely indeed!' said the general, resuming his good temper; 'and I acknowledge that I have no right to be offended with your lordship for treating me like what I used to think myself, a man of some firmness and courage. But I see my post-horses are arrived, and I must not detain your lordship from your amusement.'

'Nay, my old friend,' said Lord Woodville, 'since you cannot stay with us another day, which, indeed, I can no longer urge, give me at least half an hour more. You used to love pictures, and I have a gallery of portraits, some of them by Vandyke, representing ancestry to whom this property and castle formerly belonged. I think that several of them will strike you as possessing merit.'

General Browne accepted the invitation, though somewhat unwillingly. It was evident he was not to breathe freely or at ease till he left Woodville Castle far behind him. He could not refuse his friend's invitation, however; and the less so, that he was a little ashamed of the peevishness which he had displayed towards his well-meaning entertainer.

The general, therefore, followed Lord Woodville through several rooms, into a long gallery hung with pictures, which the latter pointed out to his guest, telling the names, and giving some account of the personages whose portraits presented themselves in progression. General Browne was but little interested in the details which these accounts conveyed to him. They were, indeed, of the kind which are usually found in an old family gallery. Here was a cavalier who had ruined the estate in the royal cause; there was a fine lady who had reinstated it by contracting a match with a wealthy Roundhead. There hung a gallant who had been in danger for corresponding with the exiled court at St Germain's; here one who had taken arms for William at the Revolution; and there a third that had thrown his weight alternately into the scale of Whig and Tory.

While Lord Woodville was cramming these words into his guest's ear, 'against the stomach of his sense', they gained the middle of the gallery, when he beheld General Browne suddenly start, and assume an attitude of the utmost surprise, not unmixed with fear, as his eyes were caught and suddenly riveted by a portrait of an old lady in a sacque, the fashionable dress of the end of the seventeenth century.

'There she is!' he exclaimed – 'there she is, in form and features, though inferior in demoniac expression to the accursed hag who visited me last night.'

'If that be the case,' said the young nobleman, 'there can remain no longer any doubt of the horrible reality of your apparition. That is the picture of a wretched ancestress of mine, of whose crimes a black and fearful catalogue is recorded in a family history in my charter-chest. The recital of them would be too horrible; it is enough to say that in yon fatal apartment incest and unnatural murder were committed. I will restore it to the solitude to which the better judgement of those who preceded me had consigned it; and never shall anyone, so long as I can prevent it, be exposed to a repetition of the supernatural horrors which could shake such courage as yours.'

Thus, the friends, who had met with such glee, parted in a very different mood – Lord Woodville to command the Tapestried Chamber to be unmantled and the door built up; and General Browne to seek in some less beautiful country, and with some less dignified friend, forgetfulness of the painful night which he had passed in Woodville Castle.

Wandering Willie's Tale

Sir Walter Scott

Ye maun have heard of Sir Robert Redgauntlet of that Ilk, who lived in these parts before the dear years. The country will lang mind him; and our fathers used to draw breath thick if ever they heard him named. He was out wi' the Hielandmen in Montrose's time; and again he was in the hills wi' Glencairn in the saxteen hundred and fifty-twa; and sae when King Charles II came in, wha was in sic favour as the Laird of Redgauntlet? He was knighted at Lonon court, wi' the king's ain sword; and being a red-hot prelatist, he came down here, rampauging like a lion, with commissions of lieutenancy (and of lunacy, for what I ken), to put down a' the Whigs and Covenanters in the country. Wild wark they made of it; for the Whigs were as dour as the Cavaliers were fierce, and it was which should first tire the other. Redgauntlet was aye for the strong hand; and his name is kend as wide in the country as Claverhouse's or Tam Dalyell's. Glen, nor dargle, nor mountain, nor cave could hide the puir hill-folk when Redgauntlet was out with bugle and bloodhound after them, as if they had been sae mony deer. And troth when they fand them, they didna mak muckle mair ceremony than a Hielandman wi' a roebuck. It was just, 'Will ye tak the test?' – if not, 'Make ready – present – fire!' – and there lay the recusant.

Far and wide was Sir Robert hated and feared. Men thought he had a direct compact with Satan – that he was proof against steel – and that bullets happed aff his buff-coat like hailstanes from a hearth – that he had a mear that would turn a hare on the side of Carrifra-gawns – and muckle to the same purpose, of whilk mair anon. The best blessing they wared on him was, 'Deil scowp wi' Redgauntlet!' He wasna a bad maister to his ain folk, though, and was weel aneugh liked by his tenants; and as for the lackies and troopers that raid out wi' him to the persecutions, as the Whigs caa'd those killing times, they wad hae drunken themsells blind to his health at ony time.

Now you are to ken that my gudesire lived on Redgauntlet's grund – they ca' the place Primrose-Knowe. We had lived on the grund, and under the Redgauntlets, since the riding days, and lang before. It was a pleasant bit: and I think the air is callerer and fresher there than onywhere else in the country. It's a' deserted now; and I sat on the broken door-cheek three days since, and was glad I couldna see the plight the place was in; but that's a' wide o' the mark. There dwelt my gudesire, Steenie Steenson; a rambling, rattling chiel' he had been in his young days, and could play weel on the pipes: he was famous at 'Hoopers and Girders' – a' Cumberland couldna touch him at 'Jockie Lattin' – and he had the finest finger for the back-lilt between Berwick and Carlisle. The like o' Steenie wasna the sort that they made Whigs o'. And so he became a Tory, as they ca' it, which we now ca' Jacobites, just out of a kind of needcessity, that he might belang to some side or other. He had nae ill-will to the Whig bodies, and liked little to see the blude rin, though, being obliged to follow Sir Robert in hunting and hosting, watching and warding, he saw muckle mischief, and maybe did some, that he couldna avoid.

Now Steenie was a kind of favourite with his master, and kend a' the folks about the castle, and was often sent for to play the pipes when they were at their merriment. Auld Dougal MacCallum, the butler that had followed Sir Robert through gude and ill, thick and thin, pool and stream, was specially fond of the pipes, and aye gae my gudesire his gude word wi' the laird; for Dougal could turn his master round his finger.

Weel, round came the Revolution, and it had like to have broken the hearts baith of Dougal and his master. But the change was not a'thegether sae great as they feared, and other folk thought for. The Whigs made an unco crawing what they wad do with their auld enemies, and in special wi' Sir Robert Redgauntlet. But there were ower mony great folks dipped in the same doings, to mak a spick and span new warld. So Parliament passed it a' ower easy; and Sir Robert, bating that he was held to hunting foxes instead of Covenanters, remained just the man he was. His revel was as loud, and his hall as weel lighted, as ever it had been, though maybe he lacked the fines of the nonconformists, that used to come to stock his larder and cellar; for it is certain he began to be keener about the rents than his tenants used to find him before, and they behoved to be prompt to the rent-day, or else the laird wasna pleased. And he was sic an awsome body, that naebody cared to anger him; for the oaths he swore, and the rage that he used to get into, and the looks that he put on, made men sometimes think him a devil incarnate.

Weel, my gudesire was nae manager – no that he was a very great misguider – but he hadna the saving gift, and he got twa terms' rent in arrear. He got the first brash at Whitsunday put ower wi' fair word and piping; but when Martinmas came, there was a summons from the grund-officer to come wi' the rent on a day preceese, or else Steenie behoved to flit. Sair wark he had to get the siller; but he was weel-freended, and at last he got the haill scraped thegether – a thousand merks – the maist of it was from a neighbour they caa'd Laurie Lapraik – a sly tod. Laurie had walth o' gear – could hunt wi the hound and rin wi' the hare – and be a Whig or Tory, saunt or sinner as the wind stood. He was a professor in this Revolution warld, but he liked an orra sough of this warld, and a tune on the pipes weel aneugh at a by-time, and abune a', he thought he had gude security for the siller he lent my gudesire ower the stocking at Primrose-Knowe.

Away trots my gudesire to Redgauntlet Castle, wi' a heavy purse and a light heart, glad to be out of the laird's danger. Weel, the first thing he learned at the castle was that Sir Robert had fretted himself into a fit of the gout, because he did not appear before twelve o'clock. It wasna a'thegether for the sake of the money, Dougal thought; but because he didna like to part wi' my gudesire aff the grund. Dougal was glad to see Steenie, and brought him into the great oak parlour, and there sat the laird his leesome lane, excepting that he had beside him a great, ill-favoured jackanapes, that was a special pet of his; a cankered beast it was, and mony an ill-natured trick it played – ill to please it was, and easily angered – ran about the haill castle, chattering and yowling, and pinching, and biting folk, especially before ill-weather or disturbances in the state. Sir Robert caa'd it Major Weir, after the warlock that was burnt; and few folk liked either the name or the conditions of the creature – they thought there was something in it by ordinar – and my gudesire was not just easy in his mind when the door shut on him, and he saw himself in the room wi' naebody but the laird, Dougal MacCallum and the major, a thing that hadna chanced to him before.

Sir Robert sat, or, I should say, lay, in a great armed chair, wi' his grand velvet gown, and his feet on a cradle; for he had baith gout and gravel, and his face looked as gash and ghastly as Satan's. Major Weir sat opposite to him, in a red laced coat, and the laird's wig on his head; and aye as Sir Robert girned wi' pain, the jackanapes girned too, like a sheep's-head between a pair of tangs – an ill-faur'd, fearsome couple they were. The laird's buff-coat was hung on a pin behind him, and his broadsword and his pistols within reach; for he keepit up the auld fashion of having the weapons ready, and a horse saddled day and night, just as he used to do when he was able to loup on horseback, and away after ony of the hill-folk he could get speerings of. Some said it was for fear of the Whigs taking vengeance, but I judge it was just his auld custom – he wasna gien to fear onything. The rental-book, wi' its black cover and brass clasps, was lying beside him; and a book of sculduddry sangs was put betwixt the leaves, to keep it open at the place where it bore evidence against the Goodman of Primrose-Knowe, as behind the hand with his mails and duties. Sir Robert gave my gudesire a look, as if he would have withered his heart in his bosom. Ye maun ken he had a way of bending his brows that men saw the visible mark of a horseshoe in his forehead, deep-dinted, as if it had been stamped there.

'Are ye come light-handed, ye son of a toom whistle?' said Sir Robert. 'Zounds! if you are – '

My gudesire, with as gude a countenance as he could put on, made a leg, and placed the bag of money on the table wi' a dash, like a man that does something clever. The laird drew it to him hastily: 'Is it all here, Steenie, man?'

'Your honour will find it right,' said my gudesire.

'Here, Dougal,' said the laird, 'gie Steenie a tass of brandy downstairs, till I count the siller and write the receipt.'

But they werena weel out of the room, when Sir Robert gied a yelloch that garr'd the castle rock. Back ran Dougal – in flew the livery-men – yell on yell gied the laird, ilk ane mair awfu' than the ither. My gudesire knew not whether to stand or flee, but he ventured back into the parlour, where a' was gaun hirdy-girdie – naebody to say 'come in' or 'gae out'. Terribly the Laird roared for cauld water to his feet and wine to cool his throat; and hell, hell, hell, and its flames, was aye the word in his mouth. They brought him water, and when they plunged his swoln feet into the tub, he cried out it was burning; and folk say that it *did* bubble and sparkle like a seething caldron. He flung the cup at Dougal's head, and said he had given him blood instead of burgundy; and, sure aneugh, the lass washed clotted blood aff the carpet the neist day. The jackanape they caa'd Major Weir, it jibbered and cried as if it was mocking its master; my gudesire's head was like to turn – he forgot baith siller and receipt, and downstairs he banged; but as he ran, the shrieks came faint and fainter; there was a deep-drawn shivering groan, and word gaed through the castle that the laird was dead.

Weel, away came my gudesire, wi' his finger in his mouth, and his best hope was that Dougal had seen the money-bag, and heard the laird speak of writing the receipt. The young laird, now Sir John, came from Edinburgh, to see things put to rights. Sir John and his father never gree'd weel. Sir John had been bred an advocate, and afterwards sat in the last Scots Parliament and voted for the Union, having gotten, it was thought, a rug of the compensations – if his father could have come out of his grave, he would have brained him for it on his awn hearthstane. Some thought it was easier counting with the auld rough knight than the fair-spoken young ane – but mair of that anon.

Dougal MacCallum, poor body, neither grat nor graned, but gaed about the house looking like a corpse, directing, as was his duty, a' the order of the grand funeral. Now, Dougal looked aye waur and waur when night was coming, and was aye the last to gang to his bed, whilk was in a little round just opposite the chamber of dais, whilk his master occupied while he was living, and where he now lay in state, as they caa'd it, weel-a-day! The night before the funeral, Dougal could keep his awn counsel nae langer; he cam doun with his proud spirit, and fairly asked auld Hutcheon to sit in his room with him for an hour. When they were in the round, Dougal took ae tass of brandy to himsell, and gave another to Hutcheon, and wished him all health, and lang life, and said that, for himsell, he wasna lang for this world; for that every night since Sir Robert's death, his silver call had sounded from the state-chamber, just as it used to do at nights in his lifetime, to call Dougal to help to turn him in his bed. Dougal said that being alone with the dead on that floor of the tower (for naebody cared to wake Sir Robert Redgauntlet like another corpse), he had never daured to answer the call, but that now his conscience checked him for neglecting his duty; for, 'Though death breaks service,' said MacCallum, 'it shall never break my service to Sir Robert; and I will answer his next whistle, so be you will stand by me, Hutcheon.'

Hutcheon had nae will to the wark, but he had stood by Dougal in battle and broil, and he wad not fail him at this pinch; so down the carles sat ower a stoup of brandy, and Hutcheon, who was something of a clerk, would have read a chapter of the Bible; but Dougal would hear naething but a blaud of Davie Lindsay, whilk was the waur preparation.

When midnight came, and the house was quiet as the grave, sure aneugh the silver whistle sounded as sharp and shrill as if Sir Robert was blowing it, and up gat the twa auld serving-men and tottered into the room where the dead man lay. Hutcheon saw aneugh at the first glance, for there were torches in the room, which showed him the foul fiend, in his ain shape, sitting on the laird's coffin! Over he cowped as if he had been dead. He could not tell how lang he lay in a trance at the door, but when he gathered himself, he cried on his neighbour, and getting nae answer, raised the house, and Dougal was found lying dead within twa steps of the bed where his master's coffin was placed. As for the whistle, it was gaen anes and aye; but mony a time was it heard at the top of the house on the bartizan, and amang the auld chimneys and turrets, where the howlets have their nests. Sir John hushed the matter up and the funeral passed over without mair bogle-wark.

But when a' was over, and the laird was beginning to settle his affairs, every tenant was called up for his arrears, and my gudesire for the full sum that stood against him in the rental-book. Weel, away he trots to the castle, to tell his story, and there he is introduced to Sir John, sitting in his father's chair, in deep mourning, with weepers and hanging cravat, and a small walking rapier by his side, instead of the auld broadsword, that had a hundredweight of steel about it, what with blade, chape and basket-hilt. I have heard their communing so often tauld ower that I almost think I was there mysell, though I couldna be born at the time.

'I wuss ye joy, sir, of the head seat, and the white loaf, and the braid lairdship. Your father was a kind man to friends and followers; muckle grace to you, Sir John, to fill his shoon – his boots, I suld say, for he seldom wore shoon, unless it were muils when he had the gout.

'Ay, Steenie,' quoth the laird, sighing deeply and putting his napkin to his een, 'his was a sudden call, and he will be missed in the country; no time to set his house in order – weel prepared Godward, no doubt, which is the root of the matter – but left us behind a tangled hesp to wind, Steenie. Hem! hem! We maun go to business, Steenie; much to do, and little time to do it in.'

Here he opened the fatal volume. I have heard of a thing they call Doomsday Book – I am clear it has been a rental of back-ganging tenants.

'Stephen,' said Sir John, still in the same soft, sleekit tone of voice, 'Stephen Stevenson, or Steenson, ye are down here for a year's rent behind the hand – due at last term.'

Stephen. 'Please your honour, Sir John, I paid it to your father.'

Sir John. 'Ye took a receipt then, doubtless, Stephen, and can produce it?'

Stephen. 'Indeed, I hadna time, an it like your honour; for nae sooner had I set doun the siller, and just as his honour Sir Robert, that's gaen, drew it till him to count it, and write out the receipt, he was ta'en wi' the pains that removed him.'

'That was unlucky,' said Sir John, after a pause. 'But ye maybe paid it in the presence of somebody. I want but a *talis qualis* evidence, Stephen. I would go ower strictly to work with no poor man.'

Stephen. 'Troth, Sir John, there was naebody in the room but Dougal MacCallum the butler. But, as your honour kens, he has e'en followed his auld master.'

'Very unlucky again, Stephen,' said Sir John, without altering his voice a single note. 'The man to whom ye paid the money is dead – and the man who witnessed the payment is dead too – and the siller, which should have been to the fore, is neither seen nor heard tell of in the repositories. How am I to believe a' this?'

Stephen. 'I dinna ken, your honour; but there is a bit memorandum note of the very coins; for, God help me! I had to borrow out of twenty purses; and I am sure that ilka man there set down will take his grit oath for what purpose I borrowed the money.'

Sir John. 'I have little doubt ye *borrowed* the money, Steenie. It is the *payment* to my father that I want to have some proof of.'

Stephen. 'The siller maun be about the house, Sir John. And since your honour never got it, and his honour that was canna have ta'en it wi' him, maybe some of the family may have seen it.'

Sir John. 'We will examine the servants, Stephen; that is but reasonable.'

But lackey and lass, and page and groom, all denied stoutly that they had ever seen such a bag of money as my gudesire described. What was waur, he had unluckily not mentioned to any living soul of them his purpose of paying his rent. Ae quean had noticed something under his arm, but she took it for the pipes.

Sir John Redgauntlet ordered the servants out of the room, and then said to my gudesire: 'Now, Steenie, ye see you have fair play; and, as I have little doubt ye ken better where to find the siller than ony other body, I beg, in fair terms, and for your own sake, that you will end this fasherie; for, Stephen, ye maun pay or flit.'

'The Lord forgie your opinion,' said Stephen, driven almost to his wit's end – 'I am an honest man.'

'So am I, Stephen,' said his honour; 'and so are all the folks in the house, I hope. But if there be a knave amongst us, it must be he that tells the story he cannot prove.' He paused, and then added, mair sternly, 'If I understand your trick, sir, you want to take advantage of some malicious reports concerning things in this family, and particularly respecting my father's sudden death, thereby to cheat me out of the money, and perhaps take away my character, by insinuating that I have received the rent I am demanding. Where do you suppose this money to be? – I insist upon knowing.'

My gudesire saw everything look sae muckle against him, that he grew nearly desperate – however, he shifted from one foot to another, looked to every corner of the room, and made no answer.

'Speak out, sirrah,' said the laird, assuming a look of his father's, a very particular ane, which he had when he was angry – it seemed as if the wrinkles of his frown made that selfsame fearful shape of a horse's shoe in the middle of his brow – 'Speak out, sir! I *will* know your thoughts; – do you suppose that I have this money?'

'Far be it frae me to say so,' said Stephen.

'Do you charge any of my people with having taken it?'

'I wad be laith to charge them that may be innocent,' said my gudesire; 'and if there be anyone that is guilty, I have nae proof.'

'Somewhere the money must be, if there is a word of truth in your story,' said Sir John; 'I ask where you think it is – and demand a correct answer?'

'In hell, if you *will* have my thoughts of it,' said my gudesire, driven to extremity – 'in hell! with your father, his jackanapes and his silver whistle.'

Down the stairs he ran (for the parlour was nae place for him after such a word), and he heard the laird swearing blood and wounds behind him, as fast as ever did Sir Robert, and roaring for the bailie and the baron-officer.

Away rode my gudesire to his chief creditor (him they caa'd Laurie Lapraik) to try if he could make onything out of him; but when he tauld his story, he got but the warst word in his wame – thief, beggar and dyvour were the saftest terms; and to the boot of these hard terms, Laurie brought up the auld story of his dipping his hand in the blood of God's saunts, just as if a tenant could have helped riding with the laird, and that a laird like Sir Robert Redgauntlet. My gudesire was, by this time, far beyond the bounds of patience, and, while he and Laurie were at deil speed the liars, he was wanchancie aneugh to abuse Lapraik's doctrine as weel as the man, and said things that garr'd folk's flesh grue that heard them – he wasna just himsell, and he had lived wi' a wild set in his day.

At last they parted, and my gudesire was to ride hame through the wood of Pitmurkie, that is a' fou of black firs, as they say. I ken the wood, but the firs may be black or white for what I can tell. At the entry of the wood there is a wild common, and on the edge of the common, a little lonely change-house, that was keepit then by an ostler-wife (they suld hae caa'd her Tibbie Faw), and there puir Steenie cried for a mutchkin of brandy, for he had had no refreshment the haill day. Tibbie was earnest wi' him to take a bite of meat, but he couldna think o't, nor would he take his foot out of the stirrup, and took off the brandy wholely at twa draughts, and named a toast at each: the first was the memory of Sir Robert Redgauntlet, and might he never lie quiet in his grave till he had righted his poor bond-tenant; and the second was a health to Man's Enemy, if he would but get him back the pock of siller, or tell him what came o't, for he saw the haill world was like to regard him as a thief and a cheat, and he took that waur than even the ruin of his house and hauld.

On he rode, little caring where. It was dark night turned, and the trees made it yet darker, and he had let the beast take its ain road through the wood when, all of a sudden, from tired and wearied that it was before, the nag began sae to spring and flee and stend that my gudesire could hardly keep the saddle. Upon the whilk, a horseman, suddenly riding up beside him, said: 'That's a mettle beast of yours, freend; will you sell him?' – So saying, he touched the horse's neck with his riding-wand, and it fell into its auld heigh-ho of a stumbling trot. 'But his spunk's soon out of him, I think,' continued the stranger, 'and that is like mony a man's courage, that thinks he wad do great things till he come to the proof.'

My gudesire scarce listened to this, but spurred his horse, with, 'Gude-e'en to you, freend.'

But it's like the stranger was ane that doesna lightly yield his point; for, ride as Steenie liked, he was aye beside him at the selfsame pace. At last, my gudesire, Steenie Steenson, grew half angry; and, to say the truth, half feared.

'What is it that ye want with me, freend?' he said. 'If ye be a robber, I have nae money; if ye be a leal man, wanting company, I have nae heart to mirth or speaking; and if ye want to ken the road, I scarce ken it mysell.'

'If you will tell me your grief,' said the stranger, 'I am one that, though I have been sair miscaa'd in the world, am the only hand for helping my freends.'

So my gudesire, to ease his ain heart, mair than from any hope of help, told him the story from beginning to end.

'It's a hard pinch,' said the stranger; 'but I think I can help you.'

'If you could lend the money, sir, and take a lang day – I ken nae other help on earth,' said my gudesire.

'But there may be some under the earth,' said the stranger. 'Come, I'll be frank wi' you; I could lend you the money on bond, but you would maybe scruple my terms. Now, I can tell you that your auld laird is disturbed in his grave by your curses, and the wailing of your family, and if ye daur venture to go to see him, he will give you the receipt.'

My gudesire's hair stood on end at this proposal, but he thought his companion might be some humoursome chield that was trying to frighten him, and might end with lending him the money. Besides, he was bauld wi' brandy and desperate wi' distress; and he said he had courage to go to the gate of hell, and a step farther, for that receipt. The stranger laughed.

Weel, they rode on through the thickest of the wood, when, all of a sudden, the horse stopped at the door of a great house; and, but that he knew the place was ten miles off, my father would have thought he was at Redgauntlet Castle. They rode into the outer courtyard, through the muckle faulding yetts, and aneath the auld portcullis; and the whole front of the house was lighted, and there were pipes and fiddles, and as much dancing and deray within as used to be in Sir Robert's house at Pace and Yule, and such high seasons. They lap off, and my gudesire, as seemed to him, fastened his horse to the very ring he had tied him to that morning, when he gaed to wait on the young Sir John.

'God!' said my gudesire, 'if Sir Robert's death be but a dream.'

He knocked at the ha' door just as he was wont, and his auld acquaintance, Dougal MacCallum – just after his wont, too – came to open the door, and said: 'Piper Steenie, are ye there, lad? Sir Robert has been crying for you.'

My gudesire was like a man in a dream – he looked for the stranger, but he was gane for the time. At last he just tried to say: 'Ha! Dougal Driveower, are ye living? I thought ye had been dead.'

'Never fash yoursell wi' me,' said Dougal, 'but look to yourself; and see ye tak naething frae onybody here, neither meat, drink or siller, except just the receipt that is your ain.'

So saying, he led the way out through halls and trances that were weel kend to my gudesire, and into the auld oak parlour; and there was as much singing of profane sangs and birling of red wine and speaking blasphemy and sculduddry as had ever been in Redgauntlet Castle when it was at the blithest.

But, Lord take us in keeping! what a set of ghastly revellers they were that sat round that table! – My gudesire kend mony that had long before gane to their place, for often had he piped to the most part in the hall of Redgauntlet. There was the fierce Middleton, and the dissolute Rothes, and the crafty Lauderdale; and Dalyell, with his bald head and a beard to his girdle; and Earlshall, with Cameron's blude on his hand; and wild Bonshaw, that tied blessed Mr Cargill's limbs till the blude sprang; and Dunbarton Douglas, the twice-turned traitor baith to country and king. There was the Bluidy Advocate MacKenyie, who, for his worldly wit and wisdom, had been to the rest as a god. And there was Claverhouse, as beautiful as when he lived, with his long, dark, curled locks, streaming down over his laced buff-coat, and his left hand always on his right spule-blade, to hide the wound that the silver bullet had made. He sat apart from them all, and looked at them with a melancholy, haughty countenance; while the rest hallooed, and sang, and laughed, that the room rang. But their smiles were fearfully contorted from time to time; and their laughter passed into such wild sounds as made my gudesire's very nails grow blue and chilled the marrow in his banes.

They that waited at the table were just the wicked serving-men and troopers that had done their work and cruel bidding on earth. There was the Lang Lad of the Nethertown, that helped to take Argyle; and the bishop's summoner, that they called the Deil's Rattlebag; and the wicked guardsmen, in their laced coats; and the savage Highland Amorites, that shed blood like water; and many a proud serving-man, haughty of heart and bloody of hand, cringing to the rich, and making them wickeder than they would be; grinding the poor to powder, when the rich had broken them to fragments. And mony, mony mair were coming and ganging, a' as busy in their vocation as if they had been alive.

Sir Robert Redgauntlet, in the midst of a' this fearful riot, cried, wi' a voice like thunder, on Steenie Piper to come to the board-head where he was sitting; his legs stretched out before him, and swathed up with flannel, with his holster pistols aside him, while the great broadsword rested against his chair, just as my gudesire had seen him the last time upon earth – the very cushion for the jackanapes was close to him, but the creature itsell was not there – it wasna its hour, it's likely; for he heard them say as he came forward, 'Is not the major come yet?' And another answered: 'The jackanapes will be here betimes the morn.' And when my gudesire came forward, Sir Robert, or his ghaist, or the deevil in his likeness, said: 'Weel, piper, hae ye settled wi' my son for the year's rent?'

With much ado my father gat breath to say that Sir John would not settle without his honour's receipt.

'Ye shall hae that for a tune of the pipes, Steenie,' said the appearance of Sir Robert. 'Play us up "Weel hoddled, Luckie".'

Now this was a tune my gudesire learned frae a warlock, that heard it when they were worshipping Satan at their meetings; and my gudesire had sometimes played it at the ranting suppers in Redgauntlet Castle, but never very willingly; and now he grew cauld at the very name of it, and said, for excuse, he hadna his pipes wi' him.

'MacCallum, ye limb of Beelzebub,' said the fearfu' Sir Robert, 'bring Steenie the pipes that I am keeping for him!'

MacCallum brought a pair of pipes might have served the piper of Donald of the Isles. But he gave my gudesire a nudge as he offered them; and looking secretly and closely, Steenie saw that the chanter was of steel, and heated to a white heat; so he had fair warning not to trust his fingers with it. So he excused himself again, and said he was faint and frightened, and had not wind aneugh to fill the bag.

'Then ye maun eat and drink, Steenie,' said the figure; 'for we do little else here; and it's ill speaking between a fou man and a fasting.'

Now these were the very words that the bloody Earl of Douglas said to keep the king's messenger in hand, while he cut the head off MacLellan of Bombie, at the Threave Castle; and that put Steenie mair and mair on his guard. So he spoke up like a man, and said he came neither to eat, or drink, or make minstrelsy; but simply for his ain – to ken what was come o' the money he had paid, and to get a discharge for it; and he was so stout-hearted by this time, that he charged Sir Robert for conscience-sake – he had no power to say the holy name – and as he hoped for peace and rest, to spread no snares for him, but just to give him his ain.

The appearance gnashed its teeth and laughed, but it took from a large pocket-book the receipt, and handed it to Steenie. 'There is your receipt, ye pitiful cur; and for the money, my dog-whelp of a son may go look for it in the Cat's Cradle.'

My gudesire uttered mony thanks, and was about to retire, when Sir Robert roared aloud: 'Stop though, thou sack-doudling son of a whore! I am not done with thee. Here we do nothing for nothing; and you must return on this very day twelvemonth, to pay your master the homage that you owe me for my protection.'

My father's tongue was loosed of a suddenty, and he said aloud: 'I refer mysell to God's pleasure, and not to yours.'

He had no sooner uttered the word than all was dark around him; and he sank on the earth with such a sudden shock that he lost both breath and sense.

How lang Steenie lay there, he could not tell; but when he came to himsell, he was lying in the auld kirkyard of Redgauntlet parochine, just at the door of the family aisle, and the scutcheon of the auld knight, Sir Robert, hanging over his head. There was a deep morning fog on grass and gravestane around him, and his horse was feeding quietly beside the minister's twa cows. Steenie would have thought the whole was a dream, but he had the receipt in his hand, fairly written and signed by the auld laird; only the last letters of his name were a little disorderly, written like one seized with sudden pain.

Sorely troubled in his mind, he left that dreary place, rode through the mist to Redgauntlet Castle, and with much ado he got speech of the laird.

'Well, you dyvour bankrupt,' was the first word, 'have you brought me my rent?'

'No,' answered my gudesire, 'I have not, but I have brought your honour Sir Robert's receipt for it.'

'How, sirrah? – Sir Robert's receipt! – You told me he had not given you one.'

'Will your honour please to see if that bit line is right?'

Sir John looked at every line, and at every letter, with much attention; and at last, at the date, which my gudesire had not observed: 'From my appointed place,' he read, 'this twenty-fifth of November. What! – That is yesterday! Villain, thou must have gone to hell for this!'

'I got it from your honour's father – whether he be in heaven or hell, I know not,' said Steenie.

'I will delate you for a warlock to the privy council!' said Sir John. 'I will send you to your master, the devil, with the help of a tar-barrel and a torch!'

'I intend to delate mysell to the presbytery,' said Steenie, 'and tell them all I have seen last night, whilk are things fitter for them to judge of than a borrel man like me.'

Sir John paused, composed himsell, and desired to hear the full history; and my gudesire told it him from point to point, as I have told it you – word for word, neither more nor less.

Sir John was silent again for a long time, and at last he said, very composedly: 'Steenie, this story of yours concerns the honour of many a noble family besides mine; and if it be a leasing-making, to keep yourself out of my danger, the least you can expect is to have a red-hot iron driven through your tongue, and that will be as bad as scauding your fingers with a red-hot chanter. But yet it may be true, Steenie; and if the money is cast up, I shall not know what to think of it. – But where shall we find the Cat's Cradle? There are cats enough about the old house, but I think they kitten without the ceremony of bed or cradle.'

'We were best ask Hutcheon,' said my gudesire; 'he kens a' the odd corners about as weel as – as another serving-man that is now gane, and that I wad not like to name.'

Aweel, Hutcheon, when he was asked, told them that a ruinous turret, lang disused, next to the clock-house, only accessible by a ladder, for the opening was on the outside, and far above the battlements, was called of old the Cat's Cradle.

'There will I go immediately,' said Sir John; and he took (with what purpose, heaven kens) one of his father's pistols from the hall-table, where they had lain since the night he died, and hastened to the battlements.

It was a dangerous place to climb, for the ladder was auld and frail, and wanted ane or twa rounds. However, up got Sir John, and entered at the turret door, where his body stopped the only little light that was in the bit turret. Something flees at him wi' a vengeance, maist dang him back ower – bang gaed the knight's pistol, and Hutcheon, that held the ladder, and my gudesire that stood beside him, hears a loud skelloch. A minute after, Sir John flings the body of the jackanapes down to them, and cries that the siller is fund, and that they should come up and help him. And there was the bag of siller, sure aneugh, and mony orra things besides that had been missing for mony a day. And Sir John, when he had riped the turret weel, led my gudesire into the dining-parlour, and took him by the hand, and spoke kindly to him, and said he was sorry he should have doubted his word, and that he would hereafter be a good master to him, to make amends.

'And now, Steenie,' said Sir John, 'although this vision of yours tends, on the whole, to my father's credit, as an honest man, that he should, even after his death, desire to see justice done to a poor man like you, yet you are sensible that ill-dispositioned men might make bad constructions upon it, concerning his soul's health. So, I think, we had better lay the haill dirdum on that ill-deedie creature, Major Weir, and say naething about your dream in the wood of Pitmurkie. You had taken ower muckle brandy to be very certain about onything; and, Steenie, this receipt – ' his hand shook while he held it out – 'it's but a queer kind of document, and we will do best, I think, to put it quietly in the fire.'

'Od, but for as queer as it is, it's a' the voucher I have for my rent,' said my gudesire, who was afraid, it may be, of losing the benefit of Sir Robert's discharge.

'I will bear the contents to your credit in the rental-book, and give you a discharge under my own hand,' said Sir John, 'and that on the spot. And, Steenie, if you can hold your tongue about this matter, you shall sit, from this term downward, at an easier rent.'

'Mony thanks to your honour,' said Steenie, who saw easily in what corner the wind was; 'doubtless I will be conformable to all your honour's commands; only I would willingly speak wi' some powerful minister on the subject, for I do not like the sort of soumons of appointment whilk your honour's father – '

'Do not call the phantom my father!' said Sir John, interrupting him.

'Weel, then, the thing that was so like him,' said my gudesire; 'he spoke of my coming back to him this time twelvemonth, and it's a weight on my conscience.'

'Aweel, then,' said Sir John, 'if you be so much distressed in mind, you may speak to our minister of the parish; he is a douce man, regards the honour of our family, and the mair that he may look for some patronage from me.'

Wi' that, my gudesire readily agreed that the receipt should be burnt, and the laird threw it into the chimney with his ain hand. Burn it would not for them, though; but away it flew up the lum, wi' a lang train of sparks at its tail, and a hissing noise like a squib.

My gudesire gaed down to the manse, and the minister, when he had heard the story, said it was his real opinion that though my gudesire had gaen very far in tampering with dangerous matters, yet, as he had refused the devil's arles (for such was the offer of meat and drink) and had refused to do homage by piping at his bidding, he hoped that, if he held a circumspect walk hereafter, Satan could take little advantage by what was come and gane. And, indeed, my gudesire, of his ain accord, long forswore baith the pipes and the brandy – it was not even till the year was out, and the fatal day passed, that he would so much as take the fiddle or drink usquebaugh or tippenny.

Sir John made up his story about the jackanapes as he liked himself; and some believe till this day there was no more in the matter than the filching nature of the brute. Indeed, ye'll no hinder some to threap that it was nane o' the Auld Enemy that Dougal and my gudesire saw in the laird's room but only that wanchancy creature, the major, capering on the coffin; and that, as to the blawing on the laird's whistle that was heard after he was dead, the filthy brute could do that as weel as the laird himself, if no better. But heaven kens the truth, whilk first came out by the minister's wife, after Sir John and her ain gudeman were baith in the moulds. And then my gudesire, wha was failed in his limbs, but not in his judgement or memory – at least, nothing to speak of – was obliged to tell the real narrative to his freends, for the credit of his good name. He might else have been charged for a warlock.

My Aunt Margaret's Mirror

Sir Walter Scott

My Aunt Margaret was one of that respected sisterhood upon whom devolve all the trouble and solicitude incidental to the possession of children, excepting only that which attends their entrance into the world. We were a large family, of very different dispositions and constitutions. Some were dull and peevish – they were sent to Aunt Margaret to be amused; some were rude, romping and boisterous – they were sent to Aunt Margaret to be kept quiet, or rather that their noise might be removed out of hearing; those who were indisposed were sent with the prospect of being nursed; those who were stubborn, with the hope of their being subdued by the kindness of Aunt Margaret's discipline; in short, she had all the various duties of a mother, without the credit and dignity of the maternal character. The busy scene of her various cares is now over. Of the invalids and the robust, the kind and the rough, the peevish and pleased children, who thronged her little parlour from morning to night, not one now remains alive but myself, who, afflicted by early infirmity, was one of the most delicate of her nurslings, yet, nevertheless, have outlived them all.

It is still my custom, and shall be so while I have the use of my limbs, to visit my respected relation at least three times a week. Her abode is about half a mile from the suburbs of the town in which I reside, and is accessible, not only by the highroad, from which it stands at some distance, but by means of a greensward footpath leading through some pretty meadows. I have so little left to torment me in life, that it is one of my greatest vexations to know that several of these sequestered fields have been devoted as sites for building. In that which is nearest the town, wheelbarrows have been at work for several weeks in such numbers that I verily believe its whole surface, to the depth of at least eighteen inches, was mounted in these monotrochs at the same moment and in the act of being transported from one place to another. Huge triangular piles of planks are also reared in different parts of the devoted messuage; and a little group of trees that still grace the eastern end, which rises in a gentle ascent, have just received warning to quit, expressed by a daub of white paint, and are to give place to a curious grove of chimneys.

It would, perhaps, hurt others in my situation to reflect that this little range of pasturage once belonged to my father (whose family was of some consideration in the world), and was sold by patches to remedy distresses in which he involved himself in an attempt by commercial adventure to redeem his diminished fortune. While the building scheme was in full operation, this circumstance was often pointed out to me by the class of friends who are anxious that no part of your misfortunes should escape your observation. 'Such pasture-ground! – lying at the very town's end – in turnips and potatoes, the parks would bring £20 per acre; and if leased for building – oh, it was a gold mine! And all sold for an old song out of the ancient possessor's hands!' My comforters cannot bring me to repine much on this subject. If I could be allowed to look back on the past without interruption, I could willingly give up the enjoyment of present income and the hope of future profit to those who have purchased what my father sold. I regret the alteration of the ground only because it destroys associations, and I would more willingly (I think) see the Earl's Closes in the hands of strangers, retaining their silvan appearance, than know them for my own, if torn up by agriculture or covered with buildings. Mine are the sensations of poor Logan:

> The horrid plough has rased the green
> Where yet a child I strayed;
> The axe has fell'd the hawthorn screen,
> The schoolboy's summer shade.

I hope, however, the threatened devastation will not be consummated in my day. Although the adventurous spirit of times short while since passed gave rise to the undertaking, I have been encouraged to think that the subsequent changes have so far damped the spirit of speculation that the rest of the woodland footpath leading to Aunt Margaret's retreat will be left undisturbed for her time and mine. I am interested in this, for every step of the way, after I have passed through the green already mentioned, has for me something of early remembrance. There is the stile at which I can recollect a cross child's-maid upbraiding me with my infirmity as she lifted me coarsely and carelessly over the flinty steps, which my brothers traversed with shout and bound. I remember the suppressed bitterness of the moment, and, conscious of my own inferiority, the feeling of envy with which I regarded the easy movements and elastic steps of my more happily formed brethren. Alas! these goodly barks have all perished on life's wide ocean, and only that which seemed so little seaworthy, as the naval phrase goes, has reached the port when the tempest is over. Then there is the pool, where, manoeuvring our little navy, constructed out of the broad water-flags, my elder brother fell in, and was scarce saved from the watery element to die under Nelson's banner. There is the hazel copse also, in which my brother Henry used to gather nuts, thinking little that he was to die in an Indian jungle in quest of rupees.

There is so much more of remembrance about the little walk, that – as I stop, rest on my crutch-headed cane, and look round with that species of comparison between the thing I was and that which I now am – it almost induces me to doubt my own identity; until I find myself in face of the honeysuckle porch of Aunt Margaret's dwelling, with its irregularity of front, and its odd, projecting latticed windows, where the workmen seem to have made it a study that no one of them should resemble another in form, size, or in the old-fashioned stone entablature and labels which adorn them. This tenement, once the manor house of the Earl's Closes, we still retain a slight hold upon; for, in some family arrangements, it had been settled upon Aunt Margaret during the term of her life. Upon this frail tenure depends, in a great measure, the last shadow of the family of Bothwell of Earl's Closes, and their last slight connection with their paternal inheritance. The only representative will then be an infirm old man, moving not unwillingly to the grave, which has devoured all that were dear to his affections.

When I have indulged such thoughts for a minute or two, I enter the mansion, which is said to have been the gatehouse only of the original building, and find one being on whom time seems to have made little impression; for the Aunt Margaret of today bears the same proportional age to the Aunt Margaret of my early youth that the boy of ten years old does to the man of (by'r Lady!) some fifty-six years. The old lady's invariable costume has doubtless some share in confirming one in the opinion that time has stood still with Aunt Margaret.

The brown or chocolate-coloured silk gown, with ruffles of the same stuff at the elbow, within which are others of Mechlin lace; the black silk gloves, or mitts; the white hair combed back upon a roll; and the cap of spotless cambric, which closes around the venerable countenance – as they were not the costume of 1780, so neither were they that of 1826; they are altogether a style peculiar to the individual Aunt Margaret. There she still sits, as she sat thirty years since, with her wheel or the stocking, which she works by the fire in winter and by the window in summer; or, perhaps, venturing as far as the porch in an unusually fine summer evening. Her frame, like some well-constructed piece of mechanics, still performs the operations for which it had seemed destined – going its round with an activity which is gradually diminished, yet indicating no probability that it will soon come to a period.

The solicitude and affection which had made Aunt Margaret the willing slave to the inflictions of a whole nursery, have now for their object the health and comfort of one old and infirm man – the last remaining relative of her family, and the only one who can still find interest in the traditional stores which she hoards, as some miser hides the gold which he desires that no one should enjoy after his death.

My conversation with Aunt Margaret generally relates little either to the present or to the future. For the passing day we possess as much as we require, and we neither of us wish for more; and for that which is to follow, we have, on this side of the grave, neither hopes, nor fears, nor anxiety. We therefore naturally look back to the past, and forget the present fallen fortunes and declined importance of our family in recalling the hours when it was wealthy and prosperous.

With this slight introduction, the reader will know as much of Aunt Margaret and her nephew as is necessary to comprehend the following conversation and narrative.

Last week, when, late in a summer evening, I went to call on the old lady to whom my reader is now introduced, I was received by her with all her usual affection and benignity, while, at the same time, she seemed abstracted and disposed to silence. I asked her the reason. 'They have been clearing out the old chapel,' she said; 'John Clayhudgeons having, it seems, discovered that the stuff within – being, I suppose, the remains of our ancestors – was excellent for top-dressing the meadows.'

Here I started up with more alacrity than I have displayed for some years; but sat down while my aunt added, laying her hand upon my sleeve, 'The chapel has been long considered as common ground, my dear, and used for a pinfold, and what objection can we have to the man for employing what is his own to his own profit? Besides, I did speak to him, and he very readily and civilly promised that if he found bones or monuments, they should be carefully respected and reinstated; and what more could I ask? So, the first stone they found bore the name of Margaret Bothwell, 1585, and I have caused it to be laid carefully aside, as I think it betokens death, and having served my namesake two hundred years, it has just been cast up in time to do me the same good turn. My house has been long put in order, as far as the small earthly concerns require it; but who shall say that their account with heaven is sufficiently revised?'

'After what you have said, aunt,' I replied, 'perhaps I ought to take my hat and go away; and so I should, but that there is on this occasion a little alloy mingled with your devotion. To think of death at all times is a duty – to suppose it nearer from the finding an old gravestone is superstition; and you, with your strong, useful common sense, which was so long the prop of a fallen family, are the last person whom I should have suspected of such weakness.'

'Neither would I deserve your suspicions, kinsman,' answered Aunt Margaret, 'if we were speaking of any incident occurring in the actual business of human life. But for all this, I have a sense of superstition about me, which I do not wish to part with. It is a feeling which separates me from this age, and links me with that to which I am hastening; and even when it seems, as now, to lead me to the brink of the grave, and bid me gaze on it, I do not love that it should be dispelled. It soothes my imagination, without influencing my reason or conduct.'

'I profess, my good lady,' replied I, 'that had anyone but you made such a declaration, I should have thought it as capricious as that of the clergyman, who, without vindicating his false reading, preferred, from habit's sake, his old Mumpsimus to the modern Sumpsimus.'

'Well,' answered my aunt, 'I must explain my inconsistency in this particular by comparing it to another. I am, as you know, a piece of that old-fashioned thing called a Jacobite; but I am so in sentiment and feeling only, for a more loyal subject never joined in prayers for the health and wealth of George IV, whom God long preserve! But I dare say that kind-hearted sovereign would not deem that an old woman did him much injury if she leaned back in her armchair, just in such a twilight as this, and thought of the high-mettled men whose sense of duty called them to arms against his great-grandfather; and how, in a cause which they deemed that of their rightful prince and country,

> They fought till their hand to the broadsword was glued,
> They fought against fortune with hearts unsubdued.

Do not come at such a moment, when my head is full of plaids, pibrochs and claymores, and ask my reason to admit what, I am afraid, it cannot deny – I mean, that the public advantage peremptorily demanded that these things should cease to exist. I cannot, indeed, refuse to allow the justice of your reasoning; but yet, being convinced against my will, you will gain little by your motion. You might as well read to an infatuated lover the catalogue of his mistress's imperfections; for when he has been compelled to listen to the summary, you will only get for answer that "he lo'es her a' the better". '

I was not sorry to have changed the gloomy train of Aunt Margaret's thoughts, and replied in the same tone, 'Well, I can't help being persuaded that our good king is the more sure of Mrs Bothwell's loyal affection that he has the Stewart right of birth as well as the Act of Succession in his favour.'

'Perhaps my attachment, were its source of consequence, might be found warmer for the union of the rights you mention,' said Aunt Margaret; 'but, upon my word, it would be as sincere if the king's right were founded only on the will of the nation, as declared at the Revolution. I am none of your *Jure Divino* folks.'

'And a Jacobite notwithstanding.'

'And a Jacobite notwithstanding – or rather, I will give you leave to call me one of the party which, in Queen Anne's time, were called, *whimsicals*, because they were sometimes operated upon by feelings, sometimes by principle. After all, it is very hard that you will not allow an old woman to be as inconsistent in her political sentiments as mankind in general show themselves in all the various courses of life; since you cannot point out one of them in which the passions and prejudices of those who pursue it are not perpetually carrying us away from the path which our reason points out.'

'True, aunt; but you are a wilful wanderer, who should be forced back into the right path.'

'Spare me, I entreat you,' replied Aunt Margaret. 'You remember the Gaelic song, though I dare say I mispronounce the words – "Hatil mohatil, na dowski mi." [I am asleep, do not waken me.] I tell you, kinsman, that the sort of waking dreams which my imagination spins out, in what your favourite Wordsworth calls 'moods of my own mind', are worth all the rest of my more active days. Then, instead of looking forward, as I did in youth, and forming for myself fairy palaces, upon the verge of the grave I turn my eyes backward upon the days and manners of my better time; and the sad, yet soothing recollections come so close and interesting, that I almost think it sacrilege to be wiser or more rational or less prejudiced than those to whom I looked up in my younger years.'

'I think I now understand what you mean,' I answered, 'and can comprehend why you should occasionally prefer the twilight of illusion to the steady light of reason.'

'Where there is no task,' she rejoined, 'to be performed, we may sit in the dark if we like it; if we go to work, we must ring for candles.'

'And amidst such shadowy and doubtful light,' continued I, 'imagination frames her enchanted and enchanting visions, and sometimes passes them upon the senses for reality.'

'Yes,' said Aunt Margaret, who is a well-read woman, 'to those who resemble the translator of Tasso –

> Prevailing poet, whose undoubting mind
> Believed the magic wonders which he sung.

It is not required for this purpose that you should be sensible of the painful horrors which an actual belief in such prodigies inflicts. Such a belief nowadays belongs only to fools and children. It is not necessary that your ears should tingle and your complexion change, like that of Theodore at the approach of the spectral huntsman. All that is indispensable for the enjoyment of the milder feeling of supernatural awe is that you should be susceptible of the slight shuddering which creeps over you when you hear a tale of terror – that well-vouched tale which the narrator, having first expressed his general disbelief of all such legendary lore, selects and produces, as having something in it which he has been always obliged to give up as inexplicable. Another symptom is a momentary hesitation to look round you, when the interest of the narrative is at the highest; and the third, a desire to avoid looking into a mirror when you are alone in your chamber for the evening. I mean such are signs which indicate the crisis, when a female imagination is in due temperature to enjoy a ghost story. I do not pretend to describe those which express the same disposition in a gentleman.'

'That last symptom, dear aunt, of shunning the mirror seems likely to be a rare occurrence amongst the fair sex.'

'You are a novice in toilet fashions, my dear cousin. All women consult the looking-glass with anxiety before they go into company; but when they return home, the mirror has not the same charm. The die has been cast – the party has been successful or unsuccessful in the impression which she desired to make. But, without going deeper into the mysteries of the dressing-table, I will tell you that I myself, like many other honest folks, do not like to see the blank, black front of a large mirror in a room dimly lighted, and where the reflection of the candle seems rather to lose itself in the deep obscurity of the glass than to be reflected back again into the apartment, That space of inky darkness seems to be a field for Fancy to play her revels in. She may call up other features to meet us, instead of the reflection of our own; or, as in the spells of Hallowe'en, which we learned in childhood, some unknown form may be seen peeping over our shoulder. In short, when I am in a ghost-seeing humour, I make my handmaiden draw the green curtains over the mirror before I go into the room, so that she may have the first shock of the apparition, if there be any to be seen, But, to tell you the truth, this dislike to look into a mirror in particular times and places has, I believe, its original foundation in a story which came to me by tradition from my grandmother, who was a party concerned in the scene of which I will now tell you.'

I

You are fond [said my aunt] of sketches of the society which has passed away. I wish I could describe to you Sir Philip Forester, the 'chartered libertine' of Scottish good company, about the end of the last century. I never saw him indeed; but my mother's traditions were full of his wit, gallantry and dissipation. This gay knight flourished about the end of the seventeenth and beginning of the eighteenth century. He was the Sir Charles Easy and the Lovelace of his day and country – renowned for the number of duels he had fought, and the successful intrigues which he had carried on. The supremacy which he had attained in the fashionable world was absolute; and when we combine it with one or two anecdotes, for which, 'if laws were made for every degree', he ought certainly to have been hanged, the popularity of such a person really serves to show, either that the present times are much more decent, if not more virtuous, than they formerly were, or that high-breeding then was of more difficult attainment than that which is now so called, and consequently entitled the successful professor to a proportional degree of plenary indulgences and privileges. No beau of this day could have borne out so ugly a story as that of Pretty Peggy Grindstone, the miller's daughter at Sillermills – it had well-nigh made work for the Lord Advocate. But it hurt Sir Philip Forester no more than the hail hurts the hearthstone. He was as well received in society as ever, and dined with the Duke of A— the day the poor girl was buried. She died of heartbreak. But that has nothing to do with my story.

Now, you must listen to a single word upon kith, kin and ally; I promise you I will not be prolix. But it is necessary to the authenticity of my legend that you should know that Sir Philip Forester, with his handsome person, elegant accomplishments and fashionable manners, married the younger Miss Falconer of King's Copland. The elder sister of this lady had previously become the wife of my grandfather, Sir Geoffrey Bothwell, and brought into our family a good fortune. Miss Jemima, or Miss Jemmie Falconer, as she was usually called, had also about ten thousand pounds sterling – then thought a very handsome portion indeed.

The two sisters were extremely different, though each had their admirers while they remained single. Lady Bothwell had some touch of the old King's Copland blood about her. She was bold, though not to the degree of audacity, ambitious and desirous to raise her house and family; and was, as has been said, a considerable spur to my grandfather, who was otherwise an indolent man, but whom, unless he has been slandered, his lady's influence involved in some political matters which had been more wisely let alone. She was a woman of high principle, however, and masculine good sense, as some of her letters testify, which are still in my wainscot cabinet.

Jemmie Falconer was the reverse of her sister in every respect. Her understanding did not reach above the ordinary pitch, if, indeed, she could be said to have attained it. Her beauty, while it lasted, consisted, in a great measure, of delicacy of complexion and regularity of features, without any peculiar force of expression. Even these charms faded under the sufferings attendant on an ill-assorted match. She was passionately attached to her husband, by whom she was treated with a callous yet polite indifference, which, to one whose heart was as tender as her judgement was weak, was more painful perhaps than absolute ill-usage. Sir Philip was a voluptuary – that is, a completely selfish egotist – whose disposition and character resembled the rapier he wore, polished, keen and brilliant, but inflexible and unpitying. As he observed carefully all the usual forms towards his lady, he had the art to deprive her even of the compassion of the world; and useless and unavailing as that may be while actually possessed by the sufferer, it is, to a mind like Lady Forester's, most painful to know she has it not.

The tattle of society did its best to place the peccant husband above the suffering wife. Some called her a poor, spiritless thing, and declared that, with a little of her sister's spirit, she might have brought to reason any Sir Philip whatsoever, were it the termagant

Falconbridge himself. But the greater part of their acquaintance affected candour, and saw faults on both sides – though, in fact, there only existed the oppressor and the oppressed. The tone of such critics was, 'To be sure, no one will justify Sir Philip Forester, but then we all know Sir Philip, and Jemmie Falconer might have known what she had to expect from the beginning. What made her set her cap at Sir Philip? He would never have looked at her if she had not thrown herself at his head, with her poor ten thousand pounds. I am sure, if it is money he wanted, she spoiled his market. I know where Sir Philip could have done much better. And then, if she *would* have the man, could not she try to make him more comfortable at home, and have his friends oftener, and not plague him with the squalling children, and take care all was handsome and in good style about the house? I declare I think Sir Philip would have made a very domestic man, with a woman who knew how to manage him.'

Now these fair critics, in raising their profound edifice of domestic felicity, did not recollect that the cornerstone was wanting, and that to receive good company with good cheer, the means of the banquet ought to have been furnished by Sir Philip, whose income (dilapidated as it was) was not equal to the display of the hospitality required, and at the same time to the supply of the good knight's *menus plaisirs*. So, in spite of all that was so sagely suggested by female friends, Sir Philip carried his good-humour everywhere abroad, and left at home a solitary mansion and a pining spouse.

At length, inconvenienced in his money affairs, and tired even of the short time which he spent in his own dull house, Sir Philip Forester determined to take a trip to the Continent, in the capacity of a volunteer. It was then common for men of fashion to do so; and our knight perhaps was of opinion that a touch of the military character, just enough to exalt, but not render pedantic, his qualities as a *beau garçon*, was necessary to maintain possession of the elevated situation which he held in the ranks of fashion.

Sir Philip's resolution threw his wife into agonies of terror; by which the worthy baronet was so much annoyed that, contrary to his wont, he took some trouble to soothe her apprehensions, and once more brought her to shed tears, in which sorrow was not altogether unmingled with pleasure. Lady Bothwell asked, as a favour, Sir Philip's permission to receive her sister and her family into her own house during his absence on the Continent. Sir Philip readily assented to a proposition which saved expense, silenced the foolish people who might have talked of a deserted wife and family, and gratified Lady Bothwell, for whom he felt some respect, as for one who often spoke to him, always with freedom and sometimes with severity, without being deterred either by his raillery or the prestige of his reputation.

A day or two before Sir Philip's departure, Lady Bothwell took the liberty of asking him, in her sister's presence, the direct question, which his timid wife had often desired, but never ventured, to put to him: 'Pray, Sir Philip, what route do you take when you reach the Continent?'

'I go from Leith to Helvoet by a packet with advices.'

'That I comprehend perfectly,' said Lady Bothwell dryly; 'but you do not mean to remain long at Helvoet, I presume, and I should like to know what is your next object.'

'You ask me, my dear lady,' answered Sir Philip, 'a question which I have not dared to ask myself. The answer depends on the fate of war. I shall, of course, go to headquarters, wherever they may happen to be for the time; deliver my letters of introduction; learn as much of the noble art of war as may suffice a poor interloping amateur; and then take a glance at the sort of thing of which we read so much in the *Gazette*.'

'And I trust, Sir Philip,' said Lady Bothwell, 'that you will remember that you are a husband and a father; and that, though you think fit to indulge this military fancy, you will not let it hurry you into dangers which it is certainly unnecessary for any save professional persons to encounter.'

'Lady Bothwell does me too much honour,' replied the adventurous knight, 'in regarding such a circumstance with the slightest interest. But to soothe your flattering anxiety, I trust your ladyship will recollect that I cannot expose to hazard the venerable and paternal character which you so obligingly recommend to my protection, without putting in some peril an honest fellow called Philip Forester, with whom I have kept company for thirty years, and with whom, though some folks consider him a coxcomb, I have not the least desire to part.'

'Well, Sir Philip, you are the best judge of your own affairs. I have little right to interfere – you are not my husband.'

'God forbid!' said Sir Philip hastily; instantly adding, however, 'God forbid that I should deprive my friend Sir Geoffrey of so inestimable a treasure.'

'But you are my sister's husband,' replied the lady; 'and I suppose you are aware of her present distress of mind – '

'If hearing of nothing else from morning to night can make me aware of it,' said Sir Philip, 'I should know something of the matter.'

'I do not pretend to reply to your wit, Sir Philip,' answered Lady Bothwell; 'but you must be sensible that all this distress is on account of apprehensions for your personal safety.'

'In that case, I am surprised that Lady Bothwell, at least, should give herself so much trouble upon so insignificant a subject.'

'My sister's interest may account for my being anxious to learn something of Sir Philip Forester's motions; about which, otherwise, I know he would not wish me to concern myself. I have a brother's safety too to be anxious for.'

'You mean Major Falconer, your brother by the mother's side? What can he possibly have to do with our present agreeable conversation?'

'You have had words together, Sir Philip,' said Lady Bothwell.

'Naturally; we are connections,' replied Sir Philip, 'and as such have always had the usual intercourse.'

'That is an evasion of the subject,' answered the lady. 'By words, I mean angry words, on the subject of your usage of your wife.'

'If,' replied Sir Philip Forester, 'you suppose Major Falconer simple enough to intrude his advice upon me, Lady Bothwell, in my domestic matters, you are indeed warranted in believing that I might possibly be so far displeased with the interference as to request him to reserve his advice till it was asked.'

'And being on these terms, you are going to join the very army in which my brother Falconer is now serving?'

'No man knows the path of honour better than Major Falconer,' said Sir Philip. 'An aspirant after fame, like me, cannot choose a better guide than his footsteps.'

Lady Bothwell rose and went to the window, the tears gushing from her eyes.

'And this heartless raillery,' she said, 'is all the consideration that is to be given to our apprehensions of a quarrel which may bring on the most terrible consequences? Good God! of what can men's hearts be made, who can thus dally with the agony of others?'

Sir Philip Forester was moved; he laid aside the mocking tone in which he had hitherto spoken.

'Dear Lady Bothwell,' he said, taking her reluctant hand, 'we are both wrong. You are too deeply serious; I, perhaps, too little so. The dispute I had with Major Falconer was of no earthly consequence. Had anything occurred betwixt us that ought to have been settled *par voie du fait*, as we say in France, neither of us are persons that are likely to postpone such a meeting. Permit me to say that were it generally known that you or my Lady Forester are apprehensive of such a catastrophe, it might be the very means of bringing about what would not otherwise be likely to happen. I know your good sense, Lady Bothwell, and that you will understand me when I say that really my affairs require my absence for some months. This Jemima cannot understand. It is a perpetual recurrence of questions, why can you not do this, or that, or the third thing? and, when you have proved to her that her expedients are totally ineffectual, you have just to begin the whole round again. Now, do you tell her, dear Lady Bothwell, that *you* are satisfied. She is, you must confess, one of those persons with whom authority goes farther than reasoning. Do but repose a little confidence in me, and you shall see how amply I will repay it.'

Lady Bothwell shook her head, as one but half satisfied. 'How difficult it is to extend confidence, when the basis on which it ought to rest has been so much shaken! But I will do my best to make Jemima easy; and further, I can only say that for keeping your present purpose I hold you responsible both to God and man,'

'Do not fear that I will deceive you,' said Sir Philip. 'The safest conveyance to me will be through the general post-office, Helvoet-sluys, where I will take care to leave orders for forwarding my letters. As for Falconer, our only encounter will be over a bottle of Burgundy; so make yourself perfectly easy on his score.'

Lady Bothwell could *not* make herself easy; yet she was sensible that her sister hurt her own cause by *taking on*, as the maidservants call it, too vehemently, and by showing before every stranger, by manner, and sometimes by words also, a dissatisfaction with her husband's journey that was sure to come to his ears, and equally certain to displease him. But there was no help for this domestic dissension, which ended only with the day of separation.

I am sorry I cannot tell, with precision, the year in which Sir Philip Forester went over to Flanders; but it was one of those in which the campaign opened with extraordinary fury, and many bloody, though indecisive, skirmishes were fought between the French on the one side and the Allies on the other. In all our modern improvements, there are none, perhaps, greater than in the accuracy and speed with which intelligence is transmitted from any scene of action to those in this country whom it may concern. During Marlborough's campaigns, the sufferings of the many who had relations in, or along with, the army were greatly augmented by the suspense in which they were detained for weeks after they had heard of bloody battles, in which, in all probability, those for whom their bosoms throbbed with anxiety had been personally engaged. Amongst those who were most agonised by this state of uncertainty was the – I had almost said deserted – wife of the gay Sir Philip Forester. A single letter had informed her of his arrival on the Continent; no others were received. One notice occurred in the newspapers, in which Volunteer Sir Philip Forester was mentioned as having been entrusted with a dangerous reconnaissance, which he had executed with the greatest courage, dexterity and intelligence, and received the thanks of the commanding officer. The sense of his having acquired distinction brought a momentary glow into the lady's pale cheek; but it was instantly lost in ashen whiteness at the recollection of his danger. After this, they had no news whatever, neither from Sir Philip, nor even from their brother Falconer. The case of Lady Forester was not indeed different from that of hundreds in the same situation; but a feeble mind is necessarily an irritable one, and the suspense which some bear with constitutional indifference or philosophical resignation, and some with a disposition to believe and hope the best, was intolerable to Lady Forester, at once solitary and sensitive, low-spirited, and devoid of strength of mind, whether natural or acquired.

2

As she received no further news of Sir Philip, whether directly or indirectly, his unfortunate lady began now to feel a sort of consolation even in those careless habits which had so often given her pain. 'He is so thoughtless,' she repeated a hundred times a day to her sister, 'he never writes when things are going on smoothly. It is his way. Had anything happened, he would have informed us.'

Lady Bothwell listened to her sister without attempting to console her. Probably she might be of opinion that even the worst intelligence which could be received from Flanders might not be without some touch of consolation; and that the Dowager Lady Forester, if so she was doomed to be called, might have a source of happiness unknown to the wife of the gayest and finest gentleman in Scotland. This conviction became stronger as they learned from enquiries made at headquarters that Sir Philip was no longer with the army – though whether he had been taken or slain in some of those skirmishes which were perpetually occurring, and in which he loved to distinguish himself, or whether he had, for some unknown reason or capricious change of mind, voluntarily left the service, none of his countrymen in the camp of the Allies could form even a conjecture. Meantime his creditors at home became clamorous, entered into possession of his property, and threatened his person, should he be rash enough to return to Scotland. These additional disadvantages aggravated Lady Bothwell's displeasure against the fugitive husband; while her sister saw nothing in any of them, save what tended to increase her grief for the absence of him whom her imagination now represented – as it had before marriage – gallant, gay and affectionate.

About this period there appeared in Edinburgh a man of singular appearance and pretensions. He was commonly called the Paduan doctor, from having received his education at that famous university. He was supposed to possess some rare receipts in medicine, with which, it was affirmed, he had wrought remarkable cures. But though, on the one hand, the physicians of Edinburgh termed him an empiric, there were many persons, and among them some of the clergy, who, while they admitted the truth of the cures and the force of his remedies, alleged that Dr Baptista Damiotti made use of charms and unlawful arts in order to obtain success in his practice. The resorting to him was even solemnly preached against, as a seeking of health from idols, and a trusting to the help which was to come from Egypt. But the protection which the Paduan doctor received from some friends of interest and consequence enabled him to set these imputations at defiance, and to assume, even in the city of Edinburgh, famed as it was for abhorrence of witches and necromancers, the dangerous character of an expounder of futurity. It was at length rumoured that, for a certain gratification, which of course was not an inconsiderable one, Dr Baptista Damiotti could tell the fate of the absent, and even show his visitors the personal form of their absent friends, and the action in which they were engaged at the moment. This rumour came to the ears of Lady Forester, who had reached that pitch of mental agony in which the sufferer will do anything, or endure anything, that suspense may be converted into certainty.

Gentle and timid in most cases, her state of mind made her equally obstinate and reckless, and it was with no small surprise and alarm that her sister, Lady Bothwell, heard her express a resolution to visit this man of art, and learn from him the fate of her husband. Lady Bothwell remonstrated on the improbability that such pretensions as those of this foreigner could be founded in anything but imposture.

'I care not,' said the deserted wife, 'what degree of ridicule I may incur; if there be any one chance out of a hundred that I may obtain some certainty of my husband's fate, I would not miss that chance for whatever else the world can offer me.'

Lady Bothwell next urged the unlawfulness of resorting to such sources of forbidden knowledge.

'Sister,' replied the sufferer, 'he who is dying of thirst cannot refrain from drinking even poisoned water. She who suffers under suspense must seek information, even were the powers which offer it unhallowed and infernal. I go to learn my fate alone, and this very evening will I know it; the sun that rises tomorrow shall find me, if not more happy, at least more resigned.'

'Sister,' said Lady Bothwell, 'if you are determined upon this wild step, you shall not go alone. If this man be an impostor, you may be too much agitated by your feelings to detect his villainy. If, which I cannot believe, there be any truth in what he pretends, you shall not be exposed alone to a communication of so extraordinary a nature. I will go with you, if indeed you determine to go. But yet reconsider your project, and renounce enquiries which cannot be prosecuted without guilt, and perhaps without danger.'

Lady Forester threw herself into her sister's arms, and, clasping her to her bosom, thanked her a hundred times for the offer of her company, while she declined with a melancholy gesture the friendly advice with which it was accompanied.

When the hour of twilight arrived – which was the period when the Paduan doctor was understood to receive the visits of those who came to consult with him – the two ladies left their apartments in the Canongate of Edinburgh, having their dress arranged like that of women of an inferior description, and their plaids disposed around their faces as they were worn by the same class; for in those days of aristocracy the quality of the wearer was generally indicated by the manner in which her plaid was disposed, as well as by the fineness of its texture. It was Lady Bothwell who had suggested this species of disguise, partly to avoid observation as they should go to the conjurer's house, and partly in order to make trial of his penetration, by appearing before him in a feigned character. Lady Forester's servant, of tried fidelity, had been employed by her to propitiate the doctor by a suitable fee, and a story intimating that a soldier's wife desired to know the fate of her husband – a subject upon which, in all probability, the sage was very frequently consulted.

To the last moment, when the palace clock struck eight, Lady Bothwell earnestly watched her sister, in hopes that she might retreat from her rash undertaking; but as mildness, and even timidity, is capable at times of vehement and fixed purposes, she found Lady Forester resolutely unmoved and determined when the moment of departure arrived. Ill satisfied with the expedition, but determined not to leave her sister at such a crisis, Lady Bothwell accompanied Lady Forester through more than one obscure street and lane, the servant walking before, and acting as their guide. At length he suddenly turned into a narrow court, and knocked at an arched door which seemed to belong to a building of some antiquity. It opened, though no one appeared to act as porter; and the servant, stepping aside from the entrance, motioned the ladies to enter. They had no sooner done so than it shut, and excluded their guide. The two ladies found themselves in a small vestibule, illuminated by a dim lamp, and having, when the door was closed, no communication with the external light or air. The door of an inner apartment, partly open, was at the farther side of the vestibule.

'We must not hesitate now, Jemima,' said Lady Bothwell, and walked forwards into the inner room, where, surrounded by books, maps, philosophical utensils and other implements of peculiar shape and appearance, they found the man of art.

There was nothing very peculiar in the Italian's appearance. He had the dark complexion and marked features of his country, seemed about fifty years old, and was handsomely but plainly dressed in a full suit of black clothes, which was then the universal costume of the medical profession. Large wax-lights, in silver sconces, illuminated the apartment, which was reasonably furnished. He rose as the ladies entered, and, notwithstanding the inferiority of their dress, received them with the marked respect due to their quality, and which foreigners are usually punctilious in rendering to those to whom such honours are due.

Lady Bothwell endeavoured to maintain her proposed incognito, and, as the doctor ushered them to the upper end of the room, made a motion declining his courtesy, as unfitted for their condition. 'We are poor people, sir,' she said; 'only my sister's distress has brought us to consult your worship whether – '

He smiled as he interrupted her – 'I am aware, madam, of your sister's distress, and its cause; I am aware, also, that I am honoured with a visit from two ladies of the highest consideration – Lady Bothwell and Lady Forester. If I could not distinguish them from the class of society which their present dress would indicate, there would be small possibility of my being able to gratify them by giving the information which they come to seek.'

'I can easily understand – ' said Lady Bothwell.

'Pardon my boldness to interrupt you, milady,' cried the Italian; 'your ladyship was about to say that you could easily understand that I had got possession of your names by means of your domestic. But in thinking so, you do injustice to the fidelity of your servant, and, I may add, to the skill of one who is also not less your humble servant – Baptista Damiotti.'

'I have no intention to do either, sir,' said Lady Bothwell, maintaining a tone of composure, though somewhat surprised; 'but the situation is something new to me. If you know who we are, you also know, sir, what brought us here.'

'Curiosity to know the fate of a Scottish gentleman of rank, now, or lately, upon the Continent,' answered the seer. 'His name is Il Cavaliero Philippo Forester, a gentleman who has the honour to be husband to this lady, and, with your ladyship's permission for using plain language, the misfortune not to value as it deserves that inestimable advantage.'

Lady Forester sighed deeply, and Lady Bothwell replied: 'Since you know our object without our telling it, the only question that remains is whether you have the power to relieve my sister's anxiety?'

'I have, madam,' answered the Paduan scholar; 'but there is still a previous enquiry. Have you the courage to behold with your own eyes what the Cavaliero Philippo Forester is now doing? or will you take it on my report?'

'That question my sister must answer for herself,' said Lady Bothwell.

'With my own eyes will I endure to see whatever you have power to show me,' said Lady Forester, with the same determined spirit which had stimulated her since her resolution was taken upon this subject.

'There may be danger in it.'

'If gold can compensate the risk – ' said Lady Forester, taking out her purse.

'I do not such things for the purpose of gain,' answered the foreigner; 'I dare not turn my art to such a purpose. If I take the gold of the wealthy, it is but to bestow it on the poor; nor do I ever accept more than the sum I have already received from your servant. Put up your purse, madam; an adept needs not your gold,'

Lady Bothwell, considering this rejection of her sister's offer as a mere trick of an empiric to induce her to press a larger sum upon him, and willing that the scene should be commenced and ended, offered some gold in turn, observing that it was only to enlarge the sphere of his charity.

'Let Lady Bothwell enlarge the sphere of her own charity,' said the Paduan, 'not merely in giving of alms, in which I know she is not deficient, but in judging the character of others; and let her oblige Baptista Damiotti by believing him honest, till she shall discover him to be a knave. Do not be surprised, madam, if I speak in answer to your thoughts rather than your expressions; and tell me once more whether you have courage to look on what I am prepared to show?'

'I own, sir,' said Lady Bothwell, 'that your words strike me with some sense of fear; but whatever my sister desires to witness, I will not shrink from witnessing along with her.'

'Nay, the danger only consists in the risk of your resolution failing you. The sight can only last for the space of seven minutes; and should you interrupt the vision by speaking a single word, not only would the charm be broken, but some danger might result to the spectators. But if you can remain steadily silent for the seven minutes, your curiosity will be gratified without the slightest risk; and for this I will engage my honour.'

Internally Lady Bothwell thought the security was but an indifferent one; but she suppressed the suspicion, as if she had believed that the adept, whose dark features wore a half-formed smile, could in reality read even her most secret reflections. A solemn pause then ensued, until Lady Forester gathered courage enough to reply to the physician, as he termed himself, that she would abide with firmness and silence the sight which he had promised to exhibit to them. Upon this, he made them a low obeisance, and saying he went to prepare matters to meet their wish, left the apartment. The two sisters, hand in hand, as if seeking by that close union to divert any danger which might threaten them, sat down on two seats in immediate contact with each other – Jemima seeking support in the manly and habitual courage of Lady Bothwell; and she, on the other hand, more agitated than she had expected, endeavouring to fortify herself by the desperate resolution which circumstances had forced her sister to assume. The one perhaps said to herself that her sister never feared anything; and the other might reflect that what so feeble-minded a woman as Jemima did not fear could not properly be a subject of apprehension to a person of firmness and resolution like her own.

In a few moments the thoughts of both were diverted from their own situation by a strain of music so singularly sweet and solemn that, while it seemed calculated to avert or dispel any feeling unconnected with its harmony, increased, at the same time, the solemn excitation which the preceding interview was calculated to produce. The music was that of some instrument with which they were unacquainted; but circumstances afterwards led my ancestress to believe that it was that of the harmonica, which she heard at a much later period in life.

When these heaven-born sounds had ceased, a door opened in the upper end of the apartment, and they saw Damiotti, standing at the head of two or three steps, sign to them to advance. His dress was so different from that which he had worn a few minutes before that they could hardly recognise him; and the deadly paleness of his countenance, and a certain stern rigidity of muscles, like that of one whose mind is made up to some strange and daring action, had totally changed the somewhat sarcastic expression with which he had previously regarded them both, and particularly Lady Bothwell. He was barefooted, excepting a species of sandals in the antique fashion; his legs were naked beneath the knees; above them he wore hose, and a doublet of dark crimson silk close to his body; and over that a flowing loose robe, something resembling a surplice, of snow-white linen. His throat and neck were uncovered, and his long, straight, black hair was carefully combed down at full length.

As the ladies approached at his bidding, he showed no gesture of that ceremonious courtesy of which he had been formerly lavish. On the contrary, he made the signal of advance with an air of command; and when, arm in arm, and with insecure steps, the sisters approached the spot where he stood, it was with a warning frown that he pressed his finger to his lips, as if reiterating his condition of absolute silence, while, stalking before them, he led the way into the next apartment.

This was a large room, hung with black, as if for a funeral. At the upper end was a table, or rather a species of altar, covered with the same lugubrious colour, on which lay divers objects resembling the usual implements of sorcery. These objects were not indeed visible as they advanced into the apartment; for the light which displayed them, being only that of two expiring lamps, was extremely faint. The master – to use the Italian phrase for persons of this description –

approached the upper end of the room, with a genuflection like that of a Catholic to the crucifix, and at the same time crossed himself. The ladies followed in silence, and arm in arm. Two or three low broad steps led to a platform in front of the altar, or what resembled such. Here the sage took his stand, and placed the ladies beside him, once more earnestly repeating by signs his injunctions of silence. The Italian then, extending his bare arm from under his linen vestment, pointed with his forefinger to five large flambeaux, or torches, placed on each side of the altar. They took fire successively at the approach of his hand, or rather of his finger, and spread a strong light through the room. By this the visitors could discern that, on the seeming altar, were disposed two naked swords laid crosswise; a large open book, which they conceived to be a copy of the Holy Scriptures, but in a language to them unknown; and beside this mysterious volume was placed a human skull. But what struck the sisters most was a very tall and broad mirror, which occupied all the space behind the altar, and, illumined by the lighted torches, reflected the mysterious articles which were laid upon it.

The master then placed himself between the two ladies, and, pointing to the mirror, took each by the hand, but without speaking a syllable. They gazed intently on the polished and sable space to which he had directed their attention. Suddenly the surface assumed a new and singular appearance. It no longer simply reflected the objects placed before it, but, as if it had self-contained scenery of its own, objects began to appear within it, at first in a disorderly, indistinct and miscellaneous manner, like form arranging itself out of chaos; at length, in distinct and defined shape and symmetry. It was thus that, after some shifting of light and darkness over the face of the wonderful glass, a long perspective of arches and columns began to arrange itself on its sides, and a vaulted roof on the upper part of it, till, after many oscillations, the whole vision gained a fixed and stationary appearance, representing the interior of a foreign church. The pillars were stately, and hung with scutcheons; the arches were lofty and magnificent; the floor was lettered with funeral inscriptions. But there were no separate shrines, no images, no display of chalice or crucifix on the altar. It was, therefore, a Protestant church upon the Continent. A clergyman dressed in the Geneva gown and band stood by the communion table, and, with the Bible opened before him and his clerk awaiting in the background, seemed prepared to perform some service of the church to which he belonged.

At length, there entered the middle aisle of the building a numerous party, which appeared to be a bridal one, as a lady and gentleman walked first, hand in hand, followed by a large concourse of persons of both sexes, gaily, nay richly, attired. The bride, whose features they could distinctly see, seemed not more than sixteen years old, and extremely beautiful. The bridegroom, for some seconds, moved rather with his shoulder towards them, and his face averted; but his elegance of form and step struck the sisters at once with the same apprehension. As he turned his face suddenly, it was frightfully realised, and they saw, in the gay bridegroom before them, Sir Philip Forester. His wife uttered an imperfect exclamation, at the sound of which the whole scene stirred and seemed to separate.

'I could compare it to nothing,' said Lady Bothwell, while recounting the wonderful tale, 'but to the dispersion of the reflection offered by a deep and calm pool when a stone is suddenly cast into it, and the shadows become dissipated and broken.' The master pressed both the ladies' hands severely, as if to remind them of their promise, and of the danger which they incurred. The exclamation died away on Lady Forester's tongue, without attaining perfect utterance, and the scene in the glass, after the fluctuation of a minute, again resumed to the eye its former appearance of a real scene, existing within the mirror, as if represented in a picture, save that the figures were movable instead of being stationary.

The representation of Sir Philip Forester, now distinctly visible in form and feature, was seen to lead on towards the clergyman that beautiful girl, who advanced at once with diffidence and with a species of affectionate pride. In the meantime, and just as the clergyman had arranged the bridal company before him, and seemed about to commence the service, another group of persons, of whom two or three were officers, entered the church. They moved, at first, forward, as though they came to witness the bridal ceremony; but suddenly one of the officers, whose back was towards the spectators, detached himself from his companions, and rushed hastily towards the marriage party, when the whole of them turned towards him, as if attracted by some exclamation which had accompanied his advance. Suddenly the intruder drew his sword; the bridegroom unsheathed his own, and made towards him; swords were also drawn by other individuals, both of the marriage party and of those who had last entered. They fell into a sort of confusion, the clergyman, and some elder and graver persons, labouring apparently to keep the peace, while the hotter spirits on both sides brandished their weapons. But now, the period of the brief space during which the soothsayer, as he pretended, was permitted to exhibit his art, was arrived. The fumes again mixed together, and dissolved gradually from observation; the vaults and columns of the church rolled asunder, and disappeared; and the front of the mirror reflected nothing save the blazing torches and the melancholy apparatus placed on the altar or table before it.

The doctor led the ladies, who greatly required his support, into the apartment from whence they came, where wine, essences and other means of restoring suspended animation had been provided during his absence. He motioned them to chairs, which they occupied in silence – Lady Forester, in particular, wringing her hands, and casting her eyes up to heaven, but without speaking a word, as if the spell had been still before her eyes.

'And what we have seen is even now acting?' said Lady Bothwell, collecting herself with difficulty.

'That,' answered Baptista Damiotti, 'I cannot justly, or with certainty, say. But it is either now acting, or has been acted during a short space before this. It is the last remarkable transaction in which the Cavalier Forester has been engaged.'

Lady Bothwell then expressed anxiety concerning her sister, whose altered countenance and apparent unconsciousness of what passed around her excited her apprehensions how it might be possible to convey her home.

'I have prepared for that,' answered the adept. 'I have directed the servant to bring your equipage as near to this place as the narrowness of the street will permit. Fear not for your sister, but give her, when you return home, this composing draught, and she will be better tomorrow morning. Few,' he added in a melancholy tone, 'leave this house as well in health as they entered it. Such being the consequence of seeking knowledge by mysterious means, I leave you to judge the condition of those who have the power of gratifying such irregular curiosity. Farewell, and forget not the potion.'

'I will give her nothing that comes from you,' said Lady Bothwell; 'I have seen enough of your art already. Perhaps you would poison us both to conceal your own necromancy. But we are persons who want neither the means of making our wrongs known, nor the assistance of friends to right them.'

'You have had no wrongs from me, madam,' said the adept. 'You sought one who is little grateful for such honour. He seeks no one, and only gives responses to those who invite and call upon him. After all, you have but learned a little sooner the evil which you must still be doomed to endure. I hear your servant's step at the door, and will detain your ladyship and Lady Forester no longer. The next packet from the Continent will explain what you have already partly witnessed. Let it not, if I may advise, pass too suddenly into your sister's hands.'

So saying, he bid Lady Bothwell good-night. She went, lighted by the adept, to the vestibule, where he hastily threw a black cloak over his singular dress, and opening the door, entrusted his visitors to the care of the servant. It was with difficulty that Lady Bothwell sustained her sister to the carriage, though it was only twenty steps distant. When they arrived at home, Lady Forester required medical assistance. The physician of the family attended, and shook his head on feeling her pulse.

'Here has been,' he said, 'a violent and sudden shock on the nerves. I must know how it has happened.'

Lady Bothwell admitted they had visited the conjurer, and that Lady Forester had received some bad news respecting her husband, Sir Philip.

'That rascally quack would make my fortune, were he to stay in Edinburgh,' said the graduate; 'this is the seventh nervous case I have heard of his making for me, and all by effect of terror.' He next examined the composing draught which Lady Bothwell had unconsciously brought in her hand, tasted it, and pronounced it very germain to the matter, and what would save an application to the apothecary. He then paused, and looking at Lady Bothwell very significantly, at length added, 'I suppose I must not ask your ladyship anything about this Italian warlock's proceedings?'

'Indeed, doctor,' answered Lady Bothwell, 'I consider what passed as confidential; and though the man may be a rogue, yet, as we were fools enough to consult him, we should, I think, be honest enough to keep his counsel.'

'*May* be a knave! Come,' said the doctor, 'I am glad to hear your ladyship allows such a possibility in anything that comes from Italy.'

'What comes from Italy may be as good as what comes from Hanover, doctor. But you and I will remain good friends; and that it may be so, we will say nothing of Whig and Tory.'

'Not I,' said the doctor, receiving his fee, and taking his hat; 'a Carolus serves my purpose as well as a Willielmus. But I should like to know why old Lady St Ringan, and all that set, go about wasting their decayed lungs in puffing this foreign fellow.'

'Ay – you had best set him down a Jesuit, as Scrub says.' On these terms they parted.

The poor patient – whose nerves, from an extraordinary state of tension, had at length become relaxed in as extraordinary a degree – continued to struggle with a sort of imbecility, the growth of superstitious terror, when the shocking tidings were brought from Holland which fulfilled even her worst expectations.

They were sent by the celebrated Earl of Stair, and contained the melancholy event of a duel betwixt Sir Philip Forester and his wife's half-brother, Captain Falconer, of the Scotch-Dutch, as they were then called, in which the latter had been killed. The cause of quarrel rendered the incident still more shocking. It seemed that Sir Philip had left the army suddenly, in consequence of being unable to pay a very considerable sum which he had lost to another volunteer at play. He had changed his name, and taken up his residence at Rotterdam, where he had insinuated himself into the good graces of an ancient and rich burgomaster, and, by his handsome person and graceful manners, captivated the affections of his only child, a very young person, of great beauty, and the heiress of much wealth. Delighted with the specious attractions of his proposed son-in-law, the wealthy merchant – whose idea of the British character was too high to admit of his taking any precaution to acquire evidence of his condition and circumstances – gave his consent to the marriage. It was about to be celebrated in the principal church of the city, when it was interrupted by a singular occurrence.

Captain Falconer having been detached to Rotterdam to bring up a part of the brigade of Scottish auxiliaries who were in quarters there, a person of consideration in the town, to whom he had been formerly known, proposed to him for amusement to go to the high church to see a countryman of his own married to the daughter of a wealthy burgomaster. Captain Falconer went accordingly, accompanied by his Dutch acquaintance, with a party of his friends, and two or three officers of the Scotch brigade. His astonishment may be conceived when he saw his own brother-in-law, a married man, on the point of leading to the altar the innocent and beautiful creature upon whom he was about to practise a base and unmanly deceit. He proclaimed his villainy on the spot, and the marriage was interrupted, of course. But against the opinion of more thinking men, who considered Sir Philip Forester as having thrown himself out of the rank of men of honour, Captain Falconer admitted him to the privilege of such, accepted a challenge from him, and in the rencounter received a mortal wound. Such are the ways of heaven, mysterious in our eyes. Lady Forester never recovered from the shock of this dismal intelligence.

*   *   *

'And did this tragedy,' said I, 'take place exactly at the time when the scene in the mirror was exhibited?'

'It is hard to be obliged to maim one's story,' answered my aunt, 'but to speak the truth, it happened some days sooner than the apparition was exhibited.'

'And so there remained a possibility,' said I, 'that by some secret and speedy communication the artist might have received early intelligence of that incident.'

'The incredulous pretended so,' replied my aunt.

'What became of the adept?' demanded I.

'Why, a warrant came down shortly afterwards to arrest him for high treason, as an agent of the Chevalier St George; and Lady Bothwell, recollecting the hints which had escaped the doctor, an ardent friend of the Protestant succession, did then call to remembrance that this man was chiefly *prone* among the ancient matrons of her own political persuasion. It certainly seemed probable that intelligence from the Continent, which could easily have been transmitted by an active and powerful agent, might have enabled him to prepare such a scene of phantasmagoria as she had herself witnessed. Yet there were so many difficulties in assigning a natural explanation that, to the day of her death, she remained in great doubt on the subject, and much disposed to cut the Gordian knot by admitting the existence of a supernatural agency.'

'But, my dear aunt,' said I, 'what became of the man of skill?'

'Oh, he was too good a fortune-teller not to be able to foresee that his own destiny would be tragical if he waited the arrival of the man with the silver greyhound upon his sleeve. He made, as we say, a moonlight flitting, and was nowhere to be seen or heard of. Some noise there was about papers or letters found in the house; but it died away, and Dr Baptista Damiotti was soon as little talked of as Galen or Hippocrates.'

'And Sir Philip Forester,' said I, 'did he too vanish for ever from the public scene?'

'No,' replied my kind informer. 'He was heard of once more, and it was upon a remarkable occasion. It is said that we Scots, when there was such a nation in existence, have, among our full peck of virtues, one or two little barley-corns of vice. In particular, it is alleged that we rarely forgive, and never forget, any injuries received – that we make an idol of our resentment, as poor Lady Constance did of her grief, and are addicted, as Burns says, to "nursing our wrath to keep it warm". Lady Bothwell was not without this feeling; and, I believe, nothing whatever, scarce the restoration of the Stewart line, could have happened so delicious to her feelings as an opportunity of being revenged on Sir Philip Forester for the deep and double injury which had deprived her of a sister and of a brother. But nothing of him was heard or known till many a year had passed away.

'At length – it was on a Fastern's E'en [Shrovetide] assembly, at which the whole fashion of Edinburgh attended, full and frequent, and when Lady Bothwell had a seat amongst the lady patronesses, that one of the attendants on the company whispered into her ear that a gentleman wished to speak with her in private.

' "In private? and in an assembly room? – he must be mad. Tell him to call upon me tomorrow morning."

' "I said so, my lady," answered the man, "but he desired me to give you this paper."

'She undid the billet, which was curiously folded and sealed. It only bore the words 'On business of life and death', written in a hand which she had never seen before. Suddenly it occurred to her that it might concern the safety of some of her political friends. She therefore followed the messenger to a small apartment where the refreshments were prepared, and from which the general company was excluded. She found an old man, who, at her approach, rose up and bowed profoundly. His appearance indicated a broken constitution, and his dress, though sedulously rendered conforming to the etiquette of a ballroom, was worn and tarnished, and hung in folds about his emaciated person. Lady Bothwell was about to feel for her purse, expecting to get rid of the supplicant at the expense of a little money, but some fear of a mistake arrested her purpose. She therefore gave the man leisure to explain himself.

' "I have the honour to speak with the Lady Bothwell?"

' "I am Lady Bothwell; allow me to say that this is no time or place for long explanations. What are your commands with me?"

' "Your ladyship," said the old man, "had once a sister."

' "True; whom I loved as my own soul."

' "And a brother."

' "The bravest, the kindest, the most affectionate!" said Lady Bothwell.

' "Both these beloved relatives you lost by the fault of an unfortunate man," continued the stranger.

' "By the crime of an unnatural, bloody-minded murderer," said the lady.

' "I am answered," replied the old man, bowing, as if to withdraw.

' "Stop, sir, I command you," said Lady Bothwell. "Who are you that, at such a place and time, come to recall these horrible recollections? I insist upon knowing."

' "I am one who intends Lady Bothwell no injury, but, on the contrary, to offer her the means of doing a deed of Christian charity, which the world would wonder at, and which heaven would reward; but I find her in no temper for such a sacrifice as I was prepared to ask."

' "Speak out, sir; what is your meaning?" said Lady Bothwell.

' "The wretch that has wronged you so deeply," rejoined the stranger, "is now on his deathbed. His days have been days of misery, his nights have been sleepless hours of anguish – yet he cannot die without your forgiveness. His life has been an unremitting penance – yet he dares not part from his burden while your curses load his soul."

' "Tell him," said Lady Bothwell sternly, "to ask pardon of that Being whom he has so greatly offended, not of an erring mortal like himself. What could my forgiveness avail him?"

' "Much," answered the old man. "It will be an earnest of that which he may then venture to ask from his Creator, lady, and from yours. Remember, Lady Bothwell, you too have a deathbed to look forward to. Your soul may – all human souls must – feel the awe of facing the judgement-seat, with the wounds of an untented conscience, raw and rankling – what thought would it be then that should whisper, 'I have given no mercy, how then shall I ask it?' "

' "Man, whosoever thou mayest be," replied Lady Bothwell, "urge me not so cruelly. It would be but blasphemous hypocrisy to utter with my lips the words which every throb of my heart protests against. They would open the earth and give to light the wasted form of my sister, the bloody form of my murdered brother. Forgive him? – never, never!"

' "Great God!" cried the old man, holding up his hands, "is it thus the worms which Thou hast called out of dust obey the commands of their Maker? Farewell, proud and unforgiving woman. Exult that thou hast added to a death in want and pain the agonies of religious despair; but never again mock heaven by petitioning for the pardon which thou hast refused to grant."

'He was turning from her.

' "Stop," she exclaimed; "I will try – yes, I will try to pardon him."

' "Gracious lady," said the old man, "you will relieve the over-burdened soul which dare not sever itself from its sinful companion of earth without being at peace with you. What do I know – your forgiveness may perhaps preserve for penitence the dregs of a wretched life."

' "Ha!" said the lady, as a sudden light broke on her, "it is the villain himself!" And grasping Sir Philip Forester – for it was he, and no other – by the collar, she raised a cry of, "Murder, murder! seize the murderer!"

'At an exclamation so singular, in such a place, the company thronged into the apartment; but Sir Philip Forester was no longer there. He had forcibly extricated himself from Lady Bothwell's hold, and had run out of the apartment, which opened on the landing-place of the stair. There seemed no escape in that direction, for there were several persons coming up the steps, and others descending. But the unfortunate man was desperate. He threw himself over the balustrade, and alighted safely in the lobby, though a leap of fifteen feet at least, then dashed into the street, and was lost in darkness. Some of the Bothwell family made pursuit, and had they come up with the fugitive they might perhaps have slain him; for in those days men's blood ran warm in their veins. But the police did not interfere, the matter most criminal having happened long since, and in a foreign land. Indeed it was always thought that this extraordinary scene originated in a hypocritical experiment, by which Sir Philip desired to ascertain whether he might return to his native country in safety from the resentment of a family which he had injured so deeply. As the result fell out so contrary to his wishes, he is believed to have returned to the Continent, and there died in exile.'

Ticonderoga: A Legend of the West Highlands*

Robert Louis Stevenson

This is the tale of the man
Who heard a word in the night
In the land of the heathery hills,
In the days of the feud and the fight.
By the sides of the rainy sea,
Where never a stranger came,
On the awful lips of the dead,
He heard the outlandish name.
It sang in his sleeping ears,
It hummed in his waking head:
The name – Ticonderoga,
The utterance of the dead.

I

The Saying of the Name

On the loch-sides of Appin,
When the mist blew from the sea,
A Stewart stood with a Cameron:
An angry man was he.
The blood beat in his ears,
The blood ran hot to his head,
The mist blew from the sea,
And there was the Cameron dead.
'Oh, what have I done to my friend,
Oh, what have I done to mysel',
That he should be cold and dead,
And I in the danger of all?

---

* See Andrew Lang's collected version on pages 194–7.

Nothing but danger about me,
Danger behind and before,
Death at wait in the heather
In Appin and Mamore,
Hate at all of the ferries
And death at each of the fords,
Camerons priming gunlocks
And Camerons sharpening swords.'

But this was a man of counsel,
This was a man of a score,
There dwelt no pawkier Stewart
In Appin or Mamore.
He looked on the blowing mist,
He looked on the awful dead,
And there came a smile on his face
And there slipped a thought in his head.

Out over cairn and moss,
Out over scrog and scaur,
He ran as runs the clansman
That bears the cross of war.
His heart beat in his body,
His hair clove to his face,
When he came at last in the gloaming
To the dead man's brother's place.
The east was white with the moon,
The west with the sun was red,
And there, in the house-doorway,
Stood the brother of the dead.

'I have slain a man to my danger,
I have slain a man to my death.
I put my soul in your hands,'
The panting Stewart saith.
'I lay it bare in your hands,
For I know your hands are leal;
And be you my targe and bulwark
From the bullet and the steel.'

Then up and spoke the Cameron,
And gave him his hand again:
'There shall never a man in Scotland
Set faith in me in vain;
And whatever man you have slaughtered,
Of whatever name or line,
By my sword and yonder mountain,
I make your quarrel mine.
I bid you in to my fireside,
I share with you house and hall;
It stands upon my honour
To see you safe from all.'

It fell in the time of midnight,
When the fox barked in the den
And the plaids were over the faces
In all the houses of men,
That as the living Cameron
Lay sleepless on his bed,
Out of the night and the other world,
Came in to him the dead.

'My blood is on the heather,
My bones are on the hill;
There is joy in the home of ravens
That the young shall eat their fill.
My blood is poured in the dust,
My soul is spilled in the air;
And the man that has undone me
Sleeps in my brother's care.'

'I'm wae for your death, my brother,
But if all of my house were dead,
I couldnae withdraw the plighted hand,
Nor break the word once said.'

'Oh, what shall I say to our father,
In the place to which I fare?
Oh, what shall I say to our mother,
Who greets to see me there?

And to all the kindly Camerons
That have lived and died long-syne –
Is this the word you send them,
Fause-hearted brother mine?'

'It's neither fear nor duty,
It's neither quick nor dead
Shall gar me withdraw the plighted hand,
Or break the word once said.'

Thrice in the time of midnight,
When the fox barked in the den,
And the plaids were over the faces
In all the houses of men,
Thrice as the living Cameron
Lay sleepless on his bed,
Out of the night and the other world
Came in to him the dead,
And cried to him for vengeance
On the man that laid him low;
And thrice the living Cameron
Told the dead Cameron, no.

'Thrice have you seen me, brother,
But now shall see me no more,
Till you meet your angry fathers
Upon the farther shore.
Thrice have I spoken, and now,
Before the cock be heard,
I take my leave for ever
With the naming of a word.
It shall sing in your sleeping ears,
It shall hum in your waking head,
The name – Ticonderoga,
And the warning of the dead.'

Now when the night was over
And the time of people's fears,
The Cameron walked abroad,
And the word was in his ears.

'Many a name I know,
But never a name like this;
Oh, where shall I find a skilly man
Shall tell me what it is?'
With many a man he counselled
Of high and low degree,
With the herdsmen on the mountains
And the fishers of the sea.
And he came and went unweary,
And read the books of yore,
And the runes that were written of old
On stones upon the moor.
And many a name he was told,
But never the name of his fears –
Never, in east or west,
The name that rang in his ears:
Names of men and of clans;
Names for the grass and the tree,
For the smallest tarn in the mountains,
The smallest reef in the sea;
Names for the high and low,
The names of the craig and the flat;
But in all the land of Scotland,
Never a name like that.

2

The Seeking of the Name

And now there was speech in the south,
And a man of the south that was wise,
A periwig'd lord of London,
Called on the clans to rise.
And the riders rode, and the summons
Came to the western shore,
To the land of the sea and the heather,
To Appin and Mamore.
It called on all to gather
From every scrog and scaur,
That loved their fathers' tartan
And the ancient game of war.

And down the watery valley
And up the windy hill,
Once more, as in the olden,
The pipes were sounding shrill;
Again in Highland sunshine
The naked steel was bright;
And the lads, once more in tartan
Went forth again to fight.

'Oh, why should I dwell here
With a weird upon my life,
When the clansmen shout for battle
And the war-swords clash in strife?
I cannae joy at feast,
I cannae sleep in bed,
For the wonder of the word
And the warning of the dead.
It sings in my sleeping ears,
It hums in my waking head,
The name – Ticonderoga,
The utterance of the dead.
Then up, and with the fighting men
To march away from here,
Till the cry of the great war-pipe
Shall drown it in my ear!'

Where flew King George's ensign
The plaided soldiers went:
They drew the sword in Germany,
In Flanders pitched the tent.
The bells of foreign cities
Rang far across the plain:
They passed the happy Rhine,
They drank the rapid Main.
Through Asiatic jungles
The Tartans filed their way,
And the neighing of the war-pipes
Struck terror in Cathay.

'Many a name have I heard,' he thought,
'In all the tongues of men,

Full many a name both here and there,
Full many both now and then.
When I was at home in my father's house
In the land of the naked knee,
Between the eagles that fly in the lift
And the herrings that swim in the sea,
And now that I am a captain-man
With a braw cockade in my hat -
Many a name have I heard,' he thought,
'But never a name like that.'

3

The Place of the Name

There fell a war in a woody place,
Lay far across the sea,
A war of the march in the mirk midnight
And the shot from behind the tree,
The shaven head and the painted face,
The silent foot in the wood,
In a land of a strange, outlandish tongue
That was hard to be understood.

It fell about the gloaming
The general stood with his staff,
He stood and he looked east and west
With little mind to laugh.
'Far have I been and much have I seen,
And kent both gain and loss,
But here we have woods on every hand
And a kittle water to cross.
Far have I been and much have I seen,
But never the beat of this;
And there's one must go down to that waterside
To see how deep it is.'

It fell in the dusk of the night
When unco things betide,
The skilly captain, the Cameron,

Went down to that waterside.
Canny and soft the captain went;
And a man of the woody land,
With the shaven head and the painted face,
Went down at his right hand.
It fell in the quiet night,
There was never a sound to ken;
But all of the woods to the right and the left
Lay filled with the painted men.

'Far have I been and much have I seen,
Both as a man and boy,
But never have I set forth a foot
On so perilous an employ.'
It fell in the dusk of the night
When unco things betide,
That he was aware of a captain-man
Drew near to the waterside.
He was aware of his coming
Down in the gloaming alone;
And he looked in the face of the man
And lo! the face was his own.
'This is my weird,' he said,
'And now I ken the worst;
For many shall fall the morn,
But I shall fall with the first.
Oh, you of the outland tongue,
You of the painted face,
This is the place of my death;
Can you tell me the name of the place?'
'Since the Frenchmen have been here
They have called it Sault-Marie;
But that is a name for priests,
And not for you and me.
It went by another word,'
Quoth he of the shaven head,
'It was called Ticonderoga
In the days of the great dead.'

And it fell on the morrow's morning,
In the fiercest of the fight,

That the Cameron bit the dust
As he foretold at night;
And far from the hills of heather
Far from the isles of the sea,
He sleeps in the place of the name
As it was doomed to be.

Markheim

Robert Louis Stevenson

'Yes,' said the dealer, 'our windfalls are of various kinds. Some customers are ignorant and then I touch a dividend on my superior knowledge. Some are dishonest,' and here he held up the candle, so that the light fell strongly on his visitor, 'and in that case,' he continued, 'I profit by my virtue.'

Markheim had but just entered from the daylight streets and his eyes had not yet grown familiar with the mingled shine and darkness in the shop. At these pointed words and before the near presence of the flame, he blinked painfully and looked aside.

The dealer chuckled. 'You come to see me on Christmas Day,' he resumed, 'when you know that I am alone in my house, put up my shutters and make a point of refusing business. Well, you will have to pay for that; you will have to pay for my loss of time, when I should be balancing my books; you will have to pay, besides, for a kind of manner that I remark in you today very strongly. I am the essence of discretion and ask no awkward questions; but when a customer cannot look me in the eye, he has to pay for it.' The dealer once more chuckled; and then, changing to his usual business voice, though still with a note of irony, 'You can give, as usual, a clear account of how you came into the possession of the object?' he continued. 'Still your uncle's cabinet? A remarkable collector, sir!'

And the little pale, round-shouldered dealer stood almost on tip-toe, looking over the top of his gold spectacles and nodding his head with every mark of disbelief. Markheim returned his gaze with one of infinite pity and a touch of horror.

'This time,' said he, 'you are in error. I have not come to sell, but to buy. I have no curios to dispose of; my uncle's cabinet is bare to the wainscot; even were it still intact, I have done well on the Stock Exchange and should more likely add to it than otherwise and my errand today is simplicity itself. I seek a Christmas present for a lady,' he continued, waxing more fluent as he struck into the speech he had prepared; 'and certainly I owe you every excuse for thus disturbing you upon so small a matter. But the thing was neglected yesterday; I must produce my little compliment at dinner; and, as you very well know, a rich marriage is not a thing to be neglected.'

There followed a pause, during which the dealer seemed to weigh this statement incredulously. The ticking of many clocks among the curious lumber of the shop and the faint rushing of the cabs in a near thoroughfare filled up the interval of silence.

'Well, sir,' said the dealer, 'be it so. You are an old customer after all; and if, as you say, you have the chance of a good marriage, far be it from me to be an obstacle. Here is a nice thing for a lady now,' he went on, 'this hand-glass – fifteenth-century, warranted; comes from a good collection, too; but I reserve the name, in the interests of my customer, who was just like yourself, my dear sir, the nephew and sole heir of a remarkable collector.'

The dealer, while he thus ran on in his dry and biting voice, had stooped to take the object from its place; and, as he had done so, a shock had passed through Markheim, a start both of hand and foot, a sudden leap of many tumultuous passions to the face. It passed as swiftly as it came and left no trace beyond a certain trembling of the hand that now received the glass.

'A glass,' he said hoarsely and then paused and repeated it more clearly. 'A glass? For Christmas? Surely not?'

'And why not?' cried the dealer. 'Why not a glass?'

Markheim was looking upon him with an indefinable expression. 'You ask me why not?' he said. 'Why, look here – look in it – look at yourself! Do you like to see it? No! nor I – nor any man.'

The little man had jumped back when Markheim had so suddenly confronted him with the mirror; but now, perceiving there was nothing worse on hand, he chuckled. 'Your future lady, sir, must be pretty hard favoured,' said he.

'I ask you,' said Markheim, 'for a Christmas present and you give me this – this damned reminder of years and sins and follies – this hand-conscience! Did you mean it? Had you a thought in your mind? Tell me. It will be better for you if you do. Come, tell me about yourself. I hazard a guess now, that you are in secret a very charitable man?'

The dealer looked closely at his companion. It was very odd, Markheim did not appear to be laughing; there was something in his face like an eager sparkle of hope, but nothing of mirth.

'What are you driving at?' the dealer asked.

'Not charitable?' returned the other gloomily. 'Not charitable; not pious; not scrupulous; unloving, unbeloved; a hand to get money, a safe to keep it. Is that all? Dear God, man, is that all?'

'I will tell you what it is,' began the dealer, with some sharpness, and then broke off again into a chuckle. 'But I see this is a love-match of yours and you have been drinking the lady's health.'

'Ah!' cried Markheim, with a strange curiosity. 'Ah, have you been in love? Tell me about that.'

'I,' cried the dealer. 'I in love! I never had the time, nor have I the time today for all this nonsense. Will you take the glass?'

'Where is the hurry?' returned Markheim. 'It is very pleasant to stand here talking; and life is so short and insecure that I would not hurry away from any pleasure – no, not even from so mild a one as this. We should rather cling, cling to what little we can get, like a man at a cliff's edge. Every second is a cliff, if you think upon it – a cliff a mile high – high enough, if we fall, to dash us out of every feature of humanity. Hence it is best to talk pleasantly. Let us talk of each other: why should we wear this mask? Let us be confidential. Who knows, we might become friends?'

'I have just one word to say to you,' said the dealer. 'Either make your purchase or walk out of my shop!'

'True, true,' said Markheim. 'Enough fooling. To business. Show me something else.'

The dealer stooped once more, this time to replace the glass upon the shelf, his thin blond hair falling over his eyes as he did so. Markheim moved a little nearer, with one hand in the pocket of his greatcoat; he drew himself up and filled his lungs; at the same time many different emotions were depicted together on his face – terror, horror and resolve, fascination and a physical repulsion; and through a haggard lift of his upper lip, his teeth looked out.

'This, perhaps, may suit,' observed the dealer: and then, as he began to re-arise, Markheim bounded from behind upon his victim. The long, skewerlike dagger flashed and fell. The dealer struggled like a hen, striking his temple on the shelf, and then tumbled on the floor in a heap.

Time had some score of small voices in that shop, some stately and slow as was becoming to their great age; others garrulous and hurried. All these told out the seconds in an intricate chorus of tickings. Then the passage of a lad's feet, heavily running on the pavement, broke in upon these smaller voices and startled Markheim into the consciousness of his surroundings. He looked about him awfully. The candle stood on the counter, its flame solemnly wagging in a draught;

and by that inconsiderable movement, the whole room was filled with noiseless bustle and kept heaving like a sea; the tall shadows nodding, the gross blots of darkness swelling and dwindling as with respiration, the faces of the portraits and the china gods changing and wavering like images in water. The inner door stood ajar and peered into that leaguer of shadows with a long slit of daylight like a pointing finger.

From these fear-stricken rovings Markheim's eyes returned to the body of his victim, where it lay both humped and sprawling, incredibly small and strangely meaner than in life. In these poor, miserly clothes, in that ungainly attitude, the dealer lay like so much sawdust. Markheim had feared to see it and lo! it was nothing. And yet, as he gazed, this bundle of old clothes and pool of blood began to find eloquent voices. There it must lie; there was none to work the cunning hinges or direct the miracle of locomotion – there it must lie till it was found. Found! ay, and then? Then would his dead flesh lift up a cry that would ring over England and fill the world with the echoes of pursuit. Ay, dead or not, this was still the enemy. 'Time was that when the brains were out,' he thought; and the first word struck into his mind. Time, now that the deed was accomplished – time, which had closed for the victim, had become instant and momentous for the slayer.

The thought was yet in his mind, when, first one and then another, with every variety of pace and voice – one deep as the bell from a cathedral turret, another ringing on its treble notes the prelude of a waltz – the clocks began to strike the hour of three in the afternoon.

The sudden outbreak of so many tongues in that dumb chamber staggered him. He began to bestir himself, going to and fro with the candle, beleaguered by moving shadows and startled to the soul by chance reflections. In many rich mirrors, some of home design, some from Venice or Amsterdam, he saw his face repeated and repeated, as it were an army of spies; his own eyes met and detected him; and the sound of his own steps, lightly as they fell, vexed the surrounding quiet. And still, as he continued to fill his pockets, his mind accused him with a sickening iteration of the thousand faults of his design. He should have chosen a more quiet hour; he should have prepared an alibi; he should not have used a knife; he should have been more cautious and only bound and gagged the dealer and not killed him; he should have been more bold and killed the servant also; he should have done all things otherwise; poignant regrets, weary, incessant toiling of the mind to change what was unchangeable, to plan what was now useless, to be the architect of the irrevocable past.

Meanwhile, and behind all this activity, brute terrors, like the scurrying of rats in a deserted attic, filled the more remote chambers of his brain with riot; the hand of the constable would fall heavy on his shoulder and his nerves would jerk like a hooked fish; or he beheld, in galloping defile, the dock, the prison, the gallows and the black coffin.

Terror of the people in the street sat down before his mind like a besieging army. It was impossible, he thought, but that some rumour of the struggle must have reached their ears and set on edge their curiosity; and now, in all the neighbouring houses, he divined them sitting motionless and with uplifted ear – solitary people, condemned to spend Christmas dwelling alone on memories of the past and now startingly recalled from that tender exercise; happy family parties, struck into silence round the table, the mother still with raised finger: every degree and age and humour, but all, by their own hearths, prying and hearkening and weaving the rope that was to hang him. Sometimes it seemed to him he could not move too softly; the clink of the tall Bohemian goblets rang out loudly like a bell; and alarmed by the bigness of the ticking, he was tempted to stop the clocks. And then, again, with a swift transition of his terrors, the very silence of the place appeared a source of peril and a thing to strike and freeze the passer-by; and he would step more boldly and bustle aloud among the contents of the shop and imitate, with elaborate bravado, the movements of a busy man at ease in his own house.

But he was now so pulled about by different alarms that, while one portion of his mind was still alert and cunning, another trembled on the brink of lunacy. One hallucination in particular took a strong hold on his credulity. The neighbour hearkening with white face beside his window, the passer-by arrested by a horrible surmise on the pavement – these could at worst suspect, they could not know; through the brick walls and shuttered windows only sounds could penetrate. But here, within the house, was he alone? He knew he was; he had watched the servant set forth sweethearting, in her poor best, 'out for the day' written in every ribbon and smile. Yes, he was alone, of course; and yet, in the bulk of empty house above him, he could surely hear a stir of delicate footing – he was surely conscious, inexplicably conscious of some presence. Ay, surely; to every room and corner of the house his imagination followed it; and now it was a faceless thing and yet had eyes to see with; and again it was a shadow of himself; and yet again behold the image of the dead dealer, re-inspired with cunning and hatred.

At times, with a strong effort, he would glance at the open door which still seemed to repel his eyes. The house was tall, the skylight small and dirty, the day blind with fog; and the light that filtered down to the ground storey was exceedingly faint and showed dimly on the threshold of the shop. And yet, in that strip of doubtful brightness, did there not hang wavering a shadow?

Suddenly, from the street outside, a very jovial gentleman began to beat with a staff on the shop-door, accompanying his blows with shouts and railleries in which the dealer was continually called upon by name. Markheim, smitten into ice, glanced at the dead man. But no! he lay quite still; he was fled away far beyond earshot of these blows and shoutings; he was sunk beneath seas of silence; and his name, which would once have caught his notice above the howling of a storm, had become an empty sound. And presently the jovial gentleman desisted from his knocking and departed.

Here was a broad hint to hurry what remained to be done, to get forth from this accusing neighbourhood, to plunge into a bath of London multitudes and to reach, on the other side of day, that haven of safety and apparent innocence – his bed. One visitor had come: at any moment another might follow and be more obstinate. To have done the deed and yet not to reap the profit, would be too abhorrent a failure. The money, that was now Markheim's concern; and as a means to that, the keys.

He glanced over his shoulder at the open door, where the shadow was still lingering and shivering; and with no conscious repugnance of the mind, yet with a tremor of the belly, he drew near the body of his victim. The human character had quite departed. Like a suit half-stuffed with bran, the limbs lay scattered, the trunk doubled, on the floor; and yet the thing repelled him. Although so dingy and inconsiderable to the eye, he feared it might have more significance to the touch. He took the body by the shoulders and turned it on its back. It was strangely light and supple and the limbs, as if they had been broken, fell into the oddest postures. The face was robbed of all expression; but it was as pale as wax and shockingly smeared with blood about one temple. That was, for Markheim, the one displeasing circumstance. It carried him back, upon the instant, to a certain fair-day in a fishers' village: a grey day, a piping wind, a crowd upon the street, the blare of brasses, the booming of drums, the nasal voice of a ballad singer; and a boy going to and fro, buried over head in the crowd and divided between interest and fear, until, coming out on the chief place of concourse, he beheld a booth and a great screen with pictures, dismally designed, garishly coloured: Brownrigg with her apprentice; the Mannings with their murdered guest; Weare in the death-grip of Thurtell; and a score besides of famous crimes. The thing was as clear as an illusion; he was once again that little boy; he was looking once again and with the same sense of physical revolt, at these vile pictures; he was still stunned by the thumping of the drums. A bar of that day's music returned upon his memory; and at that, for the first time, a qualm came over him, a breath of nausea, a sudden weakness of the joints, which he must instantly resist and conquer.

He judged it more prudent to confront than to flee from these considerations; looking the more hardily in the dead face, bending his mind to realise the nature and greatness of his crime. So little a while ago that face had moved with every change of sentiment, that pale mouth had spoken, that body had been all on fire with governable energies; and now, and by his act, that piece of life had been arrested, as the horologist, with interjected finger, arrests the beating of the clock. So he reasoned in vain; he could rise to no more remorseful consciousness; the same heart which had shuddered before the painted effigies of crime, looked on its reality unmoved. At best, he felt a gleam of pity for one who had been endowed in vain with all those faculties that can make the world a garden of enchantment, one who had never lived and who was now dead. But of penitence, no, not a tremor.

With that, shaking himself clear of these considerations, he found the keys and advanced towards the open door of the shop. Outside, it had begun to rain smartly; and the sound of the shower upon the roof had banished silence. Like some dripping cavern, the chambers of the house were haunted by an incessant echoing, which filled the ear and mingled with the ticking of the clocks. And, as Markheim approached the door, he seemed to hear, in answer to his own cautious tread, the steps of another foot withdrawing up the stair. The shadow still palpitated loosely on the threshold. He threw a ton's weight of resolve upon his muscles and drew back the door.

The faint, foggy daylight glimmered dimly on the bare floor and stairs; on the bright suit of armour posted, halbert in hand, upon the landing; and on the dark wood-carvings and framed pictures that hung against the yellow panels of the wainscot. So loud was the beating of the rain through all the house, that, in Markheim's ears, it began to be distinguished into many different sounds. Footsteps and sighs, the tread of regiments marching in the distance, the chink of money in the counting and the creaking of doors held stealthily ajar appeared to mingle with the patter of the drops upon the cupola and the gushing of the water in the pipes. The sense that he was not alone grew upon him to the verge of madness. On every side he was haunted and begirt by presences. He heard them moving in the upper chambers; from the shop, he heard the dead man getting to his legs; and as he began with a great effort to mount the stairs, feet fled quietly before him and followed stealthily behind. If he were but deaf, he thought, how tranquilly he would possess his soul! And then again, and hearkening with ever fresh attention, he blessed himself for that unresting sense which held the outposts and stood a trusty sentinel upon his life. His head turned continually on his neck; his eyes, which seemed starting from their orbits, scouted on every side and on every side were half-rewarded as with the tail of something nameless vanishing. The four-and-twenty steps to the first floor were four-and-twenty agonies.

On that first storey the doors stood ajar, three of them like three ambushes, shaking his nerves like the throats of cannon. He could never again, he felt, be sufficiently immured and fortified from men's observing eyes; he longed to be home, girt in by walls, buried among bed-clothes and invisible to all but God. And at that thought he wondered a little, recollecting tales of other murderers and the fear they were said to entertain of heavenly avengers. It was not so, at least, with him. He feared the laws of nature, lest in their callous and immutable procedure they should preserve some damning evidence of his crime. He feared tenfold more, with a slavish, superstitious terror, some scission in the continuity of man's experience, some wilful illegality of nature. He played a game of skill, depending on the rules, calculating consequence from cause; and what if nature, as the defeated tyrant overthrew the chess-board, should break the mould of their succession? The like had befallen Napoleon (so writers said) when the winter changed the time of its appearance. The like might befall Markheim; the solid walls might become transparent and reveal his doings like those of bees in a glass hive; the stout planks might yield under his foot like quicksands and detain him in their clutch; ay, and there were soberer accidents that might destroy him; if, for instance, the house should fall and imprison him beside the body of his victim; or the house next door should fly on fire and the firemen invade him from all sides. These things he feared; and, in a sense, these things might be called the hands of God reached forth against sin. But about God Himself he was at ease; his act was doubtless exceptional, but so were his excuses, which God knew; it was there, and not among men, that he felt sure of justice.

When he had got safe into the drawing-room and shut the door behind him, he was aware of a respite from alarms. The room was quite dismantled, uncarpeted besides and strewn with packing-cases and incongruous furniture; several great pier-glasses, in which he beheld himself at various angles, like an actor on a stage; many pictures, framed and unframed, standing with their faces to the wall; a fine Sheraton sideboard, a cabinet of marquetry and a great old bed, with tapestry hangings. The windows opened to the floor; but by great good fortune the lower part of the shutters had been closed and this concealed him from the neighbours. Here, then, Markheim drew in a packing-case before the cabinet and began to search among the keys. It was a long business, for there were many and it was irksome, besides; for, after all, there might be nothing in the cabinet and time was on the wing. But the closeness of the occupation sobered him. With the tail of his eye he saw the door – even glanced at it from time to time directly, like a besieged commander pleased to verify the good estate of his defences. But in truth he was at peace. The rain falling in the street sounded natural and pleasant. Presently, on the other side, the notes of a piano were wakened to the music of a hymn and the voices of many children took up the air and words. How stately, how comfortable was the melody! How fresh the youthful voices! Markheim gave ear to it smilingly, as he sorted out the keys; and his mind was thronged with answerable ideas and images; church-going children and the pealing of the high organ; children afield, bathers by the brookside, ramblers on the brambly common, kite-flyers in the windy and cloud-navigated sky; and then, at another cadence of the hymn, back again to church and the somnolence of summer Sundays and the high genteel voice of the parson (which he smiled a little to recall) and the painted Jacobean tombs and the dim lettering of the Ten Commandments in the chancel.

And as he sat thus, at once busy and absent, he was startled to his feet. A flash of ice, a flash of fire, a bursting gush of blood, went over him and then he stood transfixed and thrilling. A step mounted the stair slowly and steadily, and presently a hand was laid upon the knob and the lock clicked and the door opened.

Fear held Markheim in a vice. What to expect he knew not, whether the dead man walking or the official ministers of human justice or some chance witness blindly stumbling in to consign him to the gallows. But when a face was thrust into the aperture, glanced round the room, looked at him, nodded and smiled as if in friendly recognition and then withdrew again and the door closed behind it, his fear broke loose from his control in a hoarse cry.

At the sound of this the visitant returned. 'Did you call me?' he asked pleasantly, and with that he entered the room and closed the door behind him.

Markheim stood and gazed at him with all his eyes. Perhaps there was a film upon his sight, but the outlines of the newcomer seemed to change and waver like those of the idols in the wavering candlelight of the shop; and at times he thought he knew him; and at times he thought he bore a likeness to himself; and always, like a lump of living terror, there lay in his bosom the conviction that this thing was not of the earth and not of God.

And yet the creature had a strange air of the commonplace, as he stood looking on Markheim with a smile; and when he added: 'You are looking for the money, I believe?' it was in the tones of everyday politeness.

Markheim made no answer.

'I should warn you,' resumed the other, 'that the maid has left her sweetheart earlier than usual and will soon be here. If Mr Markheim be found in this house, I need not describe to him the consequences.'

'You know me?' cried the murderer.

The visitor smiled. 'You have long been a favourite of mine,' he said; 'and I have long observed and often sought to help you.'

'What are you?' cried Markheim: 'the Devil?'

'What I may be,' returned the other, 'cannot affect the service I propose to render you.'

'It can,' cried Markheim; 'it does! Be helped by you? No, never; not by you! You do not know me yet; thank God, you do not know me!'

'I know you,' replied the visitant, with a sort of kind severity or rather firmness. 'I know you to the soul.'

'Know me!' cried Markheim. 'Who can do so? My life is but a travesty and slander on myself. I have lived to belie my nature. All men do; all men are better than this disguise that grows about and stifles them. You see each dragged away by life, like one whom braves have seized and muffled in a cloak. If they had their own control – if you could see their faces, they would be altogether different, they would shine out for heroes and saints! I am worse than most; my self is more overlaid; my excuse is known to me and God. But, had I the time, I could disclose myself.'

'To me?' enquired the visitant.

'To you before all,' returned the murderer. 'I supposed you were intelligent. I thought – since you exist – you would prove a reader of the heart. And yet you would propose to judge me by my acts! Think of it; my acts! I was born and I have lived in a land of giants; giants have dragged me by the wrists since I was born out of my mother – the giants of circumstance. And you would judge me by my acts! But can you not look within? Can you not understand that evil is hateful to me? Can you not see within me the clear writing of conscience, never blurred by any wilful sophistry, although too often disregarded? Can you not read me for a thing that surely must be common as humanity – the unwilling sinner?'

'All this is very feelingly expressed,' was the reply, 'but it regards me not. These points of consistency are beyond my province and I care not in the least by what compulsion you may have been dragged away, so as you are but carried in the right direction. But time flies; the servant delays, looking in the faces of the crowd and at the pictures on the hoardings, but still she keeps moving nearer; and remember, it is as if the gallows itself was striding towards you through the Christmas streets! Shall I help you; I, who know all? Shall I tell you where to find the money?'

'For what price?' asked Markheim.

'I offer you the service for a Christmas gift,' returned the other.

Markheim could not refrain from smiling with a kind of bitter triumph. 'No,' said he, 'I will take nothing at your hands; if I were dying of thirst and it was your hand that put the pitcher to my lips, I should find the courage to refuse. It may be credulous, but I will do nothing to commit myself to evil.'

'I have no objection to a death-bed repentance,' observed the visitant.

'Because you disbelieve their efficacy!' Markheim cried.

'I do not say so,' returned the other; 'but I look on these things from a different side and when the life is done my interest falls. The man has lived to serve me, to spread black looks under colour of religion or to sow tares in the wheatfield, as you do, in a course of weak compliance with desire. Now that he draws so near to his deliverance, he can add but one act of service, to repent, to die smiling and thus to build up in confidence and hope the more timorous of my surviving followers. I am not so hard a master. Try me. Accept my help. Please yourself in life as you have done hitherto; please yourself more amply, spread your elbows at the board; and when the night begins to fall and the curtains to be drawn, I tell you, for your greater comfort, that you will find it even easy to compound your quarrel with your conscience and to make a truckling peace with God. I came but now from such a death-bed and the room was full of sincere mourners, listening to the man's last words: and when I looked into that face, which had been set as a flint against mercy, I found it smiling with hope.'

'And do you, then, suppose me such a creature?' asked Markheim. 'Do you think I have no more generous aspirations than to sin and sin and sin and, at the last, sneak into heaven? My heart rises at the thought. Is this, then, your experience of mankind? or is it because you find me with red hands that you presume such baseness? and is this crime of murder indeed so impious as to dry up the very springs of good?'

'Murder is to me no special category,' replied the other. 'All sins are murder, even as all life is war. I behold your race, like starving mariners on a raft, plucking crusts out of the hands of famine and feeding on each other's lives. I follow sins beyond the moment of their acting; I find in all that the last consequence is death; and to my eyes, the pretty maid who thwarts her mother with such taking graces on a question of a ball, drips no less visibly with human gore than such a murderer as yourself. Do I say that I follow sins? I follow virtues also; they differ not by the thickness of a nail, they are both scythes for the reaping angel of Death. Evil, for which I live, consists not in action but in character. The bad man is dear to me; not the bad act, whose fruits, if we could follow them far enough down the hurtling cataract of the ages, might yet be found more blessed than those of the rarest virtues. And it is not because you have killed a dealer but because you are Markheim that I offer to forward your escape.'

'I will lay my heart open to you,' answered Markheim. 'This crime on which you find me is my last. On my way to it I have learned many lessons; itself is a lesson, a momentous lesson. Hitherto I have been driven with revolt to what I would not; I was a bond-slave to poverty, driven and scourged. There are robust virtues that can stand in these temptations; mine was not so: I had a thirst of pleasure. But today, and out of this deed, I pluck both warning and riches – both the power and a fresh resolve to be myself. I become in all things a free actor in the world; I begin to see myself all changed, these hands the agents of good, this heart at peace. Something comes over me out of the past; something of what I have dreamed on Sabbath evenings to the sound of the church organ, of what I forecast when I shed tears over noble books or talked, an innocent child, with my mother.

There lies my life; I have wandered a few years, but now I see once more my city of destination.'

'You are to use this money on the Stock Exchange, I think?' remarked the visitor; 'and there, if I mistake not, you have already lost some thousands?'

'Ah,' said Markheim, 'but this time I have a sure thing.'

'This time, again, you will lose,' replied the visitor quietly.

'Ah, but I keep back the half!' cried Markheim.

'That also you will lose,' said the other.

The sweat started upon Markheim's brow. 'Well, then, what matter?' he exclaimed. 'Say it be lost, say I am plunged again in poverty, shall one part of me, and that the worse, continue until the end to override the better? Evil and good run strong in me, haling me both ways. I do not love the one thing, I love all. I can conceive great deeds, renunciations, martyrdoms; and though I be fallen to such a crime as murder, pity is no stranger to my thoughts. I pity the poor; who knows their trials better than myself? I pity and help them; I prize love, I love honest laughter; there is no good thing nor true thing on earth but I love it from my heart. And are my vices only to direct my life and my virtues to lie without effect, like some passive lumber of the mind? Not so; good, also, is a spring of acts.'

But the visitant raised his finger. 'For the six-and-thirty years that you have been in this world,' said he, 'through many changes of fortune and varieties of humour, I have watched you steadily fall. Fifteen years ago you would have started at a theft. Three years back you would have blenched at the name of murder. Is there any crime, is there any cruelty or meanness, from which you still recoil? – five years from now I shall detect you in the fact! Downward, downward, lies your way; nor can anything but death avail to stop you.'

'It is true,' Markheim said huskily, 'I have in some degree complied with evil. But it is so with all; the very saints, in the mere exercise of living, grow less dainty and take on the tone of their surroundings.'

'I will propound to you one simple question,' said the other; 'and as you answer, I shall read to you your moral horoscope. You have grown in many things more lax; possibly you do right to be so; and at any account, it is the same with all men. But, granting that, are you in any one particular, however trifling, more difficult to please with your own conduct or do you go in all things with a looser rein?'

'In any one?' repeated Markheim, with an anguish of consideration. 'No,' he added, with despair, 'in none! I have gone down in all.'

'Then,' said the visitor, 'content yourself with what you are, for you will never change; and the words of your part on this stage are irrevocably written down.'

Markheim stood for a long while silent and indeed it was the visitor who first broke the silence. 'That being so,' he said, 'shall I show you the money?'

'And grace?' cried Markheim.

'Have you not tried it?' returned the other. 'Two or three years ago, did I not see you on the platform of revival meetings and was not your voice the loudest in the hymn?'

'It is true,' said Markheim; 'and I see clearly what remains for me by way of duty. I thank you for these lessons from my soul; my eyes are opened and I behold myself at last for what I am.'

At this moment the sharp note of the doorbell rang through the house; and the visitant, as though this were some concerted signal for which he had been waiting, changed at once in his demeanour.

'The maid!' he cried. 'She has returned, as I forewarned you, and there is now before you one more difficult passage. Her master, you must say, is ill; you must let her in, with an assured but rather serious countenance – no smiles, no overacting and I promise you success! Once the girl is within and the door closed, the same dexterity that has already rid you of the dealer will relieve you of this last danger in your path. Thenceforward you have the whole evening – the whole night, if needful – to ransack the treasures of the house and to make good your safety. This is help that comes to you with the mask of danger. Up!' he cried; 'up, friend; your life hangs trembling in the scales: up and act!'

Markheim steadily regarded his counsellor. 'If I be condemned to evil acts,' he said, 'there is still one door of freedom open – I can cease from action. If my life be an ill thing, I can lay it down. Though I be, as you say truly, at the beck of every small temptation, I can yet, by one decisive gesture, place myself beyond the reach of all. My love of good is damned to barrenness; it may, and let it be! But I have still my hatred of evil; and from that, to your galling disappointment, you shall see that I can draw both energy and courage.'

The features of the visitor began to undergo a wonderful and lovely change: they brightened and softened with a tender triumph and, even as they brightened, faded and dislimned. But Markheim did not pause to watch or understand the transformation. He opened the door and went downstairs very slowly, thinking to himself. His past went soberly before him; he beheld it as it was, ugly and strenuous like a dream, random as chance-medley – a scene of defeat. Life, as he thus reviewed it, tempted him no longer; but on the farther side he perceived a quiet haven for his bark. He paused in the passage and looked into the shop, where the candle still burned by the dead body. It was strangely silent. Thoughts of the dealer swarmed into his mind as he stood gazing. And then the bell once more broke out into impatient clamour.

He confronted the maid upon the threshold with something like a smile.

'You had better go for the police,' said he: 'I have killed your master.'

Thrawn Janet

ROBERT LOUIS STEVENSON

The Reverend Murdoch Soulis was long minister of the moorland parish of Balweary, in the vale of Dule. A severe, bleak-faced old man, dreadful to his hearers, he dwelt in the last years of his life, without relative or servant or any human company, in the small and lonely manse under the Hanging Shaw. In spite of the iron composure of his features, his eye was wild, scared and uncertain; and when he dwelt, in private admonitions, on the future of the impenitent, it seemed as if his eye pierced through the storms of time to the terrors of eternity. Many young persons coming to prepare themselves against the season of the holy communion were dreadfully affected by his talk. He had a sermon on 1 Peter 5:8, 'the devil, as a roaring lion', on the Sunday after every seventeenth of August, and he was accustomed to surpass himself upon that text both by the appalling nature of the matter and the terror of his bearing in the pulpit. The children were frightened into fits, and the old looked more than usually oracular, and were, all that day, full of those hints that Hamlet deprecated. The manse itself, where it stood by the water of Dule among some thick trees, with the Shaw overhanging it on the one side, and on the other many cold, moorish hilltops rising towards the sky, had begun, at a very early period of Mr Soulis's ministry, to be avoided in the dusk hours by all who valued themselves upon their prudence; and guidmen sitting at the clachan alehouse shook their heads together at the thought of passing late by that uncanny neighbourhood. There was one spot, to be more particular, which was regarded with especial awe. The manse stood between the high road and the water of Dule, with a gable to each; its back was towards the kirk-town of Balweary, nearly half a mile away; in front of it, a bare garden, hedged with thorn, occupied the land between the river and the road. The house was two storeys high, with two large rooms on each. It opened not directly on the garden, but on a causewayed path or passage, giving on the road on the one hand and closed on the other by the tall willows and elders that bordered on the stream. And it was this strip of causeway that enjoyed among the young parishioners of Balweary so infamous a reputation. The minister walked there often after dark, sometimes groaning aloud in the instancy of his unspoken prayers; and when he was from home, and the manse door was locked, the more daring schoolboys ventured, with beating hearts, to 'follow my leader' across that legendary spot.

This atmosphere of terror, surrounding, as it did, a man of God of spotless character and orthodoxy, was a common cause of wonder and subject of enquiry among the few strangers who were led by chance or business into that unknown, outlying country. But many even of the people of the parish were ignorant of the strange events which had marked the first year of Mr Soulis's ministrations; and among those who were better informed, some were naturally reticent, and others shy of that particular topic. Now and again, only, one of the older folk would warm into courage over his third tumbler, and recount the cause of the minister's strange looks and solitary life.

Fifty years syne, when Mr Soulis cam' first into Ba'weary, he was still a young man – a callant, the folk said – fu' o' book learnin' and grand at the exposition, but, as was natural in sae young a man, wi' nae leevin' experience in religion. The younger sort were greatly taken wi' his gifts and his gab; but auld, concerned, serious men and women were moved even to prayer for the young man, whom they took to be a self-deceiver, and the parish that was like to be sae ill-supplied. It was before the days o' the Moderates – weary fa' them; but ill things are like guid – they baith come bit by bit, a pickle at a time; and there were folk even then that said the Lord had left the college professors to their ain devices, an' the lads that went to study wi' them wad hae done mair and better sittin' in a peat-bog, like their forebears of the persecution, wi' a Bible under their oxter and a speerit o' prayer in their heart. There was nae doubt, onyway, but that Mr Soulis had been ower lang at the college. He was careful and troubled for mony things besides the ae thing needful. He had a feck o' books wi' him – mair than had ever been seen before in a' that presbytery; and a sair wark the carrier had wi' them, for they were a' like to have smoored in the Deil's Hag between this and Kilmackerlie. They were books o' divinity, to be sure, or so they ca'd them; but the serious were o' opinion there was little service for sae mony, when the hail o' God's Word would gang in the neuk of a plaid. Then he wad sit half the day and half the nicht forbye, which was scant decent – writin', nae less; and first, they were feared he wad read his sermons; and syne it was proved he was writin' a book himsel', which was surely no fittin' for ane of his years an' sma' experience.

Onyway it behoved him to get an auld, decent wife to keep the manse for him an' see to his bit denners; and he was recommended to an auld limmer – Janet M'Clour, they ca'd her – and sae far left to himsel' as to be ower persuaded. There was mony advised him to the contrar, for Janet was mair than suspeckit by the best folk in Ba'weary. Lang or that, she had had a wean to a dragoon; she hadnae come forrit for maybe thretty year; and bairns had seen her mumblin' to hersel' up on Key's Loan in the gloamin', whilk was an unco time an' place for a God-fearin' woman. Howsoever, it was the laird himsel' that had first tauld the minister o' Janet; and in thae days he wad have gane a far gate to pleesure the laird. When folk tauld him that Janet was sib to the deil, it was a' superstition by his way of it; an' when they cast up the Bible to him an' the witch of Endor, he wad threep it doun their thrapples that thir days were a' gane by, and the deil was mercifully restrained.

Weel, when it got about the clachan that Janet M'Clour was to be servant at the manse, the folk were fair mad wi' her an' him thegether; and some of the guidwives had nae better to dae than get round her door cheeks and chairge her wi' a' that was ken't again her, frae the sodger's bairn to John Tamson's twa kye. She was nae great speaker; folk usually let her gang her ain gate, an' she let them gang theirs, wi' neither Fair-guid-een nor Fair-guid-day; but when she buckled to, she had a tongue to deave the miller. Up she got, an' there wasnae an auld story in Ba'weary but she gart somebody lowp for it that day; they couldnae say ae thing but she could say twa to it; till, at the hinder end, the guidwives up and claught haud of her, and clawed the coats aff her back, and pu'd her doun the clachan to the water o' Dule, to see if she were a witch or no, soum or droun. The carline skirled till ye could hear her at the Hangin' Shaw, and she focht like ten; there was mony a guidwife bure the mark of her neist day an' mony a lang day after; and just in the hettest o' the collieshangie, wha suld come up (for his sins) but the new minister.

'Women,' said he (and he had a grand voice), 'I charge you in the Lord's name to let her go.'

Janet ran to him – she was fair wud wi' terror – an' clang to him, an' prayed him, for Christ's sake, save her frae the cummers; an' they, for their pairt, tauld him a' that was ken't, and maybe mair.

'Woman,' says he to Janet, 'is this true?'

'As the Lord sees me,' says she, 'as the Lord made me, no a word o't. Forbye the bairn,' says she, 'I've been a decent woman a' my days.'

'Will you,' says Mr Soulis, 'in the name of God, and before me, His unworthy minister, renounce the devil and his works?'

Weel, it wad appear that when he askit that, she gave a girn that fairly frichtit them that saw her, an' they could hear her teeth play dirl thegether in her chafts; but there was naething for it but the ae way or the ither; an' Janet lifted up her hand and renounced the deil before them a'.

'And now,' says Mr Soulis to the guidwives, 'home with ye, one and all, and pray to God for His forgiveness.'

And he gied Janet his arm, though she had little on her but a sark, and took her up the clachan to her ain door like a leddy of the land; an' her screighin' and laughin' as was a scandal to be heard.

There were mony grave folk lang ower their prayers that nicht; but when the morn cam' there was sic a fear fell upon a' Ba'weary that the bairns hid theirsels, and even the menfolk stood and keekit frae their doors. For there was Janet comin' doun the clachan – her or her likeness, nane could tell – wi' her neck thrawn, and her heid on ae side, like a body that has been hangit, and a girn on her face like an unstreakit corp. By an' by they got used wi' it, and even speered at her to ken what was wrang; but frae that day forth she couldnae speak like a Christian woman, but slavered and played click wi' her teeth like a pair o' shears; and frae that day forth the name o' God cam' never on her lips. Whiles she would try to say it, but it michtnae be. Them that kenned best said least; but they never gied that Thing the name o' Janet M'Clour; for the auld Janet, by their way o't, was in muckle hell that day. But the minister was neither to haud nor to bind; he preached about naething but the folk's cruelty that had gi'en her a stroke of the palsy; he skelpt the bairns that meddled her; and he had her up to the manse that same nicht, and dwalled there a' his lane wi' her under the Hangin' Shaw.

Weel, time gaed by; and the idler sort commenced to think mair lichtly o' that black business. The minister was weel thocht o'; he was aye late at the writing, folk wad see his can'le doun by the Dule water after twal' at e'en; and he seemed pleased wi' himsel' and upsitten as at first, though a' body could see that he was dwining. As for Janet she cam' an' she gaed; if she didnae speak muckle afore, it was reason she should speak less then; she meddled naebody; but she was an eldritch thing to see, an' nane wad hae mistrysted wi' her for Ba'weary glebe.

About the end o' July there cam' a spell o' weather, the like o't never was in that countryside; it was lown an' het an' heartless; the herds couldnae win up the Black Hill, the bairns were ower weariet to play; an' yet it was gousty too, wi' claps o' het wund that rumm'led in the glens, and bits o' shouers that slockened naething. We aye thocht it but to thun'er on the morn; but the morn cam', an' the morn's morning, and it was aye the same uncanny weather, sair on folks and bestial. Of a' that were the waur, nane suffered like Mr Soulis; he could neither sleep, nor eat, he tauld his elders; an' when he wasnae writin' at his weary book, he wad be stravaguin' ower a' the countryside like a man possessed, when a' body else was blythe to keep caller ben the house.

Abune Hangin' Shaw, in the bield o' the Black Hill, there's a bit enclosed grund wi' an iron yett; and it seems, in the auld days, that was the kirkyaird o' Ba'weary, and consecrated by the papists before the blessed licht shone upon the kingdom. It was a great howff o' Mr Soulis's onyway; there he would sit an' consider his sermons; and indeed it's a bieldy bit. Weel, as he cam' ower the wast end o' the Black Hill, ae day, he saw first twa, an' syne fower, an' syne seeven corbie craws fleein' round an' round abune the auld kirkyaird. They flew laigh and heavy, an' squawked to ither as they gaed; and it was clear to Mr Soulis that something had put them frae their ordinar. He wasnae easy fleyed, an' gaed straucht up to the wa's; an' what suld he find there but a man, or the appearance of a man, sittin' in the inside upon a grave. He was of a great stature, an' black as hell, and his e'en were singular to see. Mr Soulis had heard tell o' black men, mony's the time; but there was something unco about this black man that daunted him. Het as he was, he took a kind o' cauld grue in the marrow o' his banes; but up he spak for a' that, an' says he: 'My friend, are you a stranger in this place?' The black man answered never a word; he got upon his feet, an' begude to hirsle to the wa' on the far side; but he aye lookit at the minister; an' the minister stood an' lookit back; till a' in a meenute the black man was ower the wa' an' rinnin' for the bield o' the trees. Mr Soulis, he hardly kenned why, ran after him; but he was sair forjaskit wi' his walk an' the het, unhalesome weather; and rin as he likit, he got nae mair than a glisk o' the black man amang the birks, till he won doun to the foot o' the hillside, an' there he saw him ance mair, gaun hap, step an' lowp ower Dule water to the manse.

Mr Soulis wasnae weel pleased that this fearsome gangrel suld mak' sae free wi' Ba'weary manse; an' he ran the harder, an', wet shoon, ower the burn an' up the walk; but the deil a black man was there to see. He stepped out upon the road, but there was naebody there; he gaed a' ower the gairden, but na, nae black man. At the hinder end, and a bit feared as was but natural, he lifted the hasp and into the manse; and there was Janet M'Clour before his een, wi' her thrawn craig, and nane sae pleased to see him. And he aye minded sinsyne, when first he set his een upon her, he had the same cauld and deidly grue.

'Janet,' says he, 'have you seen a black man?'

'A black man?' quo' she. 'Save us a'! Ye're no wise, minister. There's nae black man in a' Ba'weary.'

But she didnae speak plain, ye maun understand; but yammered, like a powney wi' the bit in its moo.

'Weel,' says he, 'Janet, if there was nae black man, I have spoken with the Accuser of the Brethren.'

And he sat down like ane wi' a fever, an' his teeth chittered in his heid.

'Hoots,' says she, 'think shame to yoursel', minister,' an' gied him a drap brandy that she keepit aye by her.

Syne Mr Soulis gaed into his study amang a' his books. It's a lang, laigh, mirk chalmer, perishin' cauld in winter, an' no very dry even in the tap o' the simmer, for the manse stands near the burn. Sae doun he sat, and thocht of a' that had come an' gane since he was in Ba'weary, an' his hame, an' the days when he was a bairn an' ran daffin' on the braes; and that black man aye ran in his heid like the owercome of a sang. Aye the mair he thocht, the mair he thocht o' the black man. He tried the prayer, an' the words wouldnae come to him; an' he tried, they say, to write at his book, but he could nae mak' nae mair o' that. There was whiles he thocht the black man was at his oxter, an' the swat stood upon him cauld as well-water; and there was other whiles, when he cam' to himsel' like a christened bairn and minded naething.

The upshot was that he gaed to the window an' stood glowrin' at Dule Water. The trees are unco thick, an' the water lies deep an' black under the manse; an' there was Janet washin' the cla'es wi' her coats kilted. She had her back to the minister, an' he, for his pairt, hardly kenned what he was lookin' at. Syne she turned round, an' shawed her face; Mr Soulis had the same cauld grue as twice that day afore, an' it was borne in upon him what folk said, that Janet was deid lang syne, an' this was a bogle in her clay-cauld flesh. He drew back a pickle and he scanned her narrowly. She was tramp-trampin' in the cla'es, croonin' to hersel'; and eh! Gude guide us, but it was a fearsome face. Whiles she sang louder, but there was nae man born o' woman that could tell the words o' her sang; an' whiles she lookit sidelang doun, but there was naething there for her to look at. There gaed a scunner through the flesh upon his banes; and that was heeven's advertisement. But Mr Soulis just blamed himsel', he said, to think sae ill of a puir auld afflicted wife that hadnae a freend forbye himsel'; an' he put up a bit prayer for him and her, an' drank a little caller water – for his heart rose again the meat – an' gaed up to his naked bed in the gloaming.

That was a nicht that has never been forgotten in Ba'weary, the nicht o' the seventeenth of August, seventeen hun'er' an' twal'. It had been het afore, as I hae said, but that nicht it was hetter than ever. The sun gaed doun among unco-lookin' clouds; it fell as mirk as the pit; no a star, no a breath o' wund; ye couldnae see your han' afore your face, and even the auld folk cuist the covers frae their beds and lay pechin' for their breath. Wi' a' that he had upon his mind, it was gey and unlikely Mr Soulis wad get muckle sleep. He lay an' he tummled; the gude, caller bed that he got into brunt his very banes; whiles he slept, and whiles he waukened; whiles he heard the time o' nicht, and whiles a tyke yowlin' up the muir, as if somebody was deid; whiles he thocht he heard bogles claverin' in his lug, an' whiles he saw spunkies in the room. He behoved, he judged, to be sick; an' sick he was – little he jaloosed the sickness.

At the hinder end, he got a clearness in his mind, sat up in his sark on the bedside, and fell thinkin' ance mair o' the black man an' Janet. He couldnae weel tell how – maybe it was the cauld to his feet – but it cam' in upon him wi' a spate that there was some connection between thir twa, an' that either or baith o' them were bogles. And just at that moment, in Janet's room, which was neist to his, there cam' a stramp o' feet as if men were wars'lin', an' then a loud bang; an' then a wund gaed reishling round the fower quarters of the house; an' then a' was aince mair as seelent as the grave.

Mr Soulis was feared for neither man nor deevil. He got his tinderbox, an' lit a can'le, an' made three steps o't ower to Janet's door. It was on the hasp, an' he pushed it open, an' keeked bauldly in. It was a big room, as big as the minister's ain, an' plenished wi' grand auld solid gear, for he had naething else. There was a fower-posted bed wi' auld tapestry; and a braw cabinet of aik, that was fu' o' the minister's divinity books, an' put there to be out o' the gate; an' a wheen duds o' Janet's lying here and there about the floor. But nae Janet could Mr Soulis see; nor ony sign of a contention. In he gaed (an' there's few that wad ha'e followed him) an' lookit a' round, an' listened. But there was naethin' to be heard, neither inside the manse nor in a' Ba'weary parish, an' naethin' to be seen but the muckle shadows turnin' round the can'le. An' then a' at aince, the minister's heart played dunt an' stood stock-still; an' a cauld wund blew amang the hairs o' his heid. Whaten a weary sicht was that for the puir man's een! For there was Janet hangin' frae a nail beside the auld aik cabinet: her heid aye lay on her shoother, her een were steeked, the tongue projekit frae her mouth, and her heels were twa feet clear abune the floor.

'God forgive us all!' thocht Mr Soulis; 'poor Janet's dead.'

He cam' a step nearer to the corp; an' then his heart fair whammled in his inside. For by what cantrip it wad ill-beseem a man to judge, she was hingin' frae a single nail an' by a single wursted thread for darnin' hose.

It's an awfu' thing to be your lane at nicht wi' siccan prodigies o' darkness; but Mr Soulis was strong in the Lord. He turned an' gaed his ways oot o' that room, and lockit the door ahint him; and step by step, down the stairs, as heavy as leed; and set doon the can'le on the table at the stairfoot. He couldnae pray, he couldnae think, he was dreepin' wi' caul' swat, an' naething could he hear but the dunt-dunt-duntin' o' his ain heart. He micht maybe have stood there an hour, or maybe twa, he minded sae little; when a' o' a sudden, he heard a laigh, uncanny steer upstairs; a foot gaed to an' fro in the cha'mer whaur the corp was hingin'; syne the door was opened, though he minded weel that he had lockit it; an' syne there was a step upon the landin', an' it seemed to him as if the corp was lookin' ower the rail and doun upon him whaur he stood.

He took up the can'le again (for he couldnae want the licht), and as saftly as ever he could, gaed straucht out o' the manse an' to the far end o' the causeway. It was aye pit-mirk; the flame o' the can'le, when he set it on the grund, brunt steedy and clear as in a room; naething moved, but the Dule Water seepin' and sabbin' doon the glen, an' yon unhaly footstep that cam' ploddin' doun the stairs inside the manse. He kenned the foot over weel, for it was Janet's; and at ilka step that cam' a wee thing nearer, the cauld got deeper in his vitals. He commended his soul to Him that made an' keepit him; 'and O Lord,' said he, 'give me strength this night to war against the powers of evil.'

By this time the foot was comin' through the passage for the door;

he could hear a hand skirt alang the wa', as if the fearsome thing was feelin' for its way. The saughs tossed an' maned thegether, a lang sigh cam' ower the hills, the flame o' the can'le was blawn aboot; an' there stood the corp of Thrawn Janet, wi' her grogram goun an' her black mutch, wi' the heid aye upon the shouther, an' the girn still upon the face o't – leevin', ye wad hae said – deid, as Mr Soulis weel kenned, upon the threshold o' the manse.

It's a strange thing that the saul of man should be that thirled into his perishable body; but the minister saw that, an' his heart didnae break.

She didnae stand there lang; she began to move again an' cam' slowly towards Mr Soulis whaur he stood under the saughs. A' the life o' his body, a' the strength o' his speerit, were glowerin' frae his een. It seemed she was gaun to speak, but wanted words, an' made a sign wi' the left hand. There cam' a clap o' wund, like a cat's fuff; oot gaed the can'le, the saughs skreighed like folk; an' Mr Soulis kenned that, live or die, this was the end o't.

'Witch, beldame, devil!' he cried, 'I charge you, by the power of God, begone – if you be dead, to the grave – if you be damned, to hell.'

An' at that moment the Lord's ain hand out o' the heevens struck the horror whaur it stood; the auld, deid, desecrated corp o' the witch-wife, sae lang keepit frae the grave and hirsled round by deils, lowed up like a brunstane spunk and fell in ashes to the grund; the thunder followed, peal on dirling peal, the rairing rain upon the back o' that; and Mr Soulis lowped through the garden hedge, and ran, wi' skelloch upon skelloch, for the clachan.

That same mornin', John Christie saw the black man pass the Muckle Cairn as it was chappin' six; before eicht, he gaed by the change-house at Knockdow; an' no lang after, Sandy M'Lellan saw him gaun linkin' doun the braes frae Kilmackerlie. There's little doubt but it was him that dwalled sae lang in Janet's body; but he was awa' at last; and sinsyne the deil has never fashed us in Ba'weary.

But it was a sair dispensation for the minister; lang, lang he lay ravin' in his bed; and frae that hour to this, he was the man ye ken the day.

The Body-Snatchers

ROBERT LOUIS STEVENSON

Every night in the year, four of us sat in the small parlour of the George at Debenham – the undertaker and the landlord and Fettes and myself. Sometimes there would be more; but blow high, blow low, come rain or snow or frost, we four would be each planted in his own particular armchair. Fettes was an old drunken Scotchman, a man of education obviously, and a man of some property, since he lived in idleness. He had come to Debenham years ago, while still young, and by a mere continuance of living had grown to be an adopted townsman. His blue camlet cloak was a local antiquity, like the church-spire. His place in the parlour at the George, his absence from church, his old, crapulous, disreputable vices, were all things of course in Debenham. He had some vague radical opinions and some fleeting infidelities, which he would now and again set forth and emphasise with tottering slaps upon the table. He drank rum – five glasses regularly every evening; and for the greater portion of his nightly visit to the George sat, with his glass in his right hand, in a state of melancholy alcoholic saturation. We called him the Doctor, for he was supposed to have some special knowledge of medicine, and had been known, upon a pinch, to set a fracture or reduce a dislocation; but beyond these slight particulars, we had no knowledge of his character and antecedents.

One dark winter night – it had struck nine some time before the landlord joined us – there was a sick man in the George, a great neighbouring proprietor suddenly struck down with apoplexy on his way to Parliament; and the great man's still greater London doctor had been telegraphed to his bedside. It was the first time that such a thing had happened in Debenham, for the railway was but newly open, and we were all proportionately moved by the occurrence.

'He's come,' said the landlord, after he had filled and lighted his pipe.

'He?' said I. 'Who? – not the doctor?'

'Himself,' replied our host.

'What is his name?'

'Dr Macfarlane,' said the landlord.

Fettes was far through his third tumbler, stupidly fuddled, now nodding over, now staring mazily around him; but at the last word he seemed to awaken, and repeated the name 'Macfarlane' twice, quietly enough the first time, but with sudden emotion at the second.

'Yes,' said the landlord, 'that's his name, Dr Wolfe Macfarlane.'

Fettes became instantly sober; his eyes awoke, his voice became clear, loud and steady, his language forcible and earnest. We were all startled by the transformation, as if a man had risen from the dead.

'I beg your pardon,' he said, 'I am afraid I have not been paying much attention to your talk. Who is this Wolfe Macfarlane?' And then, when he had heard the landlord out, 'It cannot be, it cannot be,' he added; 'and yet I would like well to see him face to face.'

'Do you know him, Doctor?' asked the undertaker, with a gasp.

'God forbid!' was the reply. 'And yet the name is a strange one; it were too much to fancy two. Tell me, landlord, is he old?'

'Well,' said the host, 'he's not a young man, to be sure, and his hair is white; but he looks younger than you.'

'He is older, though; years older. But,' with a slap upon the table, 'it's the rum you see in my face – rum and sin. This man, perhaps, may have an easy conscience and a good digestion. Conscience! Hear me speak. You would think I was some good, old, decent Christian, would you not? But no, not I; I never canted. Voltaire might have canted if he'd stood in my shoes; but the brains' – with a rattling fillip on his bald head – 'the brains were clear and active, and I saw and made no deductions.'

'If you know this doctor,' I ventured to remark, after a somewhat awful pause, 'I should gather that you do not share the landlord's good opinion.'

Fettes paid no regard to me.

'Yes,' he said, with sudden decision, 'I must see him face to face.'

There was another pause, and then a door was closed rather sharply on the first floor and a step was heard upon the stair.

'That's the doctor,' cried the landlord. 'Look sharp, and you can catch him.'

It was but two steps from the small parlour to the door of the old George Inn; the wide oak staircase landed almost in the street; there was room for a Turkey rug and nothing more between the threshold and the last round of the descent; but this little space was every evening brilliantly lit up, not only by the light upon the stair and the great signal lamp below the sign, but by the warm radiance of the bar-room window. The George thus brightly advertised itself to passers-by in the cold street. Fettes walked steadily to the spot, and we, who were hanging behind, beheld the two men meet, as one of them had phrased it, face to face. Dr Macfarlane was alert and vigorous. His white hair set off his pale and placid, although energetic, countenance. He was richly dressed in the finest of broadcloth and the whitest of linen, with a great gold watch-chain, and studs and spectacles of the same precious material. He wore a broad-folded tie, white and speckled with lilac, and he carried on his arm a comfortable driving-coat of fur. There was no doubt but he became his years, breathing, as he did, of wealth and consideration; and it was a surprising contrast to see our parlour sot – bald, dirty, pimpled and robed in his old camlet cloak – confront him at the bottom of the stairs.

'Macfarlane!' he said somewhat loudly, more like a herald than a friend.

The great doctor pulled up short on the fourth step, as though the familiarity of the address surprised and somewhat shocked his dignity.

'Toddy Macfarlane!' repeated Fettes.

The London man almost staggered. He stared for the swiftest of seconds at the man before him, glanced behind him with a sort of scare, and then in a startled whisper, 'Fettes!' he said, 'you!'

'Ay,' said the other, 'me! Did you think I was dead too? We are not so easy shut of our acquaintance.'

'Hush, hush!' exclaimed the doctor. 'Hush, hush! this meeting is so unexpected – I can see you are unmanned. I hardly knew you, I confess, at first; but I am overjoyed – overjoyed to have this opportunity. For the present it must be how-d'ye-do and goodbye in one, for my fly is waiting, and I must not fail the train; but you shall – let me see – yes – you shall give me your address, and you can count on early news of me. We must do something for you, Fettes. I fear you are out at elbows; but we must see to that for auld lang syne, as once we sang at suppers.'

'Money!' cried Fettes; 'money from you! The money that I had from you is lying where I cast it in the rain.'

Dr Macfarlane had talked himself into some measure of superiority and confidence, but the uncommon energy of this refusal cast him back into his first confusion.

A horrible, ugly look came and went across his almost venerable countenance. 'My dear fellow,' he said, 'be it as you please; my last thought is to offend you. I would intrude on none. I will leave you my address, however – '

'I do not wish it – I do not wish to know the roof that shelters you,' interrupted the other. 'I heard your name; I feared it might be you; I wished to know if, after all, there were a God; I know now that there is none. Begone!'

He still stood in the middle of the rug, between the stair and doorway; and the great London physician, in order to escape, would be forced to step to one side. It was plain that he hesitated before the thought of this humiliation. White as he was, there was a dangerous glitter in his spectacles; but while he still paused uncertain, he became aware that the driver of his fly was peering in from the street at this unusual scene and caught a glimpse at the same time of our little body in the parlour, huddled by the corner of the bar. The presence of so many witnesses decided him at once to flee. He crouched together, brushing on the wainscot, and made a dart like a serpent, striking for the door. But his tribulation was not entirely at an end, for even as he was passing, Fettes clutched him by the arm and these words came in a whisper, and yet painfully distinct, 'Have you seen it again?'

The great rich London doctor cried out aloud with a sharp, throttling cry; he dashed his questioner across the open space, and, with his hands over his head, fled out of the door like a detected thief. Before it had occurred to one of us to make a movement, the fly was already rattling towards the station. The scene was over like a dream, but the dream had left proofs and traces of its passage. Next day the servant found the fine gold spectacles broken on the threshold, and that very night we were all standing breathless by the bar-room window, and Fettes at our side, sober, pale and resolute in look.

'God protect us, Mr Fettes!' said the landlord, coming first into possession of his customary senses. 'What in the universe is all this? These are strange things you have been saying.'

Fettes turned towards us; he looked us each in succession in the face. 'See if you can hold your tongues,' said he. 'That man Macfarlane is not safe to cross; those that have done so already have repented it too late.'

And then, without so much as finishing his third glass, far less waiting for the other two, he bade us goodbye and went forth, under the lamp of the hotel, into the black night.

We three turned to our places in the parlour, with the big red fire and four clear candles; and as we recapitulated what had passed, the first chill of our surprise soon changed into a glow of curiosity. We sat late; it was the latest session I have known in the old George. Each man, before we parted, had his theory that he was bound to prove; and none of us had any nearer business in this world than to track out the past of our condemned companion, and surprise the secret that he shared with the great London doctor. It is no great boast, but I believe I was a better hand at worming out a story than either of my fellows at the George; and perhaps there is now no other man alive who could narrate to you the following foul and unnatural events.

In his young days Fettes studied medicine in the schools of Edinburgh. He had talent of a kind, the talent that picks up swiftly what it hears and readily retails it for its own. He worked little at home; but he was civil, attentive and intelligent in the presence of his masters. They soon picked him out as a lad who listened closely and remembered well; nay, strange as it seemed to me when I first heard it, he was in those days well favoured, and pleased by his exterior. There was, at that period, a certain extramural teacher of anatomy, whom I shall here designate by the letter K. His name was subsequently too well known. The man who bore it skulked through the streets of Edinburgh in disguise, while the mob that applauded at the execution of Burke called loudly for the blood of his employer. But Mr K— was then at the top of his vogue; he enjoyed a popularity due partly to his own talent and address, partly to the incapacity of his rival, the university professor. The students, at least, swore by his name, and Fettes believed himself, and was believed by others, to have laid the foundations of success when he acquired the favour of this meteorically famous man. Mr K— was a *bon vivant* as well as an accomplished teacher; he liked a sly illusion no less than a careful preparation. In both capacities Fettes enjoyed and deserved his notice, and by the second year of his attendance he held the half-regular position of second demonstrator, or sub-assistant, in his class.

In this capacity the charge of the theatre and lecture-room devolved in particular upon his shoulders. He had to answer for the cleanliness of the premises and the conduct of the other students, and it was a part of his duty to supply, receive and divide the various subjects. It was with a view to this last – at that time very delicate – affair that he was lodged by Mr K— in the same wynd, and at last in the same building, with the dissecting-rooms. Here, after a night of turbulent pleasures, his hand still tottering, his sight still misty and confused, he would be called out of bed in the black hours before the winter dawn by the unclean and desperate interlopers who supplied the table. He would open the door to these men, since infamous throughout the land. He would help them with their tragic burden, pay them their sordid price, and remain alone, when they were gone, with the unfriendly relics of humanity. From such a scene he would return to snatch another hour or two of slumber, to repair the abuses of the night and refresh himself for the labours of the day.

Few lads could have been more insensible to the impressions of a life thus passed among the ensigns of mortality. His mind was closed against all general considerations. He was incapable of interest in the fate and fortunes of another, the slave of his own desires and low ambitions. Cold, light and selfish in the last resort, he had that modicum of prudence, miscalled morality, which keeps a man from inconvenient drunkenness or punishable theft. He coveted, besides, a measure of consideration from his masters and his fellow-pupils, and he had no desire to fail conspicuously in the external parts of life. Thus he made it his pleasure to gain some distinction in his studies, and day after day rendered unimpeachable eye-service to his employer, Mr K—. For his day of work he indemnified himself by nights of roaring, blackguardly enjoyment; and when that balance had been struck, the organ that he called his conscience declared itself content.

The supply of subjects was a continual trouble to him as well as to his master. In that large and busy class, the raw material of the anatomist kept perpetually running out; and the business thus rendered necessary was not only unpleasant in itself, but threatened dangerous consequences to all who were concerned. It was the policy of Mr K— to ask no questions in his dealings with the trade. 'They bring the body, and we pay the price,' he used to say, dwelling on the alliteration – '*quid pro quo*.' And, again, and somewhat profanely, 'Ask no questions,' he would tell his assistants, 'for conscience' sake.' There was no understanding that the subjects were provided by the crime of murder. Had that idea been broached to him in words, he would have recoiled in horror; but the lightness of his speech upon so grave a matter was, in itself, an offence against good manners, and a temptation to the men with whom he dealt. Fettes, for instance, had often remarked to himself upon the singular freshness of the bodies. He had been struck again and again by the hangdog, abominable looks of the ruffians who came to him before the dawn; and putting things together clearly in his private thoughts, he perhaps attributed a meaning too immoral and too categorical to the unguarded counsels of his master. He understood his duty, in short, to have three branches: to take what was brought, to pay the price and to avert the eye from any evidence of crime.

One November morning this policy of silence was put sharply to the test. He had been awake all night with a racking toothache – pacing his room like a caged beast or throwing himself in fury on his bed – and had fallen at last into that profound, uneasy slumber that so often follows on a night of pain, when he was awakened by the third or fourth angry repetition of the concerted signal. There was a thin, bright moonshine; it was bitter cold, windy and frosty; the town had not yet awakened, but an indefinable stir already preluded the noise and business of the day. The ghouls had come later than usual, and they seemed more than usually eager to be gone. Fettes, sick with sleep, lighted them upstairs. He heard their grumbling Irish voices through a dream; and as they stripped the sack from their sad merchandise he leaned dozing, with his shoulder propped against the wall; he had to shake himself to find the men their money. As he did so his eyes lighted on the dead face. He started; he took two steps nearer, with the candle raised.

'God almighty!' he cried. 'That is Jane Galbraith!'

The men answered nothing, but they shuffled nearer the door.

'I know her, I tell you,' he continued. 'She was alive and hearty yesterday. It's impossible she can be dead; it's impossible you should have got this body fairly.'

'Sure, sir, you're mistaken entirely,' said one of the men.

But the other looked Fettes darkly in the eyes, and demanded the money on the spot.

It was impossible to misconceive the threat or to exaggerate the danger. The lad's heart failed him. He stammered some excuses, counted out the sum, and saw his hateful visitors depart. No sooner were they gone than he hastened to confirm his doubts. By a dozen unquestionable marks he identified the girl he had jested with the day before. He saw, with horror, marks upon her body that might well betoken violence. A panic seized him, and he took refuge in his room. There he reflected at length over the discovery that he had made; considered soberly the bearing of Mr K—'s instructions and the danger to himself of interference in so serious a business; and at last, in sore perplexity, determined to wait for the advice of his immediate superior, the class assistant.

This was a young doctor, Wolfe Macfarlane, a high favourite

among all the reckless students, clever, dissipated and unscrupulous to the last degree. He had travelled and studied abroad. His manners were agreeable and a little forward. He was an authority on the stage; skilful on the ice or the links with skate or golf-club; he dressed with nice audacity and, to put the finishing touch upon his glory, he kept a gig and a strong trotting-horse. With Fettes he was on terms of intimacy; indeed, their relative positions called for some community of life; and when subjects were scarce the pair would drive far into the country in Macfarlane's gig, visit and desecrate some lonely grave-yard, and return before dawn with their booty to the door of the dissecting-room.

On that particular morning, Macfarlane arrived somewhat earlier than his wont. Fettes heard him, and met him on the stairs, told him his story, and showed him the cause of his alarm. Macfarlane examined the marks on her body.

'Yes,' he said, with a nod, 'it looks fishy.'

'Well, what should I do?' asked Fettes.

'Do?' repeated the other. 'Do you want to do anything? Least said soonest mended, I should say.'

'Someone else might recognise her,' objected Fettes. 'She was as well known as the Castle Rock.'

'We'll hope not,' said Macfarlane, 'and if anybody does – well, you didn't, don't you see, and there's an end. The fact is, this has been going on too long. Stir up the mud, and you'll get K— into the most unholy trouble; you'll be in a shocking box yourself. So will I, if you come to that. I should like to know how any one of us would look, or what the devil we should have to say for ourselves, in any Christian witness-box. For me, you know there's one thing certain – that, practically speaking, all our subjects have been murdered.'

'Macfarlane!' cried Fettes.

'Come now!' sneered the other. 'As if you hadn't suspected it yourself!'

'Suspecting is one thing – '

'And proof another. Yes, I know; and I'm as sorry as you are this should have come here,' tapping the body with his cane. 'The next best thing for me is not to recognise it; and,' he added coolly, 'I don't. You may, if you please. I don't dictate, but I think a man of the world would do as I do; and I may add, I fancy that is what K— would look for at our hands. The question is, Why did he choose us two for his assistants? And I answer, Because he didn't want old wives.'

This was the tone of all others to affect the mind of a lad like Fettes.

He agreed to imitate Macfarlane. The body of the unfortunate girl was duly dissected, and no one remarked or appeared to recognise her.

One afternoon, when his day's work was over, Fettes dropped into a popular tavern and found Macfarlane sitting with a stranger. This was a small man, very pale and dark, with coal-black eyes. The cut of his features gave a promise of intellect and refinement which was but feebly realised in his manners, for he proved, upon a nearer acquaintance, coarse, vulgar and stupid. He exercised, however, a very remarkable control over Macfarlane; issued orders like the Great Bashaw; became inflamed at the least discussion or delay and commented rudely on the servility with which he was obeyed. This most offensive person took a fancy to Fettes on the spot, plied him with drinks and honoured him with unusual confidences on his past career. If a tenth part of what he confessed were true, he was a very loathsome rogue; and the lad's vanity was tickled by the attention of so experienced a man.

'I'm a pretty bad fellow myself,' the stranger remarked, 'but Macfarlane is the boy – Toddy Macfarlane I call him. Toddy, order your friend another glass.' Or it might be, 'Toddy, you jump up and shut the door.' 'Toddy hates me,' he said again. 'Oh, yes, Toddy, you do!'

'Don't you call me that confounded name,' growled Macfarlane.

'Hear him! Did you ever see the lads play knife? He would like to do that all over my body,' remarked the stranger.

'We medicals have a better way than that,' said Fettes. 'When we dislike a dead friend of ours, we dissect him.'

Macfarlane looked up sharply, as though this jest were scarcely to his mind.

The afternoon passed. Gray, for that was the stranger's name, invited Fettes to join them at dinner, ordered a feast so sumptuous that the tavern was thrown into commotion, and when all was done, commanded Macfarlane to settle the bill. It was late before they separated; the man Gray was incapably drunk. Macfarlane, sobered by his fury, chewed the cud of the money he had been forced to squander and the slights he had been obliged to swallow. Fettes, with various liquors singing in his head, returned home with devious footsteps and a mind entirely in abeyance. Next day Macfarlane was absent from the class, and Fettes smiled to himself as he imagined him still squiring the intolerable Gray from tavern to tavern. As soon as the hour of liberty had struck, he posted from place to place in quest of his last night's companions. He could find them, however, nowhere; so returned early to his rooms, went early to bed, and slept the sleep of the just.

At four in the morning he was awakened by the well-known signal. Descending to the door, he was filled with astonishment to find Macfarlane with his gig, and in the gig one of those long and ghastly packages with which he was so well acquainted.

'What?' he cried. 'Have you been out alone? How did you manage?'

But Macfarlane silenced him roughly, bidding him turn to business. When they had got the body upstairs and laid it on the table, Macfarlane made at first as if he were going away. Then he paused and seemed to hesitate; and then, 'You had better look at the face,' said he, in tones of some constraint. 'You had better,' he repeated, as Fettes only stared at him in wonder.

'But where, and how, and when did you come by it?' cried the other.

'Look at the face,' was the only answer.

Fettes was staggered; strange doubts assailed him. He looked from the young doctor to the body, and then back again. At last, with a start, he did as he was bidden. He had almost expected the sight that met his eyes, and yet the shock was cruel. To see, fixed in the rigidity of death and naked on that coarse layer of sack-cloth, the man whom he had left well clad and full of meat and sin upon the threshold of a tavern, awoke, even in the thoughtless Fettes, some of the terrors of the conscience. It was a *cras tibi* which re-echoed in his soul, that two whom he had known should have come to lie upon these icy tables. Yet these were only secondary thoughts. His first concern regarded Wolfe. Unprepared for a challenge so momentous, he knew not how to look his comrade in the face. He durst not meet his eye, and he had neither words nor voice at his command.

It was Macfarlane himself who made the first advance. He came up quietly behind and laid his hand gently but firmly on the other's shoulder.

'Richardson,' said he, 'may have the head.'

Now Richardson was a student who had long been anxious for that portion of the human subject to dissect. There was no answer, and the murderer resumed: 'Talking of business, you must pay me; your accounts, you see, must tally.'

Fettes found a voice, the ghost of his own: 'Pay you!' he cried. 'Pay you for that?'

'Why, yes, of course you must. By all means and on every possible account, you must,' returned the other. 'I dare not give it for nothing, you dare not take it for nothing; it would compromise us both. This is another case like Jane Galbraith's. The more things are wrong the more we must act as if all were right. Where does old K— keep his money?'

'There,' answered Fettes hoarsely, pointing to a cupboard in the corner.

'Give me the key, then,' said the other calmly, holding out his hand.

There was an instant's hesitation, and the die was cast. Macfarlane could not suppress a nervous twitch, the infinitesimal mark of an immense relief, as he felt the key between his fingers. He opened the cupboard, brought out pen and ink and a paper-book that stood in one compartment, and separated from the funds in a drawer a sum suitable to the occasion.

'Now, look here,' he said, 'there is the payment made – first proof of your good faith: first step to your security. You have now to clinch it by a second. Enter the payment in your book, and then you for your part may defy the devil.'

The next few seconds were for Fettes an agony of thought; but in balancing his terrors it was the most immediate that triumphed. Any future difficulty seemed almost welcome if he could avoid a present quarrel with Macfarlane. He set down the candle which he had been carrying all this time, and with a steady hand entered the date, the nature and the amount of the transaction.

'And now,' said Macfarlane, 'it's only fair that you should pocket the lucre. I've had my share already. By the by, when a man of the world falls into a bit of luck, has a few shillings extra in his pocket – I'm ashamed to speak of it, but there's a rule of conduct in the case. No treating, no purchase of expensive class-books, no squaring of old debts; borrow, don't lend.'

'Macfarlane,' began Fettes, still somewhat hoarsely, 'I have put my neck in a halter to oblige you.'

'To oblige me?' cried Wolfe. 'Oh, come! You did, as near as I can see the matter, what you downright had to do in self-defence. Suppose I got into trouble, where would you be? This second little matter flows clearly from the first. Mr Gray is the continuation of Miss Galbraith. You can't begin and then stop. If you begin, you must keep on beginning; that's the truth. No rest for the wicked.'

A horrible sense of blackness and the treachery of fate seized hold upon the soul of the unhappy student.

'My God!' he cried, 'but what have I done? and when did I begin? To be made a class assistant – in the name of reason, where's the harm in that? Service wanted the position; Service might have got it. Would *he* have been where *I* am now?'

'My dear fellow,' said Macfarlane, 'what a boy you are! What harm *has* come to you? What harm *can* come to you if you hold your tongue? Why, man, do you know what this life is? There are two squads of us – the lions and the lambs. If you're a lamb, you'll come to lie upon these tables like Gray or Jane Galbraith; if you're a lion, you'll live and drive a horse like me, like K—, like all the world with any wit or courage. You're staggered at the first. But look at K—! My dear fellow, you're clever, you have pluck. I like you, and K— likes you. You were born to lead the hunt; and I tell you, on my honour and my experience of life, three days from now you'll laugh at all these scarecrows like a high-school boy at a farce.'

And with that Macfarlane took his departure and drove off up the wynd in his gig to get under cover before daylight. Fettes was thus left alone with his regrets. He saw the miserable peril in which he stood involved. He saw, with inexpressible dismay, that there was no limit to his weakness, and that, from concession to concession, he had fallen from the arbiter of Macfarlane's destiny to his paid and helpless accomplice. He would have given the world to have been a little braver at the time, but it did not occur to him that he might still be brave. The secret of Jane Galbraith and the cursed entry in the day-book closed his mouth.

Hours passed; the class began to arrive; the members of the unhappy Gray were dealt out to one and to another, and received without remark. Richardson was made happy with the head; and before the hour of freedom rang Fettes trembled with exultation to perceive how far they had already gone towards safety.

For two days he continued to watch, with increasing joy, the dreadful process of disguise.

On the third day Macfarlane made his appearance. He had been ill, he said; but he made up for lost time by the energy with which he directed the students. To Richardson in particular he extended the most valuable assistance and advice, and that student, encouraged by the praise of the demonstrator, burned high with ambitious hopes, and saw the medal already in his grasp.

Before the week was out Macfarlane's prophecy had been fulfilled. Fettes had outlived his terrors and had forgotten his baseness. He began to plume himself upon his courage, and had so arranged the story in his mind that he could look back on these events with an unhealthy pride. Of his accomplice he saw but little. They met, of course, in the business of the class; they received their orders together from Mr K—. At times they had a word or two in private, and Macfarlane was from first to last particularly kind and jovial. But it was plain that he avoided any reference to their common secret; and even when Fettes whispered to him that he had cast in his lot with the lions and forsworn the lambs, he only signed to him smilingly to hold his peace.

At length an occasion arose which threw the pair once more into a closer union. Mr K— was again short of subjects; pupils were eager, and it was a part of this teacher's pretensions to be always well supplied. At the same time there came the news of a burial in the rustic graveyard of Glencorse. Time has little changed the place in question. It stood then, as now, upon a crossroads, out of call of human habitations and buried fathom deep in the foliage of six cedar trees. The cries of the sheep upon the neighbouring hills, the streamlets upon either hand, one loudly singing among pebbles, the other dripping furtively from pond to pond, the stir of the wind in mountainous old flowering chestnuts and, once in seven days, the voice of the bell and the old tunes of the precentor were the only sounds that disturbed the silence around the rural church. The Resurrection Man – to use a byname of the period – was not to be deterred by any of the sanctities of customary piety. It was part of his trade to despise and desecrate the scrolls and trumpets of old tombs, the paths worn by the feet of worshippers and mourners and the offerings and the inscriptions of bereaved affection. To rustic neighbourhoods, where love is more than commonly tenacious and where some bonds of blood or fellowship unite the entire society of a parish, the body-snatcher, far from being repelled by natural respect, was attracted by the ease and safety of the task. To bodies that had been laid in earth, in joyful expectation of a far different awakening, there came that hasty, lamp-lit, terror-haunted resurrection of the spade and mattock. The coffin was forced, the cerements torn, and the melancholy relics, clad in sackcloth, after being rattled for hours on moonless byways, were at length exposed to uttermost indignities before a class of gaping boys.

Somewhat as two vultures may swoop upon a dying lamb, Fettes and Macfarlane were to be let loose upon a grave in that green and quiet resting-place. The wife of a farmer, a woman who had lived for sixty years and been known for nothing but good butter and a godly conversation, was to be rooted from her grave at midnight and carried, dead and naked, to that faraway city that she had always honoured with her Sunday's best; the place beside her family was to be empty till the crack of doom; her innocent and almost venerable members were to be exposed to that last curiosity of the anatomist.

Late one afternoon the pair set forth, well wrapped in cloaks and furnished with a formidable bottle. It rained without remission – a cold, dense, lashing rain. Now and again there blew a puff of wind, but these sheets of falling water kept it down. Bottle and all, it was a sad and silent drive as far as Penicuik, where they were to spend the evening. They stopped once, to hide their implements in a thick bush not far from the churchyard, and once again at the Fisher's Tryst, to have a toast before the kitchen fire and vary their nips of whisky with a glass of ale. When they reached their journey's end the gig was housed, the horse was fed and comforted, and the two young doctors in a private room sat down to the best dinner and the best wine the house afforded. The lights, the fire, the beating rain upon the window, the cold, incongruous work that lay before them, added zest to their enjoyment of the meal. With every glass their cordiality increased. Soon Macfarlane handed a little pile of gold to his companion.

'A compliment,' he said. 'Between friends these little damned accommodations ought to fly like pipe-lights.'

Fettes pocketed the money, and applauded the sentiment to the echo. 'You are a philosopher,' he cried. 'I was an ass till I knew you. You and K— between you, by the Lord Harry! but you'll make a man of me.'

'Of course we shall,' applauded Macfarlane. 'A man? I tell you, it required a man to back me up the other morning. There are some big, brawling, forty-year-old cowards who would have turned sick at the look of the damned thing; but not you – you kept your head. I watched you.'

'Well, and why not?' Fettes thus vaunted himself. 'It was no affair of mine. There was nothing to gain on the one side but disturbance, and on the other I could count on your gratitude, don't you see?' And he slapped his pocket till the gold pieces rang.

Macfarlane somehow felt a certain touch of alarm at these unpleasant words. He may have regretted that he had taught his young companion so successfully, but he had no time to interfere, for the other noisily continued in this boastful strain: 'The great thing is not to be afraid. Now, between you and me, I don't want to hang –

that's practical; but for all cant, Macfarlane, I was born with a contempt. Hell, God, Devil, right, wrong, sin, crime, and all the old gallery of curiosities – they may frighten boys, but men of the world, like you and me, despise them. Here's to the memory of Gray!'

It was by this time growing somewhat late. The gig, according to order, was brought round to the door with both lamps brightly shining, and the young men had to pay their bill and take the road. They announced that they were bound for Peebles, and drove in that direction till they were clear of the last houses of the town; then, extinguishing the lamps, they returned upon their course, and followed a byroad towards Glencorse. There was no sound but that of their own passage, and the incessant, strident pouring of the rain. It was pitch dark; here and there a white gate or a white stone in the wall guided them for a short space across the night; but for the most part it was at a foot pace, and almost groping, that they picked their way through that resonant blackness to their solemn and isolated destination. In the sunken woods that traverse the neighbourhood of the burying-ground the last glimmer failed them, and it became necessary to kindle a match and reillumine one of the lanterns of the gig. Thus, under the dripping trees and environed by huge and moving shadows, they reached the scene of their unhallowed labours.

They were both experienced in such affairs, and powerful with the spade, and they had scarce been twenty minutes at their task before they were rewarded by a dull rattle on the coffin lid. At the same moment, Macfarlane, having hurt his hand upon a stone, flung it carelessly above his head. The grave, in which they now stood almost to the shoulders, was close to the edge of the plateau of the graveyard, and the gig lamp had been propped, the better to illuminate their labours, against a tree and on the immediate verge of the steep bank descending to the stream. Chance had taken a sure aim with the stone. There came a clang of broken glass; night fell upon them; sounds alternately dull and ringing announced the bounding of the lantern down the bank, and its occasional collision with the trees. A stone or two, which it had dislodged in its descent, rattled behind it into the profundities of the glen; and then silence, like night, resumed its sway; and they might bend their hearing to its utmost pitch, but naught was to be heard except the rain, now marching to the wind, now steadily falling over miles of open country.

They were so nearly at an end of their abhorred task that they judged it wisest to complete it in the dark. The coffin was exhumed and broken open; the body inserted in the dripping sack and carried between them to the gig; one mounted to keep it in its place, and the other, taking the horse by the mouth, groped along by wall and bush until they reached the wider road by the Fisher's Tryst. Here was a faint, diffused radiancy, which they hailed like daylight; by that they pushed the horse to a good pace and began to rattle along merrily in the direction of the town.

They had both been wetted to the skin during their operations, and now, as the gig jumped among the deep ruts, the thing that stood propped between them fell now upon one and now upon the other. At every repetition of the horrid contact each instinctively repelled it with the greater haste; and the process, natural although it was, began to tell upon the nerves of the companions. Macfarlane made some ill-favoured jest about the farmer's wife, but it came hollowly from his lips and was allowed to drop in silence. Still their unnatural burden bumped from side to side; and now the head would be laid, as if in confidence, upon their shoulders, and now the drenching sackcloth would flap icily about their faces. A creeping chill began to possess the soul of Fettes. He peered at the bundle, and it seemed somehow larger than at first. All over the countryside, and from every degree of distance, the farm dogs accompanied their passage with tragic ululations; and it grew and grew upon his mind that some unnatural miracle had been accomplished, that some nameless change had befallen the dead body and that it was in fear of their unholy burden that the dogs were howling.

'For God's sake,' said he, making a great effort to arrive at speech, 'for God's sake, let's have a light!'

Seemingly Macfarlane was affected in the same direction; for, though he made no reply, he stopped the horse, passed the reins to his companion, got down, and proceeded to kindle the remaining lamp. They had by that time got no farther than the crossroad down to Auchenclinny. The rain still poured as though the Deluge were returning, and it was no easy matter to make a light in such a world of wet and darkness. When at last the flickering blue flame had been transferred to the wick and began to expand and clarify, and shed a wide circle of misty brightness round the gig, it became possible for the two young men to see each other and the thing they had along with them. The rain had moulded the rough sacking to the outlines of the body underneath; the head was distinct from the trunk, the shoulders plainly modelled; something at once spectral and human riveted their eyes upon the ghastly comrade of their drive.

For some time Macfarlane stood motionless, holding up the lamp. A nameless dread was swathed, like a wet sheet, about the body, and tightened the white skin upon the face of Fettes; a fear that was meaningless, a horror of what could not be, kept mounting to his brain. Another beat of the watch, and he had spoken. But his comrade forestalled him.

'That is not a woman,' said Macfarlane, in a hushed voice.

'It was a woman when we put her in,' whispered Fettes.

'Hold that lamp,' said the other. 'I must see her face.'

And as Fettes took the lamp his companion untied the fastenings of the sack and drew down the cover from the head. The light fell very clear upon the dark, well-moulded features and smooth-shaven cheeks of a too familiar countenance, often beheld in dreams by both of these young men. A wild yell rang up into the night; each leaped from his own side into the roadway: the lamp fell, broke, and was extinguished; and the horse, terrified by this unusual commotion, bounded and went off towards Edinburgh at a gallop, bearing along with it, sole occupant of the gig, the body of the dead and long-dissected Gray.

Olalla

Robert Louis Stevenson

'Now,' said the doctor, 'my part is done, and, I may say, with some vanity, well done. It remains only to get you out of this cold and poisonous city, and to give you two months of a pure air and an easy conscience. The last is your affair. To the first I think I can help you. It falls indeed rather oddly; it was but the other day the padre came in from the country; and as he and I are old friends, although of contrary professions, he applied to me in a matter of distress among some of his parishioners. This was a family – but you are ignorant of Spain, and even the names of our grandees are hardly known to you; suffice it, then, that they were once great people, and are now fallen to the brink of destitution. Nothing now belongs to them but the *residencia*, and certain leagues of desert mountain, in the greater part of which not even a goat could support life. But the house is a fine old place, and stands at a great height among the hills, and most salubriously; and I had no sooner heard my friend's tale than I remembered you. I told him I had a wounded officer, wounded in the good cause, who was now able to make a change; and I proposed that his friends should take you for a lodger. Instantly the padre's face grew dark, as I had maliciously foreseen it would. It was out of the question, he said. Then let them starve, said I, for I have no sympathy with tatterdemalion pride. Thereupon we separated, not very content with one another; but yesterday, to my wonder, the padre returned and made a submission: the difficulty, he said, he had found upon enquiry to be less than he had feared; or, in other words, these proud people had put their pride in their pocket. I closed with the offer; and, subject to your approval, I have taken rooms for you in the *residencia*. The air of these mountains will renew your blood; and the quiet in which you will there live is worth all the medicines in the world.'

'Doctor,' said I, 'you have been throughout my good angel, and your advice is a command. But tell me, if you please, something of the family with which I am to reside.'

'I am coming to that,' replied my friend; 'and, indeed, there is a difficulty in the way. These beggars are, as I have said, of very high descent and swollen with the most baseless vanity; they have lived for some generations in a growing isolation, drawing away, on either hand, from the rich who had now become too high for them, and from the poor, whom they still regarded as too low; and even today, when poverty forces them to unfasten their door to a guest, they cannot do so without a most ungracious stipulation. You are to remain, they say, a stranger; they will give you attendance, but they refuse from the first the idea of the smallest intimacy.'

I will not deny that I was piqued, and perhaps the feeling strengthened my desire to go, for I was confident that I could break down that barrier if I desired. 'There is nothing offensive in such a stipulation,' said I; 'and I even sympathise with the feeling that inspired it.'

'It is true they have never seen you,' returned the doctor politely; 'and if they knew you were the handsomest and the most pleasant man that ever came from England (where I am told that handsome men are common, but pleasant ones not so much so), they would doubtless make you welcome with a better grace. But since you take the thing so well, it matters not. To me, indeed, it seems discourteous. But you will find yourself the gainer. The family will not much tempt you. A mother, a son and a daughter; an old woman said to be half-witted, a country lout and a country girl, who stands very high with her confessor, and is, therefore,' chuckled the physician, 'most likely plain; there is not much in that to attract the fancy of a dashing officer.'

'And yet you say they are high-born,' I objected.

'Well, as to that, I should distinguish,' returned the doctor. 'The mother is; not so the children. The mother was the last representative of a princely stock, degenerate both in parts and fortune. Her father was not only poor, he was mad; and the girl ran wild about the *residencia* till his death. Then, much of the fortune having died with him, and the family being quite extinct, the girl ran wilder than ever, until at last she married, heaven knows whom; a muleteer some say, others a smuggler; while there are some who uphold there was no marriage at all, and that Felipe and Olalla are bastards. The union, such as it was, was tragically dissolved some years ago; but they live in such seclusion, and the country at that time was in so much disorder, that the precise manner of the man's end is known only to the priest – if even to him.'

'I begin to think I shall have strange experiences,' said I.

'I would not romance, if I were you,' replied the doctor; 'you will find, I fear, a very grovelling and commonplace reality. Felipe, for instance, I have seen. And what am I to say? He is very rustic, very cunning, very loutish, and, I should say, an innocent; the others are probably to match. No, no, señor commandante, you must seek congenial society among the great sights of our mountains; and in these at least, if you are at all a lover of the works of nature, I promise you will not be disappointed.'

The next day Felipe came for me in a rough country cart, drawn by a mule; and a little before the stroke of noon, after I had said farewell to the doctor, the innkeeper, and different good souls who had befriended me during my sickness, we set forth out of the city by the eastern gate, and began to ascend into the sierra. I had been so long a prisoner, since I was left behind for dying after the loss of the convoy, that the mere smell of the earth set me smiling. The country through which we went was wild and rocky, partially covered with rough woods, now of the cork tree and now of the great Spanish chestnut, and frequently intersected by the beds of mountain torrents. The sun shone, the wind rustled joyously, and we had advanced some miles, and the city had already shrunk into an inconsiderable knoll upon the plain behind us, before my attention began to be diverted to the companion of my drive. To the eye, he seemed but a diminutive, loutish, well-made country lad, such as the doctor had described, mighty quick and active, but devoid of any culture; and this first impression was with most observers final. What began to strike me was his familiar, chattering talk; so strangely inconsistent with the terms on which I was to be received; and partly from his imperfect enunciation, partly from the sprightly incoherence of the matter, so very difficult to follow clearly without an effort of the mind. It is true I had before talked with persons of a similar mental constitution; persons who seemed to live (as he did) by the senses, taken and possessed by the visual object of the moment and unable to discharge their minds of that impression. His seemed to me (as I sat, distantly giving ear) a kind of conversation proper to drivers, who pass much of their time in a great vacancy of the intellect and threading the sights of a familiar country. But this was not the case with Felipe; by his own account, he was a home-keeper; 'I wish I was there now,' he said; and then, spying a tree by the wayside, he broke off to tell me that he had once seen a crow among its branches.

'A crow?' I repeated, struck by the ineptitude of the remark, and thinking I had heard imperfectly.

But by this time he was already filled with a new idea, hearkening with a rapt intentness, his head on one side, his face puckered; and he struck me rudely, to make me hold my peace. Then he smiled and shook his head.

'What did you hear?' I asked.

'Oh, it is all right,' he said; and began encouraging his mule with cries that echoed unhumanly up the mountain walls.

I looked at him more closely. He was superlatively well-built, light, and lithe and strong; he was well-featured; his yellow eyes were very large, though, perhaps, not very expressive; take him altogether, he was a pleasant-looking lad, and I had no fault to find with him, beyond that he was of a dusky hue, and inclined to hairiness; two characteristics that I disliked. It was his mind that puzzled and yet attracted me. The doctor's phrase – an innocent – came back to me; and I was wondering if that were, after all, the true description, when the road began to go down into the narrow and naked chasm of a torrent. The waters thundered tumultuously in the bottom; and the ravine was filled full of the sound, the thin spray and the claps of wind that accompanied their descent. The scene was certainly impressive; but the road was in that part very securely walled in; the mule went steadily forward; and I was astonished to perceive the paleness of terror in the face of my companion. The voice of that wild river was inconstant, now sinking lower as if in weariness, now doubling its hoarse tones; momentary freshets seemed to swell its volume, sweeping down the gorge, raving and booming against the barrier walls; and I observed it was at each of these accessions to the clamour that my driver more particularly winced and blanched. Some thoughts of Scottish superstition and the River Kelpie passed across my mind; I wondered if perchance the like were prevalent in that part of Spain; and turning to Felipe, sought to draw him out.

'What is the matter?' I asked.

'Oh, I am afraid,' he replied.

'Of what are you afraid?' I returned. 'This seems one of the safest places on this very dangerous road.'

'It makes a noise,' he said, with a simplicity of awe that set my doubts at rest.

The lad was but a child in intellect; his mind was like his body, active and swift, but stunted in development; and I began from that time forth to regard him with a measure of pity, and to listen at first with indulgence, and at last even with pleasure, to his disjointed babble.

By about four in the afternoon we had crossed the summit of the mountain line, said farewell to the western sunshine, and began to go down upon the other side, skirting the edge of many ravines and moving through the shadow of dusky woods. There rose upon all sides the voice of falling water, not condensed and formidable as in the gorge of the river, but scattered and sounding gaily and musically from glen to glen. Here, too, the spirits of my driver mended, and he began to sing aloud in a falsetto voice, and with a singular bluntness of musical perception, never true either to melody or key, but wandering at will, and yet somehow with an effect that was natural and pleasing, like that of the song of birds. As the dusk increased, I fell more and more under the spell of this artless warbling, listening and waiting for some articulate air, and still disappointed; and when at last I asked him what it was he sang – 'Oh,' cried he, 'I am just singing!' Above all, I was taken with a trick he had of unweariedly repeating the same note at little intervals; it was not so monotonous as you would think, or, at least, not disagreeable; and it seemed to breathe a wonderful contentment with what is, such as we love to fancy in the attitude of trees or the quiescence of a pool.

Night had fallen dark before we came out upon a plateau, and drew up a little after before a certain lump of superior blackness which I could only conjecture to be the *residencia*. Here, my guide, getting down from the cart, hooted and whistled for a long time in vain; until at last an old peasant man came towards us from somewhere in the surrounding dark, carrying a candle in his hand. By the light of this I was able to perceive a great arched doorway of a Moorish character: it was closed by iron-studded gates, in one of the leaves of which Felipe opened a wicket. The peasant carried off the cart to some out-building; but my guide and I passed through the wicket, which was closed again behind us; and by the glimmer of the candle, passed through a court, up a stone stair, along a section of an open gallery, and up more stairs again, until we came at last to the door of a great and somewhat bare apartment. This room, which I understood was to be mine, was pierced by three windows, lined with some lustrous wood disposed in panels, and carpeted with the skins of many savage animals. A bright fire burned in the chimney, and shed abroad a changeful flicker; close up to the blaze there was drawn a table, laid for supper; and in the far end a bed stood ready. I was pleased by these preparations, and said so to Felipe; and he, with the same simplicity of disposition that I had already remarked in him, warmly re-echoed my praises. 'A fine room,' he said; 'a very fine room. And fire, too; fire is good; it melts out the pleasure in your bones. And the bed,' he continued, carrying over the candle in that direction – 'see what fine sheets – how soft, how smooth, smooth'; and he passed his hand again and again over their texture, and then laid down his head and rubbed his cheeks among them with a grossness of content that somehow offended me. I took the candle from his hand (for I feared he would set the bed on fire) and walked back to the supper-table, where, perceiving a measure of wine, I poured out a cup and called to him to come and drink of it. He started to his feet at once and ran to me with a strong expression of hope; but when he saw the wine, he visibly shuddered.

'Oh, no,' he said, 'not that; that is for you. I hate it.'

'Very well, señor,' said I; 'then I will drink to your good health, and to the prosperity of your house and family. Speaking of which,' I added, after I had drunk, 'shall I not have the pleasure of laying my salutations in person at the feet of the señora, your mother?'

But at these words all the childishness passed out of his face and was succeeded by a look of indescribable cunning and secrecy. He backed away from me at the same time, as though I were an animal about to leap or some dangerous fellow with a weapon, and when he had got near the door, glowered at me sullenly with contracted pupils. 'No,' he said at last, and the next moment was gone noiselessly out of the room; and I heard his footing die away downstairs as light as rainfall, and silence closed over the house.

After I had supped I drew up the table nearer to the bed and began to prepare for rest; but in the new position of the light, I was struck by a picture on the wall. It represented a woman, still young. To judge by her costume and the mellow unity which reigned over the canvas, she had long been dead; to judge by the vivacity of the attitude, the eyes and the features, I might have been beholding in a mirror the image of life. Her figure was very slim and strong, and of a just proportion; red tresses lay like a crown over her brow; her eyes, of a very golden brown, held mine with a look; and her face, which was perfectly shaped, was yet marred by a cruel, sullen and sensual expression. Something in both face and figure, something exquisitely intangible, like the echo of an echo, suggested the features and bearing of my guide; and I stood awhile, unpleasantly attracted and wondering at the oddity of the resemblance. The common carnal stock of that race, which had been originally designed for such high dames as the one now looking on me from the canvas, had fallen to baser uses, wearing country clothes, sitting on the shaft and holding the reins of a mule cart, to bring home a lodger. Perhaps an actual link subsisted; perhaps some scruple of the delicate flesh that was once clothed upon with the satin and brocade of the dead lady, now winced at the rude contact of Felipe's frieze.

The first light of the morning shone full upon the portrait, and, as I lay awake, my eyes continued to dwell upon it with growing complacency; its beauty crept about my heart insidiously, silencing my scruples one after another; and while I knew that to love such a woman were to sign and seal one's own sentence of degeneration, I still knew that, if she were alive, I should love her. Day after day the double knowledge of her wickedness and of my weakness grew clearer. She came to be the heroine of many day-dreams, in which her eyes led on to, and sufficiently rewarded, crimes. She cast a dark shadow on my fancy; and when I was out in the free air of heaven, taking vigorous exercise and healthily renewing the current of my blood, it was often a glad thought to me that my enchantress was safe in the grave, her wand of beauty broken, her lips closed in silence, her philtre spilt. And yet I had a half-lingering terror that she might not be dead after all, but re-arisen in the body of some descendant.

Felipe served my meals in my own apartment; and his resemblance to the portrait haunted me. At times it was not; at times, upon some change of attitude or flash of expression, it would leap out upon me like a ghost. It was above all in his ill-tempers that the likeness triumphed. He certainly liked me; he was proud of my notice, which he sought to engage by many simple and childlike devices; he loved to sit close before my fire, talking his broken talk or singing his odd, endless, wordless songs, and sometimes drawing his hand over my clothes with an affectionate manner of caressing that never failed to cause in me an embarrassment of which I was ashamed. But for all that, he was capable of flashes of causeless anger and fits of sturdy sullenness. At a word of reproof, I have seen him upset the dish of which I was about to eat, and this not surreptitiously, but with defiance; and similarly at a hint of inquisition. I was not unnaturally curious, being in a strange place and surrounded by strange people; but at the shadow of a question, he shrank back, lowering and dangerous. Then it was that, for a fraction of a second, this rough lad might have been the brother of the lady in the frame. But these humours were swift to pass; and the resemblance died along with them.

In these first days I saw nothing of anyone but Felipe, unless the portrait is to be counted; and since the lad was plainly of weak mind, and had moments of passion, it may be wondered that I bore his dangerous neighbourhood with equanimity. As a matter of fact, it was for some time irksome; but it happened before long that I obtained over him so complete a mastery as set my disquietude at rest.

It fell in this way. He was by nature slothful, and much of a vagabond, and yet he kept by the house, and not only waited upon my wants, but laboured every day in the garden or small farm to the south of the *residencia*. Here he would be joined by the peasant whom I had seen on the night of my arrival, and who dwelt at the far end of the enclosure, about half a mile away, in a rude out-house; but it was plain to me that, of these two, it was Felipe who did most; and though I would sometimes see him throw down his spade and go to sleep among the very plants he had been digging, his constancy and energy were admirable in themselves, and still more so since I was well assured they were foreign to his disposition and the fruit of an ungrateful effort. But while I admired, I wondered what had called forth in a lad so shuttle-witted this enduring sense of duty. How was it sustained, I asked myself, and to what length did it prevail over his instincts? The priest was possibly his inspirer. But the priest came one day to the *residencia*; I saw him both come and go after an interval of close upon an hour, from a knoll where I was sketching, and all that time Felipe continued to labour undisturbed in the garden.

At last, in a very unworthy spirit, I determined to debauch the lad from his good resolutions and, waylaying him at the gate, easily persuaded him to join me in a ramble. It was a fine day, and the woods to which I led him were green and pleasant and sweet-smelling and alive with the hum of insects. Here he discovered himself in a fresh character, mounting up to heights of gaiety that abashed me, and displaying an energy and grace of movement that delighted the eye. He leaped, he ran round me in mere glee; he would stop, and look and listen, and seem to drink in the world like a cordial; and then he would suddenly spring into a tree with one bound, and hang and gambol there like one at home. Little as he said to me, and that of not much import, I have rarely enjoyed more stirring company; the sight of his delight was a continual feast; the speed and accuracy of his movements pleased me to the heart; and I might have been so thoughtlessly unkind as to make a habit of these walks, had not chance prepared a very rude conclusion to my pleasure. By some swiftness or dexterity the lad captured a squirrel in a tree-top. He was then some way ahead of me, but I saw him drop to the ground and crouch there, crying aloud for pleasure like a child. The sound stirred my sympathies, it was so fresh and innocent; but as I bettered my pace to draw near, the cry of the squirrel knocked upon my heart. I have heard and seen much of the cruelty of lads, and above all of peasants; but what I now beheld struck me into a passion of anger. I thrust the fellow aside, plucked the poor brute out of his hands, and with swift mercy killed it. Then I turned upon the torturer, spoke to him long out of the heat of my indignation, calling him names at which he seemed to wither; and at length, pointing towards the *residencia*, bade him begone and leave me, for I chose to walk with men, not with vermin. He fell upon his knees and, the words coming to him with more clearness than usual, poured out a stream of the most touching supplications, begging me in mercy to forgive him, to forget what he had done, to look to the future. 'Oh, I try so hard,' he said. 'O commandante, bear with Felipe this once; he will never be a brute again!' Thereupon, much more affected than I cared to show, I suffered myself to be persuaded, and at last shook hands with him and made it up. But the squirrel, by way of penance, I made him bury; speaking of the poor thing's beauty, telling him what pains it had suffered, and how base a thing was the abuse of strength. 'See, Felipe,' said I, 'you are strong indeed; but in my hands you are as helpless as that poor thing of the trees. Give me your hand in mine. You cannot remove it. Now suppose that I were cruel like you, and took a pleasure in pain. I only tighten my hold, and see how you suffer.' He screamed aloud, his face stricken ashy and dotted with needle points of sweat; and when I set him free he fell to the earth and nursed his hand and moaned over it like a baby. But he took the lesson in good part; and whether from that, or from what I had said to him, or the higher notion he now had of my bodily strength, his original affection was changed into a dog-like, adoring fidelity.

Meanwhile I gained rapidly in health. The *residencia* stood on the crown of a stony plateau; on every side the mountains hemmed it about; only from the roof, where was a bartizan, there might be seen between two peaks a small segment of plain, blue with extreme distance. The air in these altitudes moved freely and largely; great clouds congregated there, and were broken up by the wind and left in tatters on the hilltops; a hoarse and yet faint rumbling of torrents rose from all round; and one could there study all the ruder and more ancient characters of nature in something of their pristine force. I delighted from the first in the vigorous scenery and changeful weather; nor less in the antique and dilapidated mansion where I dwelt. This was a large oblong, flanked at two opposite corners by bastion-like projections, one of which commanded the door, while both were loopholed for musketry. The lower storey was, besides, naked of windows, so that the building, if garrisoned, could not be carried without artillery. It enclosed an open court planted with pomegranate trees. From this a broad flight of marble stairs ascended to an open gallery, running all round and resting, towards the court, on slender pillars. Thence again, several enclosed stairs led to the upper storeys of the house, which were thus broken up into distinct divisions. The windows, both within and without, were closely shuttered; some of the stonework in the upper parts had fallen; the roof in one place had been wrecked in one of the flurries of wind which were common in these mountains; and the whole house, in the strong, beating sunlight, and standing out above a grove of stunted cork trees, thickly laden and discoloured with dust, looked like the sleeping palace of the legend. The court, in particular, seemed the very home of slumber. A hoarse cooing of doves haunted about the eaves; the winds were excluded, but when they blew outside, the mountain dust fell here as thick as rain, and veiled the red bloom of the pomegranates; shuttered windows and the closed doors of numerous cellars, and the vacant arches of the gallery, enclosed it; and all day long the sun made broken profiles on the four sides, and paraded the shadow of the pillars on the gallery floor. At the ground level there was, however, a certain pillared recess, which bore the marks of human habitation. Though it was open in front upon the court, it was yet provided with a chimney, where a wood fire would be always prettily blazing; and the tile floor was littered with the skins of animals.

It was in this place that I first saw my hostess. She had drawn one of the skins forward and sat in the sun, leaning against a pillar. It was her dress that struck me first of all, for it was rich and brightly coloured, and shone out in that dusty courtyard with something of the same relief as the flowers of the pomegranates. At a second look it was her beauty of person that took hold of me. As she sat back – watching me, I thought, though with invisible eyes – and wearing at the same time an expression of almost imbecile good-humour and contentment, she showed a perfectness of feature and a quiet nobility of attitude that were beyond a statue's. I took off my hat to her in passing, and her face puckered with suspicion as swiftly and lightly as a pool ruffles in the breeze; but she paid no heed to my courtesy. I went forth on my customary walk a trifle daunted, her idol-like impassivity haunting me; and when I returned, although she was still in much the same posture, I was half surprised to see that she had moved as far as the next pillar, following the sunshine. This time, however, she addressed me with some trivial salutation, civilly enough conceived, and uttered in the same deep-chested and yet indistinct and lisping tones that had already baffled the utmost niceness of my hearing of her son. I answered rather at a venture; for not only did I fail to take her meaning with precision, but the sudden disclosure of her eyes disturbed me. They were unusually large, the iris golden like Felipe's, but the pupil at that moment so distended that they seemed almost black; and what affected me was not so much their size as (what was perhaps its consequence) the singular insignificance of their regard. A look more blankly stupid I have never met. My eyes dropped before it even as I spoke, and I went on my way upstairs to my own room, at once baffled and embarrassed. Yet, when I came there and saw the face of the portrait, I was again reminded of the miracle of family descent. My hostess was, indeed, both older and fuller in person; her eyes were of a different colour; her face, besides, was not only free from the ill-significance that offended and attracted me in the painting; it was devoid of either good or bad – a moral blank expressing literally naught. And yet there was a likeness, not so much speaking as immanent, not so much in any particular feature as upon the whole. It should seem, I thought, as if when the master set his signature to that grave canvas, he had not only caught the image of one smiling and false-eyed woman, but stamped the essential quality of a race.

From that day forth, whether I came or went, I was sure to find the señora seated in the sun against a pillar, or stretched on a rug before the fire; only at times she would shift her station to the top round of the stone staircase, where she lay with the same nonchalance right across my path. In all these days, I never knew her to display the least spark of energy beyond what she expended in brushing and re-brushing her copious copper-coloured hair, or in lisping out, in the rich and broken hoarseness of her voice, her customary idle salutations to myself. These, I think, were her two chief pleasures, beyond that of mere quiescence. She seemed always proud of her remarks, as though they had been witticisms; and, indeed, though they were empty enough, like the conversation of many respectable persons, and turned on a very narrow range of subjects, they were never meaningless or incoherent; nay, they had a certain beauty of their own, breathing, as they did, of her entire contentment. Now she would speak of the warmth, in which (like her son) she greatly delighted; now of the flowers of the pomegranate trees; and now of the white doves and long-winged swallows that fanned the air of the court. The birds excited her. As they raked the eaves in their swift flight, or skimmed sidelong past her with a rush of wind, she would sometimes stir and sit a little up, and seem to awaken from her doze of satisfaction. But for the rest of her days she lay luxuriously folded on herself and sunk in sloth and pleasure. Her invincible content at first annoyed me, but I came gradually to find repose in the spectacle, until at last it grew to be my habit to sit down beside her four times in the day both coming and going, and to talk with her sleepily, I scarce knew of what. I had come to like her dull, almost animal neigh-bourhood; her beauty and her stupidity soothed and amused me. I began to find a kind of transcendental good sense in her remarks, and her unfathomable good nature moved me to admiration and envy. The liking was returned; she enjoyed my presence half-unconsciously, as a man in deep meditation may enjoy the babbling of a brook. I can scarce say she brightened when I came, for satisfaction was written on her face eternally, as on some foolish statue's; but I was made conscious of her pleasure by some more intimate communication than the sight. And one day, as I sat within reach of her on the marble step, she suddenly shot forth one of her hands and patted mine. The thing was done, and she was back in her accustomed attitude, before my mind had received intelligence of the caress; and when I turned to look her in the face I could perceive no answerable sentiment. It was plain she attached no moment to the act, and I blamed myself for my own more uneasy consciousness.

The sight and (if I may so call it) the acquaintance of the mother confirmed the view I had already taken of the son. The family blood had been impoverished, perhaps by long inbreeding, which I knew to be a common error among the proud and the exclusive. No decline, indeed, was to be traced in the body, which had been handed down unimpaired in shapeliness and strength; and the faces of today were struck as sharply from the mint as the face of two centuries ago that smiled upon me from the portrait. But the intelligence (that more precious heirloom) was degenerate; the treasure of ancestral memory ran low; and it had required the potent, plebeian crossing of a muleteer or mountain contrabandist to raise what approached hebetude in the mother into the active oddity of the son. Yet of the two, it was the mother I preferred. Of Felipe, vengeful and placable, full of starts and shyings, inconstant as a hare, I could even conceive as a creature possibly noxious. Of the mother I had no thoughts but those of kindness. And indeed, as spectators are apt ignorantly to take sides, I grew something of a partisan in the enmity which I perceived to smoulder between them. True, it seemed mostly on the mother's part. She would sometimes draw in her breath as he came near, and the pupils of her vacant eyes would contract as if with horror or fear. Her emotions, such as they were, were much upon the surface and readily shared; and this latent repulsion occupied my mind, and kept me wondering on what grounds it rested, and whether the son was certainly in fault.

I had been about ten days in the *residencia*, when there sprang up a high and harsh wind, carrying clouds of dust. It came out of malarious lowlands and over several snowy sierras. The nerves of those on whom it blew were strung and jangled; their eyes smarted with the dust; their legs ached under the burthen of their body; and the touch of one hand upon another grew to be odious. The wind, besides, came down the gullies of the hills and stormed about the house with a great, hollow buzzing and whistling that was wearisome to the ear and dismally depressing to the mind. It did not so much blow in gusts as with the steady sweep of a waterfall, so that there was no remission of discomfort while it blew. But higher upon the mountain it was probably of a more variable strength, with accesses of fury; for there came down at times a far-off wailing, infinitely grievous to hear; and at times, on one of the high shelves or terraces, there would start up and then disperse a tower of dust, like the smoke of an explosion.

I no sooner awoke in bed than I was conscious of the nervous tension and depression of the weather, and the effect grew stronger as the day proceeded. It was in vain that I resisted; in vain that I set forth upon my customary morning's walk; the irrational, unchanging fury of the storm had soon beat down my strength and wrecked my temper; and I returned to the *residencia*, glowing with dry heat and foul and gritty with dust. The court had a forlorn appearance; now and then a glimmer of sun fled over it; now and then the wind swooped down upon the pomegranates and scattered the blossoms and set the window-shutters clapping on the wall. In the recess the señora was pacing to and fro with a flushed countenance and bright eyes; I thought, too, she was speaking to herself, like one in anger. But when I addressed her with my customary salutation she only replied by a sharp gesture and continued her walk. The weather had distempered even this impassive creature; and as I went on upstairs I was the less ashamed of my own discomposure.

All day the wind continued; and I sat in my room and made a feint of reading, or walked up and down and listened to the riot overhead. Night fell and I had not so much as a candle. I began to long for some society and stole down to the court. It was now plunged in the blue of the first darkness, but the recess was redly lighted by the fire. The wood had been piled high and was crowned by a shock of flames, which the draught of the chimney brandished to and fro. In this strong and shaken brightness the señora continued pacing from wall to wall with disconnected gestures, clasping her hands, stretching forth her arms, throwing back her head as in appeal to heaven. In these disordered movements the beauty and grace of the woman showed more clearly; but there was a light in her eye that struck on me unpleasantly; and when I had looked on awhile in silence, and seemingly unobserved, I turned tail as I had come, and groped my way back again to my own chamber.

By the time Felipe brought my supper and lights, my nerve was utterly gone; and, had the lad been such as I was used to seeing him, I should have kept him (even by force had that been necessary) to take off the edge from my distasteful solitude. But on Felipe, also, the wind had exercised its influence. He had been feverish all day; now that the night had come he was fallen into a low and tremulous humour that reacted on my own. The sight of his scared face, his starts and pallors and sudden hearkenings, unstrung me; and when he dropped and broke a dish, I fairly leaped out of my seat.

'I think we are all mad today,' said I, affecting to laugh.

'It is the black wind,' he replied dolefully. 'You feel as if you must do something, and you don't know what it is.'

I noted the aptness of the description; but, indeed, Felipe had sometimes a strange felicity in rendering into words the sensations of the body. 'And your mother, too,' said I; 'she seems to feel this weather much. Do you not fear she may be unwell?'

He stared at me a little, and then said, 'No,' almost defiantly and the next moment, carrying his hand to his brow, cried out lamentably on the wind and the noise that made his head go round like a mill-wheel. 'Who can be well?' he cried; and, indeed, I could only echo his question, for I was disturbed enough myself.

I went to bed early, wearied with day-long restlessness, but the poisonous nature of the wind, and its ungodly and unintermittent uproar, would not suffer me to sleep. I lay there and tossed, my nerves and senses on the stretch. At times I would doze, dream horribly, and wake again; and these snatches of oblivion confused me as to time. But it must have been late on in the night, when I was suddenly startled by an outbreak of pitiable and hateful cries. I leaped from my bed, supposing I had dreamed; but the cries still continued to fill the house, cries of pain, I thought, but certainly of rage also, and so savage and discordant that they shocked the heart. It was no illusion; some living thing, some lunatic or some wild animal, was being foully tortured. The thought of Felipe and the squirrel flashed into my mind, and I ran to the door, but it had been locked from the outside; and I might shake it as I pleased, I was a fast prisoner. Still the cries continued. Now they would dwindle down into a moaning that seemed to be articulate, and at these times I made sure they must be human; and again they would break forth and fill the house with ravings worthy of hell. I stood at the door and gave ear to them, till at last they died away. Long after that I still lingered and still continued to hear them mingle in fancy with the storming of the wind; and when at last I crept to my bed, it was with a deadly sickness and a blackness of horror on my heart.

It was little wonder if I slept no more. Why had I been locked in? What had passed? Who was the author of these indescribable and shocking cries? A human being? It was unconceivable. A beast? The cries were scarce quite bestial; and what animal, short of a lion or a tiger, could thus shake the solid walls of the *residencia*? And while I was thus turning over the elements of the mystery, it came into my mind that I had not yet set eyes upon the daughter of the house. What was more probable than that the daughter of the señora, and the sister of Felipe, should be herself insane? Or, what more likely than that these ignorant and half-witted people should seek to manage an afflicted kinswoman by violence? Here was a solution; and yet when I called to mind the cries (which I never did without a shuddering chill) it seemed altogether insufficient: not even cruelty could wring such cries from madness. But of one thing I was sure: I could not live in a house where such a thing was half conceivable and not probe the matter home and, if necessary, interfere.

The next day came, the wind had blown itself out, and there was nothing to remind me of the business of the night. Felipe came to my bedside with obvious cheerfulness; as I passed through the court, the señora was sunning herself with her accustomed immobility; and when I issued from the gateway, I found the whole face of nature austerely smiling, the heavens of a cold blue, and sown with great cloud islands, and the mountainsides mapped forth into provinces of light and shadow. A short walk restored me to myself, and renewed within me the resolve to plumb this mystery; and when, from the vantage of my knoll, I had seen Felipe pass forth to his labours in the garden, I returned at once to the *residencia* to put my design in practice. The señora appeared plunged in slumber; I stood awhile and marked her, but she did not stir; even if my design were indiscreet, I had little to fear from such a guardian; and turning away, I mounted to the gallery and began my exploration of the house.

All morning I went from one door to another, and entered spacious and faded chambers, some rudely shuttered, some receiving their full charge of daylight, all empty and unhomely. It was a rich house, on which Time had breathed his tarnish and dust had scattered disillusion. The spider swung there; the bloated tarantula scampered on the cornices; ants had their crowded highways on the floor of halls of audience; the big and foul fly, that lives on carrion and is often the messenger of death, had set up his nest in the rotten woodwork, and buzzed heavily about the rooms. Here and there a stool or two, a couch, a bed, or a great carved chair remained behind, like islets on the bare floors, to testify to man's bygone habitation; and everywhere the walls were set with the portraits of the dead. I could judge, by these decaying effigies, in the house of what a great and what a handsome race I was then wandering. Many of the men wore orders on their breasts and had the port of noble offices; the women were all richly attired; the canvases most of them by famous hands. But it was not so much these evidences of greatness that took hold upon my mind, even contrasted, as they were, with the present depopulation and decay of that great house. It was rather the parable of family life that I read in this succession of fair faces and shapely bodies. Never before had I so realised the miracle of the continued race, the creation and re-creation, the weaving and changing and handing down of fleshly elements. That a child should be born of its mother, that it should grow and clothe itself (we know not how) with humanity, and put on inherited looks, and turn its head with the manner of one ascendant, and offer its hand with the gesture of another, are wonders dulled for us by repetition. But in the singular unity of look, in the common features and common bearing, of all these painted generations on the walls of the *residencia*, the miracle stared out and looked me in the face. And an ancient mirror falling opportunely in my way, I stood and read my own features a long while, tracing out on either hand the filaments of descent and the bonds that knit me with my family.

At last, in the course of these investigations, I opened the door of a

chamber that bore the marks of habitation. It was of large proportions and faced to the north, where the mountains were most
wildly figured. The embers of a fire smouldered and smoked upon
the hearth, to which a chair had been drawn close. And yet the aspect
of the chamber was ascetic to the degree of sternness; the chair was
uncushioned; the floor and walls were naked; and beyond the books
which lay here and there in some confusion, there was no instrument
of either work or pleasure. The sight of books in the house of such a
family exceedingly amazed me; and I began with a great hurry, and in
momentary fear of interruption, to go from one to another and
hastily inspect their character. They were of all sorts, devotional,
historical and scientific, but mostly of a great age and in the Latin
tongue. Some I could see to bear the marks of constant study; others
had been torn across and tossed aside as if in petulance or dis-
approval. Lastly, as I cruised about that empty chamber, I espied
some papers written upon with pencil on a table near the window. An
unthinking curiosity led me to take one up. It bore a copy of verses,
very roughly metred in the original Spanish, and which I may render
somewhat thus:

> Pleasure approached with Pain and Shame,
> Grief with a wreath of lilies came.
> Pleasure showed the lovely sun;
> Jesu dear, how sweet it shone!
> Grief with her worn hand pointed on,
> Jesu dear, to thee!

Shame and confusion at once fell on me; and, laying down the
paper, I beat an immediate retreat from the apartment. Neither
Felipe nor his mother could have read the books nor written these
rough but feeling verses. It was plain I had stumbled with sacrilegious
feet into the room of the daughter of the house. God knows, my own
heart most sharply punished me for my indiscretion. The thought
that I had thus secretly pushed my way into the confidence of a girl so
strangely situated, and the fear that she might somehow come to hear
of it, oppressed me like guilt. I blamed myself besides for my
suspicions of the night before; wondered that I should ever have
attributed those shocking cries to one of whom I now conceived as of
a saint, spectral of mien, wasted with maceration, bound up in the
practices of a mechanical devotion, and dwelling in a great isolation of
soul with her incongruous relatives; and as I leaned on the balustrade
of the gallery and looked down into the bright close of pomegranates

and at the gaily dressed and somnolent woman, who just then stretched herself and delicately licked her lips as in the very sensuality of sloth, my mind swiftly compared the scene with the cold chamber looking northward on the mountains, where the daughter dwelt.

That same afternoon, as I sat upon my knoll, I saw the padre enter the gates of the *residencia*. The revelation of the daughter's character had struck home to my fancy, and almost blotted out the horrors of the night before; but at sight of this worthy man the memory revived. I descended, then, from the knoll, and making a circuit among the woods, posted myself by the wayside to await his passage. As soon as he appeared I stepped forth and introduced myself as the lodger of the *residencia*. He had a very strong, honest countenance, on which it was easy to read the mingled emotions with which he regarded me – as a foreigner, a heretic, and yet one who had been wounded for the good cause. Of the family at the *residencia* he spoke with reserve, and yet with respect. I mentioned that I had not yet seen the daughter, whereupon he remarked that that was as it should be, and looked at me a little askance. Lastly, I plucked up courage to refer to the cries that had disturbed me in the night. He heard me out in silence, and then stopped and partly turned about, as though to mark beyond doubt that he was dismissing me.

'Do you take tobacco powder?' said he, offering his snuff-box; and then, when I had refused, 'I am an old man,' he added, 'and I may be allowed to remind you that you are a guest.'

'I have, then, your authority,' I returned, firmly enough, although I flushed at the implied reproof, 'to let things take their course, and not to interfere?'

He said, 'Yes,' and with a somewhat uneasy salute turned and left me where I was. But he had done two things: he had set my conscience at rest, and he had awakened my delicacy. I made a great effort, once more dismissed the recollections of the night, and fell again to brooding on my saintly poetess. At the same time, I could not quite forget that I had been locked in, and that night when Felipe brought me my supper I attacked him warily on both points of interest.

'I never see your sister,' said I casually.

'Oh, no,' said he; 'she is a good, good girl,' and his mind instantly veered to something else.

'Your sister is pious, I suppose?' I asked in the next pause.

'Oh!' he cried, joining his hands with extreme fervour, 'a saint; it is she that keeps me up.'

'You are very fortunate,' said I, 'for the most of us, I am afraid, and myself among the number, are better at going down.'

'Señor,' said Felipe earnestly, 'I would not say that. You should not tempt your angel. If one goes down, where is he to stop?'

'Why, Felipe,' said I, 'I had no guess you were a preacher, and I may say a good one; but I suppose that is your sister's doing?'

He nodded at me with round eyes.

'Well, then,' I continued, 'she has doubtless reproved you for your sin of cruelty?'

'Twelve times!' he cried; for this was the phrase by which the odd creature expressed the sense of frequency. 'And I told her you had done so – I remembered that,' he added proudly – 'and she was pleased.'

'Then, Felipe,' said I, 'what were those cries that I heard last night? for surely they were cries of some creature in suffering.'

'The wind,' returned Felipe, looking in the fire.

I took his hand in mine, at which, thinking it to be a caress, he smiled with a brightness of pleasure that came near disarming my resolve. But I trod the weakness down. 'The wind,' I repeated; 'and yet I think it was this hand,' holding it up, 'that had first locked me in.' The lad shook visibly, but answered never a word. 'Well,' said I, 'I am a stranger and a guest. It is not my part either to meddle or to judge in your affairs; in these you shall take your sister's counsel, which I cannot doubt to be excellent. But in so far as concerns my own, I will be no man's prisoner, and I demand that key.' Half an hour later my door was suddenly thrown open, and the key tossed ringing on the floor.

A day or two after I came in from a walk a little before the point of noon. The señora was lying lapped in slumber on the threshold of the recess; the pigeons dozed below the eaves like snowdrifts; the house was under a deep spell of noontide quiet; and only a wandering and gentle wind from the mountain stole round the galleries, rustled among the pomegranates, and pleasantly stirred the shadows. Something in the stillness moved me to imitation, and I went very lightly across the court and up the marble staircase. My foot was on the topmost round, when a door opened, and I found myself face to face with Olalla. Surprise transfixed me; her loveliness struck to my heart; she glowed in the deep shadow of the gallery a gem of colour; her eyes took hold upon mine and clung there, and bound us together like the joining of hands; and the moments we thus stood face to face, drinking each other in, were sacramental and the wedding of souls. I know not how long it was before I awoke out of a deep trance, and, hastily bowing, passed on into the upper stair. She did not move, but followed me with her great, thirsting eyes; and as I passed out of sight it seemed to me as if she paled and faded.

In my own room, I opened the window and looked out, and could not think what change had come upon that austere field of mountains that it should thus sing and shine under the lofty heaven. I had seen her – Olalla! And the stone crags answered, Olalla! and the dumb, unfathomable azure answered, Olalla! The pale saint of my dreams had vanished for ever; and in her place I beheld this maiden on whom God had lavished the richest colours and the most exuberant energies of life, whom He had made active as a deer, slender as a reed, and in whose great eyes He had lighted the torches of the soul. The thrill of her young life, strung like a wild animal's, had entered into me; the force of soul that had looked out from her eyes and conquered mine, mantled about my heart and sprang to my lips in singing. She passed through my veins: she was one with me.

I will not say that this enthusiasm declined; rather my soul held out in its ecstasy as in a strong castle, and was there besieged by cold and sorrowful considerations. I could not doubt but that I loved her at first sight, and already with a quivering ardour that was strange to my experience. What then was to follow? She was the child of an afflicted house, the señora's daughter, the sister of Felipe; she bore it even in her beauty. She had the lightness and swiftness of the one, swift as an arrow, light as dew; like the other, she shone on the pale background of the world with the brilliancy of flowers. I could not call by the name of brother that half-witted lad, nor by the name of mother that immovable and lovely thing of flesh, whose silly eyes and perpetual simper now recurred to my mind like something hateful. And if I could not marry, what then? She was helplessly unprotected; her eyes, in that single and long glance which had been all our intercourse, had confessed a weakness equal to my own; but in my heart I knew her for the student of the cold northern chamber, and the writer of the sorrowful lines; and this was a knowledge to disarm a brute. To flee was more than I could find courage for; but I registered a vow of unsleeping circumspection.

As I turned from the window, my eyes alighted on the portrait. It had fallen dead, like a candle after sunrise; it followed me with eyes of paint. I knew it to be like, and marvelled at the tenacity of type in that declining race; but the likeness was swallowed up in difference. I remembered how it had seemed to me a thing unapproachable in the life, a creature rather of the painter's craft than of the modesty of nature, and I marvelled at the thought, and exulted in the image of Olalla. Beauty I had seen before, and not been charmed, and I had been often drawn to women who were not beautiful except to me; but in Olalla all that I desired and had not dared to imagine was united.

I did not see her the next day, and my heart ached and my eyes longed for her, as men long for morning. But the day after, when I returned, about my usual hour, she was once more on the gallery, and our looks once more met and embraced. I would have spoken, I would have drawn near to her; but strongly as she plucked at my heart, drawing me like a magnet, something yet more imperious withheld me; and I could only bow and pass by; and she, leaving my salutation unanswered, only followed me with her noble eyes.

I had now her image by rote, and as I conned the traits in memory it seemed as if I read her very heart. She was dressed with something of her mother's coquetry, and love of positive colour. Her robe, which I knew she must have made with her own hands, clung about her with a cunning grace. After the fashion of that country, besides, her bodice stood open in the middle, in a long slit, and here, in spite of the poverty of the house, a gold coin, hanging by a ribbon, lay on her brown bosom. These were proofs, had any been needed, of her inborn delight in life and her own loveliness. On the other hand, in her eyes that hung upon mine, I could read depth beyond depth of passion and sadness, lights of poetry and hope, blacknesses of despair, and thoughts that were above the earth. It was a lovely body, but the inmate, the soul, was more than worthy of that lodging. Should I leave this incomparable flower to wither unseen on these rough mountains? Should I despise the great gift offered me in the eloquent silence of her eyes? Here was a soul immured; should I not burst its prison? All side considerations fell off from me; were she the child of Herod I swore I should make her mine; and that very evening I set myself, with a mingled sense of treachery and disgrace, to captivate the brother. Perhaps I read him with more favourable eyes, perhaps the thought of his sister always summoned up the better qualities of that imperfect soul; but he had never seemed to be so amiable, and his very likeness to Olalla, while it annoyed, yet softened me.

A third day passed in vain – an empty desert of hours. I would not lose a chance, and loitered all afternoon in the court where (to give myself a countenance) I spoke more than usual with the señora. God knows it was with a most tender and sincere interest that I now studied her; and even as for Felipe, so now for the mother, I was conscious of a growing warmth of toleration. And yet I wondered. Even while I spoke with her, she would doze off into a little sleep, and presently awake again without embarrassment; and this composure staggered me. And again, as I marked her make infinitesimal changes in her posture, savouring and lingering on the bodily pleasure of the movement, I was driven to wonder at this depth of passive sensuality. She lived in her body; and her consciousness was all sunk into and disseminated through her members, where it luxuriously dwelt. Lastly, I could not grow accustomed to her eyes. Each time she turned on me these great beautiful and meaningless orbs, wide open to the day, but closed against human enquiry – each time I had occasion to observe the lively changes of her pupils which expanded and contracted in a breath – I know not what it was came over me, I can find no name for the mingled feeling of disappointment, annoyance and distaste that jarred along my nerves. I tried her on a variety of subjects, equally in vain; and at last led the talk to her daughter. But even there she proved indifferent; said she was pretty, which (as with children) was her highest word of commendation, but was plainly incapable of any higher thought; and when I remarked that Olalla seemed silent, merely yawned in my face and replied that speech was of no great use when you had nothing to say. 'People speak much, very much,' she added, looking at me with expanded pupils; and then again yawned, and again showed me a mouth that was as dainty as a toy. This time I took the hint, and, leaving her to her repose, went up into my own chamber to sit by the open window, looking on the hills and not beholding them, sunk in lustrous and deep dreams, and hearkening in fancy to the note of a voice that I had never heard.

I awoke on the fifth morning with a brightness of anticipation that seemed to challenge fate. I was sure of myself, light of heart and foot, and resolved to put my love incontinently to the touch of knowledge. It should lie no longer under the bonds of silence, a dumb thing, living by the eye only, like the love of beasts; but should now put on the spirit, and enter upon the joys of the complete human intimacy. I thought of it with wild hopes, like a voyager to El Dorado; into that unknown and lovely country of her soul, I no longer trembled to adventure. Yet when I did encounter her, the same force of passion descended on me and at once submerged my mind; speech seemed to drop away from me like a childish habit; and I but drew near to her as the giddy man draws near to the margin of a gulf. She drew back from me a little as I came; but her eyes did not waver from mine, and these lured me forward. At last, when I was already within reach of her, I stopped. Words were denied me; if I advanced I could but clasp her to my heart in silence; and all that was sane in me, all that was still unconquered, revolted against the thought of such an accost. So we stood for a second, all our life in our eyes, exchanging salvos of attraction and yet each resisting; and then, with a great effort of the will, and conscious at the same time of a sudden bitterness of disppointment, I turned and went away in the same silence.

What power lay upon me that I could not speak? And she, why was she also silent? Why did she draw away before me dumbly, with fascinated eyes? Was this love? or was it a mere brute attraction, mindless and inevitable, like that of the magnet for the steel? We had never spoken, we were wholly strangers; and yet an influence, strong as the grasp of a giant, swept us silently together. On my side it filled me with impatience; and yet I was sure that she was worthy; I had seen her books, read her verses, and thus, in a sense, divined the soul of my mistress. But on her side it struck me almost cold. Of me she knew nothing but my bodily favour; she was drawn to me as stones fall to the earth; the laws that rule the earth conducted her, unconsenting, to my arms; and I drew back at the thought of such a bridal, and began to be jealous for myself. It was not thus that I desired to be loved. And then I began to fall into a great pity for the girl herself. I thought how sharp must be her mortification, that she, the student, the recluse, Felipe's saintly monitress, should have thus confessed an overweening weakness for a man with whom she had never exchanged a word. And at the coming of pity, all other thoughts were swallowed up; and I longed only to find and console and reassure her; to tell her how wholly her love was returned on my side, and how her choice, even if blindly made, was not unworthy.

The next day it was glorious weather; depth upon depth of blue over-canopied the mountains; the sun shone wide; and the wind in the trees and the many falling torrents in the mountains filled the air with delicate and haunting music. Yet I was prostrated with sadness. My heart wept for the sight of Olalla, as a child weeps for its mother. I sat down on a boulder on the verge of the low cliffs that bound the plateau to the north. Thence I looked down into the wooded valley of a stream, where no foot came. In the mood I was in, it was even touching to behold the place untenanted; it lacked Olalla; and I thought of the delight and glory of a life passed wholly with her in that strong air, and among these rugged and lovely surroundings, at first with a whimpering sentiment, and then again with such a fiery joy that I seemed to grow in strength and stature, like a Samson.

And then suddenly I was aware of Olalla drawing near. She appeared out of a grove of cork trees, and came straight towards me; and I stood up and waited. She seemed in her walking a creature of such life and fire and lightness as amazed me; yet she came quietly and slowly. Her energy was in the slowness; but for inimitable strength, I felt she would have run, she would have flown to me. Still, as she approached, she kept her eyes lowered to the ground; and when she had drawn quite near, it was without one glance that she addressed me. At the first note of her voice I started. It was for this I had been waiting; this was the last test of my love. And lo, her enunciation was precise and clear, not lisping and incomplete like that of her family; and the voice, though deeper than usual with women, was still both youthful and womanly. She spoke in a rich chord; golden contralto strains mingled with hoarseness, as the red threads were mingled with the brown among her tresses. It was not only a voice that spoke to my heart directly; but it spoke to me of her. And yet her words immediately plunged me back upon despair.

'You will go away,' she said, 'today.'

Her example broke the bonds of my speech; I felt as lightened of a weight, or as if a spell had been dissolved. I know not in what words I answered; but, standing before her on the cliffs, I poured out the whole ardour of my love, telling her I lived upon the thought of her, slept only to dream of her loveliness, and would gladly forswear my country, my language and my friends, to live for ever by her side. And then, strongly commanding myself, I changed the note; I reassured, I comforted her; I told her I had divined in her a pious and heroic spirit, with which I was worthy to sympathise, and which I longed to share and lighten. 'Nature,' I told her, 'is the voice of God, which men disobey at peril; and if we are thus dumbly drawn together, ay, even as by a miracle of love, it must imply a divine fitness in our souls; we must be made,' I said – 'made for one another. We should be mad rebels,' I cried out – 'mad rebels against God, not to obey this instinct.'

She shook her head. 'You will go today,' she repeated, and then with a gesture, and in a sudden, sharp note – 'no, not today,' she cried, 'tomorrow!'

But at this sign of relenting, power came in upon me in a tide. I stretched out my arms and called upon her name; and she leaped to me and clung to me. The hills rocked about us, the earth quailed; a shock as of a blow went through me and left me blind and dizzy. And the next moment she had thrust me back, broken rudely from my arms, and fled with the speed of a deer among the cork trees.

I stood and shouted to the mountains; I turned and went back towards the *residencia*, walking upon air. She sent me away, and yet I had but to call upon her name and she came to me. These were but the weaknesses of girls, from which even she, the strangest of her sex, was not exempted. Go? not I, Olalla – oh, not I, Olalla, my Olalla! A bird sang near by; and in that season birds were rare. It bade me be of good cheer. And once more the whole countenance of nature, from the ponderous and stable mountains down to the lightest leaf and the smallest darting fly in the shadow of the groves, began to stir before me and to put on the lineaments of life and wear a face of awful joy. The sunshine struck upon the hills, strong as a hammer on the anvil, and the hills shook; the earth, under that vigorous insolation, yielded up heady scents; the woods smouldered in the blaze. I felt the thrill of travail and delight run through the earth. Something elemental, something rude, violent and savage in the love that sang in my heart, was like a key to nature's secrets; and the very stones that rattled under my feet appeared alive and friendly. Olalla! Her touch had quickened, and renewed, and strung me up to the old pitch of concert with the rugged earth, to a swelling of the soul that men learned to forget in their polite assemblies. Love burned in me like rage; tenderness waxed fierce; I hated, I adored, I pitied, I revered her with ecstasy. She seemed the link that bound me in with dead things on the one hand, and with our pure and pitying God upon the other: a thing brutal and divine, and akin at once to the innocence and to the unbridled forces of the earth.

My head thus reeling, I came into the courtyard of the *residencia*, and the sight of the mother struck me like a revelation. She sat there, all sloth and contentment, blinking under the strong sunshine, branded with a passive enjoyment, a creature set quite apart, before whom my ardour fell away like a thing ashamed. I stopped a moment, and, commanding such shaken tones as I was able, said a word or two. She looked at me with her unfathomable kindness; her voice in reply sounded vaguely out of the realm of peace in which she slumbered, and there fell on my mind, for the first time, a sense of respect for one so uniformly innocent and happy, and I passed on in a kind of wonder at myself, that I should be so much disquieted.

On my table there lay a piece of the same yellow paper I had seen in the north room; it was written on with pencil in the same hand,

Olalla's hand, and I picked it up with a sudden sinking of alarm, and read: 'If you have any kindness for Olalla, if you have any chivalry for a creature sorely wrought, go from here today; in pity, in honour, for the sake of Him who died, I supplicate that you shall go.' I looked at this awhile in mere stupidity, then I began to awaken to a weariness and horror of life; the sunshine darkened outside on the bare hills, and I began to shake like a man in terror. The vacancy thus suddenly opened in my life unmanned me like a physical void. It was not my heart, it was not my happiness, it was life itself that was involved. I could not lose her. I said so, and stood repeating it. And then, like one in a dream, I moved to the window, put forth my hand to open the casement, and thrust it through the pane. The blood spurted from my wrist; and with an instantaneous quietude and command of myself, I pressed my thumb on the little leaping fountain and reflected what to do. In that empty room there was nothing to my purpose; I felt, besides, that I required assistance. There shot into my mind a hope that Olalla herself might be my helper, and I turned and went downstairs, still keeping my thumb upon the wound.

There was no sign of either Olalla or Felipe, and I addressed myself to the recess, whither the señora had now drawn quite back and sat dozing close before the fire, for no degree of heat appeared too much for her.

'Pardon me,' said I, 'if I disturb you, but I must apply to you for help.'

She looked up sleepily and asked me what it was, and with the very words I thought she drew in her breath with a widening of the nostrils and seemed to come suddenly and fully alive.

'I have cut myself,' I said, 'and rather badly. See!' And I held out my two hands from which the blood was oozing and dripping.

Her great eyes opened wide, the pupils shrank into points; a veil seemed to fall from her face, and leave it sharply expressive and yet inscrutable. And as I still stood, marvelling a little at her disturbance, she came swiftly up to me, and stooped and caught me by the hand; and the next moment my hand was at her mouth, and she had bitten me to the bone. The pang of the bite, the sudden spurting of blood and the monstrous horror of the act flashed through me all in one and I beat her back; and she sprang at me again and again, with bestial cries, cries that I recognised, such cries as had awakened me on the night of the high wind. Her strength was like that of madness; mine was rapidly ebbing with the loss of blood; my mind besides was whirling with the abhorrent strangeness of the onslaught, and I was already forced against the wall, when Olalla ran betwixt us, and Felipe, following at a bound, pinned down his mother on the floor.

A trance-like weakness fell upon me; I saw, heard and felt, but I was incapable of movement. I heard the struggle roll to and fro upon the floor, the yells of that catamount ringing up to heaven as she strove to reach me. I felt Olalla clasp me in her arms, her hair falling on my face, and, with the strength of a man, raise and half drag, half carry me upstairs into my own room, where she cast me down upon the bed. Then I saw her hasten to the door and lock it, and stand an instant listening to the savage cries that shook the *residencia*. And then, swift and light as a thought, she was again beside me, binding up my hand, laying it in her bosom, moaning and mourning over it with dove-like sounds. They were not words that came to her, they were sounds more beautiful than speech, infinitely touching, infinitely tender; and yet as I lay there, a thought stung to my heart, a thought wounded me like a sword, a thought, like a worm in a flower, profaned the holiness of my love. Yes, they were beautiful sounds, and they were inspired by human tenderness; but was their beauty human?

All day I lay there. For a long time the cries of that nameless female thing, as she struggled with her half-witted whelp, resounded through the house, and pierced me with despairing sorrow and disgust. They were the death-cry of my love; my love was murdered; it was not only dead, but an offence to me; and yet, think as I pleased, feel as I must, it still swelled within me like a storm of sweetness, and my heart melted at her looks and touch. This horror that had sprung out, this doubt upon Olalla, this savage and bestial strain that ran not only through the whole behaviour of her family, but found a place in the very foundations and story of our love – though it appalled, though it shocked and sickened me, was yet not of power to break the knot of my infatuation.

When the cries had ceased, there came a scraping at the door, by which I knew Felipe was without; and Olalla went and spoke to him – I know not what. With that exception, she stayed close beside me, now kneeling by my bed and fervently praying, now sitting with her eyes upon mine. So then, for these six hours I drank in her beauty, and silently perused the story in her face. I saw the golden coin hover on her breasts; I saw her eyes darken and brighten, and still speak no language but that of an unfathomable kindness; I saw the faultless face, and, through the robe, the lines of the faultless body. Night came at last, and in the growing darkness of the chamber, the sight of her slowly melted; but even then the touch of her smooth hand lingered in mine and talked with me. To lie thus in deadly weakness and drink in the traits of the beloved is to reawake to love from whatever shock of disillusion. I reasoned with myself, and I shut my eyes on horrors, and again I was very bold to accept the worst. What mattered it if that imperious sentiment survived; if her eyes still beckoned and attached me; if now, even as before, every fibre of my dull body yearned and turned to her? Late on in the night some strength revived in me, and I spoke: 'Olalla,' I said, 'nothing matters; I ask nothing; I am content; I love you.'

She knelt down awhile and prayed, and I devoutly respected her devotions. The moon had begun to shine in upon one side of each of the three windows, and make a misty clearness in the room, by which I saw her indistinctly. When she re-arose she made the sign of the cross.

'It is for me to speak,' she said, 'and for you to listen. I know; you can but guess. I prayed, how I prayed for you to leave this place! I begged it of you, and I know you would have granted me even this; or if not, oh, let me think so!'

'I love you,' I said.

'And yet you have lived in the world,' she said; after a pause, 'you are a man and wise; and I am but a child. Forgive me, if I seem to teach, who am as ignorant as the trees of the mountain; but those who learn much do but skim the face of knowledge; they seize the laws, they conceive the dignity of the design – the horror of the living fact fades from their memory. It is we who sit at home with evil who remember, I think, and are warned and pity. Go, rather, go now, and keep me in mind. So I shall have a life in the cherished places of your memory: a life as much my own as that which I lead in this body.'

'I love you,' I said once more; and reaching out my weak hand, took hers, and carried it to my lips and kissed it. Nor did she resist, but winced a little; and I could see her look upon me with a frown that was not unkindly, only sad and baffled. And then it seemed she made a call upon her resolution; plucked my hand towards her, herself at the same time leaning somewhat forward, and laid it on the beating of her heart. 'There,' she cried, 'you feel the very footfall of my life. It only moves for you; it is yours. But is it even mine? It is mine indeed to offer you, as I might take the coin from my neck, as I might break a live branch from a tree and give it you. And yet not mine! I dwell, or I think I dwell (if I exist at all), somewhere apart, an impotent prisoner, and carried about and deafened by a mob that I disown. This capsule, such as throbs against the sides of animals, knows you at a touch for its master; ay, it loves you! But my soul, does my soul? I think not; I know not, fearing to ask. Yet when you spoke to me, your words were of the soul; it is of the soul that you ask – it is only from the soul that you would take me.'

'Olalla,' I said, 'the soul and the body are one, and mostly so in love. What the body chooses, the soul loves; where the body clings, the soul cleaves; body for body, soul to soul, they come together at God's signal; and the lower part (if we can call aught low) is only the footstool and foundation of the highest.'

'Have you,' she said, 'seen the portraits in the house of my fathers? Have you looked at my mother or at Felipe? Have your eyes never rested on that picture that hangs by your bed? She who sat for it died ages ago; and she did evil in her life. But, look again: there is my hand to the least line, there are my eyes and my hair. What is mine, then, and what am I? If not a curve in this poor body of mine (which you love, and for the sake of which you dotingly dream that you love me), not a gesture that I can frame, not a tone of my voice, not any look from my eyes, no, not even now when I speak to him I love, but has belonged to others? Others, ages dead, have wooed other men with my eyes; other men have heard the pleading of the same voice that now sounds in your ears. The hands of the dead are in my bosom; they move me, they pluck me, they guide me; I am a puppet at their command; and I but reinform features and attributes that have long been laid aside from evil in the quiet of the grave. Is it me you love, friend? or the race that made me? The girl who does not know and cannot answer for the least portion of herself? or the stream of which she is a transitory eddy, the tree of which she is the passing fruit? The race exists; it is old, it is ever young, it carries its eternal destiny in its bosom; upon it, like waves upon the sea, individual succeeds to individual, mocked with a semblance of self-control, but they are nothing. We speak of the soul, but the soul is in the race.'

'You fret against the common law,' I said. 'You rebel against the voice of God, which He has made so winning to convince, so imperious to command. Hear it, and how it speaks between us! Your hand clings to mine, your heart leaps at my touch, the unknown elements of which we are compounded awake and run together at a look; the clay of the earth remembers its independent life and yearns to join us; we are drawn together as the stars are turned about in space, or as the tides ebb and flow, by things older and greater than we ourselves.'

'Alas!' she said, 'what can I say to you? My fathers, eight hundred years ago, ruled all this province: they were wise, great, cunning and cruel; they were a picked race of the Spanish; their flags led in war; the king called them his cousin; the people, when the rope was slung for them or when they returned and found their hovels smoking, blasphemed their name. Presently a change began. Man has risen; if he has sprung from the brutes, he can descend again to the same level. The breath of weariness blew on their humanity and the cords relaxed; they began to go down; their minds fell on sleep, their passions awoke in gusts, heady and senseless like the wind in the gutters of the mountains; beauty was still handed down, but no longer the guiding wit nor the human heart; the seed passed on, it was wrapped in flesh, the flesh covered the bones, but they were the bones and the flesh of brutes, and their mind was as the mind of flies. I speak to you as I dare; but you have seen for yourself how the wheel has gone backward with my doomed race. I stand, as it were, upon a little rising ground in this desperate descent, and see both before and behind, both what we have lost and to what we are condemned, to go farther downward. And shall I – I that dwell apart in the house of the dead, my body, loathing its ways – shall I repeat the spell? Shall I bind another spirit, reluctant as my own, into this bewitched and tempest-broken tenement that I now suffer in? Shall I hand down this cursed vessel of humanity, charge it with fresh life as with fresh poison, and dash it, like a fire, in the faces of posterity? But my vow has been given; the race shall cease from off the earth. At this hour my brother is making ready; his foot will soon be on the stair; and you will go with him and pass out of my sight for ever. Think of me sometimes as one to whom the lesson of life was very harshly told, but who heard it with courage; as one who loved you indeed, but who hated herself so deeply that her love was hateful to her; as one who sent you away and yet would have longed to keep you for ever; who had no dearer hope than to forget you, and no greater fear than to be forgotten.'

She had drawn towards the door as she spoke, her rich voice sounding softer and farther away; and with the last word she was gone, and I lay alone in the moonlit chamber. What I might have done had not I lain bound by my extreme weakness, I know not; but as it was there fell upon me a great and blank despair. It was not long before there shone in at the door the ruddy glimmer of a lantern, and Felipe coming, charged me without a word upon his shoulders, and carried me down to the great gate, where the cart was waiting. In the moonlight the hills stood out sharply, as if they were of cardboard; on the glimmering surface of the plateau, and from among the low trees which swung together and sparkled in the wind, the great black cube of the *residencia* stood out bulkily, its mass only broken by three dimly lighted windows in the northern front above the gate. They were Olalla's windows, and as the cart jolted onwards I kept my eyes fixed upon them till, where the road dipped into a valley, they were lost to my view for ever. Felipe walked in silence beside the shafts, but from time to time he would check the mule and seem to look back upon me; and at length drew quite near and laid his hand upon my head. There was such kindness in the touch, and such a simplicity, as of the brutes, that tears broke from me like the bursting of an artery.

'Felipe,' I said, 'take me where they will ask no questions.'

He said never a word, but he turned his mule about, end for end, retraced some part of the way we had gone, and, striking into another path, led me to the mountain village, which was, as we say in Scotland, the kirkton of that thinly peopled district. Some broken memories dwell in my mind of the day breaking over the plain, of the cart stopping, of arms that helped me down, of a bare room into which I was carried and of a swoon that fell upon me like sleep.

The next day and the days following the old priest was often at my side with his snuff-box and prayer-book, and after a while, when I began to pick up strength, he told me that I was now on a fair way to recovery, and must as soon as possible hurry my departure; where-upon, without naming any reason, he took snuff and looked at me sideways. I did not affect ignorance; I knew he must have seen Olalla. 'Sir,' said I, 'you know that I do not ask in wantonness. What of that family?'

He said they were very unfortunate; that it seemed a declining race, and that they were very poor and had been much neglected.

'But she has not,' I said. 'Thanks, doubtless, to yourself, she is instructed and wise beyond the use of women.'

'Yes,' he said; 'the señorita is well informed. But the family has been neglected.'

'The mother?' I queried.

'Yes, the mother too,' said the padre, taking snuff. 'But Felipe is a well-intentioned lad.'

'The mother is odd?' I asked.

'Very odd,' replied the priest.

'I think, sir, we beat about the bush,' said I. 'You must know more of my affairs than you allow. You must know my curiosity to be justified on many grounds. Will you not be frank with me?'

'My son,' said the old gentleman, 'I will be very frank with you on matters within my competence; on those of which I know nothing it does not require much discretion to be silent. I will not fence with you, I take your meaning perfectly; and what can I say, but that we are all in God's hands, and that His ways are not as our ways? I have even advised with my superiors in the Church, but they, too, were dumb. It is a great mystery.'

'Is she mad?' I asked.

'I will answer you according to my belief. She is not,' returned the padre, 'or she was not. When she was young – God help me, I fear I neglected that wild lamb – she was surely sane; and yet, although it did not run to such heights, the same strain was already notable; it had been so before her in her father, ay, and before him, and this inclined me, perhaps, to think too lightly of it. But these things go on growing, not only in the individual but in the race.'

'When she was young,' I began, and my voice failed me for a moment, and it was only with a great effort that I was able to add, 'was she like Olalla?'

'Now God forbid!' exclaimed the padre. 'God forbid that any man should think so slightingly of my favourite penitent. No, no; the señorita (but for her beauty, which I wish most honestly she had less of) has not a hair's resemblance to what her mother was at the same age. I could not bear to have you think so; though, heaven knows, it were, perhaps, better that you should.'

At this, I raised myself in bed and opened my heart to the old man; telling him of our love and of her decision, owning my own horrors, my own passing fancies, but telling him that these were at an end, and with something more than a purely formal submission, appealing to his judgement.

He heard me very patiently and without surprise; and when I had done, he sat for some time silent. Then he began: 'The Church – ' and instantly broke off again to apologise. 'I had forgotten, my child, that you were not a Christian,' said he. 'And indeed, upon a point so highly unusual, even the Church can scarce be said to have decided. But would you have my opinion? The señorita is, in a matter of this kind, the best judge; I would accept her judgement.'

On the back of that he went away, nor was he thenceforward so assiduous in his visits; indeed, even when I began to get about again, he plainly feared and deprecated my society, not as in distaste but much as a man might be disposed to flee from the riddling sphinx. The villagers, too, avoided me; they were unwilling to be my guides upon the mountain. I thought they looked at me askance, and I made sure that the more superstitious crossed themselves on my approach. At first I set this down to my heretical opinions; but it began at length to dawn upon me that if I was thus redoubted it was because I had stayed at the *residencia*. All men despise the savage notions of such peasantry; and yet I was conscious of a chill shadow that seemed to fall and dwell upon my love. It did not conquer, but I may not deny that it restrained my ardour.

Some miles westward of the village there was a gap in the sierra, from which the eye plunged direct upon the *residencia*, and thither it became my daily habit to repair. A wood crowned the summit, and just where the pathway issued from its fringes it was overhung by a considerable shelf of rock, and that, in its turn, was surmounted by a crucifix of the size of life and more than usually painful in design. This was my perch; thence, day after day, I looked down upon the plateau and the great old house, and could see Felipe, no bigger than a fly, going to and fro about the garden. Sometimes mists would draw across the view, and be broken up again by mountain winds; sometimes the plain slumbered below me in unbroken sunshine; it would sometimes be all blotted out by rain. This distant post, these interrupted sights of the place where my life had been so strangely changed, suited the indecision of my humour. I passed whole days there, debating with myself the various elements of our position; now leaning to the suggestions of love, now giving an ear to prudence, and in the end halting irresolute between the two.

One day, as I was sitting on my rock, there came by that way a somewhat gaunt peasant wrapped in a mantle. He was a stranger, and plainly did not know me even by repute; for, instead of keeping the other side, he drew near and sat down beside me, and we had soon fallen into talk. Among other things he told me he had been a muleteer, and in former years had much frequented these mountains; later on, he had followed the army with his mules, had realised a competence, and was now living retired with his family.

'Do you know that house?' I enquired at last, pointing to the *residencia*, for I readily wearied of any talk that kept me from the thought of Olalla.

He looked at me darkly and crossed himself.

'Too well,' he said, 'it was there that one of my comrades sold himself to Satan; the Virgin shield us from temptations! He has paid the price; he is now burning in the reddest place in Hell!'

A fear came upon me; I could answer nothing; and presently the man resumed, as if to himself: 'Yes,' he said, 'oh yes, I know it. I have passed its doors. There was snow upon the pass, the wind was driving it; sure enough there was death that night upon the mountains, but there was worse beside the hearth. I took him by the arm, señor, and dragged him to the gate; I conjured him, by all he loved and respected, to go forth with me; I went on my knees before him in the snow, and I could see he was moved by my entreaty. And just then she came out on the gallery and called him by his name; and he turned, and there was she standing with a lamp in her hand and smiling on him to come back. I cried out aloud to God, and threw my arms about him, but he put me by and left me alone. He had made his choice; God help us. I would pray for him, but to what end? there are sins that not even the Pope can loose.'

'And your friend,' I asked, 'what became of him?'

'Nay, God knows,' said the muleteer. 'If all be true that we hear, his end was like his sin, a thing to raise the hair.'

'Do you mean that he was killed?' I asked.

'Sure enough, he was killed,' returned the man. 'But how? Ay, how? But these are things that it is sin to speak of.'

'The people of that house . . . ' I began.

But he interrupted me with a savage outburst. 'The people?' he cried. 'What people? There are neither men nor women in that house of Satan's! What? have you lived here so long and never heard?' And here he put his mouth to my ear and whispered, as if even the fowls of the mountain might have overheard and been stricken with horror.

What he told me was not true, nor was it even original; being, indeed, but a new edition, vamped up again by village ignorance and superstition, of stories nearly as ancient as the race of man. It was rather the application that appalled me. In the old days, he said, the Church would have burned out that nest of basilisks; but the arm of the Church was now shortened; his friend Miguel had been unpunished by the hands of men, and left to the more awful judgement of an offended God. This was wrong; but it should be so no more. The padre was sunk in age; he was even bewitched himself; but the eyes of his flock were now awake to their own danger; and someday – ay, and before long – the smoke of that house should go up to heaven.

He left me filled with horror and fear. Which way to turn I knew not; whether first to warn the padre, or to carry my ill-news direct to the threatened inhabitants of the *residencia*. Fate was to decide for me, for, while I was still hesitating, I beheld the veiled figure of a woman drawing near to me up the pathway. No veil could deceive my penetration; by every line and every movement I recognised Olalla; and keeping hidden behind a corner of the rock, I suffered her to gain the summit. Then I came forward. She knew me and paused, but did not speak; I, too, remained silent, and we continued for some time to gaze upon each other with a passionate sadness.

'I thought you had gone,' she said at length. 'It is all that you can do for me – to go. It is all I ever asked of you. And you still stay. But do you know that every day heaps up the peril of death, not only on your head, but on ours? A report has gone about the mountain; it is thought you love me, and the people will not suffer it.'

I saw she was already informed of her danger, and I rejoiced at it. 'Olalla,' I said, 'I am ready to go this day, this very hour, but not alone.'

She stepped aside and knelt down before the crucifix to pray, and I stood by and looked now at her and now at the object of her adoration, now at the living figure of the penitent, and now at the ghastly daubed countenance, the painted wounds and the projected ribs of the image. The silence was only broken by the wailing of some large birds that circled sidelong, as if in surprise or alarm, about the summit of the hills. Presently Olalla rose again, turned towards me, raised her veil, and, still leaning with one hand on the shaft of the crucifix, looked upon me with a pale and sorrowful countenance.

'I have laid my hand upon the cross,' she said. 'The padre says you are no Christian; but look up for a moment with my eyes, and behold the face of the Man of Sorrows. We are all such as He was – the inheritors of sin; we must all bear and expiate a past which was not ours; there is in all of us – ay, even in me – a sparkle of the divine. Like Him, we must endure for a little while, until morning returns bringing peace. Suffer me to pass on upon my way alone; it is thus that I shall be least lonely, counting for my friend Him who is the friend of all the distressed; it is thus that I shall be the most happy, having taken my farewell of earthly happiness, and willingly accepted sorrow for my portion.'

I looked at the face of the crucifix, and, though I was no friend to images, and despised that imitative and grimacing art of which it was a rude example, some sense of what the thing implied was carried home to my intelligence. The face looked down upon me with a painful and deadly contraction; but the rays of a glory encircled it, and reminded me that the sacrifice was voluntary. It stood there, crowning the rock, as it still stands on so many highway sides, vainly preaching to passers-by, an emblem of sad and noble truths, that pleasure is not an end, but an accident; that pain is the choice of the magnanimous; that it is best to suffer all things and do well. I turned and went down the mountain in silence; and when I looked back for the last time before the wood closed about my path, I saw Olalla still leaning on the crucifix.

ANONYMOUS

The Ghost of Craig-Aulnaic

Two celebrated ghosts existed, once on a time, in the wilds of Craig-Aulnaic, a romantic place in the district of Strathdown, Banffshire. The one was a male and the other a female. The male was called Fhuna Mhoir Ben Baynac, after one of the mountains of Glenavon, where at one time he resided; and the female was called Clashnichd Aulnaic, from her having had her abode in Craig-Aulnaic. But although the great ghost of Ben Baynac was bound by the common ties of nature and of honour to protect and cherish his weaker companion, Clashnichd Aulnaic, yet he often treated her in the most cruel and unfeeling manner. In the dead of night, when the surrounding hamlets were buried in deep repose, and when nothing else disturbed the solemn stillness of the midnight scene, oft would the shrill shrieks of poor Clashnichd burst upon the slumberer's ears, and awake him to anything but pleasant reflections.

But of all those who were incommoded by the noisy and unseemly quarrels of these two ghosts, James Owre or Gray, the tenant of the farm of Balbig of Delnabo, was the greatest sufferer. From the proximity of his abode to their haunts, it was the misfortune of himself and family to be the nightly audience of Clashnichd's cries and lamentations, which they considered anything but agreeable entertainment.

One day as James Gray was on his rounds looking after his sheep, he happened to fall in with Clashnichd, the ghost of Aulnaic, with whom he entered into a long conversation. In the course of it he took occasion to remonstrate with her on the very disagreeable disturbance she caused himself and family by her wild and unearthly cries – cries which, he said, few mortals could relish in the dreary hours of midnight. Poor Clashnichd, by way of apology for her conduct, gave James Gray a sad account of her usage, detailing at full length the series of cruelties committed upon her by Ben Baynac. From this account, it appeared that her living with the latter was by no means a matter of choice with Clashnichd; on the contrary, it seemed that she had, for a long time, lived apart with much comfort, residing in a snug dwelling, as already mentioned, in the wilds of Craig-Aulnaic; but Ben Baynac having unfortunately taken into his head to pay her a visit, took a fancy, not to herself, but her dwelling, of which, in his own name and authority, he took immediate possession, and soon after he expelled poor Clashnichd, with many stripes, from her natural inheritance. Not satisfied with invading and depriving her of her just rights, he was in the habit of following her into her private haunts, not with the view of offering her any endearments, but for the purpose of inflicting on her person every torment which his brain could invent.

Such a moving relation could not fail to affect the generous heart of James Gray, who determined from that moment to risk life and limb in order to vindicate the rights and avenge the wrongs of poor Clashnichd, the ghost of Craig-Aulnaic. He, therefore, took good care to interrogate his new *protégée* touching the nature of her oppressor's constitution, whether he was of that *killable* species of ghost that could be shot with a silver sixpence or if there was any other weapon that could possibly accomplish his annihilation. Clashnichd informed him that she had occasion to know that Ben Baynac was wholly invulnerable to all the weapons of man, with the exception of a large mole on his left breast, which was no doubt penetrable by silver or steel; but that, from the specimens she had of his personal prowess and strength, it were vain for mere man to attempt to combat him. Confiding, however, in his expertness as an archer – for he was allowed to be the best marksman of the age – James Gray told Clashnichd he did not fear him with all his might – that *he* was a man; and desired her, moreover, next time the ghost chose to repeat his incivilities to her, to apply to him, James Gray, for redress.

It was not long ere he had an opportunity of fulfilling his promises. Ben Baynac having one night, in the want of better amusement, entertained himself by inflicting an inhuman castigation on Clashnichd, she lost no time in waiting on James Gray, with a full and particular account of it. She found him smoking his cutty, for it was night when she came to him; but, notwithstanding the inconvenience of the hour, James needed no great persuasion to induce him to proceed directly along with Clashnichd to hold a communing with their friend, Ben Baynac, the great ghost. Clashnichd was stout and sturdy, and understood the knack of travelling much better than our women do. She expressed a wish that, for the sake of expedition,

James Gray would suffer her to bear him along, a motion to which the latter agreed; and a few minutes brought them close to the scene of Ben Baynac's residence. As they approached his haunt, he came forth to meet them, with looks and gestures which did not at all indicate a cordial welcome. It was a fine moonlight night, and they could easily observe his actions. Poor Clashnichd was now sorely afraid of the great ghost. Apprehending instant destruction from his fury, she exclaimed to James Gray that they would be both dead people, and that immediately, unless James Gray hit with an arrow the mole which covered Ben Baynac's heart. This was not so difficult a task as James had hitherto apprehended it. The mole was as large as a common bonnet, and yet nowise disproportioned to the natural size of the ghost's body, for he certainly was a great and a mighty ghost. Ben Baynac cried out to James Gray that he would soon make eagle's meat of him; and certain it is, such was his intention, had not the shepherd so effectually stopped him from the execution of it. Raising his bow to his eye when within a few yards of Ben Baynac, he took deliberate aim; the arrow flew – it hit – a yell from Ben Baynac announced the result. A hideous howl re-echoed from the surrounding mountains, responsive to the groans of a thousand ghosts; and Ben Baynac, like the smoke of a shot, vanished into air.

Clashnichd, the ghost of Aulnaic, now found herself emancipated from the most abject state of slavery and restored to freedom and liberty, through the invincible courage of James Gray. Overpowered with gratitude, she fell at his feet, and vowed to devote the whole of her time and talents towards his service and prosperity. Meanwhile, being anxious to have her remaining goods and furniture removed to her former dwelling, whence she had been so iniquitously expelled by Ben Baynac, the great ghost, she requested of her new master the use of his horses to remove them. James observing on the adjacent hill a flock of deer, and wishing to have a trial of his new servant's sagacity or expertness, told her those were his horses – she was welcome to the use of them – desiring that when she had done with them, she would enclose them in his stable. Clashnichd then proceeded to make use of the horses, and James Gray returned home to enjoy his night's rest.

Scarce had he reached his armchair, and reclined his cheek on his hand, to ruminate over the bold adventure of the night, when Clashnichd entered, with her 'breath in her throat', and venting the bitterest complaints at the unruliness of his horses, which had broken one-half of her furniture, and caused her more trouble in the stabling of them than their services were worth.

'Oh! they are stabled, then?' enquired James Gray. Clashnichd replied in the affirmative. 'Very well,' rejoined James, 'they shall be tame enough tomorrow.'

From this specimen of Clashnichd the ghost of Craig-Aulnaic's expertness, it will be seen what a valuable acquisition her service proved to James Gray and his young family. They were, however, speedily deprived of her assistance by a most unfortunate accident. From the sequel of the story, from which the foregoing is an extract, it appears that poor Clashnichd was deeply addicted to propensities which at that time rendered her kin so obnoxious to their human neighbours. She was constantly in the habit of visiting her friends much oftener than she was invited, and, in the course of such visits, was never very scrupulous in making free with any eatables which fell within the circle of her observation.

One day, while engaged on a foraging expedition of this description, she happened to enter the Mill of Delnabo, which was inhabited in those days by the miller's family. She found his wife engaged in roasting a large gridiron of fine savoury fish, the agreeable smell proceeding from which perhaps occasioned her visit. With the usual enquiries after the health of the miller and his family, Clashnichd proceeded with the greatest familiarity and good-humour to make herself comfortable at their expense. But the miller's wife, enraged at the loss of her fish, and not relishing such unwelcome familiarity, punished the unfortunate Clashnichd rather too severely for her freedom. It happened that there was at the time a large caldron of boiling water suspended over the fire, and this caldron the enraged wife overturned in Clashnichd's bosom!

Scalded beyond recovery, she fled up the wilds of Craig-Aulnaic, uttering the most melancholy lamentations, nor has she been ever heard of since.

The Doomed Rider

'The Conan is as bonny a river as we hae in a' the north country. There's mony a sweet sunny spot on its banks, an' mony a time an' aft hae I waded through its shallows, whan a boy, to set my little scautling-line for the trouts an' the eels, or to gather the big pearl-mussels that lie sae thick in the fords. But its bonny wooded banks are places for enjoying the day in – no for passing the nicht. I kenna how it is; it's nane o' your wild streams that wander desolate through a desert country, like the Aven, or that come rushing down in foam and thunder, ower broken rocks, like the Foyers, or that wallow in darkness, deep, deep in the bowels o' the earth, like the fearfu' Auldgraunt; an' yet no ane o' these rivers has mair or frightfuller stories connected wi' it than the Conan. Ane can hardly saunter ower half a mile in its course, frae where it leaves Coutin till where it enters the sea, without passing ower the scene o' some frightful auld legend o' the kelpie or the waterwraith. And ane o' the most frightful looking o' these places is to be found among the woods of Conan House. Ye enter a swampy meadow that waves wi' flags an' rushes like a cornfield in harvest, an' see a hillock covered wi' willows rising like an island in the midst. There are thick mirk-woods on ilka side; the river, dark an' awesome, an' whirling round an' round in mossy eddies, sweeps away behind it; an' there is an auld burying-ground, wi' the broken ruins o' an auld Papist kirk, on the tap. Ane can see amang the rougher stanes the rose-wrought mullions of an arched window, an' the trough that ance held the holy water. About twa hunder years ago – a wee mair maybe, or a wee less, for ane canna be very sure o' the date o' thae old stories – the building was entire; an' a spot near it, whar the wood now grows thickest, was laid out in a cornfield. The marks o' the furrows may still be seen amang the trees.

'A party o' Highlanders were busily engaged, ae day in harvest, in cutting down the corn o' that field; an' just aboot noon, when the sun shone brightest an' they were busiest in the work, they heard a voice frae the river exclaim: "The hour but not the man has come." Sure enough, on looking round, there was the kelpie stan'in' in what they ca' a fause ford, just fornent the auld kirk. There is a deep black pool baith aboon an' below, but i' the ford there's a bonny ripple, that shows, as ane might think, but little depth o' water; an' just i' the middle o' that, in a place where a horse might swim, stood the kelpie. An' it again repeated its words: "The hour but not the man has come," an' then flashing through the water like a drake, it disappeared in the lower pool. When the folk stood wondering what the creature might mean, they saw a man on horseback come spurring down the hill in hot haste, making straight for the fause ford. They could then understand her words at ance; an' four o' the stoutest o' them sprang oot frae amang the corn to warn him o' his danger, an' keep him back. An' sae they tauld him what they had seen an' heard, an' urged him either to turn back an' tak' anither road, or stay for an hour or sae where he was. But he just wadna hear them, for he was baith unbelieving an' in haste, an' wauld hae taen the ford for a' they could say, hadna the Highlanders, determined on saving him whether he would or no, gathered round him an' pulled him frae his horse, an' then, to mak' sure o' him, locked him up in the auld kirk. Weel, when the hour had gone by – the fatal hour o' the kelpie – they flung open the door, an' cried to him that he might noo gang on his journey. Ah! but there was nae answer, though; an' sae they cried a second time, an' there was nae answer still; an' then they went in, an' found him lying stiff an' cauld on the floor, wi' his face buried in the water o' the very stone trough that we may still see amang the ruins. His hour had come, an' he had fallen in a fit, as 'twould seem, head-foremost amang the water o' the trough, where he had been smothered – an' sae ye see, the prophecy o' the kelpie availed naething.'

The Weird of the Three Arrows

Sir James Douglas, the companion of Bruce, and well known by his appellation of the 'Black Douglas', was once, during the hottest period of the exterminating war carried on by him and his colleague Randolph, against the English, stationed at Linthaughlee, near Jedburgh. He was resting himself and his men after the toils of many days' fighting-marches through Teviotdale; and, according to his custom, had walked round the tents, previous to retiring to the unquiet rest of a soldier's bed. He stood for a few minutes at the entrance to his tent contemplating the scene before him, rendered more interesting by a clear moon, whose silver beams fell, in the silence of a night without a breath of wind, calmly on the slumbers of mortals destined to mix in the mêlée of dreadful war, perhaps on the morrow. As he stood gazing, irresolute whether to retire to rest or indulge longer in a train of thought not very suitable to a warrior who delighted in the spirit-stirring scenes of his profession, his eye was attracted by the figure of an old woman, who approached him with a trembling step, leaning on a staff and holding in her left hand three English cloth-shaft arrows.

'You are he who is ca'ed the guid Sir James?' said the old woman.

'I am, good woman,' replied Sir James. 'Why hast thou wandered from the sutler's camp?'

'I dinna belang to the camp o' the hoblers,' answered the woman. 'I hae been a residenter in Linthaughlee since the day when King Alexander passed the door o' my cottage wi' his bonny French bride, wha was terrified awa' frae Jedburgh by the death's-head whilk appeared to her on the day o' her marriage. What I hae suffered sin' that day' (looking at the arrows in her hand) 'lies between me an' heaven.'

'Some of your sons have been killed in the wars, I presume?' said Sir James.

'Ye hae guessed a pairt o' my waes,' replied the woman. 'That arrow' (holding out one of the three) 'carries on its point the bluid o' my first born; that is stained wi' the stream that poured frae the heart o' my second; and that is red wi' the gore in which my youngest weltered, as he gae up the life that made me childless. They were a' shot by English hands, in different armies, in different battles. I am an honest woman, and wish to return to the English what belongs to the English; but that in the same fashion in which they were sent. The Black Douglas has the strongest arm an' the surest ee in auld Scotland; an' wha can execute my commission better than he?'

'I do not use the bow, good woman,' replied Sir James. 'I love the grasp of the dagger or the battle-axe. You must apply to some other individual to return your arrows.'

'I canna tak' them hame again,' said the woman, laying them down at the feet of Sir James. 'Ye'll see me again on St James's E'en.'

The old woman departed as she said these words.

Sir James took up the arrows, and placed them in an empty quiver that lay amongst his baggage. He retired to rest, but not to sleep. The figure of the old woman and her strange request occupied his thoughts, and produced trains of meditation which ended in nothing but restlessness and disquietude. Getting up at daybreak, he met a messenger at the entrance of his tent, who informed him that Sir Thomas de Richmont, with a force of ten thousand men, had crossed the Borders, and would pass through a narrow defile, which he mentioned, where he could be attacked with great advantage. Sir James gave instant orders to march to the spot; and, with that genius for scheming, for which he was so remarkable, commanded his men to twist together the young birch trees on either side of the passage to prevent the escape of the enemy. This finished, he concealed his archers in a hollow way, near the gorge of the pass.

The enemy came on; and when their ranks were embarrassed by the narrowness of the road, and it was impossible for the cavalry to act with effect, Sir James rushed upon them at the head of his horsemen; and the archers, suddenly discovering themselves, poured in a flight of arrows on the confused soldiers, and put the whole army to flight. In the heat of the onset, Douglas killed Sir Thomas de Richmont with his dagger.

Not long after this, Edmund de Cailon, a knight of Gascony, and Governor of Berwick, who had been heard to vaunt that he had sought the famous Black Knight, but could not find him, was returning to England, loaded with plunder, the fruit of an inroad on Teviotdale. Sir James thought it a pity that a Gascon's vaunt should be heard unpunished in Scotland, and made long forced marches to satisfy the desire of the foreign knight, by giving him a sight of the dark countenance he had made a subject of reproach. He soon succeeded in gratifying both himself and the Gascon. Coming up in his terrible manner, he called to Cailon to stop and, before he proceeded into England, receive the respects of the Black Knight he had come to find but hitherto had not met. The Gascon's vaunt was now changed; but shame supplied the place of courage, and he ordered his men to receive Douglas's attack. Sir James assiduously sought his enemy. He at last succeeded; and a single combat ensued, of a most desperate character. But who ever escaped the arm of Douglas when fairly opposed to him in single conflict? Cailon was killed; he had met the Black Knight at last.

'So much,' cried Sir James, 'for the vaunt of a Gascon!'

Similar in every respect to the fate of Cailon, was that of Sir Ralph Neville. He, too, on hearing the great fame of Douglas's prowess, from some of Gallon's fugitive soldiers, openly boasted that he would fight with the Scottish knight if he would come and show his banner before Berwick. Sir James heard the boast and rejoiced in it. He marched to that town, and caused his men to ravage the country in front of the battlements and burn the villages. Neville left Berwick with a strong body of men; and, stationing himself on a high ground, waited till the rest of the Scots should disperse to plunder; but Douglas called in his detachment and attacked the knight. After a desperate conflict, in which many were slain, Douglas, as was his custom, succeeded in bringing the leader to a personal encounter, and the skill of the Scottish knight was again successful. Neville was slain, and his men utterly discomfited.

Having retired one night to his tent to take some rest after so much pain and toil, Sir James Douglas was surprised by the reappearance of the old woman whom he had seen at Linthaughlee.

'This is the feast o' St James,' said she, as she approached him. 'I said I would see ye again this nicht, an' I'm as guid as my word. Hae ye returned the arrows I left wi' ye to the English wha sent them to the hearts o' my sons?'

'No,' replied Sir James. 'I told ye I did not fight with the bow. Wherefore do ye importune me thus?'

'Give me back the arrows then,' said the woman.

Sir James went to bring the quiver in which he had placed them. On taking them out, he was surprised to find that they were all broken through the middle.

'How has this happened?' said he. 'I put these arrows in this quiver entire, and now they are broken.'

'The weird is fulfilled!' cried the old woman, laughing eldrichly, and clapping her hands. 'That broken shaft cam' frae a soldier o' Richmont's; that frae ane o' Cailon's, and that frae ane o' Neville's. They are a' dead, an' I am revenged!'

The old woman then departed, scattering, as she went, the broken fragments of the arrows on the floor of the tent.

The Laird of Balmachie's Wife

In the olden times, when it was the fashion for gentlemen to wear swords, the Laird of Balmachie went one day to Dundee, leaving his wife at home ill in bed. Riding home in the twilight, he had occasion to leave the high road, and when crossing between some little romantic knolls, called the Cur Hills, in the neighbourhood of Carlungy, he encountered a troop of fairies supporting a kind of litter, upon which some person seemed to be borne. Being a man of dauntless courage, and, as he said, impelled by some internal impulse, he pushed his horse close to the litter, drew his sword, laid it across the vehicle, and in a firm tone exclaimed: 'In the name of God, release your captive.'

The tiny troop immediately disappeared, dropping the litter on the ground. The laird dismounted, and found that it contained his own wife, dressed in her bedclothes. Wrapping his coat around her, he placed her on the horse before him, and, having only a short distance to ride, arrived safely at home.

Placing her in another room, under the care of an attentive friend, he immediately went to the chamber where he had left his wife in the morning, and there to all appearance she still lay, very sick of a fever. She was fretful, discontented, and complained much of having been neglected in his absence, at all of which the laird affected great concern, and pretending much sympathy, insisted upon her rising to have her bed made. She said that she was unable to rise, but her husband was peremptory, and having ordered a large wood fire to warm the room, he lifted the impostor from the bed, and bearing her across the floor as if to a chair, which had been previously prepared, he threw her on the fire, from which she bounced like a sky-rocket, and went through the ceiling, and out at the roof of the house, leaving a hole among the slates. He then brought in his own wife, a little recovered from her alarm, who said that sometime after sunset, the nurse having left her for the purpose of preparing a little caudle, a multitude of elves came in at the window, thronging like bees from a hive. They filled the room, and having lifted her from the bed carried her through the window, after which she recollected nothing further, till she saw her husband standing over her on the Cur Hills, at the back of Carlungy. The hole in the roof, by which the female fairy made her escape, was mended, but could never be kept in repair as a tempest of wind happened always once a year and uncovered that particular spot, without injuring any other part of the roof.

Michael Scott

In the early part of Michael Scott's life he was in the habit of emigrating annually to the Scottish metropolis, for the purpose of being employed in his capacity of mason. One time as he and two companions were journeying to the place of their destination for a similar object, they had occasion to pass over a high hill, the name of which is not mentioned, but which is supposed to have been one of the Grampians, and being fatigued with climbing, they sat down to rest themselves. They had no sooner done so than they were warned to take to their heels by the hissing of a large serpent, which they observed revolving itself towards them with great velocity. Terrified at the sight, Michael's two companions fled, while he, on the contrary, resolved to encounter the reptile. The appalling monster approached Michael Scott with distended mouth and forked tongue; and, throwing itself into a coil at his feet, was raising its head to inflict a mortal sting, when Michael, with one stroke of his stick, severed its body into three pieces. He then rejoined his affrighted comrades and they resumed their journey; and, on arriving at the next public-house, it being late, and the travellers being weary, they took up their quarters at it for the night. In the course of the evening's conversation, reference was naturally made to Michael's recent exploit with the serpent, when the landlady of the house, who was remarkable for her 'arts', happened to be present. Her curiosity appeared much excited by the conversation; and, after making some enquiries regarding the colour of the serpent, which she was told was white, she offered any of them that would procure her the middle piece such a tempting reward as induced one of the party instantly to go for it. The distance was not great; and on reaching the spot, he found the middle and tail piece in the place where Michael left them, but the head piece was gone.

The landlady on receiving the piece, which still vibrated with life, seemed highly gratified at her acquisition; and, over and above the promised reward, regaled her lodgers very plentifully with the choicest dainties of her house. Fired with curiosity to know the purpose for which the serpent was intended, the wily Michael Scott was immediately seized with a severe fit of indisposition, which caused him to request that he might be allowed to sleep beside the fire, the warmth of which, he affirmed, was in the highest degree beneficial to him.

Never suspecting Michael Scott's hypocrisy, and naturally supposing that a person so severely indisposed would feel very little curiosity about the contents of any cooking utensils which might lie around the fire, the landlady allowed his request. As soon as the other inmates of the house were retired to bed, the landlady resorted to her darling occupation; and, in his feigned state of indisposition, Michael had a favourable opportunity of watching most scrupulously all her actions through the keyhole of a door leading to the next apartment where she was. He could see the rites and ceremonies with which the serpent was put into the oven, along with many mysterious ingredients. After which the unsuspicious landlady placed the dish by the fireside, where lay the distressed traveller, to stove till the morning.

Once or twice in the course of the night the 'wife of the change-house', under the pretence of enquiring for her sick lodger, and administering to him some renovating cordials, the beneficial effects of which he gratefully acknowledged, took occasion to dip her finger in her saucepan, upon which the cock, perched on his roost, crowed aloud. All Michael's sickness could not prevent him considering very inquisitively the landlady's cantrips, and particularly the influence of the sauce upon the crowing of the cock. Nor could he dissipate some inward desires he felt to follow her example. At the same time, he suspected that Satan had a hand in the pie, yet he thought he would like very much to be at the bottom of the concern; and thus his reason and his curiosity clashed against each other for the space of several hours. At length passion, as is too often the case, became the conqueror. Michael, too, dipped his finger in the sauce, and applied it to the tip of his tongue, and immediately the cock perched on the *spardan* announced the circumstance in a mournful clarion. Instantly his mind received a new light to which he was formerly a stranger, and the astonished dupe of a landlady now found it her interest to admit her sagacious lodger into a knowledge of the remainder of her secrets.

Endowed with the knowledge of 'good and evil', and all the 'second sights' that can be acquired, Michael left his lodgings in the morning, with the philosopher's stone in his pocket. By daily perfecting his supernatural attainments, by new series of discoveries, he became more than a match for Satan himself. Having seduced some thousands of Satan's best workmen into his employment, he trained them up so successfully to the architective business, and inspired them with such industrious habits, that he was more than sufficient for all the architectural work of the empire. To establish this assertion, we need only refer to some remains of his workmanship still existing north of the Grampians, some of them stupendous bridges built by him in one short night, with no other visible agents than two or three workmen.

On one occasion work was getting scarce, as might have been naturally expected, and his workmen, as they were wont, flocked to his doors, perpetually exclaiming, 'Work! work! work!' Continually annoyed by their incessant entreaties, he called out to them in derision to go and make a dry road from Fortrose to Arderseir, over the Moray Firth. Immediately their cry ceased, and as Scott supposed it wholly impossible for them to execute his order, he retired to rest, laughing most heartily at the chimerical sort of employment he had given to his industrious workmen. Early in the morning, however, he got up and took a walk at the break of day down to the shore to divert himself at the fruitless labours of his zealous workmen. But on reaching the spot, what was his astonishment to find the formidable piece of work allotted to them only a few hours before already nearly finished. Seeing the great damage the commercial class of the community would sustain from the operation, he ordered the workmen to demolish the most part of their work; leaving, however, the point of Fortrose to show the traveller to this day the wonderful exploit of Michael Scott's fairies.

On being thus again thrown out of employment, their former clamour was resumed, nor could Michael Scott, with all his sagacity, devise a plan to keep them in innocent employment. He at length discovered one. 'Go,' says he, 'and manufacture me ropes that will carry me to the back of the moon; make them of these materials – miller's-sudds and sea-sand.' Michael Scott here obtained rest from his active operators, for, when other work failed them, he always despatched them to their rope manufactory. But though these agents could never make proper ropes of those materials, their efforts to that effect are far from being contemptible, for some of their ropes are seen by the seaside to this day.

We shall close our notice of Michael Scott by reciting one anecdote of him in the latter part of his life.

In consequence of a violent quarrel which Michael Scott once had with a person whom he conceived to have caused him some injury, he resolved, as the highest punishment he could inflict upon him, to send his adversary to that evil place designed only for Satan and his black companions. He accordingly, by means of his supernatural machinations, sent the poor unfortunate man thither; and had he been sent by any other means than those of Michael Scott, he would no doubt have met with a warm reception. Out of pure spite to Michael, however, when Satan learned who was his billet-master, he would no more receive him than he would receive the Wife of Bath; and instead of treating the unfortunate man with the harshness characteristic of him, he showed him considerable civilities. Introducing him to his 'Ben Taigh', he directed her to show the stranger any curiosities he might wish to see, hinting very significantly that he had provided some accommodation for their mutual friend, Michael Scott, the sight of which might afford him some gratification. The polite housekeeper accordingly conducted the stranger through the principal apartments in the house, where he saw fearful sights. But the bed of Michael Scott! – his greatest enemy could not but feel satiated with revenge at the sight of it. It was a place too horrid to be described, filled promiscuously with all the awful brutes imaginable. Toads and lions, lizards and leeches, and, amongst the rest, not the least conspicuous, a large serpent gaping for Michael Scott, with its mouth wide open. This last sight having satisfied the stranger's curiosity, he was led to the outer gate, and came away. He reached his friends, and, among other pieces of news touching his travels, he was not backward in relating the entertainment that awaited his friend Michael Scott, as soon as he would 'stretch his foot' for the other world. But Michael did not at all appear disconcerted at his friend's intelligence. He affirmed that he would disappoint all his enemies in their expectations – in proof of which he gave the following signs: 'When I am just dead,' says he, 'open my breast and extract my heart. Carry it to some place where the public may see the result. You will then transfix it upon a long pole, and if Satan will have my soul, he will come in the likeness of a black raven and carry it off; and if my soul will be saved it will be carried off by a white dove.'

His friends faithfully obeyed his instructions. Having exhibited his heart in the manner directed, a large black raven was observed to come from the east with great fleetness, while a white dove came from the west with equal velocity. The raven made a furious dash at the heart, missing which, it was unable to curb its force, till it was considerably past it; and the dove, reaching the spot at the same time, carried off the heart amidst the rejoicing and ejaculations of the spectators.

The Haunted Ships

Along the sea of Solway, romantic on the Scottish side, with its woodland, its bays, its cliffs and headlands; and interesting on the English side, with its many beautiful towns with their shadows on the water, rich pastures, safe harbours and numerous ships, there still linger many traditional stories of a maritime nature, most of them connected with superstitions singularly wild and unusual. To the curious these tales afford a rich fund of entertainment, from the many diversities of the same story: some dry and barren, and stripped of all the embellishments of poetry; others dressed out in all the riches of a superstitious belief and haunted imagination. In this they resemble the inland traditions of the peasants; but many of the oral treasures of the Galwegian or the Cumbrian coast have the stamp of the Dane and the Norseman upon them, and claim but a remote or faint affinity with the legitimate legends of Caledonia. Something like a rude prosaic outline of several of the most noted of the northern ballads, the adventures and depredations of the old ocean kings, still lends life to the evening tale; and, among others, the story of the Haunted Ships is still popular among the maritime peasantry.

One fine harvest evening I went on board the shallop of Richard Faulder, of Allanbay, and, committing ourselves to the waters, we allowed a gentle wind from the east to waft us at its pleasure towards the Scottish coast. We passed the sharp promontory of Siddick, and, skirting the land within a stonecast, glided along the shore till we came within sight of the ruined Abbey of Sweetheart. The green mountain of Criffel ascended beside us; and the bleat of the flocks from its summit, together with the winding of the evening horn of the reapers, came softened into something like music over land and sea. We pushed our shallop into a deep and wooded bay, and sat silently looking on the serene beauty of the place. The moon glimmered in her rising through the tall shafts of the pines of Caerlaverock; and the sky, with scarce a cloud, showered down on wood and headland and bay the twinkling beams of a thousand stars, rendering every object visible. The tide, too, was coming with that swift and silent swell observable when the wind is gentle; the woody curves along the land were filling with the flood, till it touched the green branches of the drooping trees; while in the centre current the roll and the plunge of a thousand pellocks told to the experienced fisherman that salmon were abundant.

As we looked, we saw an old man emerging from a path that wound to the shore through a grove of doddered hazel; he carried a halve-net on his back, while behind him came a girl, bearing a small harpoon, with which the fishers are remarkably dexterous in striking their prey. The senior seated himself on a large grey stone, which overlooked the bay, laid aside his bonnet, and submitted his bosom and neck to the refreshing sea breeze, and, taking his harpoon from his attendant, sat with the gravity and composure of a spirit of the flood, with his ministering nymph behind him. We pushed our shallop to the shore, and soon stood at their side.

'This is old Mark Macmoran the mariner, with his granddaughter Barbara,' said Richard Faulder, in a whisper that had something of fear in it; 'he knows every creek and cavern and quicksand in Solway; has seen the Spectre Hound that haunts the Isle of Man; has heard him bark, and at every bark has seen a ship sink; and he has seen, too, the Haunted Ships in full sail; and, if all tales be true, he has sailed in them himself; he's an awful person.'

Though I perceived in the communication of my friend something of the superstition of the sailor, I could not help thinking that common rumour had made a happy choice in singling out old Mark to maintain her contact with the invisible world. His hair, which seemed to have refused all intercourse with the comb, hung matted upon his shoulders; a kind of mantle, or rather blanket, pinned with a wooden skewer round his neck, fell mid-leg down, concealing all his nether garments as far as a pair of hose, darned with yarn of all conceivable colours, and a pair of shoes, patched and repaired till nothing of the original structure remained and clasped on his feet with two massy silver buckles. If the dress of the old man was rude and sordid, that of his granddaughter was gay, and even rich. She wore a bodice of fine wool, wrought round the bosom with alternate leaf and lily, and a kirtle of the same fabric, which, almost touching her white and delicate ankle, showed her snowy feet, so fairy-light and round that they scarcely seemed to touch the grass where she stood. Her hair, a natural ornament which woman seeks much to improve, was of bright glossy brown, and encumbered rather than adorned with a snood, set thick with marine productions, among which the small clear pearl found in the Solway was conspicuous. Nature had not trusted to a handsome shape and a sylph-like air for young Barbara's influence over the heart of man, but had bestowed a pair of large bright blue eyes, swimming in liquid light, so full of love and gentleness and joy that all the sailors from Annanwater to far St Bees acknowledged their power, and sang songs about the bonnie lass of Mark Macmoran. She stood holding a small gaff-hook of polished steel in her hand, and seemed not dissatisfied with the glances I bestowed on her from time to time, and which I held more than requited by a single glance of those eyes which retained so many capricious hearts in subjection.

The tide, though rapidly augmenting, had not yet filled the bay at our feet. The moon now streamed fairly over the tops of Caer-laverock pines, and showed the expanse of ocean dimpling and swelling, on which sloops and shallops came dancing, displaying at every turn their extent of white sail against the beam of the moon. I looked on old Mark the mariner, who, seated motionless on his grey stone, kept his eye fixed on the increasing waters with a look of seriousness and sorrow, in which I saw little of the calculating spirit of a mere fisherman. Though he looked on the coming tide, his eyes seemed to dwell particularly on the black and decayed hulls of two vessels, which, half immersed in the quicksand, still addressed to every heart a tale of shipwreck and desolation. The tide wheeled and foamed around them, and, creeping inch by inch up the side, at last fairly threw its waters over the top, and a long and hollow eddy showed the resistance which the liquid element received.

The moment they were fairly buried in the water, the old man clasped his hands together, and said: 'Blessed be the tide that will break over and bury ye for ever! Sad to mariners and sorrowful to maids and mothers has the time been you have choked up this deep and bonnie bay. For evil were you sent, and for evil have you continued. Every season finds from you its song of sorrow and wail, its funeral processions and its shrouded corses. Woe to the land where the wood grew that made ye! Cursed be the axe that hewed ye on the mountains, the hands that joined ye together, the bay that ye first swam in and the wind that wafted ye here! Seven times have ye put my life in peril, three fair sons have ye swept from my side, and two bonnie grand-bairns; and now, even now, your waters foam and flash for my destruction, did I venture my infirm limbs in quest of food in your deadly bay. I see by that ripple and that foam, and hear by the sound and singing of your surge, that ye yearn for another victim; but it shall not be me nor mine.'

Even as the old mariner addressed himself to the wrecked ships, a young man appeared at the southern extremity of the bay, holding his halve-net in his hand and hastening into the current. Mark rose and shouted, and waved him back from a place which, to a person unacquainted with the dangers of the bay, real and superstitious, seemed sufficiently perilous; his granddaughter, too, added her voice to his, and waved her white hands; but the more they strove, the faster advanced the peasant, till he stood to his middle in the water, while the tide increased every moment in depth and strength. 'Andrew, Andrew,' cried the young woman, in a voice quavering with emotion, 'turn, turn, I tell you! Oh the ships, the Haunted Ships!' But the appearance of a fine run of fish had more influence with the peasant than the voice of bonnie Barbara, and forward he dashed, net in hand. In a moment he was borne off his feet, and mingled like foam with the water, and hurried towards the fatal eddies which whirled and roared round the sunken ships. But he was a powerful young man, and an expert swimmer; he seized on one of the projecting ribs of the nearest hulk, and clinging to it with the grasp of despair, uttered yell after yell, sustaining himself against the prodigious rush of the current.

From a shealing of turf and straw, within the pitch of a bar from the spot where we stood, came out an old woman bent with age and leaning on a crutch. 'I heard the voice of that lad Andrew Lammie; can the chield be drowning that he skirls sae uncannily?' said the old woman, seating herself on the ground, and looking earnestly at the water. 'Ou, ay,' she continued, 'he's doomed, he's doomed; heart and hand can never save him; boats, ropes and man's strength and wit, all vain! vain! – he's doomed, he's doomed!'

By this time I had thrown myself into the shallop, followed reluctantly by Richard Faulder, over whose courage and kindness of heart superstition had great power, and with one push from the shore, and some exertion in sculling, we came within a quoit-cast of the unfortunate fisherman. He stayed not to profit by our aid; for, when he perceived us near, he uttered a piercing shriek of joy, and bounded towards us through the agitated element the full length of an oar. I saw him for a second on the surface of the water, but the eddying current sucked him down; and all I ever beheld of him again was his hand held above the flood and clutching in agony at some imaginary aid. I sat gazing in horror on the vacant sea before us; but a breathing-time before, a human being, full of youth and strength and hope, was there; his cries were still ringing in my ears, and echoing in the woods; and now nothing was seen or heard save the turbulent expanse of water, and the sound of its chafing on the shores. We pushed back our shallop, and resumed our station on the cliff beside the old mariner and his descendant.

'Wherefore sought ye to peril your own lives fruitlessly,' said Mark, 'in attempting to save the doomed? Whoso touches those infernal ships never survives to tell the tale. Woe to the man who is found nigh them at midnight when the tide has subsided, and they arise in their former beauty, with forecastle, and deck, and sail, and pennon, and shroud! Then is seen the streaming of lights along the water from their cabin windows, and then is heard the sound of mirth and the clamour of tongues, and the infernal whoop and halloo and song, ringing far and wide. Woe to the man who comes nigh them!'

To all this my Allanbay companion listened with a breathless attention. I felt something touched with a superstition to which I partly believed I had seen one victim offered up; and I enquired of the old mariner, 'How and when came these Haunted Ships there? To me they seem but the melancholy relics of some unhappy voyagers, and much more likely to warn people to shun destruction than entice and delude them to it.'

'And so,' said the old man with a smile, which had more of sorrow in it than of mirth; 'and so, young man, these black and shattered hulks seem to the eye of the multitude. But things are not what they seem: that water, a kind and convenient servant to the wants of man, which seems so smooth and so dimpling and so gentle, has swallowed up a human soul even now; and the place which it covers, so fair and so level, is a faithless quicksand, out of which none escape. Things are otherwise than they seem. Had you lived as long as I have had the sorrow to live; had you seen the storms, and braved the perils, and endured the distresses which have befallen me; had you sat gazing out on the dreary ocean at midnight on a haunted coast; had you seen comrade after comrade, brother after brother and son after son swept away by the merciless ocean from your very side; had you seen the shapes of friends, doomed to the wave and the quicksand, appearing to you in the dreams and visions of the night, then would your mind have been prepared for crediting the maritime legends of mariners; and the two haunted Danish ships would have had their terrors for you, as they have for all who sojourn on this coast.

'Of the time and the cause of their destruction,' continued the old man, 'I know nothing certain; they have stood as you have seen them for uncounted time; and while all other ships wrecked on this unhappy coast have gone to pieces and rotted and sunk away in a few years, these two haunted hulks have neither sunk in the quicksand, nor has a single spar or board been displaced. Maritime legend says that two ships of Denmark, having had permission, for a time, to work deeds of darkness and dolour on the deep, were at last condemned to the whirlpool and the sunken rock, and were wrecked in this bonnie bay, as a sign to seamen to be gentle and devout. The night when they were lost was a harvest evening of uncommon mildness and beauty: the sun had newly set; the moon came brighter and brighter out; and the reapers, laying their sickles at the root of the standing corn, stood on rock and bank, looking at the increasing magnitude of the waters, for sea and land were visible from St Bees to Barnhourie. The sails of two vessels were soon seen bent for the Scottish coast; and, with a speed outrunning the swiftest ship, they approached the dangerous quicksands and headland of Borranpoint. On the deck of the foremost ship not a living soul was seen, or shape, unless something in darkness and form resembling a human shadow could be called a shape, which flitted from extremity to extremity of the ship, with the appearance of trimming the sails and directing the vessel's course. But the decks of its companion were crowded with human shapes; the captain and mate, and sailor and cabin-boy, all seemed there; and from them the sound of mirth and minstrelsy echoed over land and water. The coast which they skirted along was one of extreme danger, and the reapers shouted to warn them to beware of sandbank and rock; but of this friendly counsel no notice was taken, except that a large and famished dog, which sat on the prow, answered every shout with a long, loud and melancholy howl. The deep sandbank of Carsethorn was expected to arrest the career of these desperate navigators; but they passed, with the celerity of waterfowl, over an obstruction which had wrecked many pretty ships.

'Old men shook their heads and departed, saying, "We have seen the fiend sailing in a bottomless ship; let us go home and pray;" but one young and wilful man said, "Fiend! I'll warrant it's nae fiend, but douce Janet Withershins the witch, holding a carouse with some of her Cumberland cummers, and mickle red wine will be spilt atween them. Dod I would gladly have a toothfu'! I'll warrant it's nane o' your cauld sour slae-water like a bottle of Bailie Skrinkie's port, but right drap-o'-my-heart's-blood stuff, that would waken a body out of their last linen. I wonder where the cummers will anchor their craft?"

"And I'll vow," said another rustic, "the wine they quaff is none of your visionary drink, such as a drouthie body has dished out to his lips in a dream; nor is it shadowy and unsubstantial, like the vessels they sail in, which are made out of a cockleshell or a cast-off slipper, or the paring of a seaman's right thumb-nail. I once got a hansel out of a witch's quaigh myself – auld Marion Mathers, of Dustiefoot, whom they tried to bury in the old kirkyard of Dunscore; but the cummer rose as fast as they laid her down, and naewhere else would she lie but in the bonnie green kirkyard of Kier, among douce and sponsible fowk. So I'll vow that the wine of a witch's cup is as fell liquor as ever did a kindly turn to a poor man's heart; and be they fiends, or be they witches, if they have red wine asteer, I'll risk a drouket sark for ae glorious tout on't."

' "Silence, ye sinners," said the minister's son of a neighbouring parish, who united in his own person his father's lack of devotion with his mother's love of liquor. "Whist! – speak as if ye had the fear of something holy before ye. Let the vessels run their own way to destruction: who can stay the eastern wind and the current of the Solway sea? I can find ye Scripture warrant for that; so let them try their strength on Blawhooly rocks, and their might on the broad quicksand. There's a surf running there would knock the ribs together of a galley built by the imps of the pit, and commanded by the Prince of Darkness. Bonnily and bravely they sail away there, but before the blast blows by they'll be wrecked; and red wine and strong brandy will be as rife as dyke-water, and we'll drink the health of bonnie Bell Blackness out of her left-foot slipper."

'The speech of the young profligate was applauded by several of his companions, and away they flew to the bay of Blawhooly, from whence they never returned. The two vessels were observed all at once to stop in the bosom of the bay, on the spot where their hulls now appear; the mirth and the minstrelsy waxed louder than ever, and the forms of maidens, with instruments of music and wine-cups in their hands, thronged the decks. A boat was lowered; and the same shadowy pilot who conducted the ships made it start towards the shore with the rapidity of lightning, and its head knocked against the bank where the four young men stood who longed for the unblest drink. They leaped in with a laugh, and with a laugh were they welcomed on deck; wine-cups were given to each, and as they raised them to their lips the vessels melted away beneath their feet, and one loud shriek, mingled with laughter still louder, was heard over land and water for many miles. Nothing more was heard or seen till the morning, when the crowd who came to the beach saw with fear and wonder the two Haunted Ships, such as they now seem, masts and tackle gone; nor mark, nor sign, by which their name, country or destination could be known was left remaining. Such is the tradition of the mariners; and its truth has been attested by many families whose sons and whose fathers have been drowned in the haunted bay of Blawhooly.'

'And trow ye,' said the old woman, who, attracted from her hut by the drowning cries of the young fisherman, had remained an auditor of the mariner's legend – 'And trow ye, Mark Macmoran, that the tale of the Haunted Ships is done? I can say no to that. Mickle have mine ears heard; but more mine eyes have witnessed since I came to dwell in this humble home by the side of the deep sea. I mind the night weel; it was on Hallowmas Eve; the nuts were cracked, and the apples were eaten, and spell and charm were tried at my fireside; till, wearied with diving into the dark waves of futurity, the lads and lasses fairly took to the more visible blessings of kind words, tender clasps and gentle courtship. Soft words in a maiden's ear, and a kindly kiss o' her lip were old-world matters to me, Mark Macmoran; though I mean not to say that I have been free of the folly of daunering and daffin with a youth in my day, and keeping tryst with him in dark and lonely places. However, as I say, these times of enjoyment were passed and gone with me – the mair's the pity that pleasure should fly sae fast away – and as I couldna make sport I thought I should not mar any; so out I sauntered into the fresh cold air, and sat down behind that old oak, and looked abroad on the wide sea. I had my ain sad thoughts, ye may think, at the time: it was in that very bay my blythe goodman perished, with seven more in his company; and on that very bank where ye see the waves leaping and foaming, I saw seven stately corses streeked, but the dearest was the eighth. It was a woful sight to me, a widow, with four bonnie boys, with nought to support them but these twa hands, and God's blessing, and a cow's grass. I have never liked to live out of sight of this bay since that time; and mony's the moonlight night I sit looking on these watery mountains and these waste shores; it does my heart good, whatever it may do to my head. So ye see it was Hallowmas Night, and looking on sea and land sat I; and my heart wandering to other thoughts soon made me forget my youthful company at hame. It might be near the howe hour of the night. The tide was making, and its singing brought strange old-world stories with it, and I thought on the dangers that sailors endure, the fates they meet with, and the fearful forms they see. My own blythe goodman had seen sights that made him grave enough at times, though he aye tried to laugh them away.

'Aweel, atween that very rock aneath us and the coming tide, I saw, or thought I saw – for the tale is so dreamlike that the whole might pass for a vision of the night – I saw the form of a man; his plaid was grey, his face was grey; and his hair, which hung low down till it nearly came to the middle of his back, was as white as the white sea-foam. He began to howk and dig under the bank; an' God be near me, thought I, this maun be the unblessed spirit of auld Adam Gowdgowpin the miser, who is doomed to dig for shipwrecked treasure, and count how many millions are hidden for ever from man's enjoyment. The form found something which in shape and hue seemed a left-foot slipper of brass; so down to the tide he marched, and, placing it on the water, whirled it thrice round, and the infernal slipper dilated at every turn, till it became a bonnie barge with its sails bent, and on board leaped the form, and scudded swiftly away. He came to one of the Haunted Ships, and striking it with his oar, a fair ship, with mast and canvas and mariners, started up; he touched the other Haunted Ship, and produced the like trans-formation; and away the three spectre ships bounded, leaving a track of fire behind them on the billows which was long unextinguished. Now wasna that a bonnie and fearful sight to see beneath the light of the Hallowmas moon? But the tale is far frae finished, for mariners say that once a year, on a certain night, if ye stand on the Borran Point, ye will see the infernal shallops coming snoring through the Solway; ye will hear the same laughter and song and mirth and minstrelsy which our ancestors heard; see them bound over the sandbanks and sunken rocks like seagulls, cast their anchor in Blawhooly Bay, while the shadowy figure lowers down the boat, and augments their numbers with the four unhappy mortals to whose memory a stone stands in the kirkyard, with a sinking ship and a shoreless sea cut upon it. Then the spectre ships vanish, and the drowning shriek of mortals and the rejoicing laugh of fiends are heard, and the old hulls are left as a memorial that the old spiritual kingdom has not departed from the earth. But I maun away, and trim my little cottage fire, and make it burn and blaze up bonnie, to warm the crickets and my cold and crazy bones that maun soon be laid aneath the green sod in the eerie kirkyard.' And away the old dame tottered to her cottage, secured the door on the inside, and soon the hearth-flame was seen to glimmer and gleam through the keyhole and window.

'I'll tell ye what,' said the old mariner, in a subdued tone, and with a shrewd and suspicious glance of his eye after the old sibyl, 'it's a word that may not very well be uttered, but there are many mistakes made in evening stories if old Moll Moray there, where she lives, knows not mickle more than she is willing to tell of the Haunted Ships and their unhallowed mariners. She lives cannily and quietly; no one knows how she is fed or supported; but her dress is aye whole, her cottage ever smokes, and her table lacks neither of wine, white and red, nor of fowl and fish, and white bread and brown. It was a dear scoff to Jock Matheson, when he called old Moll the uncanny carline of Blawhooly: his boat ran round and round in the centre of the Solway – everybody said it was enchanted – and down it went head foremost; and hadna Jock been a swimmer equal to a sheldrake, he would have fed the fish. But I'll warrant it sobered the lad's speech; and he never reckoned himself safe till he made old Moll the present of a new kirtle and a stone of cheese.'

'Oh, father!' said his granddaughter Barbara, 'ye surely wrong poor old Mary Moray; what use could it be to an old woman like her, who has no wrongs to redress, no malice to work out against mankind, and nothing to seek of enjoyment save a canny hour and a quiet grave – what use could the fellowship of fiends and the communion of evil spirits be to her? I know Jenny Primrose puts rowan tree above the door-head when she sees old Mary coming; I know the good-wife of Kittlenaket wears rowan-berry leaves in the headband of her blue kirtle, and all for the sake of averting the unsonsie glance of Mary's right ee; and I know that the auld Laird of Burntroutwater drives his seven cows to their pasture with a wand of witch tree, to keep Mary from milking them. But what has all that to do with haunted shallops, visionary mariners and bottomless boats? I have heard myself as pleasant a tale about the Haunted Ships and their unworldly crews as anyone would wish to hear on a winter evening. It was told me by young Benjie Macharg, one summer night, sitting on Arbigland bank: the lad intended a sort of love meeting; but all that he could talk of was about smearing sheep and shearing sheep, and of the wife which the Norway elves of the Haunted Ships made for his uncle Sandie Macharg. And I shall tell ye the tale as the honest lad told it to me.

'Alexander Macharg, besides being the laird of three acres of peatmoss and two kale gardens, and the owner of seven good milch cows, a pair of horses and six pet sheep, was the husband of one of the handsomest women in the seven parishes. Many a lad sighed the day he was brided; and a Nithsdale laird and two Annandale moorland farmers drank themselves to their last linen, as well as their last shilling, through sorrow for her loss. But married was the dame; and home she was carried, to bear rule over her home and her husband, as an honest woman should. Now ye maun ken that though the flesh-and-blood lovers of Alexander's bonnie wife all ceased to love and to sue her after she became another's, there were certain admirers who did not consider their claim at all abated, or their hopes lessened by the kirk's famous obstacle of matrimony. Ye have heard how the devout minister of Tinwald had a fair son carried away, and wedded against his liking to an unchristened bride, whom the elves and the fairies provided; ye have heard how the bonnie bride of the drunken Laird of Soukitup was stolen by the fairies out at the back-window of the bridal chamber, the time the bridegroom was groping his way to the chamber door; and ye have heard – but why need I multiply cases? Such things in the ancient days were as common as candlelight. So ye'll no hinder certain water elves and sea fairies, who sometimes keep festival and summer mirth in these old haunted hulks, from falling in love with the weel-faured wife of Laird Macharg; and to their plots and contrivances they went how they might accomplish to sunder man and wife; and sundering such a man and such a wife was like sundering the green leaf from the summer or the fragrance from the flower.

'So it fell on a time that Laird Macharg took his halve-net on his back, and his steel spear in his hand, and down to Blawhooly Bay gaed he, and into the water he went right between the two haunted hulks, and placing his net awaited the coming of the tide. The night, ye maun ken, was mirk, and the wind lowne, and the singing of the increasing waters among the shells and the peebles was heard for sundry miles. All at once light began to glance and twinkle on board the two Haunted Ships from every hole and seam, and presently the sound as of a hatchet employed in squaring timber echoed far and wide. But if the toil of these unearthly workmen amazed the laird, how much more was his amazement increased when a sharp shrill voice called out, "Ho, brother! what are you doing now?" A voice still shriller responded from the other haunted ship, "I'm making a wife to Sandie Macharg!" And a loud quavering laugh running from ship to ship, and from bank to bank, told the joy they expected from their labour.

'Now the laird, besides being a devout and a God-fearing man, was shrewd and bold; and in plot and contrivance, and skill in conducting his designs, was fairly an overmatch for any dozen land elves; but the water elves are far more subtle; besides, their haunts and their dwellings being in the great deep, pursuit and detection is hopeless if they succeed in carrying their prey to the waves. But ye shall hear. Home flew the laird, collected his family around the hearth, spoke of the signs and the sins of the times, and talked of mortification and prayer for averting calamity; and, finally, taking his father's Bible, brass clasps, black print and covered with calf-skin, from the shelf, he proceeded without let or stint to perform domestic worship. I should have told ye that he bolted and locked the door, shut up all inlet to the house, threw salt into the fire, and proceeded in every way like a man skilful in guarding against the plots of fairies and fiends. His wife looked on all this with wonder; but she saw something in her husband's looks that hindered her from intruding either question or advice, and a wise woman was she.

'Near the mid-hour of the night the rush of a horse's feet was heard, and the sound of a rider leaping from its back, and a heavy knock came to the door, accompanied by a voice, saying, "The cummer drink's hot, and the knave bairn is expected at Laird Laurie's tonight; sae mount, good-wife, and come."

' "Preserve me!" said the wife of Sandie Macharg, "that's news indeed; who could have thought it? The laird has been heirless for seventeen years! Now, Sandie, my man, fetch me my skirt and hood."

'But he laid his arm round his wife's neck, and said, "If all the lairds in Galloway go heirless, over this door threshold shall you not stir tonight; and I have said, and I have sworn it; seek not to know why or wherefore – but, Lord, send us thy blessed mornlight." The wife looked for a moment in her husband's eyes, and desisted from further entreaty.

' "But let us send a civil message to the gossips, Sandy; and hadna ye better say I am sair laid with a sudden sickness? though it's sinful-like to send the poor messenger a mile agate with a lie in his mouth without a glass of brandy."

' "To such a messenger, and to those who sent him, no apology is needed," said the austere laird; "so let him depart." And the clatter of a horse's hoofs was heard, and the muttered imprecations of its rider on the churlish treatment he had experienced.

' "Now, Sandie, my lad," said his wife, laying an arm particularly white and round about his neck as she spoke, "are you not a queer man and a stern? I have been your wedded wife now these three years; and, beside my dower, have brought you three as bonnie bairns as ever smiled aneath a summer sun. Oh, man, you a douce man, and fitter to be an elder than even Willie Greer himself, I have the minister's ain word for 't, to put on these hard-hearted looks, and gang waving your arms that way, as if ye said, 'I winna take the counsel of sic a hempie as you;' I'm your ain leal wife, and will and maun have an explanation."

'To all this Sandie Macharg replied, "It is written, 'Wives, obey your husbands'; but we have been stayed in our devotion, so let us pray;" and down he knelt: his wife knelt also, for she was as devout as bonnie; and beside them knelt their household, and all lights were extinguished.

' "Now this beats a'," muttered his wife to herself; "however, I shall be obedient for a time; but if I dinna ken what all this is for before the morn by sunket-time, my tongue is nae langer a tongue, nor my hands worth wearing."

'The voice of her husband in prayer interrupted this mental soliloquy; and ardently did he beseech to be preserved from the wiles of the fiends and the snares of Satan; from witches, ghosts, goblins, elves, fairies, spunkies and water-kelpies; from the spectre shallop of Solway; from spirits visible and invisible; from the Haunted Ships and their unearthly tenants; from maritime spirits that plotted against godly men and fell in love with their wives –

' "Nay, but His presence be near us!" said his wife, in a low tone of dismay. "God guide my gudeman's wits: I never heard such a prayer from human lips before. But, Sandie, my man, Lord's sake, rise. What fearful light is this? Barn and byre and stable maun be in a blaze; and Hawkie and Hurley, Doddie and Cherrie and Damson-plum will be smoored with reek and scorched with flame."

'And a flood of light, but not so gross as a common fire, which ascended to heaven and filled all the court before the house, amply justified the good-wife's suspicions. But to the terrors of fire Sandie was as immovable as he was to the imaginary groans of the barren wife of Laird Laurie; and he held his wife, and threatened the weight of his right hand – and it was a heavy one – to all who ventured abroad or even unbolted the door. The neighing and prancing of horses and the bellowing of cows augmented the horrors of the night; and to anyone who only heard the din, it seemed that the whole onstead was in a blaze, and horses and cattle perishing in the flame. All wiles, common or extraordinary, were put in practice to entice or force the honest farmer and his wife to open the door; and when the like success attended every new stratagem, silence for a little while ensued, and a long, loud and shrilling laugh wound up the dramatic efforts of the night. In the morning, when Laird Macharg went to the door, he found standing against one of the pilasters a piece of black ship oak, rudely fashioned into something like human form, and which skilful people declared would have been clothed with seeming flesh and blood, and palmed upon him by elfin adroitness for his wife, had he admitted his visitants. A synod of wise men and women sat upon the woman of timber, and she was finally ordered to be devoured by fire, and that in the open air. A fire was soon made, and into it the elfin sculpture was tossed from the prongs of two pairs of pitchforks. The blaze that arose was awful to behold; and hissings and burstings and loud cracklings and strange noises were heard in the midst of the flame; and when the whole sank into ashes, a drinking-cup of some precious metal was found; and this cup, fashioned no doubt by elfin skill, but rendered harmless by the purification of fire, the sons and daughters of Sandie Macharg and his wife drink out of to this very day. Bless all bold men, say I, and obedient wives!'

Glamis Castle

The Castle of Glamis, a venerable and majestic pile of buildings, says an old Scots gazetteer, is situate about one mile north from the village, on the flat grounds at the confluence of the Glamis Burn and the Dean. There is a print of it given by Slezer in Charles II's reign – by which it appears to have been anciently much more extensive, being a large quadrangular mass of buildings, having two courts in front, with a tower in each, and gateway through below them; and on the northern side was the principal tower, which now constitutes the central portion of the present castle upwards of a hundred feet in height. The building received the addition of a tower in one of its angles for a spiral staircase from bottom to top with conical roof. The wings were added, at the same time, by Patrick Earl of Strathmore, who repaired and modernised the structure, under the directions of Inigo Jones. One of the wings has been renovated within the last forty years, and other additions made, but not in harmony with Earl Patrick's repairs.

There are no records of the castle prior to the tenth century, when it is first noticed in connection with the death of Malcolm II in 1034. Tradition says that he was murdered in this castle, and in a room which is still pointed out, in the centre of the principal tower; and that the murderers lost their way in the darkness of the night, and, by the breaking of the ice, were drowned in the loch of Forfar. Fordun's account is, however, somewhat different and more probable. He states that the king was mortally wounded in a skirmish in the neighbourhood by some of the adherents of Kenneth V.

A lady, well known in London society, an artistic and social celebrity, wealthy beyond all doubts of the future, a cultivated, clear-headed and indeed slightly matter-of-fact woman, went to stay at Glamis Castle for the first time. She was allotted handsome apartments, just on the point of junction between the new buildings – perhaps a hundred or two hundred years old – and the very ancient part of the castle. The rooms were handsomely furnished; no gaunt carvings grinned from the walls; no grim tapestry swung to and fro, making strange figures look still stranger by the flickering firelight; all was smooth, cosy and modern, and the guest retired to bed without a thought of the mysteries of Glamis.

In the morning she appeared at the breakfast table quite cheerful and self-possessed. To the enquiry how she had slept, she replied: 'Well, thanks, very well, up to four o'clock in the morning. But your Scottish carpenters seem to come to work very early. I suppose they put up their scaffolding quickly, though, for they are quiet now.' This speech produced a dead silence, and the speaker saw with astonishment that the faces of members of the family were very pale.

She was asked, as she valued the friendship of all there, never to speak to them on that subject again; there had been no carpenters at Glamis Castle for months past. This fact, whatever it may be worth, is absolutely established, so far as the testimony of a single witness can establish anything. The lady was awakened by a loud knocking and hammering, as if somebody were putting up a scaffold, and the noise did not alarm her in the least. On the contrary, she took it for an accident, due to the presumed matutinal habits of the people. She knew, of course, that there were stories about Glamis, but had not the remotest idea that the hammering she had heard was connected with any story. She had regarded it simply as an annoyance, and was glad to get to sleep after an unrestful time; but had no notion of the noise being supernatural until informed of it at the breakfast-table.

With what particular event in the stormy annals of the Lyon family the hammering is connected is quite unknown, except to members of the family, but there is no lack of legends, possible and impossible, to account for any sights or sounds in the magnificent old feudal edifice.

It is said that once a visitor stayed at Glamis Castle for a few days, and, sitting up late one moonlight night, saw a face appear at the window opposite to him. The owner of the face – it was very pale, with great sorrowful eyes – seemed to wish to attract attention; but vanished suddenly from the window, as if plucked away by superior strength. For a long while the horror-stricken guest gazed at the window in the hope that the pale face and great sad eyes would appear again. Nothing was seen at the window, but presently horrible shrieks penetrated even the thick walls of the castle, and rent the night air. An hour later, a dark huddled figure, like that of an old decrepit woman, carrying something in a bundle, came into the waning moonlight, and presently vanished.

There is also a secret room in it, only known to two or at most three individuals at the same time, who are bound not to reveal it, unless to their successors in the secret. It has been frequently the object of search with the inquisitive, but the search has been in vain.

There is a modern story of a stonemason, who was engaged at Glamis Castle last century, and who, having discovered more than he should have done, was supplied with a handsome competency, upon the conditions that he emigrated and kept inviolable the secret he had learned.

The employment of a stonemason is explained by the conditions under which the mystery is revealed to successive heirs and factors. The abode of the dread secret is in a part of the castle also haunted by the apparition of a bearded man, who flits about at night, but without committing any other objectionable action. What connection, if any, the bearded spectre may have with the mystery is not even guessed. He hovers at night over the couches of children for an instant, and then vanishes. The secret itself abides in a room – a secret chamber – the very situation of which, beyond a general idea that it is in the most ancient part of the castle, is unknown. Where walls are fifteen feet thick, it is not impossible to have a chamber so concealed that none but the initiated can guess its position. It was once attempted by a madcap party of guests to discover the locality of the secret chamber by hanging their towels out of their windows, and thus deciding in favour of any window from which no spotless banner waved; but this escapade, which is said to have been ill-received by the owners, ended in nothing but a vague conclusion that the old square tower must be the spot sought.